nickelodeon

降击神通

AVATAR

THE LAST AIRBENDER.

A Random House SCREEN COMIX™ Book

nickelodeon

降去神通

AVATAR

THE LAST AIRBENDER™

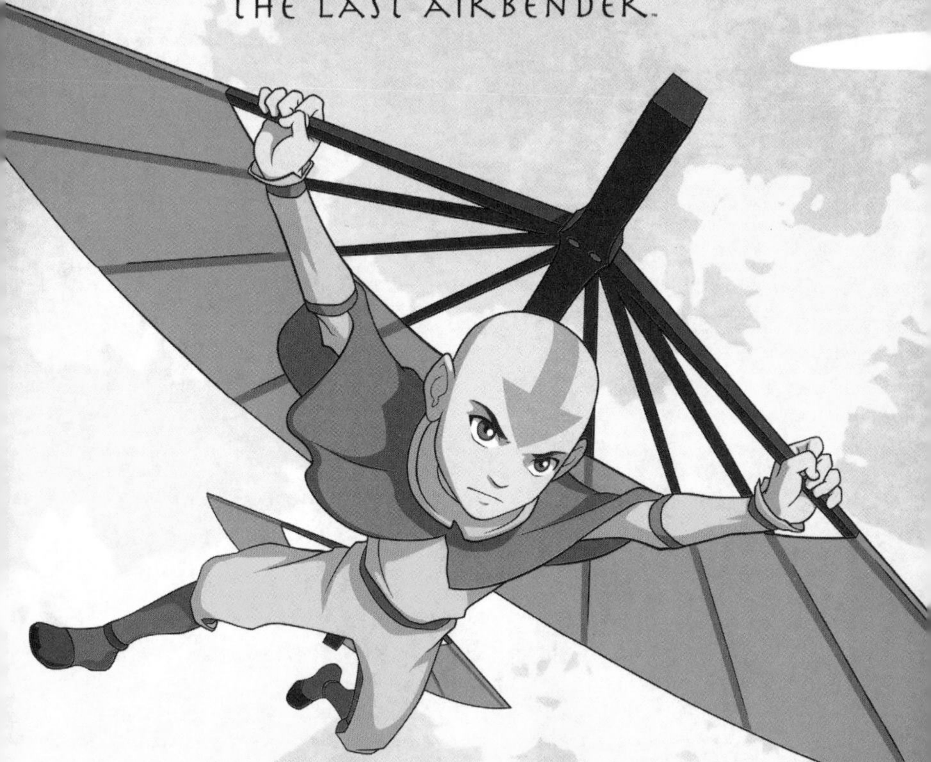

BOOK 1: WATER

VOLUME 2

Random House • New York

Published in the United States by Random House Children's Books, a division of Penguin Random House LLC, 1745 Broadway, New York, NY, 10019, and in Canada by Penguin Random House Canada Limited, Toronto.

ISBN 978-0-593-38080-2
rhcbooks.com

Printed in the United States of America
10 9 8 7 6 5 4 3 2 1

CHAPTER SEVEN

THE SPIRIT WORLD

WINTER SOLSTICE: PART ONE

SQUAWK

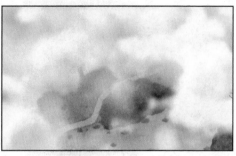

THOSE CLOUDS LOOK SO SOFT, DON'T THEY?

LIKE YOU COULD JUST JUMP DOWN AND YOU'D LAND IN A BIG, SOFT, COTTONY HEAP.

MAYBE YOU SHOULD GIVE IT A TRY.

YOU'RE HILARIOUS.

I'LL TRY IT!

HAHAHA!

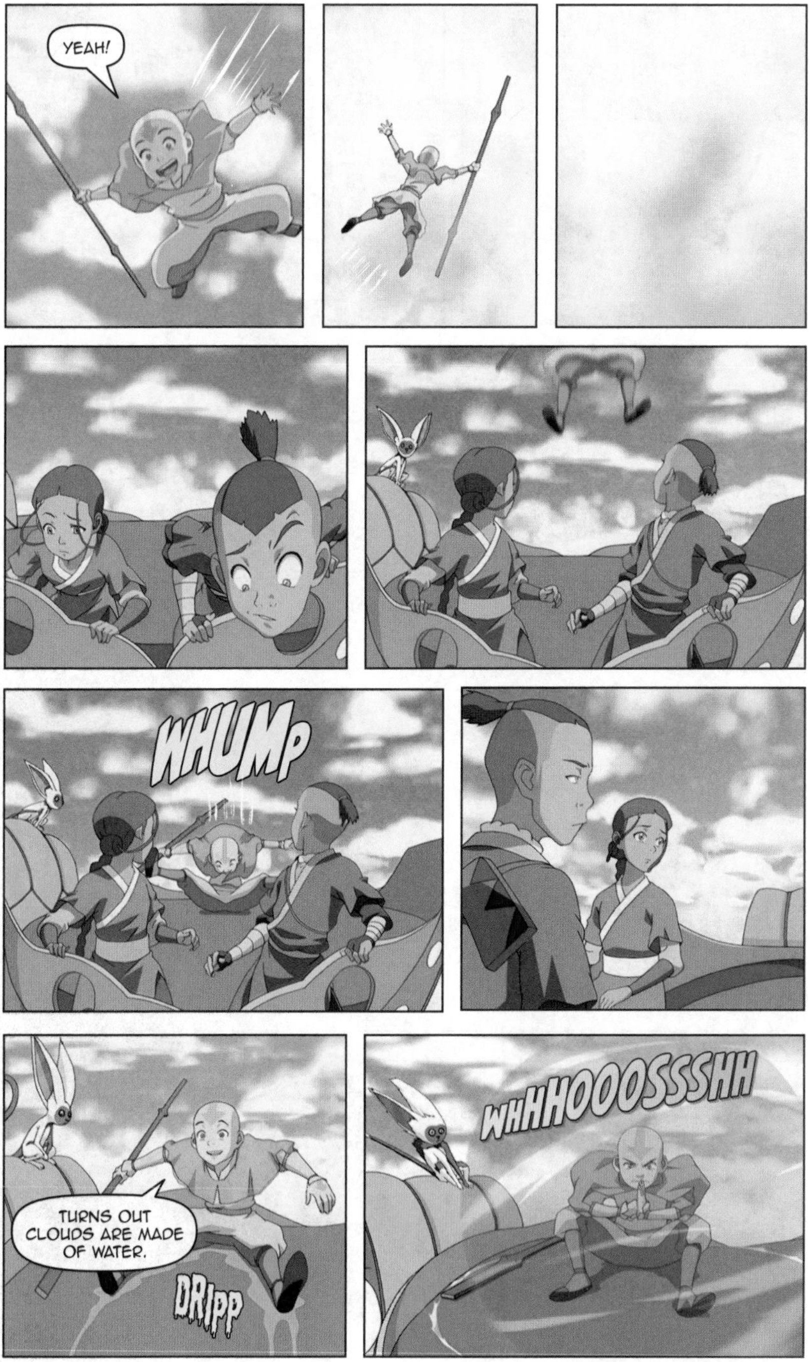
YEAH!
WHUMP
TURNS OUT CLOUDS ARE MADE OF WATER.
DRIPP
WHHHOOOSSSHH

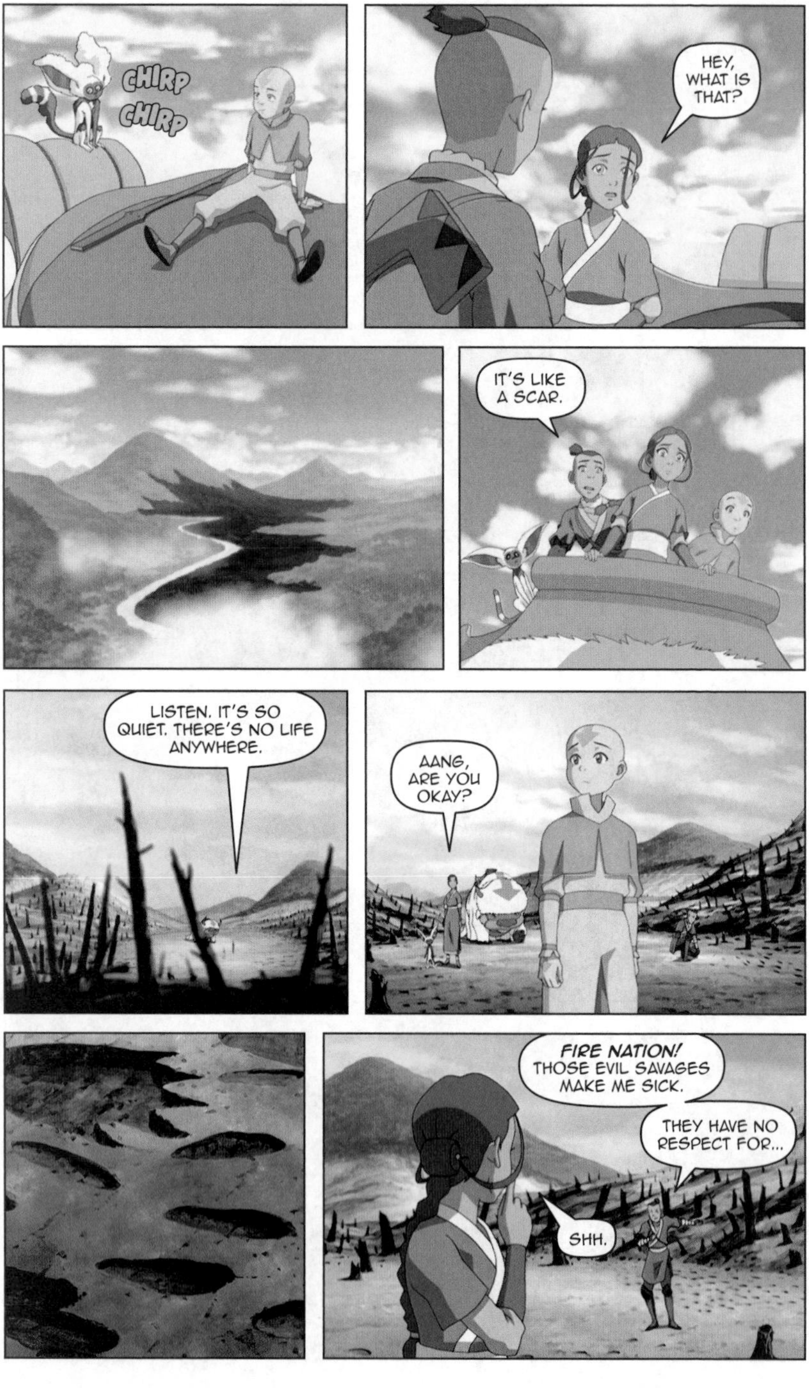
CHIRP
CHIRP
HEY, WHAT IS THAT?
IT'S LIKE A SCAR.
LISTEN. IT'S SO QUIET. THERE'S NO LIFE ANYWHERE.
AANG, ARE YOU OKAY?
FIRE NATION! THOSE EVIL SAVAGES MAKE ME SICK.
THEY HAVE NO RESPECT FOR...
SHH.

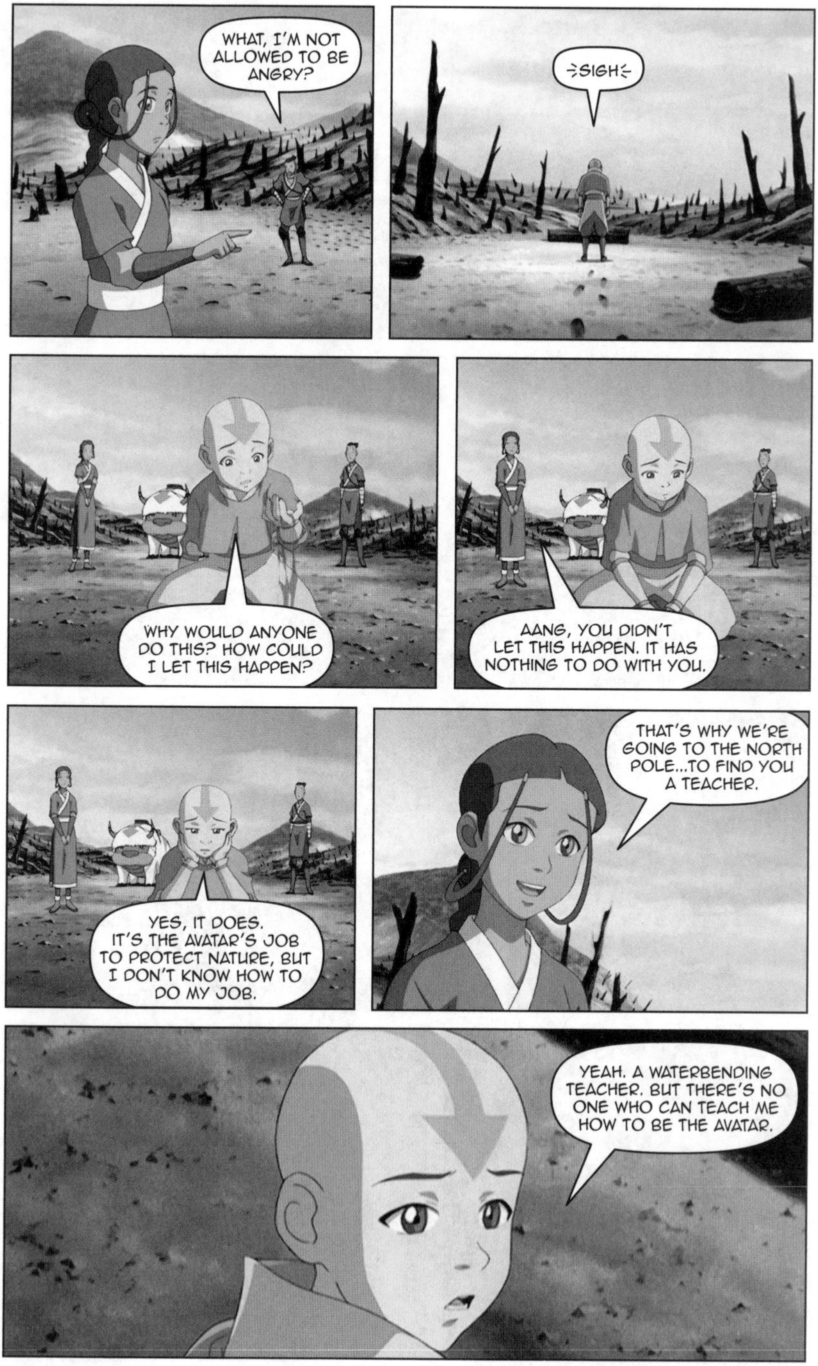
WHAT, I'M NOT ALLOWED TO BE ANGRY?
⇒SIGH⇐
WHY WOULD ANYONE DO THIS? HOW COULD I LET THIS HAPPEN?
AANG, YOU DIDN'T LET THIS HAPPEN. IT HAS NOTHING TO DO WITH YOU.
YES, IT DOES. IT'S THE AVATAR'S JOB TO PROTECT NATURE, BUT I DON'T KNOW HOW TO DO MY JOB.
THAT'S WHY WE'RE GOING TO THE NORTH POLE...TO FIND YOU A TEACHER.
YEAH. A WATERBENDING TEACHER. BUT THERE'S NO ONE WHO CAN TEACH ME HOW TO BE THE AVATAR.

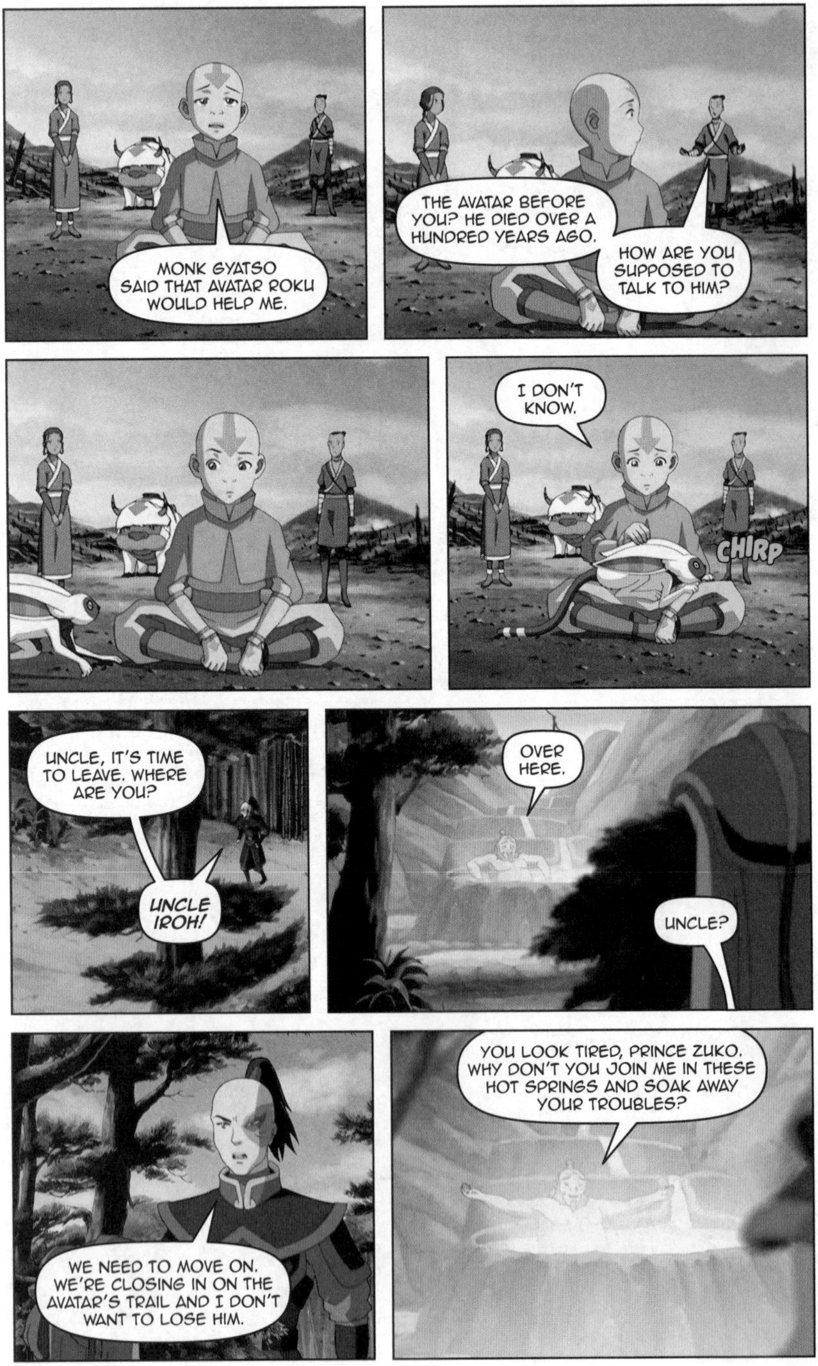
MONK GYATSO SAID THAT AVATAR ROKU WOULD HELP ME.
THE AVATAR BEFORE YOU? HE DIED OVER A HUNDRED YEARS AGO.
HOW ARE YOU SUPPOSED TO TALK TO HIM?
I DON'T KNOW.
CHIRP
UNCLE, IT'S TIME TO LEAVE. WHERE ARE YOU?
UNCLE IROH!
OVER HERE.
UNCLE?
WE NEED TO MOVE ON. WE'RE CLOSING IN ON THE AVATAR'S TRAIL AND I DON'T WANT TO LOSE HIM.
YOU LOOK TIRED, PRINCE ZUKO. WHY DON'T YOU JOIN ME IN THESE HOT SPRINGS AND SOAK AWAY YOUR TROUBLES?

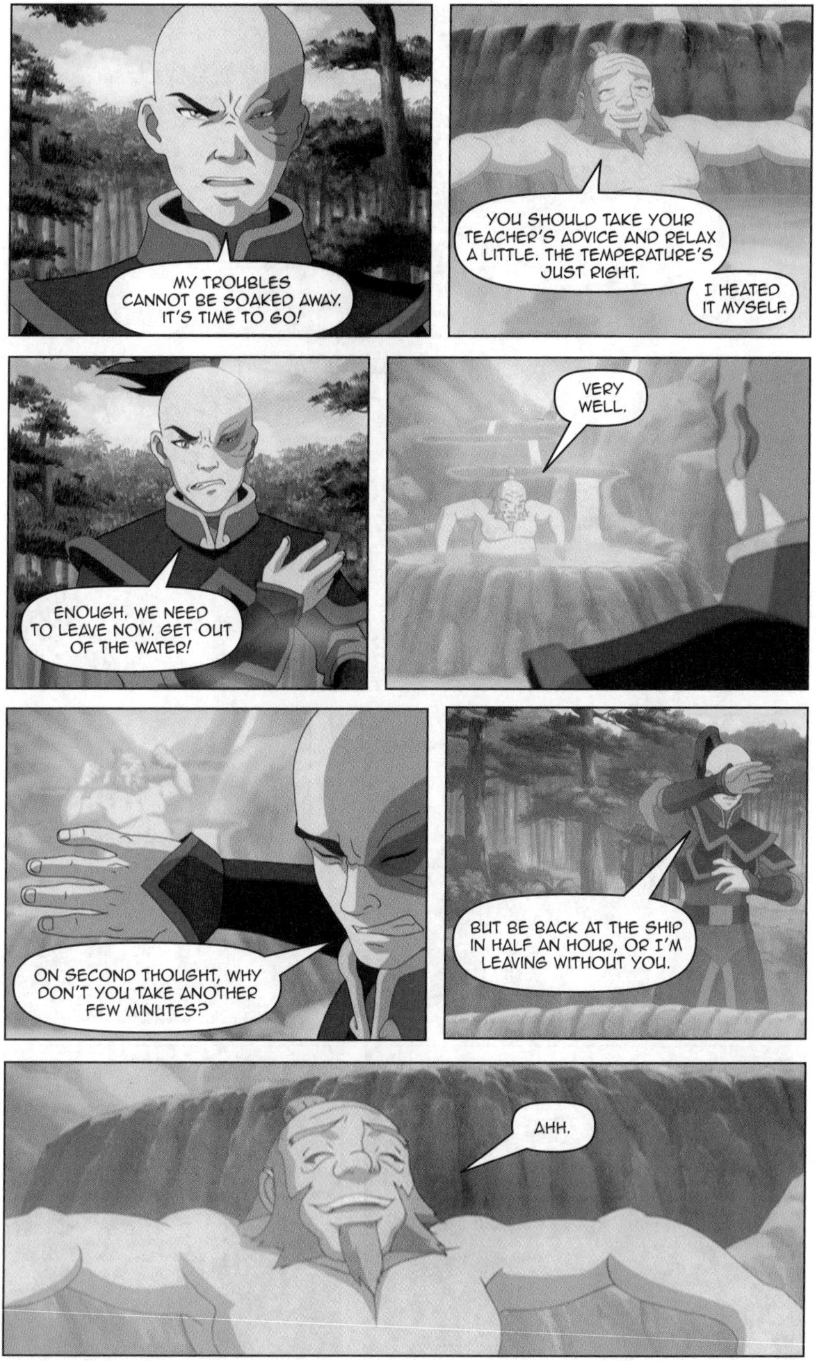
MY TROUBLES CANNOT BE SOAKED AWAY. IT'S TIME TO GO!
YOU SHOULD TAKE YOUR TEACHER'S ADVICE AND RELAX A LITTLE. THE TEMPERATURE'S JUST RIGHT.
I HEATED IT MYSELF.
ENOUGH. WE NEED TO LEAVE NOW. GET OUT OF THE WATER!
VERY WELL.
ON SECOND THOUGHT, WHY DON'T YOU TAKE ANOTHER FEW MINUTES?
BUT BE BACK AT THE SHIP IN HALF AN HOUR, OR I'M LEAVING WITHOUT YOU.
AHH.

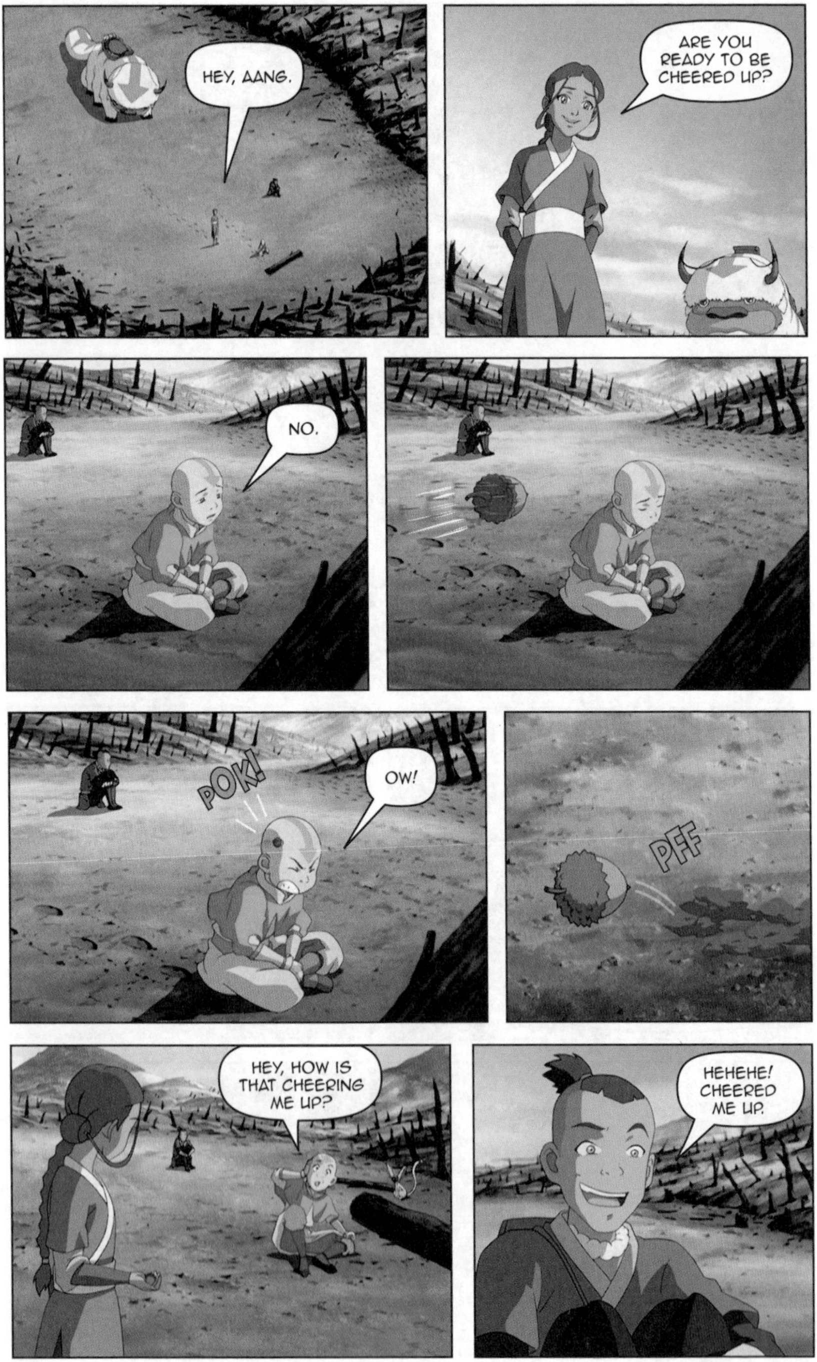
HEY, AANG.
ARE YOU READY TO BE CHEERED UP?
NO.
POK!
OW!
PFF
HEY, HOW IS THAT CHEERING ME UP?
HEHEHE! CHEERED ME UP.

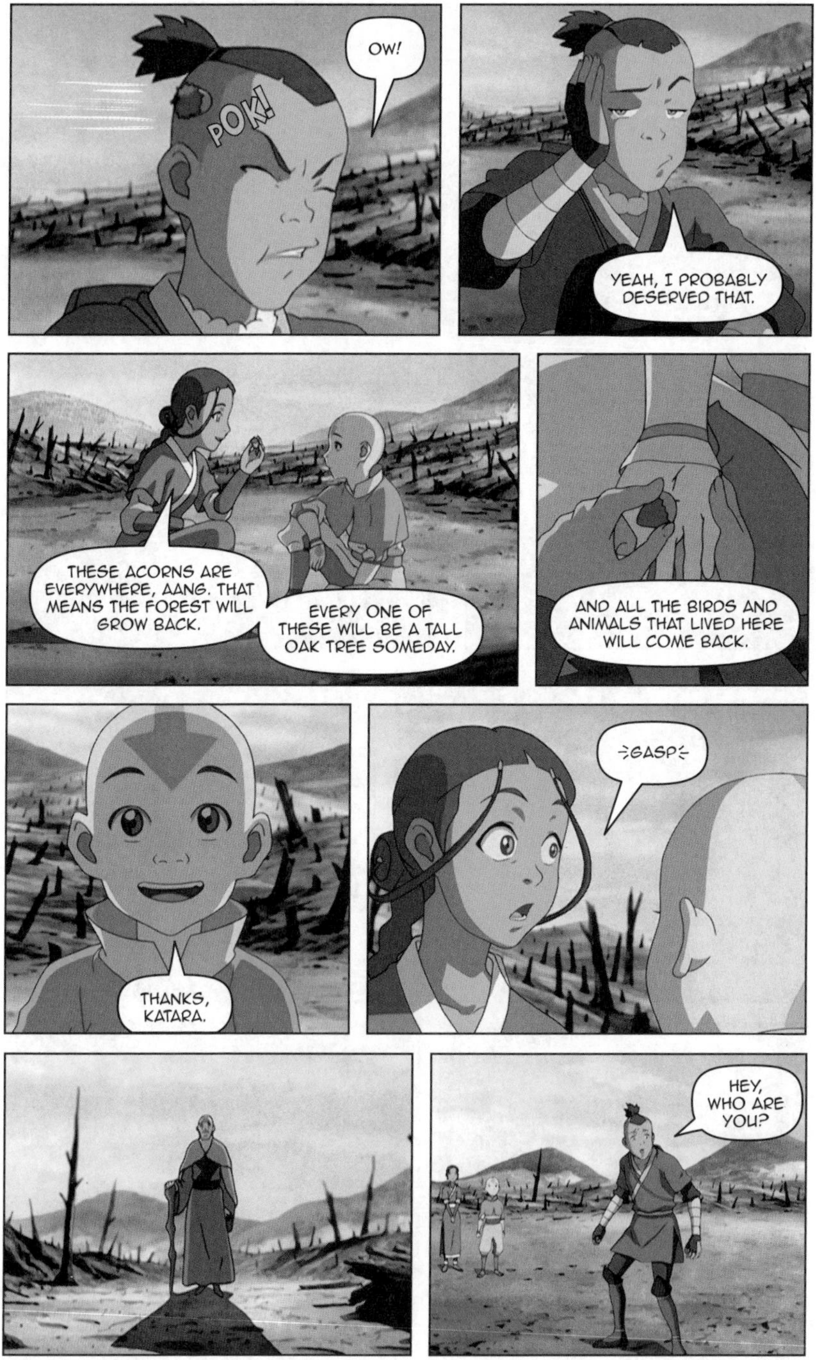
POK!
OW!
YEAH, I PROBABLY DESERVED THAT.
THESE ACORNS ARE EVERYWHERE, AANG. THAT MEANS THE FOREST WILL GROW BACK.
EVERY ONE OF THESE WILL BE A TALL OAK TREE SOMEDAY.
AND ALL THE BIRDS AND ANIMALS THAT LIVED HERE WILL COME BACK.
THANKS, KATARA.
GASP
HEY, WHO ARE YOU?

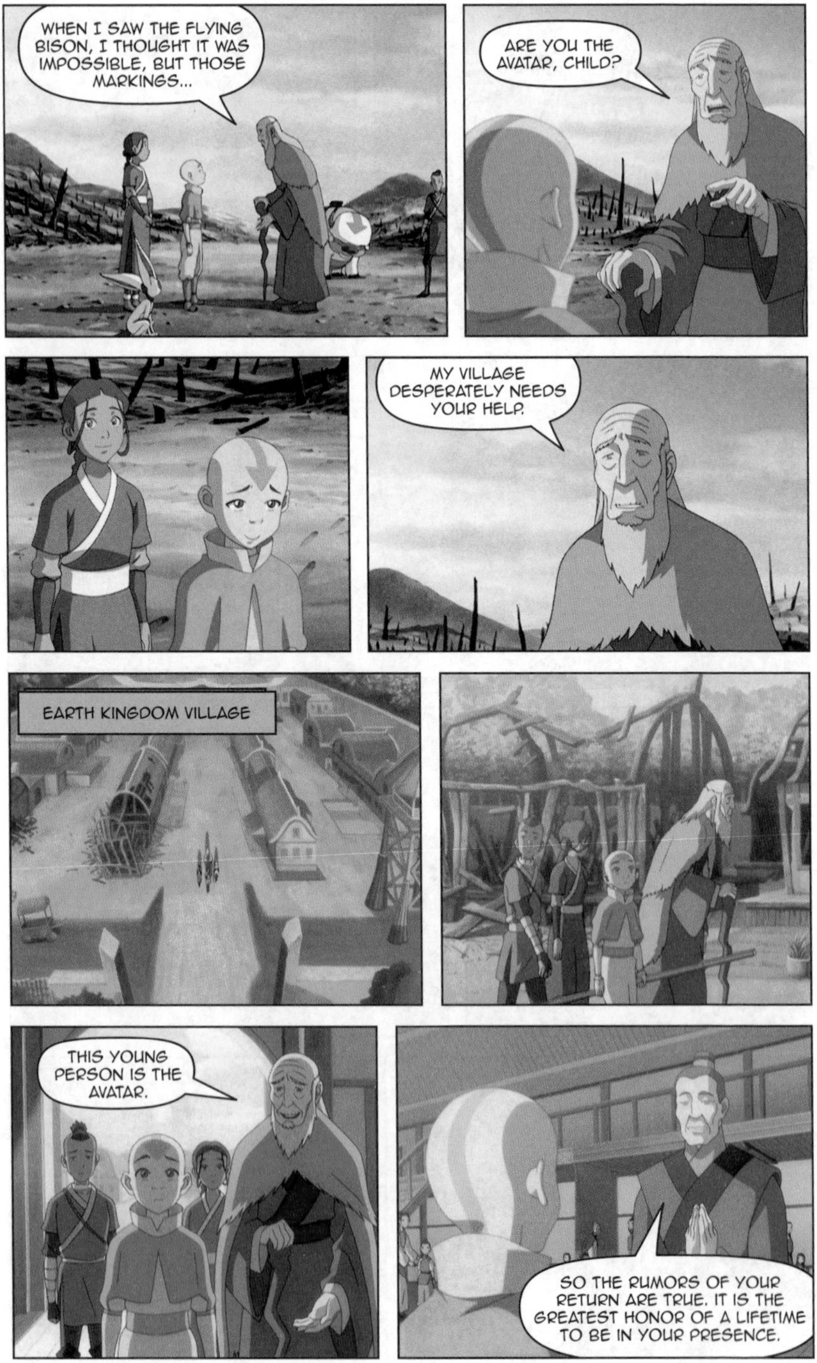
WHEN I SAW THE FLYING BISON, I THOUGHT IT WAS IMPOSSIBLE, BUT THOSE MARKINGS...
ARE YOU THE AVATAR, CHILD?
MY VILLAGE DESPERATELY NEEDS YOUR HELP.
EARTH KINGDOM VILLAGE
THIS YOUNG PERSON IS THE AVATAR.
SO THE RUMORS OF YOUR RETURN ARE TRUE. IT IS THE GREATEST HONOR OF A LIFETIME TO BE IN YOUR PRESENCE.

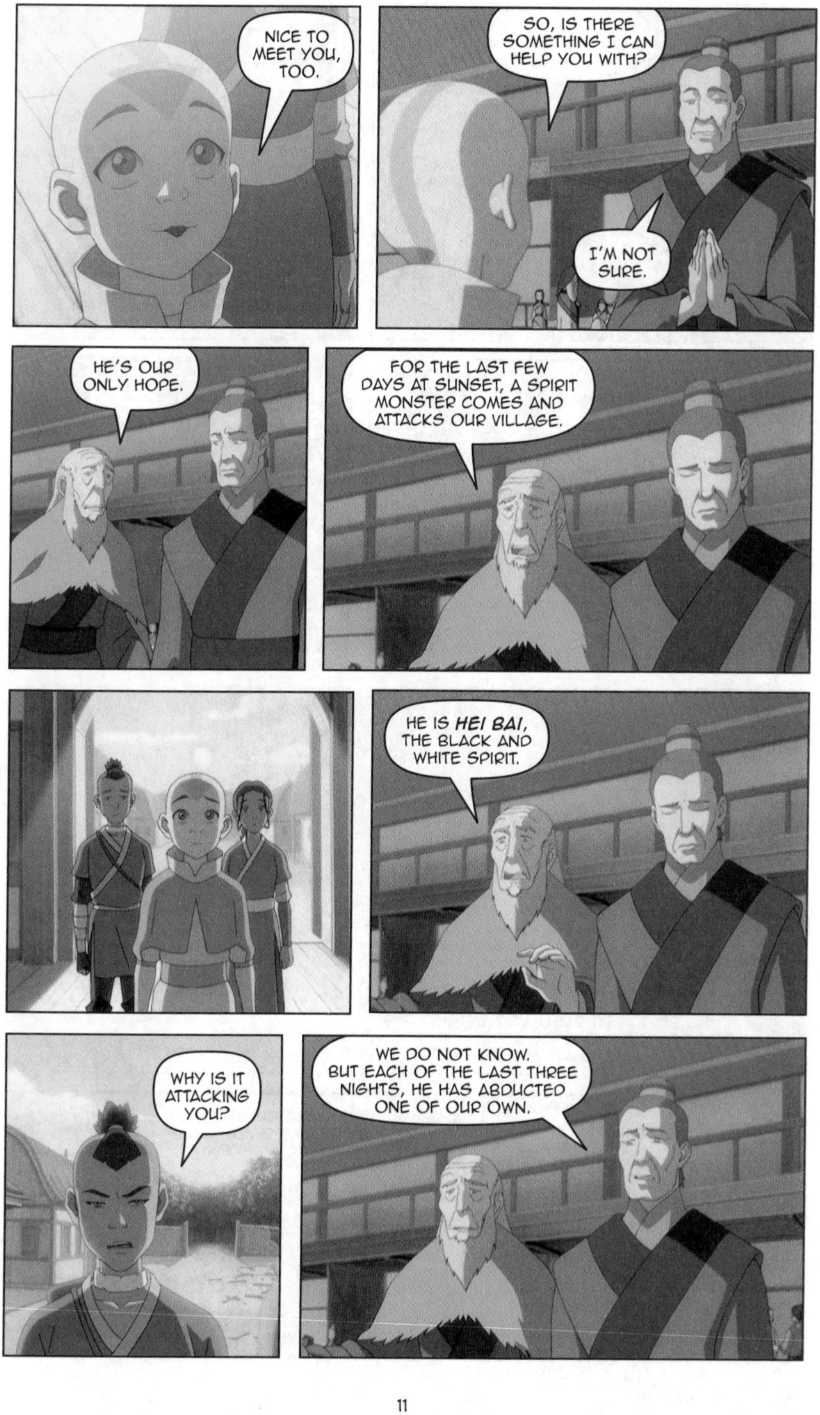
NICE TO MEET YOU, TOO.
SO, IS THERE SOMETHING I CAN HELP YOU WITH?
I'M NOT SURE.
HE'S OUR ONLY HOPE.
FOR THE LAST FEW DAYS AT SUNSET, A SPIRIT MONSTER COMES AND ATTACKS OUR VILLAGE.
HE IS ***HEI BAI***, THE BLACK AND WHITE SPIRIT.
WHY IS IT ATTACKING YOU?
WE DO NOT KNOW. BUT EACH OF THE LAST THREE NIGHTS, HE HAS ABDUCTED ONE OF OUR OWN.

WE ARE ESPECIALLY FEARFUL BECAUSE THE WINTER SOLSTICE DRAWS NEAR.

WHAT HAPPENS THEN?

AS THE SOLSTICE APPROACHES, THE NATURAL WORLD AND THE SPIRIT WORLD GROW CLOSER AND CLOSER, UNTIL THE LINE BETWEEN THEM IS BLURRED COMPLETELY.

HEI BAI IS ALREADY CAUSING DEVASTATION AND DESTRUCTION. ONCE THE SOLSTICE IS HERE, THERE IS NO TELLING WHAT WILL HAPPEN.

SO WHAT DO YOU WANT ME TO DO, EXACTLY?

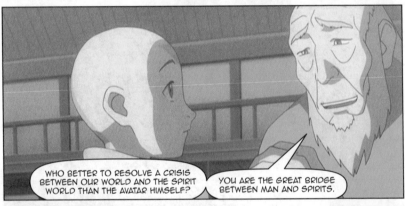

WHO BETTER TO RESOLVE A CRISIS BETWEEN OUR WORLD AND THE SPIRIT WORLD THAN THE AVATAR HIMSELF?

YOU ARE THE GREAT BRIDGE BETWEEN MAN AND SPIRITS.

RIGHT. THAT'S ME.

HEY, GREAT BRIDGE GUY. CAN I TALK TO YOU OVER HERE FOR A SECOND?

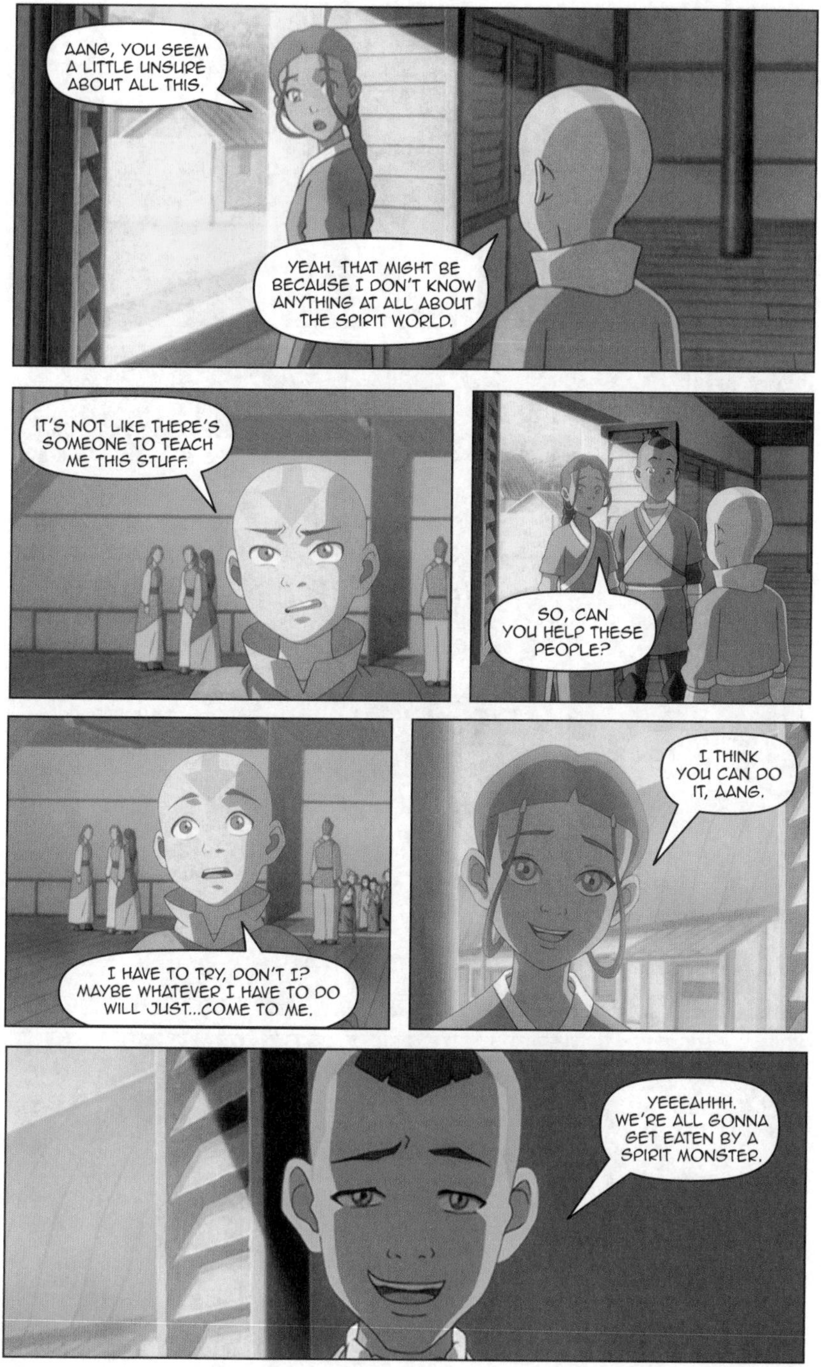
AANG, YOU SEEM A LITTLE UNSURE ABOUT ALL THIS.
YEAH. THAT MIGHT BE BECAUSE I DON'T KNOW ANYTHING AT ALL ABOUT THE SPIRIT WORLD.
IT'S NOT LIKE THERE'S SOMEONE TO TEACH ME THIS STUFF.
SO, CAN YOU HELP THESE PEOPLE?
I HAVE TO TRY, DON'T I? MAYBE WHATEVER I HAVE TO DO WILL JUST...COME TO ME.
I THINK YOU CAN DO IT, AANG.
YEEEAHHH. WE'RE ALL GONNA GET EATEN BY A SPIRIT MONSTER.

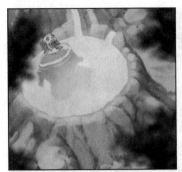

SNORE

RUSTLE RUSTLE

WHO'S THERE?

A MEADOW VOLE.

I SHOULD HAVE KNOWN. YOU STARTLED ME, LITTLE ONE.

SEEMS I DOZED OFF AND MISSED MY NEPHEW'S DEADLINE.

BUT IT WAS A VERY SWEET NAP.

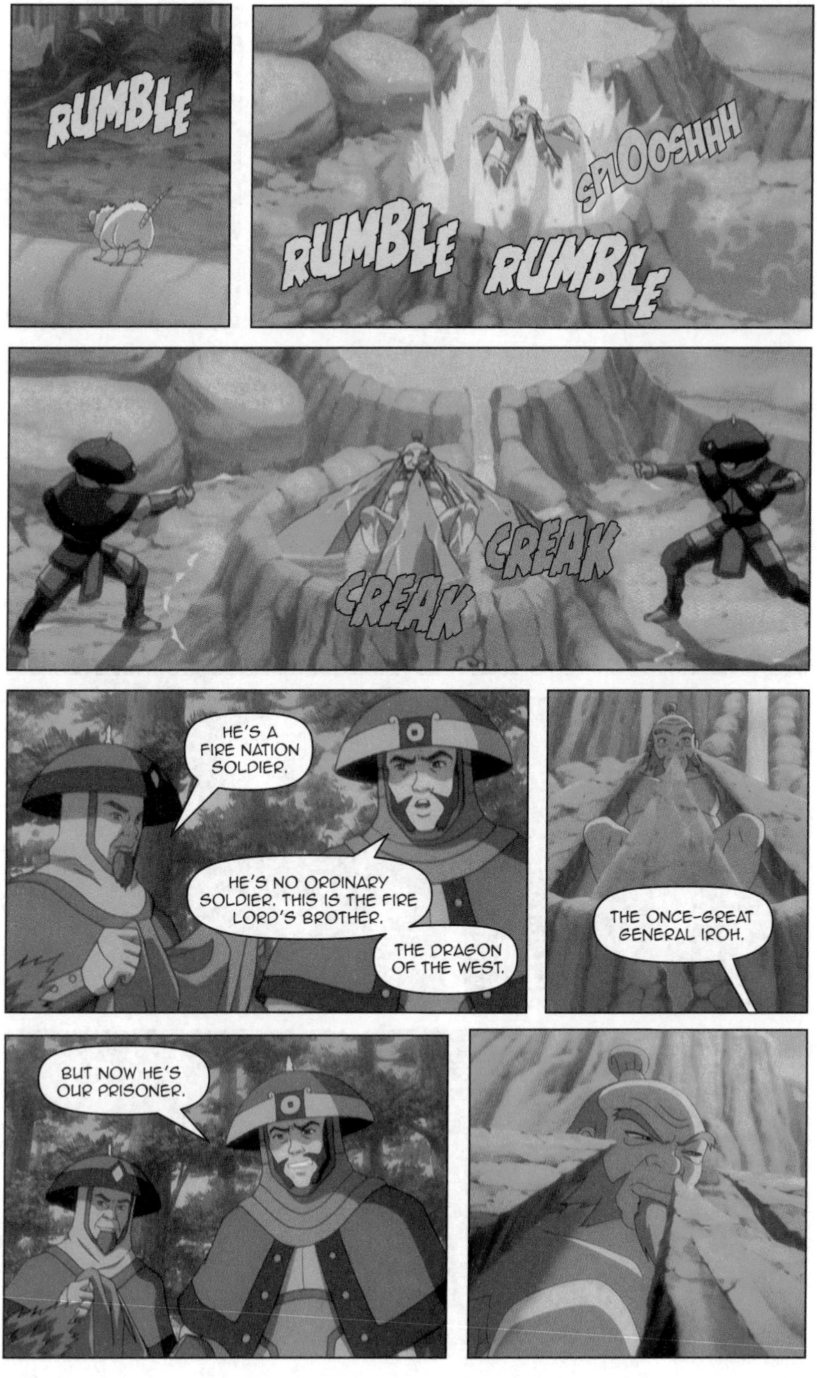
RUMBLE
SPLOOSHHH
RUMBLE
RUMBLE
CREAK
CREAK
HE'S A FIRE NATION SOLDIER.
HE'S NO ORDINARY SOLDIER. THIS IS THE FIRE LORD'S BROTHER.
THE DRAGON OF THE WEST.
THE ONCE-GREAT GENERAL IROH.
BUT NOW HE'S OUR PRISONER.

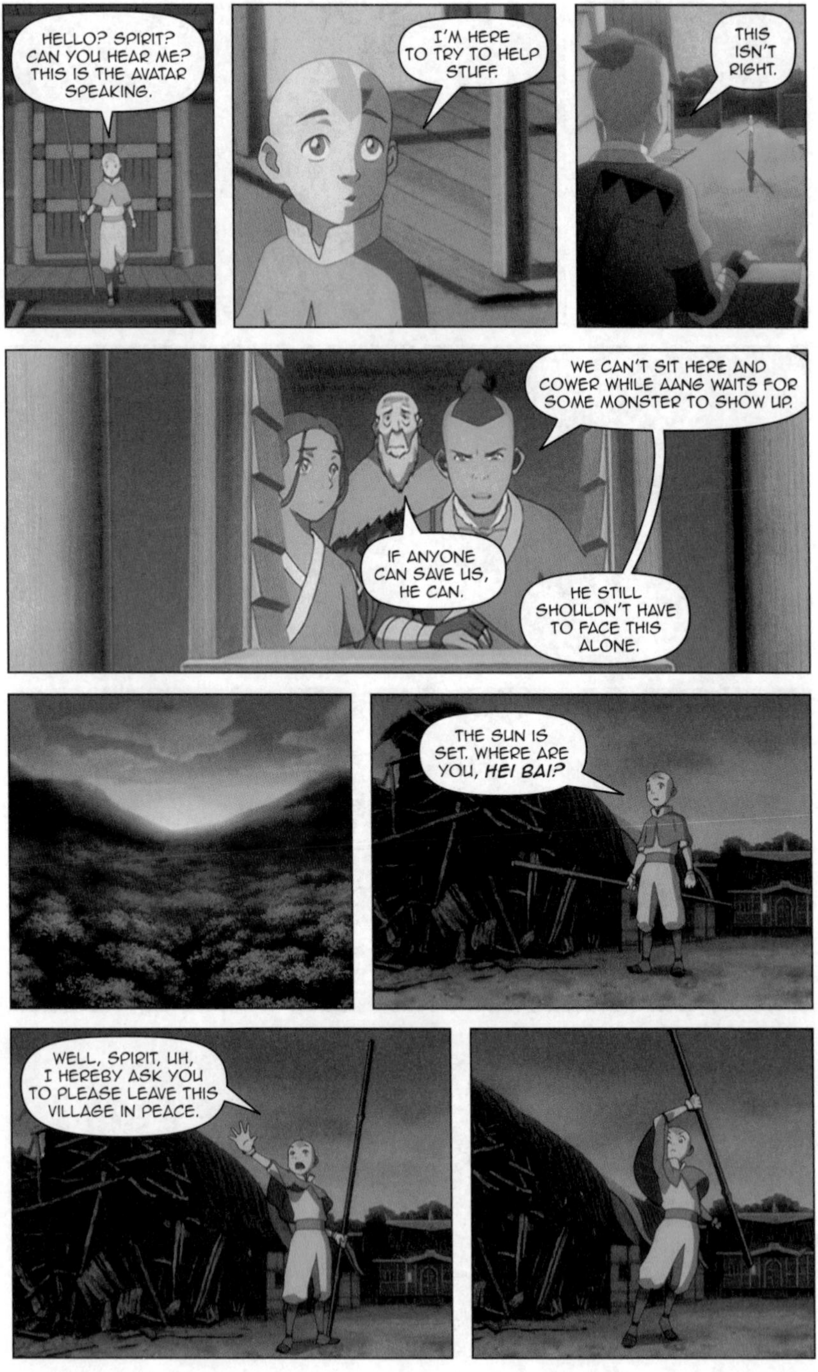
HELLO? SPIRIT? CAN YOU HEAR ME? THIS IS THE AVATAR SPEAKING.
I'M HERE TO TRY TO HELP STUFF.
THIS ISN'T RIGHT.
IF ANYONE CAN SAVE US, HE CAN.
WE CAN'T SIT HERE AND COWER WHILE AANG WAITS FOR SOME MONSTER TO SHOW UP.
HE STILL SHOULDN'T HAVE TO FACE THIS ALONE.
THE SUN IS SET. WHERE ARE YOU, *HEI BAI?*
WELL, SPIRIT, UH, I HEREBY ASK YOU TO PLEASE LEAVE THIS VILLAGE IN PEACE.

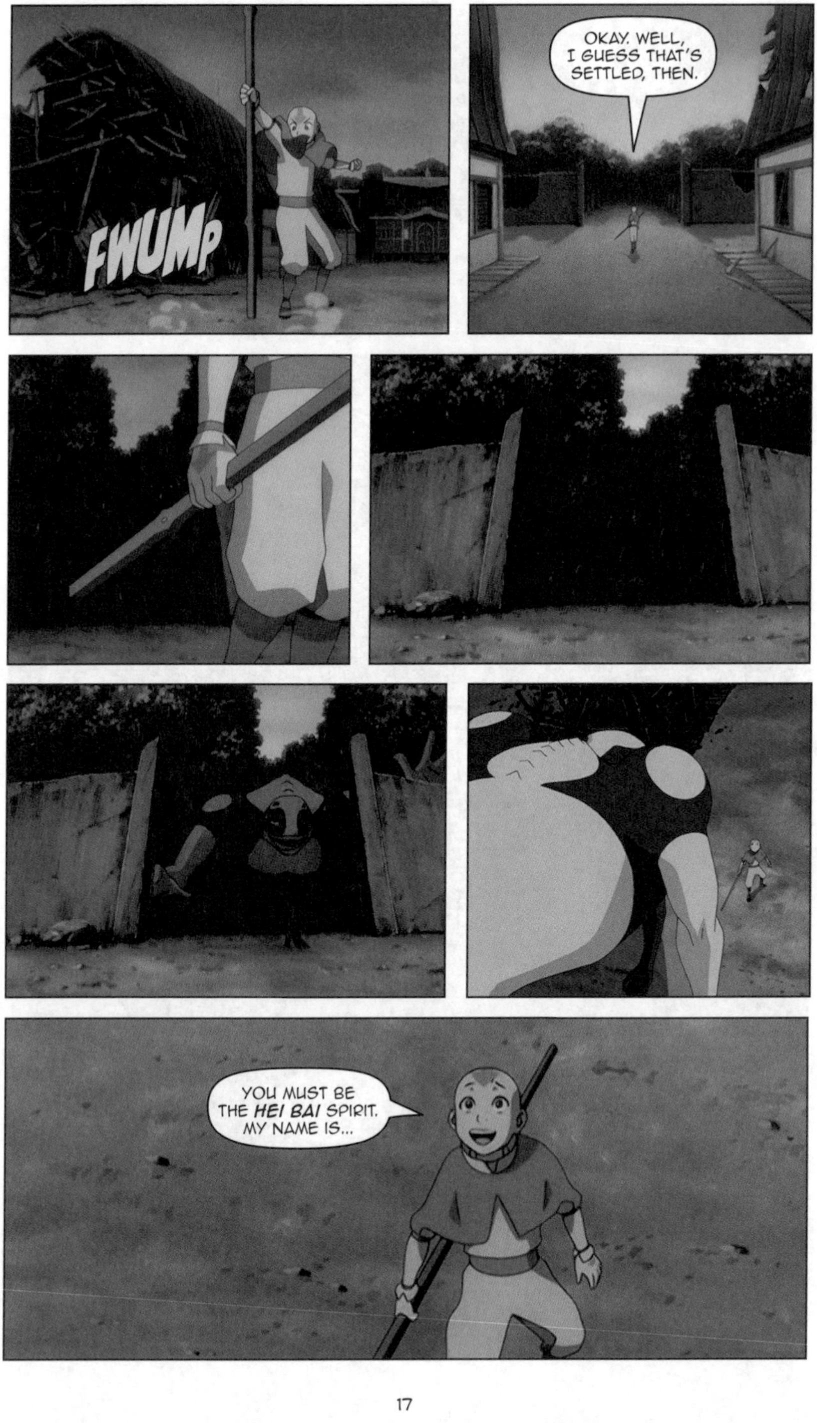
FWUMP
OKAY. WELL, I GUESS THAT'S SETTLED, THEN.
YOU MUST BE THE *HEI BAI* SPIRIT. MY NAME IS...

MY NAME IS AANG.
I'M THE AVATAR, AND I
WOULD LIKE TO HELP.

HEY,
WAIT UP!

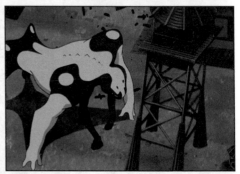

RROARRR

THE AVATAR'S
METHODS ARE...
UNUSUAL.

IT DOESN'T SEEM
TOO INTERESTED IN
WHAT HE'S SAYING.

MAYBE WE
SHOULD GO
HELP HIM.

NO. ONLY THE
AVATAR STANDS A
CHANCE AGAINST
THE *HEI BAI*.

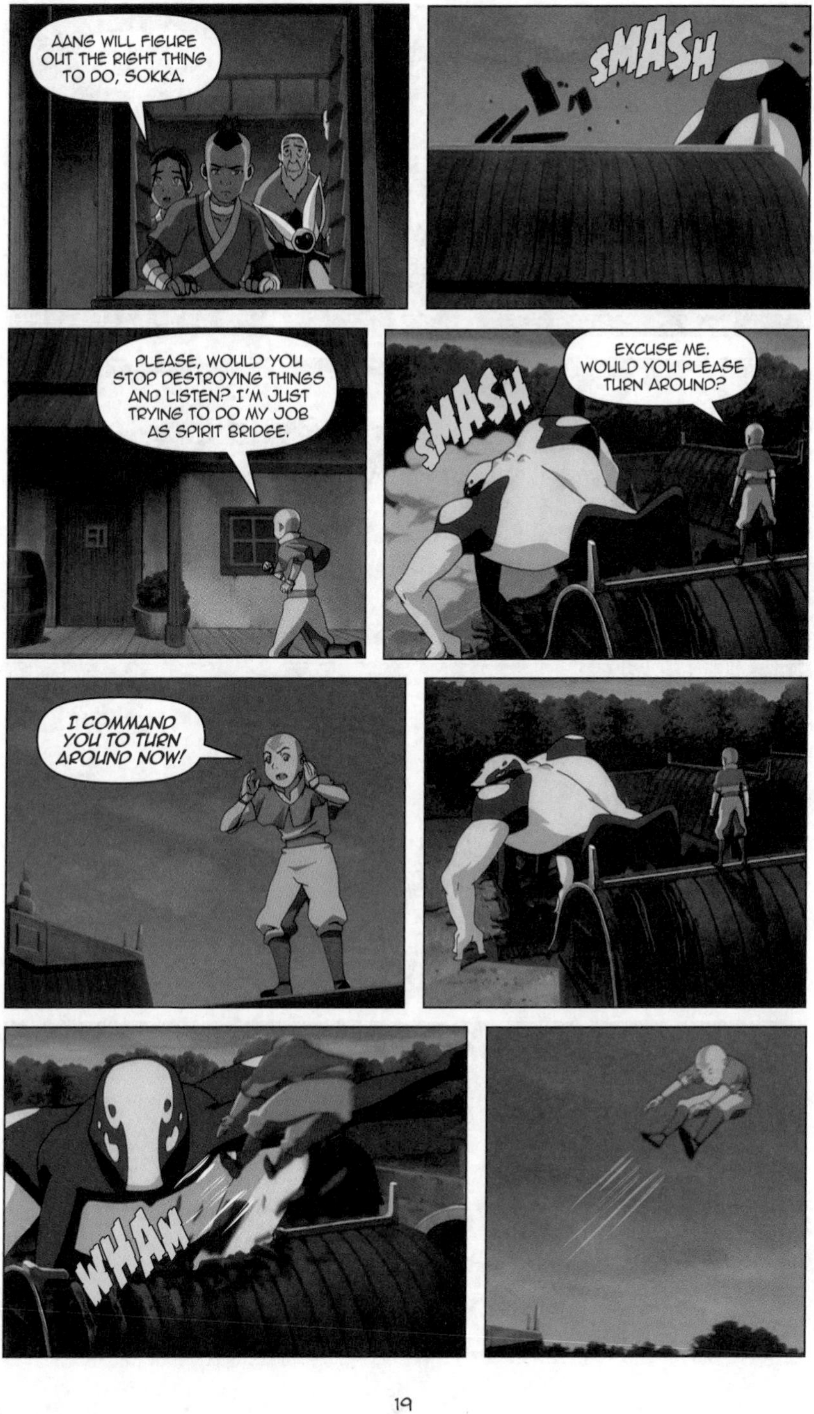
AANG WILL FIGURE OUT THE RIGHT THING TO DO, SOKKA.
SMASH
PLEASE, WOULD YOU STOP DESTROYING THINGS AND LISTEN? I'M JUST TRYING TO DO MY JOB AS SPIRIT BRIDGE.
SMASH
EXCUSE ME. WOULD YOU PLEASE TURN AROUND?
I COMMAND YOU TO TURN AROUND NOW!
WHAM

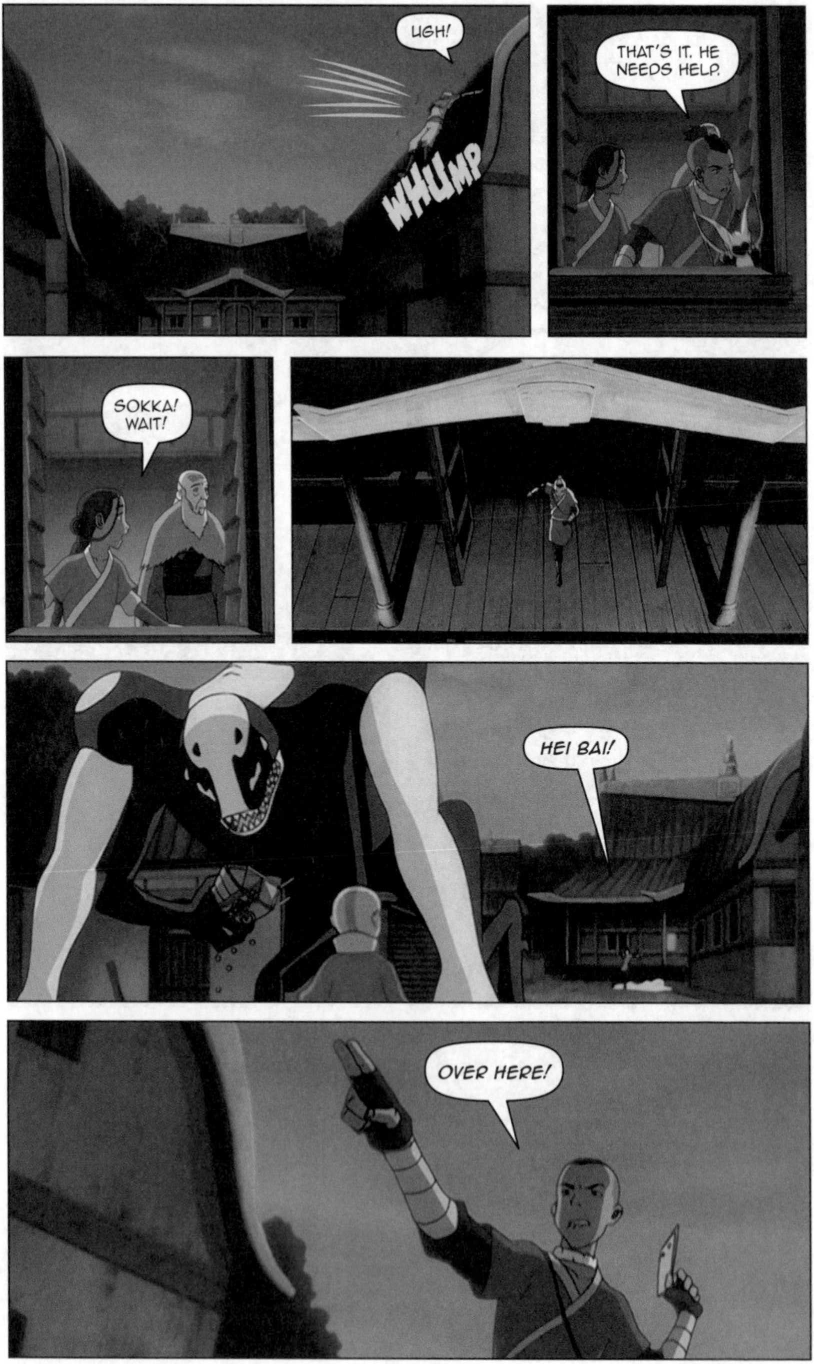
UGH!
WHUMP
THAT'S IT. HE NEEDS HELP.
SOKKA! WAIT!
HEI BAI!
OVER HERE!

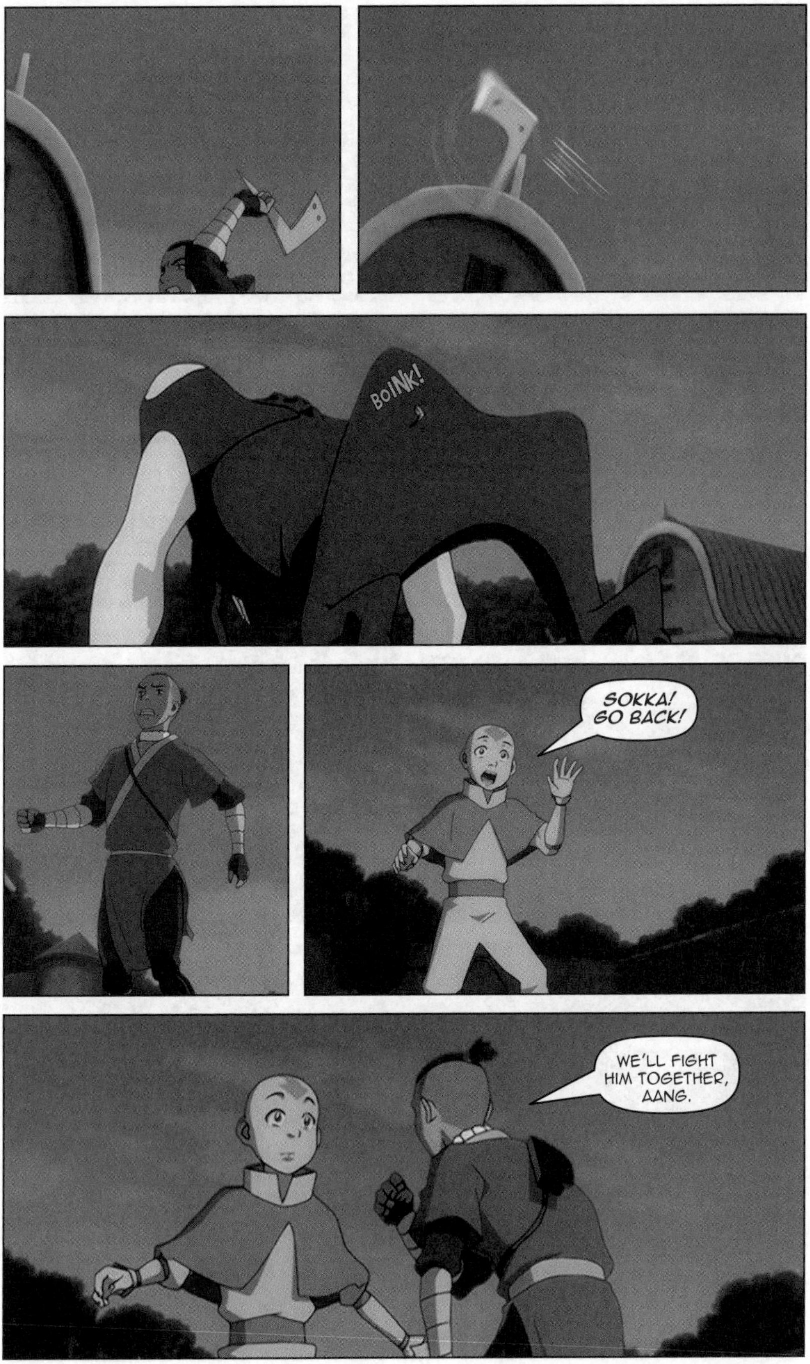
BOINK!
SOKKA! GO BACK!
WE'LL FIGHT HIM TOGETHER, AANG.

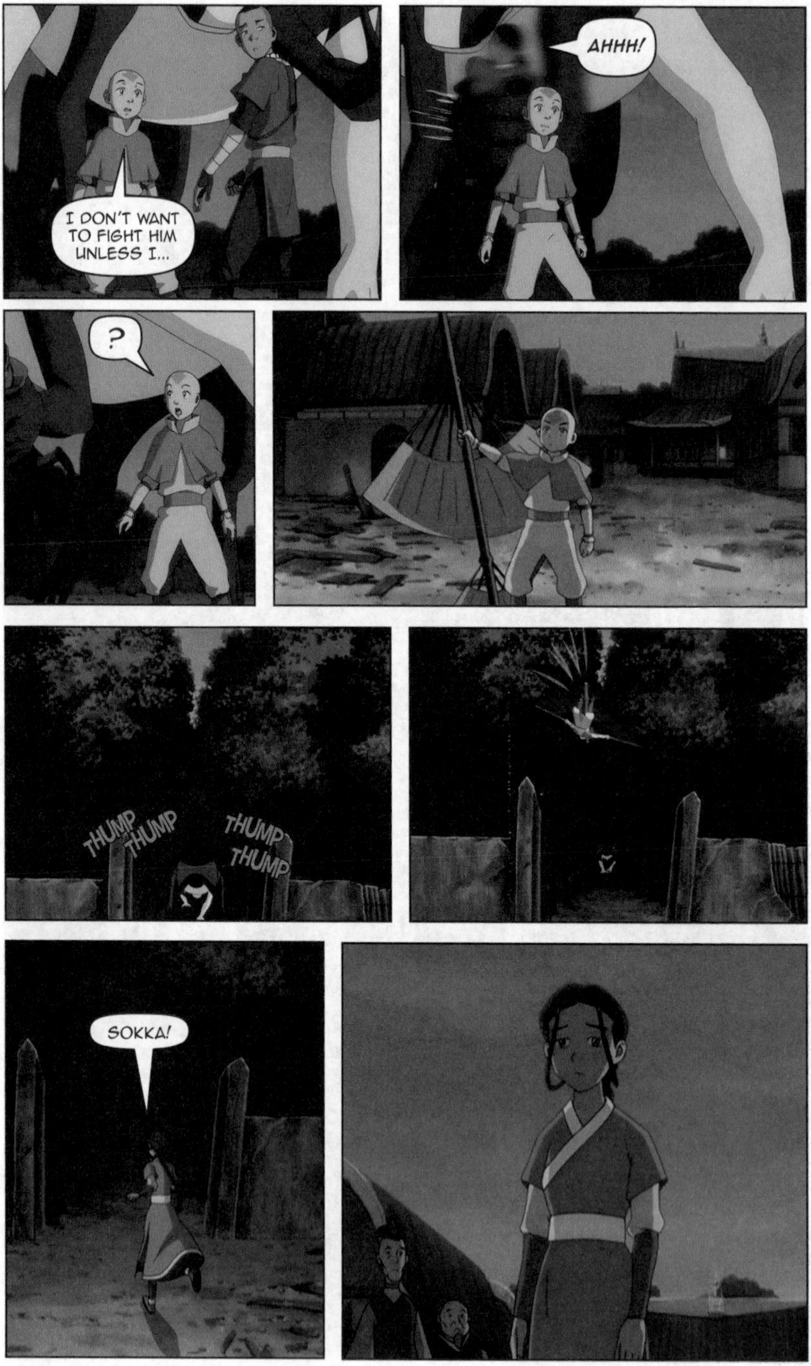
I DON'T WANT TO FIGHT HIM UNLESS I...
AHHH!
?
THUMP THUMP
THUMP THUMP
SOKKA!

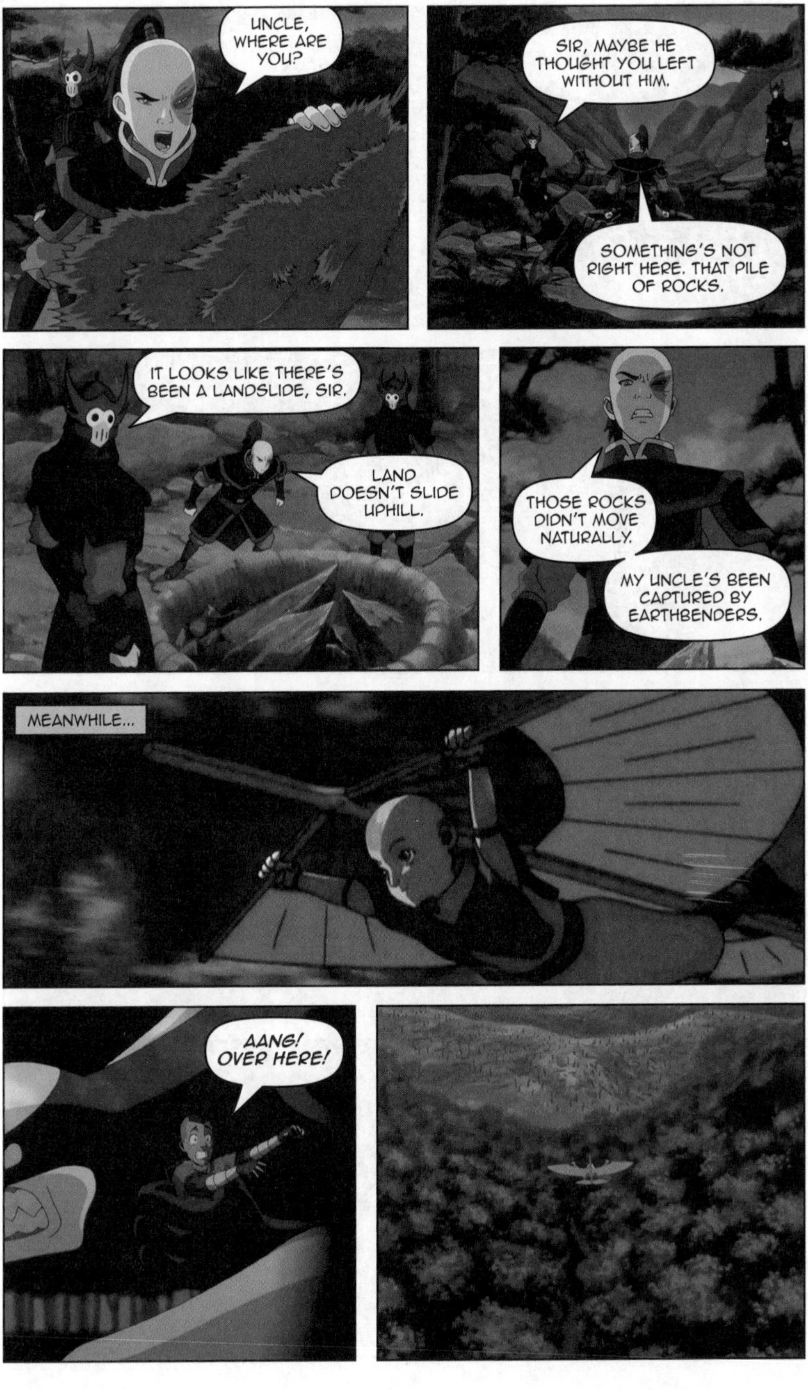
UNCLE, WHERE ARE YOU?
SIR, MAYBE HE THOUGHT YOU LEFT WITHOUT HIM.
SOMETHING'S NOT RIGHT HERE. THAT PILE OF ROCKS.
IT LOOKS LIKE THERE'S BEEN A LANDSLIDE, SIR.
LAND DOESN'T SLIDE UPHILL.
THOSE ROCKS DIDN'T MOVE NATURALLY.
MY UNCLE'S BEEN CAPTURED BY EARTHBENDERS.
MEANWHILE...
AANG! OVER HERE!

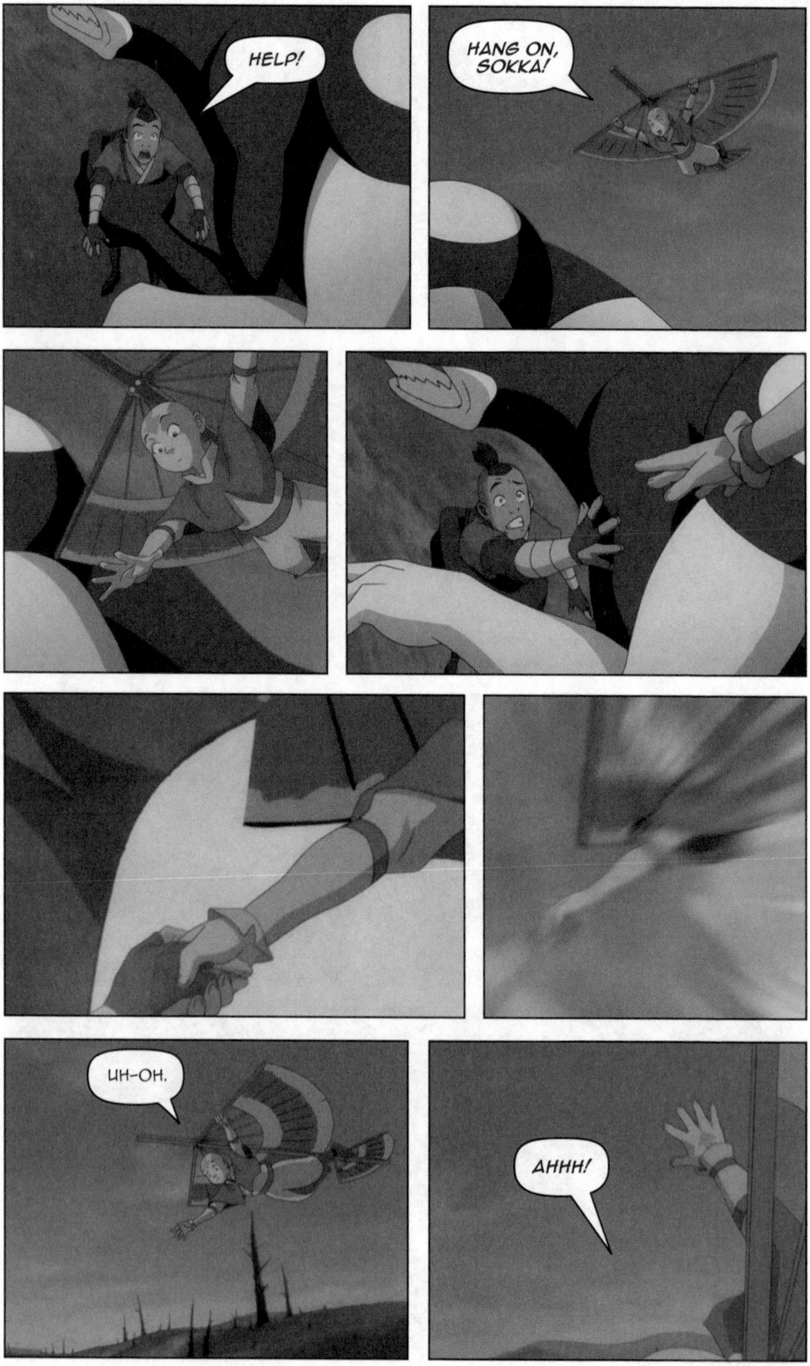
HELP!
HANG ON, SOKKA!
UH-OH.
AHHH!

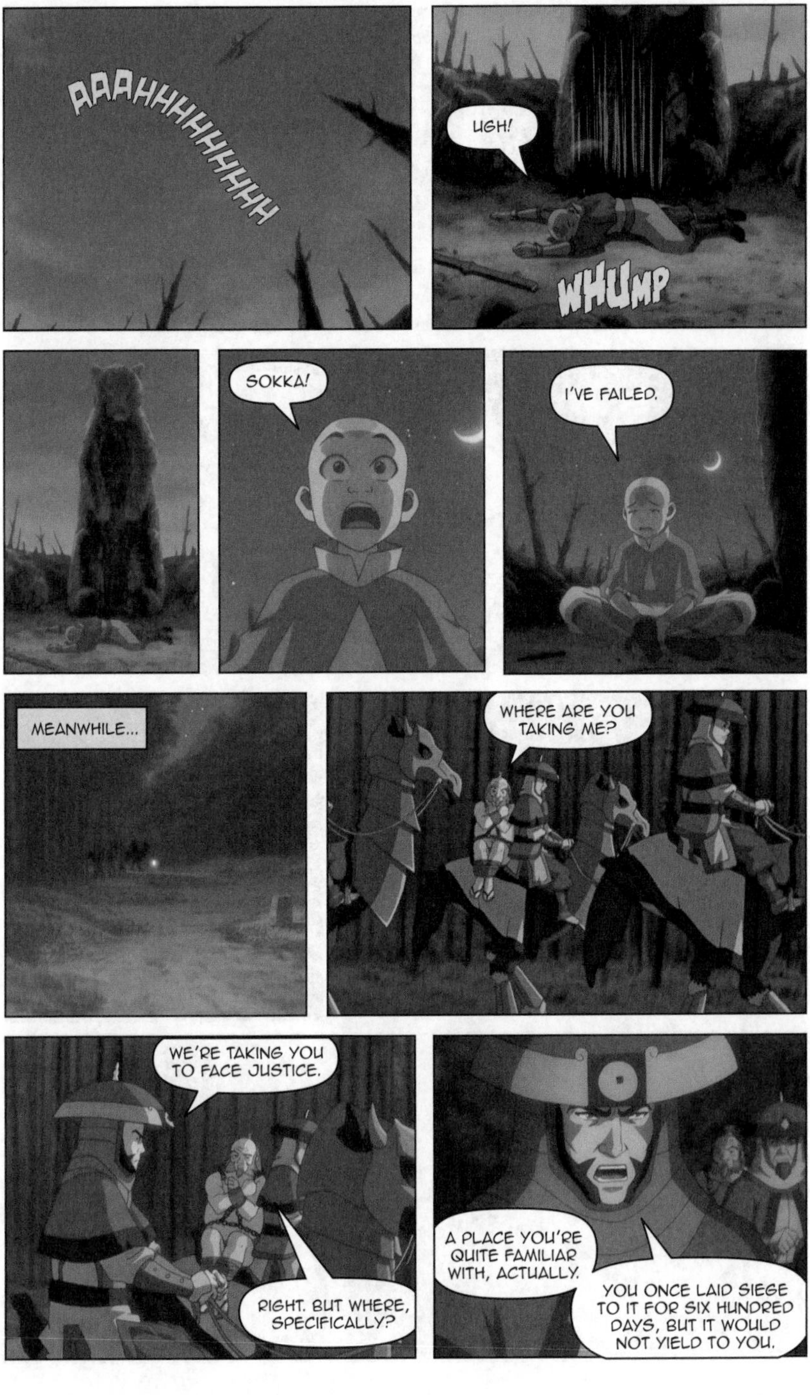
AAAHHHHHHHHHH
UGH!
WHUMP
SOKKA!
I'VE FAILED.
MEANWHILE...
WHERE ARE YOU TAKING ME?
WE'RE TAKING YOU TO FACE JUSTICE.
RIGHT. BUT WHERE, SPECIFICALLY?
A PLACE YOU'RE QUITE FAMILIAR WITH, ACTUALLY.
YOU ONCE LAID SIEGE TO IT FOR SIX HUNDRED DAYS, BUT IT WOULD NOT YIELD TO YOU.

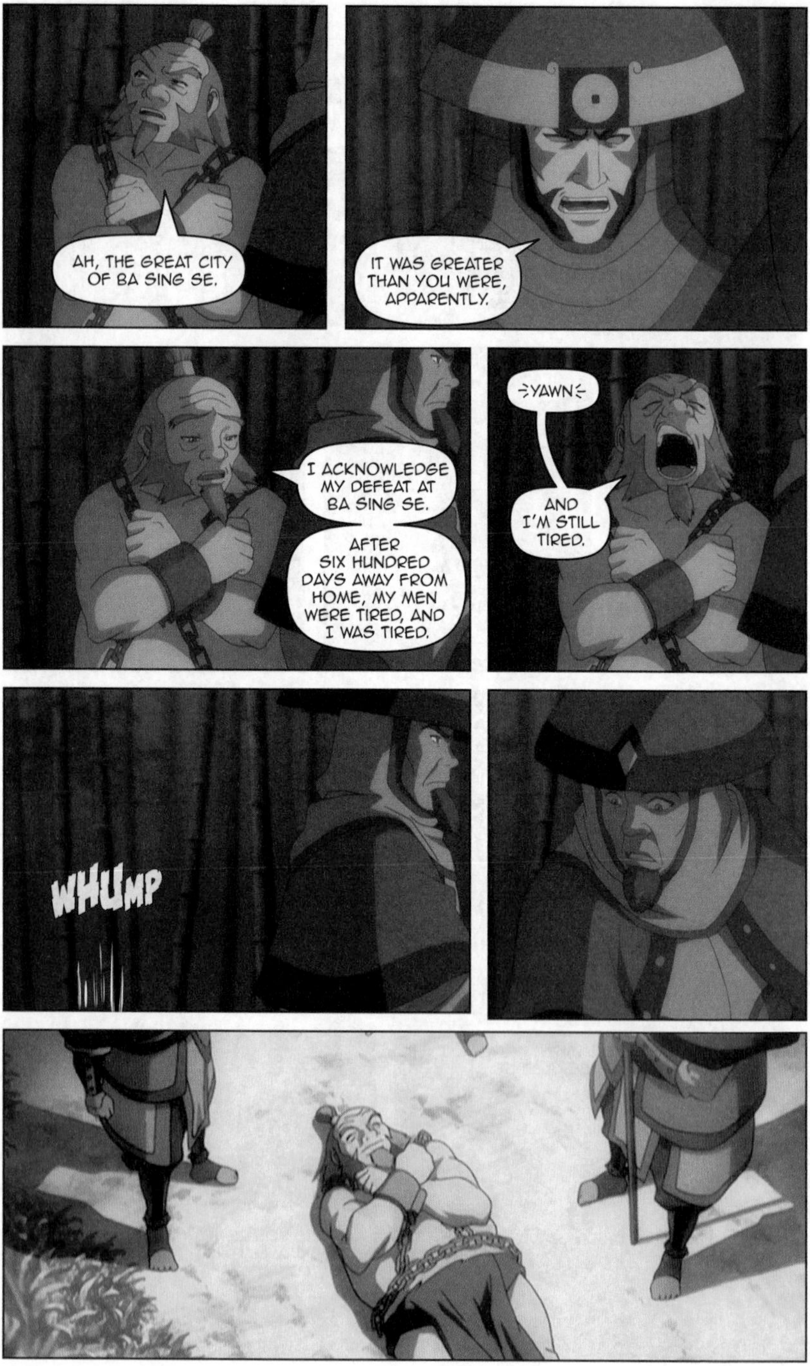
AH, THE GREAT CITY OF BA SING SE.
IT WAS GREATER THAN YOU WERE, APPARENTLY.
I ACKNOWLEDGE MY DEFEAT AT BA SING SE.
AFTER SIX HUNDRED DAYS AWAY FROM HOME, MY MEN WERE TIRED, AND I WAS TIRED.
YAWN
AND I'M STILL TIRED.
WHUMP

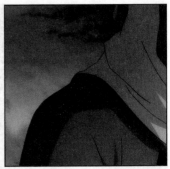

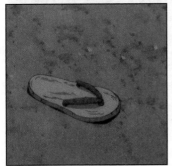

I'M SURE THEY'LL BE BACK.

I KNOW.

YOU SHOULD GET SOME REST.

EVERYTHING'S GONNA BE OKAY.

YOUR BROTHER IS IN GOOD HANDS.

I WOULD BE SHOCKED IF THE AVATAR RETURNED WITHOUT HIM.

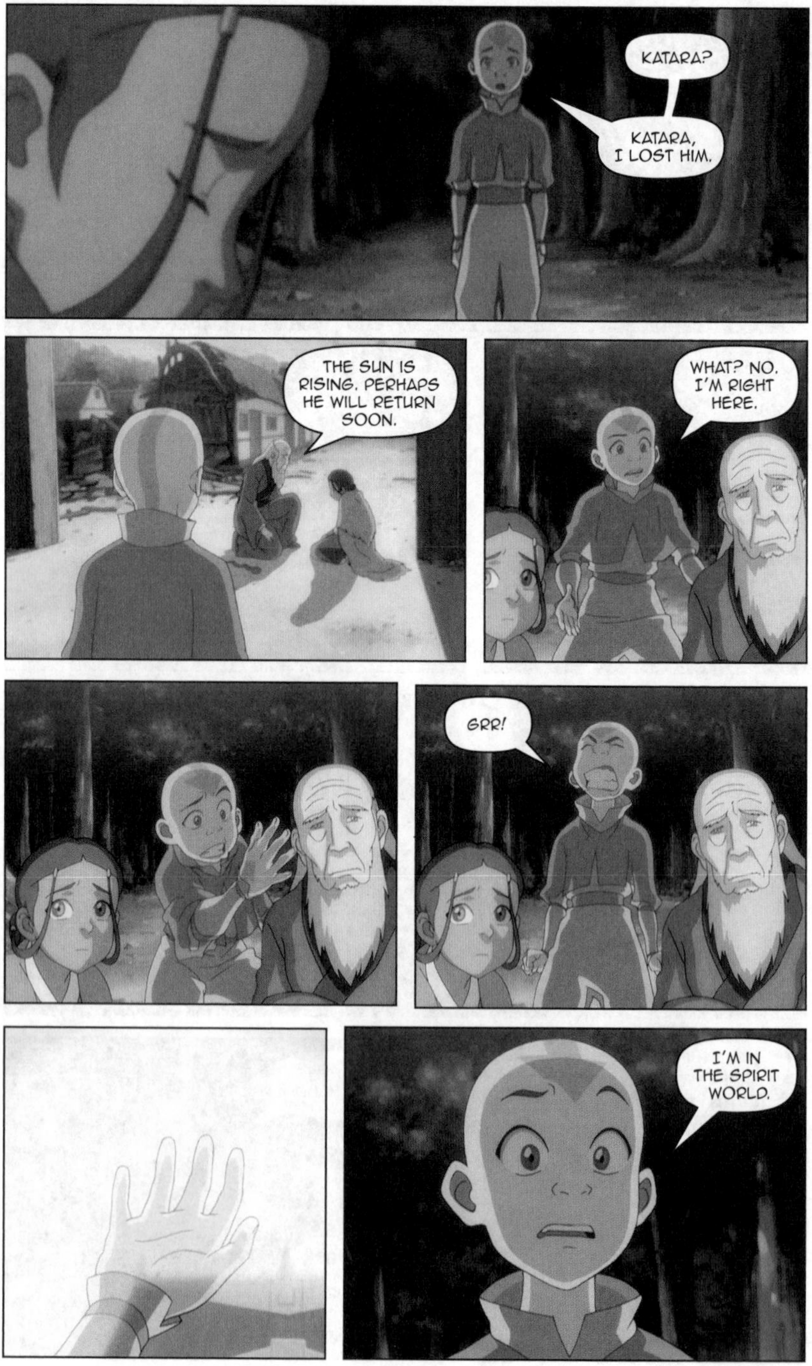
KATARA?
KATARA, I LOST HIM.
THE SUN IS RISING. PERHAPS HE WILL RETURN SOON.
WHAT? NO. I'M RIGHT HERE.
GRR!
I'M IN THE SPIRIT WORLD.

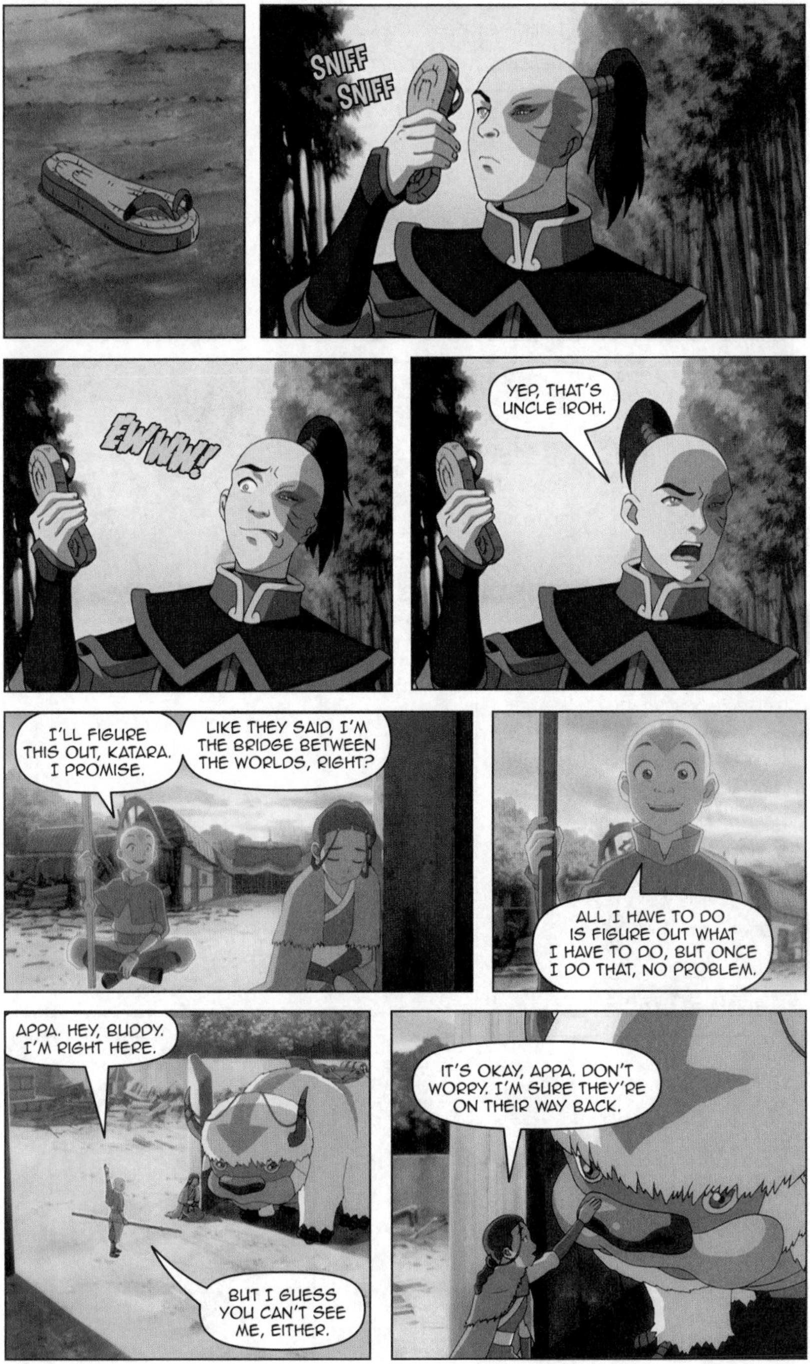
SNIFF
SNIFF
EWWW!
YEP, THAT'S UNCLE IROH.
I'LL FIGURE THIS OUT, KATARA. I PROMISE.
LIKE THEY SAID, I'M THE BRIDGE BETWEEN THE WORLDS, RIGHT?
ALL I HAVE TO DO IS FIGURE OUT WHAT I HAVE TO DO, BUT ONCE I DO THAT, NO PROBLEM.
APPA. HEY, BUDDY. I'M RIGHT HERE.
BUT I GUESS YOU CAN'T SEE ME, EITHER.
IT'S OKAY, APPA. DON'T WORRY. I'M SURE THEY'RE ON THEIR WAY BACK.

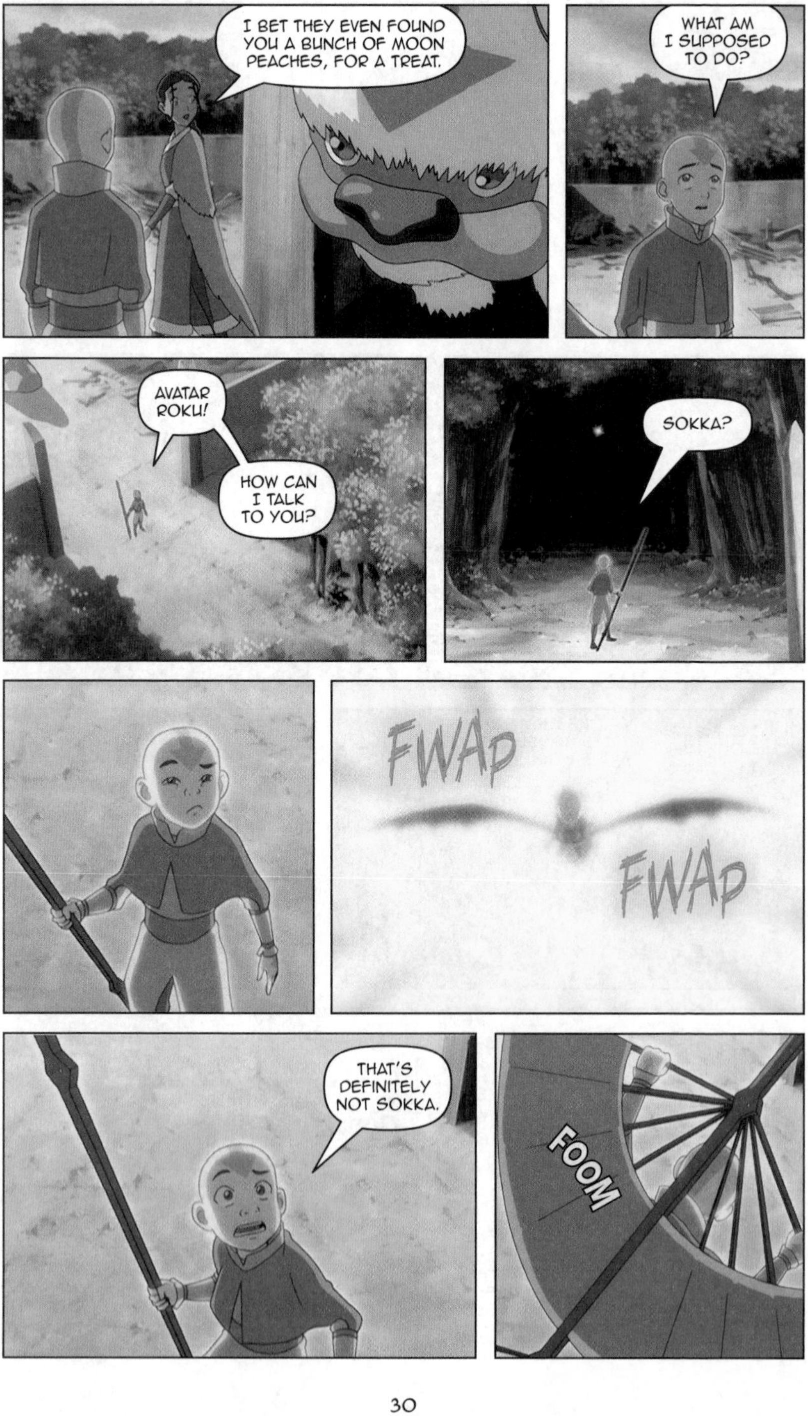
I BET THEY EVEN FOUND YOU A BUNCH OF MOON PEACHES, FOR A TREAT.
WHAT AM I SUPPOSED TO DO?
AVATAR ROKU!
HOW CAN I TALK TO YOU?
SOKKA?
FWAP
FWAP
THAT'S DEFINITELY NOT SOKKA.
FOOM

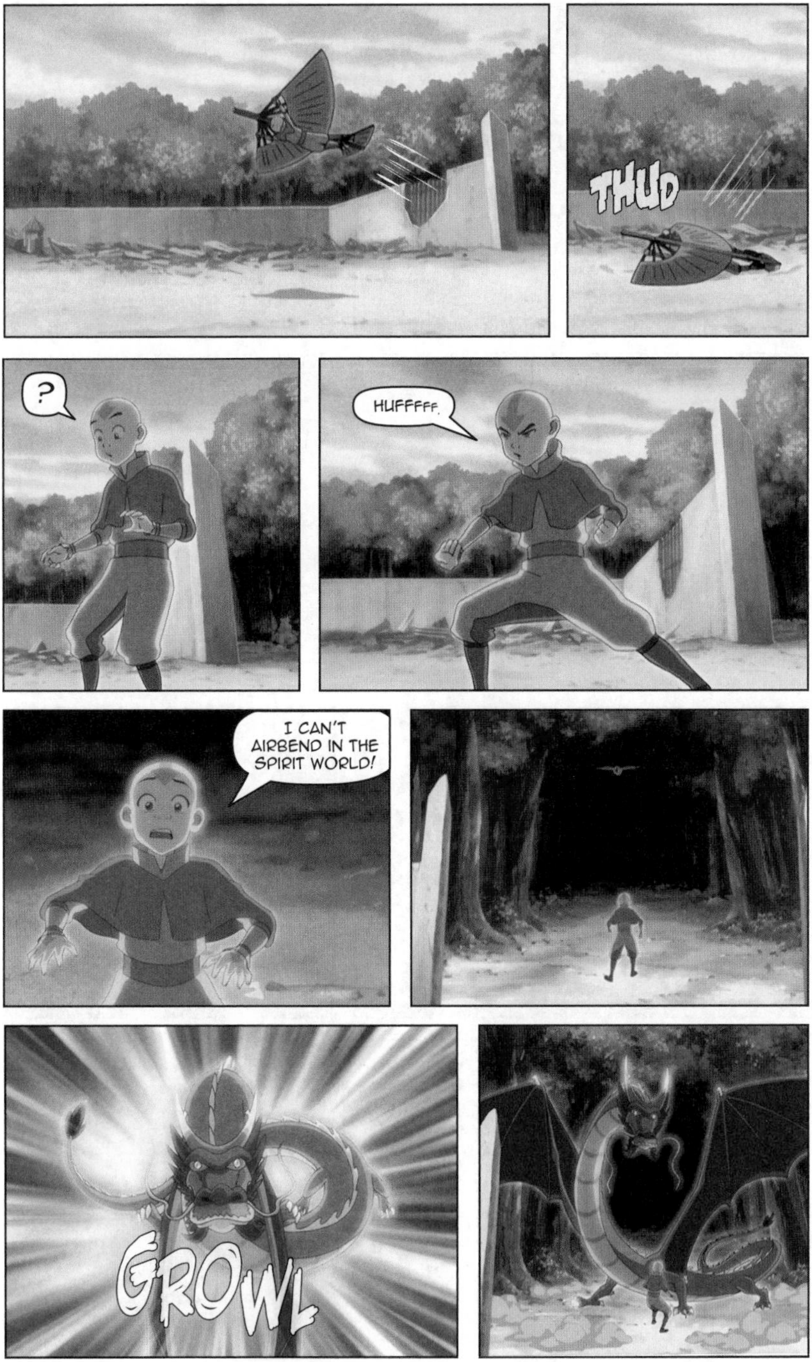
THUD
?
HUFFFFF.
I CAN'T AIRBEND IN THE SPIRIT WORLD!
GROWL

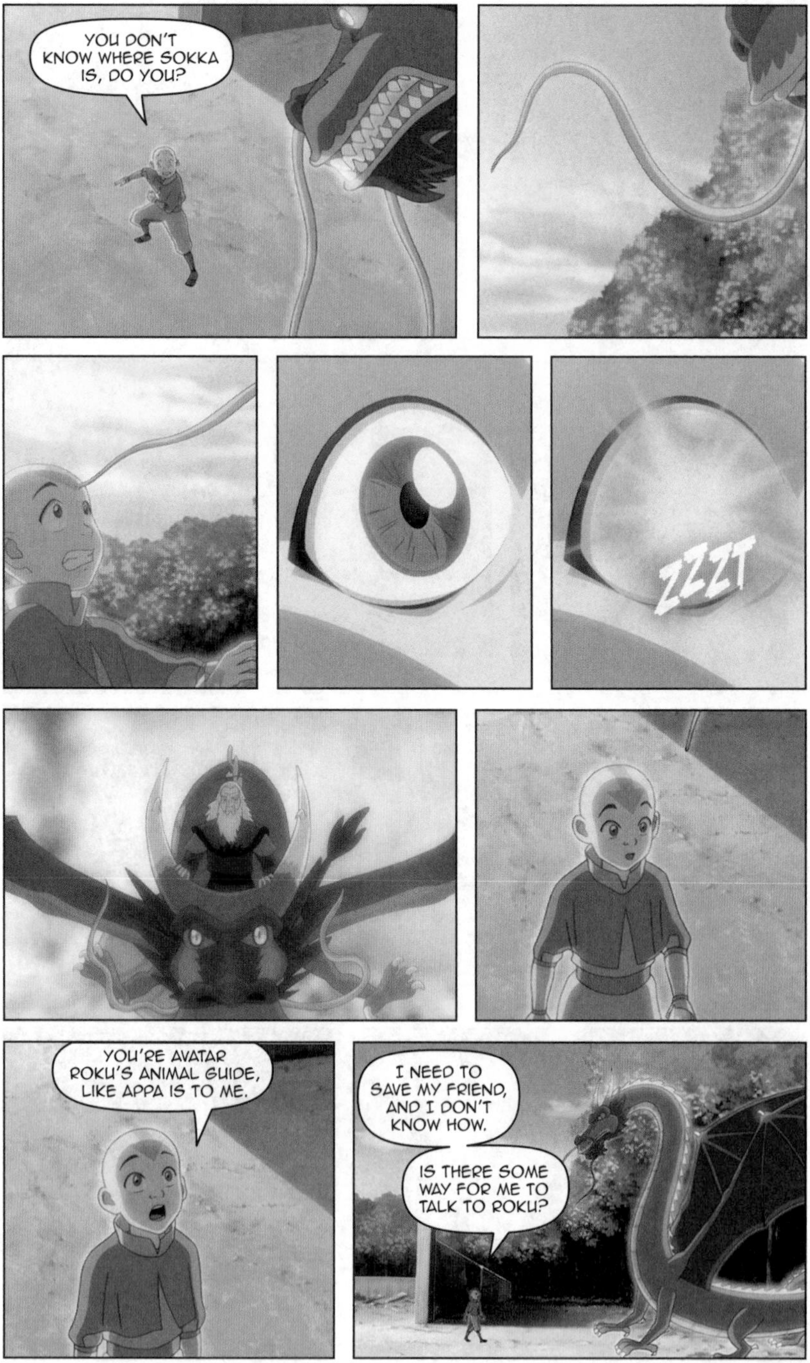
YOU DON'T KNOW WHERE SOKKA IS, DO YOU?
ZZZT
YOU'RE AVATAR ROKU'S ANIMAL GUIDE, LIKE APPA IS TO ME.
I NEED TO SAVE MY FRIEND, AND I DON'T KNOW HOW.
IS THERE SOME WAY FOR ME TO TALK TO ROKU?

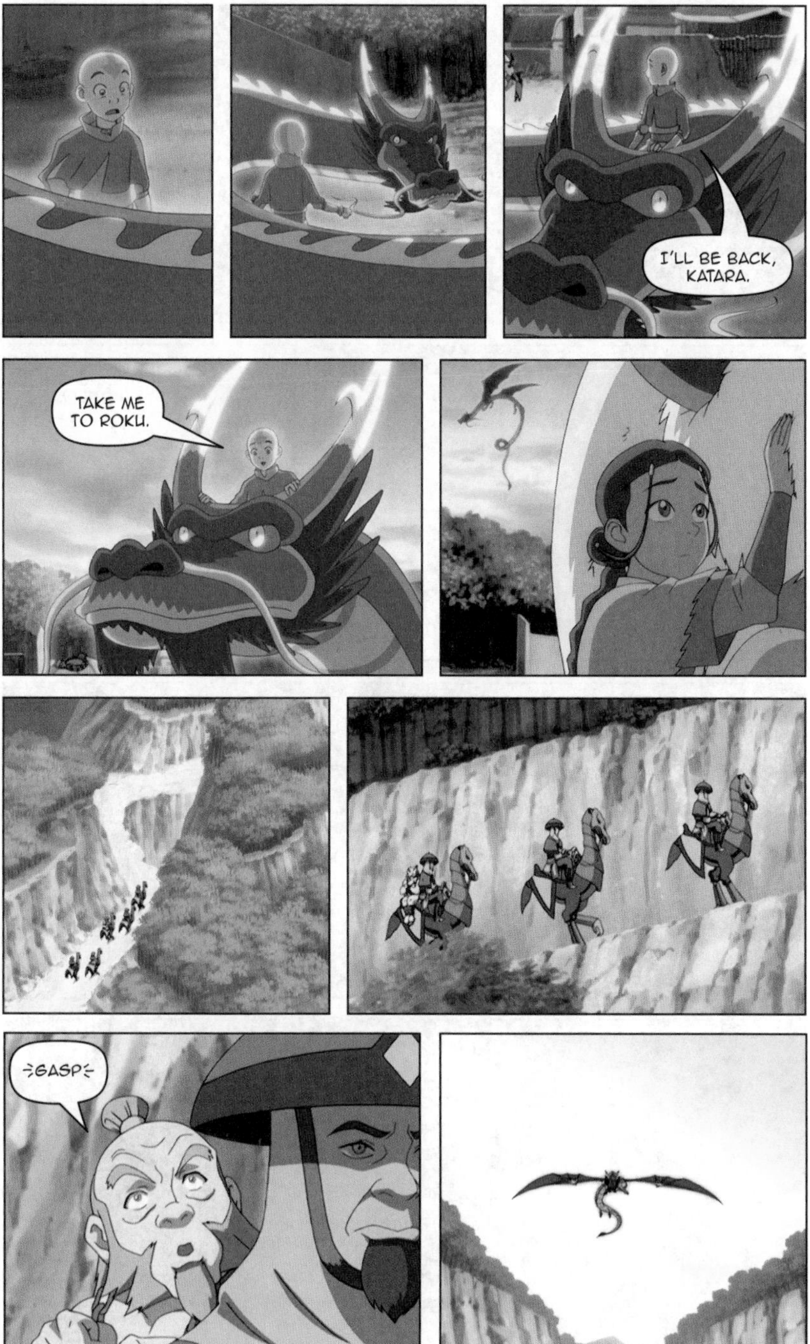
I'LL BE BACK, KATARA.
TAKE ME TO ROKU.
⇒GASP⇐

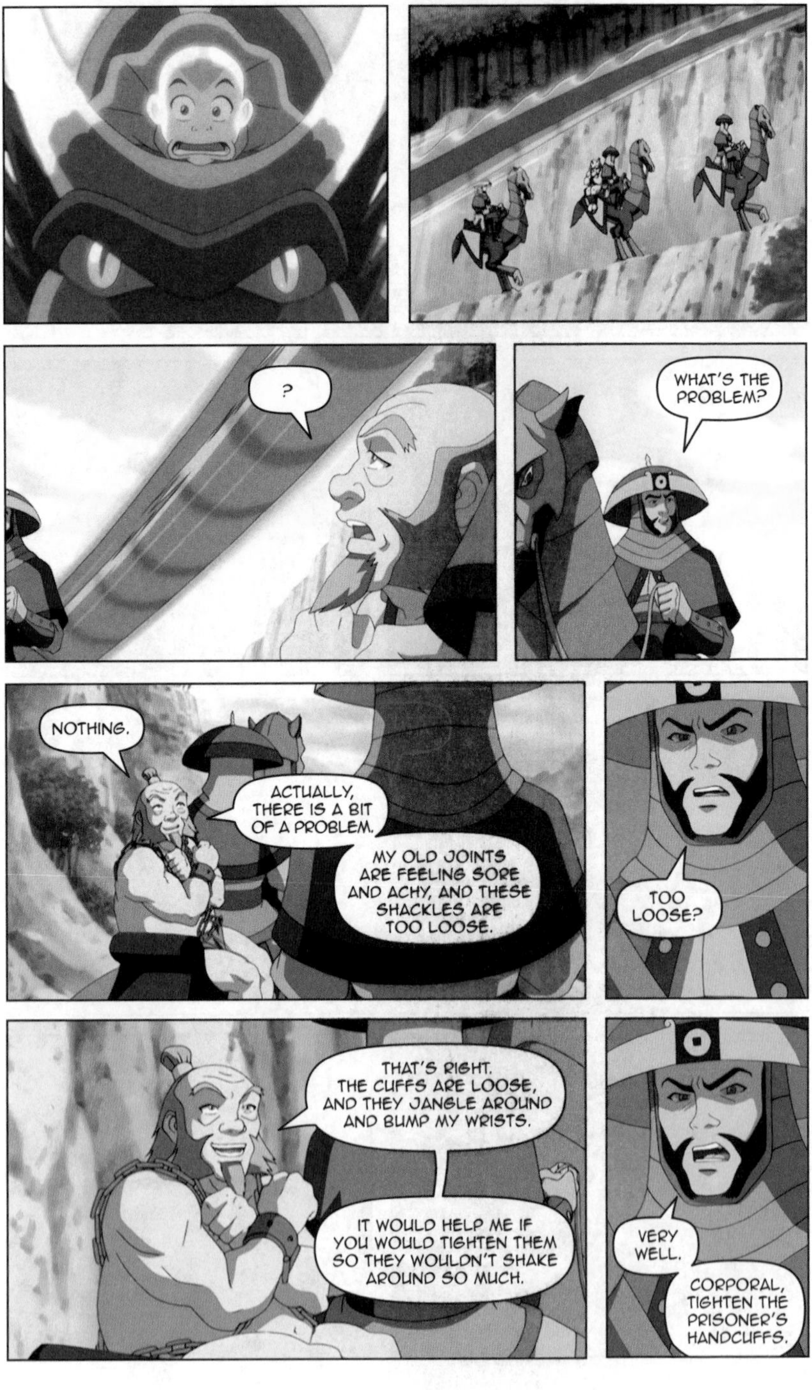

?
WHAT'S THE PROBLEM?
NOTHING.
ACTUALLY, THERE IS A BIT OF A PROBLEM.
MY OLD JOINTS ARE FEELING SORE AND ACHY, AND THESE SHACKLES ARE TOO LOOSE.
TOO LOOSE?
THAT'S RIGHT. THE CUFFS ARE LOOSE, AND THEY JANGLE AROUND AND BUMP MY WRISTS.
IT WOULD HELP ME IF YOU WOULD TIGHTEN THEM SO THEY WOULDN'T SHAKE AROUND SO MUCH.
VERY WELL.
CORPORAL, TIGHTEN THE PRISONER'S HANDCUFFS.

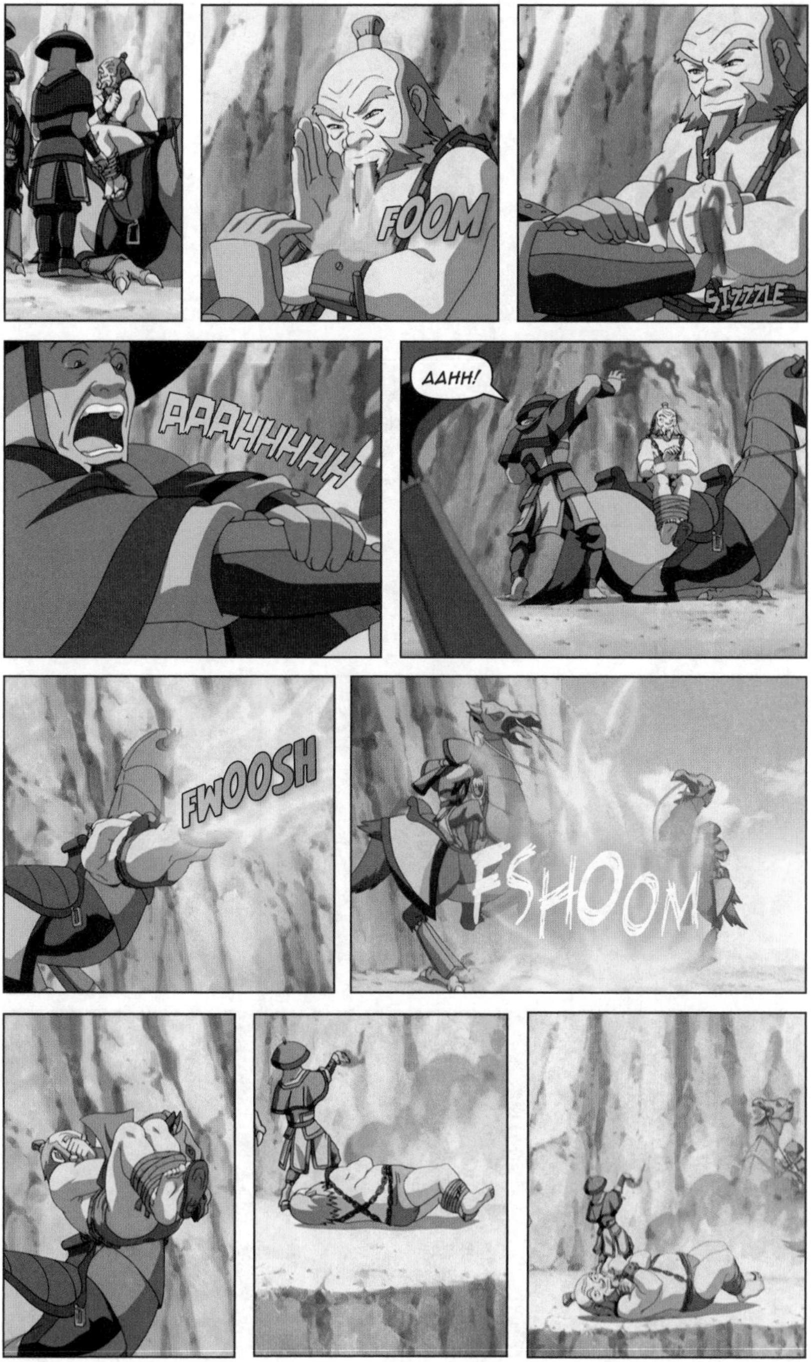
FOOM
SIZZZLE
AAAHHHHHH
AAHH!
FWOOSH
FSHOOM

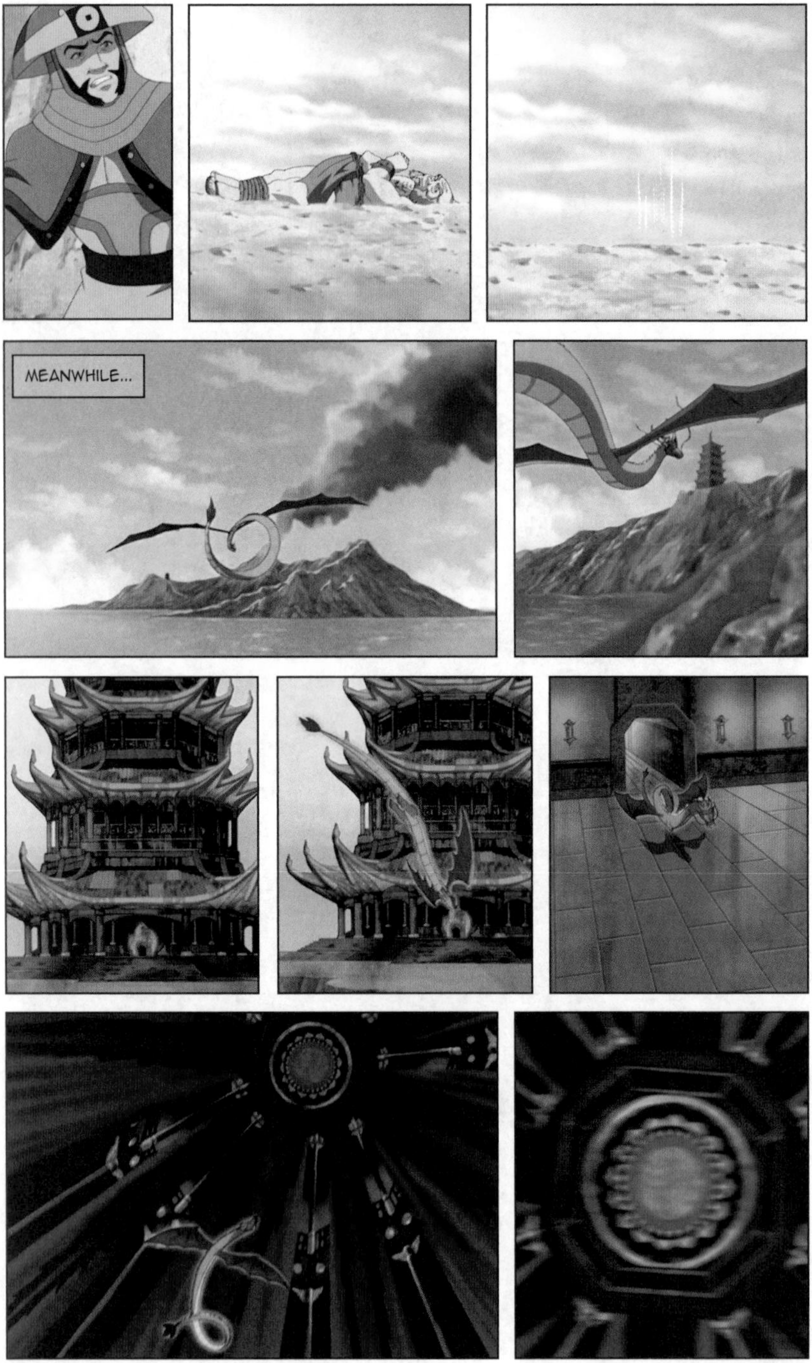
MEANWHILE...

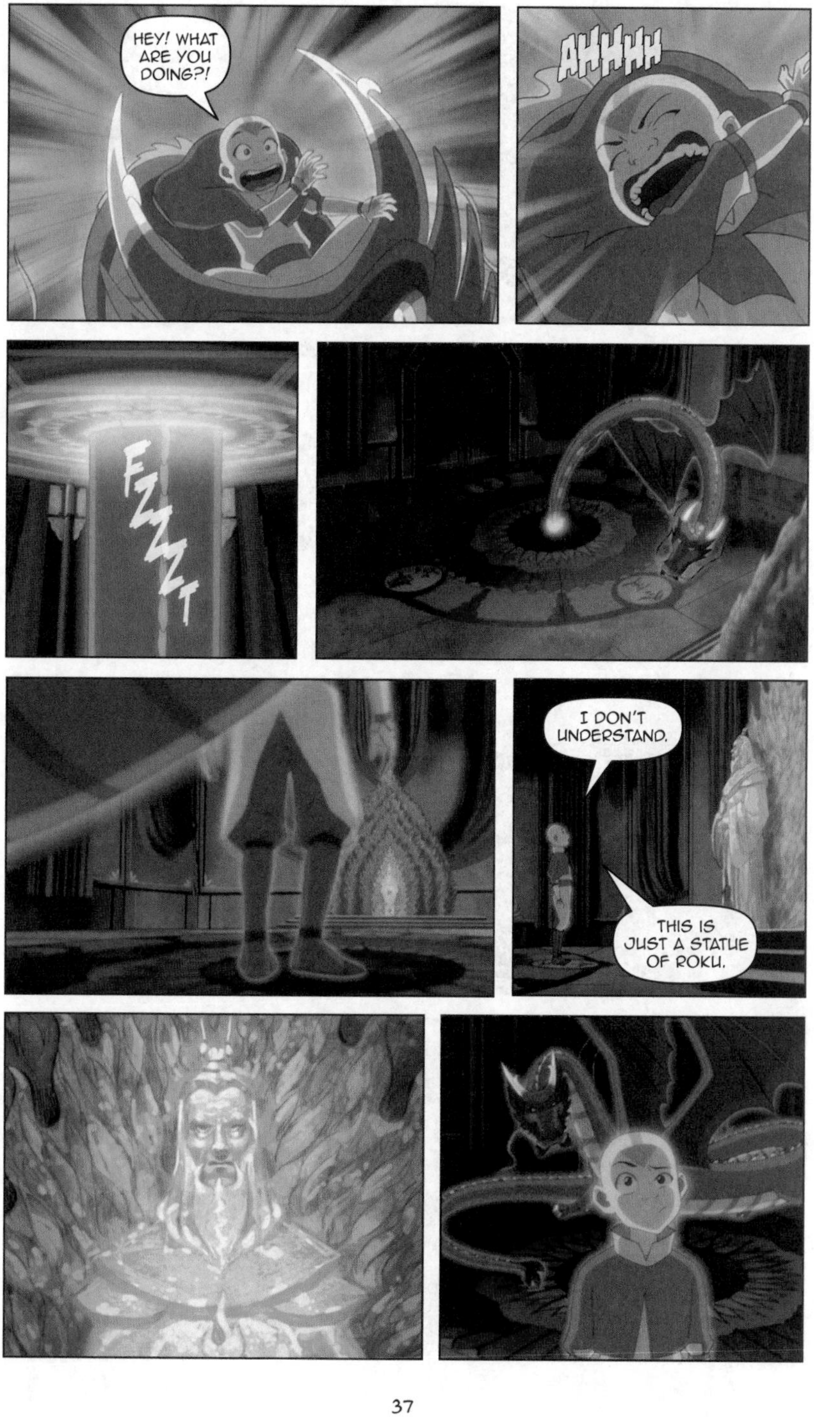
HEY! WHAT ARE YOU DOING?!
AHHHH
FZZZT
I DON'T UNDERSTAND.
THIS IS JUST A STATUE OF ROKU.

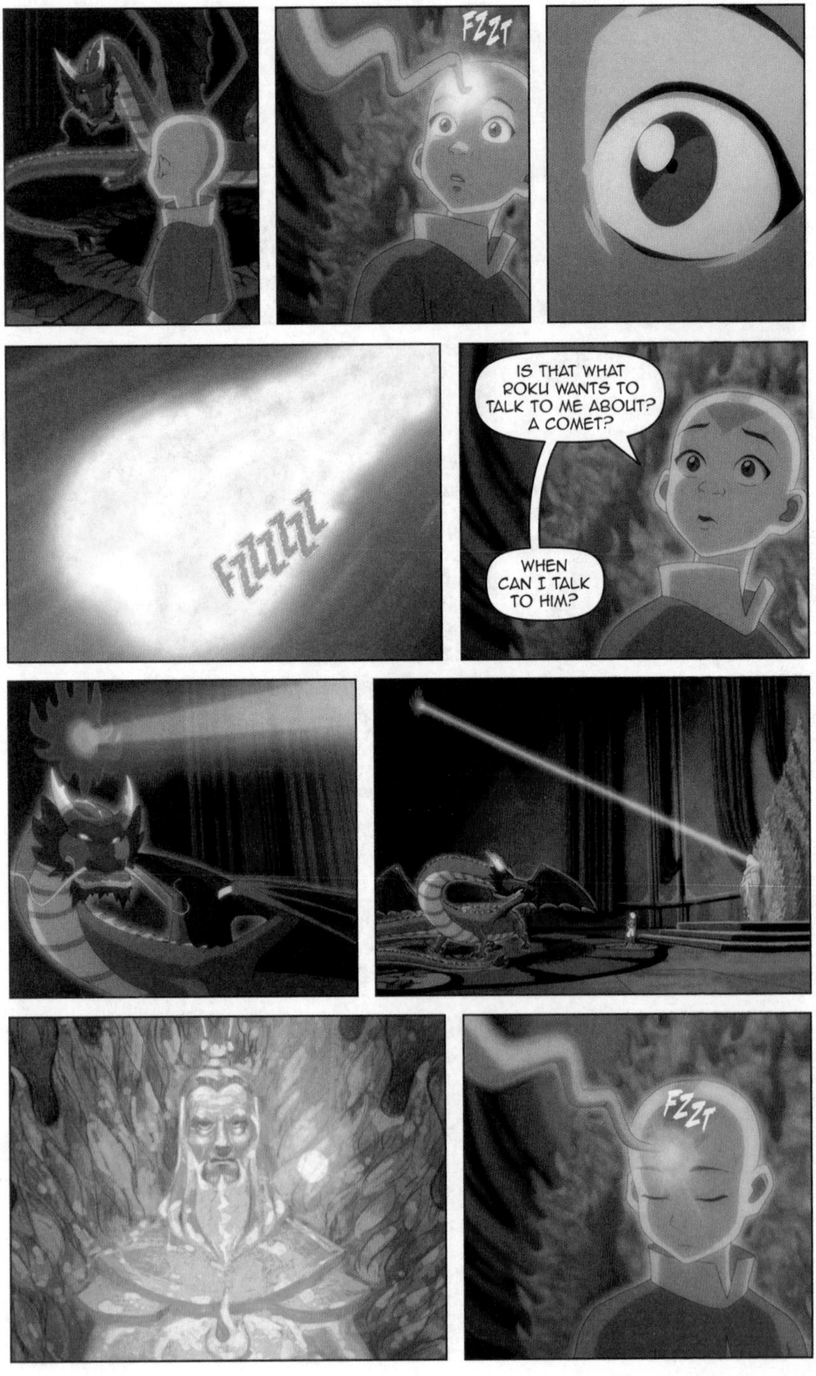
FZZT
IS THAT WHAT ROKU WANTS TO TALK TO ME ABOUT? A COMET?
WHEN CAN I TALK TO HIM?
FZZT

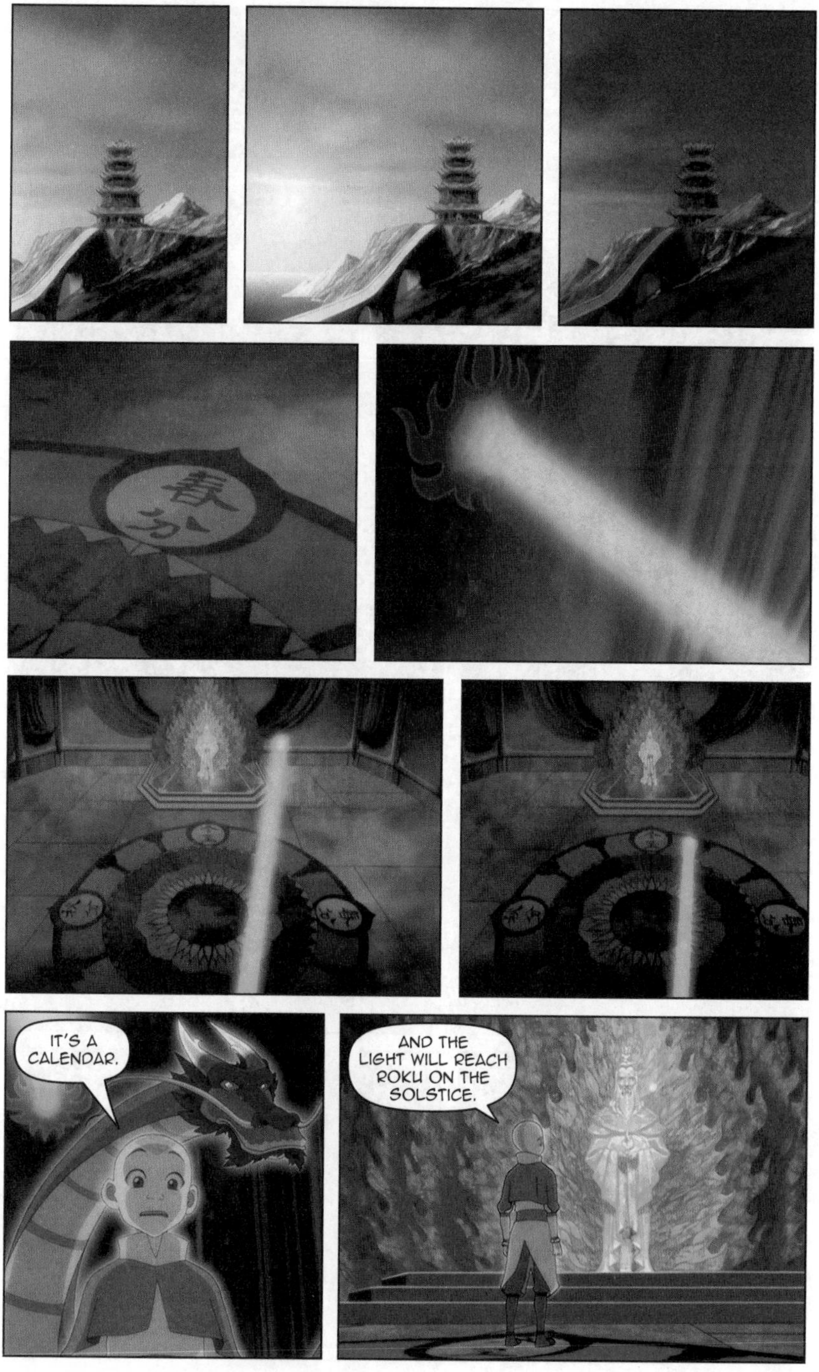
IT'S A CALENDAR.
AND THE LIGHT WILL REACH ROKU ON THE SOLSTICE.

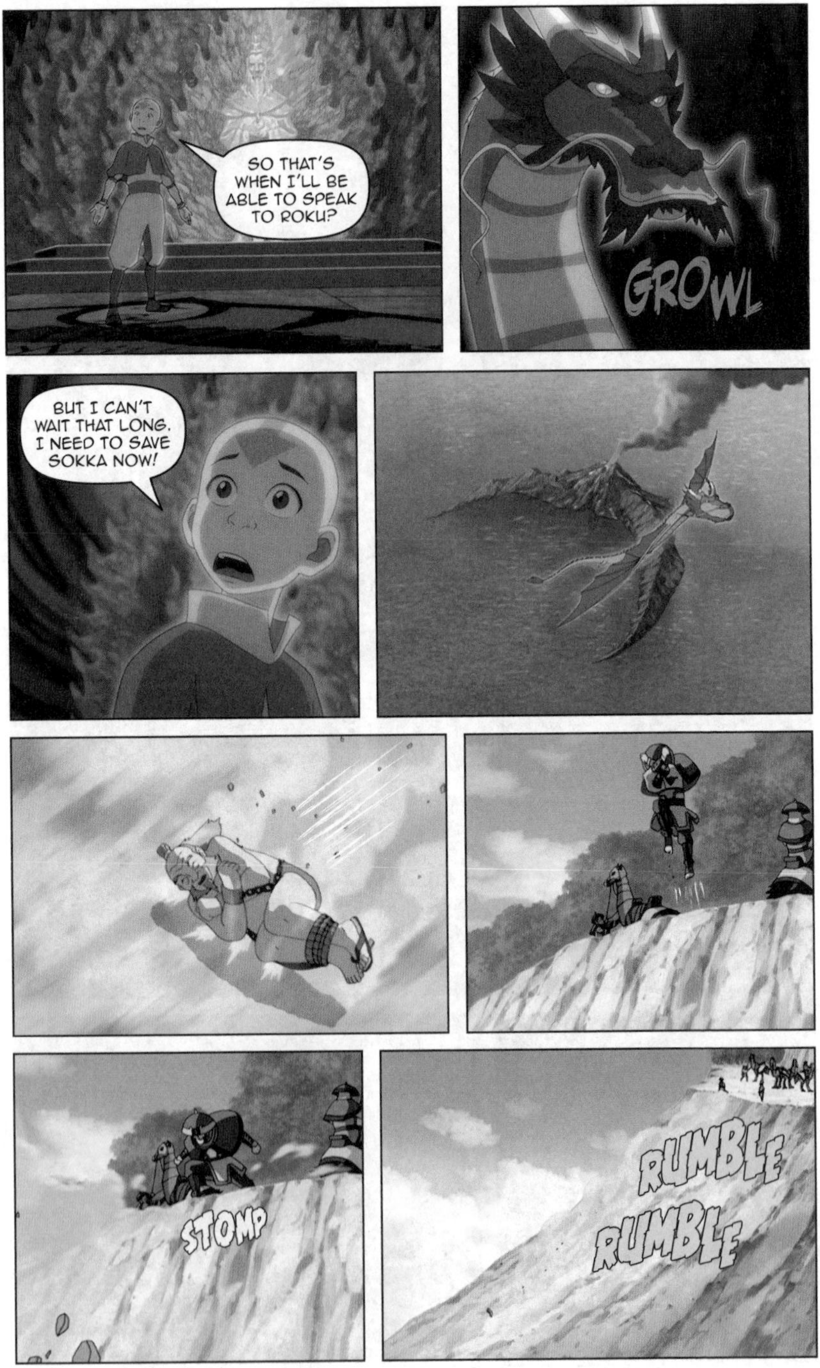
SO THAT'S WHEN I'LL BE ABLE TO SPEAK TO ROKU?
GROWL
BUT I CAN'T WAIT THAT LONG. I NEED TO SAVE SOKKA NOW!
STOMP
RUMBLE
RUMBLE

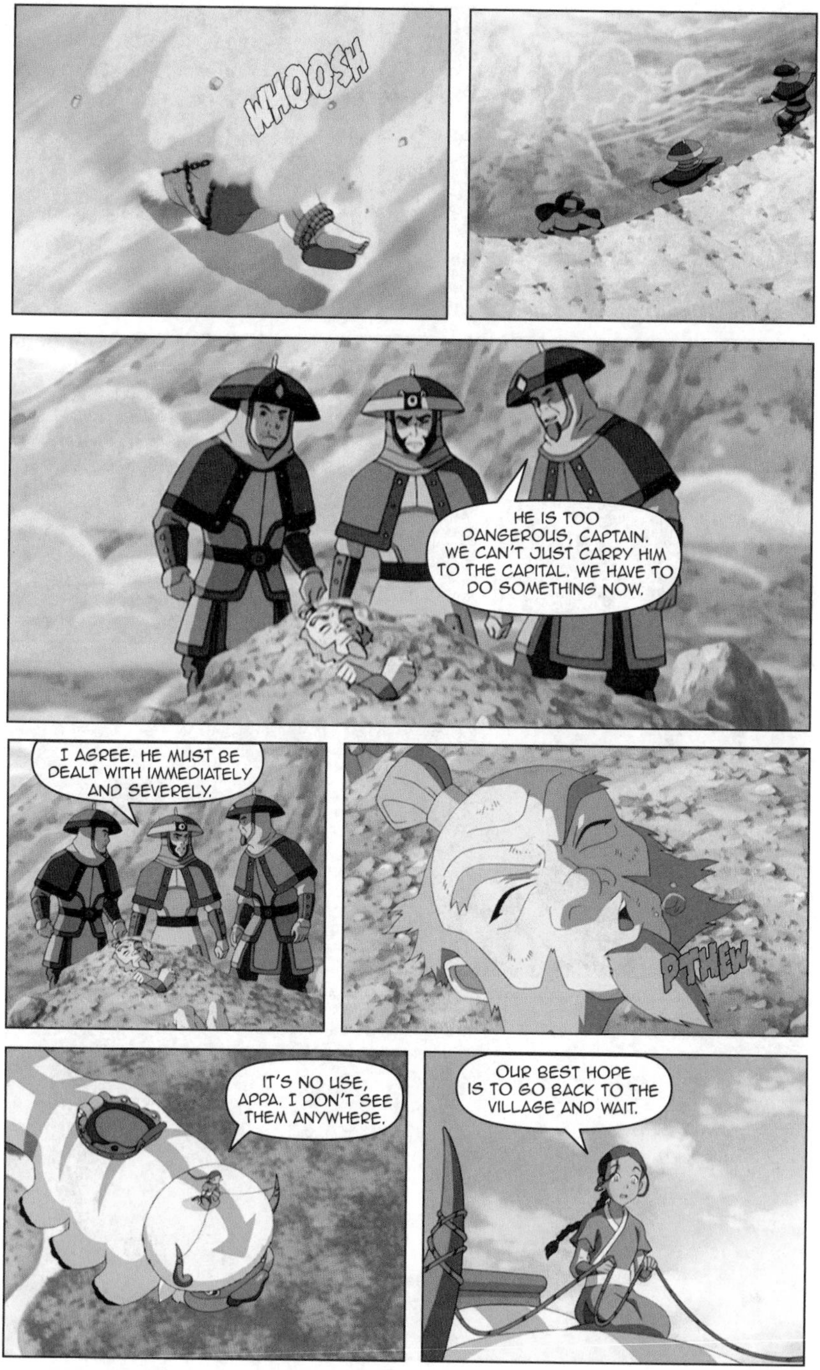
WHOOSH
HE IS TOO DANGEROUS, CAPTAIN. WE CAN'T JUST CARRY HIM TO THE CAPITAL. WE HAVE TO DO SOMETHING NOW.
I AGREE. HE MUST BE DEALT WITH IMMEDIATELY AND SEVERELY.
PTHEW
IT'S NO USE, APPA. I DON'T SEE THEM ANYWHERE.
OUR BEST HOPE IS TO GO BACK TO THE VILLAGE AND WAIT.

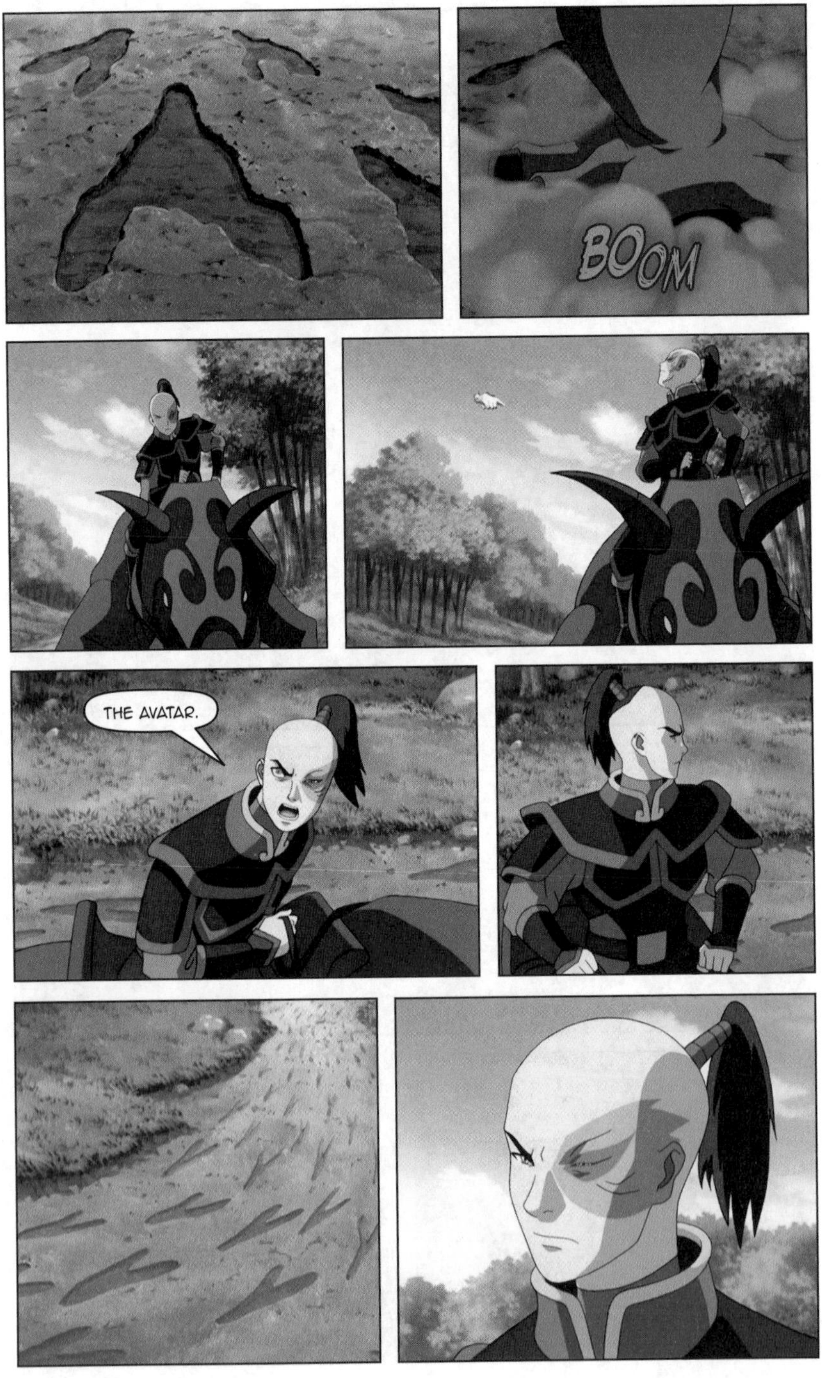
BOOM
THE AVATAR.

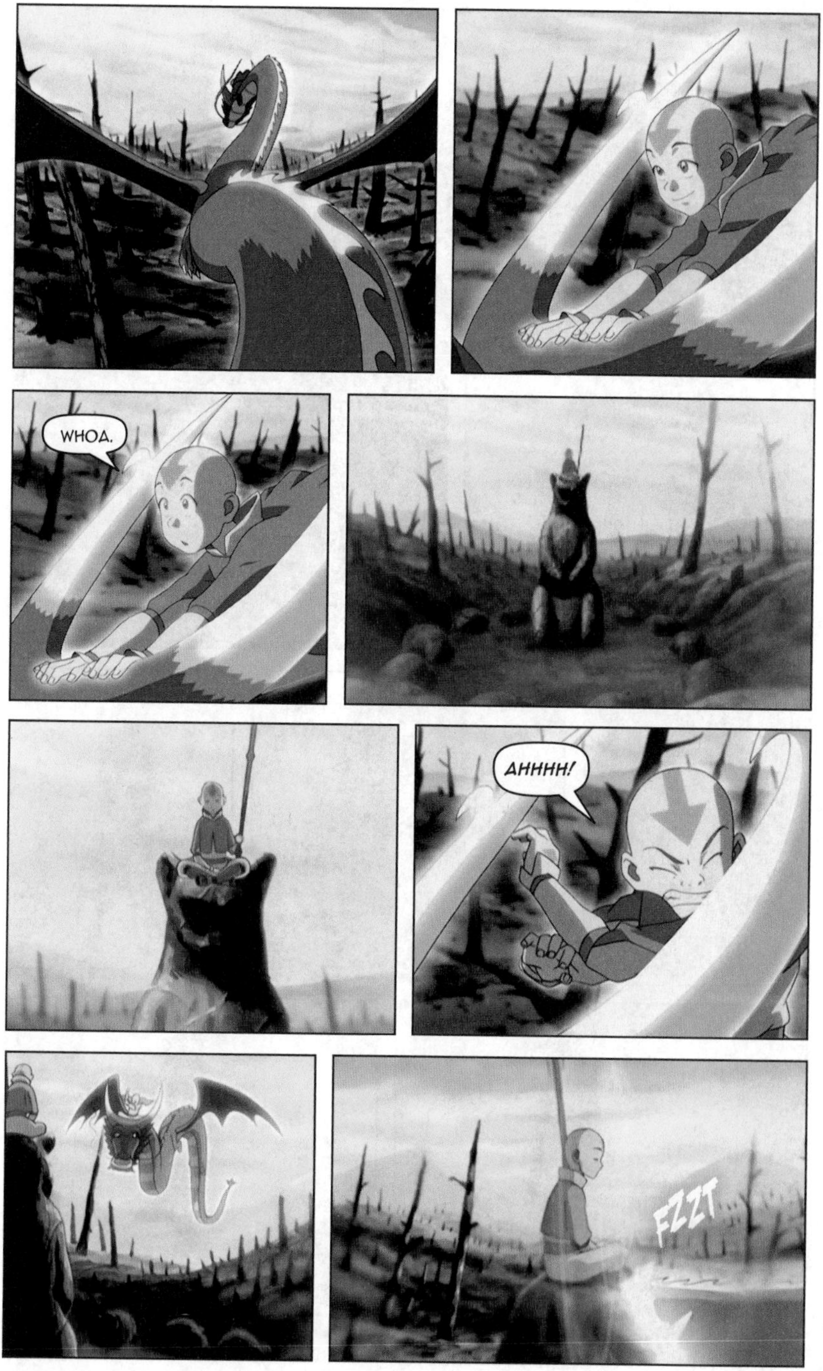
WHOA.
AHHHH!
FZZT

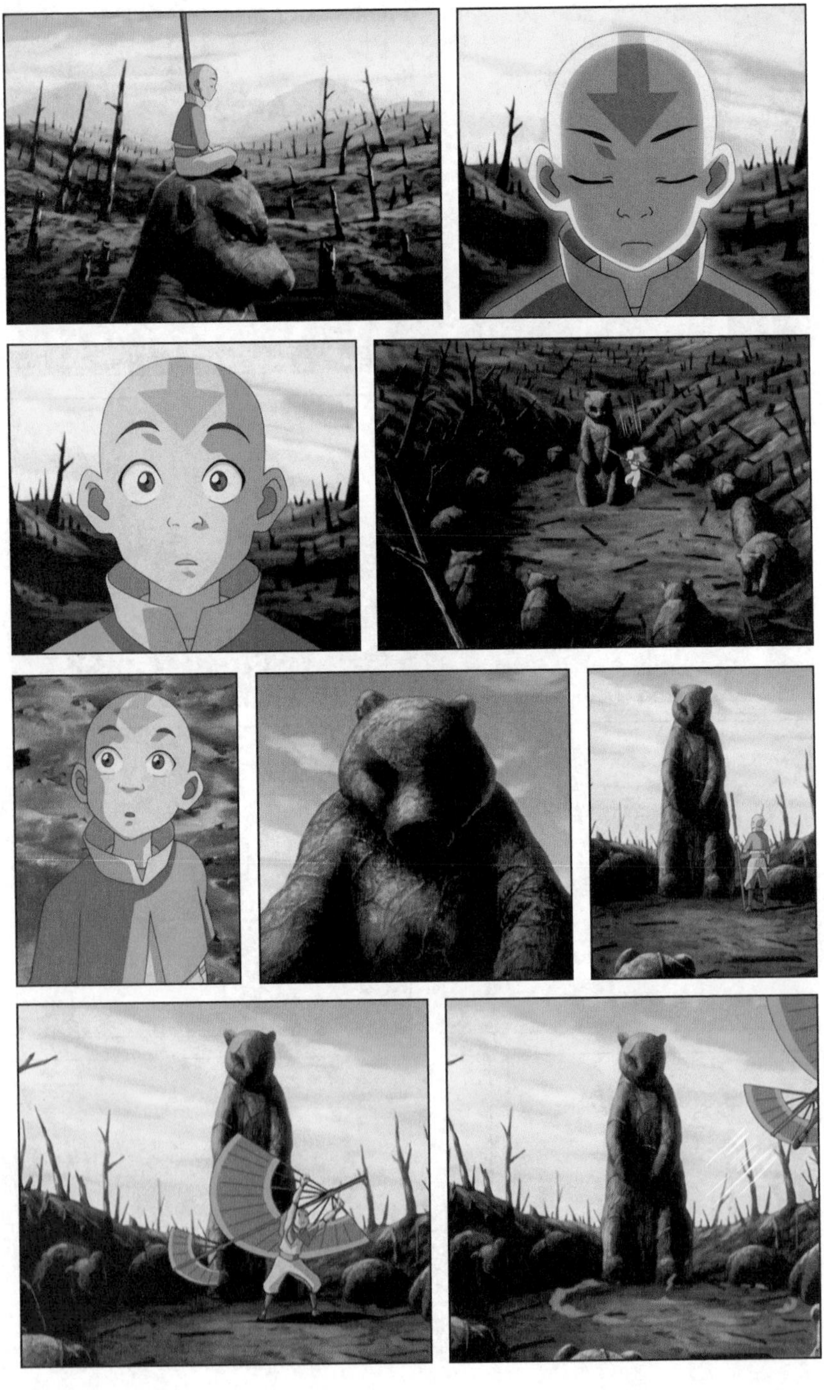

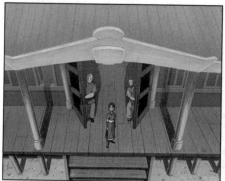

YOU'RE BACK!

WHERE'S SOKKA?

I'M NOT SURE.

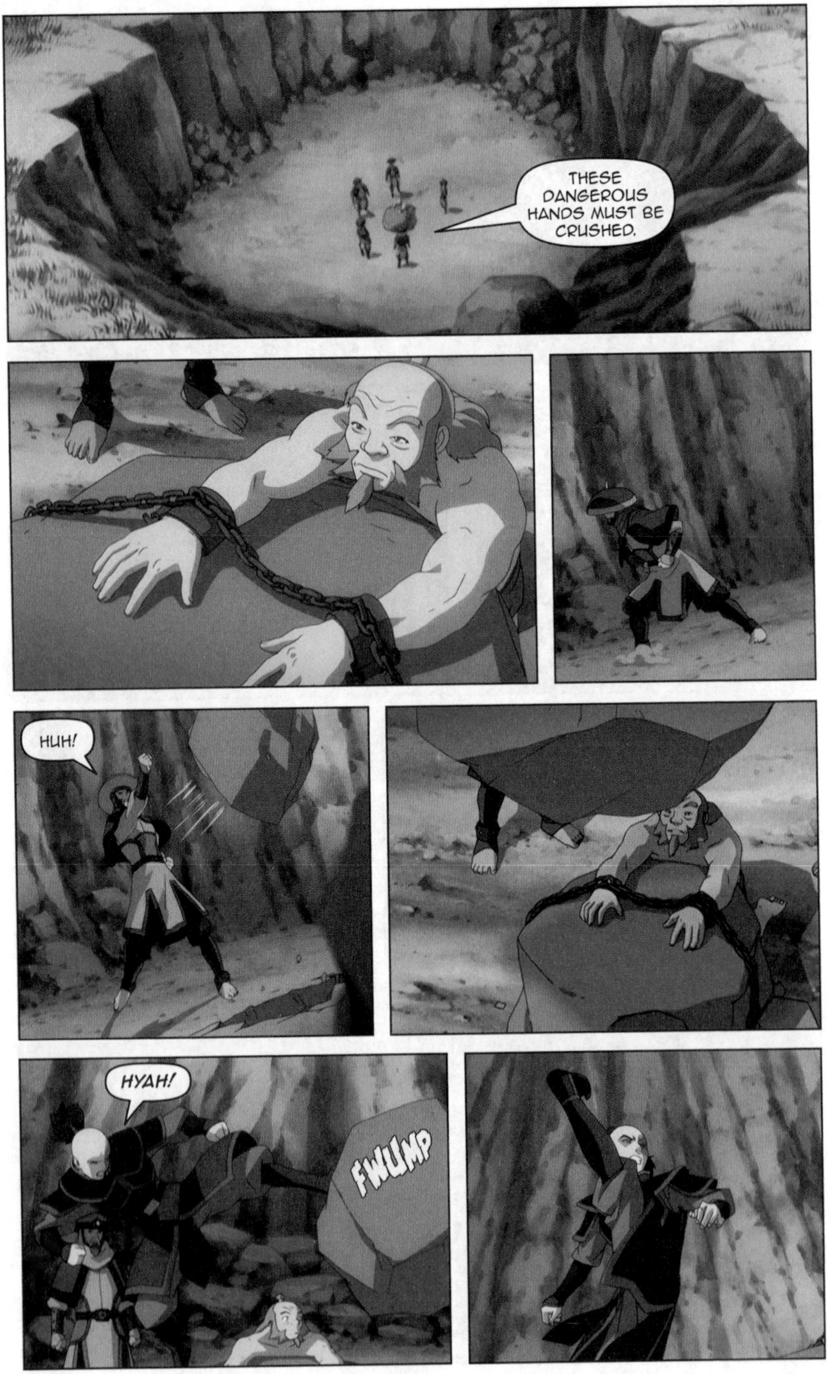
THESE DANGEROUS HANDS MUST BE CRUSHED.
HUH!
HYAH!
FWUMP

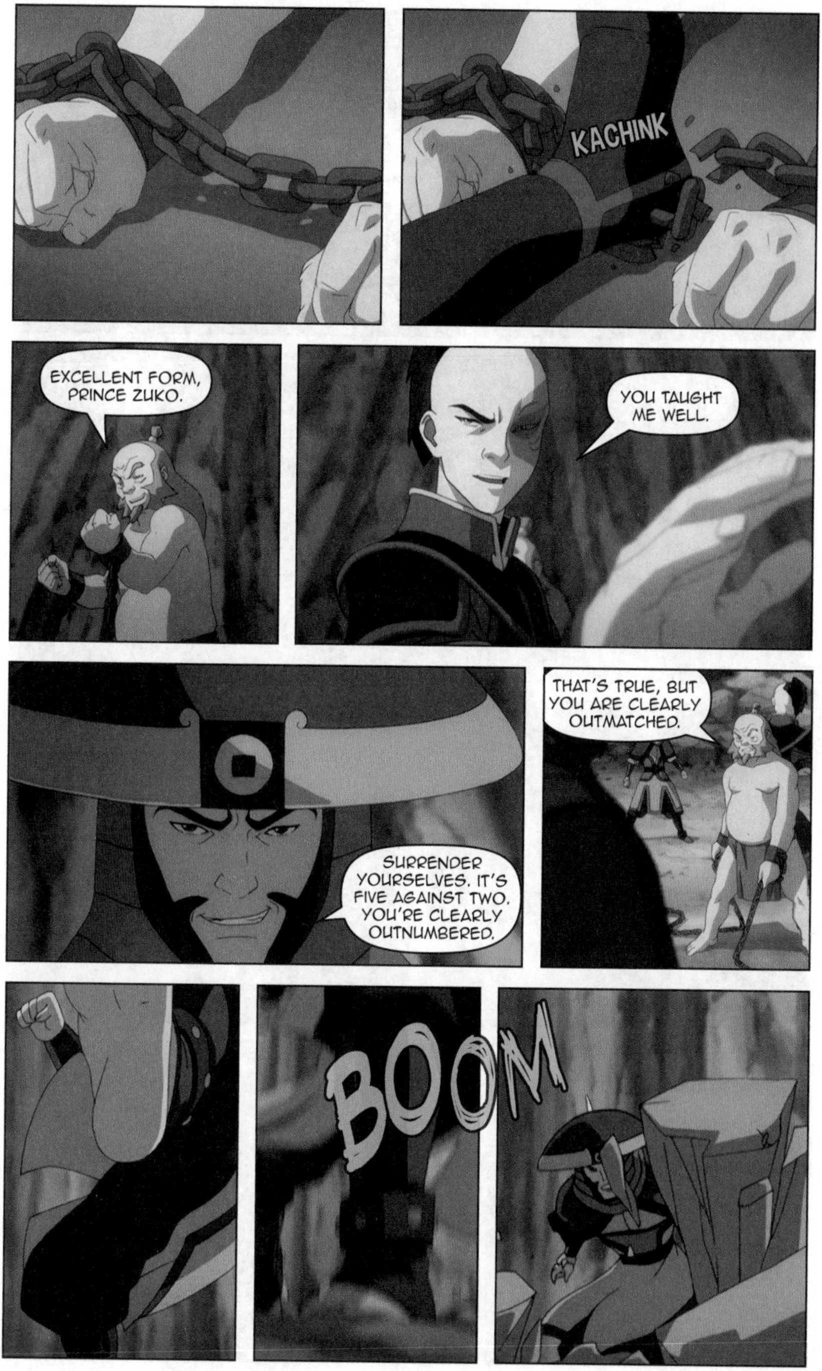
KACHINK
EXCELLENT FORM, PRINCE ZUKO.
YOU TAUGHT ME WELL.
SURRENDER YOURSELVES. IT'S FIVE AGAINST TWO. YOU'RE CLEARLY OUTNUMBERED.
THAT'S TRUE, BUT YOU ARE CLEARLY OUTMATCHED.
BOOM

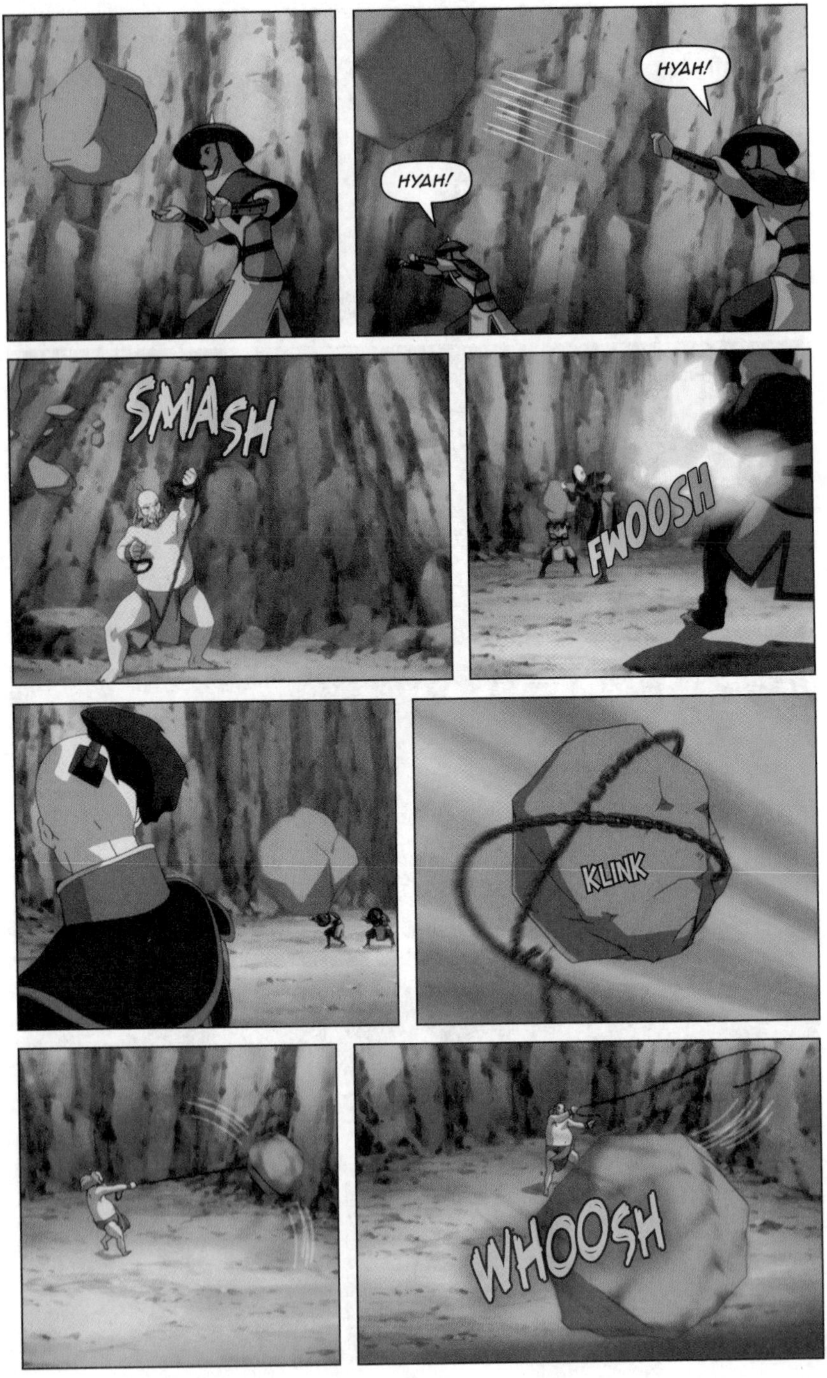
HYAH!
HYAH!
SMASH
FWOOSH
KLINK
WHOOSH

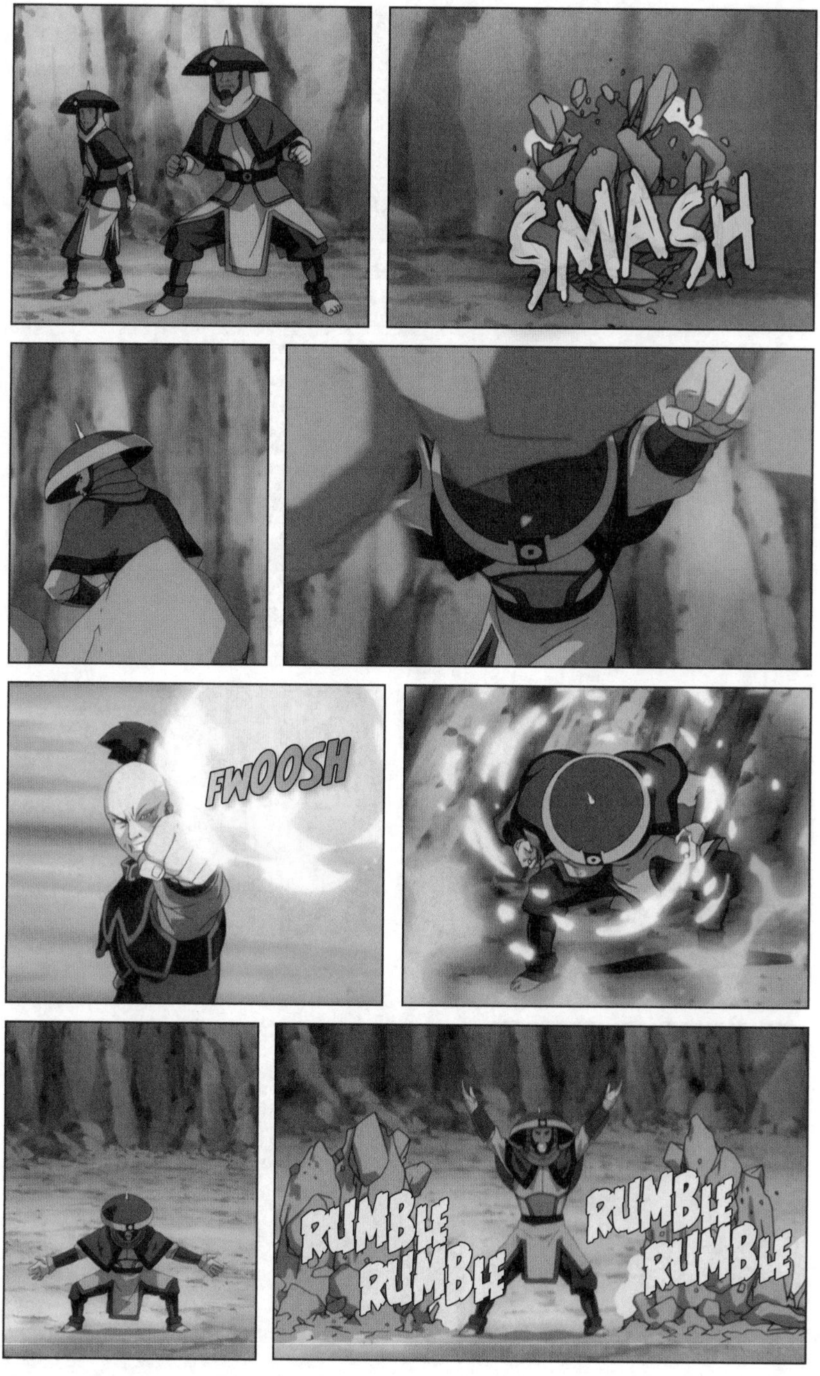
SMASH
FWOOSH
RUMBLE
RUMBLE
RUMBLE
RUMBLE

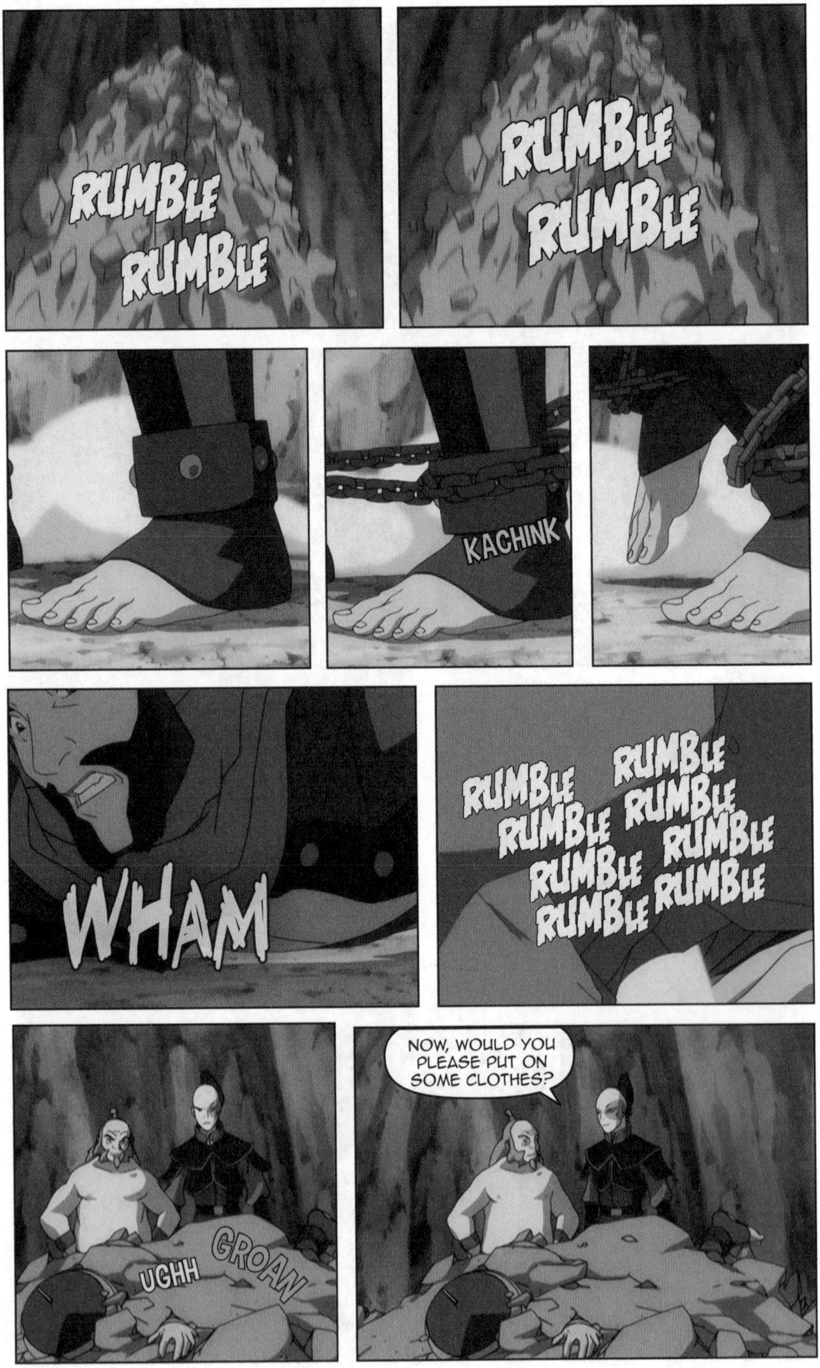
RUMBLE RUMBLE
RUMBLE RUMBLE
KACHINK
WHAM
RUMBLE RUMBLE RUMBLE RUMBLE RUMBLE RUMBLE RUMBLE RUMBLE
UGHH
GROAN
NOW, WOULD YOU PLEASE PUT ON SOME CLOTHES?

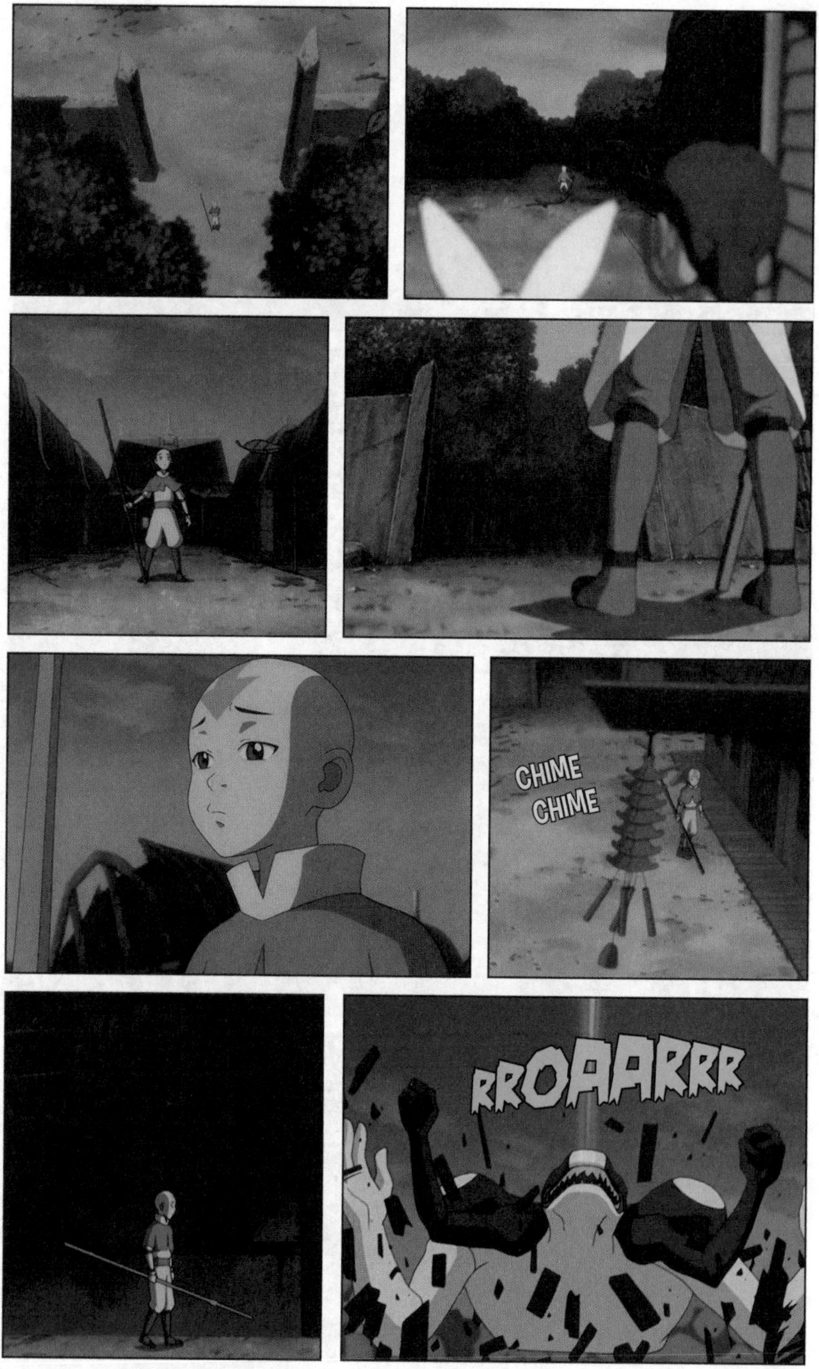
CHIME
CHIME
RROAARRR

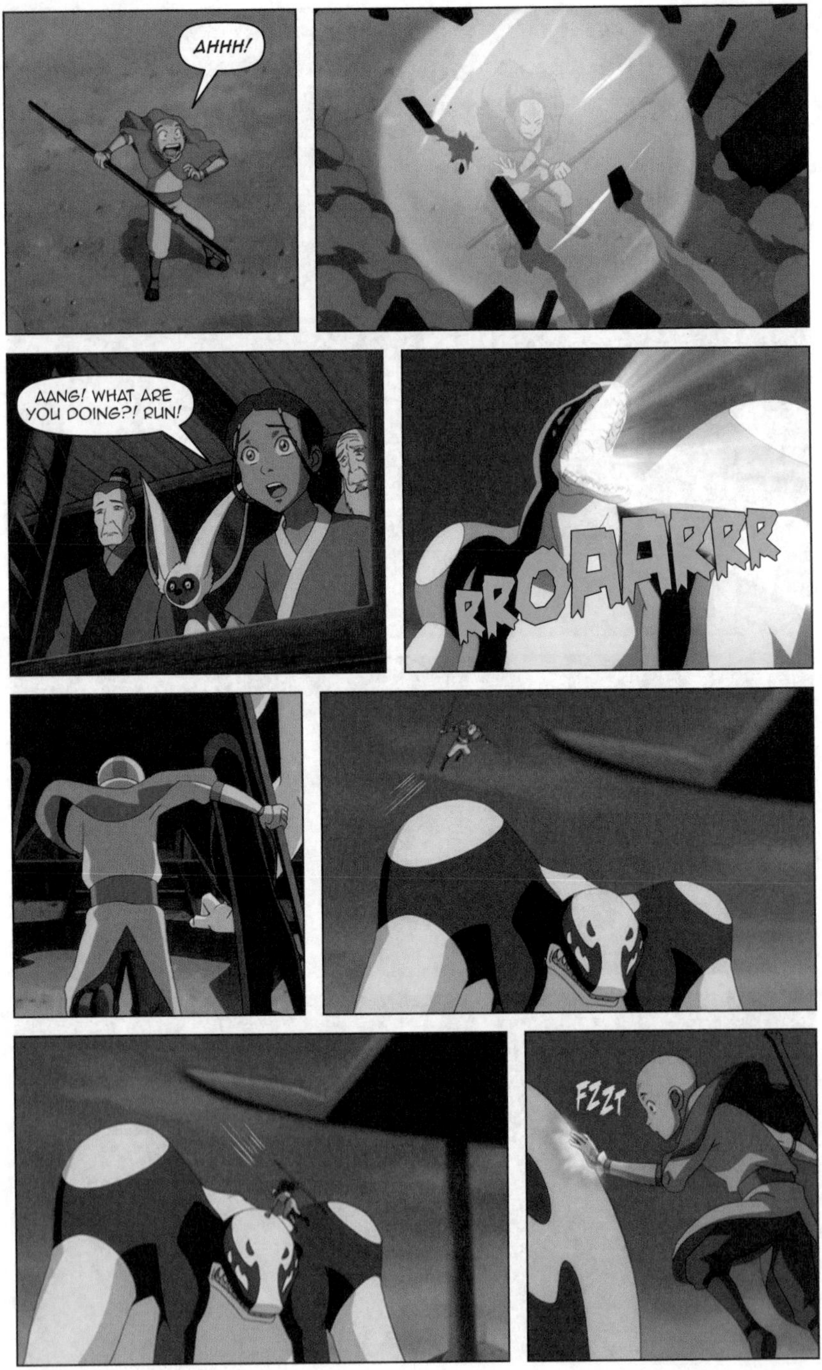
AHHH!
AANG! WHAT ARE YOU DOING?! RUN!
RROAARRR
FZZT

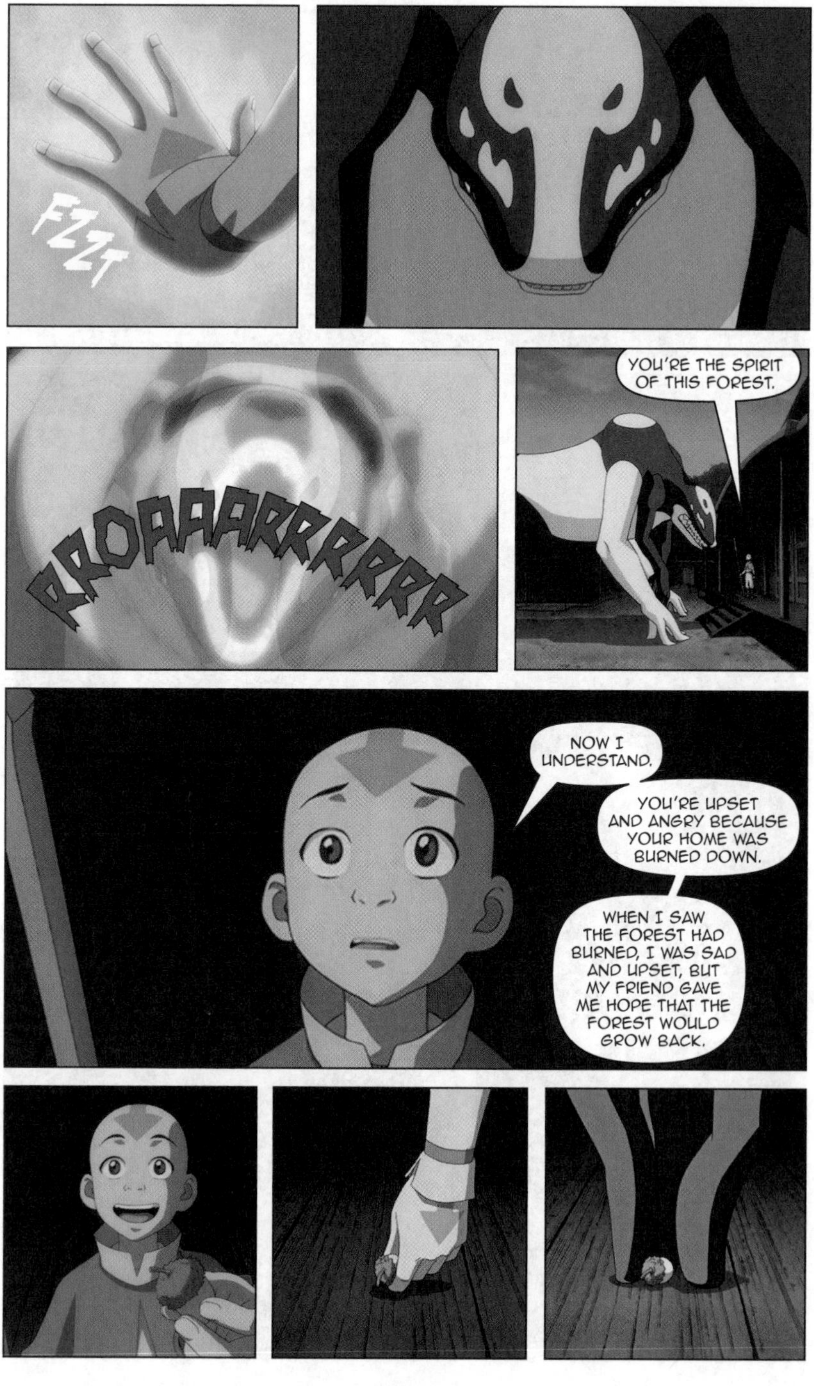
FZZT
RROAAAARRRRRR
YOU'RE THE SPIRIT OF THIS FOREST.
NOW I UNDERSTAND.
YOU'RE UPSET AND ANGRY BECAUSE YOUR HOME WAS BURNED DOWN.
WHEN I SAW THE FOREST HAD BURNED, I WAS SAD AND UPSET, BUT MY FRIEND GAVE ME HOPE THAT THE FOREST WOULD GROW BACK.

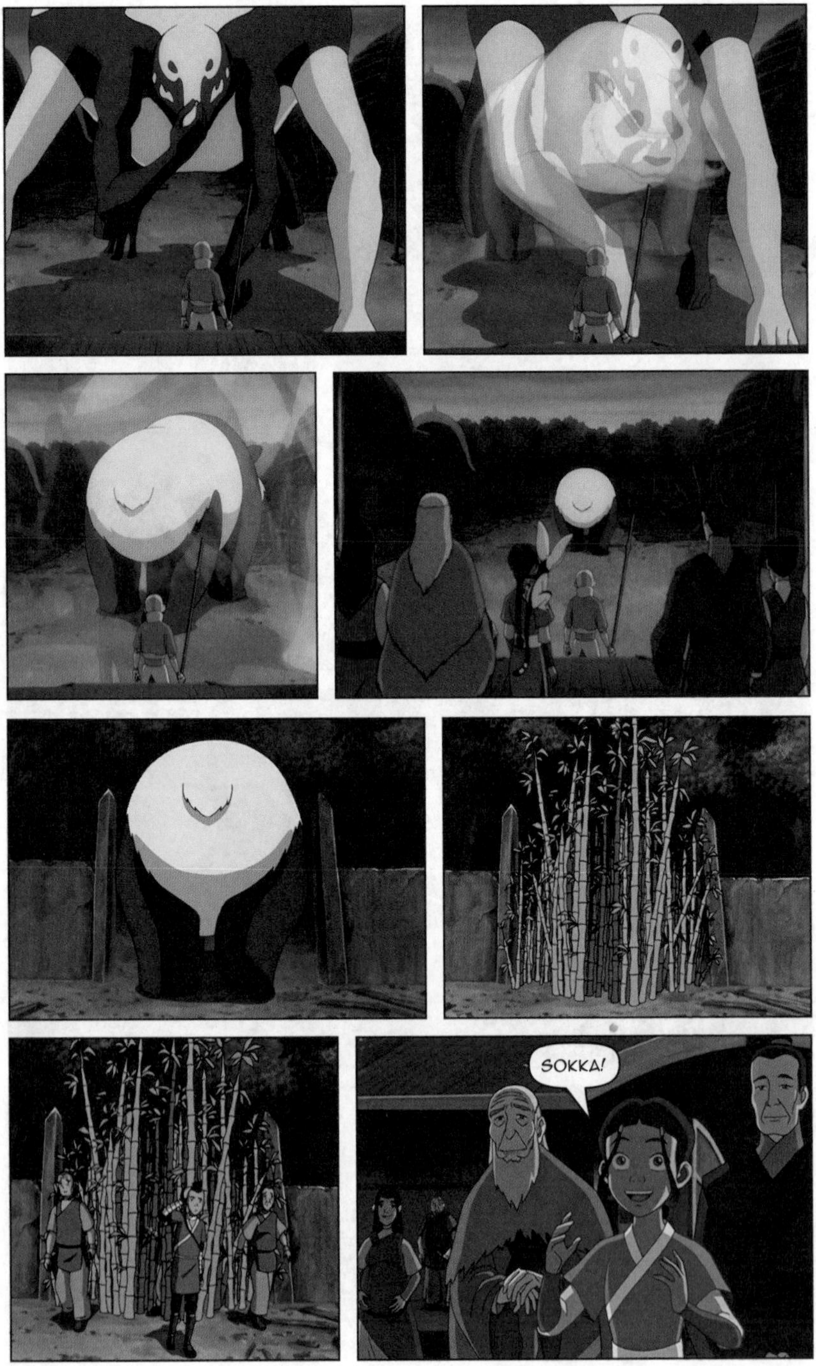
SOKKA!

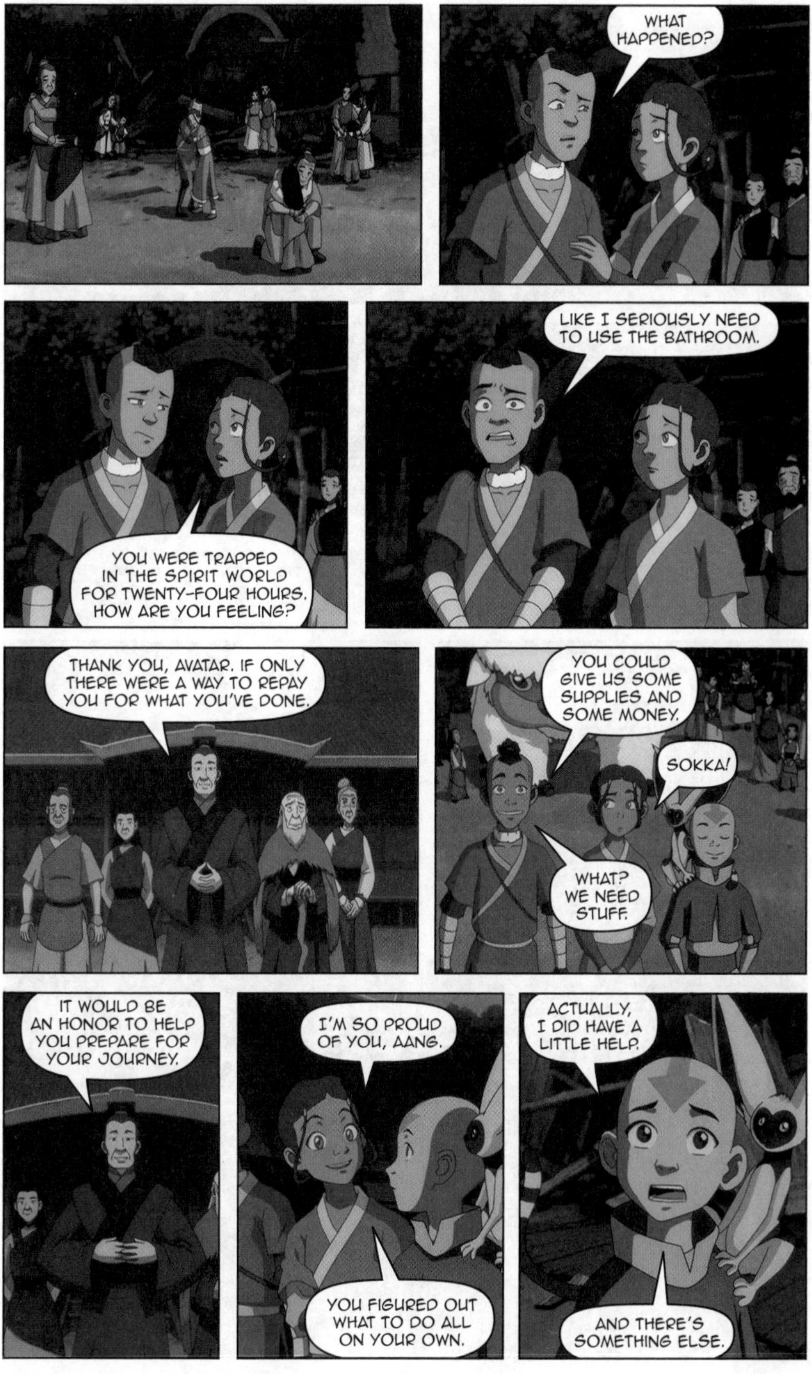
WHAT HAPPENED?
YOU WERE TRAPPED IN THE SPIRIT WORLD FOR TWENTY-FOUR HOURS. HOW ARE YOU FEELING?
LIKE I SERIOUSLY NEED TO USE THE BATHROOM.
THANK YOU, AVATAR. IF ONLY THERE WERE A WAY TO REPAY YOU FOR WHAT YOU'VE DONE.
YOU COULD GIVE US SOME SUPPLIES AND SOME MONEY.
SOKKA!
WHAT? WE NEED STUFF.
IT WOULD BE AN HONOR TO HELP YOU PREPARE FOR YOUR JOURNEY.
I'M SO PROUD OF YOU, AANG.
YOU FIGURED OUT WHAT TO DO ALL ON YOUR OWN.
ACTUALLY, I DID HAVE A LITTLE HELP.
AND THERE'S SOMETHING ELSE.

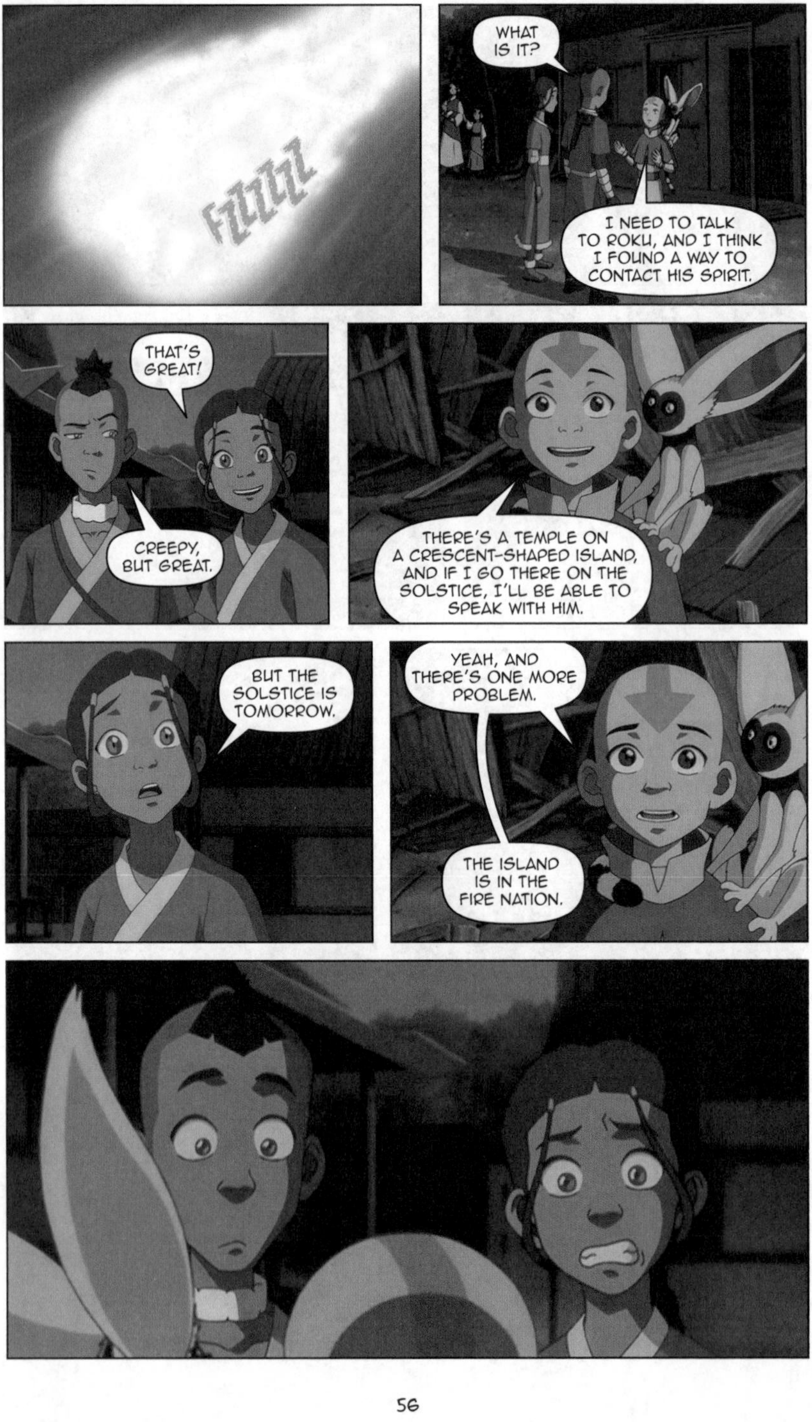
FZZZZZ
WHAT IS IT?
I NEED TO TALK TO ROKU, AND I THINK I FOUND A WAY TO CONTACT HIS SPIRIT.
THAT'S GREAT!
CREEPY, BUT GREAT.
THERE'S A TEMPLE ON A CRESCENT-SHAPED ISLAND, AND IF I GO THERE ON THE SOLSTICE, I'LL BE ABLE TO SPEAK WITH HIM.
BUT THE SOLSTICE IS TOMORROW.
YEAH, AND THERE'S ONE MORE PROBLEM.
THE ISLAND IS IN THE FIRE NATION.

CHAPTER EIGHT
AVATAR ROKU
WINTER SOLSTICE: PART TWO

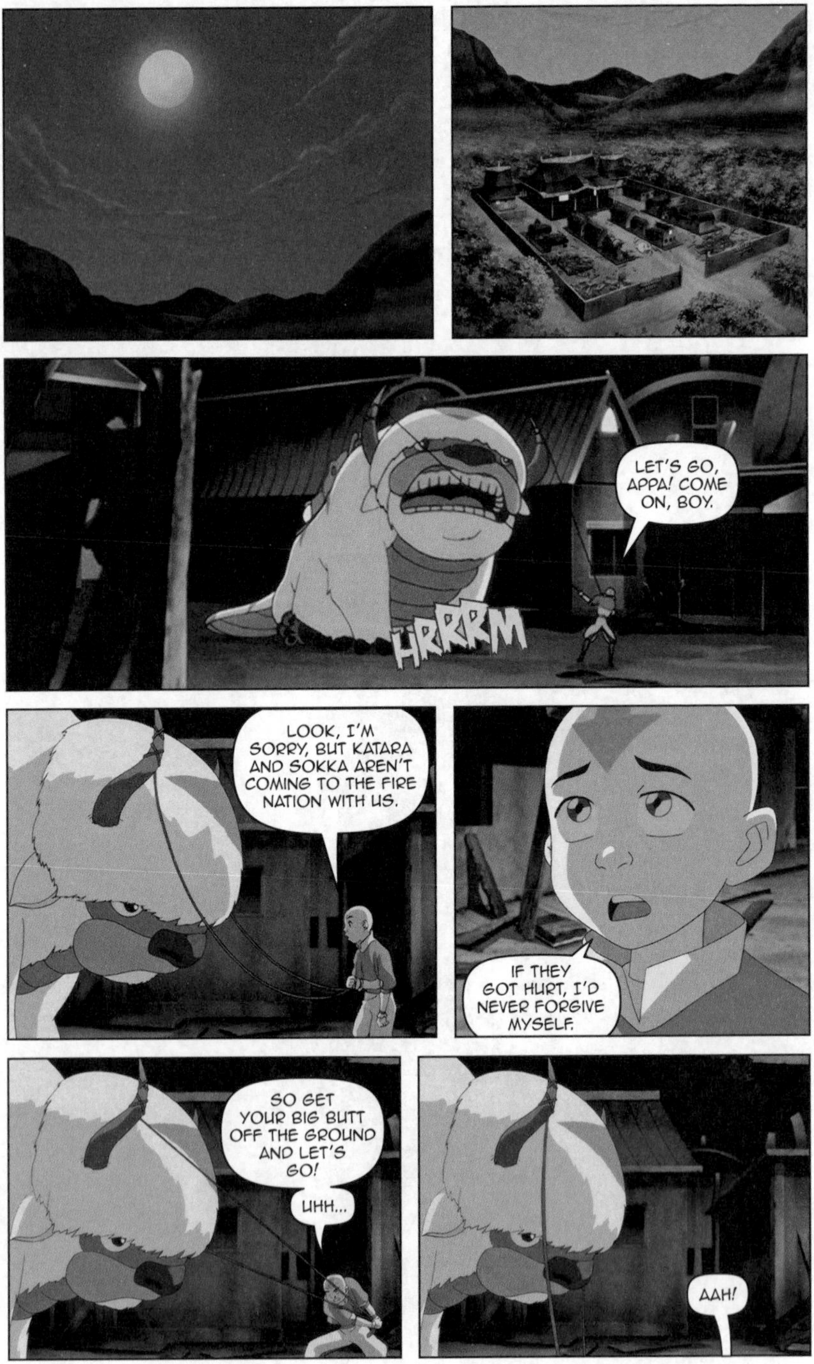
LET'S GO, APPA! COME ON, BOY.
HRRRM
LOOK, I'M SORRY, BUT KATARA AND SOKKA AREN'T COMING TO THE FIRE NATION WITH US.
IF THEY GOT HURT, I'D NEVER FORGIVE MYSELF.
SO GET YOUR BIG BUTT OFF THE GROUND AND LET'S GO!
UHH...
AAH!

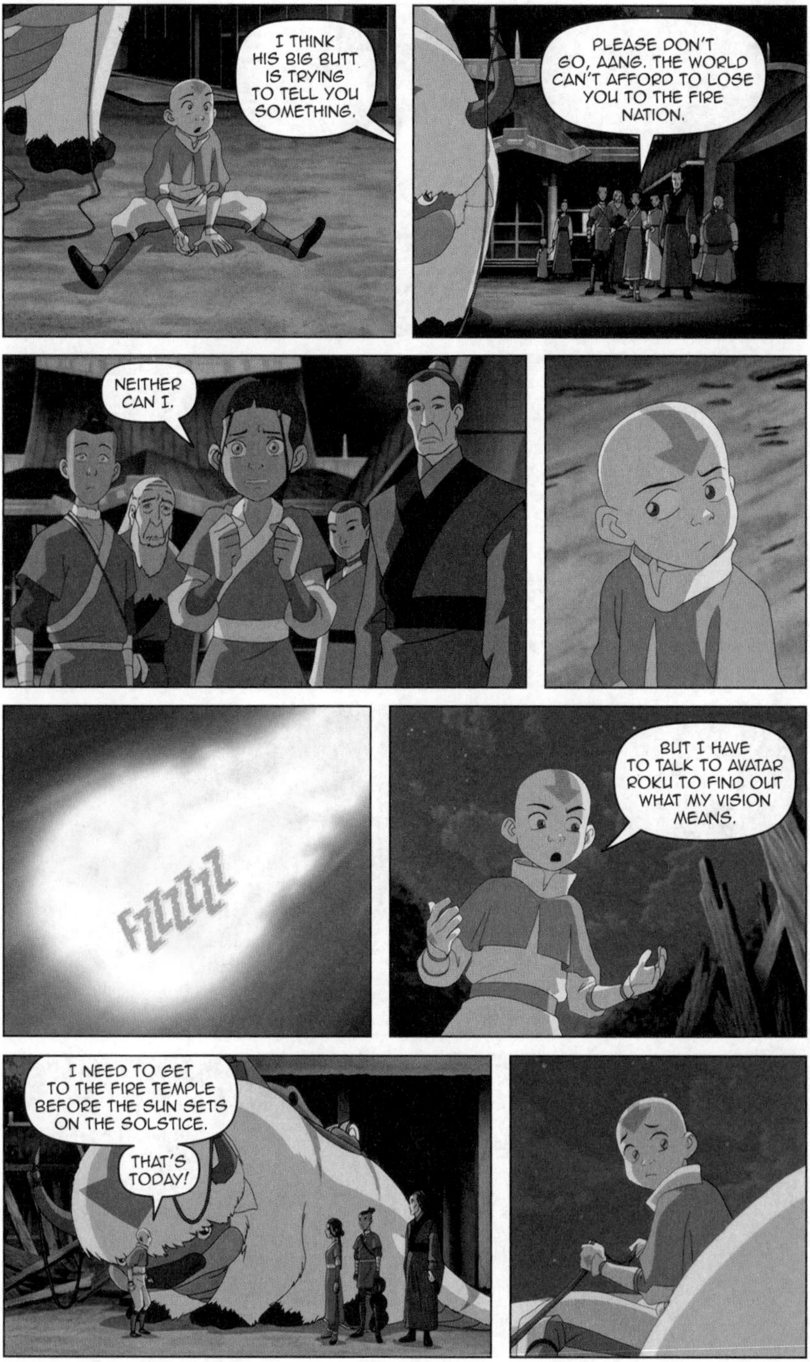
I THINK HIS BIG BUTT IS TRYING TO TELL YOU SOMETHING.
PLEASE DON'T GO, AANG. THE WORLD CAN'T AFFORD TO LOSE YOU TO THE FIRE NATION.
NEITHER CAN I.
FZZZZZ
BUT I HAVE TO TALK TO AVATAR ROKU TO FIND OUT WHAT MY VISION MEANS.
I NEED TO GET TO THE FIRE TEMPLE BEFORE THE SUN SETS ON THE SOLSTICE.
THAT'S TODAY!

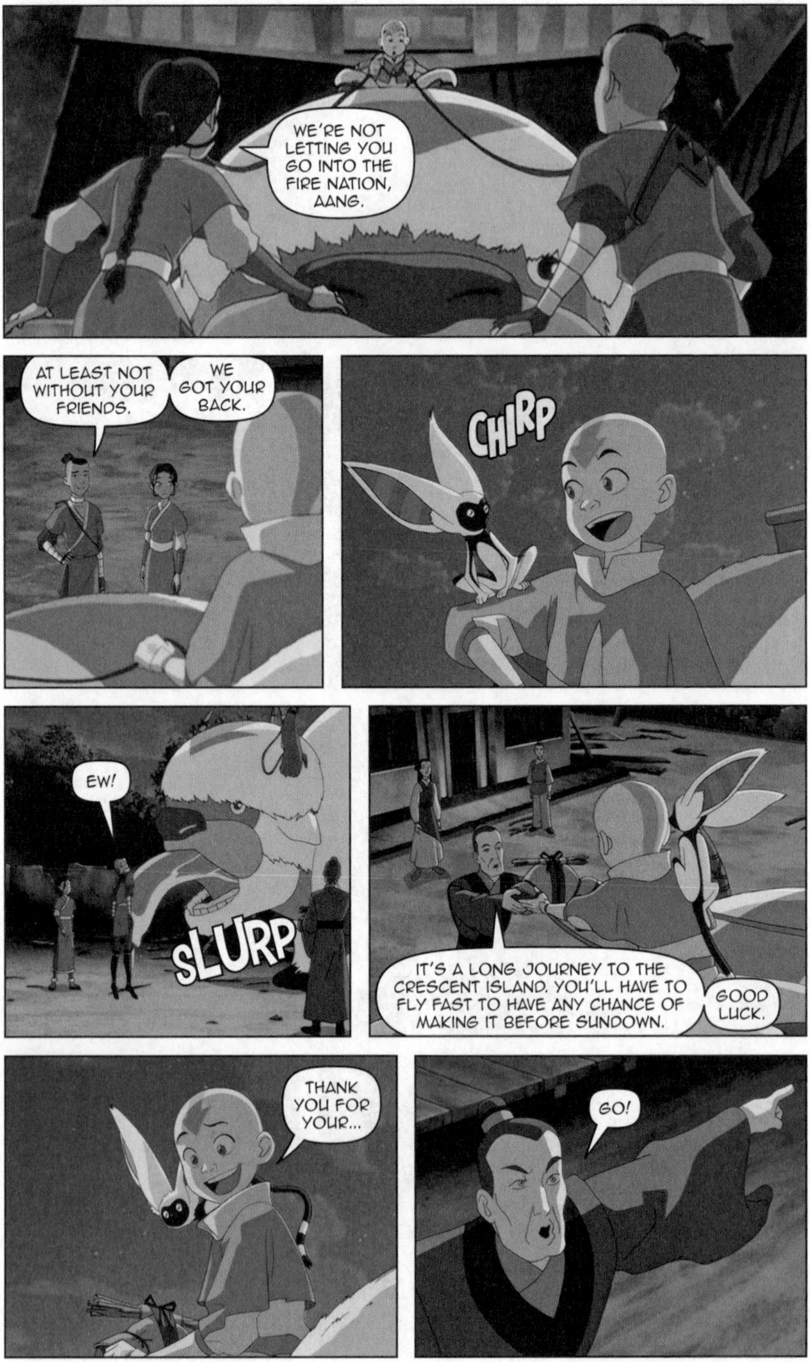
WE'RE NOT LETTING YOU GO INTO THE FIRE NATION, AANG.
AT LEAST NOT WITHOUT YOUR FRIENDS.
WE GOT YOUR BACK.
CHIRP
EW!
SLURP
IT'S A LONG JOURNEY TO THE CRESCENT ISLAND. YOU'LL HAVE TO FLY FAST TO HAVE ANY CHANCE OF MAKING IT BEFORE SUNDOWN.
GOOD LUCK.
THANK YOU FOR YOUR...
GO!

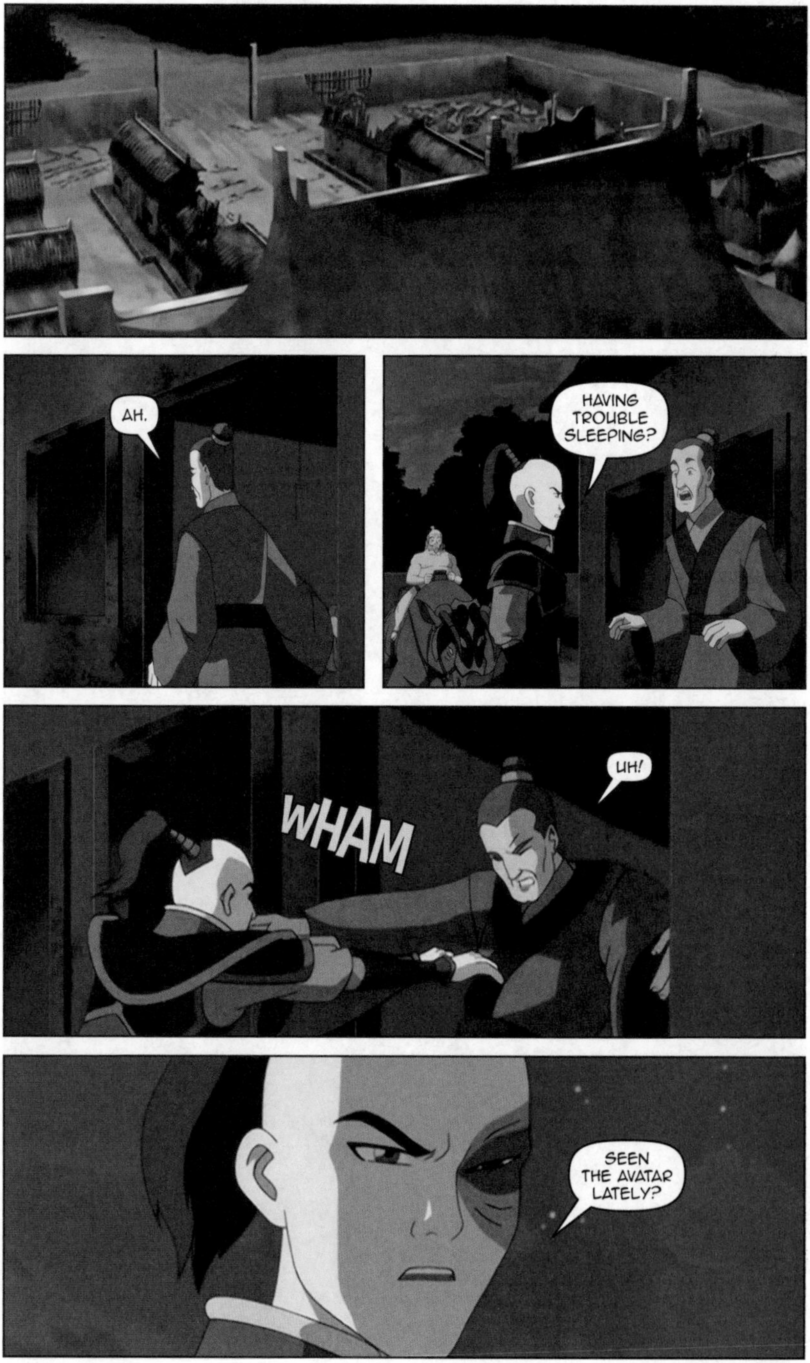
AH.
HAVING TROUBLE SLEEPING?
WHAM
UH!
SEEN THE AVATAR LATELY?

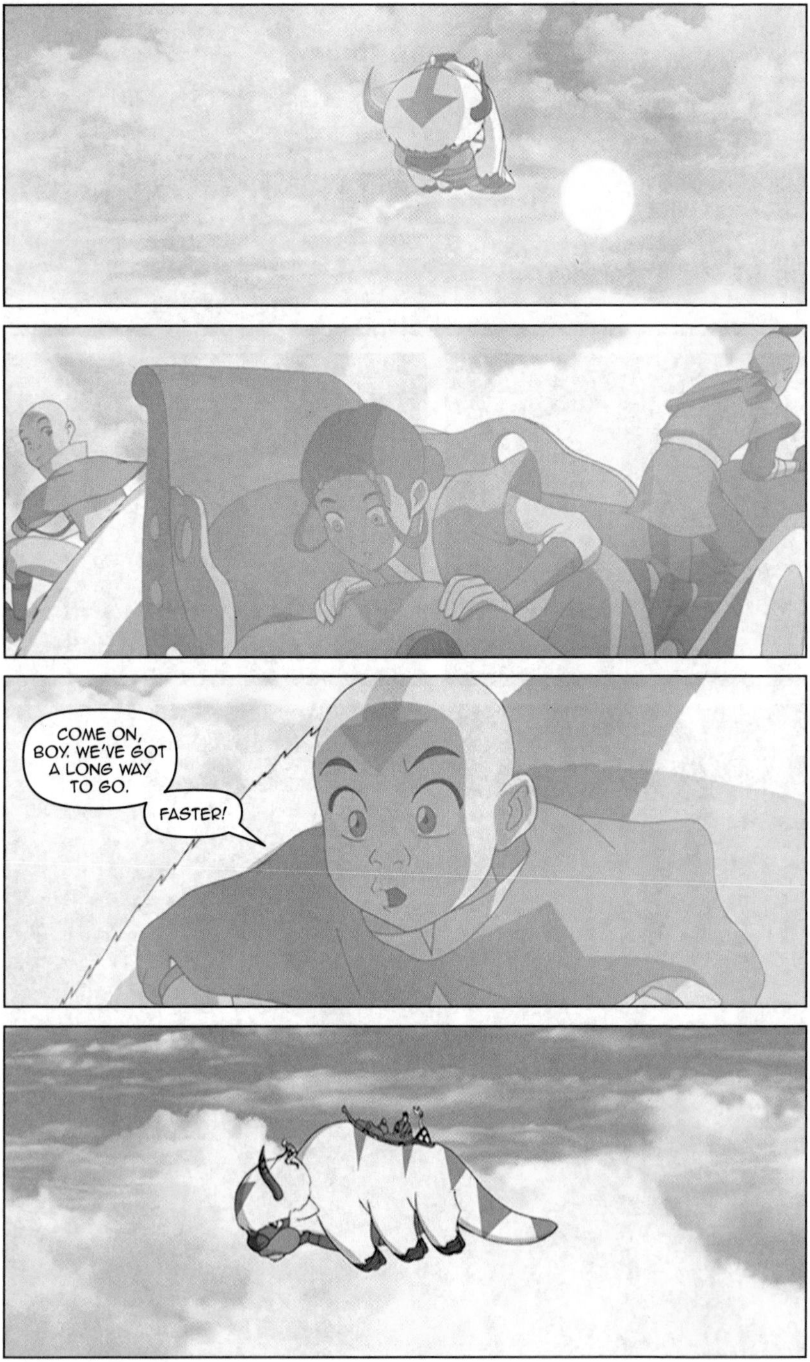
COME ON, BOY. WE'VE GOT A LONG WAY TO GO.
FASTER!

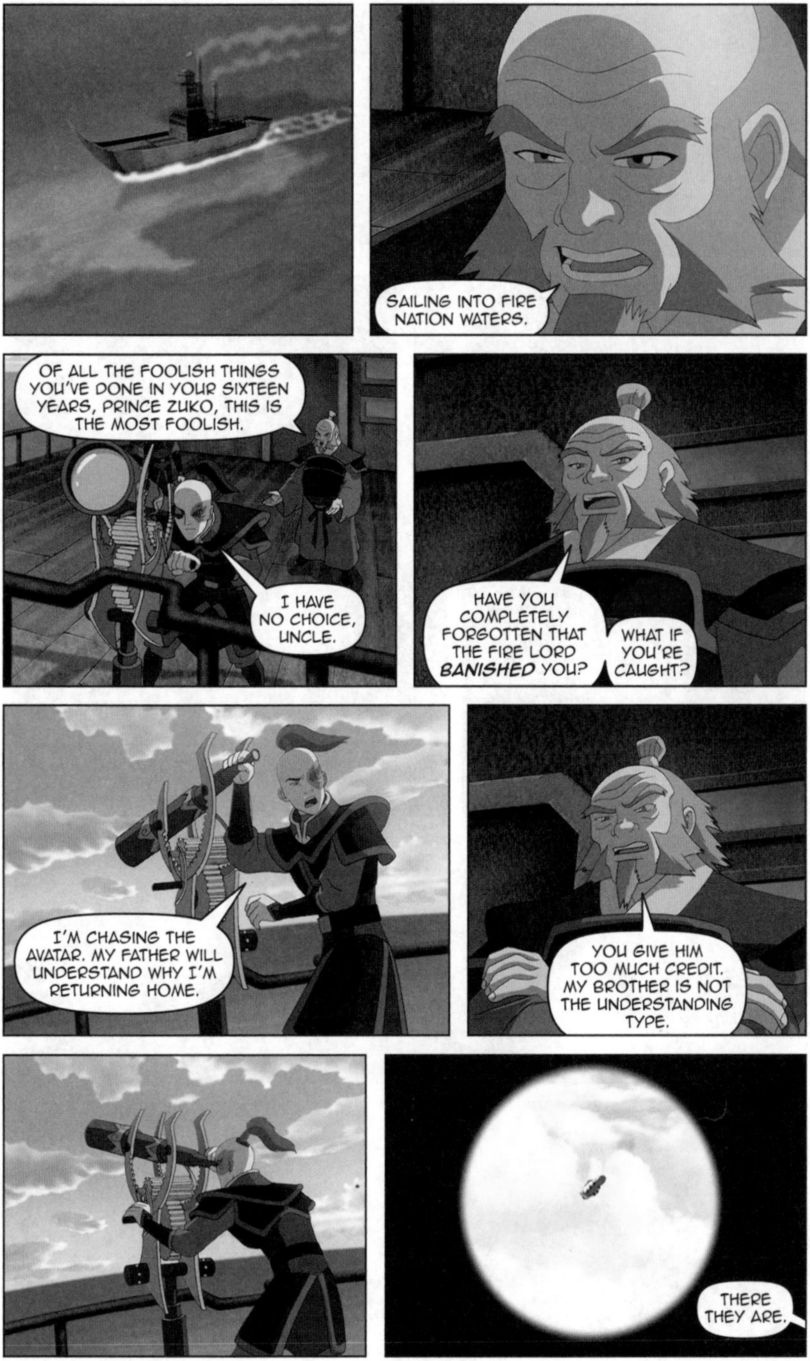
SAILING INTO FIRE NATION WATERS.
OF ALL THE FOOLISH THINGS YOU'VE DONE IN YOUR SIXTEEN YEARS, PRINCE ZUKO, THIS IS THE MOST FOOLISH.
I HAVE NO CHOICE, UNCLE.
HAVE YOU COMPLETELY FORGOTTEN THAT THE FIRE LORD ***BANISHED*** YOU?
WHAT IF YOU'RE CAUGHT?
I'M CHASING THE AVATAR. MY FATHER WILL UNDERSTAND WHY I'M RETURNING HOME.
YOU GIVE HIM TOO MUCH CREDIT. MY BROTHER IS NOT THE UNDERSTANDING TYPE.
THERE THEY ARE.

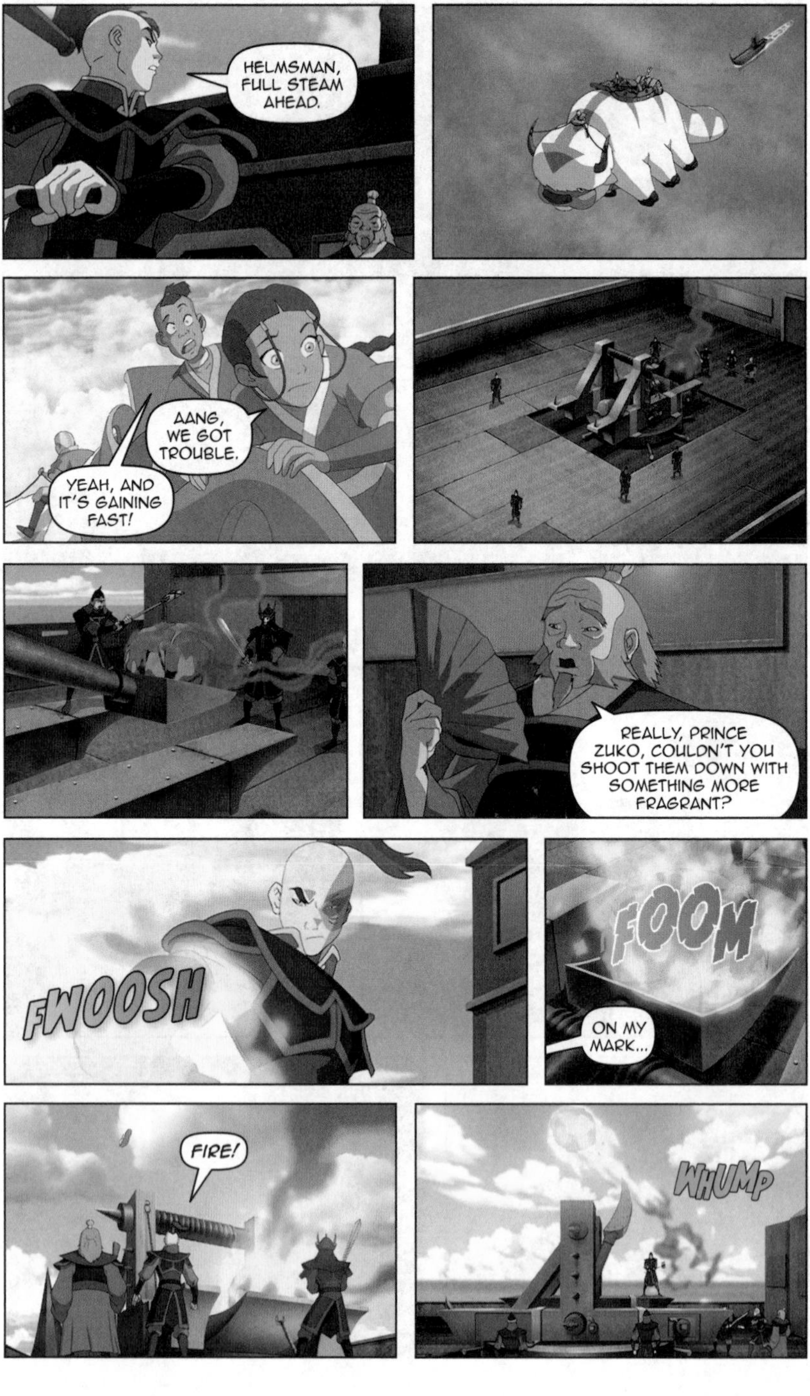
HELMSMAN, FULL STEAM AHEAD.
AANG, WE GOT TROUBLE.
YEAH, AND IT'S GAINING FAST!
REALLY, PRINCE ZUKO, COULDN'T YOU SHOOT THEM DOWN WITH SOMETHING MORE FRAGRANT?
FWOOSH
FOOM
ON MY MARK...
FIRE!
WHUMP

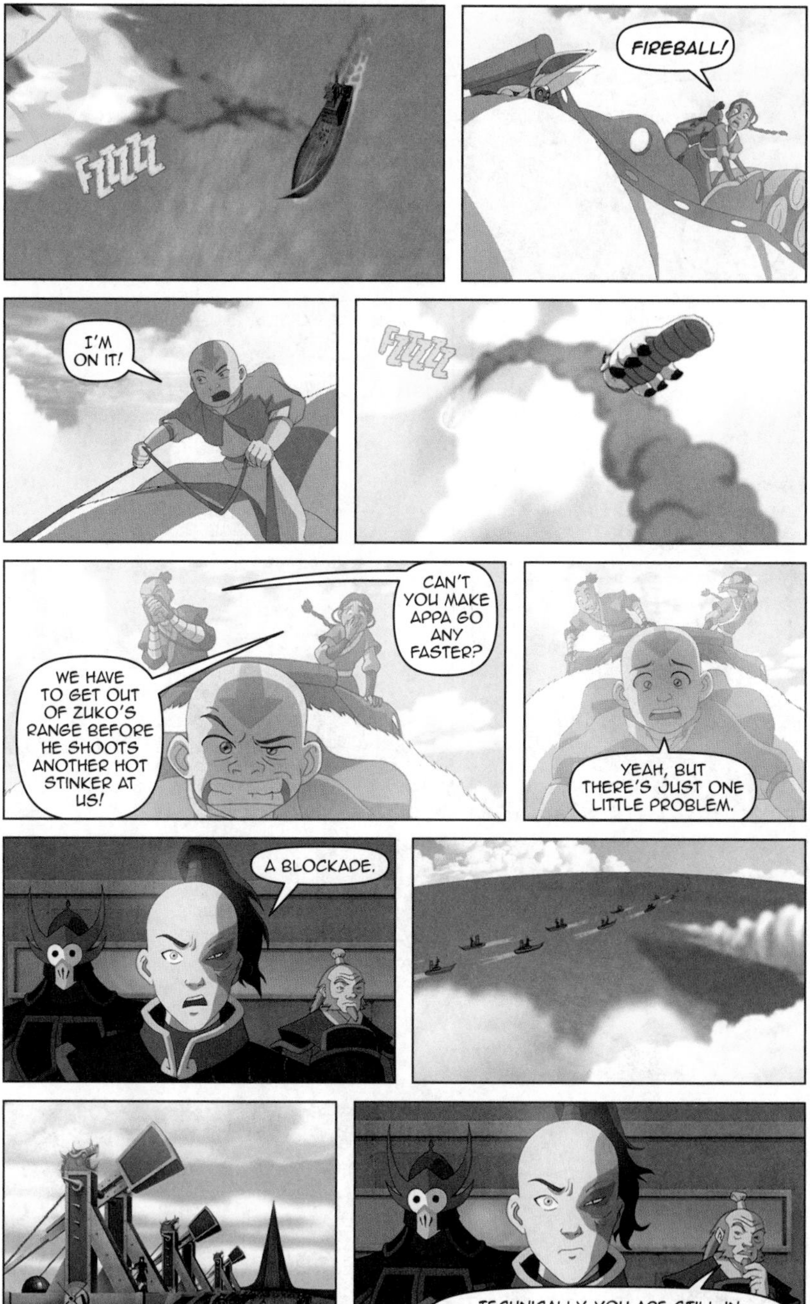
FZZZZ
FIREBALL!
I'M ON IT!
FZZZZ
CAN'T YOU MAKE APPA GO ANY FASTER?
WE HAVE TO GET OUT OF ZUKO'S RANGE BEFORE HE SHOOTS ANOTHER HOT STINKER AT US!
YEAH, BUT THERE'S JUST ONE LITTLE PROBLEM.
A BLOCKADE.
TECHNICALLY, YOU ARE STILL IN EARTH KINGDOM WATERS. TURN BACK NOW, AND THEY CANNOT ARREST YOU.

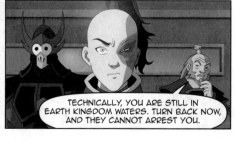

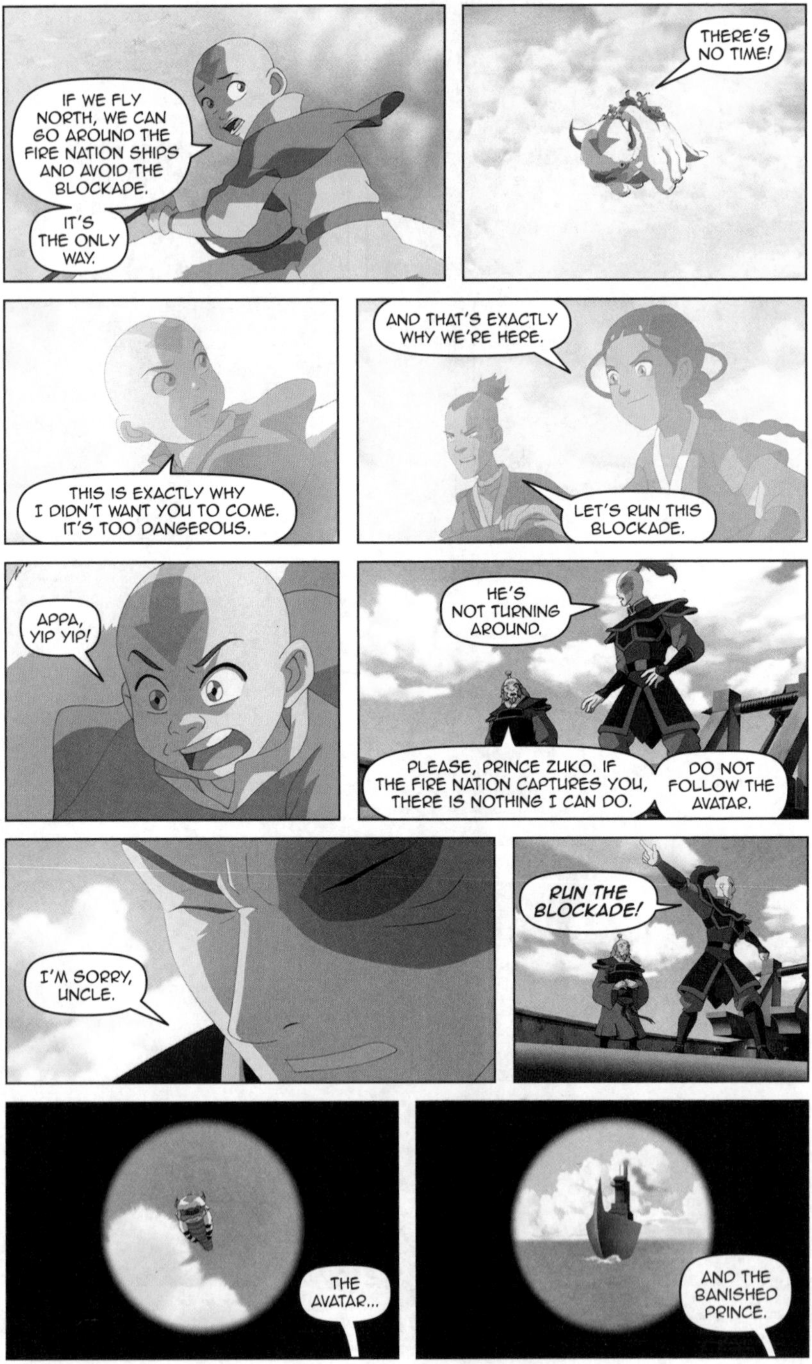
IF WE FLY NORTH, WE CAN GO AROUND THE FIRE NATION SHIPS AND AVOID THE BLOCKADE.
IT'S THE ONLY WAY.
THERE'S NO TIME!
THIS IS EXACTLY WHY I DIDN'T WANT YOU TO COME. IT'S TOO DANGEROUS.
AND THAT'S EXACTLY WHY WE'RE HERE.
LET'S RUN THIS BLOCKADE.
APPA, YIP YIP!
HE'S NOT TURNING AROUND.
PLEASE, PRINCE ZUKO. IF THE FIRE NATION CAPTURES YOU, THERE IS NOTHING I CAN DO.
DO NOT FOLLOW THE AVATAR.
I'M SORRY, UNCLE.
RUN THE BLOCKADE!
THE AVATAR...
AND THE BANISHED PRINCE.

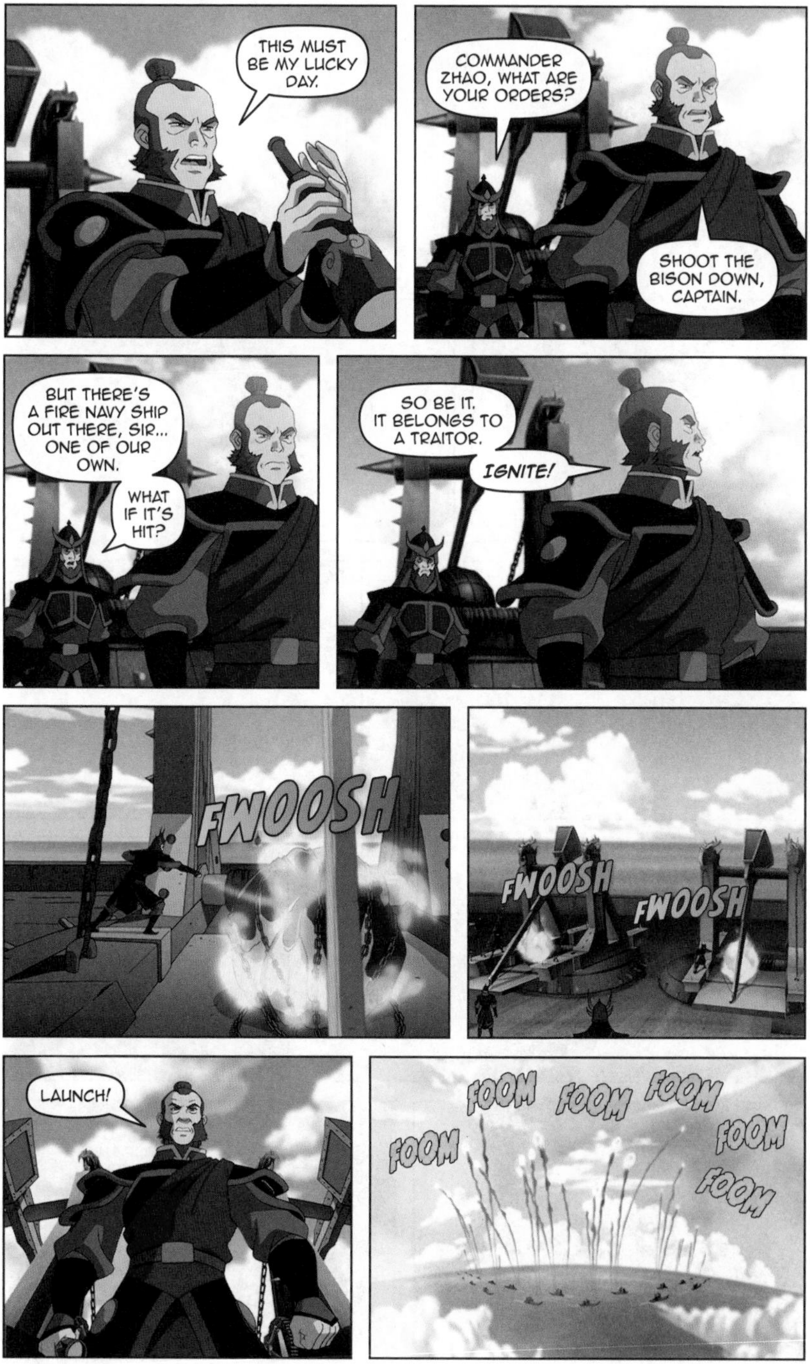
THIS MUST BE MY LUCKY DAY.
COMMANDER ZHAO, WHAT ARE YOUR ORDERS?
SHOOT THE BISON DOWN, CAPTAIN.
BUT THERE'S A FIRE NAVY SHIP OUT THERE, SIR... ONE OF OUR OWN.
WHAT IF IT'S HIT?
SO BE IT. IT BELONGS TO A TRAITOR.
IGNITE!
FWOOSH
FWOOSH
FWOOSH
LAUNCH!
FOOM
FOOM
FOOM
FOOM
FOOM
FOOM

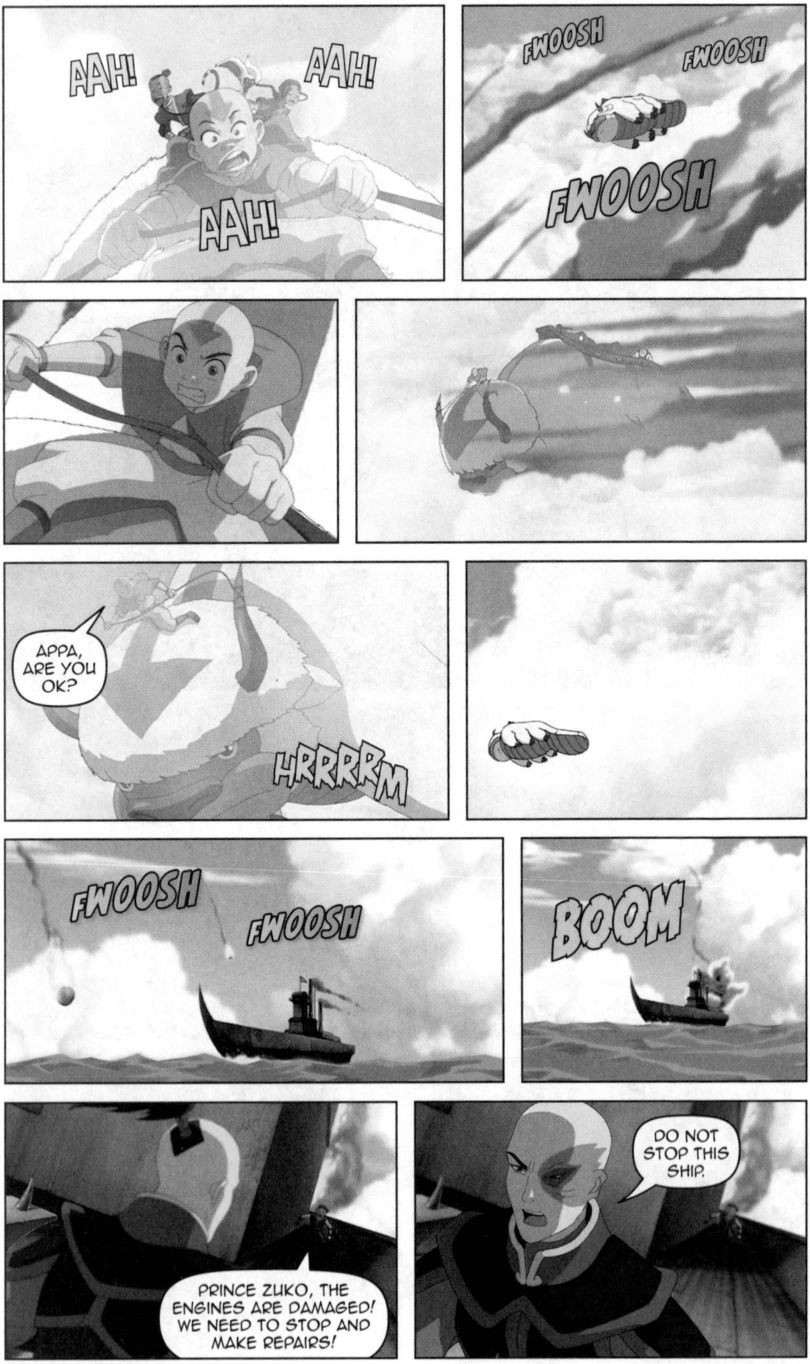
AAH!
AAH!
AAH!
FWOOSH
FWOOSH
FWOOSH
APPA, ARE YOU OK?
HRRRRM
FWOOSH
FWOOSH
BOOM
PRINCE ZUKO, THE ENGINES ARE DAMAGED! WE NEED TO STOP AND MAKE REPAIRS!
DO NOT STOP THIS SHIP.

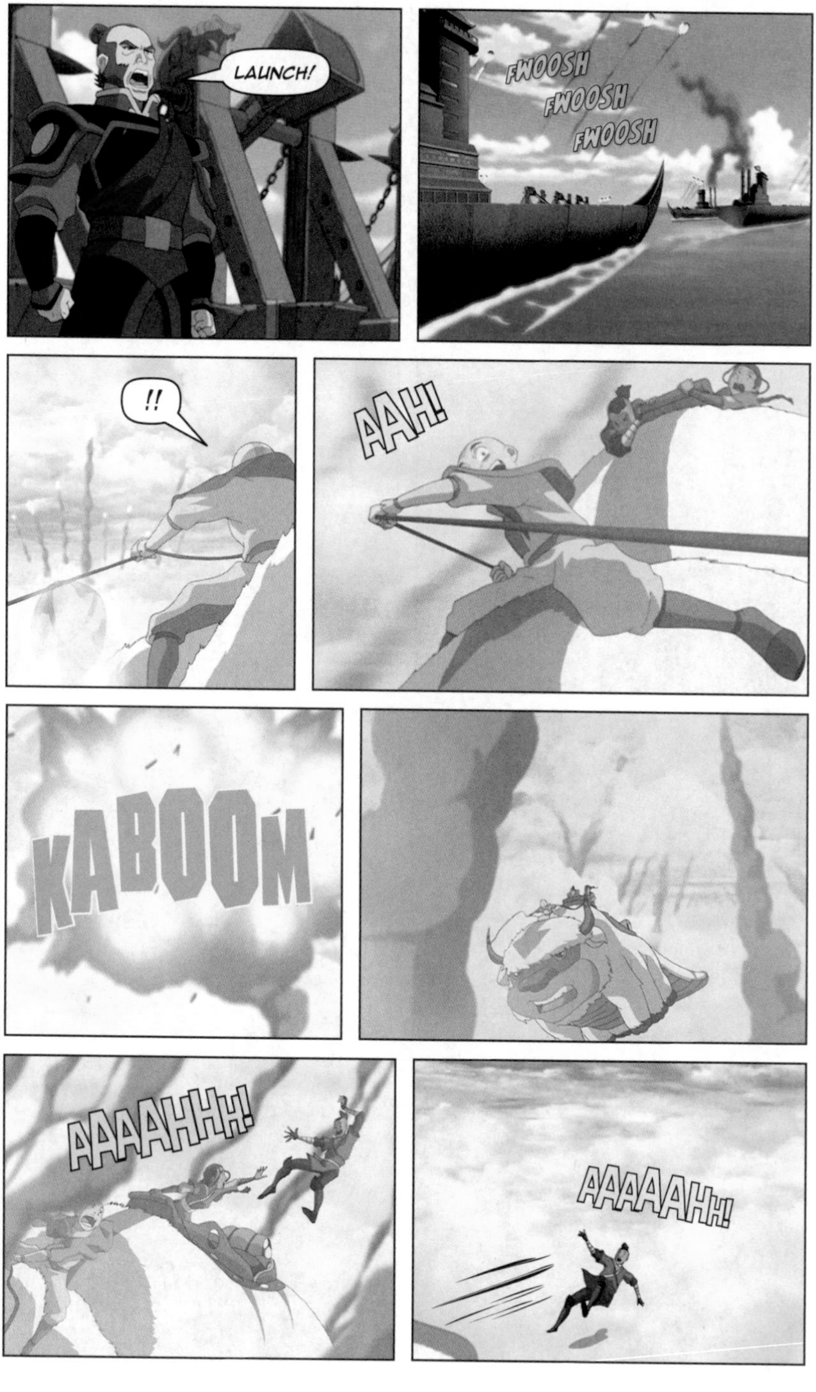
LAUNCH!
FWOOSH
FWOOSH
FWOOSH
!!
AAH!
KABOOM
AAAAHHH!
AAAAAHH!

SOKKA!

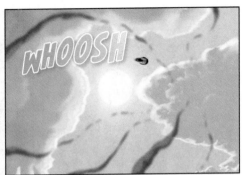

WHOOSH

AAAHHHHH

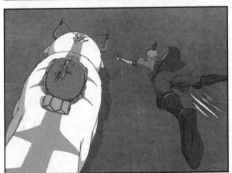

YANK

AGH!

SPLASH

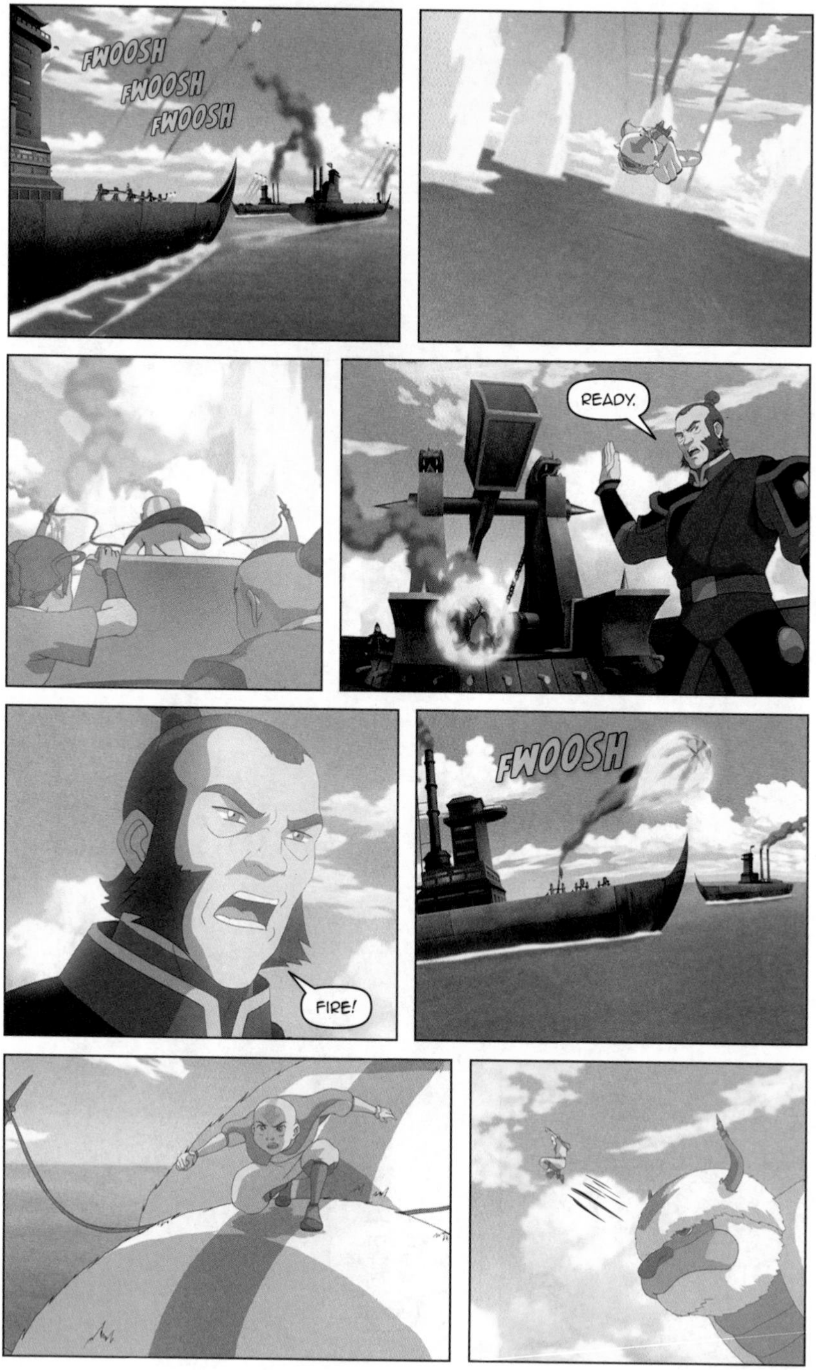
FWOOSH
FWOOSH
FWOOSH
READY.
FIRE!
FWOOSH

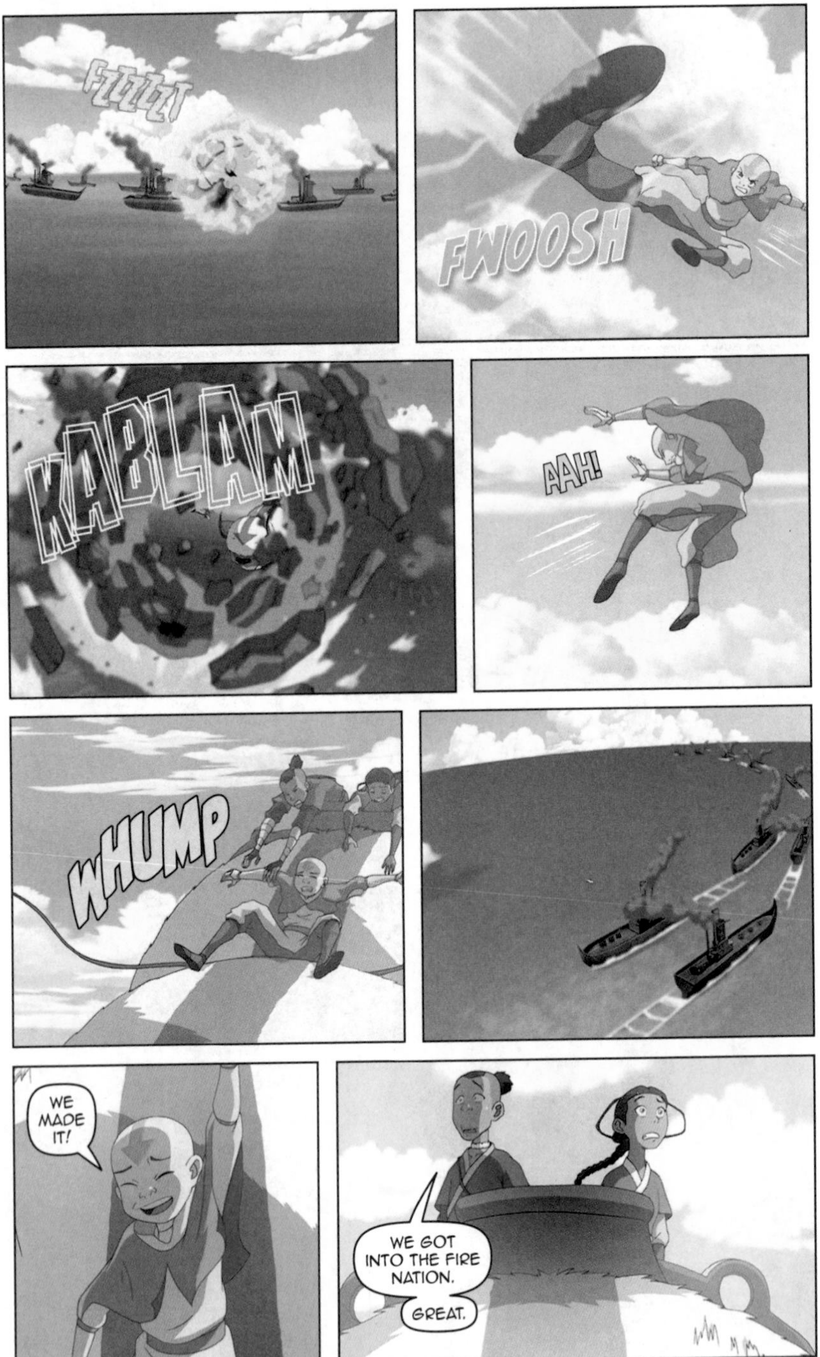
FZZZZZT
FWOOSH
KABLAM
AAH!
WHUMP
WE MADE IT!
WE GOT INTO THE FIRE NATION.
GREAT.

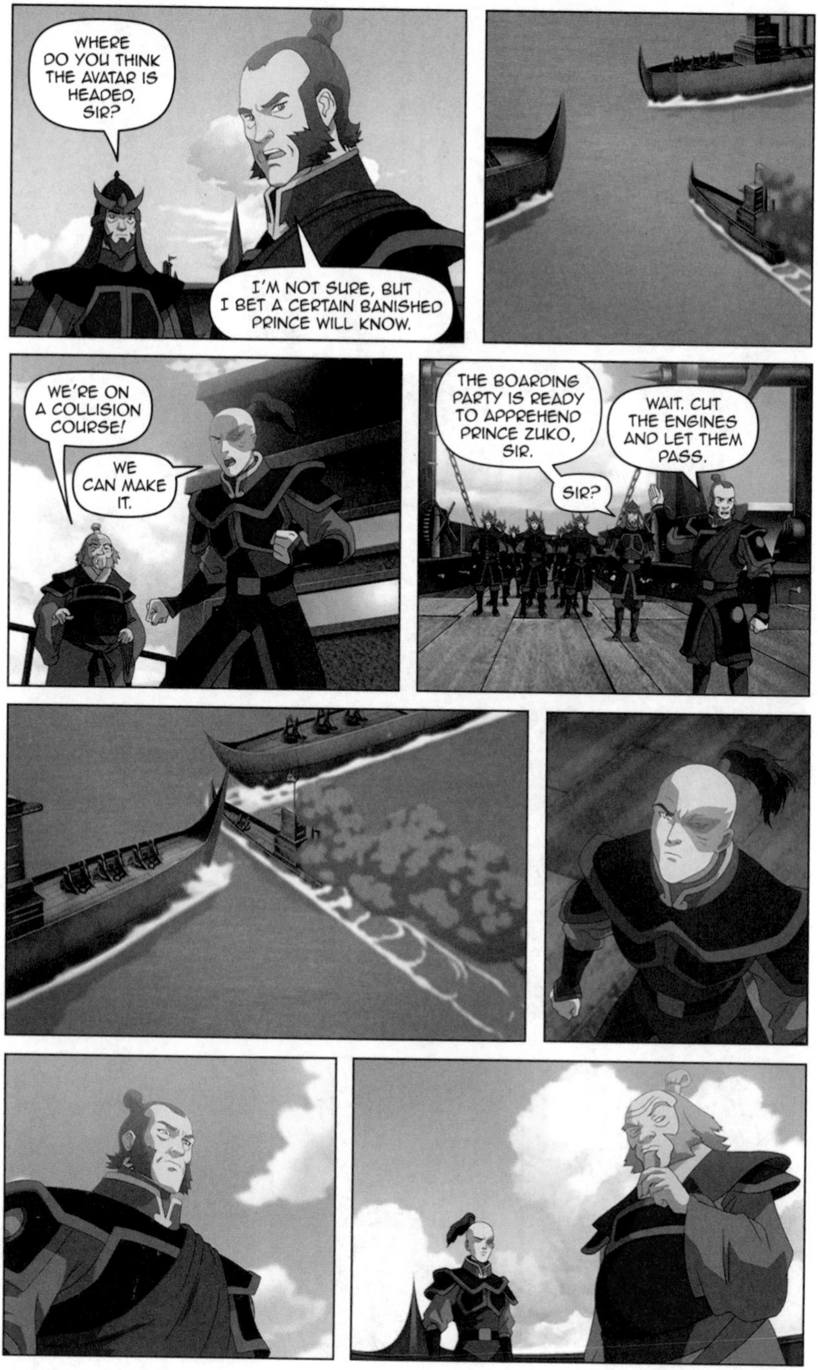
WHERE DO YOU THINK THE AVATAR IS HEADED, SIR?
I'M NOT SURE, BUT I BET A CERTAIN BANISHED PRINCE WILL KNOW.
WE'RE ON A COLLISION COURSE!
WE CAN MAKE IT.
THE BOARDING PARTY IS READY TO APPREHEND PRINCE ZUKO, SIR.
SIR?
WAIT. CUT THE ENGINES AND LET THEM PASS.

CHRRP

THERE IT IS...

THE ISLAND WHERE ROKU'S DRAGON TOOK ME.

ZZZZZ

YOU DID IT, BUDDY. NICE FLYING.

OH, YOU MUST BE TIRED.

NO, I'M GOOD. REFRESHED AND READY TO FIGHT SOME FIREBENDERS.

I WAS TALKING TO APPA.

WELL, I WAS TALKING TO MOMO.

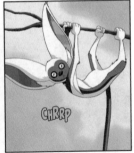
CHRRP

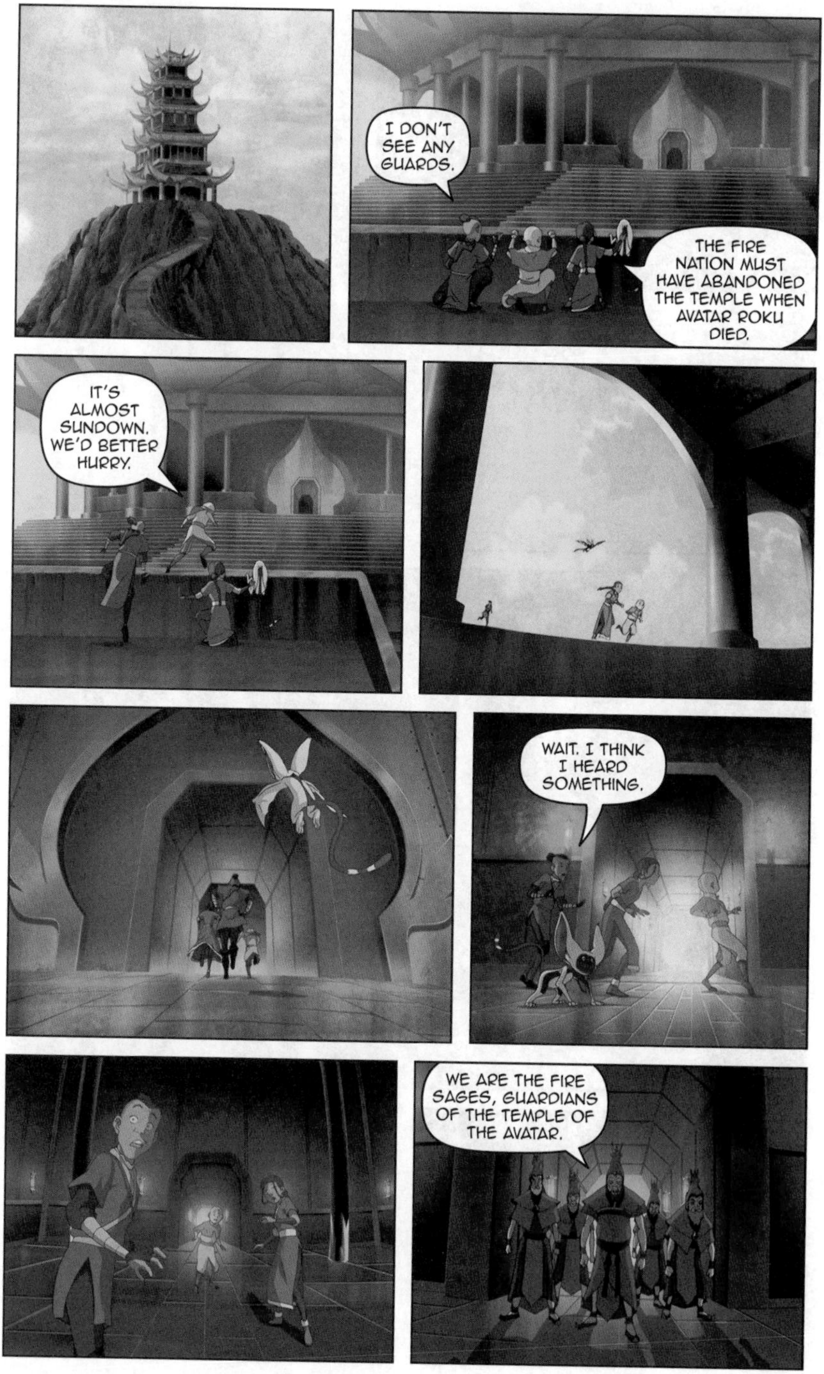
I DON'T SEE ANY GUARDS.
THE FIRE NATION MUST HAVE ABANDONED THE TEMPLE WHEN AVATAR ROKU DIED.
IT'S ALMOST SUNDOWN. WE'D BETTER HURRY.
WAIT. I THINK I HEARD SOMETHING.
WE ARE THE FIRE SAGES, GUARDIANS OF THE TEMPLE OF THE AVATAR.

GREAT. I AM THE AVATAR.

WE KNOW.

FWOOSH

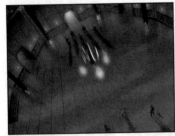

FSSSSH

I'LL HOLD THEM OFF. RUN!

FWOOSH

IF THE AVATAR CONTACTS ROKU, THERE'S NO TELLING HOW POWERFUL THE BOY WILL BECOME.

SPLIT UP AND FIND HIM.

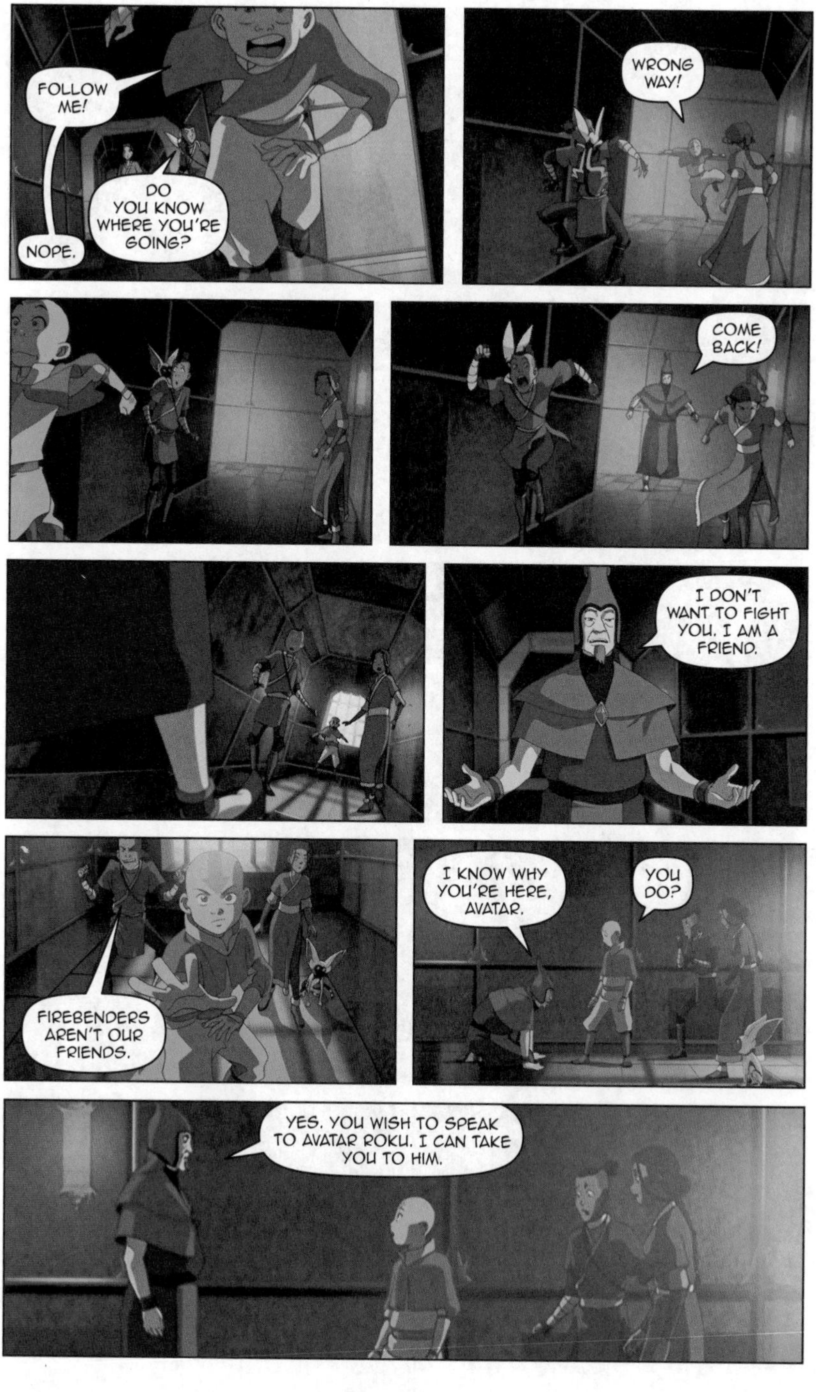
FOLLOW ME!
DO YOU KNOW WHERE YOU'RE GOING?
NOPE.
WRONG WAY!
COME BACK!
I DON'T WANT TO FIGHT YOU. I AM A FRIEND.
FIREBENDERS AREN'T OUR FRIENDS.
I KNOW WHY YOU'RE HERE, AVATAR.
YOU DO?
YES. YOU WISH TO SPEAK TO AVATAR ROKU. I CAN TAKE YOU TO HIM.

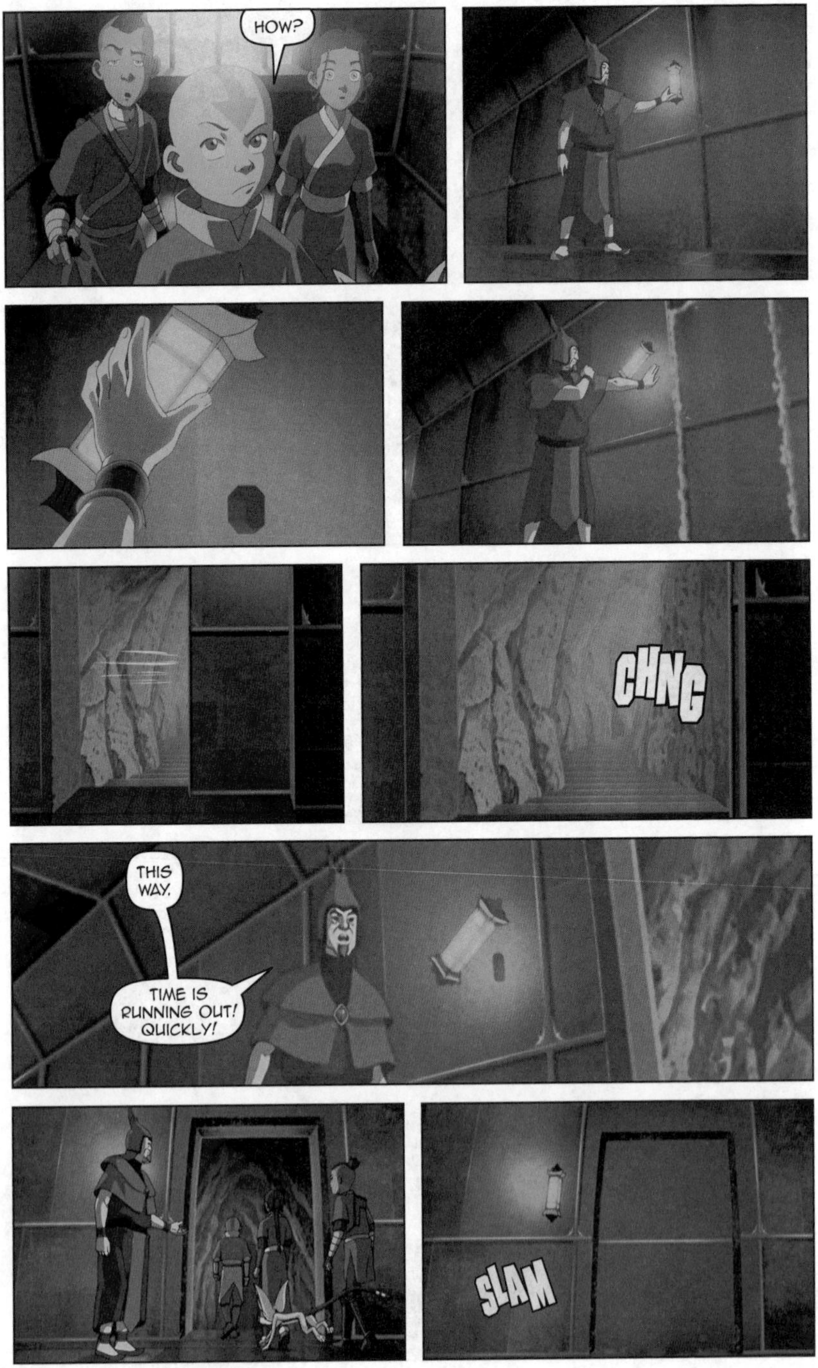
HOW?
CHNG
THIS WAY.
TIME IS RUNNING OUT! QUICKLY!
SLAM

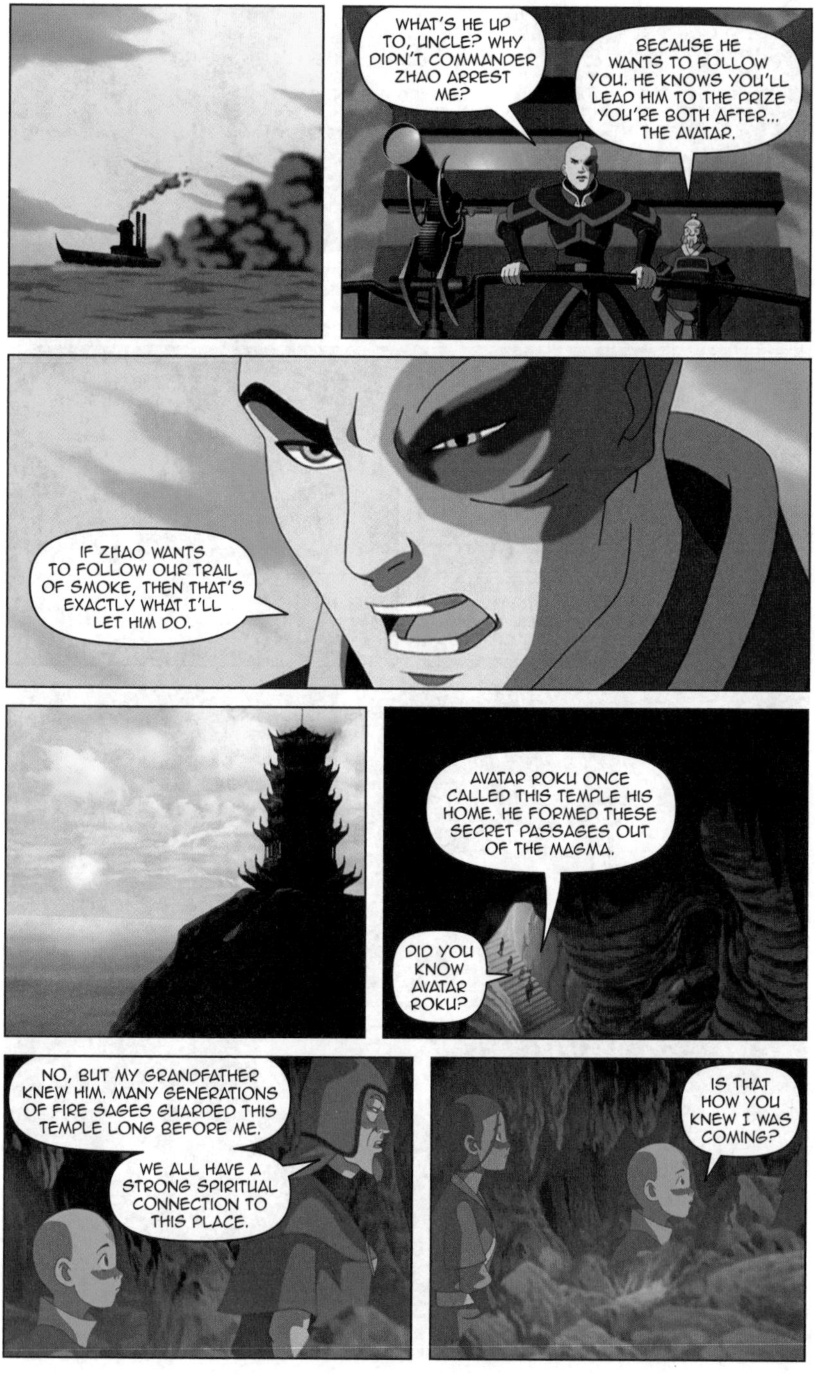
WHAT'S HE UP TO, UNCLE? WHY DIDN'T COMMANDER ZHAO ARREST ME?
BECAUSE HE WANTS TO FOLLOW YOU. HE KNOWS YOU'LL LEAD HIM TO THE PRIZE YOU'RE BOTH AFTER... THE AVATAR.
IF ZHAO WANTS TO FOLLOW OUR TRAIL OF SMOKE, THEN THAT'S EXACTLY WHAT I'LL LET HIM DO.
AVATAR ROKU ONCE CALLED THIS TEMPLE HIS HOME. HE FORMED THESE SECRET PASSAGES OUT OF THE MAGMA.
DID YOU KNOW AVATAR ROKU?
NO, BUT MY GRANDFATHER KNEW HIM. MANY GENERATIONS OF FIRE SAGES GUARDED THIS TEMPLE LONG BEFORE ME.
WE ALL HAVE A STRONG SPIRITUAL CONNECTION TO THIS PLACE.
IS THAT HOW YOU KNEW I WAS COMING?

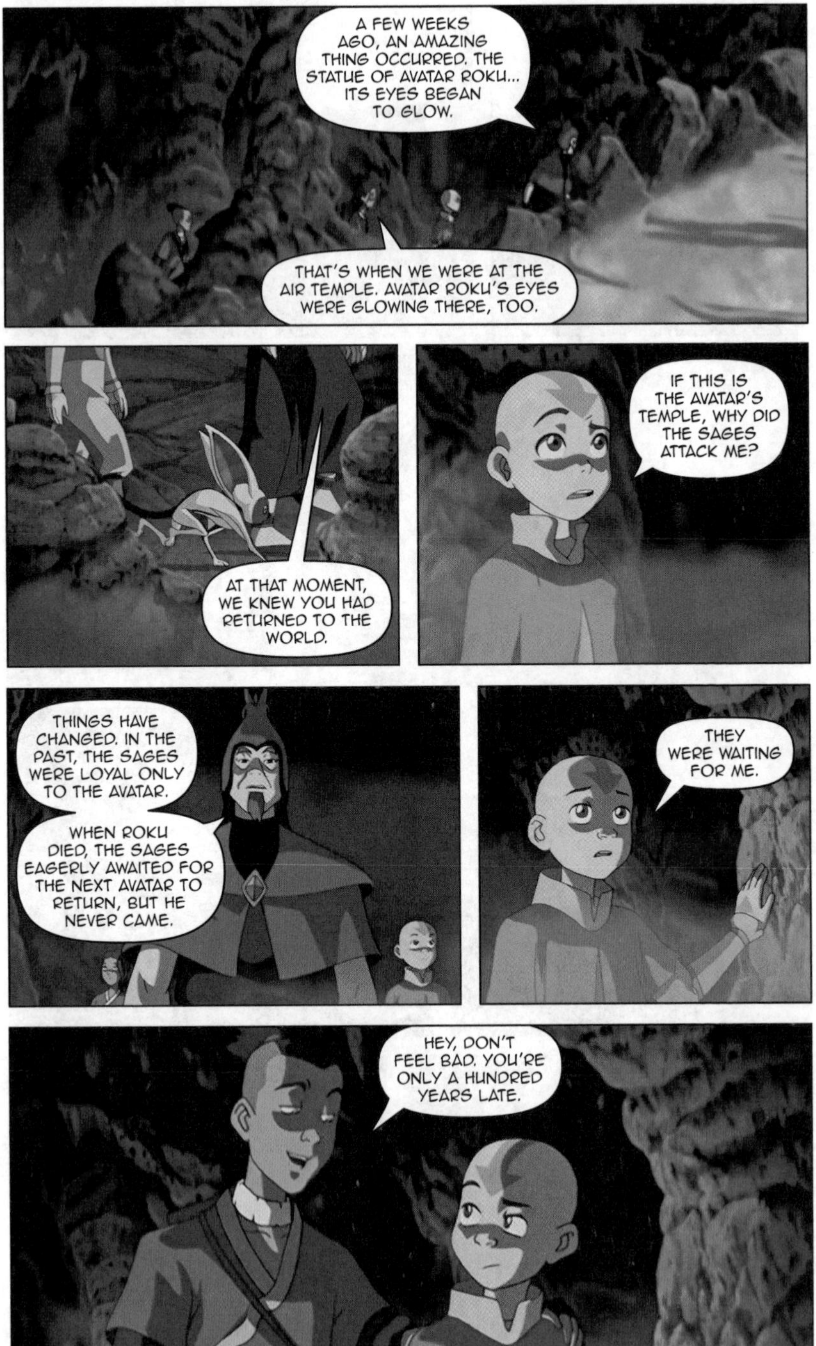
A FEW WEEKS AGO, AN AMAZING THING OCCURRED. THE STATUE OF AVATAR ROKU... ITS EYES BEGAN TO GLOW.
THAT'S WHEN WE WERE AT THE AIR TEMPLE. AVATAR ROKU'S EYES WERE GLOWING THERE, TOO.
AT THAT MOMENT, WE KNEW YOU HAD RETURNED TO THE WORLD.
IF THIS IS THE AVATAR'S TEMPLE, WHY DID THE SAGES ATTACK ME?
THINGS HAVE CHANGED. IN THE PAST, THE SAGES WERE LOYAL ONLY TO THE AVATAR.
WHEN ROKU DIED, THE SAGES EAGERLY AWAITED FOR THE NEXT AVATAR TO RETURN, BUT HE NEVER CAME.
THEY WERE WAITING FOR ME.
HEY, DON'T FEEL BAD. YOU'RE ONLY A HUNDRED YEARS LATE.

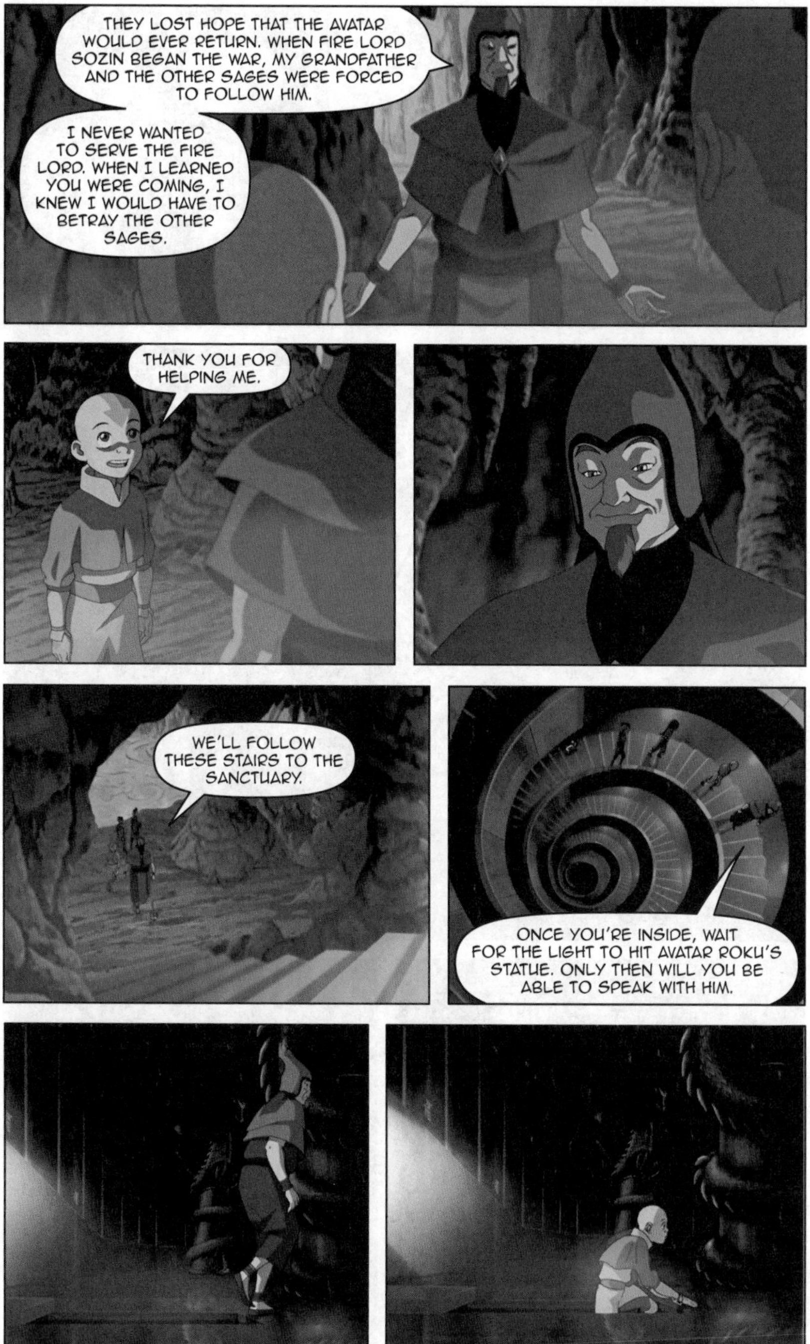
THEY LOST HOPE THAT THE AVATAR WOULD EVER RETURN. WHEN FIRE LORD SOZIN BEGAN THE WAR, MY GRANDFATHER AND THE OTHER SAGES WERE FORCED TO FOLLOW HIM.
I NEVER WANTED TO SERVE THE FIRE LORD. WHEN I LEARNED YOU WERE COMING, I KNEW I WOULD HAVE TO BETRAY THE OTHER SAGES.
THANK YOU FOR HELPING ME.
WE'LL FOLLOW THESE STAIRS TO THE SANCTUARY.
ONCE YOU'RE INSIDE, WAIT FOR THE LIGHT TO HIT AVATAR ROKU'S STATUE. ONLY THEN WILL YOU BE ABLE TO SPEAK WITH HIM.

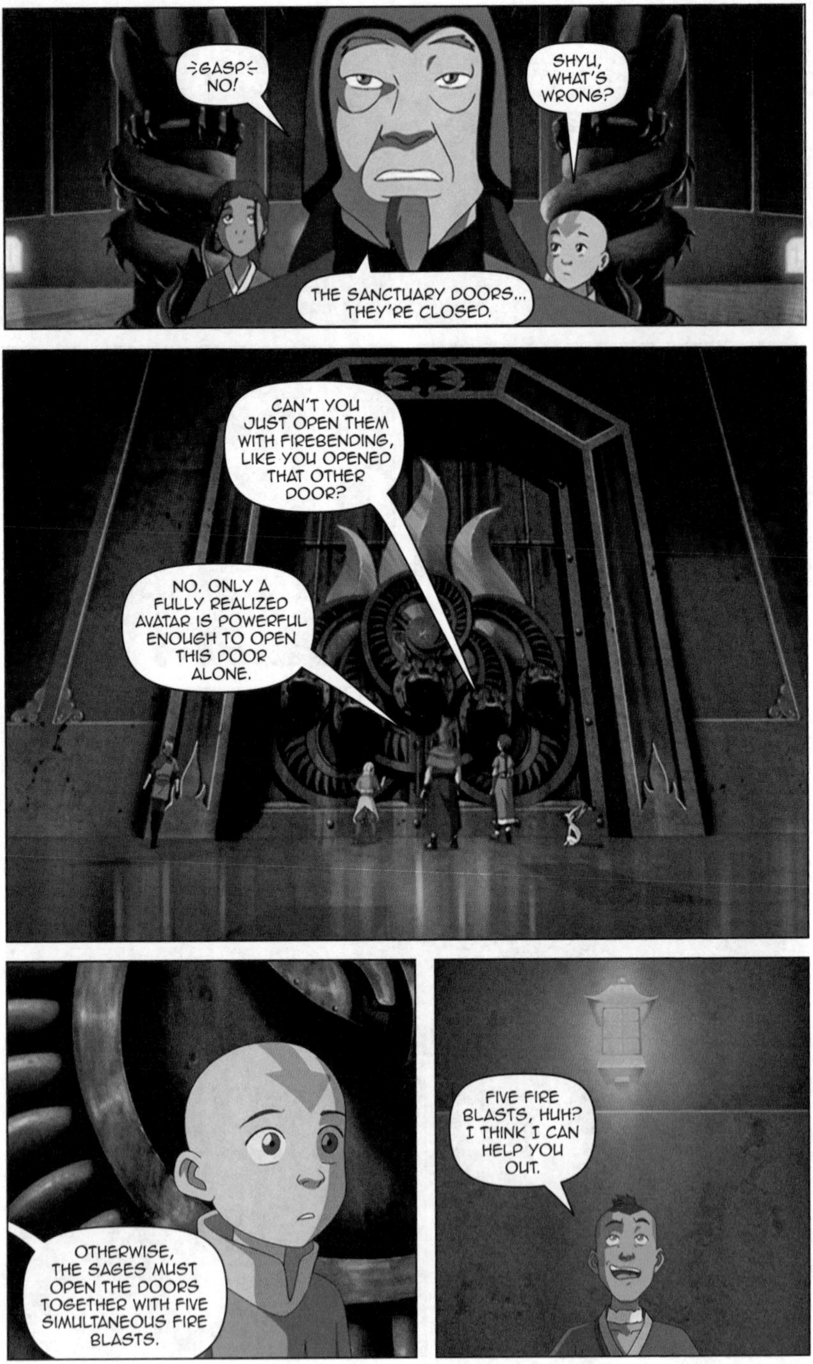
⸗GASP⸗ NO!
SHYU, WHAT'S WRONG?
THE SANCTUARY DOORS... THEY'RE CLOSED.
CAN'T YOU JUST OPEN THEM WITH FIREBENDING, LIKE YOU OPENED THAT OTHER DOOR?
NO. ONLY A FULLY REALIZED AVATAR IS POWERFUL ENOUGH TO OPEN THIS DOOR ALONE.
OTHERWISE, THE SAGES MUST OPEN THE DOORS TOGETHER WITH FIVE SIMULTANEOUS FIRE BLASTS.
FIVE FIRE BLASTS, HUH? I THINK I CAN HELP YOU OUT.

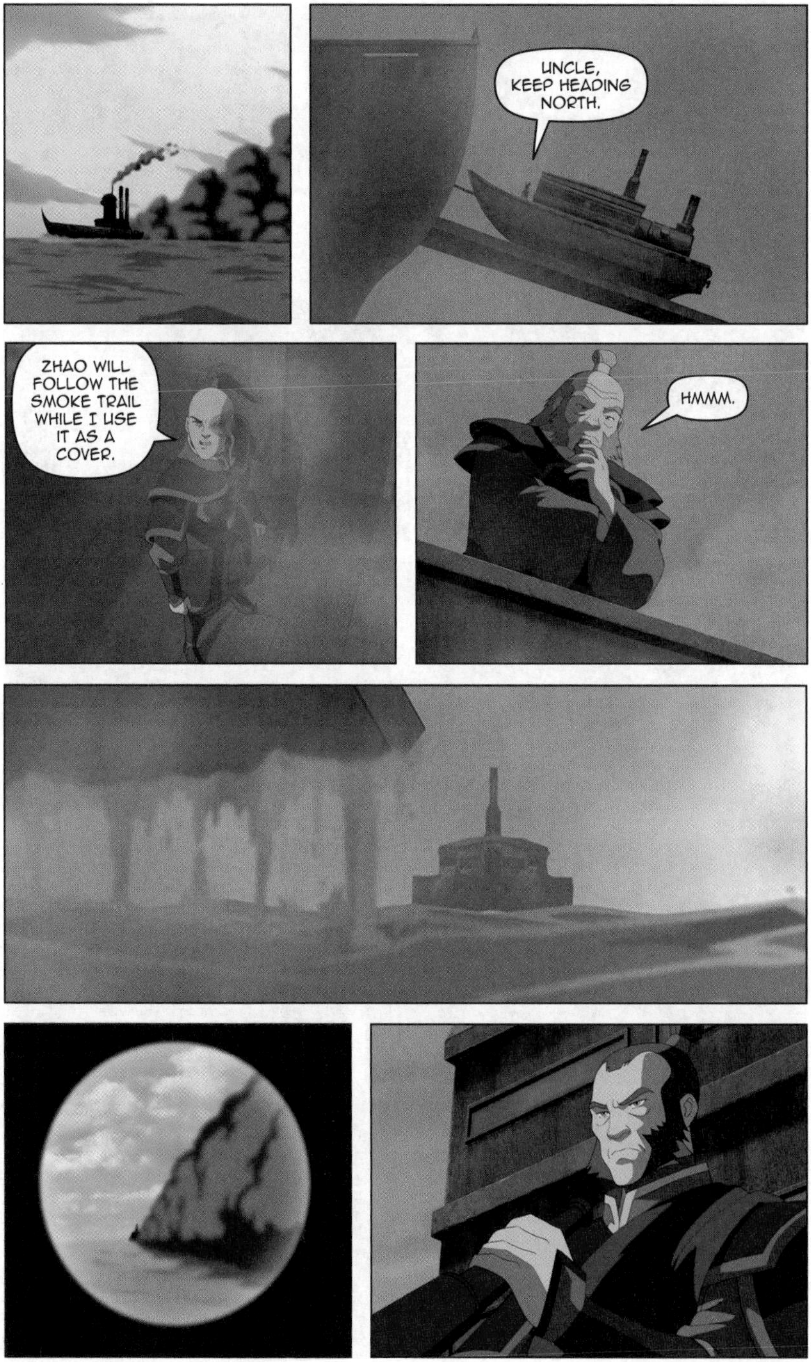
UNCLE, KEEP HEADING NORTH.
ZHAO WILL FOLLOW THE SMOKE TRAIL WHILE I USE IT AS A COVER.
HMMM.

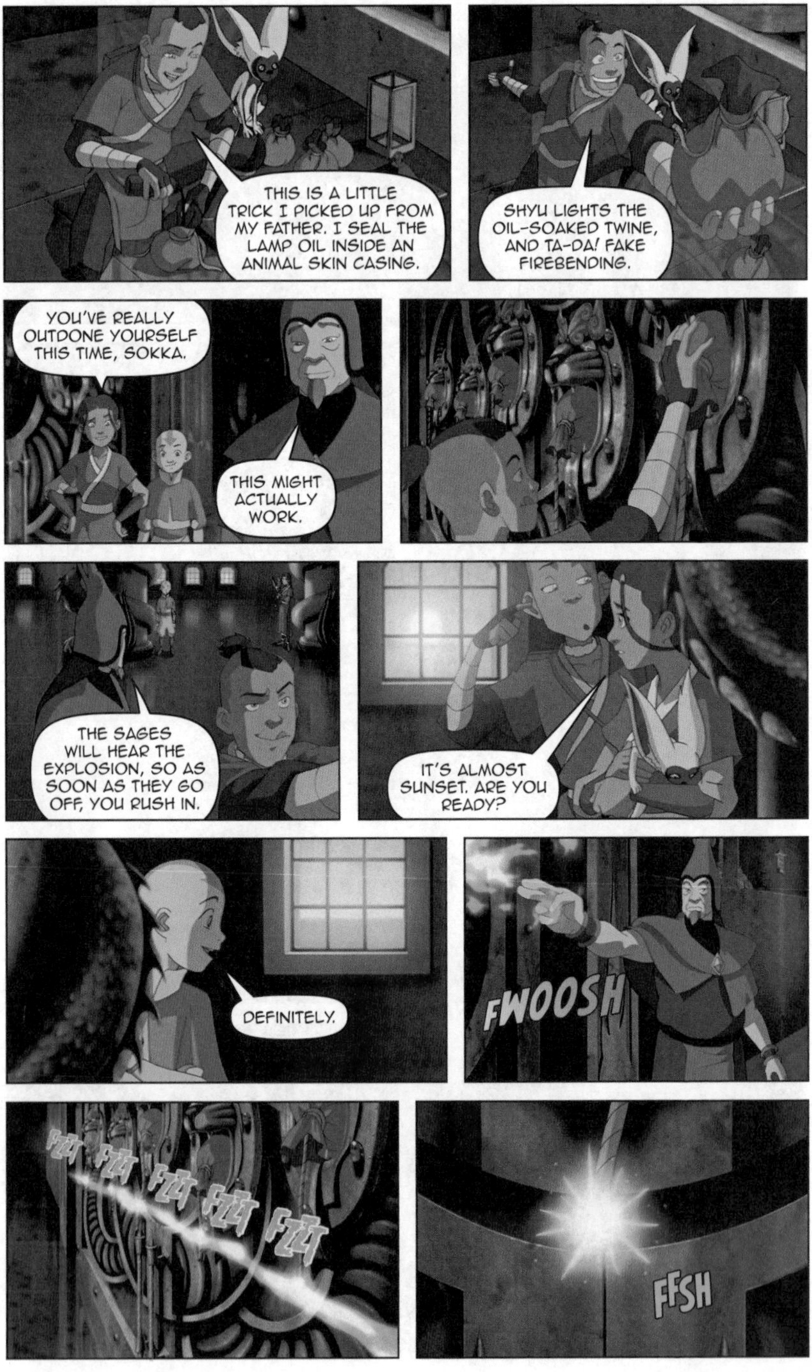
THIS IS A LITTLE TRICK I PICKED UP FROM MY FATHER. I SEAL THE LAMP OIL INSIDE AN ANIMAL SKIN CASING.
SHYU LIGHTS THE OIL-SOAKED TWINE, AND TA-DA! FAKE FIREBENDING.
YOU'VE REALLY OUTDONE YOURSELF THIS TIME, SOKKA.
THIS MIGHT ACTUALLY WORK.
THE SAGES WILL HEAR THE EXPLOSION, SO AS SOON AS THEY GO OFF, YOU RUSH IN.
IT'S ALMOST SUNSET. ARE YOU READY?
DEFINITELY.
FWOOSH
FZZT FZZT FZZT FZZT FZZT
FFSH

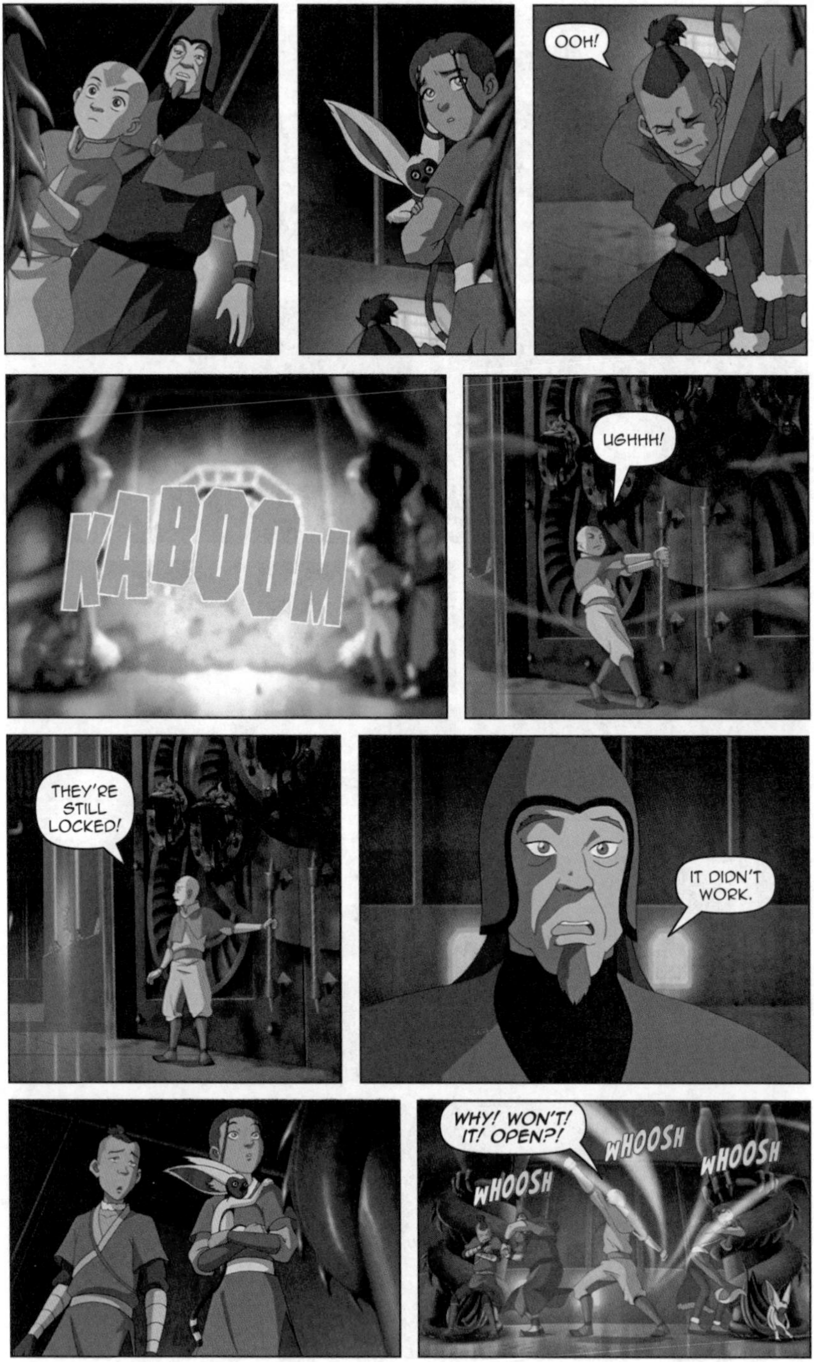
OOH!
KABOOM
UGHHH!
THEY'RE STILL LOCKED!
IT DIDN'T WORK.
WHY! WON'T! IT! OPEN?!
WHOOSH
WHOOSH
WHOOSH

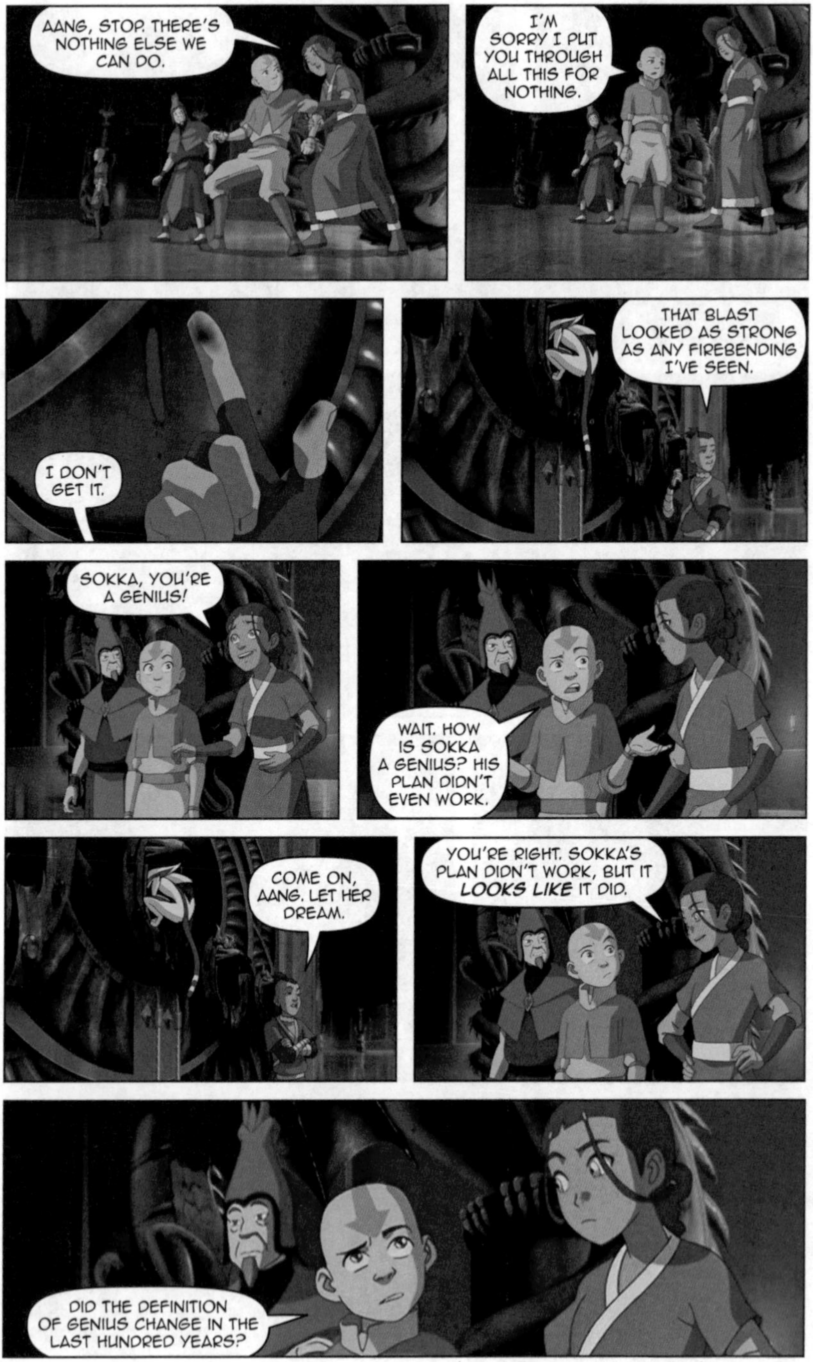
AANG, STOP. THERE'S NOTHING ELSE WE CAN DO.
I'M SORRY I PUT YOU THROUGH ALL THIS FOR NOTHING.
I DON'T GET IT.
THAT BLAST LOOKED AS STRONG AS ANY FIREBENDING I'VE SEEN.
SOKKA, YOU'RE A GENIUS!
WAIT. HOW IS SOKKA A GENIUS? HIS PLAN DIDN'T EVEN WORK.
COME ON, AANG. LET HER DREAM.
YOU'RE RIGHT. SOKKA'S PLAN DIDN'T WORK, BUT IT ***LOOKS LIKE*** IT DID.
DID THE DEFINITION OF GENIUS CHANGE IN THE LAST HUNDRED YEARS?

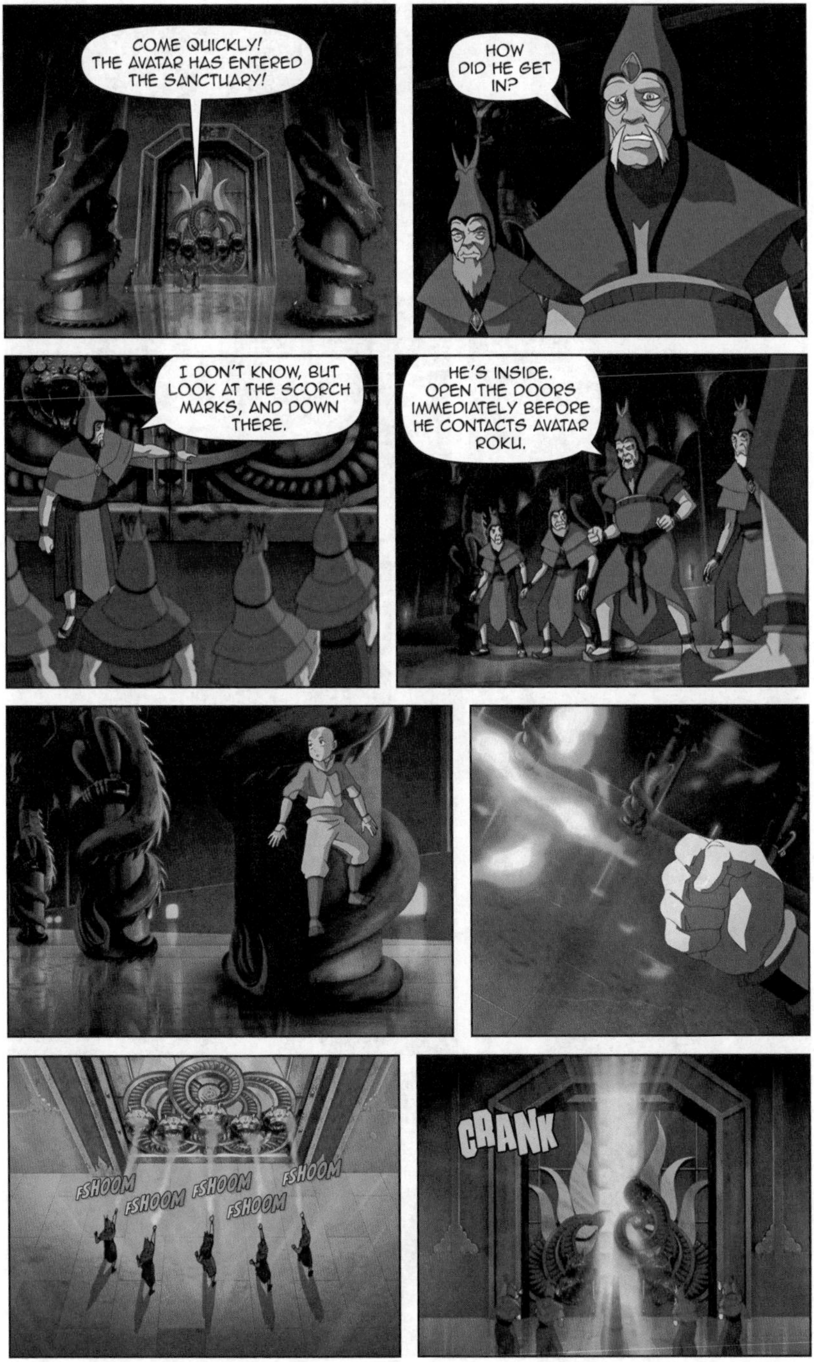
COME QUICKLY! THE AVATAR HAS ENTERED THE SANCTUARY!
HOW DID HE GET IN?
I DON'T KNOW, BUT LOOK AT THE SCORCH MARKS, AND DOWN THERE.
HE'S INSIDE. OPEN THE DOORS IMMEDIATELY BEFORE HE CONTACTS AVATAR ROKU.
FSHOOM
FSHOOM
FSHOOM
FSHOOM
FSHOOM
CRANK

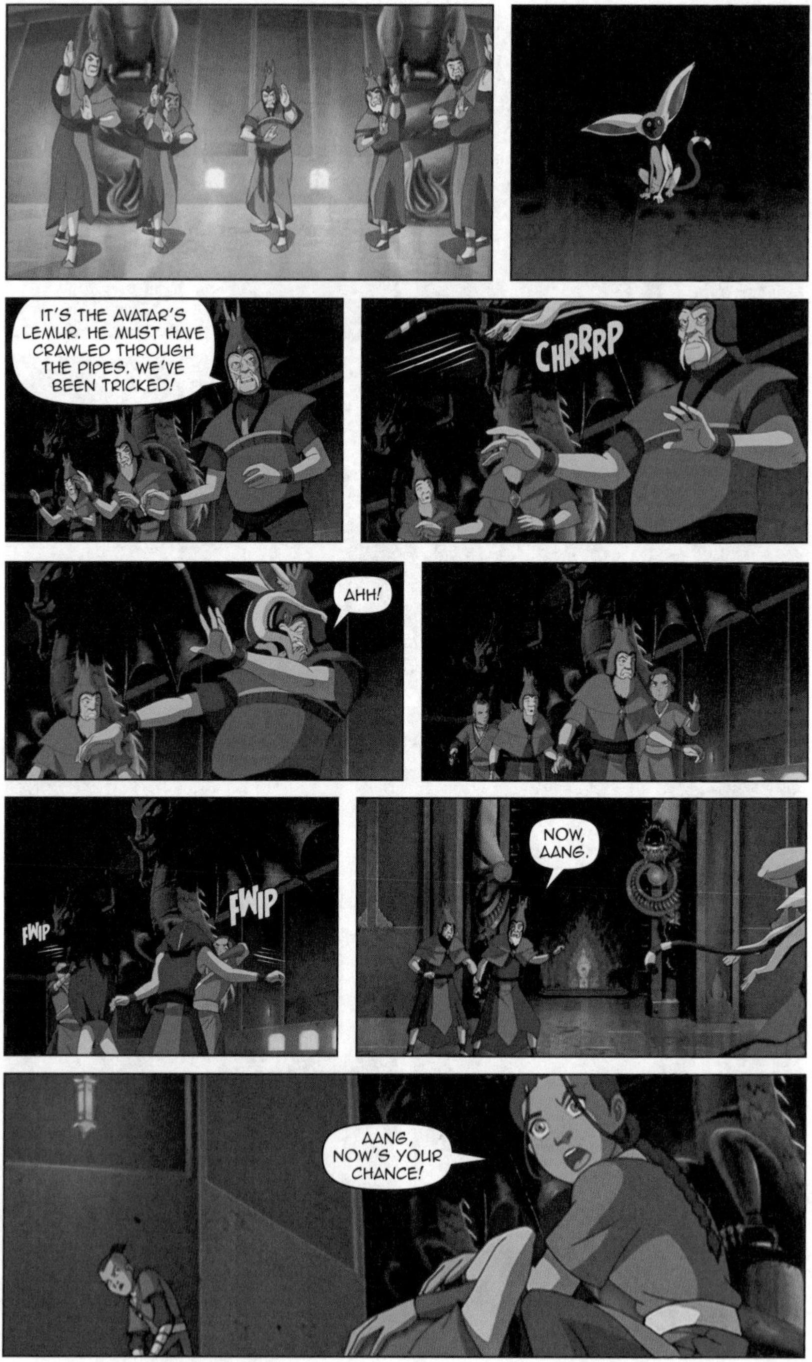
IT'S THE AVATAR'S LEMUR. HE MUST HAVE CRAWLED THROUGH THE PIPES. WE'VE BEEN TRICKED!
CHRRRP
AHH!
FWIP
FWIP
NOW, AANG.
AANG, NOW'S YOUR CHANCE!

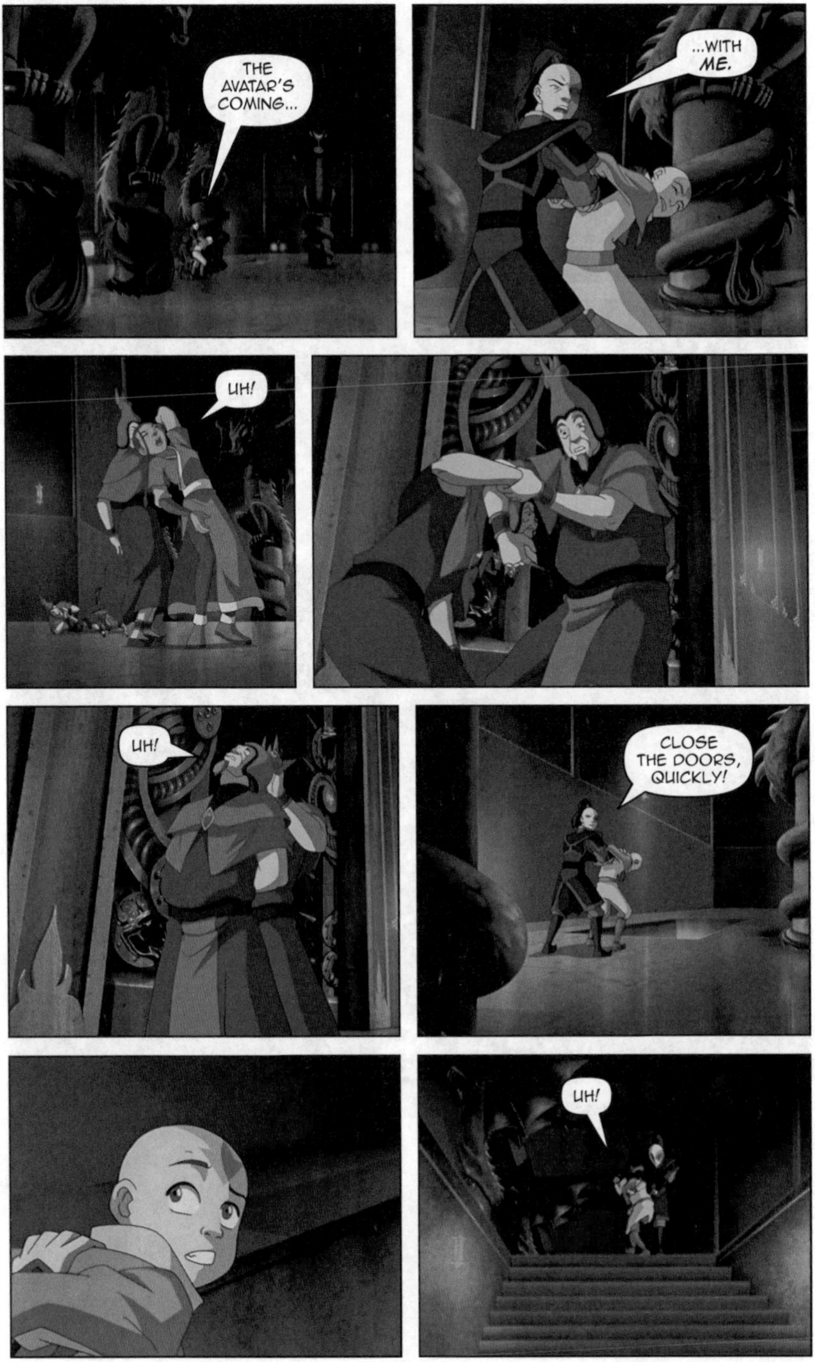
THE AVATAR'S COMING...
...WITH ME.
UH!
UH!
CLOSE THE DOORS, QUICKLY!
UH!

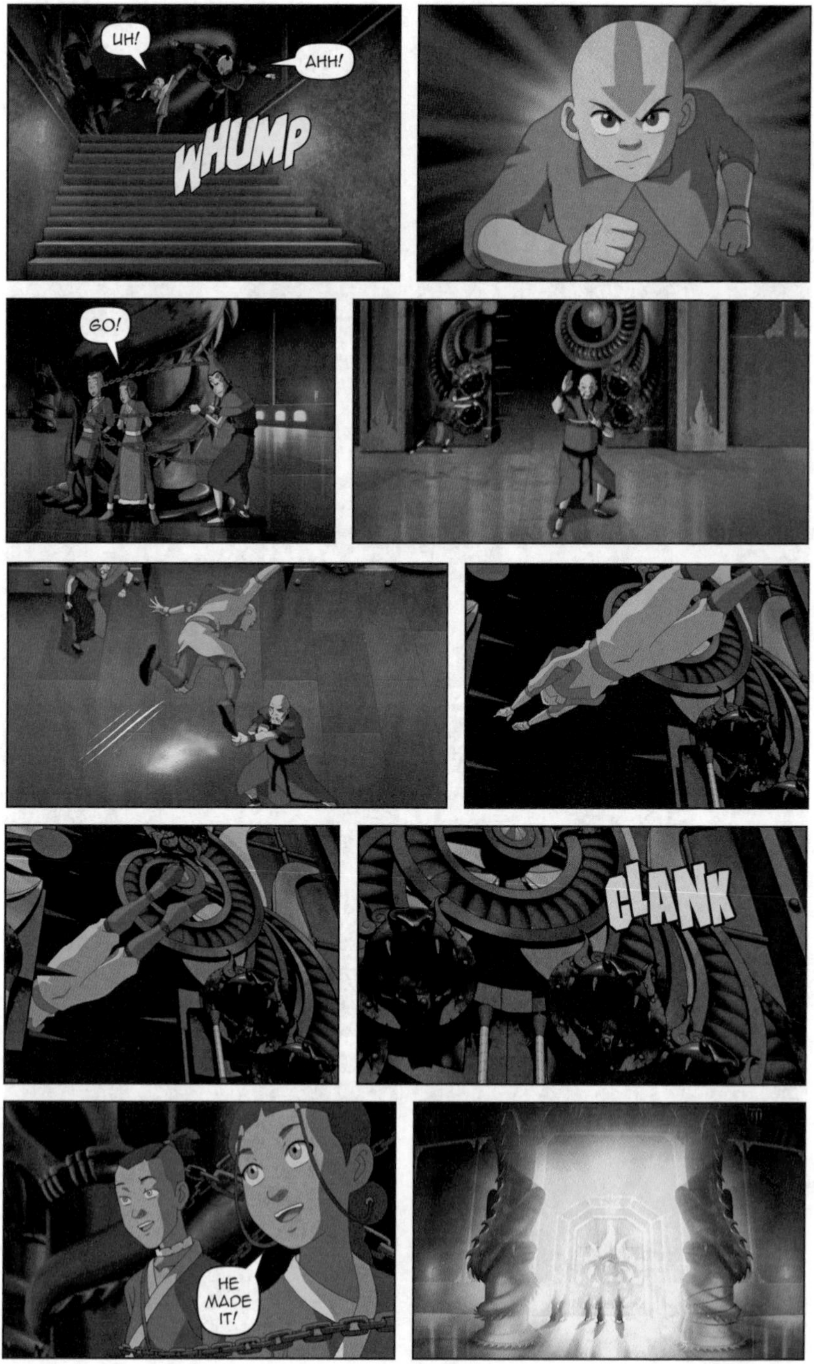
UH!
AHH!
WHUMP
GO!
CLANK
HE MADE IT!

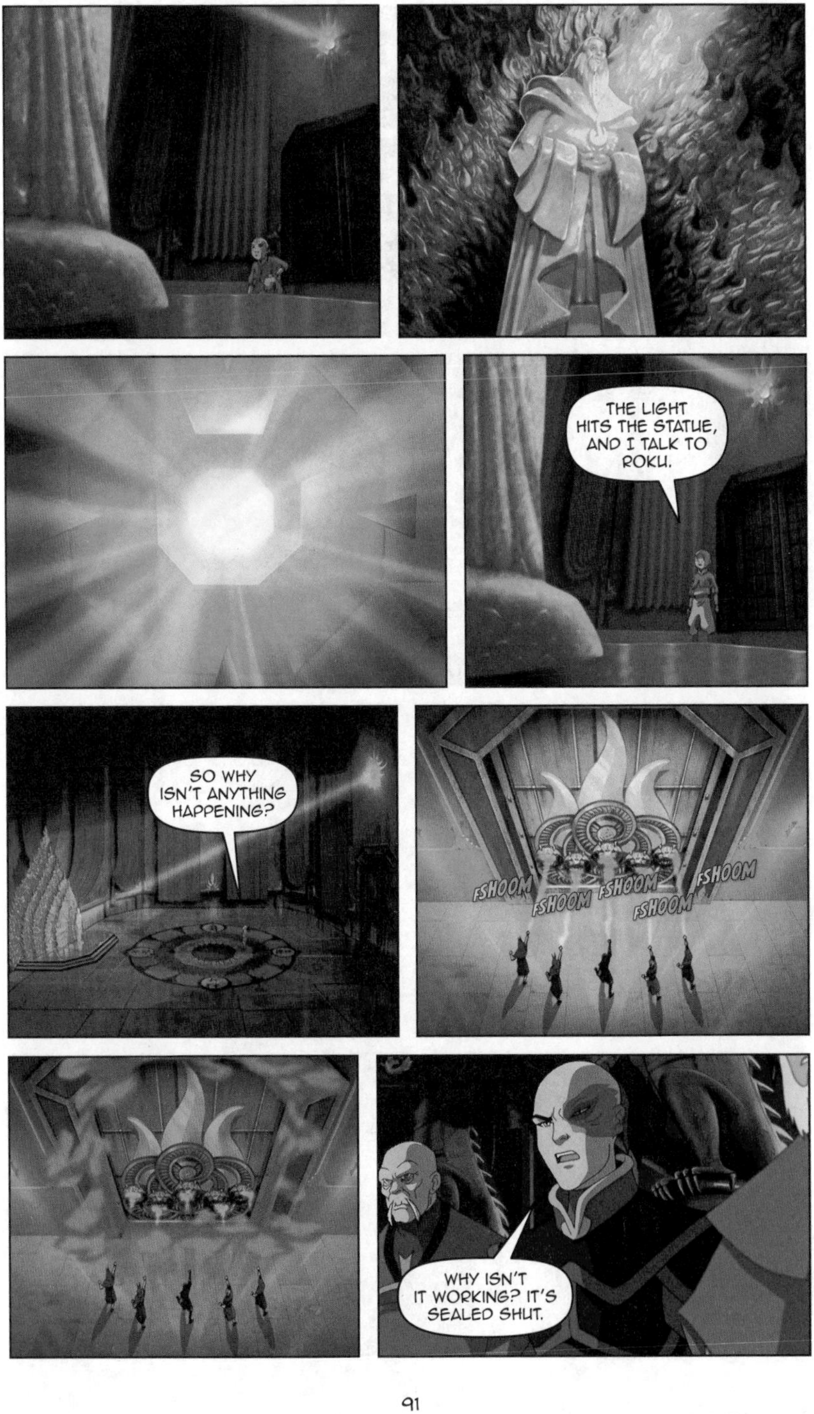
THE LIGHT HITS THE STATUE, AND I TALK TO ROKU.
SO WHY ISN'T ANYTHING HAPPENING?
FSHOOM
FSHOOM
FSHOOM
FSHOOM
FSHOOM
WHY ISN'T IT WORKING? IT'S SEALED SHUT.

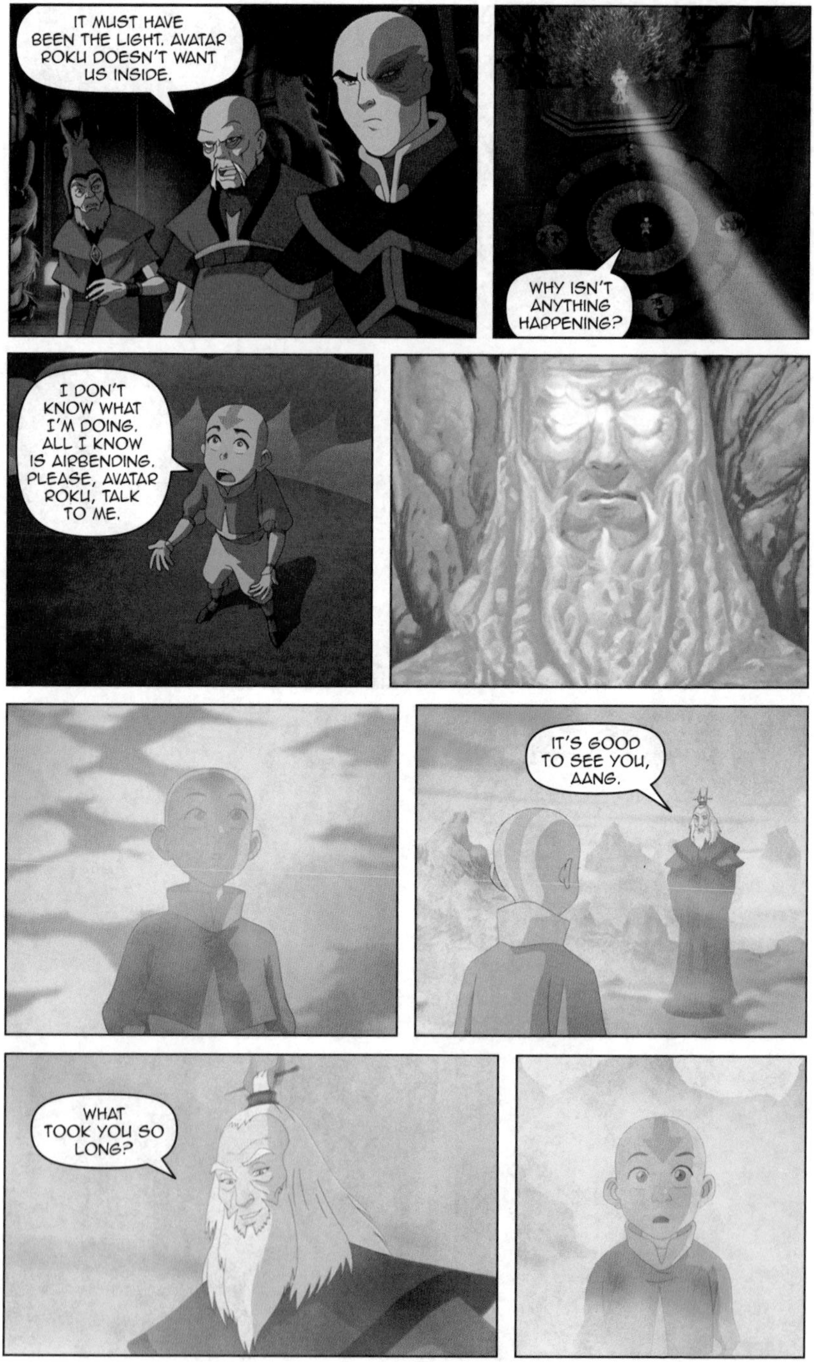
IT MUST HAVE BEEN THE LIGHT. AVATAR ROKU DOESN'T WANT US INSIDE.
WHY ISN'T ANYTHING HAPPENING?
I DON'T KNOW WHAT I'M DOING. ALL I KNOW IS AIRBENDING. PLEASE, AVATAR ROKU, TALK TO ME.
IT'S GOOD TO SEE YOU, AANG.
WHAT TOOK YOU SO LONG?

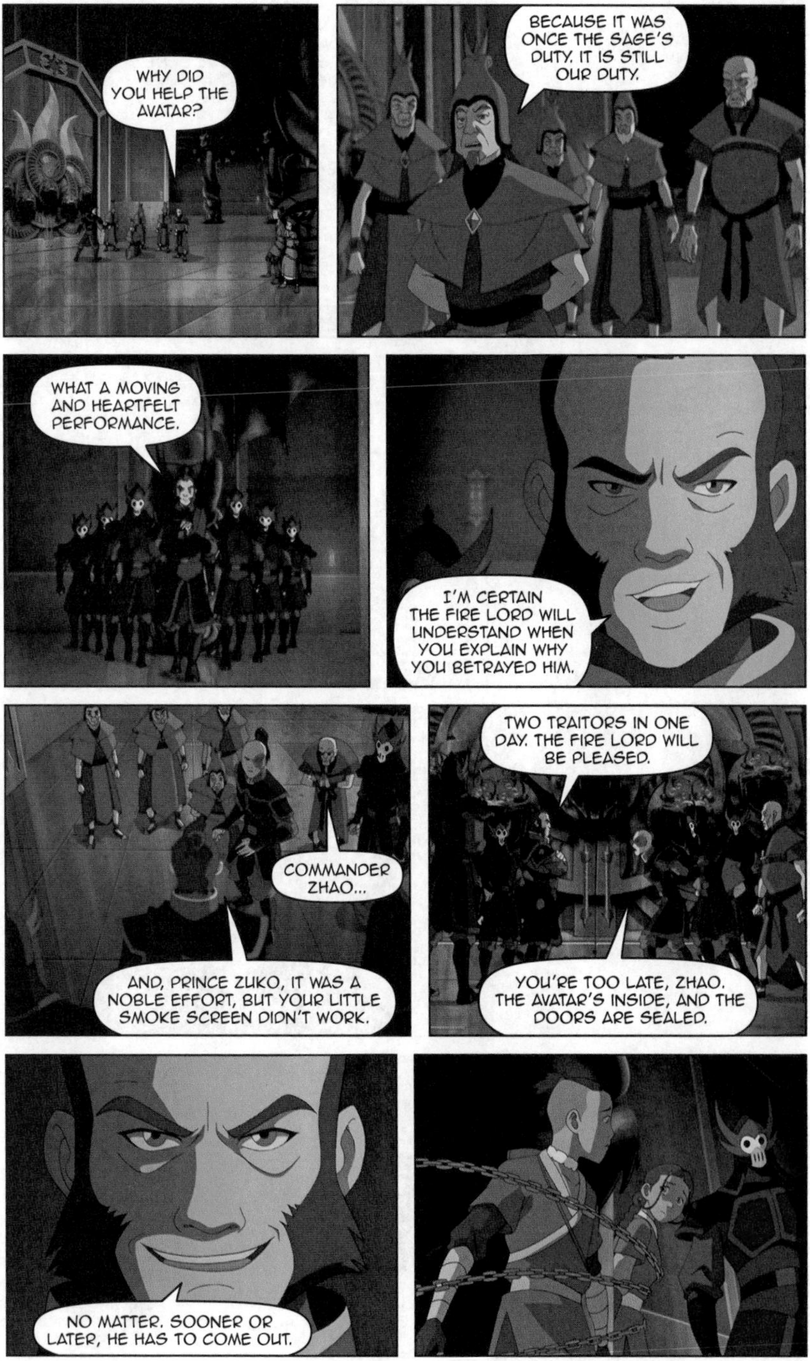
WHY DID YOU HELP THE AVATAR?
BECAUSE IT WAS ONCE THE SAGE'S DUTY. IT IS STILL OUR DUTY.
WHAT A MOVING AND HEARTFELT PERFORMANCE.
I'M CERTAIN THE FIRE LORD WILL UNDERSTAND WHEN YOU EXPLAIN WHY YOU BETRAYED HIM.
COMMANDER ZHAO...
AND, PRINCE ZUKO, IT WAS A NOBLE EFFORT, BUT YOUR LITTLE SMOKE SCREEN DIDN'T WORK.
TWO TRAITORS IN ONE DAY. THE FIRE LORD WILL BE PLEASED.
YOU'RE TOO LATE, ZHAO. THE AVATAR'S INSIDE, AND THE DOORS ARE SEALED.
NO MATTER. SOONER OR LATER, HE HAS TO COME OUT.

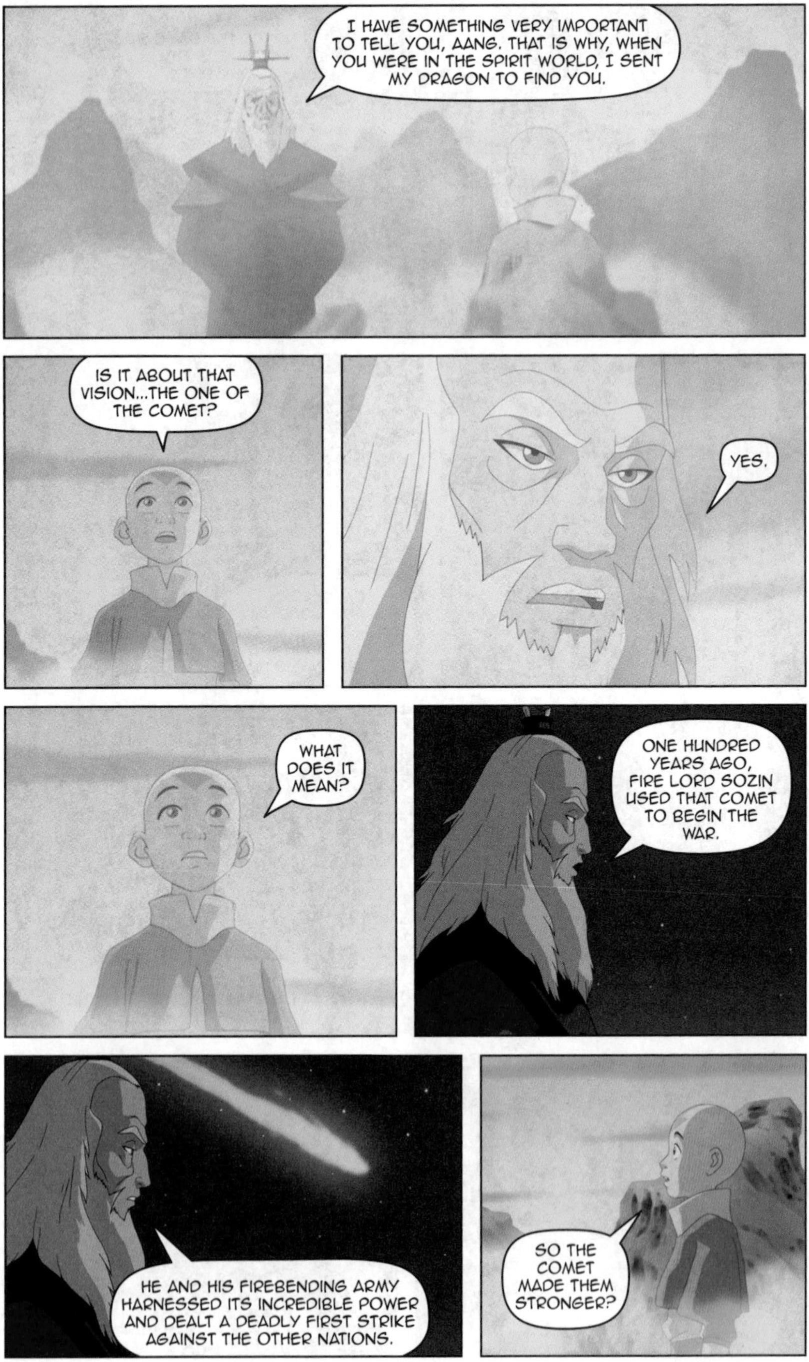
I HAVE SOMETHING VERY IMPORTANT TO TELL YOU, AANG. THAT IS WHY, WHEN YOU WERE IN THE SPIRIT WORLD, I SENT MY DRAGON TO FIND YOU.
IS IT ABOUT THAT VISION...THE ONE OF THE COMET?
YES.
WHAT DOES IT MEAN?
ONE HUNDRED YEARS AGO, FIRE LORD SOZIN USED THAT COMET TO BEGIN THE WAR.
HE AND HIS FIREBENDING ARMY HARNESSED ITS INCREDIBLE POWER AND DEALT A DEADLY FIRST STRIKE AGAINST THE OTHER NATIONS.
SO THE COMET MADE THEM STRONGER?

YES, STRONGER THAN YOU COULD EVEN IMAGINE.

BUT THAT HAPPENED A HUNDRED YEARS AGO. WHAT DOES THE COMET HAVE TO DO WITH THE WAR NOW?

"LISTEN CAREFULLY. SOZIN'S COMET WILL RETURN BY THE END OF THIS SUMMER."

AND FIRE LORD OZAI WILL USE ITS POWER TO FINISH THE WAR ONCE AND FOR ALL.

IF HE SUCCEEDS, EVEN THE AVATAR WON'T BE ABLE TO RESTORE BALANCE TO THE WORLD.

AANG, YOU MUST DEFEAT THE FIRE LORD BEFORE THE COMET ARRIVES.

MASTERING THE ELEMENTS TAKES YEARS OF DISCIPLINE AND PRACTICE. BUT IF THE WORLD IS TO SURVIVE, YOU MUST DO IT BY SUMMER'S END.

BUT I HAVEN'T EVEN STARTED LEARNING WATERBENDING, NOT TO MENTION EARTH AND FIRE.

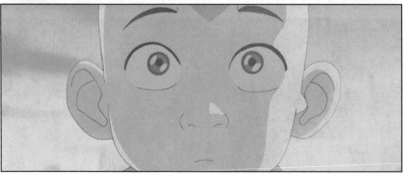

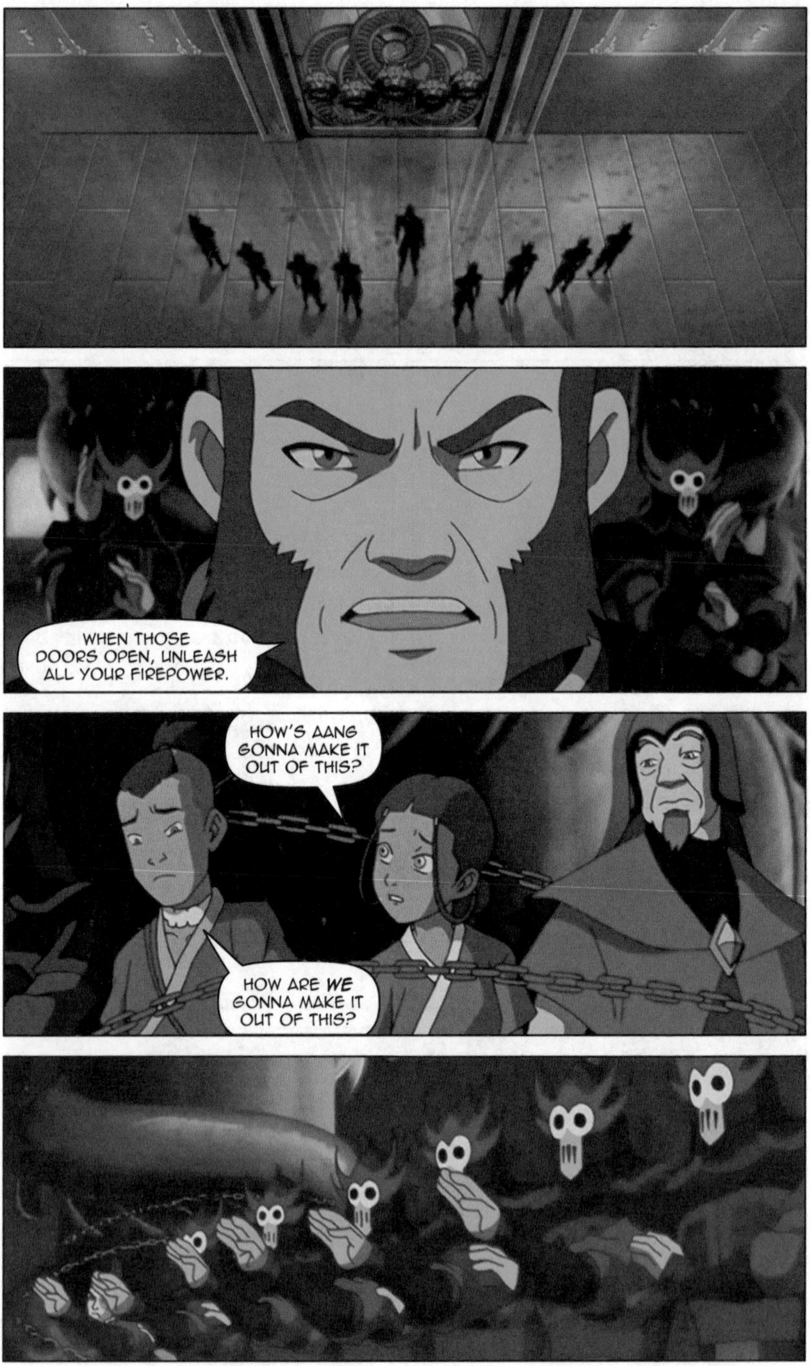
WHEN THOSE DOORS OPEN, UNLEASH ALL YOUR FIREPOWER.
HOW'S AANG GONNA MAKE IT OUT OF THIS?
HOW ARE *WE* GONNA MAKE IT OUT OF THIS?

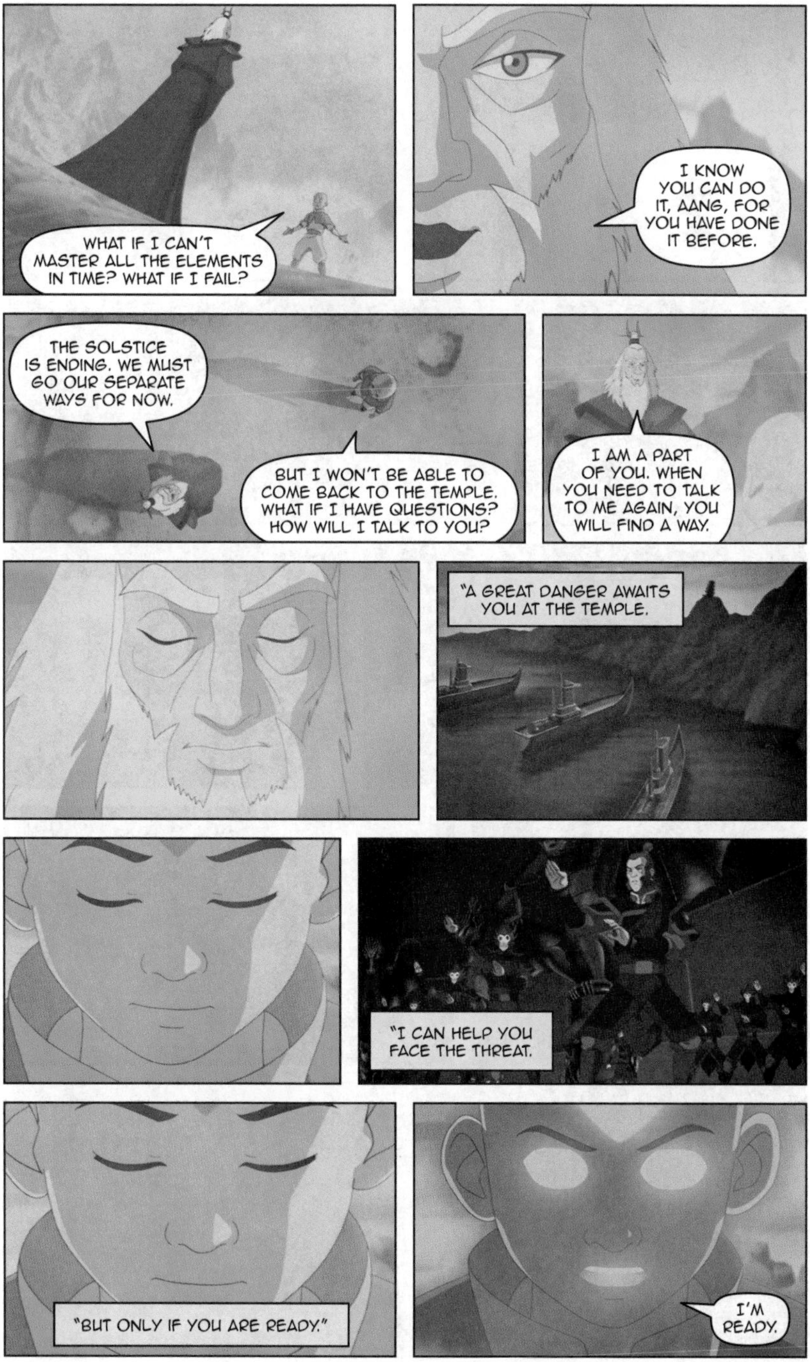
WHAT IF I CAN'T MASTER ALL THE ELEMENTS IN TIME? WHAT IF I FAIL?
I KNOW YOU CAN DO IT, AANG, FOR YOU HAVE DONE IT BEFORE.
THE SOLSTICE IS ENDING. WE MUST GO OUR SEPARATE WAYS FOR NOW.
BUT I WON'T BE ABLE TO COME BACK TO THE TEMPLE. WHAT IF I HAVE QUESTIONS? HOW WILL I TALK TO YOU?
I AM A PART OF YOU. WHEN YOU NEED TO TALK TO ME AGAIN, YOU WILL FIND A WAY.
"A GREAT DANGER AWAITS YOU AT THE TEMPLE.
"I CAN HELP YOU FACE THE THREAT.
"BUT ONLY IF YOU ARE READY."
I'M READY.

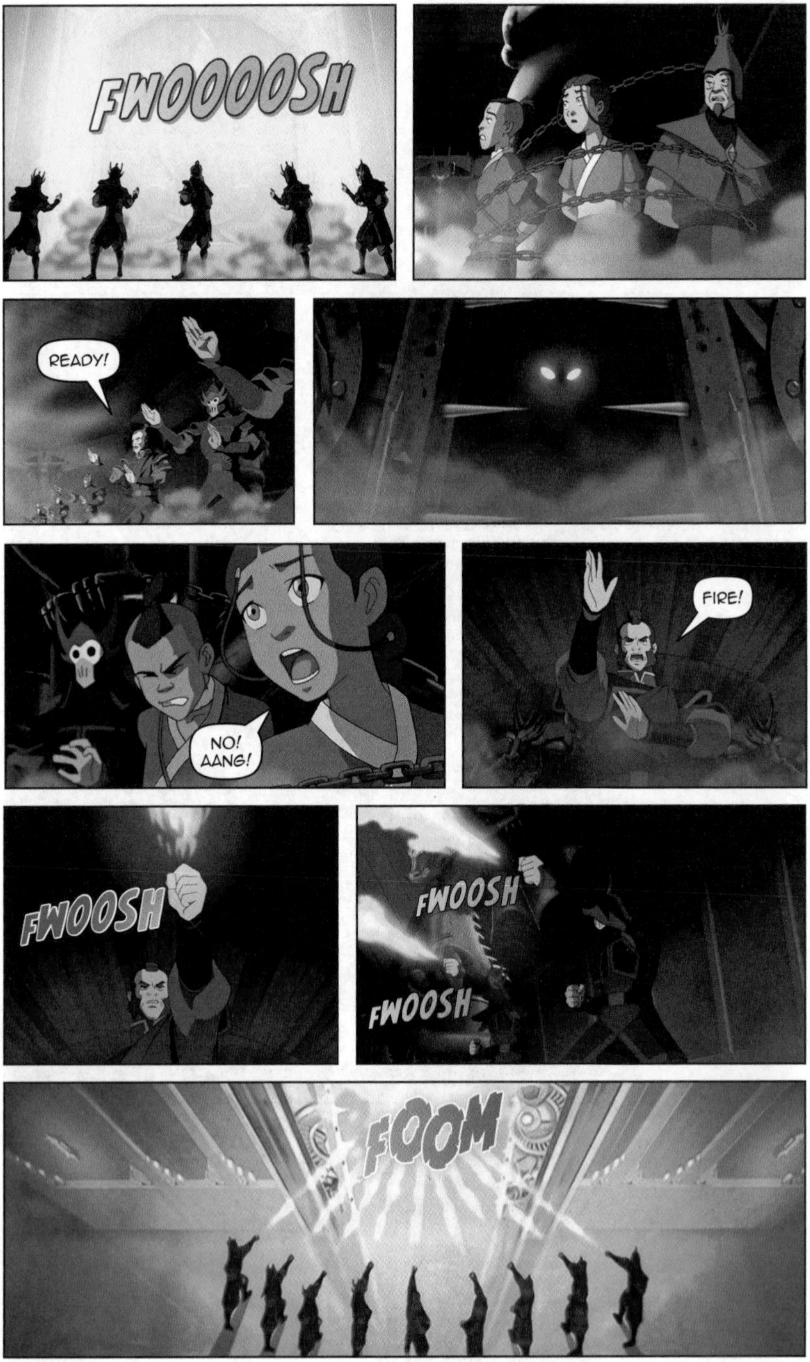
FWOOOOSH
READY!
NO! AANG!
FIRE!
FWOOSH
FWOOSH
FWOOSH
FOOM

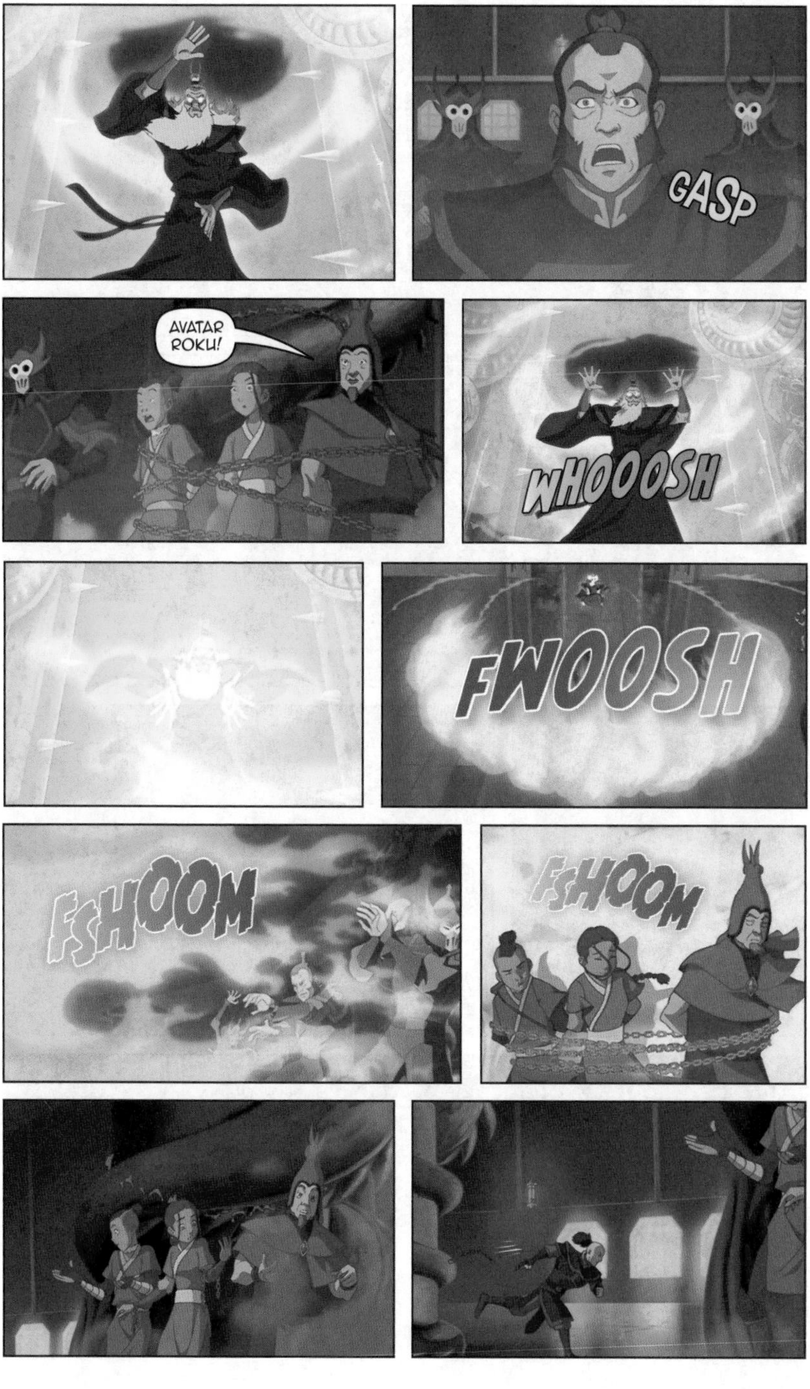
GASP
AVATAR ROKU!
WHOOOSH
FWOOSH
FSHOOM
FSHOOM

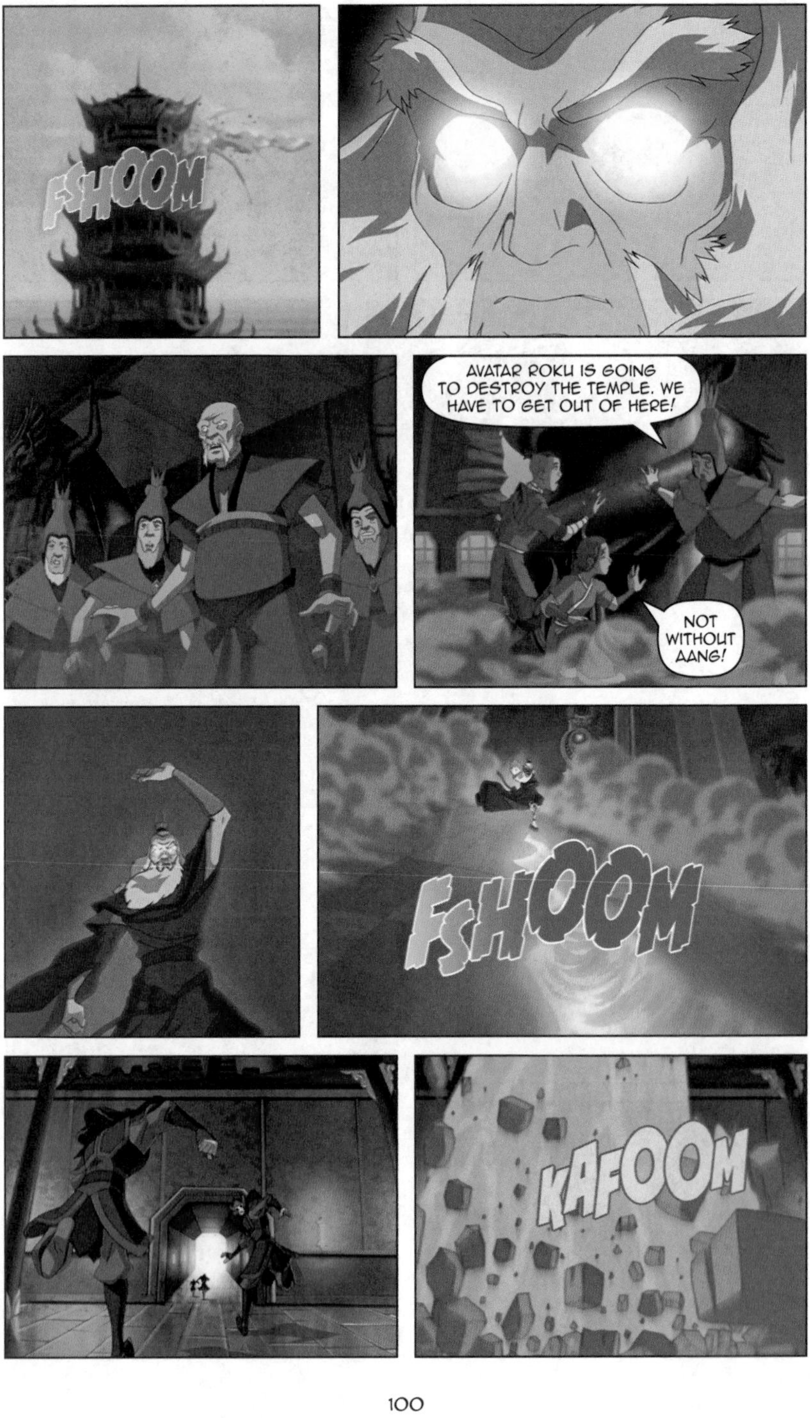
FSHOOM
AVATAR ROKU IS GOING TO DESTROY THE TEMPLE. WE HAVE TO GET OUT OF HERE!
NOT WITHOUT AANG!
FSHOOM
KAFOOM

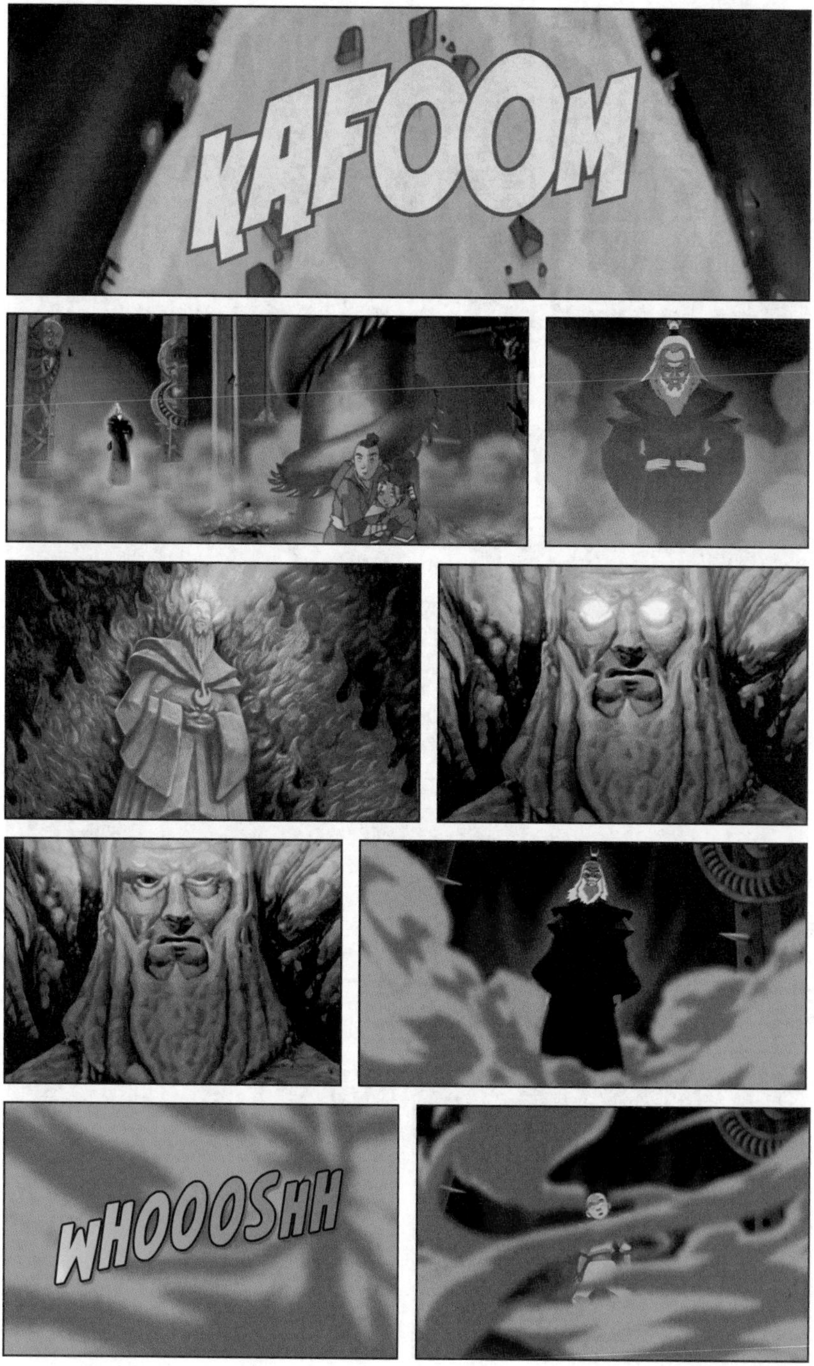
KAFOOM
WHOOOSHH

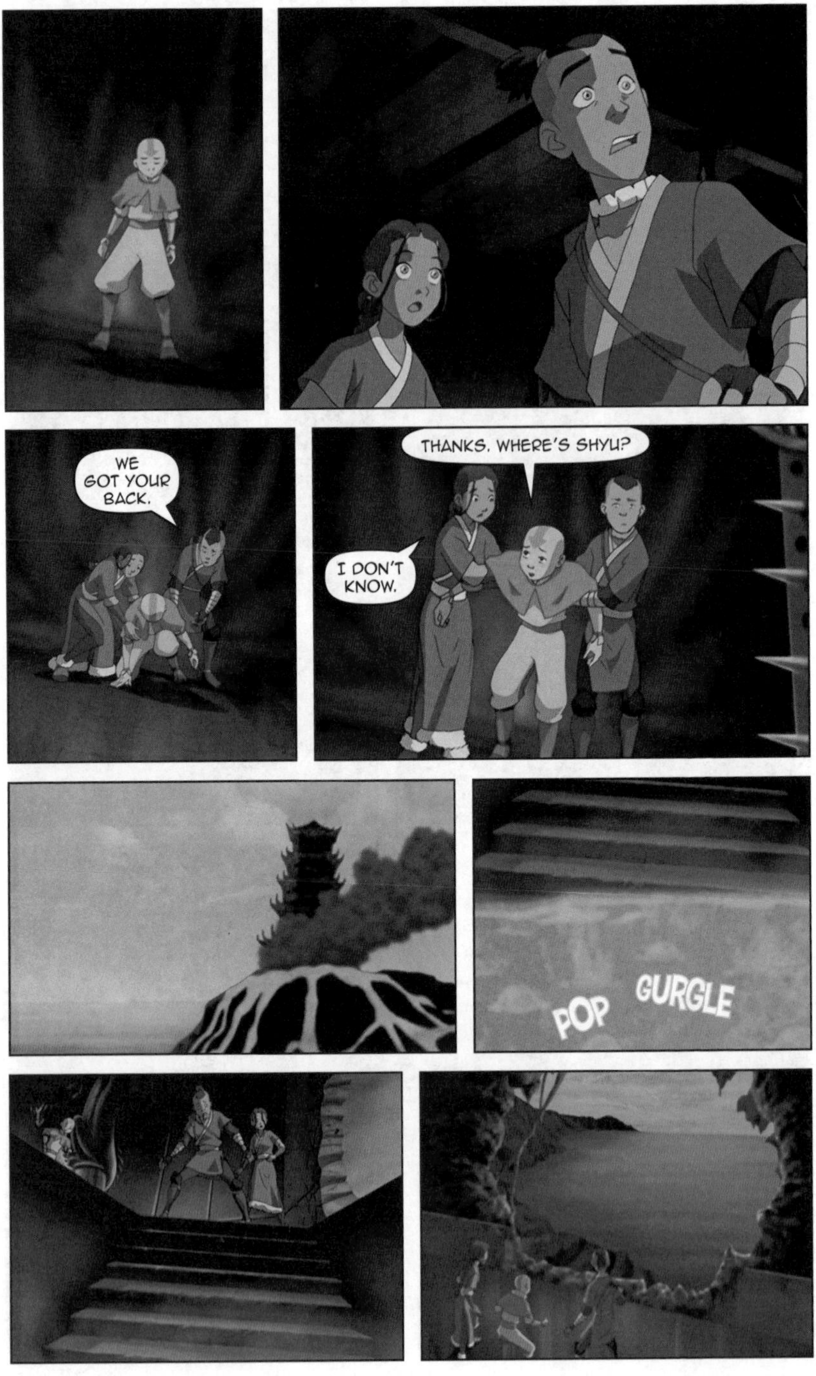
WE GOT YOUR BACK.
THANKS. WHERE'S SHYU?
I DON'T KNOW.
POP
GURGLE

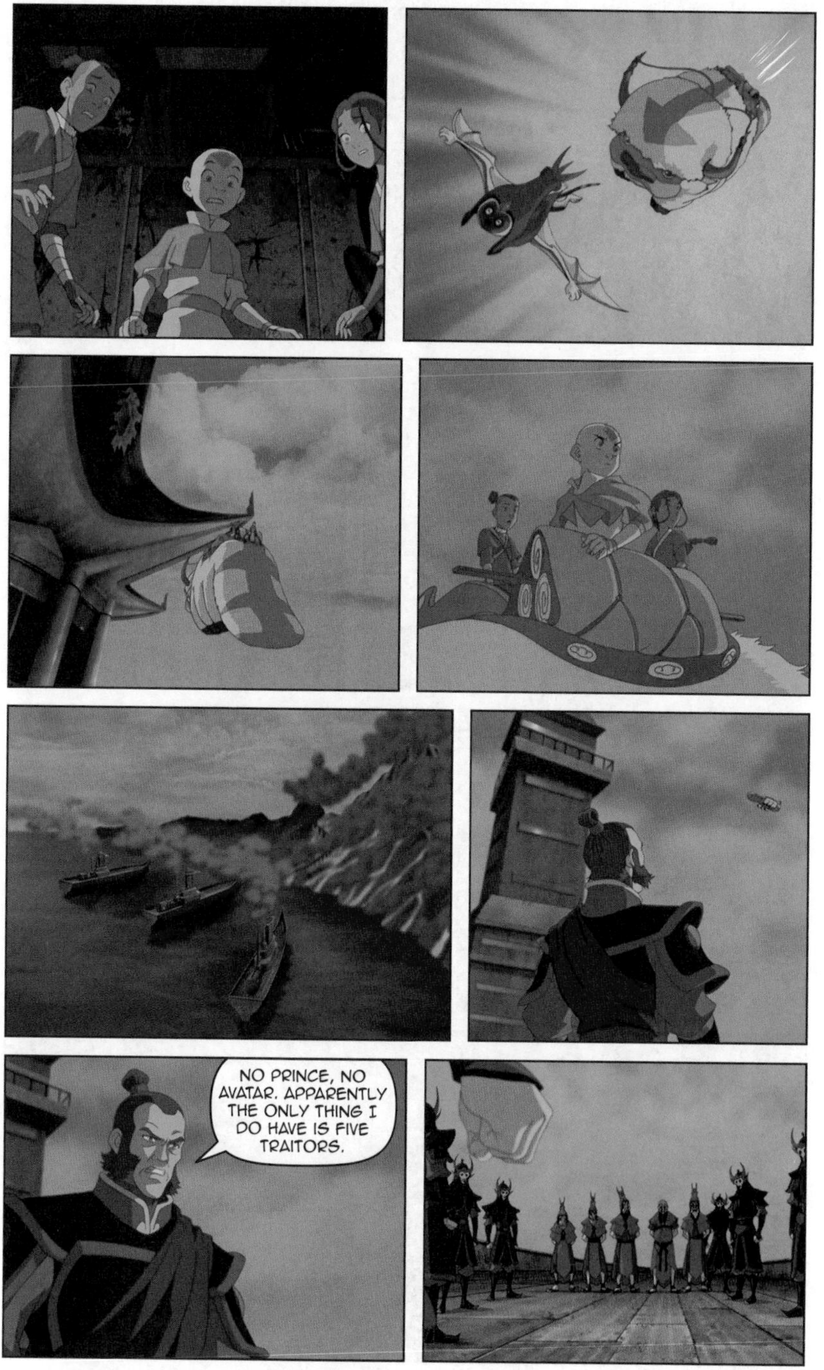
NO PRINCE, NO AVATAR. APPARENTLY THE ONLY THING I DO HAVE IS FIVE TRAITORS.

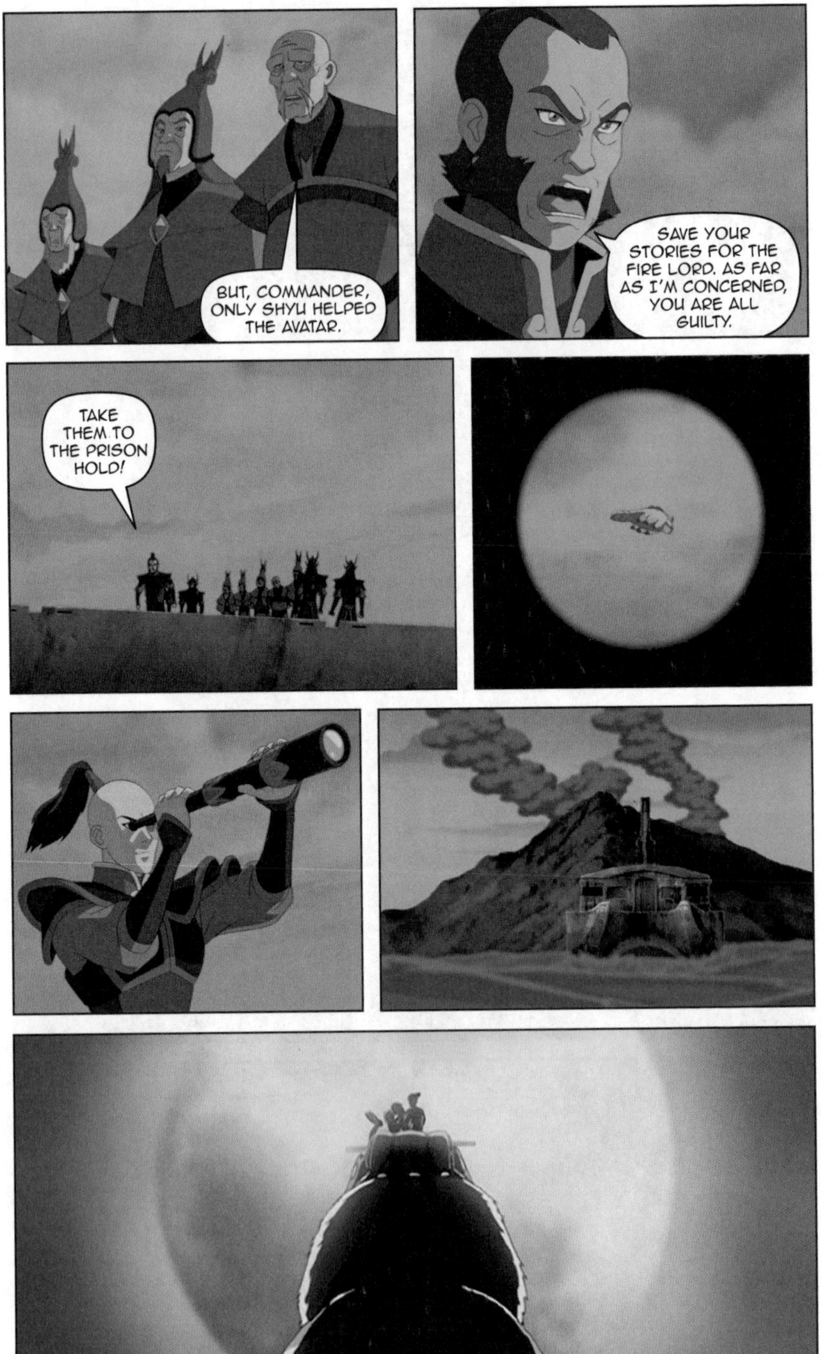
BUT, COMMANDER, ONLY SHYU HELPED THE AVATAR.
SAVE YOUR STORIES FOR THE FIRE LORD. AS FAR AS I'M CONCERNED, YOU ARE ALL GUILTY.
TAKE THEM TO THE PRISON HOLD!

CHAPTER NINE
THE WATERBENDING SCROLL

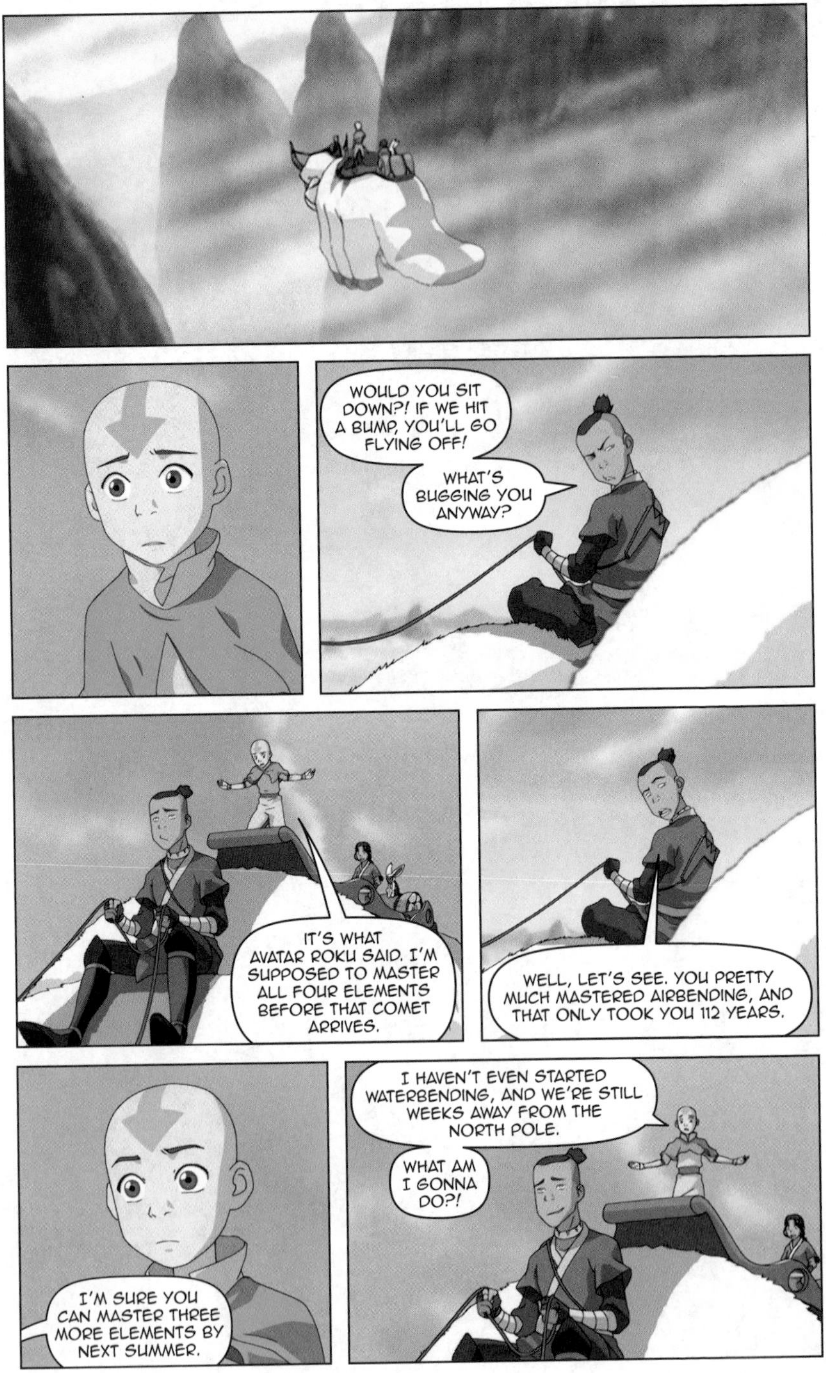
WOULD YOU SIT DOWN?! IF WE HIT A BUMP, YOU'LL GO FLYING OFF!
WHAT'S BUGGING YOU ANYWAY?
IT'S WHAT AVATAR ROKU SAID. I'M SUPPOSED TO MASTER ALL FOUR ELEMENTS BEFORE THAT COMET ARRIVES.
WELL, LET'S SEE. YOU PRETTY MUCH MASTERED AIRBENDING, AND THAT ONLY TOOK YOU 112 YEARS.
I'M SURE YOU CAN MASTER THREE MORE ELEMENTS BY NEXT SUMMER.
I HAVEN'T EVEN STARTED WATERBENDING, AND WE'RE STILL WEEKS AWAY FROM THE NORTH POLE.
WHAT AM I GONNA DO?!

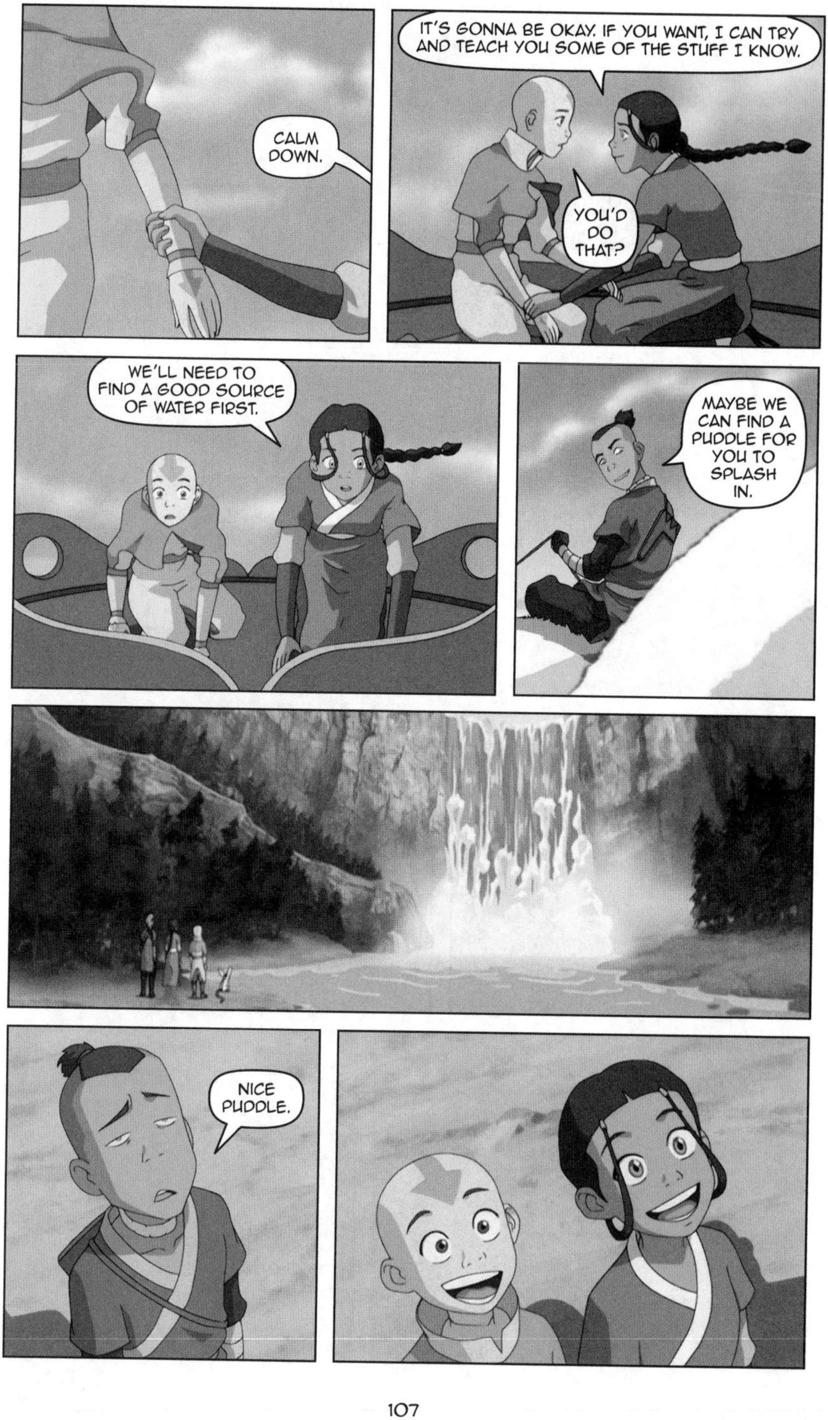
CALM DOWN.
IT'S GONNA BE OKAY. IF YOU WANT, I CAN TRY AND TEACH YOU SOME OF THE STUFF I KNOW.
YOU'D DO THAT?
WE'LL NEED TO FIND A GOOD SOURCE OF WATER FIRST.
MAYBE WE CAN FIND A PUDDLE FOR YOU TO SPLASH IN.
NICE PUDDLE.

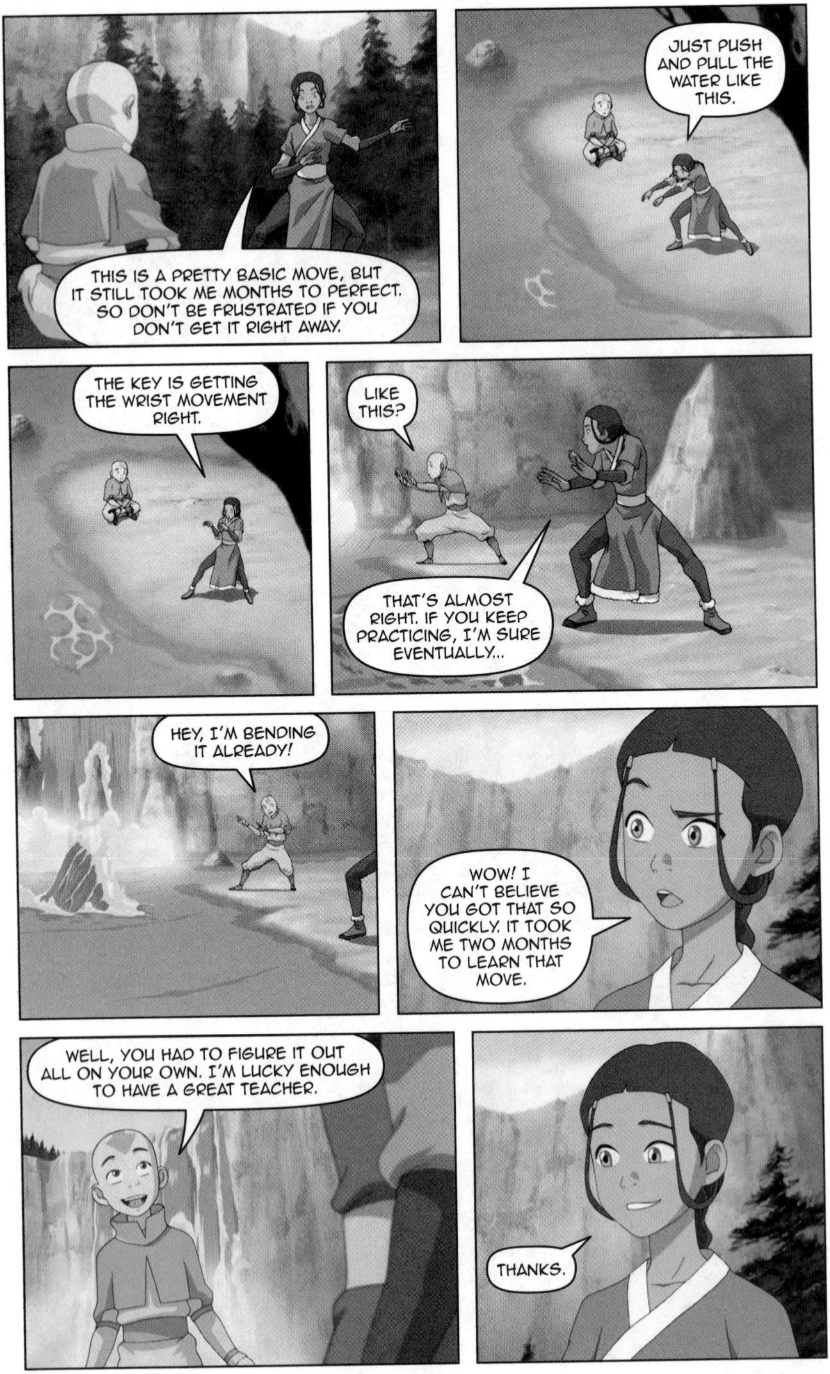
THIS IS A PRETTY BASIC MOVE, BUT IT STILL TOOK ME MONTHS TO PERFECT. SO DON'T BE FRUSTRATED IF YOU DON'T GET IT RIGHT AWAY.
JUST PUSH AND PULL THE WATER LIKE THIS.
THE KEY IS GETTING THE WRIST MOVEMENT RIGHT.
LIKE THIS?
THAT'S ALMOST RIGHT. IF YOU KEEP PRACTICING, I'M SURE EVENTUALLY...
HEY, I'M BENDING IT ALREADY!
WOW! I CAN'T BELIEVE YOU GOT THAT SO QUICKLY. IT TOOK ME TWO MONTHS TO LEARN THAT MOVE.
WELL, YOU HAD TO FIGURE IT OUT ALL ON YOUR OWN. I'M LUCKY ENOUGH TO HAVE A GREAT TEACHER.
THANKS.

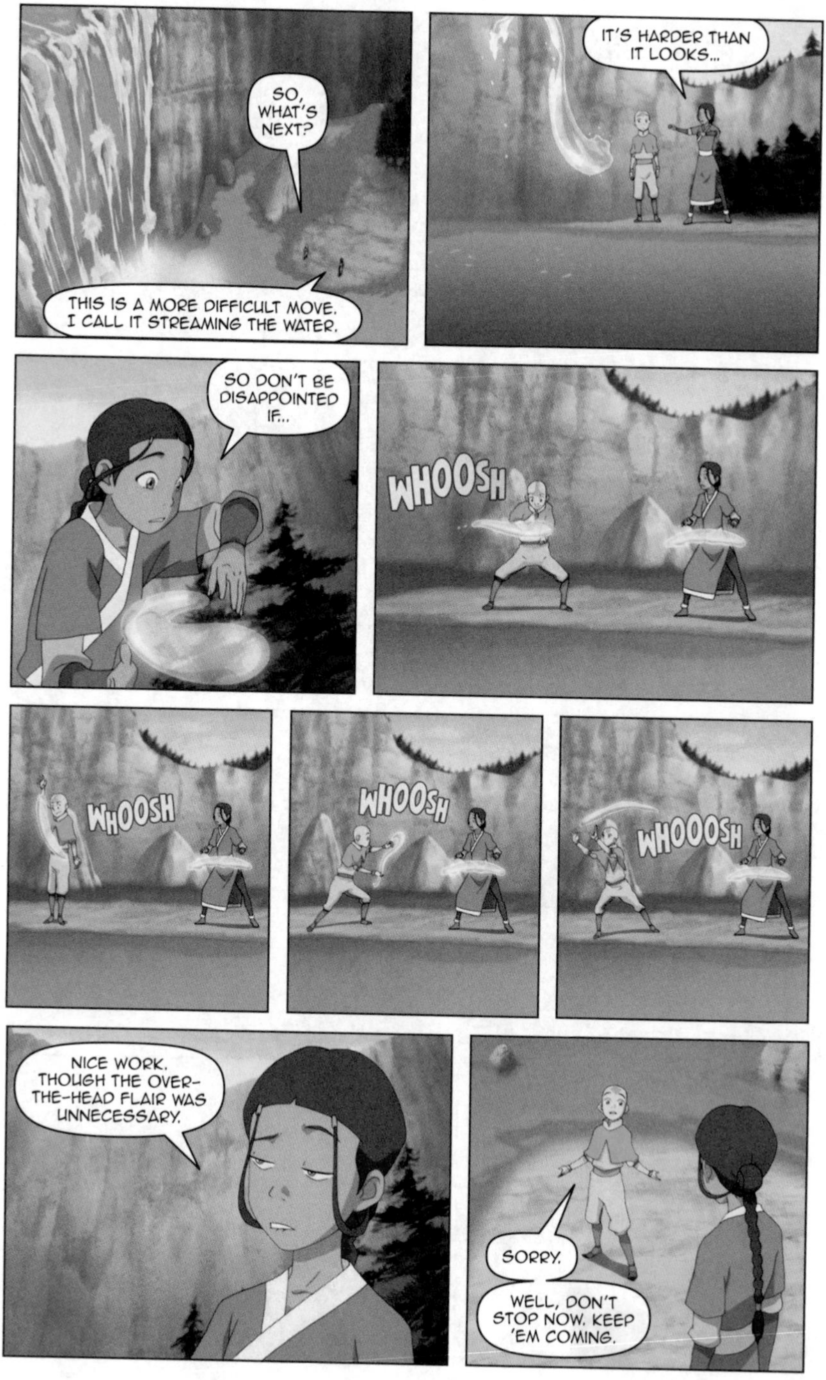
SO, WHAT'S NEXT?
THIS IS A MORE DIFFICULT MOVE. I CALL IT STREAMING THE WATER.
IT'S HARDER THAN IT LOOKS...
SO DON'T BE DISAPPOINTED IF...
WHOOSH
WHOOSH
WHOOSH
WHOOOSH
NICE WORK. THOUGH THE OVER-THE-HEAD FLAIR WAS UNNECESSARY.
SORRY.
WELL, DON'T STOP NOW. KEEP 'EM COMING.

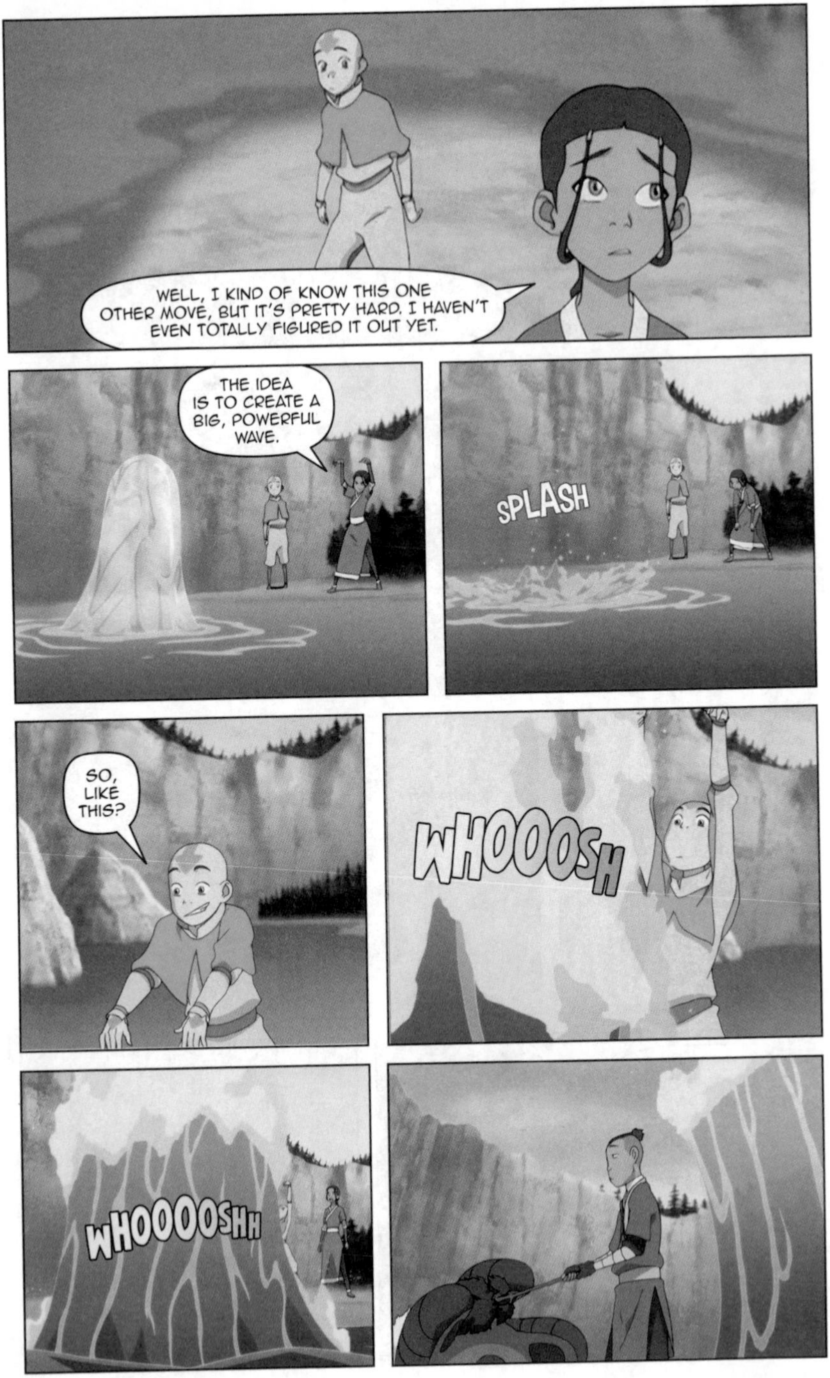
WELL, I KIND OF KNOW THIS ONE OTHER MOVE, BUT IT'S PRETTY HARD. I HAVEN'T EVEN TOTALLY FIGURED IT OUT YET.
THE IDEA IS TO CREATE A BIG, POWERFUL WAVE.
SPLASH
SO, LIKE THIS?
WHOOOSH
WHOOOOSHH

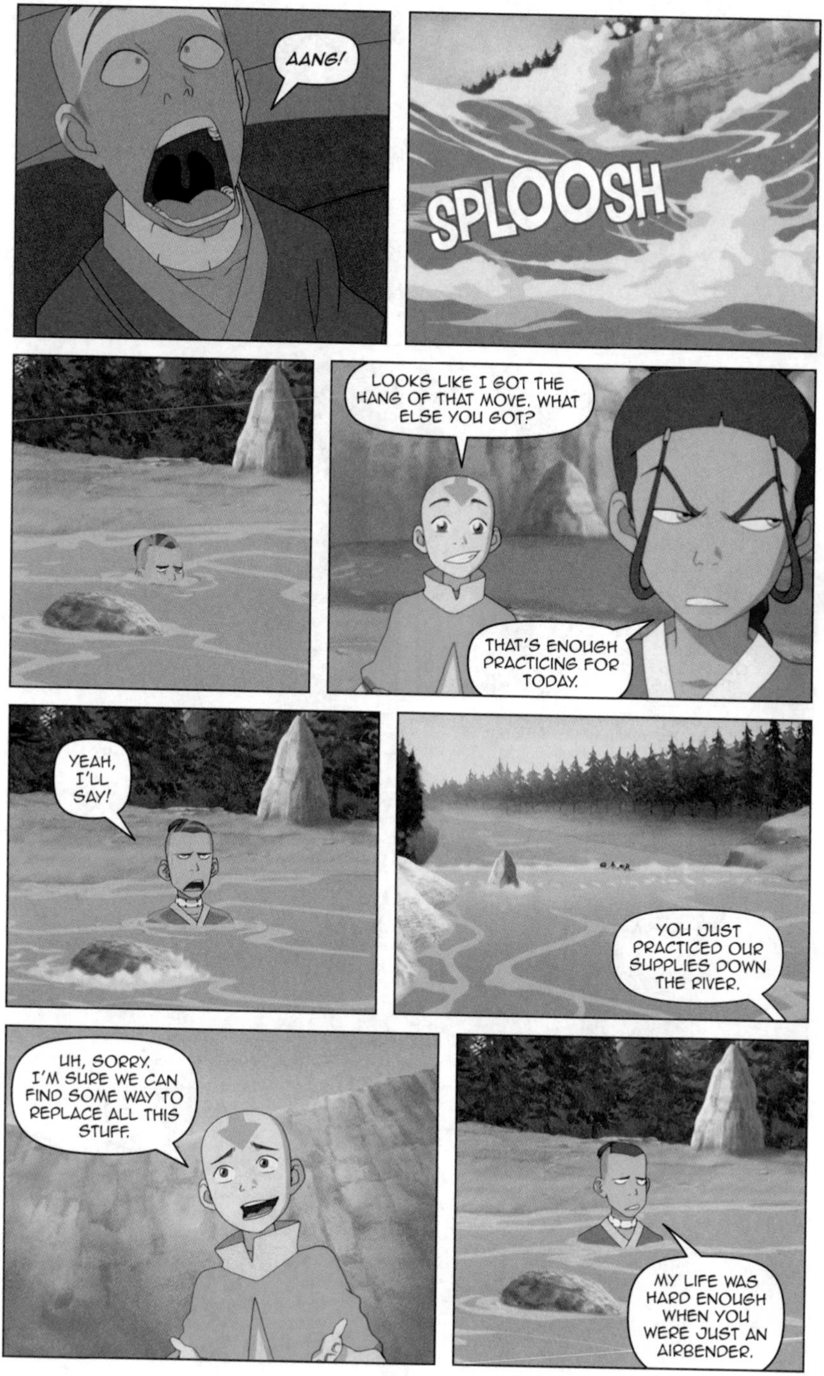
AANG!
SPLOOSH
LOOKS LIKE I GOT THE HANG OF THAT MOVE. WHAT ELSE YOU GOT?
THAT'S ENOUGH PRACTICING FOR TODAY.
YEAH, I'LL SAY!
YOU JUST PRACTICED OUR SUPPLIES DOWN THE RIVER.
UH, SORRY. I'M SURE WE CAN FIND SOME WAY TO REPLACE ALL THIS STUFF.
MY LIFE WAS HARD ENOUGH WHEN YOU WERE JUST AN AIRBENDER.

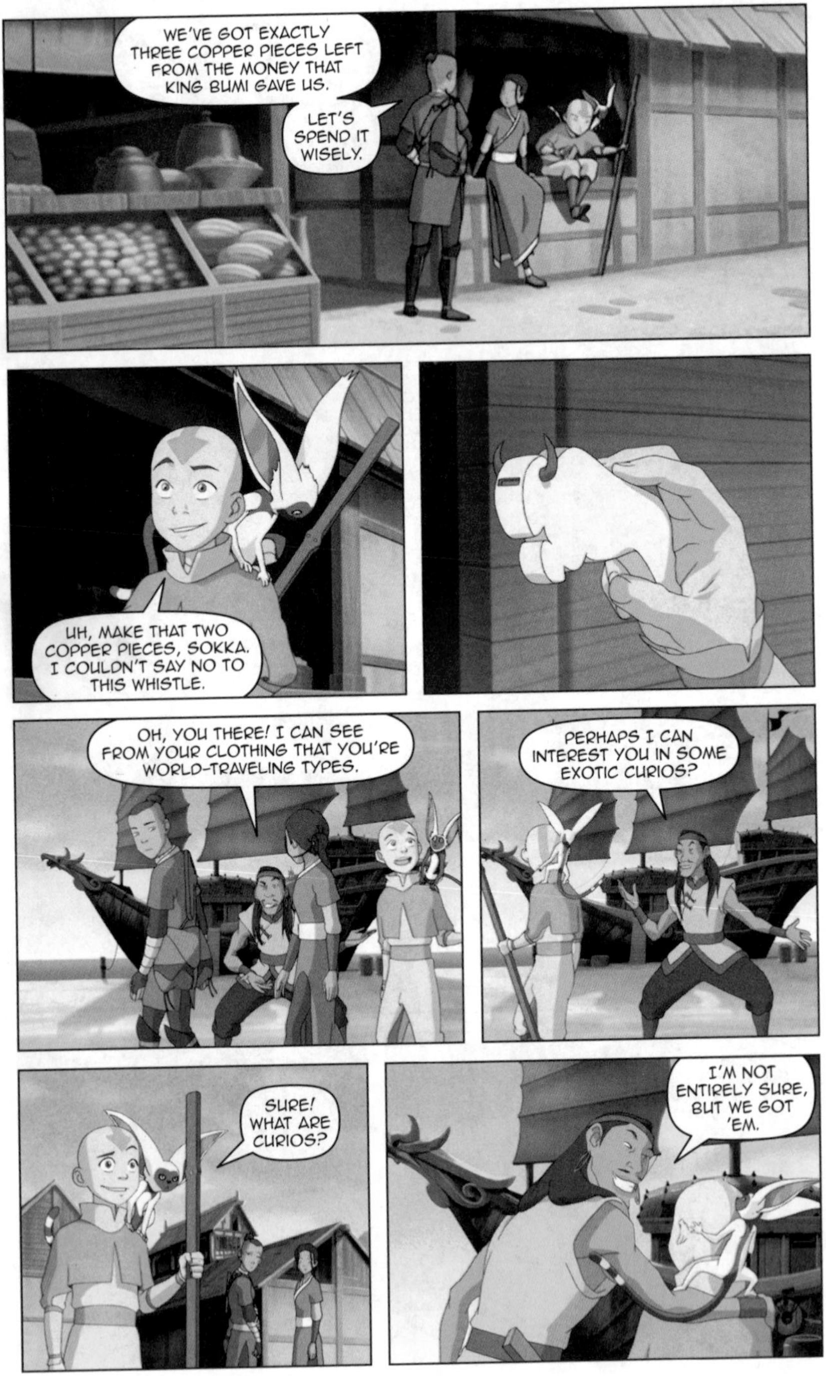
WE'VE GOT EXACTLY THREE COPPER PIECES LEFT FROM THE MONEY THAT KING BUMI GAVE US.
LET'S SPEND IT WISELY.
UH, MAKE THAT TWO COPPER PIECES, SOKKA. I COULDN'T SAY NO TO THIS WHISTLE.
OH, YOU THERE! I CAN SEE FROM YOUR CLOTHING THAT YOU'RE WORLD-TRAVELING TYPES.
PERHAPS I CAN INTEREST YOU IN SOME EXOTIC CURIOS?
SURE! WHAT ARE CURIOS?
I'M NOT ENTIRELY SURE, BUT WE GOT 'EM.

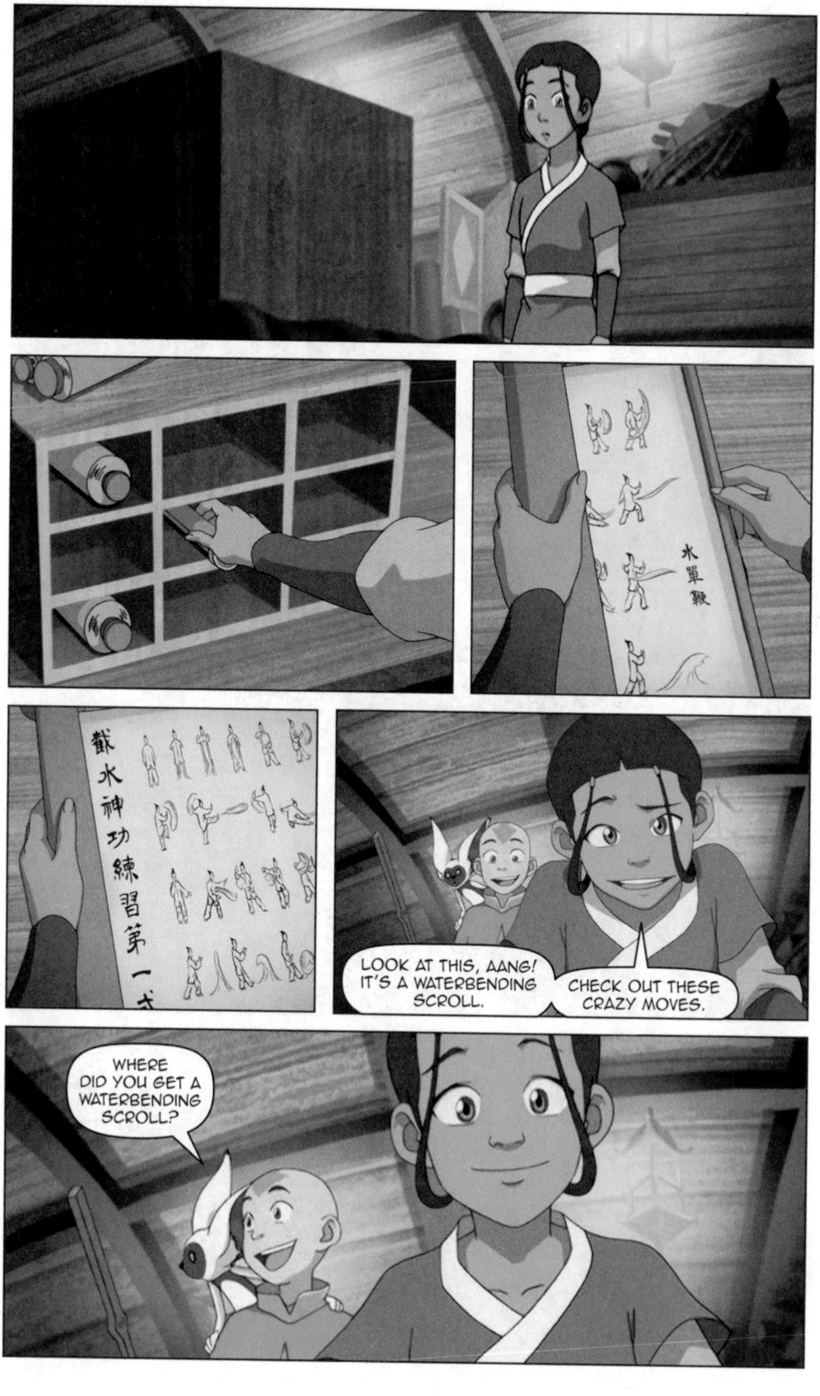
LOOK AT THIS, AANG! IT'S A WATERBENDING SCROLL.
CHECK OUT THESE CRAZY MOVES.
WHERE DID YOU GET A WATERBENDING SCROLL?

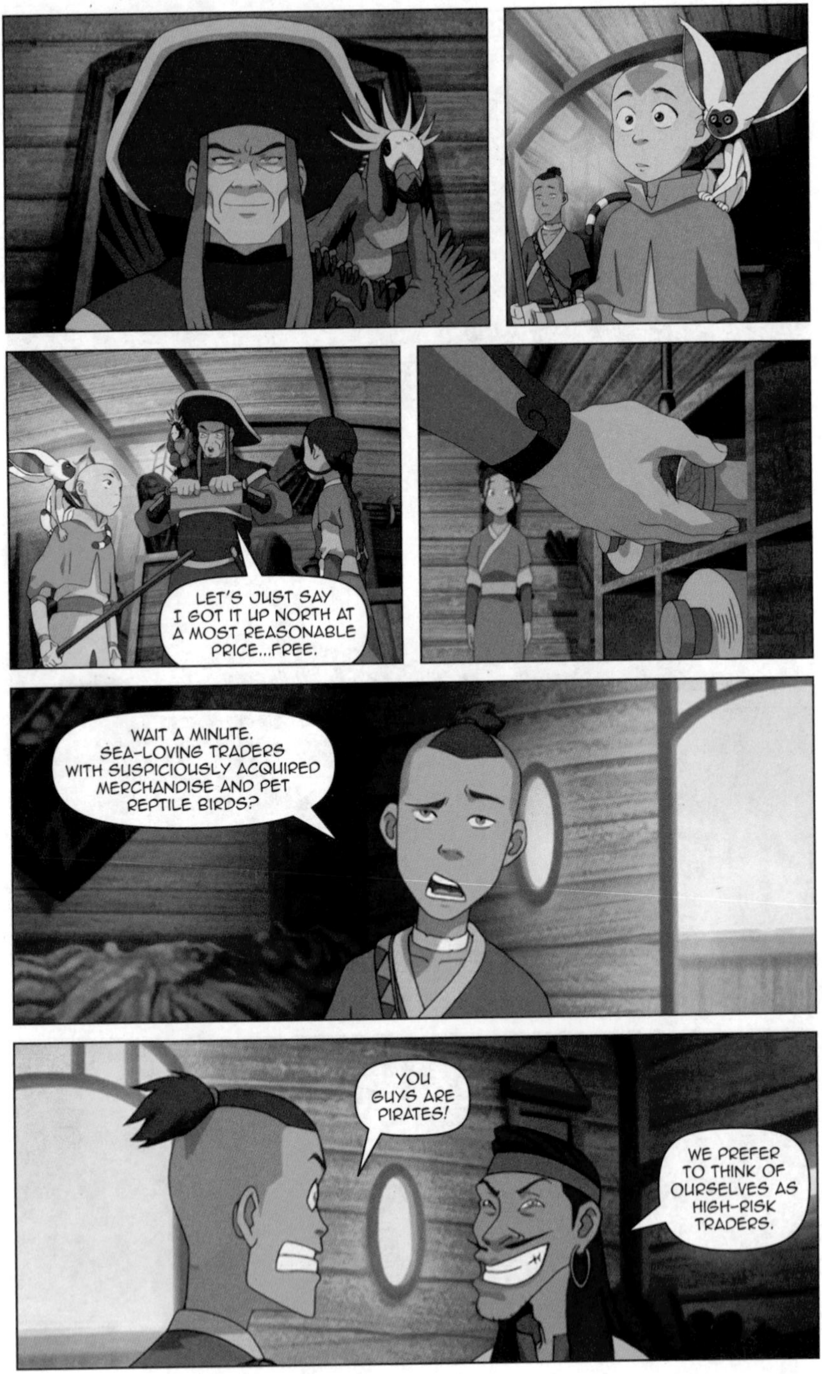
LET'S JUST SAY I GOT IT UP NORTH AT A MOST REASONABLE PRICE...FREE.
WAIT A MINUTE. SEA-LOVING TRADERS WITH SUSPICIOUSLY ACQUIRED MERCHANDISE AND PET REPTILE BIRDS?
YOU GUYS ARE PIRATES!
WE PREFER TO THINK OF OURSELVES AS HIGH-RISK TRADERS.

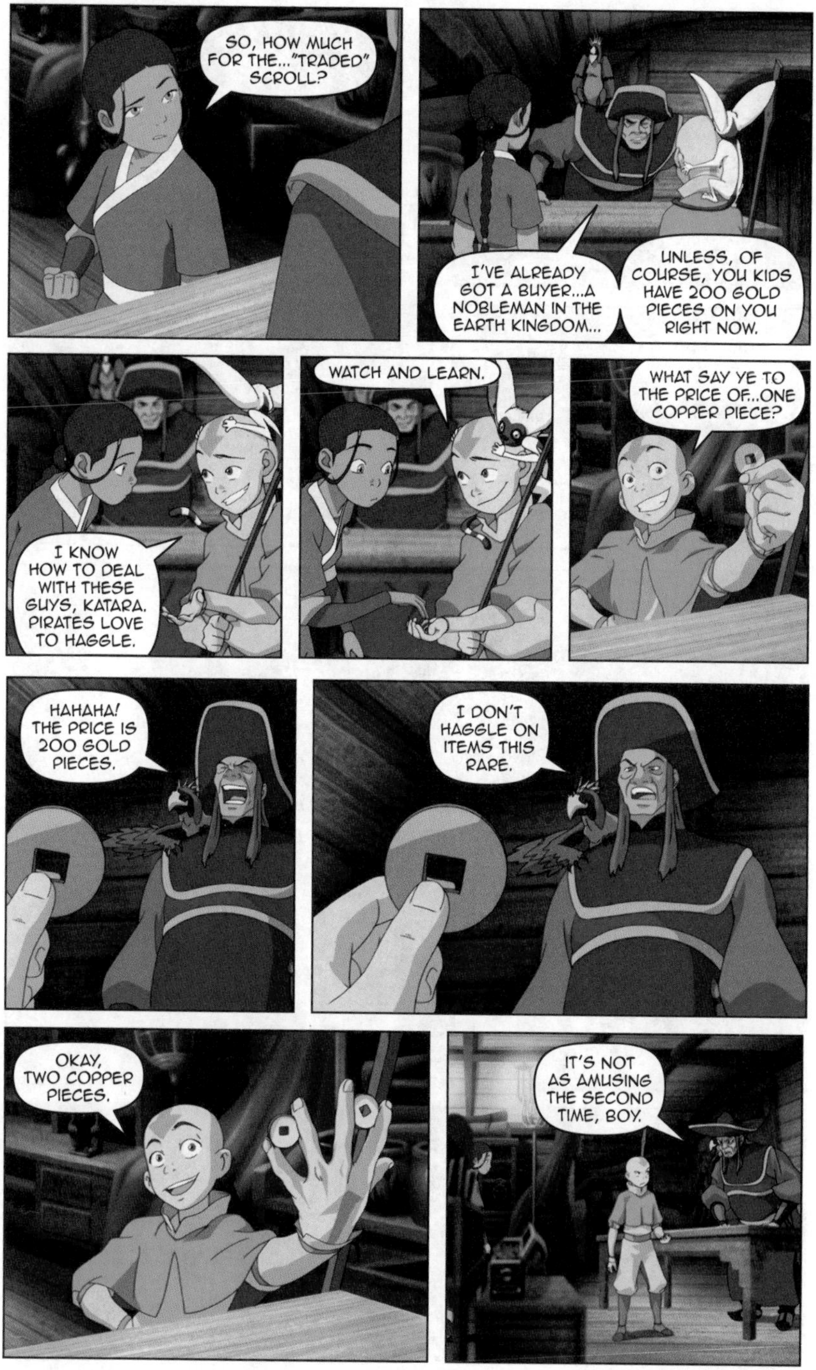

SO, HOW MUCH FOR THE..."TRADED" SCROLL?
I'VE ALREADY GOT A BUYER...A NOBLEMAN IN THE EARTH KINGDOM...
UNLESS, OF COURSE, YOU KIDS HAVE 200 GOLD PIECES ON YOU RIGHT NOW.
I KNOW HOW TO DEAL WITH THESE GUYS, KATARA. PIRATES LOVE TO HAGGLE.
WATCH AND LEARN.
WHAT SAY YE TO THE PRICE OF...ONE COPPER PIECE?
HAHAHA! THE PRICE IS 200 GOLD PIECES.
I DON'T HAGGLE ON ITEMS THIS RARE.
OKAY, TWO COPPER PIECES.
IT'S NOT AS AMUSING THE SECOND TIME, BOY.

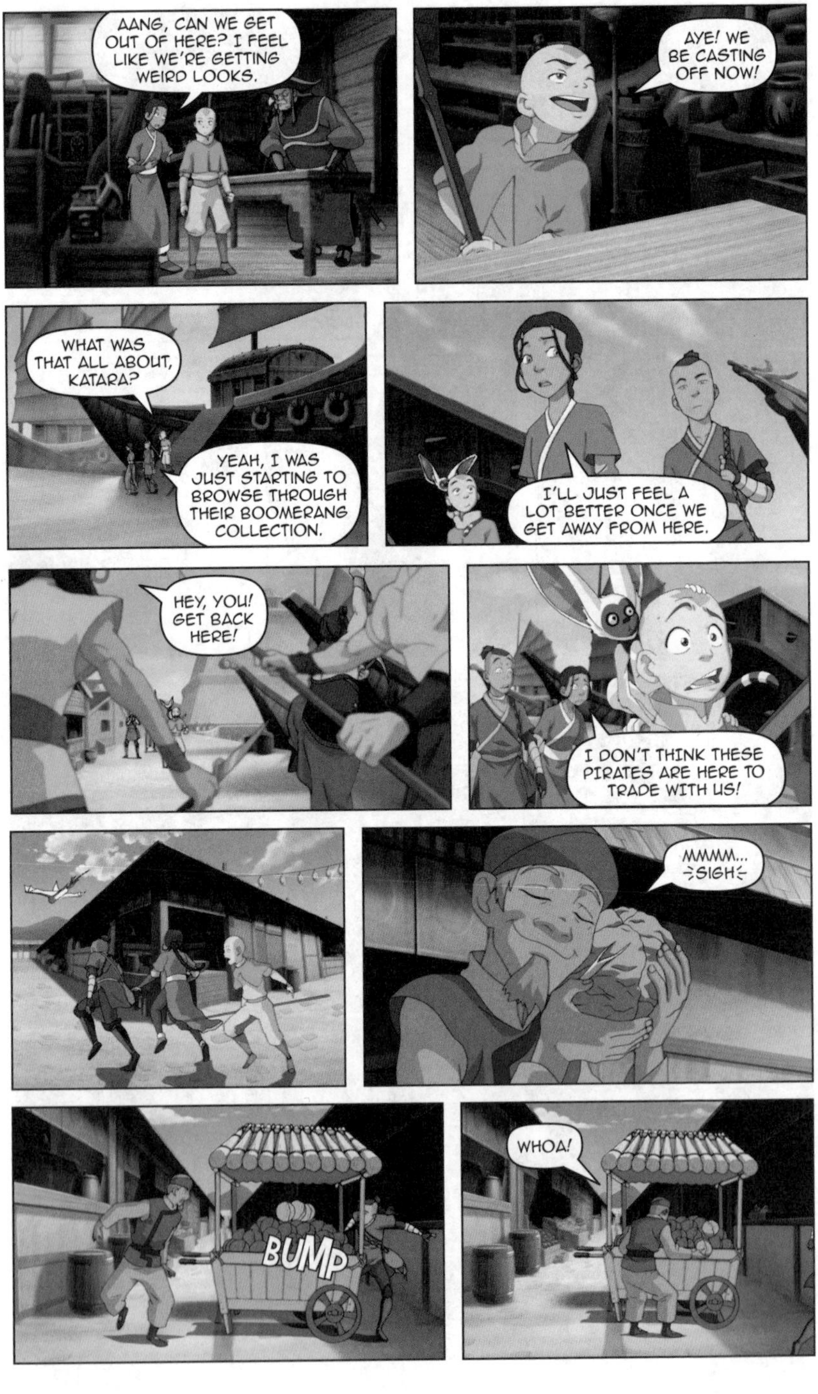
AANG, CAN WE GET OUT OF HERE? I FEEL LIKE WE'RE GETTING WEIRD LOOKS.
AYE! WE BE CASTING OFF NOW!
WHAT WAS THAT ALL ABOUT, KATARA?
YEAH, I WAS JUST STARTING TO BROWSE THROUGH THEIR BOOMERANG COLLECTION.
I'LL JUST FEEL A LOT BETTER ONCE WE GET AWAY FROM HERE.
HEY, YOU! GET BACK HERE!
I DON'T THINK THESE PIRATES ARE HERE TO TRADE WITH US!
MMMM... ⁼SIGH⁼
BUMP
WHOA!

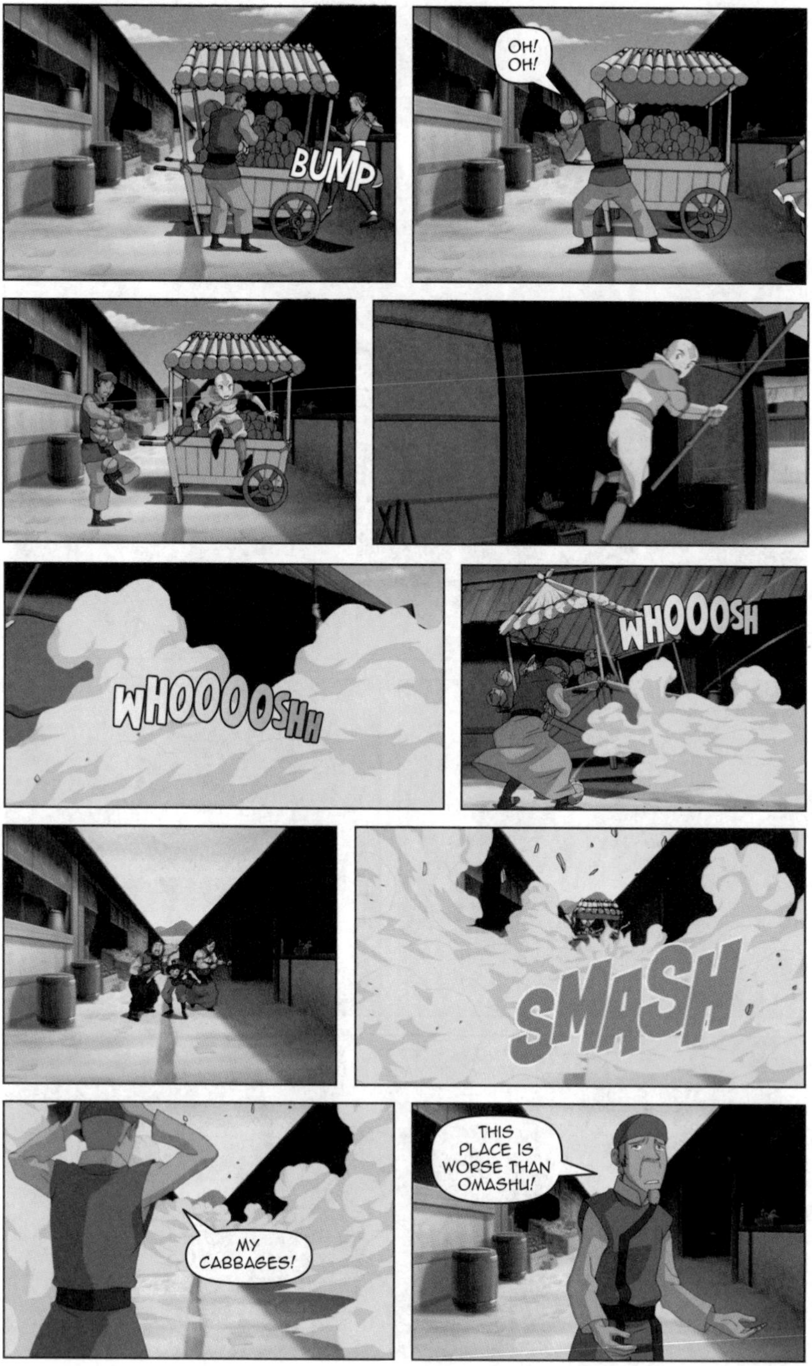
BUMP
OH! OH!
WHOOOOSHH
WHOOOSH
SMASH
MY CABBAGES!
THIS PLACE IS WORSE THAN OMASHU!

I USED TO KIND OF LOOK UP TO PIRATES, BUT THOSE GUYS ARE TERRIBLE.

I KNOW. THAT'S WHY I TOOK THIS.

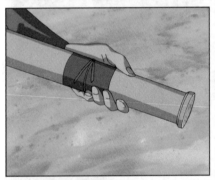

NO WAY!

ISN'T IT GREAT?!

NO WONDER THEY WERE TRYING TO HACK US UP. YOU STOLE THEIR WATERBENDING SCROLL!

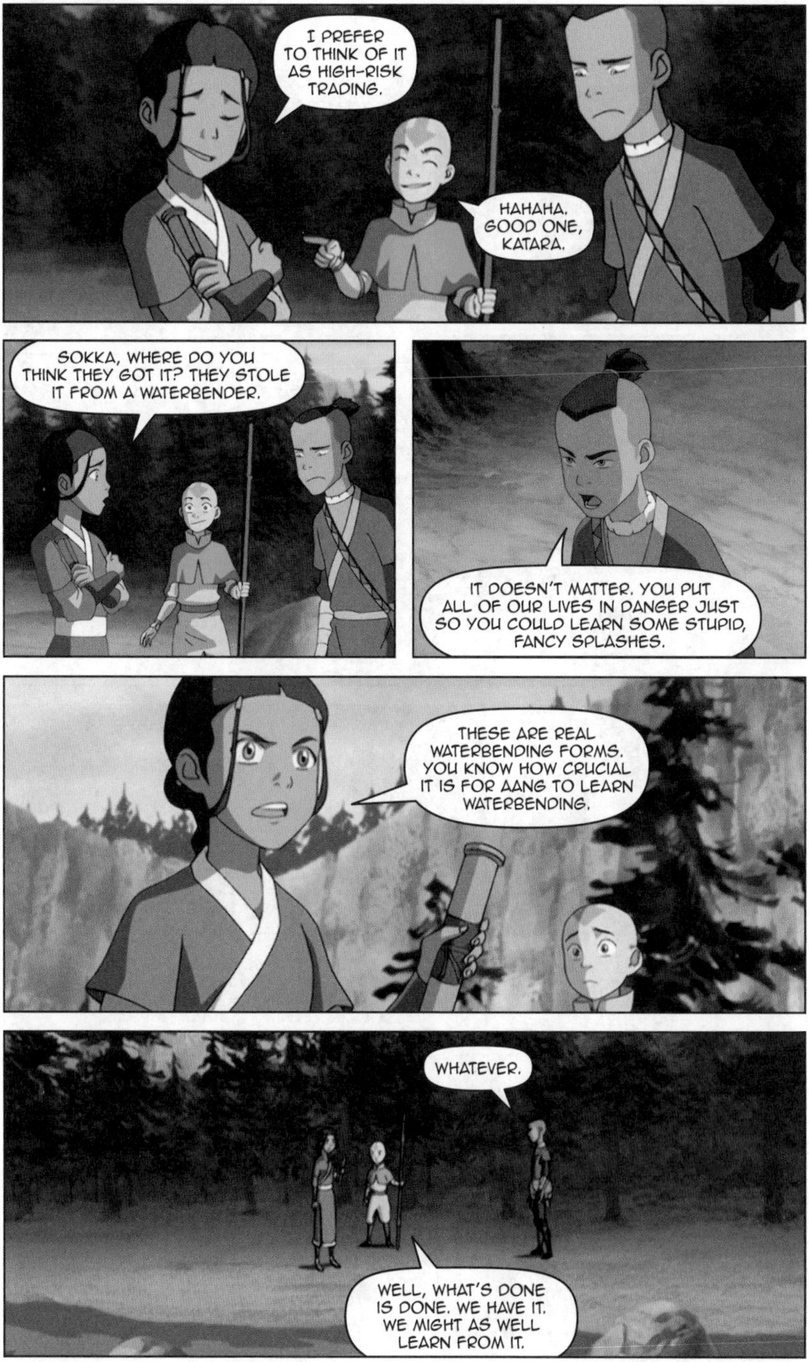
I PREFER TO THINK OF IT AS HIGH-RISK TRADING.
HAHAHA. GOOD ONE, KATARA.
SOKKA, WHERE DO YOU THINK THEY GOT IT? THEY STOLE IT FROM A WATERBENDER.
IT DOESN'T MATTER. YOU PUT ALL OF OUR LIVES IN DANGER JUST SO YOU COULD LEARN SOME STUPID, FANCY SPLASHES.
THESE ARE REAL WATERBENDING FORMS. YOU KNOW HOW CRUCIAL IT IS FOR AANG TO LEARN WATERBENDING.
WHATEVER.
WELL, WHAT'S DONE IS DONE. WE HAVE IT. WE MIGHT AS WELL LEARN FROM IT.

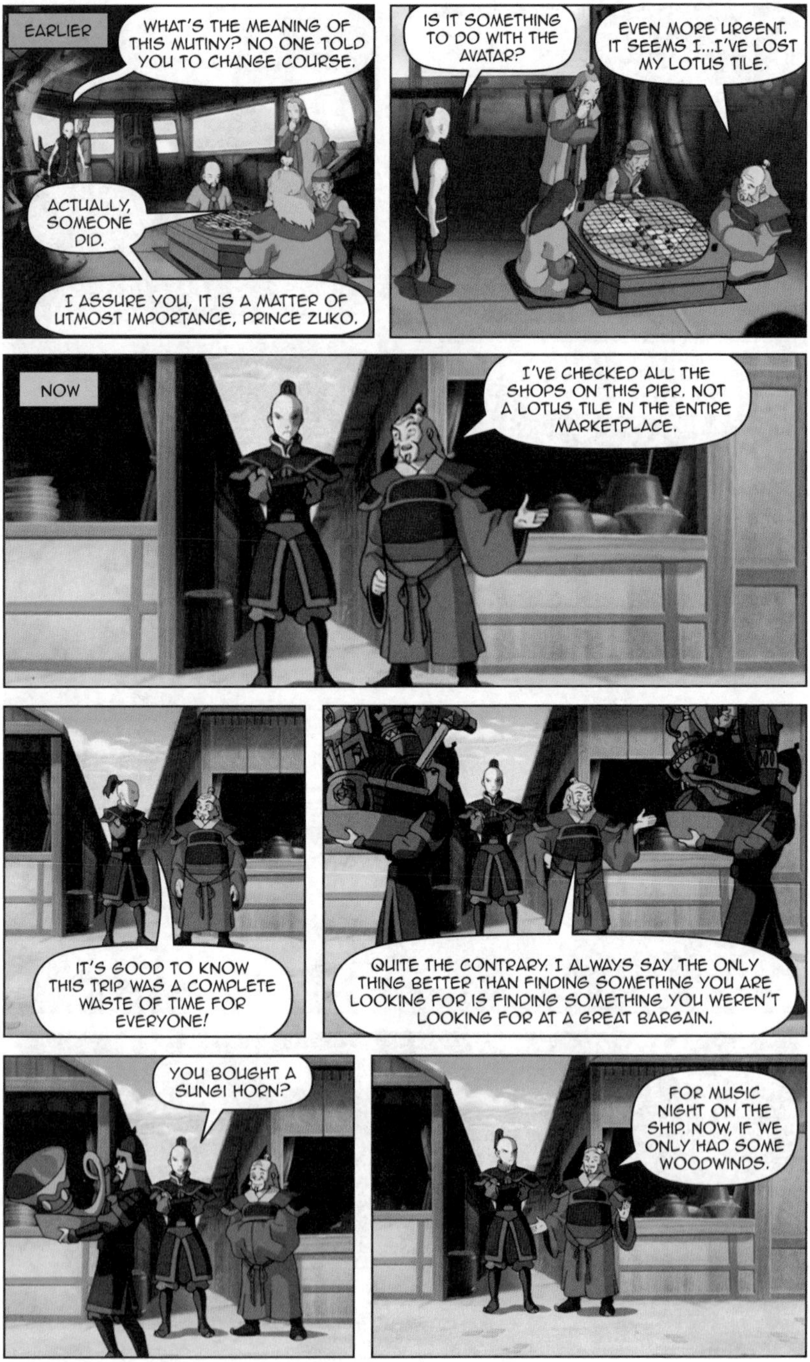
EARLIER
WHAT'S THE MEANING OF THIS MUTINY? NO ONE TOLD YOU TO CHANGE COURSE.
ACTUALLY, SOMEONE DID.
I ASSURE YOU, IT IS A MATTER OF UTMOST IMPORTANCE, PRINCE ZUKO.
IS IT SOMETHING TO DO WITH THE AVATAR?
EVEN MORE URGENT. IT SEEMS I...I'VE LOST MY LOTUS TILE.
NOW
I'VE CHECKED ALL THE SHOPS ON THIS PIER. NOT A LOTUS TILE IN THE ENTIRE MARKETPLACE.
IT'S GOOD TO KNOW THIS TRIP WAS A COMPLETE WASTE OF TIME FOR EVERYONE!
QUITE THE CONTRARY. I ALWAYS SAY THE ONLY THING BETTER THAN FINDING SOMETHING YOU ARE LOOKING FOR IS FINDING SOMETHING YOU WEREN'T LOOKING FOR AT A GREAT BARGAIN.
YOU BOUGHT A SUNGI HORN?
FOR MUSIC NIGHT ON THE SHIP. NOW, IF WE ONLY HAD SOME WOODWINDS.

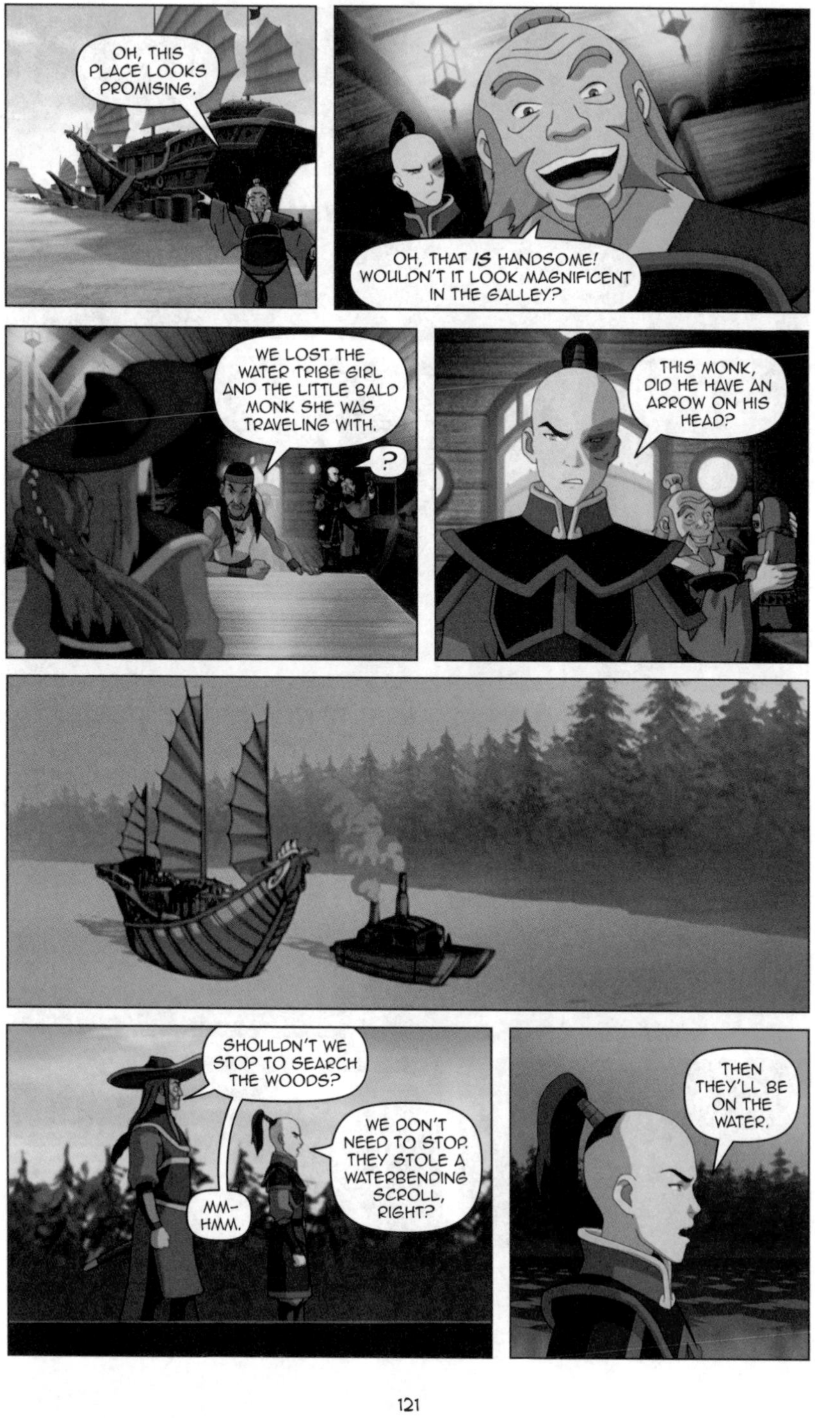
OH, THIS PLACE LOOKS PROMISING.
OH, THAT *IS* HANDSOME! WOULDN'T IT LOOK MAGNIFICENT IN THE GALLEY?
WE LOST THE WATER TRIBE GIRL AND THE LITTLE BALD MONK SHE WAS TRAVELING WITH.
?
THIS MONK, DID HE HAVE AN ARROW ON HIS HEAD?
SHOULDN'T WE STOP TO SEARCH THE WOODS?
MM-HMM.
WE DON'T NEED TO STOP. THEY STOLE A WATERBENDING SCROLL, RIGHT?
THEN THEY'LL BE ON THE WATER.

CRACKLE

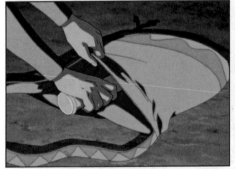

PRRRR

SHH. MOMO, GO BACK TO SLEEP.

PRRR

SHH!

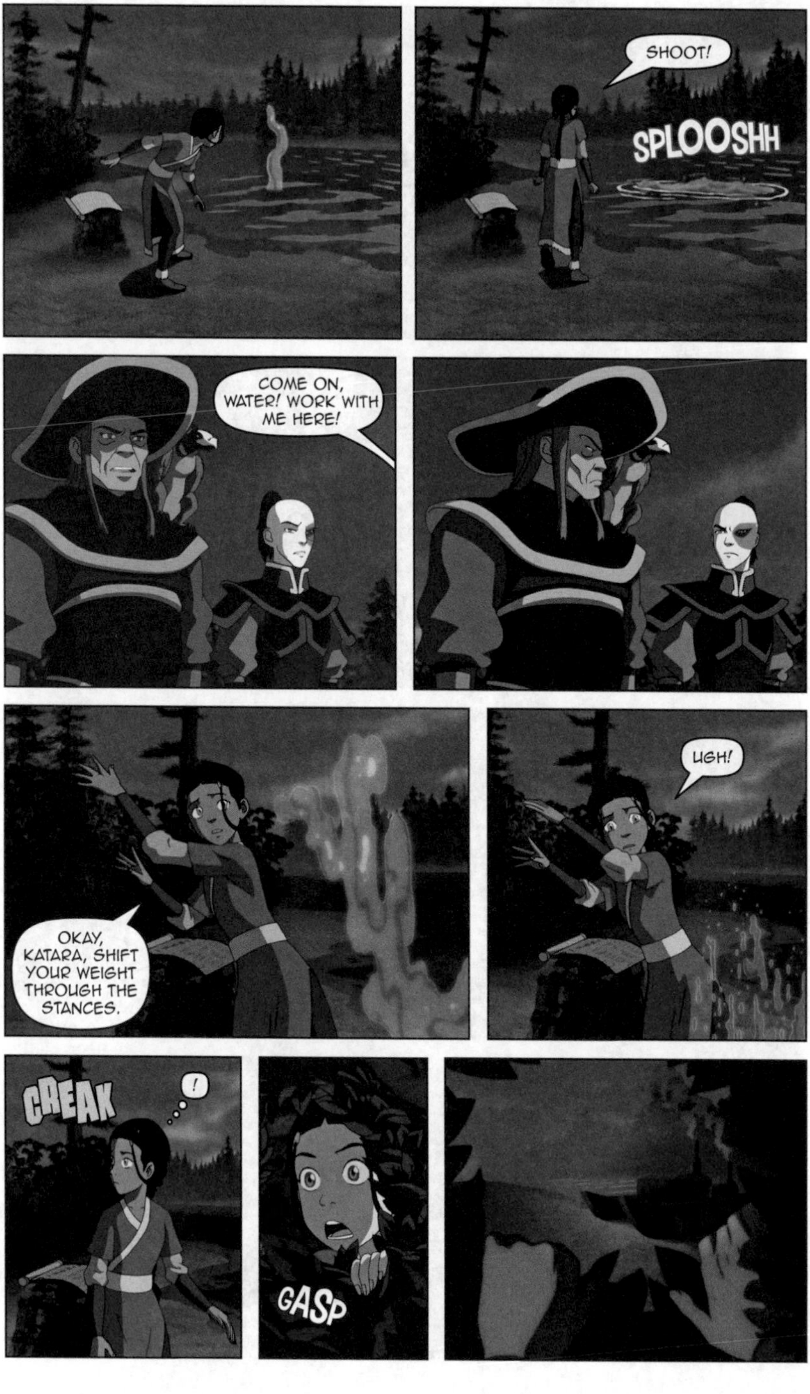
SHOOT!
SPLOOSHH
COME ON, WATER! WORK WITH ME HERE!
OKAY, KATARA, SHIFT YOUR WEIGHT THROUGH THE STANCES.
UGH!
CREAK
!
GASP

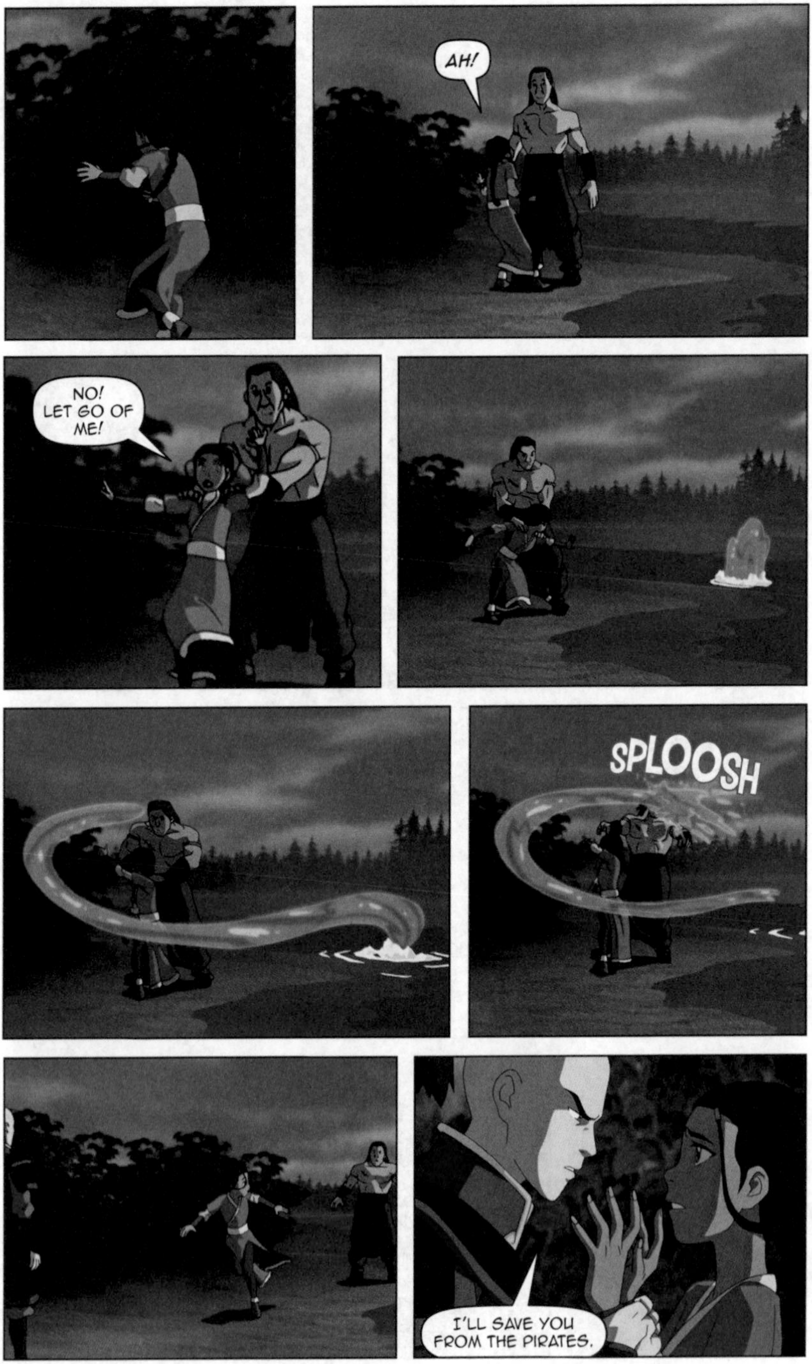
AH!
NO! LET GO OF ME!
SPLOOSH
I'LL SAVE YOU FROM THE PIRATES.

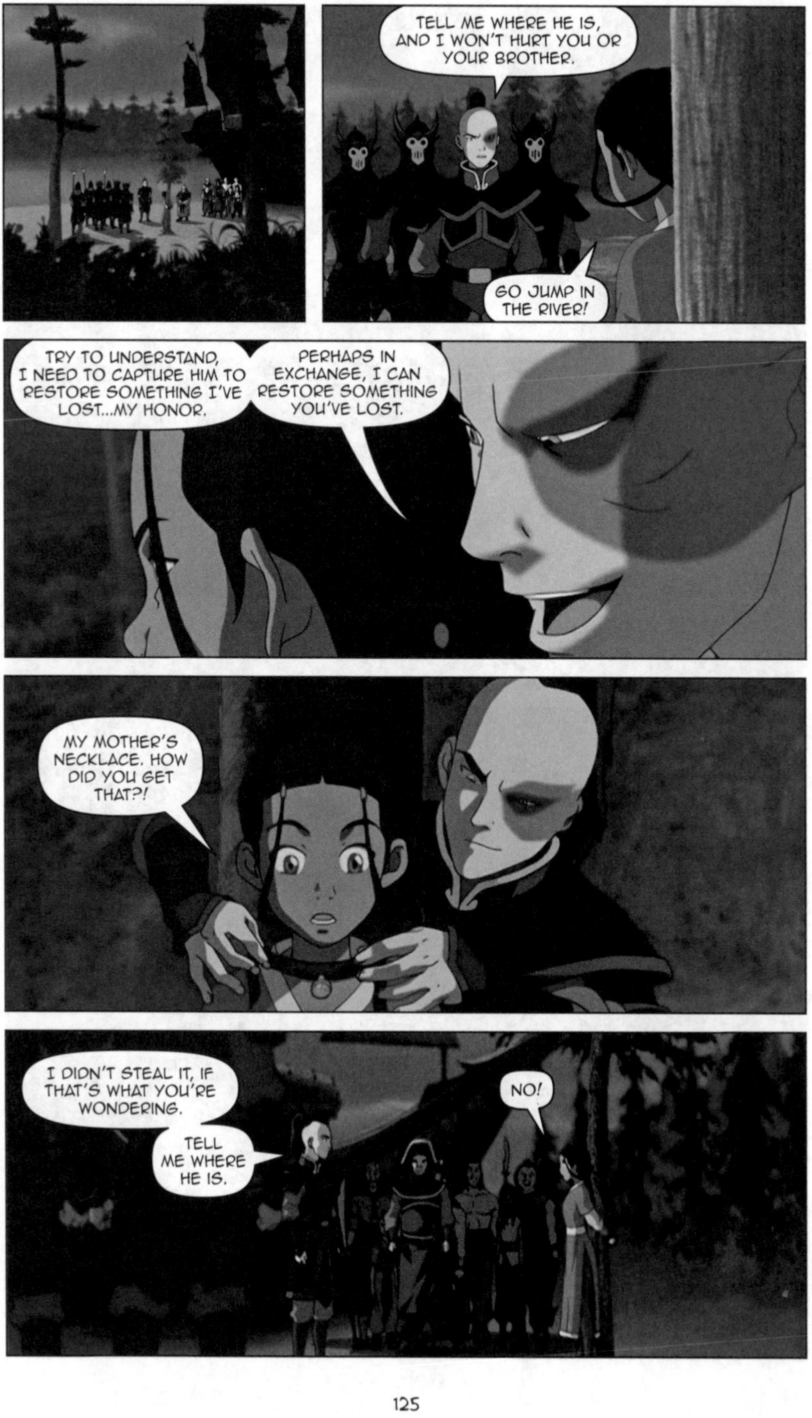
TELL ME WHERE HE IS, AND I WON'T HURT YOU OR YOUR BROTHER.
GO JUMP IN THE RIVER!
TRY TO UNDERSTAND, I NEED TO CAPTURE HIM TO RESTORE SOMETHING I'VE LOST...MY HONOR.
PERHAPS IN EXCHANGE, I CAN RESTORE SOMETHING YOU'VE LOST.
MY MOTHER'S NECKLACE. HOW DID YOU GET THAT?!
I DIDN'T STEAL IT, IF THAT'S WHAT YOU'RE WONDERING.
TELL ME WHERE HE IS.
NO!

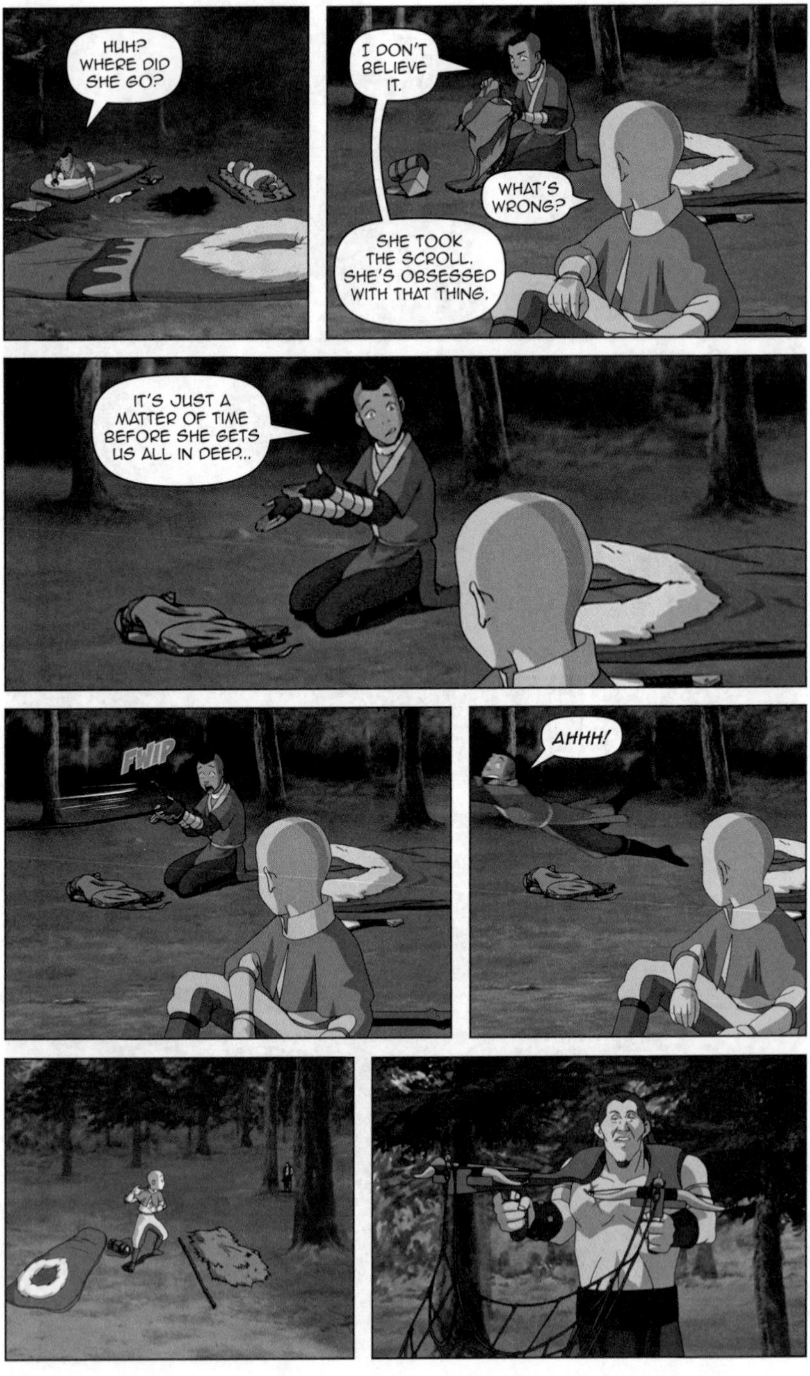
HUH? WHERE DID SHE GO?
I DON'T BELIEVE IT.
WHAT'S WRONG?
SHE TOOK THE SCROLL. SHE'S OBSESSED WITH THAT THING.
IT'S JUST A MATTER OF TIME BEFORE SHE GETS US ALL IN DEEP...
FWIP
AHHH!

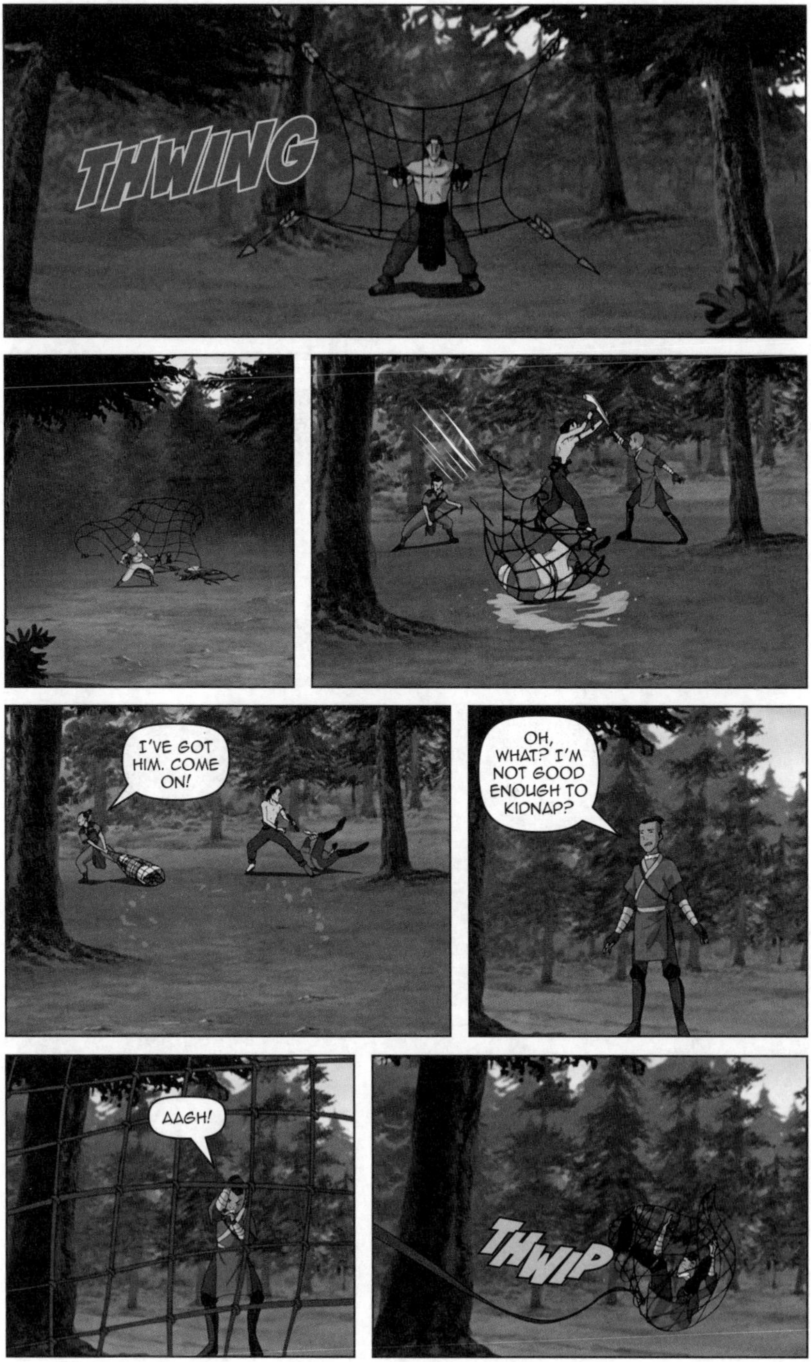
THWING
I'VE GOT HIM. COME ON!
OH, WHAT? I'M NOT GOOD ENOUGH TO KIDNAP?
AAGH!
THWIP

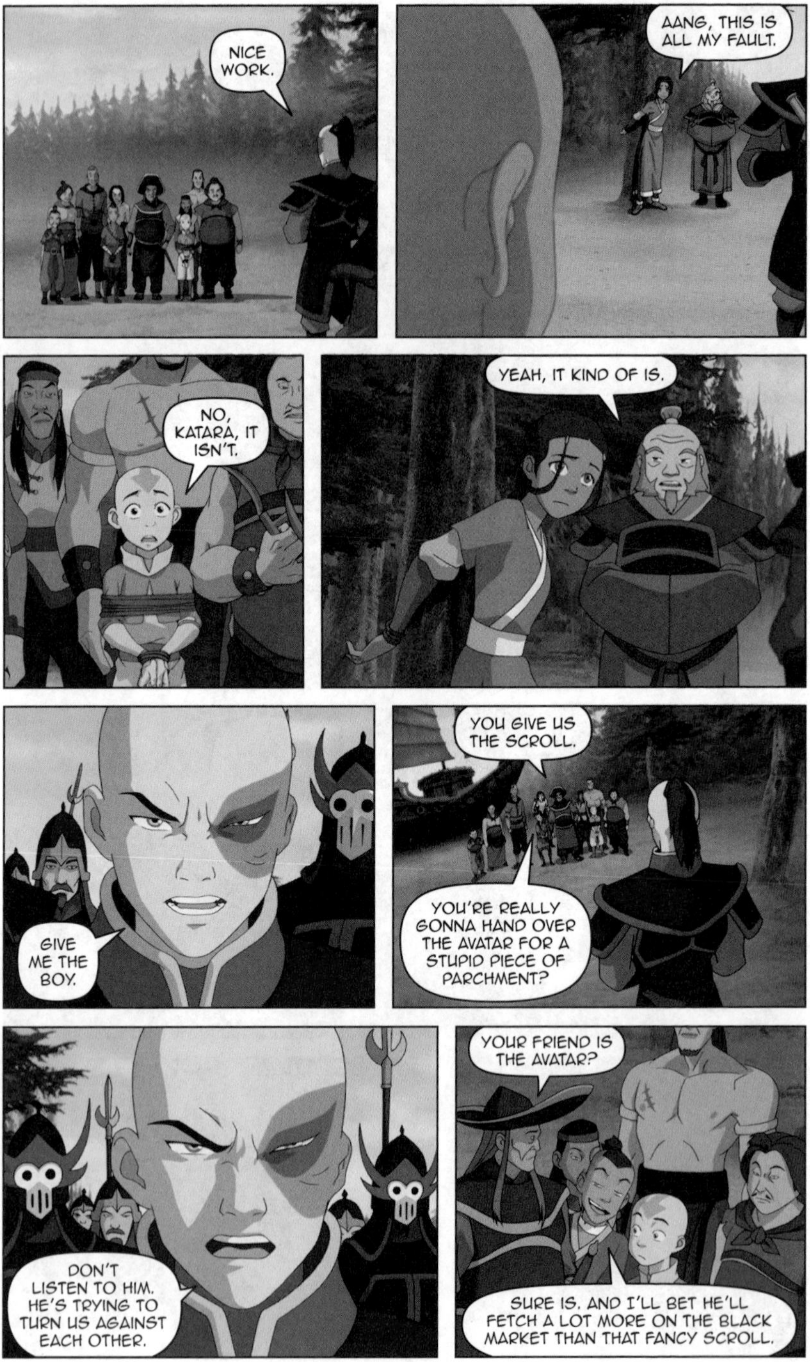
NICE WORK.
AANG, THIS IS ALL MY FAULT.
NO, KATARA, IT ISN'T.
YEAH, IT KIND OF IS.
GIVE ME THE BOY.
YOU GIVE US THE SCROLL.
YOU'RE REALLY GONNA HAND OVER THE AVATAR FOR A STUPID PIECE OF PARCHMENT?
DON'T LISTEN TO HIM. HE'S TRYING TO TURN US AGAINST EACH OTHER.
YOUR FRIEND IS THE AVATAR?
SURE IS. AND I'LL BET HE'LL FETCH A LOT MORE ON THE BLACK MARKET THAN THAT FANCY SCROLL.

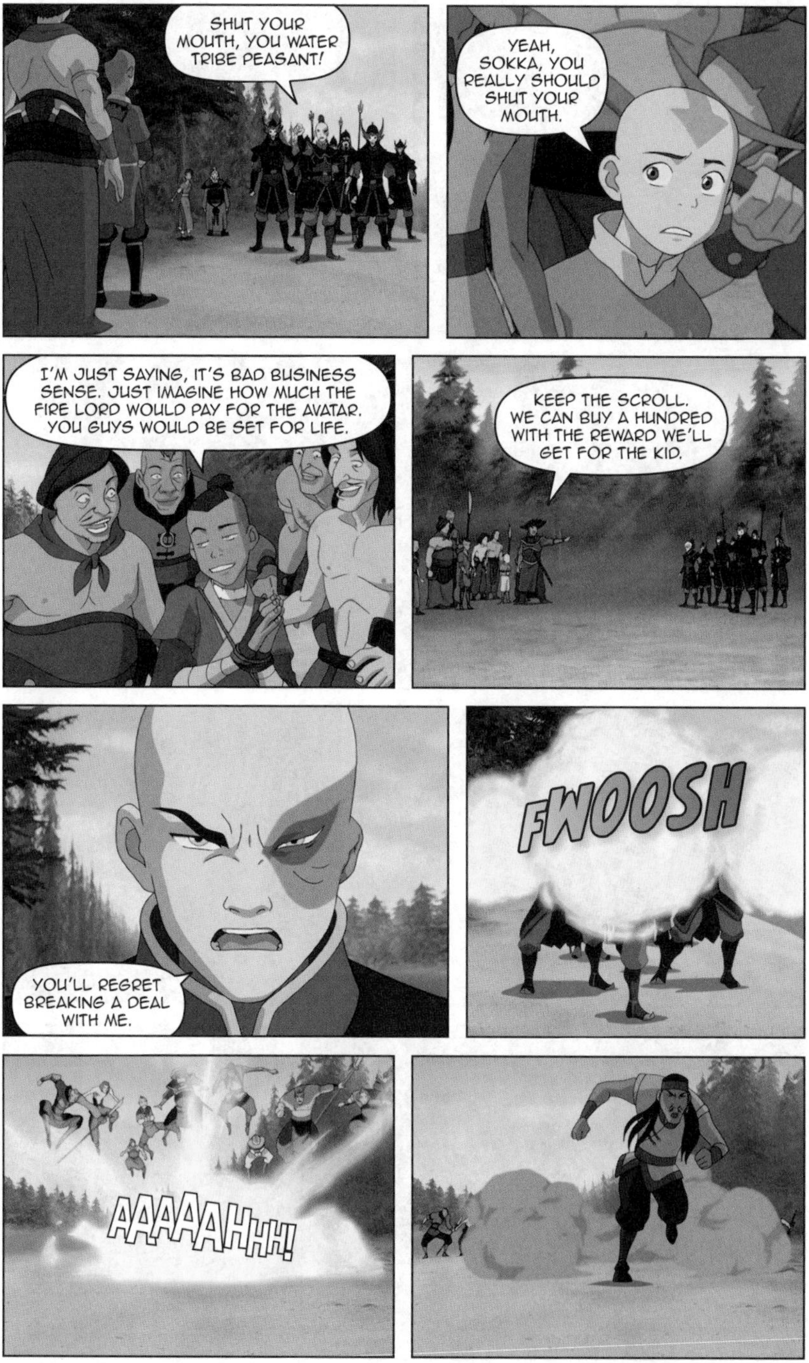
SHUT YOUR MOUTH, YOU WATER TRIBE PEASANT!
YEAH, SOKKA, YOU REALLY SHOULD SHUT YOUR MOUTH.
I'M JUST SAYING, IT'S BAD BUSINESS SENSE. JUST IMAGINE HOW MUCH THE FIRE LORD WOULD PAY FOR THE AVATAR. YOU GUYS WOULD BE SET FOR LIFE.
KEEP THE SCROLL. WE CAN BUY A HUNDRED WITH THE REWARD WE'LL GET FOR THE KID.
YOU'LL REGRET BREAKING A DEAL WITH ME.
FWOOSH
AAAAAHHH!

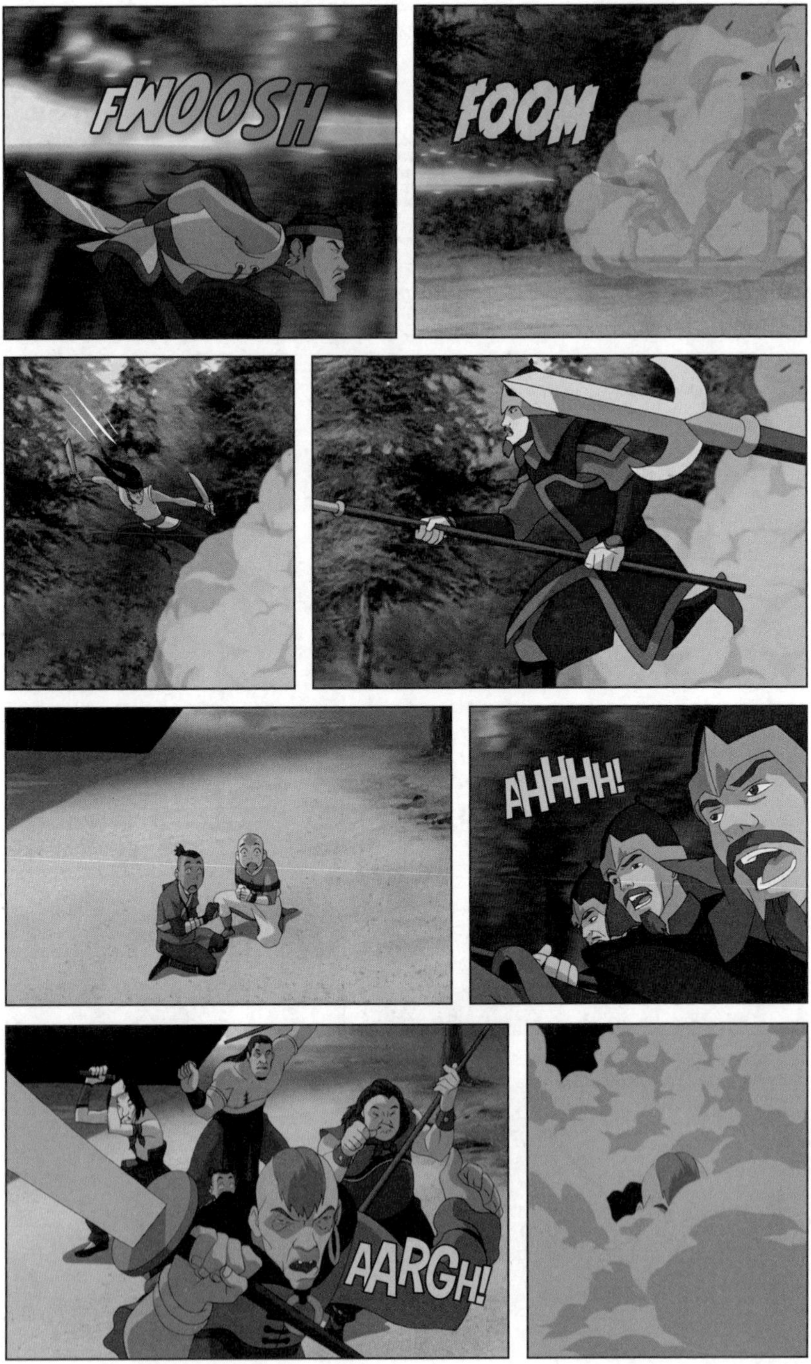
FWOOSH
FOOM
AHHHH!
AARGH!

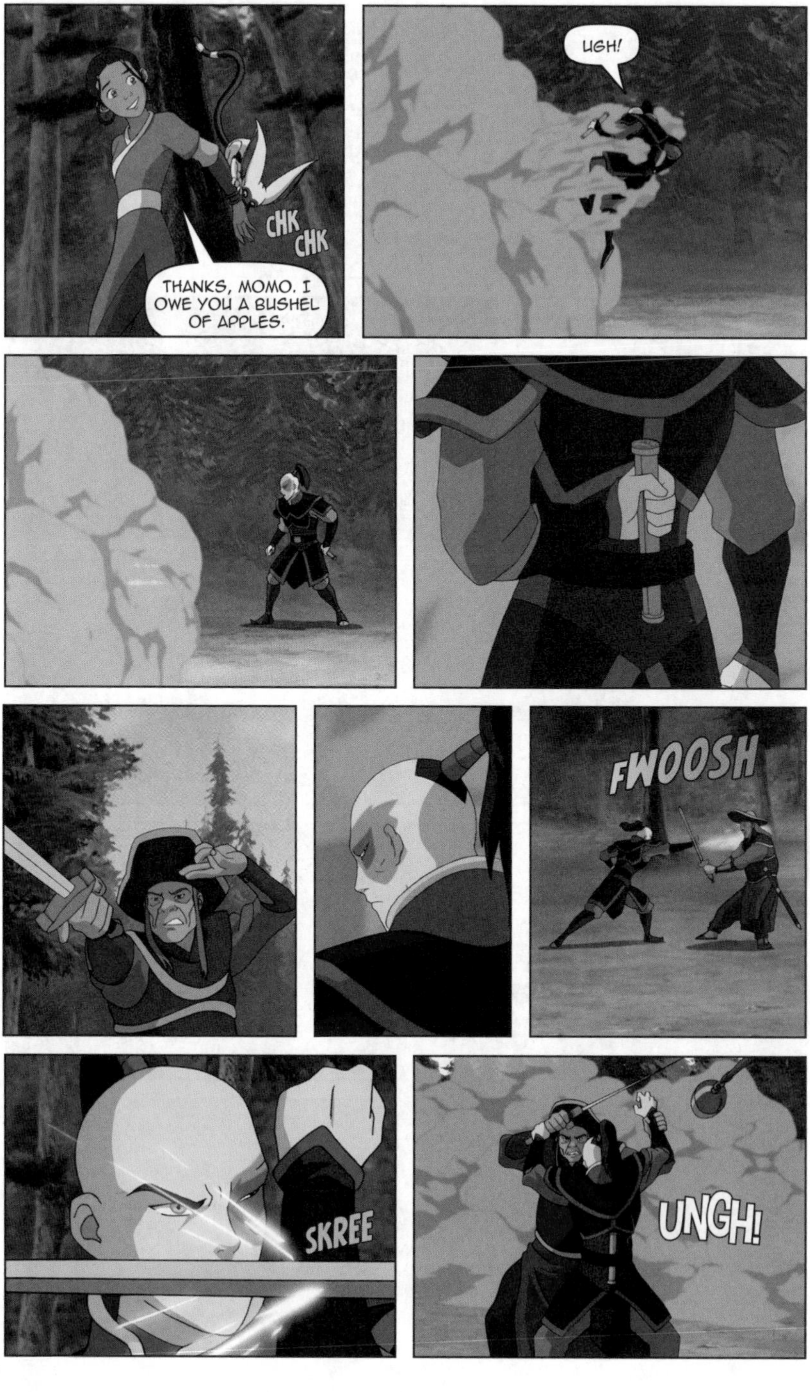
CHK
CHK
THANKS, MOMO. I OWE YOU A BUSHEL OF APPLES.
UGH!
FWOOSH
SKREE
UNGH!

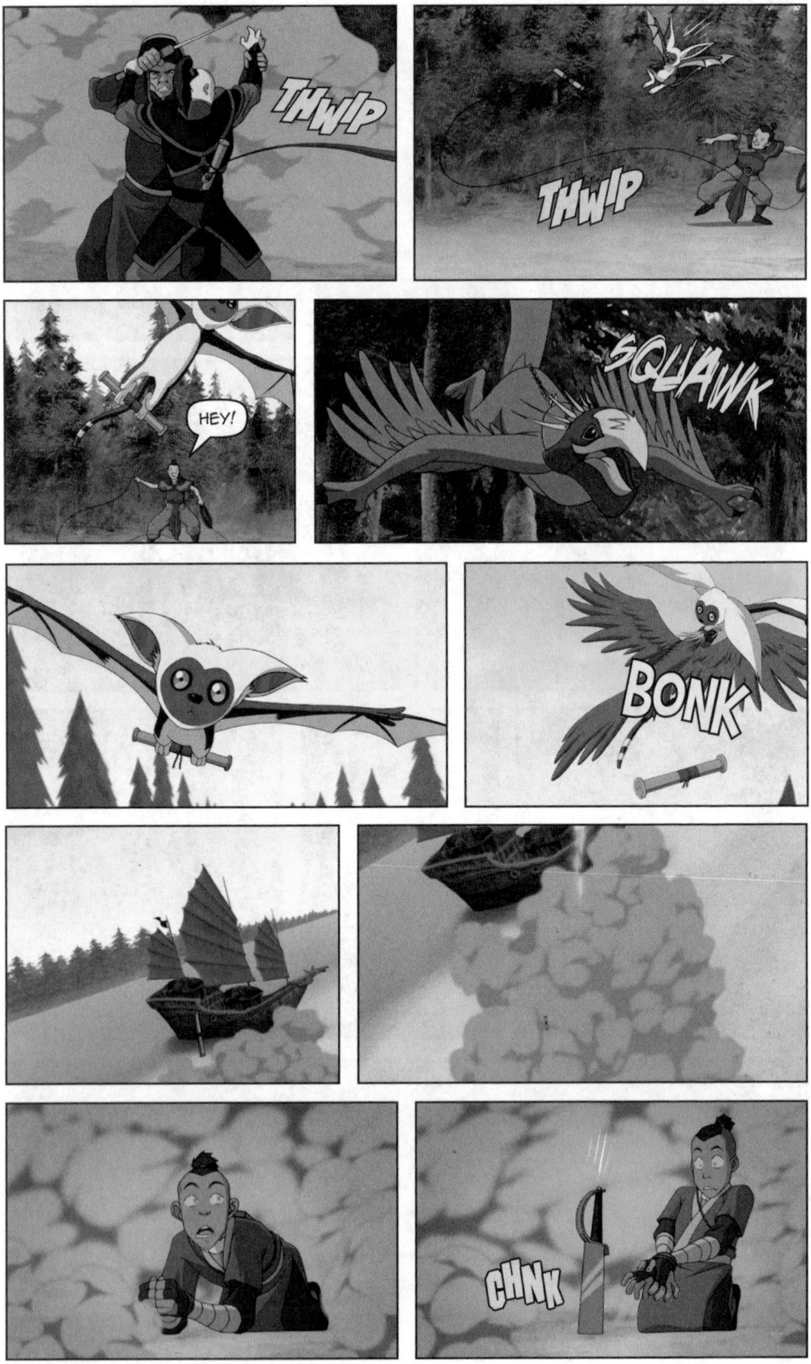
THWIP
THWIP
HEY!
SQUAWK
BONK
CHNK

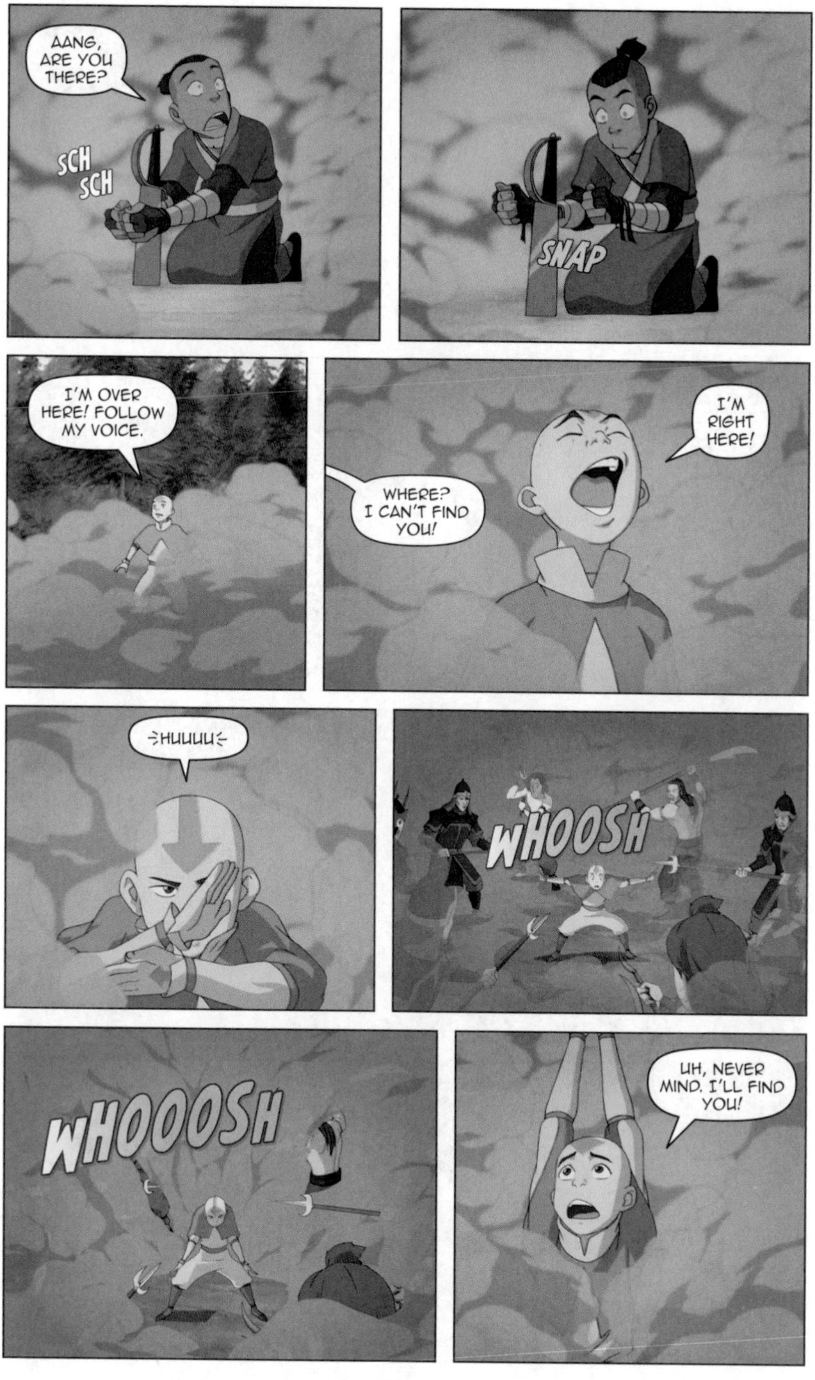
AANG, ARE YOU THERE?
SCH SCH
SNAP
I'M OVER HERE! FOLLOW MY VOICE.
WHERE? I CAN'T FIND YOU!
I'M RIGHT HERE!
HUUUU
WHOOSH
WHOOOSH
UH, NEVER MIND. I'LL FIND YOU!

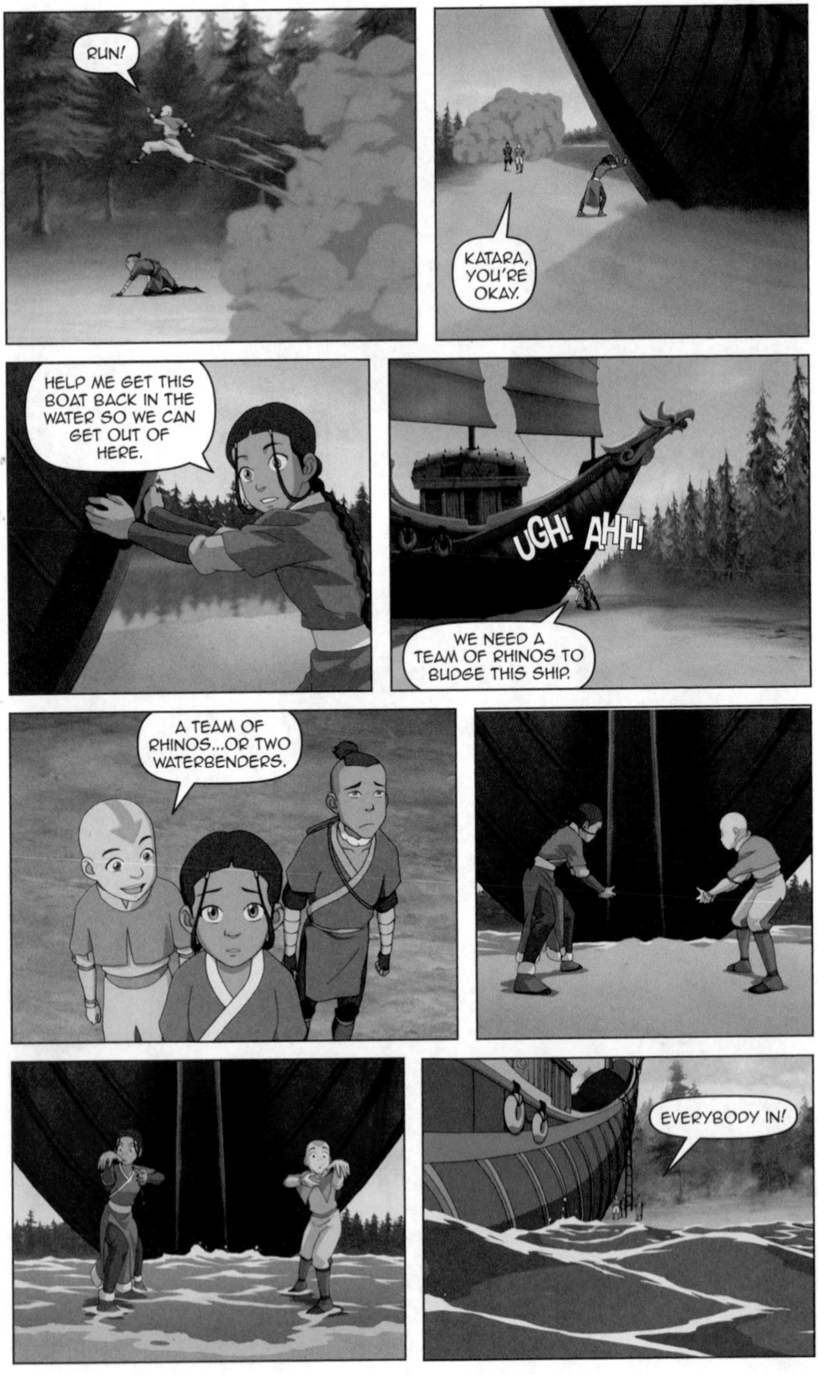
RUN!
KATARA, YOU'RE OKAY.
HELP ME GET THIS BOAT BACK IN THE WATER SO WE CAN GET OUT OF HERE.
UGH!
AHH!
WE NEED A TEAM OF RHINOS TO BUDGE THIS SHIP.
A TEAM OF RHINOS...OR TWO WATERBENDERS.
EVERYBODY IN!

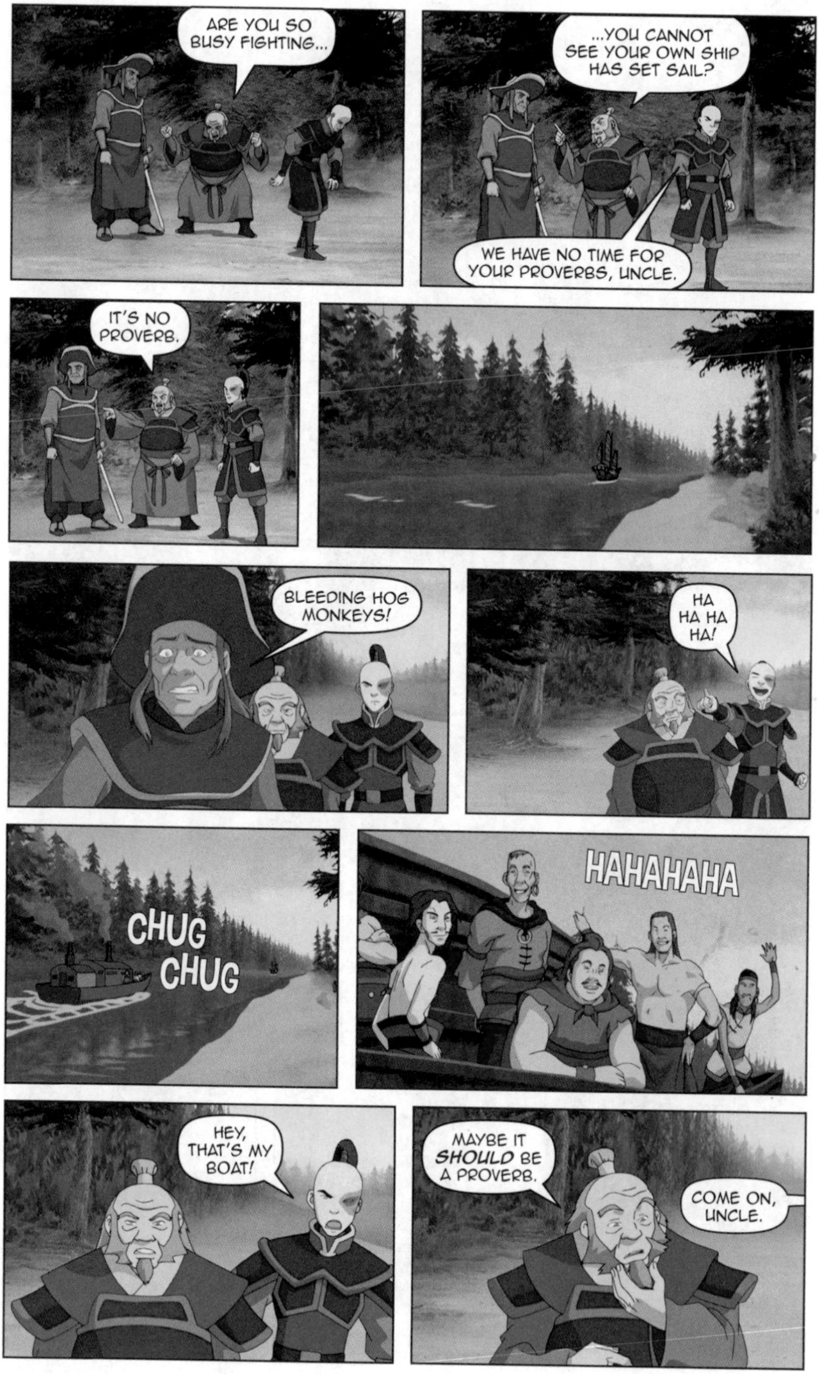
ARE YOU SO BUSY FIGHTING...
...YOU CANNOT SEE YOUR OWN SHIP HAS SET SAIL?
WE HAVE NO TIME FOR YOUR PROVERBS, UNCLE.
IT'S NO PROVERB.
BLEEDING HOG MONKEYS!
HA HA HA HA HA!
CHUG CHUG
HAHAHAHA
HEY, THAT'S MY BOAT!
MAYBE IT SHOULD BE A PROVERB.
COME ON, UNCLE.

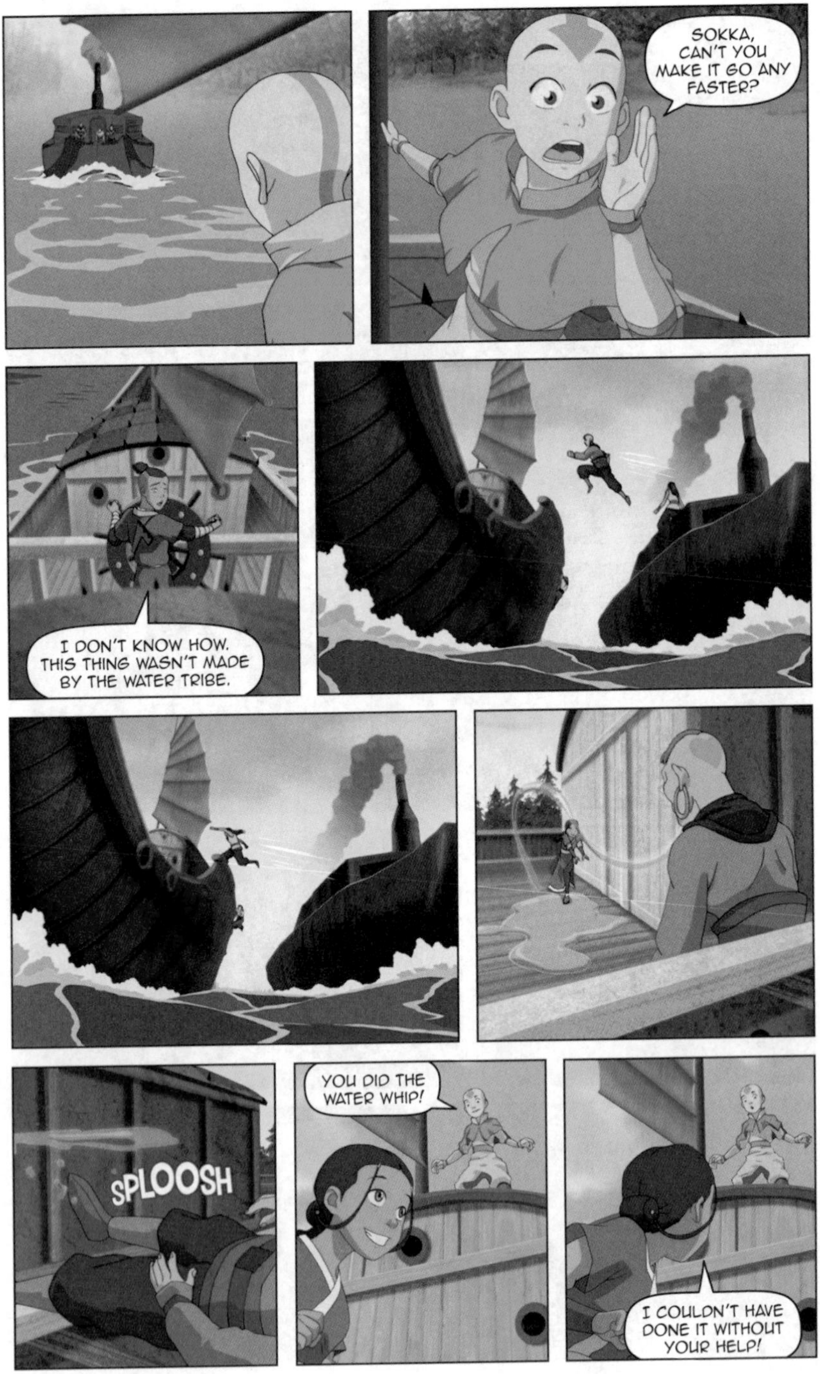
SOKKA, CAN'T YOU MAKE IT GO ANY FASTER?
I DON'T KNOW HOW. THIS THING WASN'T MADE BY THE WATER TRIBE.
SPLOOSH
YOU DID THE WATER WHIP!
I COULDN'T HAVE DONE IT WITHOUT YOUR HELP!

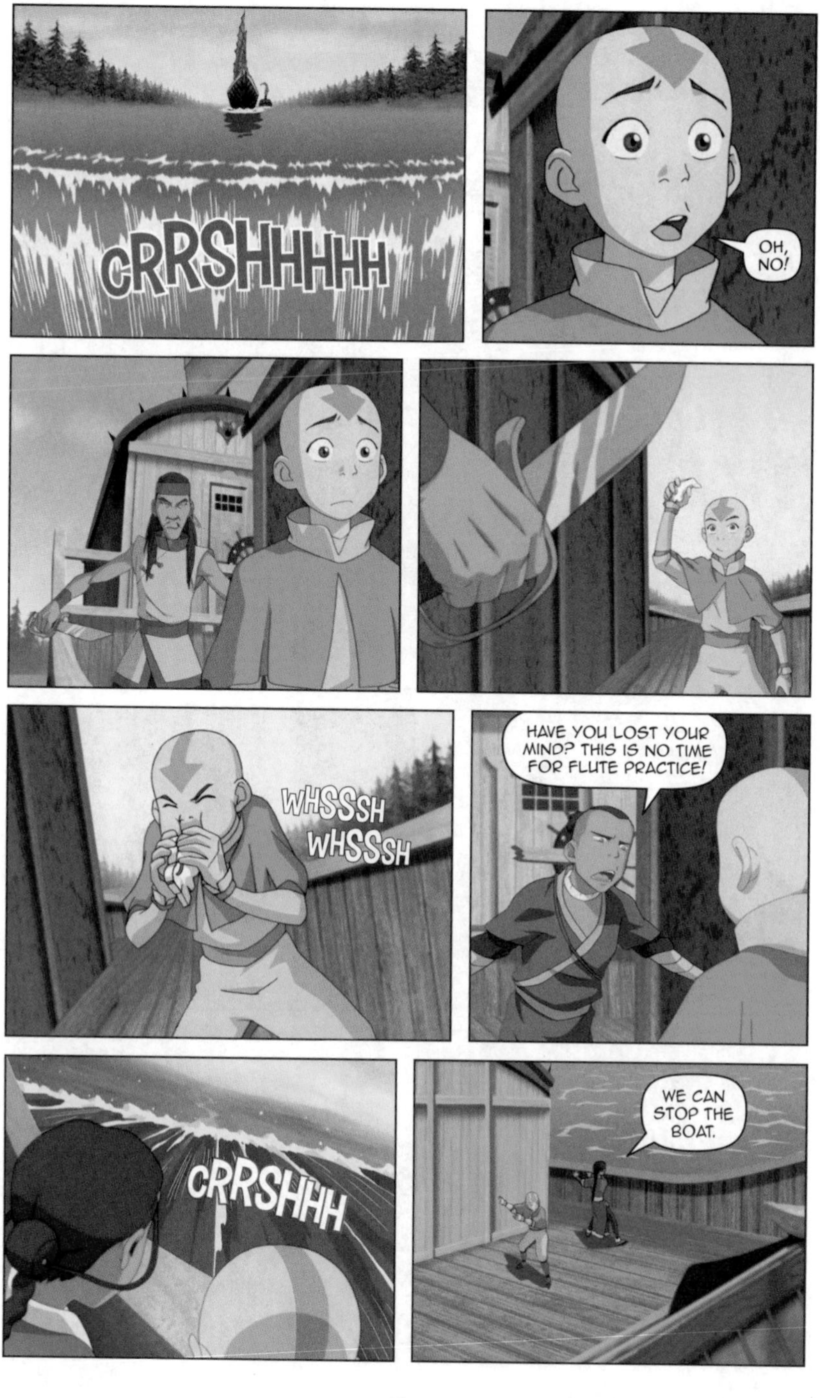
cRRSHHHHH
OH, NO!
WHSSSH WHSSSH
HAVE YOU LOST YOUR MIND? THIS IS NO TIME FOR FLUTE PRACTICE!
cRRSHHH
WE CAN STOP THE BOAT.

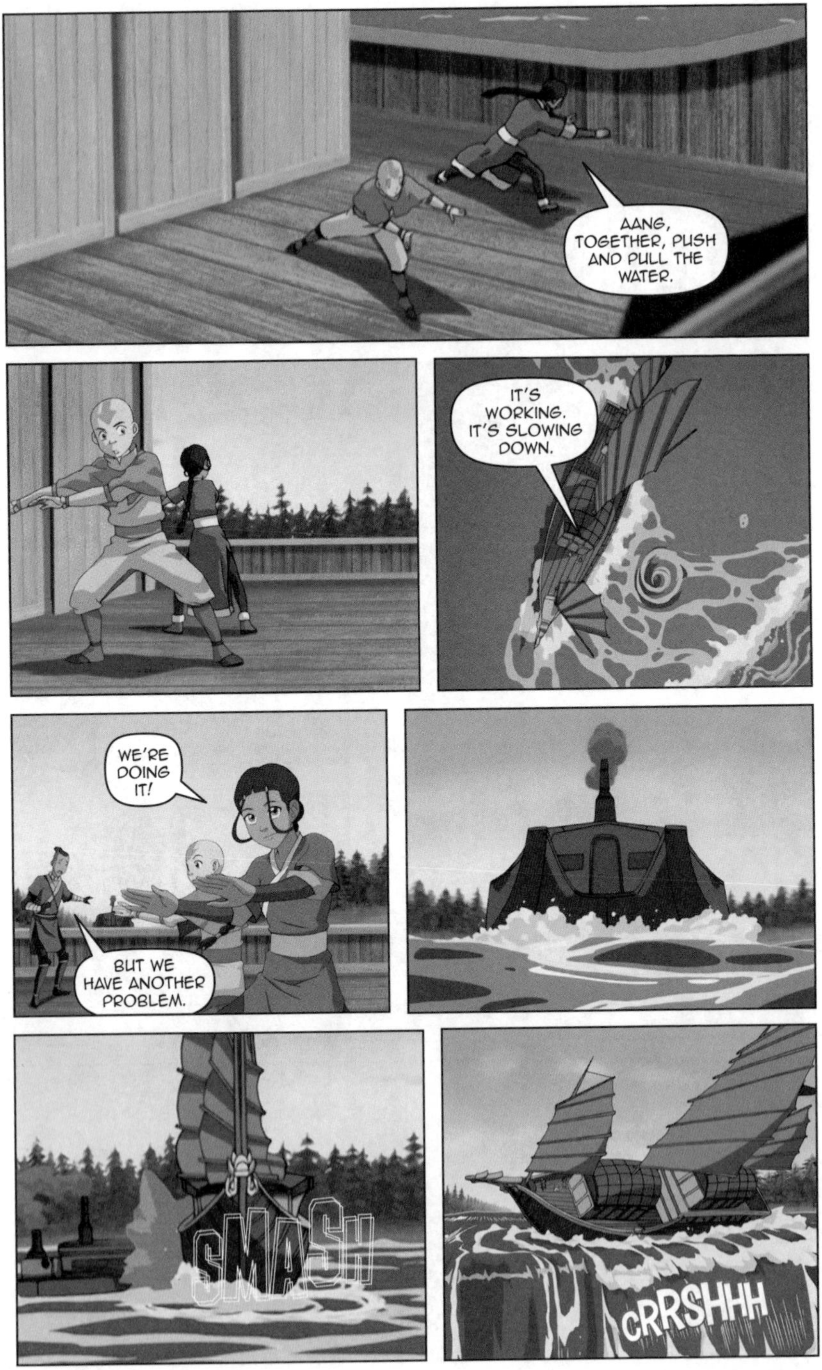
AANG, TOGETHER, PUSH AND PULL THE WATER.
IT'S WORKING. IT'S SLOWING DOWN.
WE'RE DOING IT!
BUT WE HAVE ANOTHER PROBLEM.
SMASH
cRRSHHH

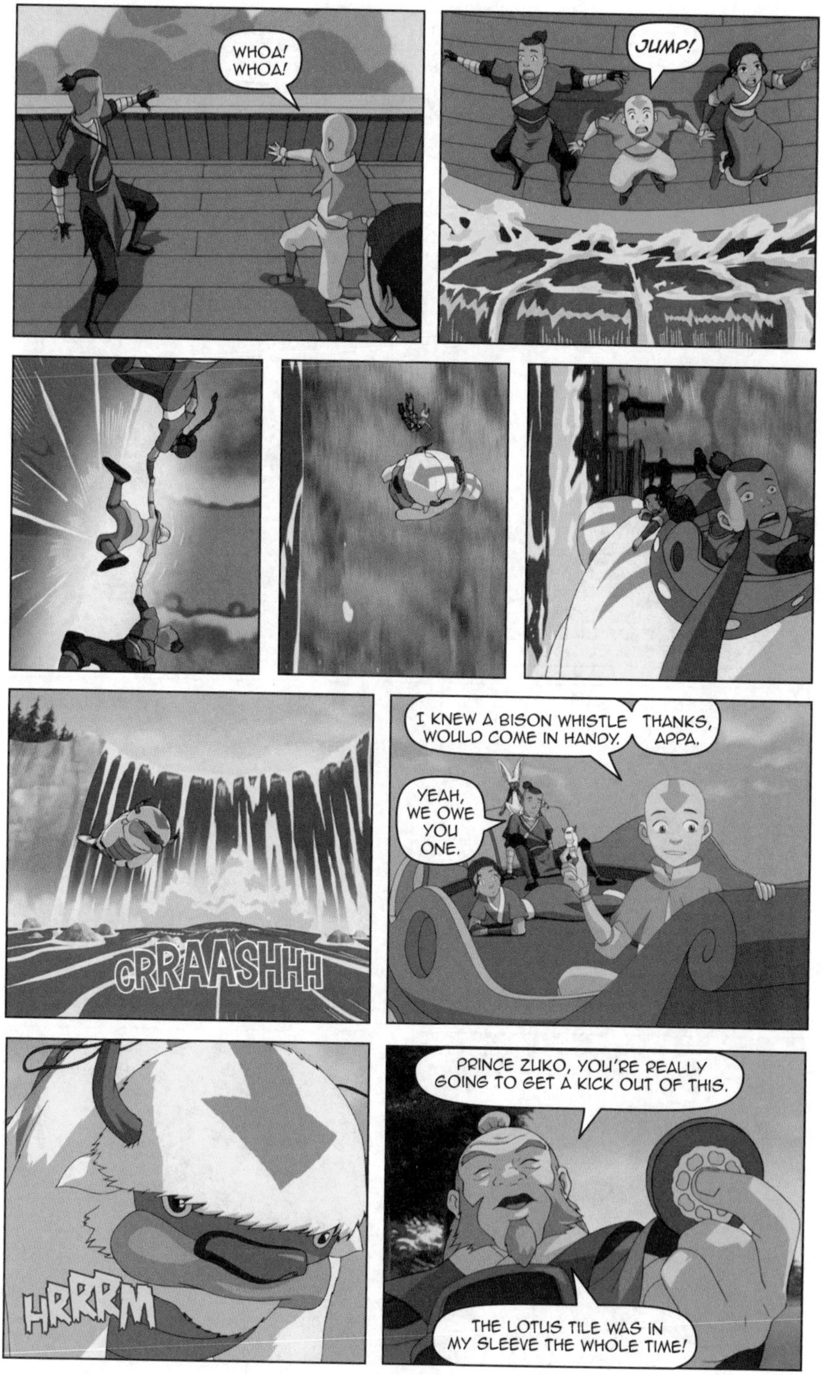
WHOA! WHOA!
JUMP!
CRRAASHHH
I KNEW A BISON WHISTLE WOULD COME IN HANDY.
THANKS, APPA.
YEAH, WE OWE YOU ONE.
HRRRM
PRINCE ZUKO, YOU'RE REALLY GOING TO GET A KICK OUT OF THIS.
THE LOTUS TILE WAS IN MY SLEEVE THE WHOLE TIME!

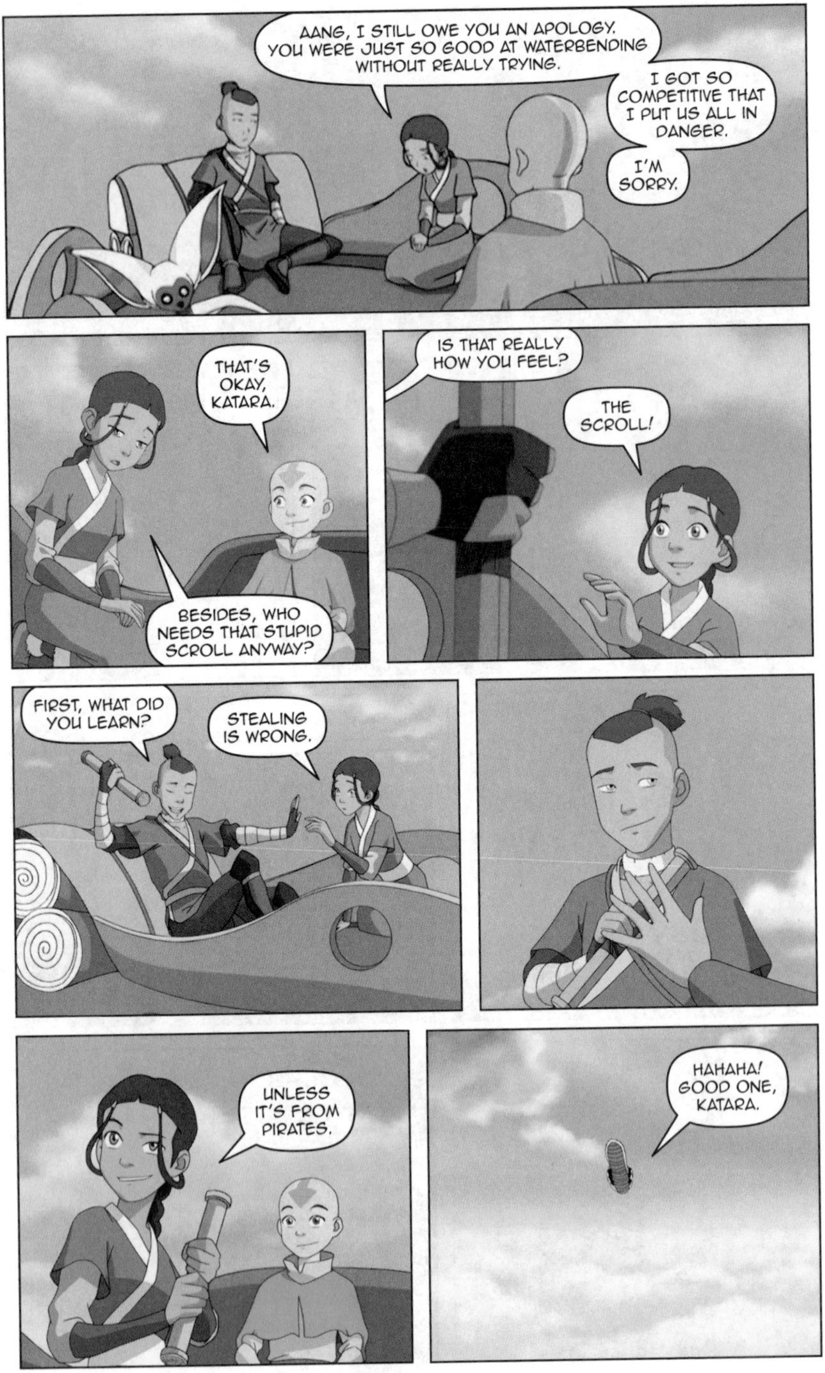
AANG, I STILL OWE YOU AN APOLOGY. YOU WERE JUST SO GOOD AT WATERBENDING WITHOUT REALLY TRYING.
I GOT SO COMPETITIVE THAT I PUT US ALL IN DANGER.
I'M SORRY.
THAT'S OKAY, KATARA.
BESIDES, WHO NEEDS THAT STUPID SCROLL ANYWAY?
IS THAT REALLY HOW YOU FEEL?
THE SCROLL!
FIRST, WHAT DID YOU LEARN?
STEALING IS WRONG.
UNLESS IT'S FROM PIRATES.
HAHAHA! GOOD ONE, KATARA.

CHAPTER TEN

JET

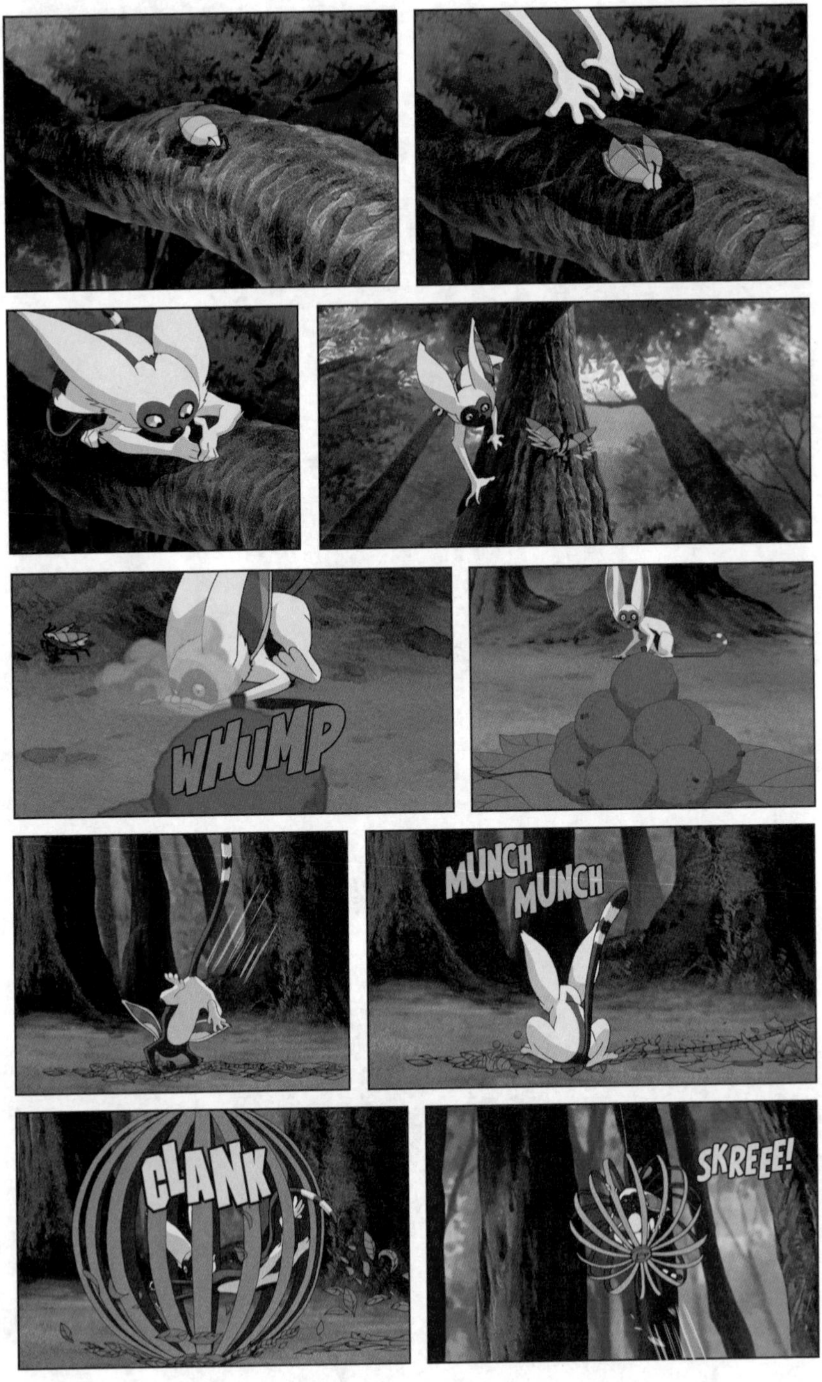
WHUMP
MUNCH
MUNCH
CLANK
SKREEE!

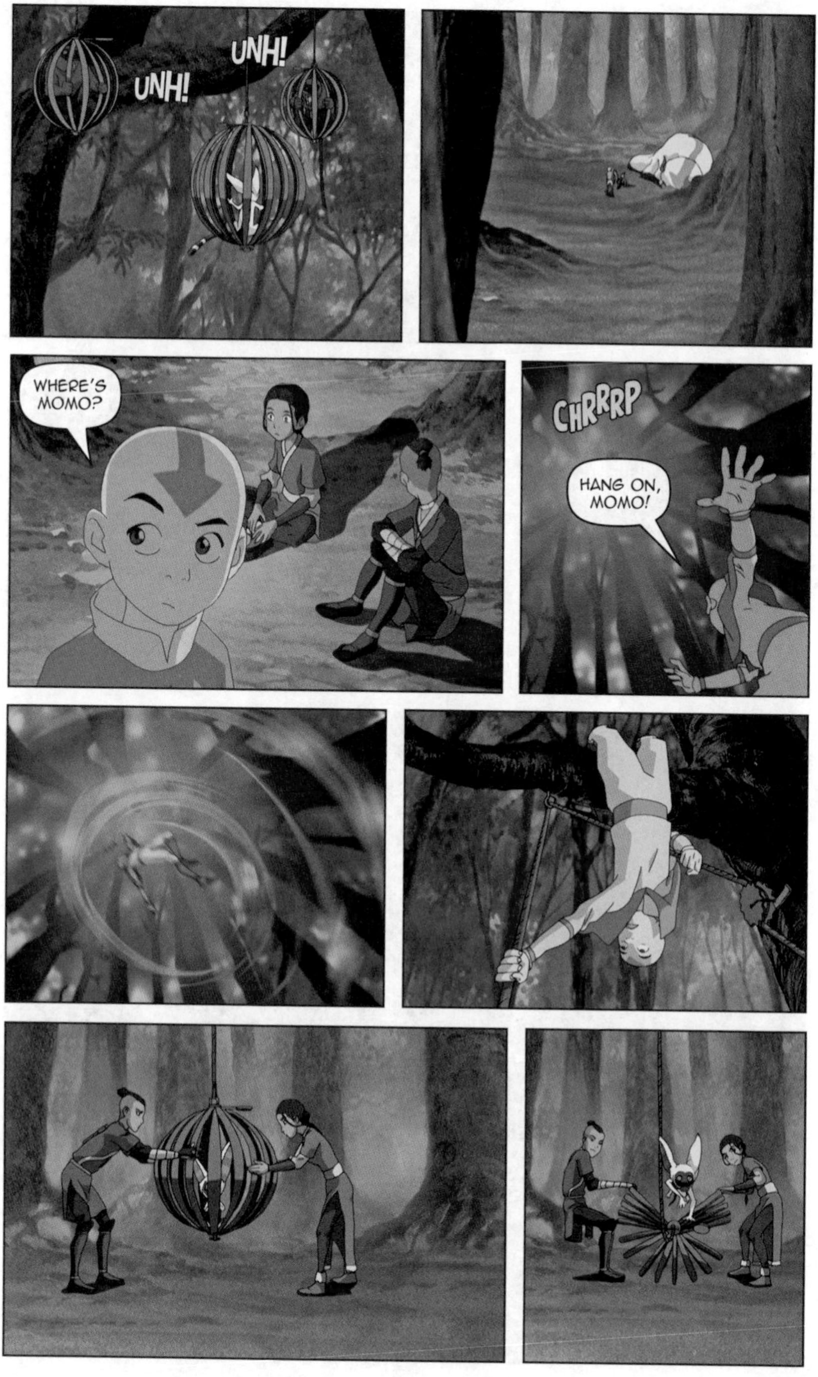
UNH!
UNH!
WHERE'S MOMO?
CHRRRP
HANG ON, MOMO!

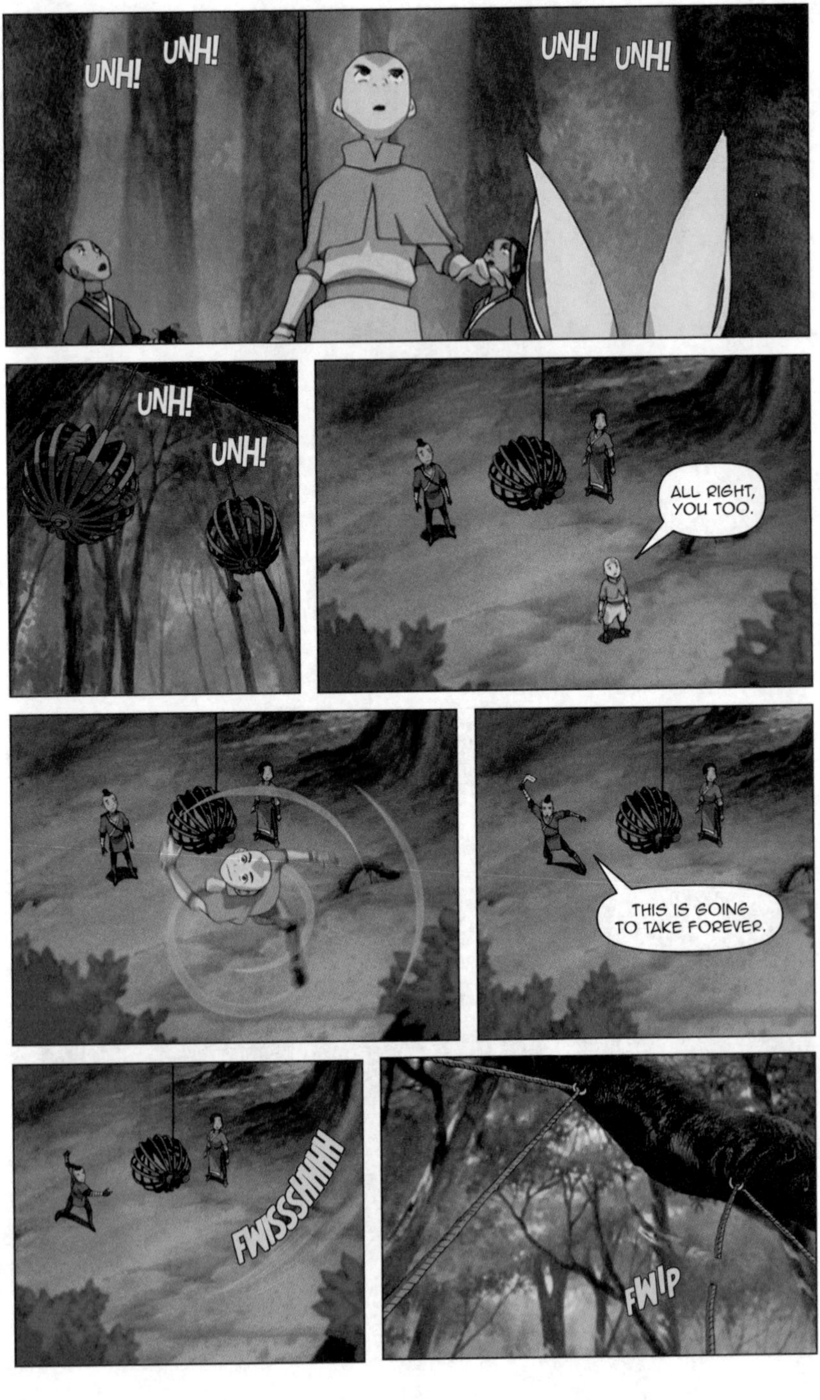
UNH!
UNH!
UNH!
UNH!
UNH!
UNH!
ALL RIGHT, YOU TOO.
THIS IS GOING TO TAKE FOREVER.
FWISSSHHHH
FWIP

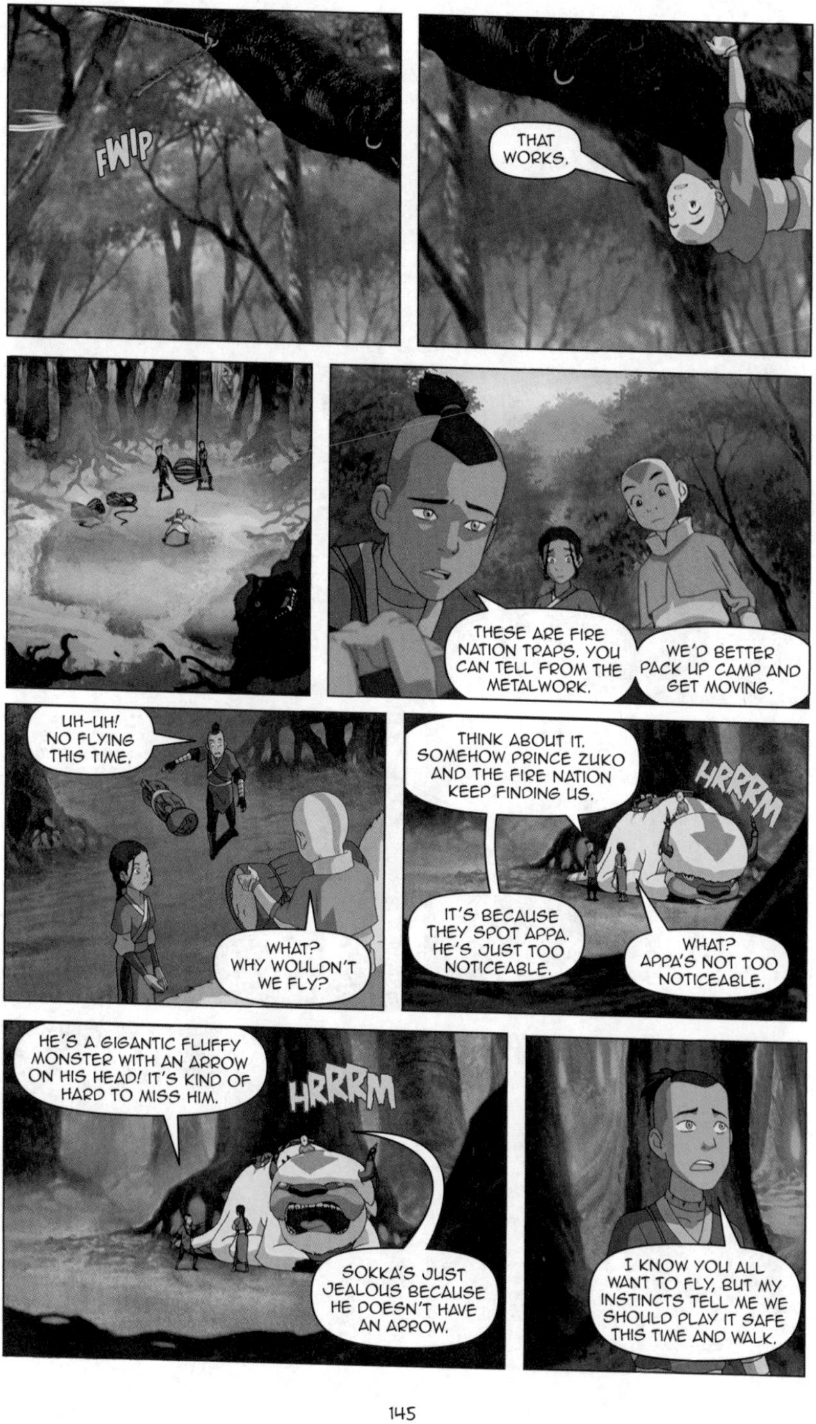
FWIP
THAT WORKS.
THESE ARE FIRE NATION TRAPS. YOU CAN TELL FROM THE METALWORK.
WE'D BETTER PACK UP CAMP AND GET MOVING.
UH-UH! NO FLYING THIS TIME.
WHAT? WHY WOULDN'T WE FLY?
THINK ABOUT IT. SOMEHOW PRINCE ZUKO AND THE FIRE NATION KEEP FINDING US.
HRRRM
IT'S BECAUSE THEY SPOT APPA. HE'S JUST TOO NOTICEABLE.
WHAT? APPA'S NOT TOO NOTICEABLE.
HE'S A GIGANTIC FLUFFY MONSTER WITH AN ARROW ON HIS HEAD! IT'S KIND OF HARD TO MISS HIM.
HRRRM
SOKKA'S JUST JEALOUS BECAUSE HE DOESN'T HAVE AN ARROW.
I KNOW YOU ALL WANT TO FLY, BUT MY INSTINCTS TELL ME WE SHOULD PLAY IT SAFE THIS TIME AND WALK.

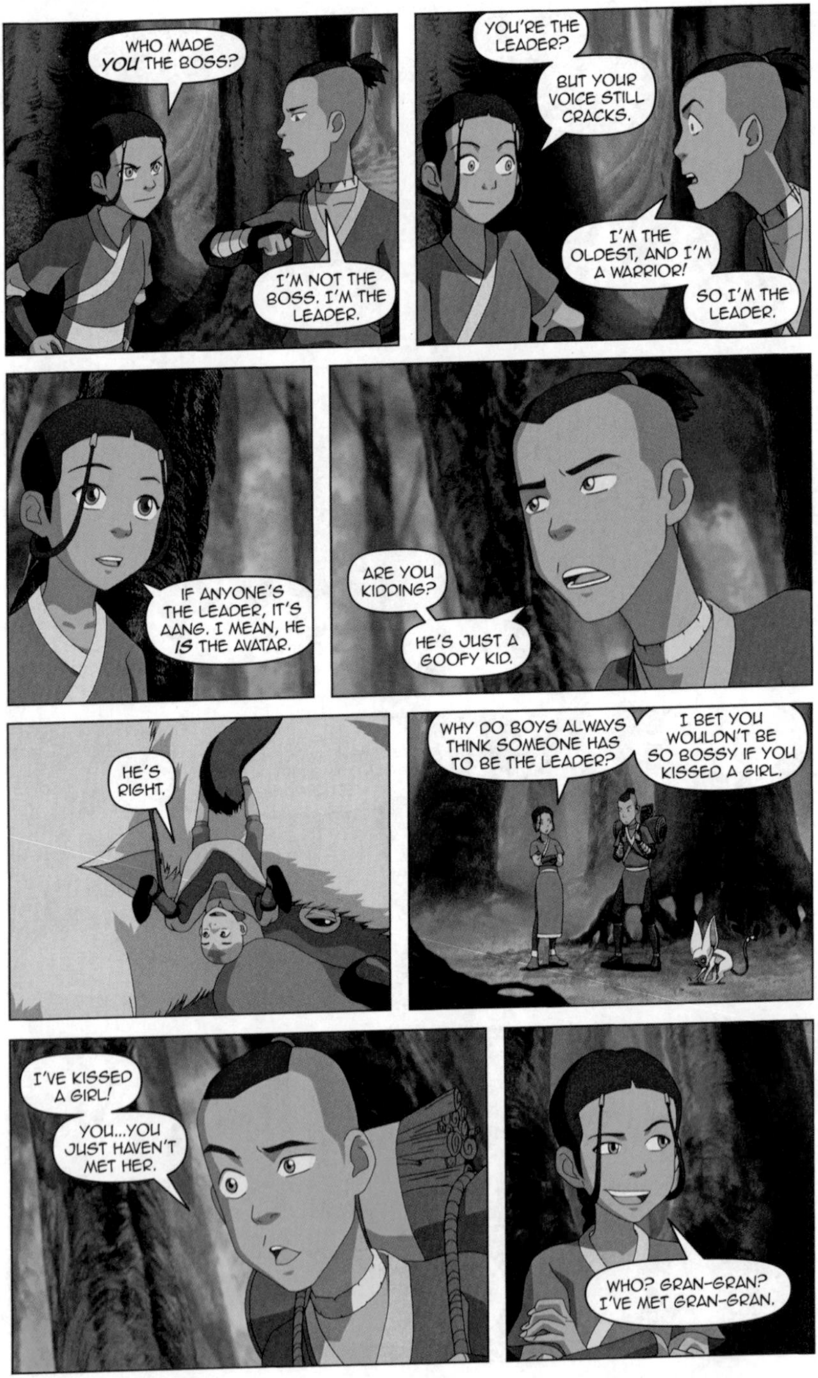
WHO MADE *YOU* THE BOSS?
I'M NOT THE BOSS. I'M THE LEADER.
YOU'RE THE LEADER?
BUT YOUR VOICE STILL CRACKS.
I'M THE OLDEST, AND I'M A WARRIOR!
SO I'M THE LEADER.
IF ANYONE'S THE LEADER, IT'S AANG. I MEAN, HE *IS* THE AVATAR.
ARE YOU KIDDING?
HE'S JUST A GOOFY KID.
HE'S RIGHT.
WHY DO BOYS ALWAYS THINK SOMEONE HAS TO BE THE LEADER?
I BET YOU WOULDN'T BE SO BOSSY IF YOU KISSED A GIRL.
I'VE KISSED A GIRL!
YOU...YOU JUST HAVEN'T MET HER.
WHO? GRAN-GRAN? I'VE MET GRAN-GRAN.

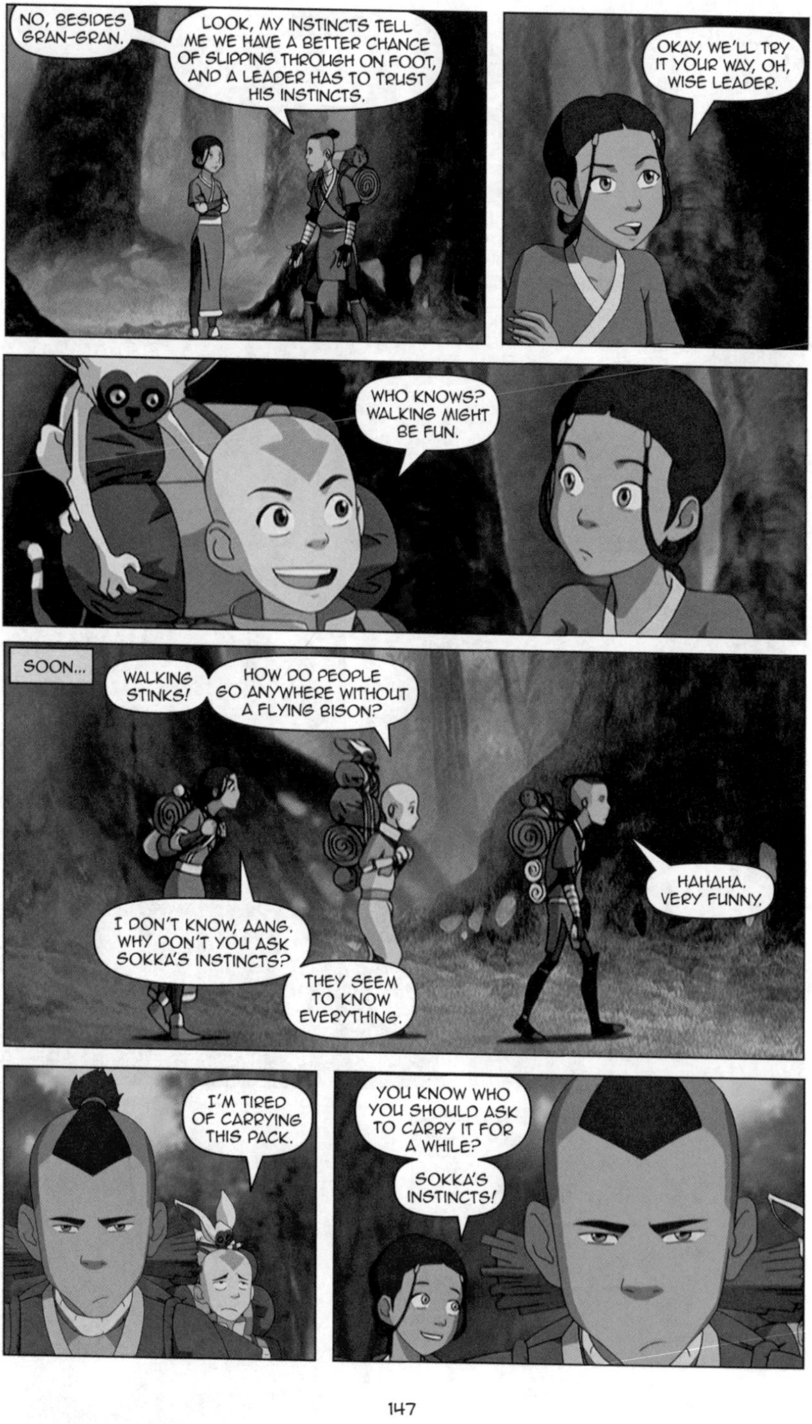
NO, BESIDES GRAN-GRAN.
LOOK, MY INSTINCTS TELL ME WE HAVE A BETTER CHANCE OF SLIPPING THROUGH ON FOOT, AND A LEADER HAS TO TRUST HIS INSTINCTS.
OKAY, WE'LL TRY IT YOUR WAY, OH, WISE LEADER.
WHO KNOWS? WALKING MIGHT BE FUN.
SOON...
WALKING STINKS!
HOW DO PEOPLE GO ANYWHERE WITHOUT A FLYING BISON?
HAHAHA. VERY FUNNY.
I DON'T KNOW, AANG. WHY DON'T YOU ASK SOKKA'S INSTINCTS?
THEY SEEM TO KNOW EVERYTHING.
I'M TIRED OF CARRYING THIS PACK.
YOU KNOW WHO YOU SHOULD ASK TO CARRY IT FOR A WHILE?
SOKKA'S INSTINCTS!

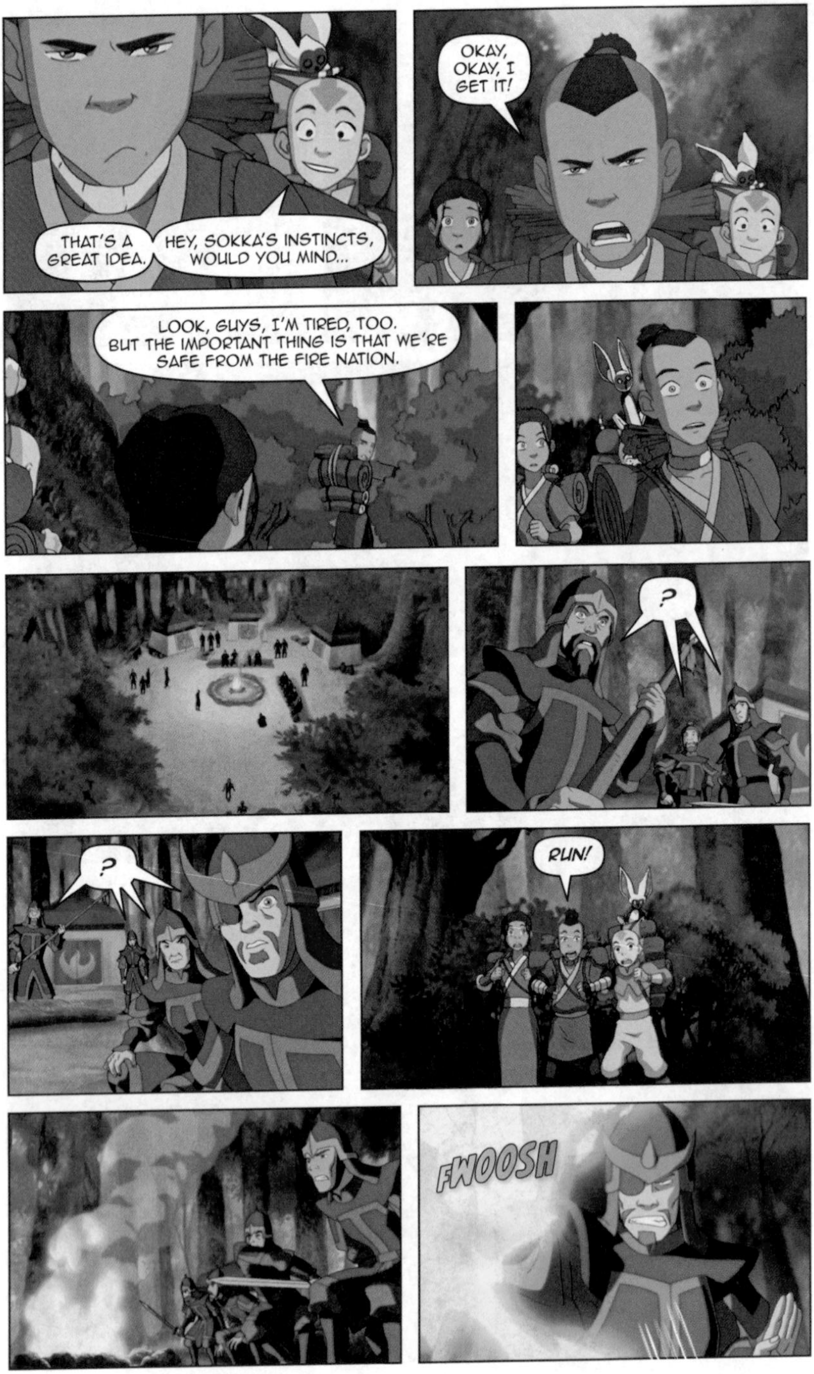
THAT'S A GREAT IDEA.
HEY, SOKKA'S INSTINCTS, WOULD YOU MIND...
OKAY, OKAY, I GET IT!
LOOK, GUYS, I'M TIRED, TOO. BUT THE IMPORTANT THING IS THAT WE'RE SAFE FROM THE FIRE NATION.
?
?
RUN!
FWOOSH

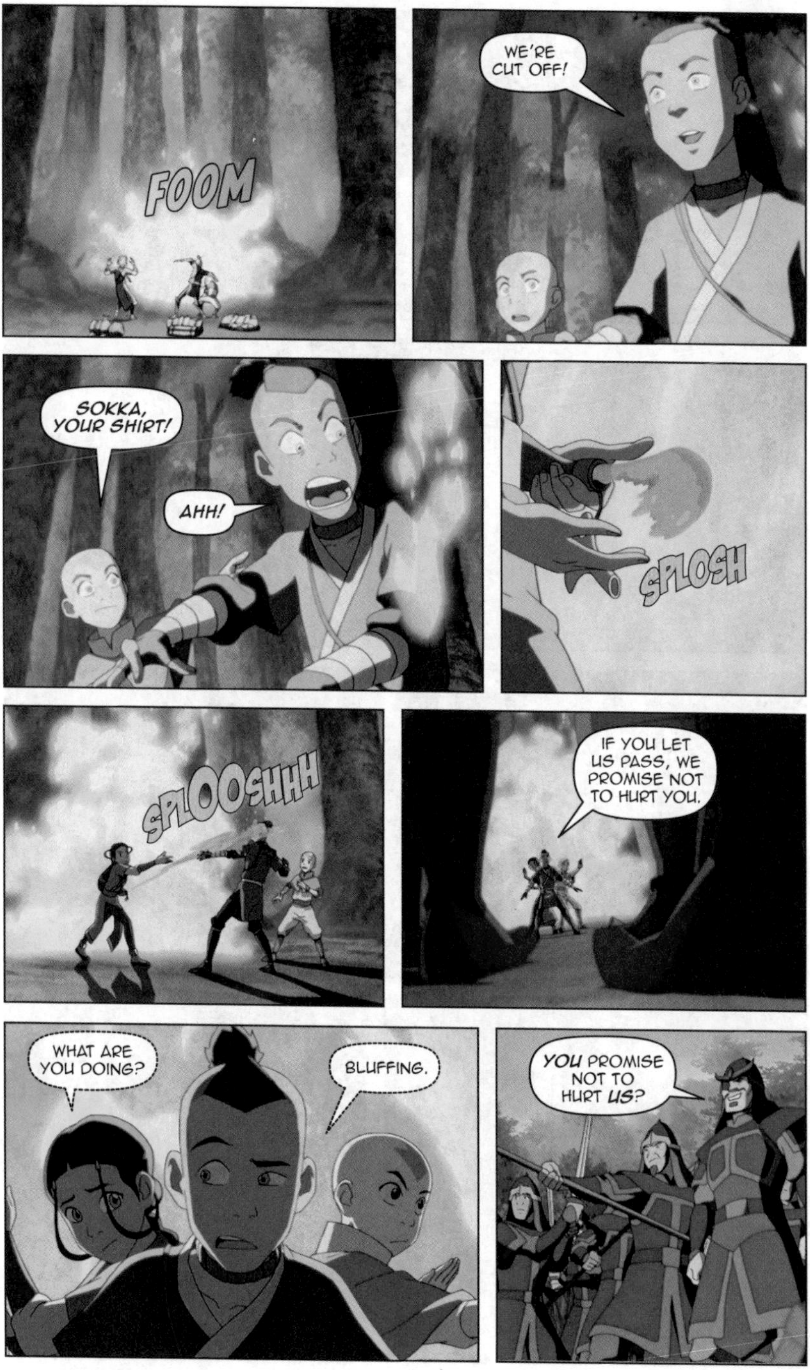
FOOM
WE'RE CUT OFF!
SOKKA, YOUR SHIRT!
AHH!
SPLOSH
SPLOOSHHH
IF YOU LET US PASS, WE PROMISE NOT TO HURT YOU.
WHAT ARE YOU DOING?
BLUFFING.
YOU PROMISE NOT TO HURT US?

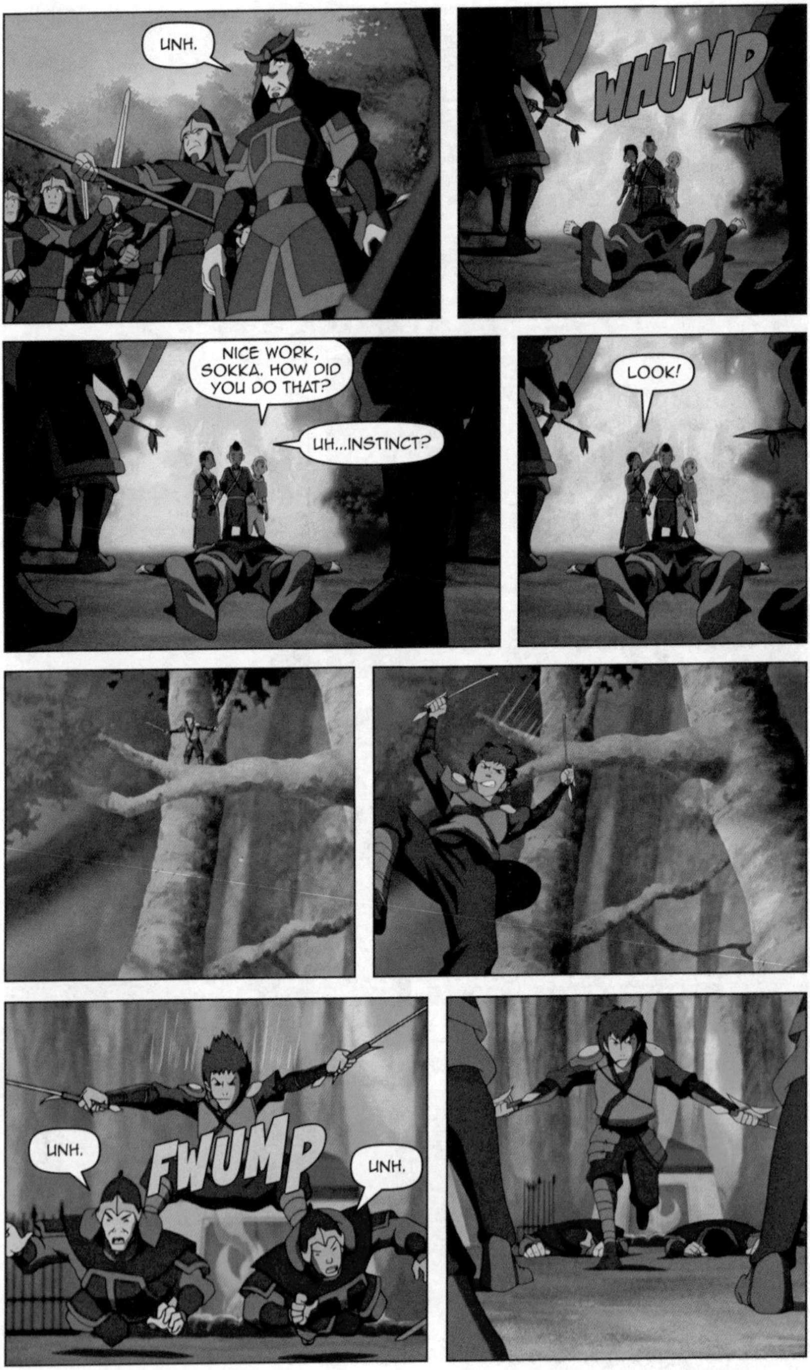
UNH.
WHUMP
NICE WORK, SOKKA. HOW DID YOU DO THAT?
UH...INSTINCT?
LOOK!
UNH.
FWUMP
UNH.

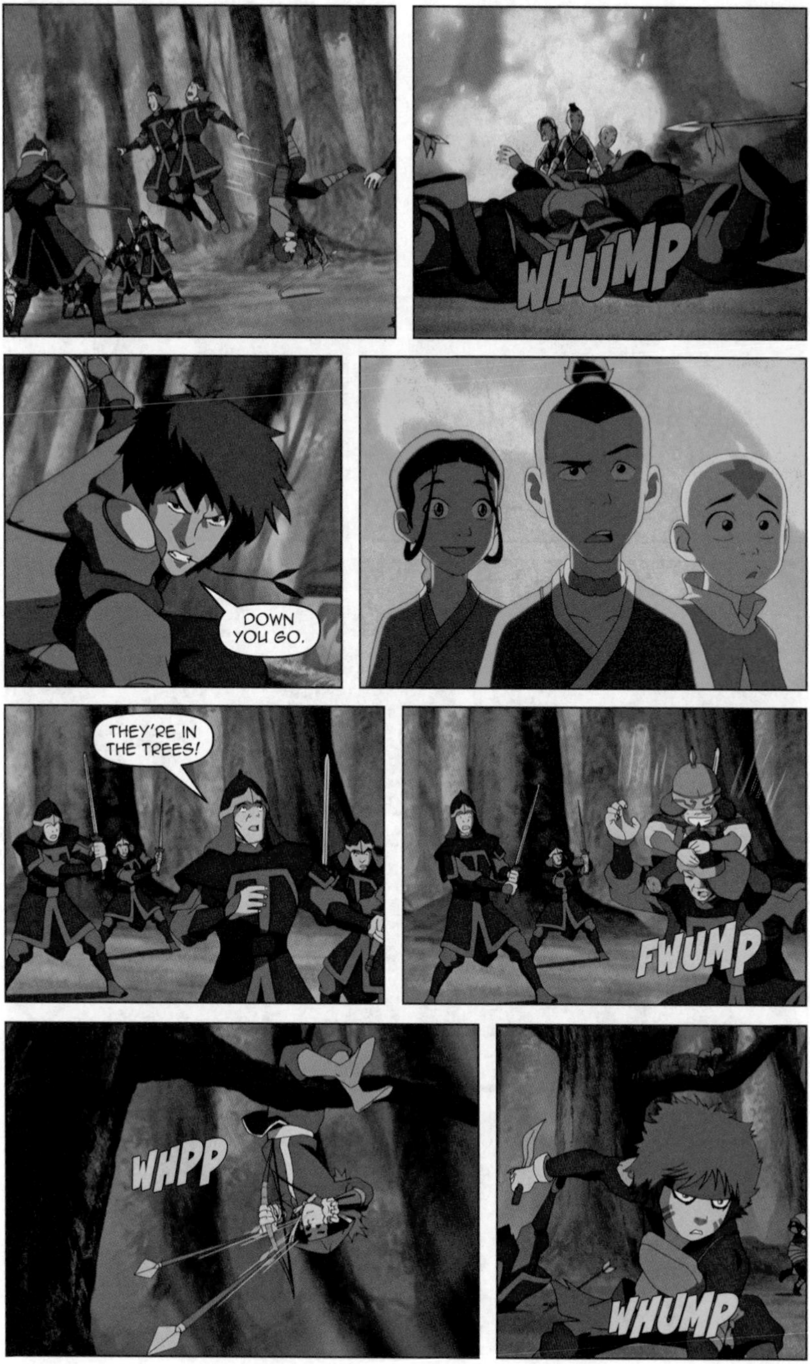

WHUMP
DOWN YOU GO.
THEY'RE IN THE TREES!
FWUMP
WHPP
WHUMP

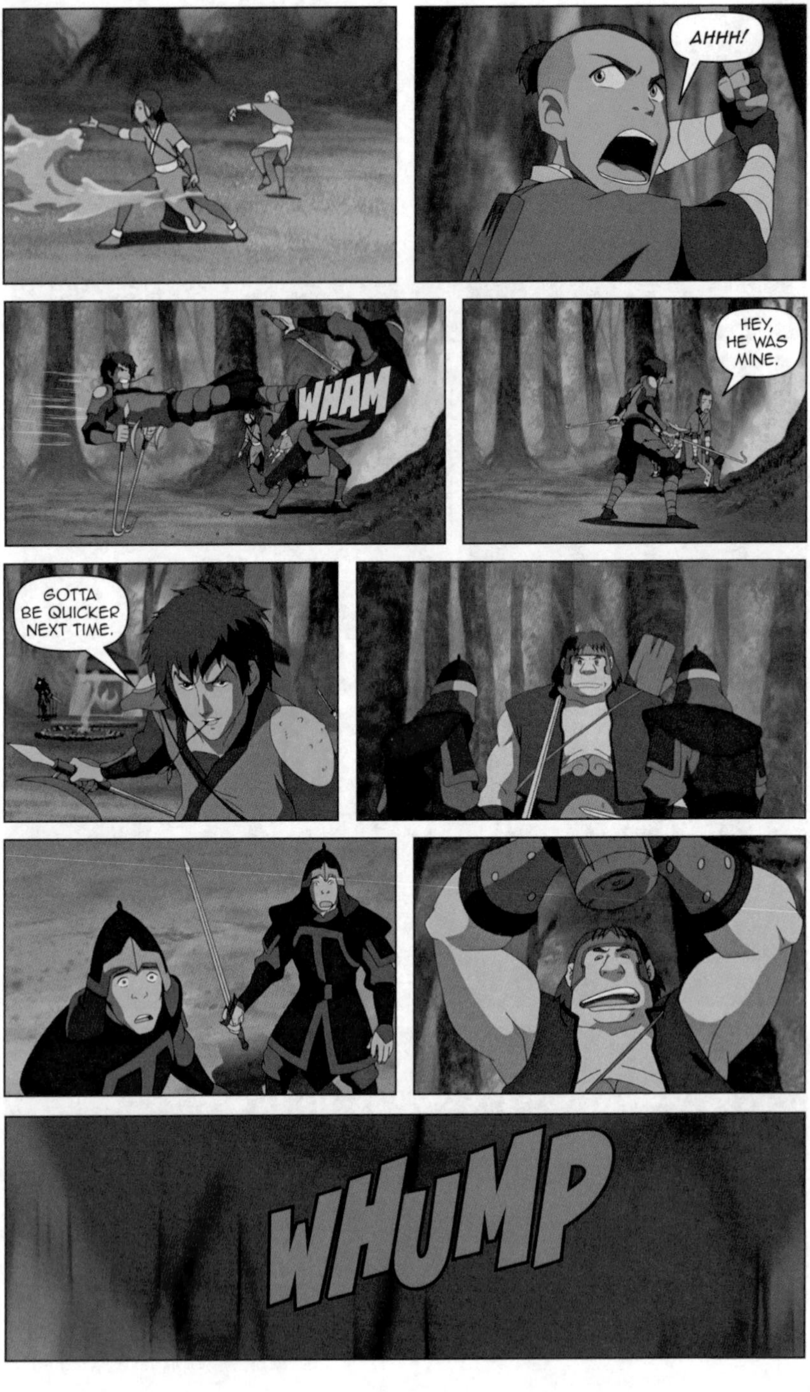
AHHH!
WHAM
HEY, HE WAS MINE.
GOTTA BE QUICKER NEXT TIME.
WHUMP

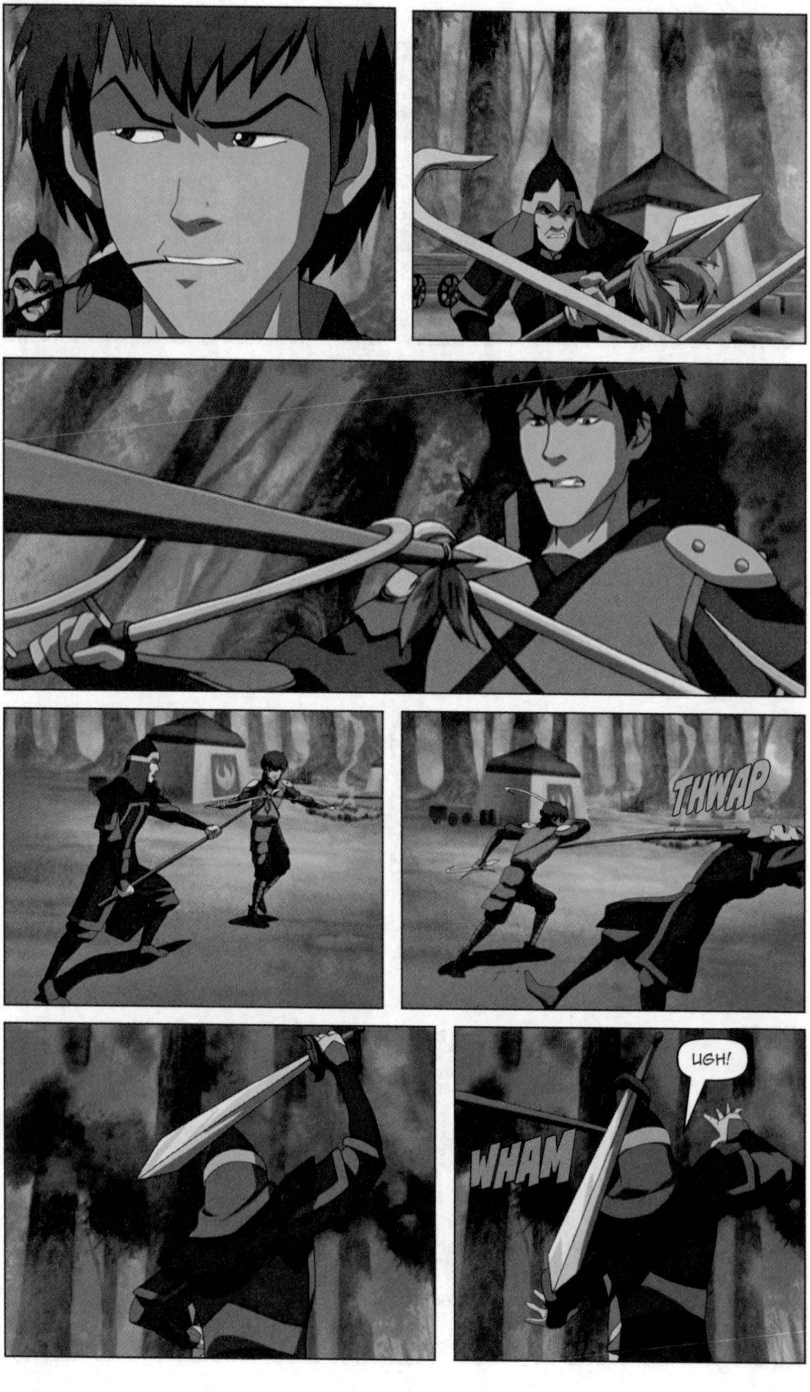
THWAP
UGH!
WHAM

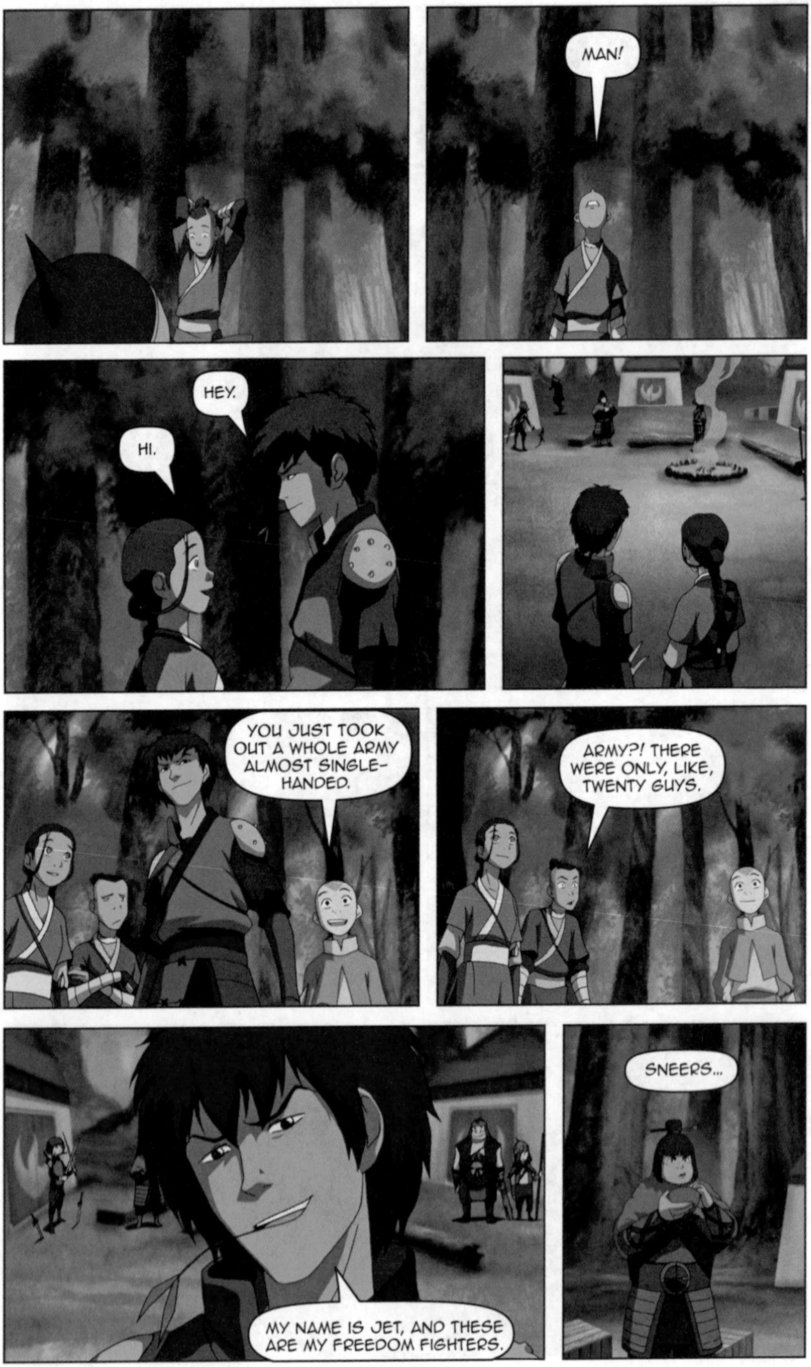
MAN!
HI.
HEY.
YOU JUST TOOK OUT A WHOLE ARMY ALMOST SINGLE-HANDED.
ARMY?! THERE WERE ONLY, LIKE, TWENTY GUYS.
MY NAME IS JET, AND THESE ARE MY FREEDOM FIGHTERS.
SNEERS...

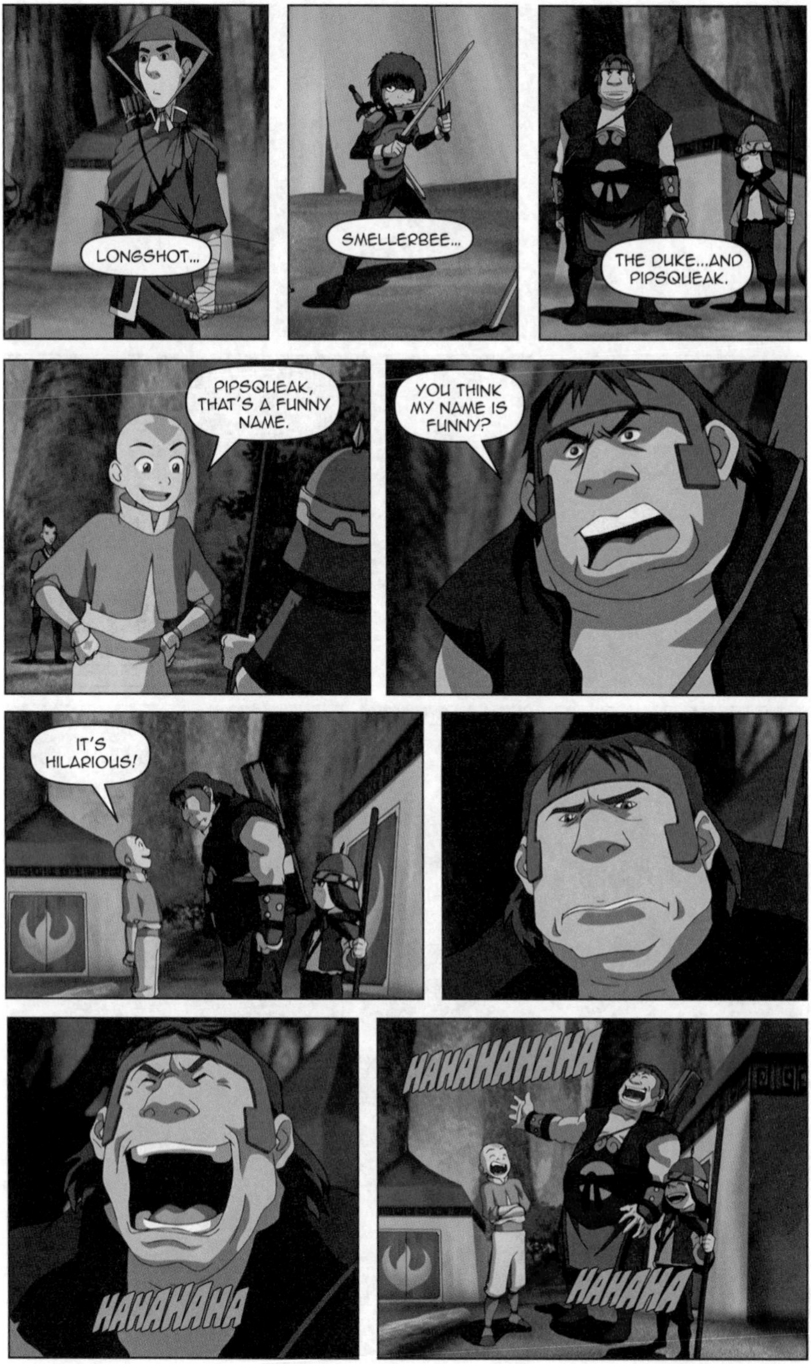
LONGSHOT...
SMELLERBEE...
THE DUKE...AND PIPSQUEAK.
PIPSQUEAK, THAT'S A FUNNY NAME.
YOU THINK MY NAME IS FUNNY?
IT'S HILARIOUS!
HAHAHAHA
HAHAHAHAHA
HAHAHA

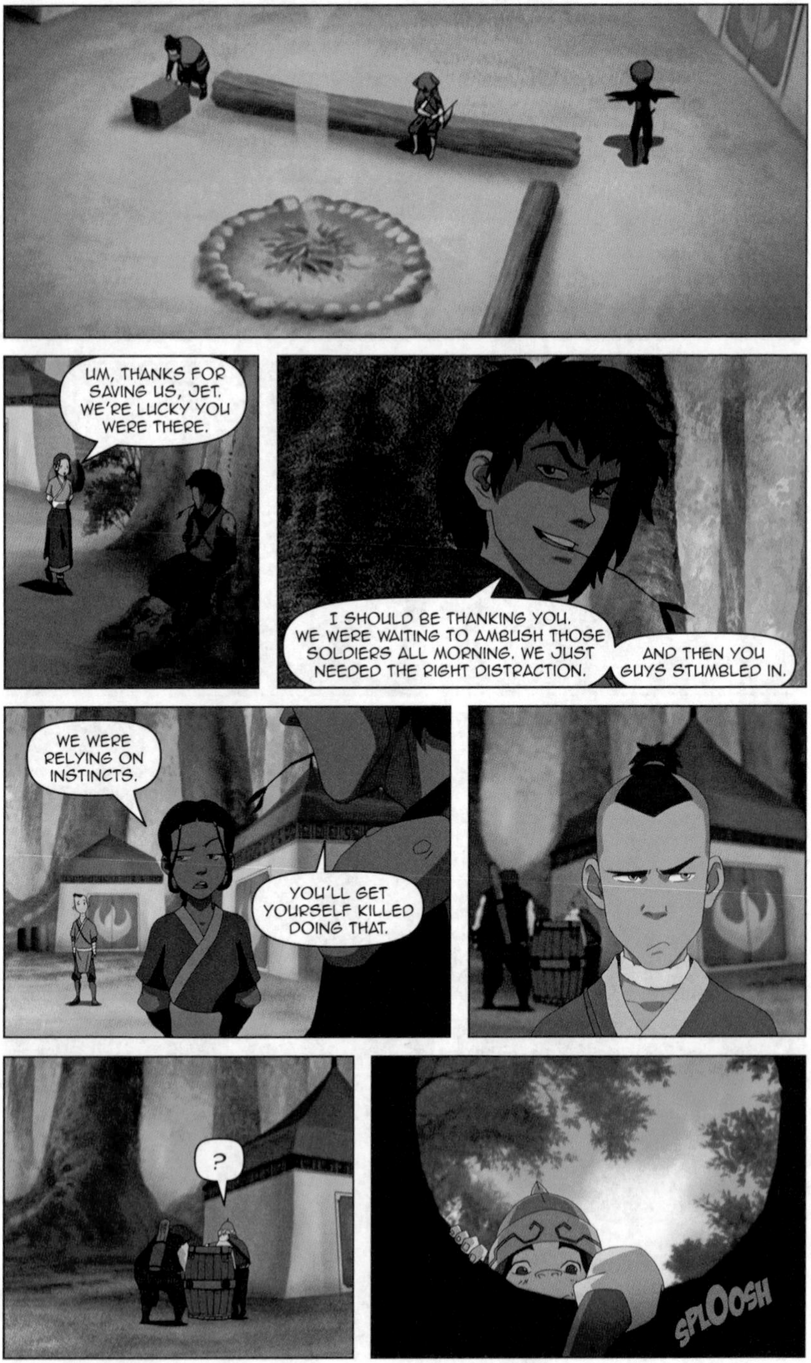
UM, THANKS FOR SAVING US, JET. WE'RE LUCKY YOU WERE THERE.
I SHOULD BE THANKING YOU. WE WERE WAITING TO AMBUSH THOSE SOLDIERS ALL MORNING. WE JUST NEEDED THE RIGHT DISTRACTION.
AND THEN YOU GUYS STUMBLED IN.
WE WERE RELYING ON INSTINCTS.
YOU'LL GET YOURSELF KILLED DOING THAT.
?
SPLOOSH

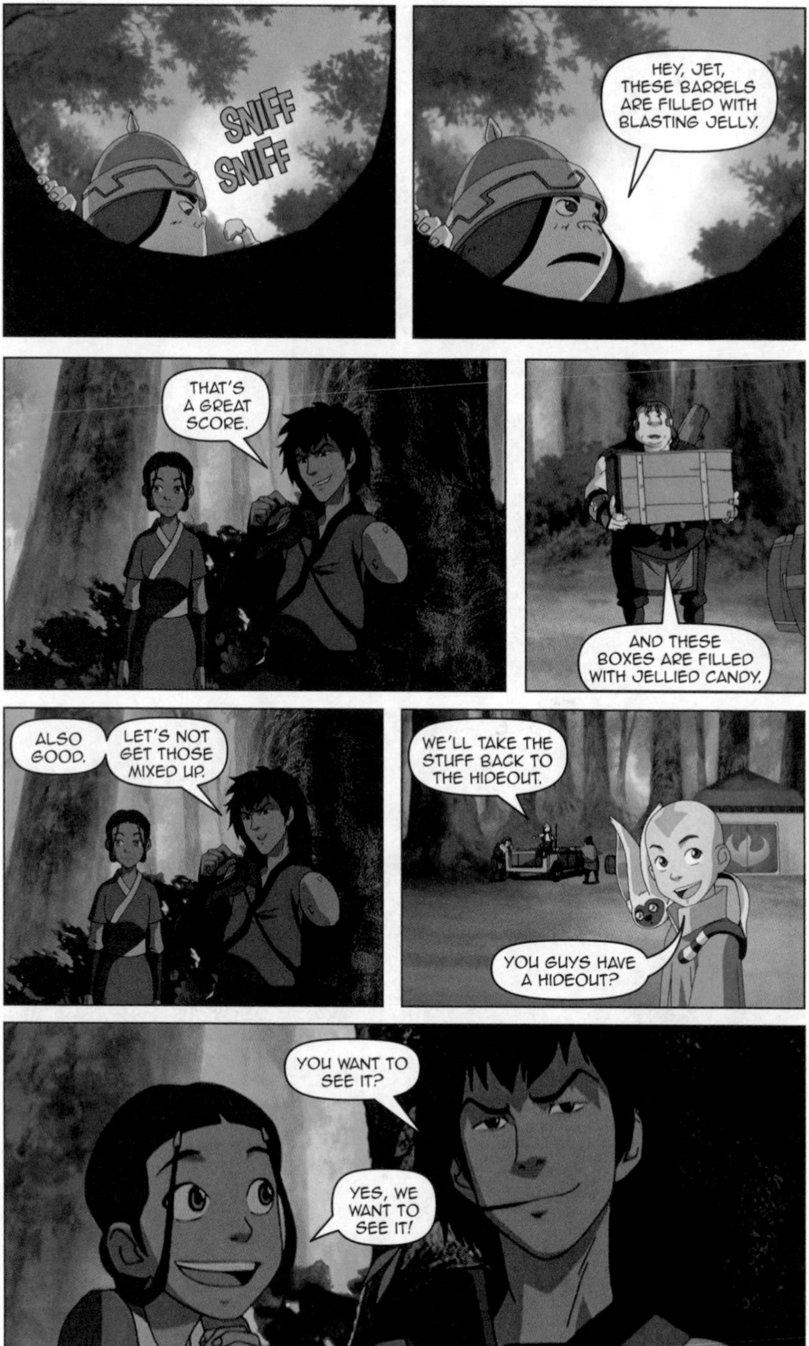
SNIFF
SNIFF
HEY, JET, THESE BARRELS ARE FILLED WITH BLASTING JELLY.
THAT'S A GREAT SCORE.
AND THESE BOXES ARE FILLED WITH JELLIED CANDY.
ALSO GOOD.
LET'S NOT GET THOSE MIXED UP.
WE'LL TAKE THE STUFF BACK TO THE HIDEOUT.
YOU GUYS HAVE A HIDEOUT?
YOU WANT TO SEE IT?
YES, WE WANT TO SEE IT!

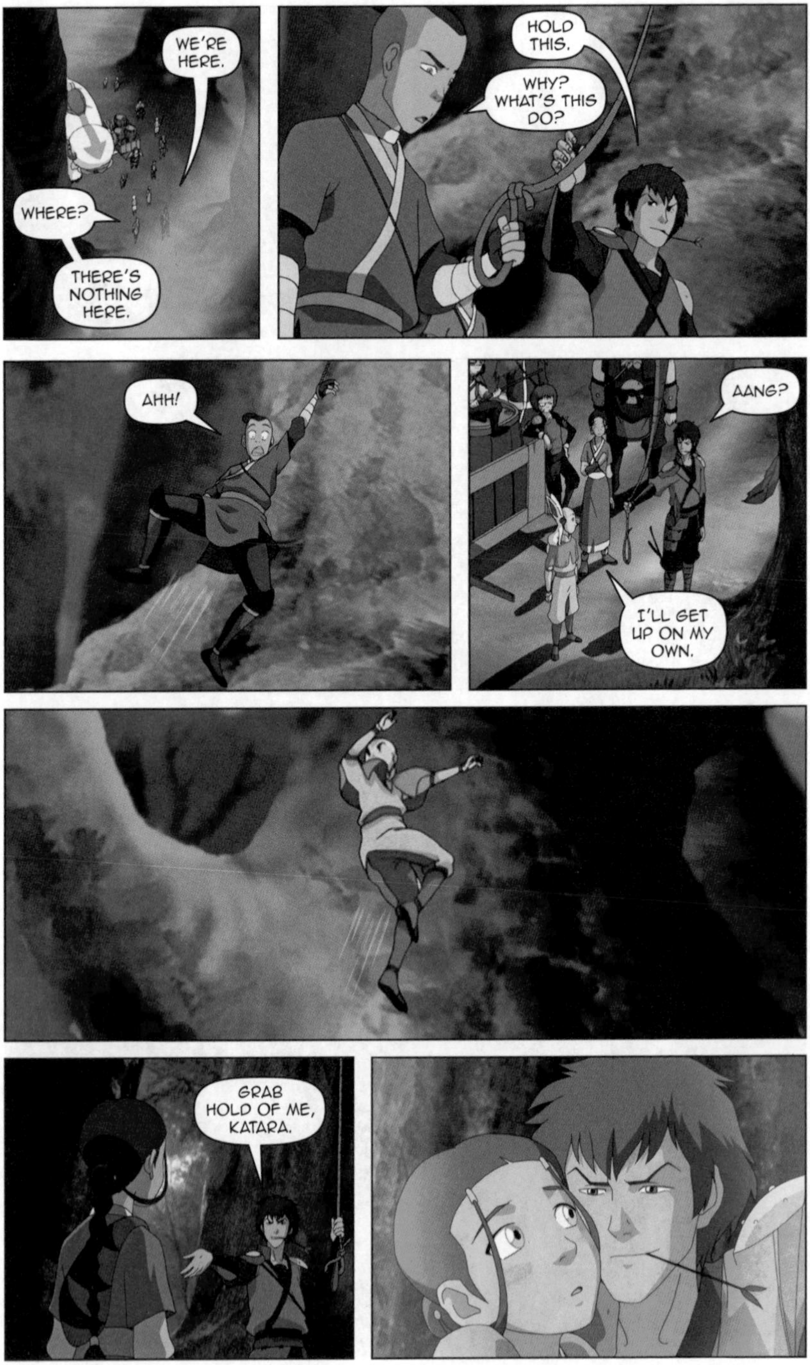
WE'RE HERE.
WHERE?
THERE'S NOTHING HERE.
HOLD THIS.
WHY? WHAT'S THIS DO?
AHH!
AANG?
I'LL GET UP ON MY OWN.
GRAB HOLD OF ME, KATARA.

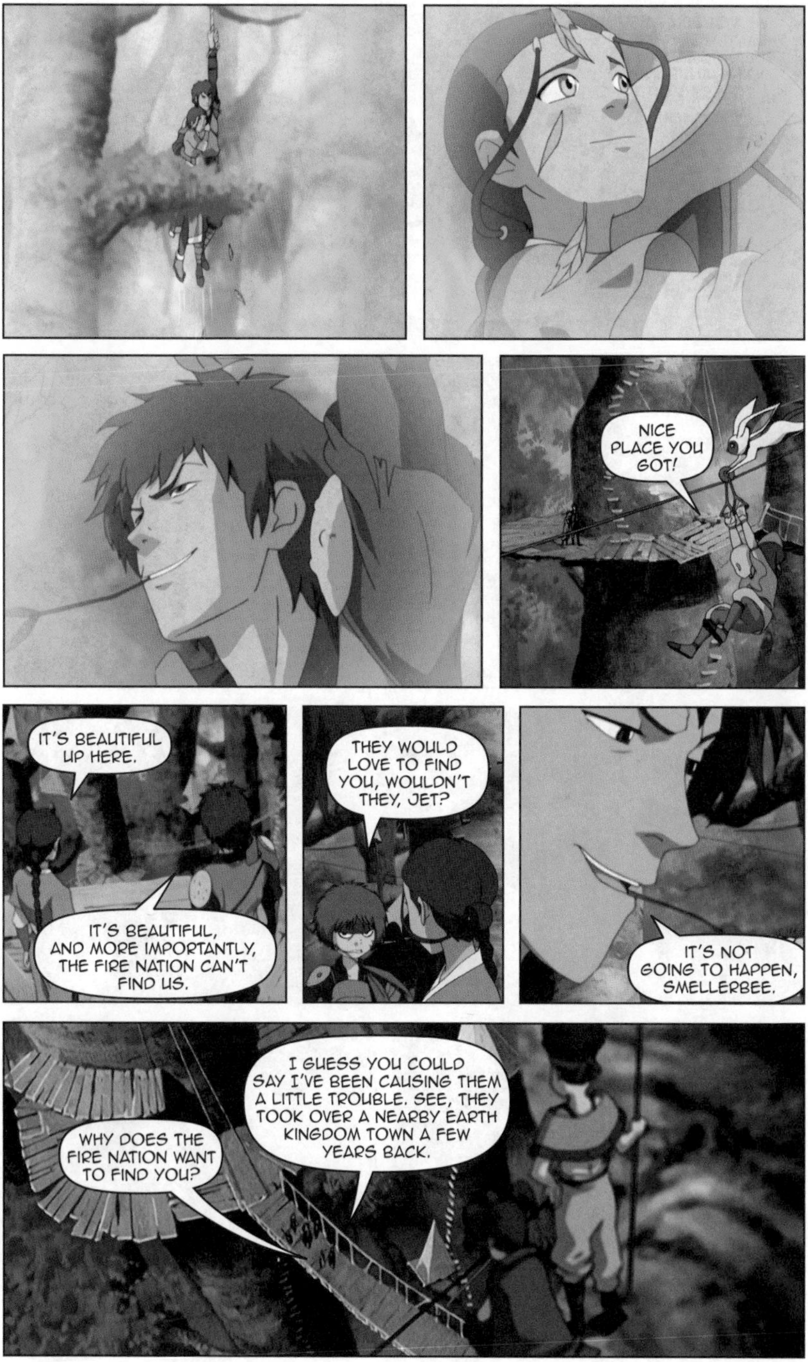
NICE PLACE YOU GOT!
IT'S BEAUTIFUL UP HERE.
IT'S BEAUTIFUL, AND MORE IMPORTANTLY, THE FIRE NATION CAN'T FIND US.
THEY WOULD LOVE TO FIND YOU, WOULDN'T THEY, JET?
IT'S NOT GOING TO HAPPEN, SMELLERBEE.
WHY DOES THE FIRE NATION WANT TO FIND YOU?
I GUESS YOU COULD SAY I'VE BEEN CAUSING THEM A LITTLE TROUBLE. SEE, THEY TOOK OVER A NEARBY EARTH KINGDOM TOWN A FEW YEARS BACK.

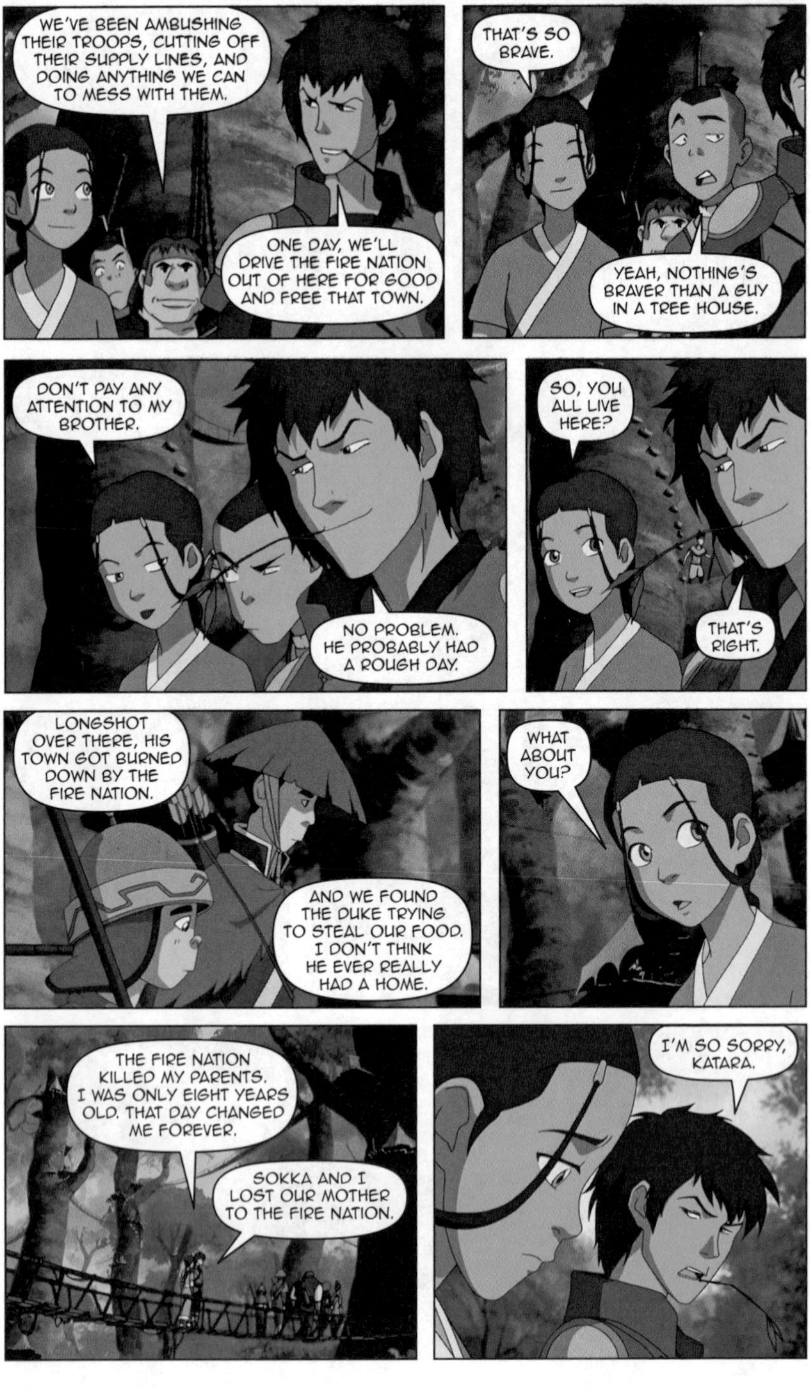
WE'VE BEEN AMBUSHING THEIR TROOPS, CUTTING OFF THEIR SUPPLY LINES, AND DOING ANYTHING WE CAN TO MESS WITH THEM.
ONE DAY, WE'LL DRIVE THE FIRE NATION OUT OF HERE FOR GOOD AND FREE THAT TOWN.
THAT'S SO BRAVE.
YEAH, NOTHING'S BRAVER THAN A GUY IN A TREE HOUSE.
DON'T PAY ANY ATTENTION TO MY BROTHER.
NO PROBLEM. HE PROBABLY HAD A ROUGH DAY.
SO, YOU ALL LIVE HERE?
THAT'S RIGHT.
LONGSHOT OVER THERE, HIS TOWN GOT BURNED DOWN BY THE FIRE NATION.
AND WE FOUND THE DUKE TRYING TO STEAL OUR FOOD. I DON'T THINK HE EVER REALLY HAD A HOME.
WHAT ABOUT YOU?
THE FIRE NATION KILLED MY PARENTS. I WAS ONLY EIGHT YEARS OLD. THAT DAY CHANGED ME FOREVER.
SOKKA AND I LOST OUR MOTHER TO THE FIRE NATION.
I'M SO SORRY, KATARA.

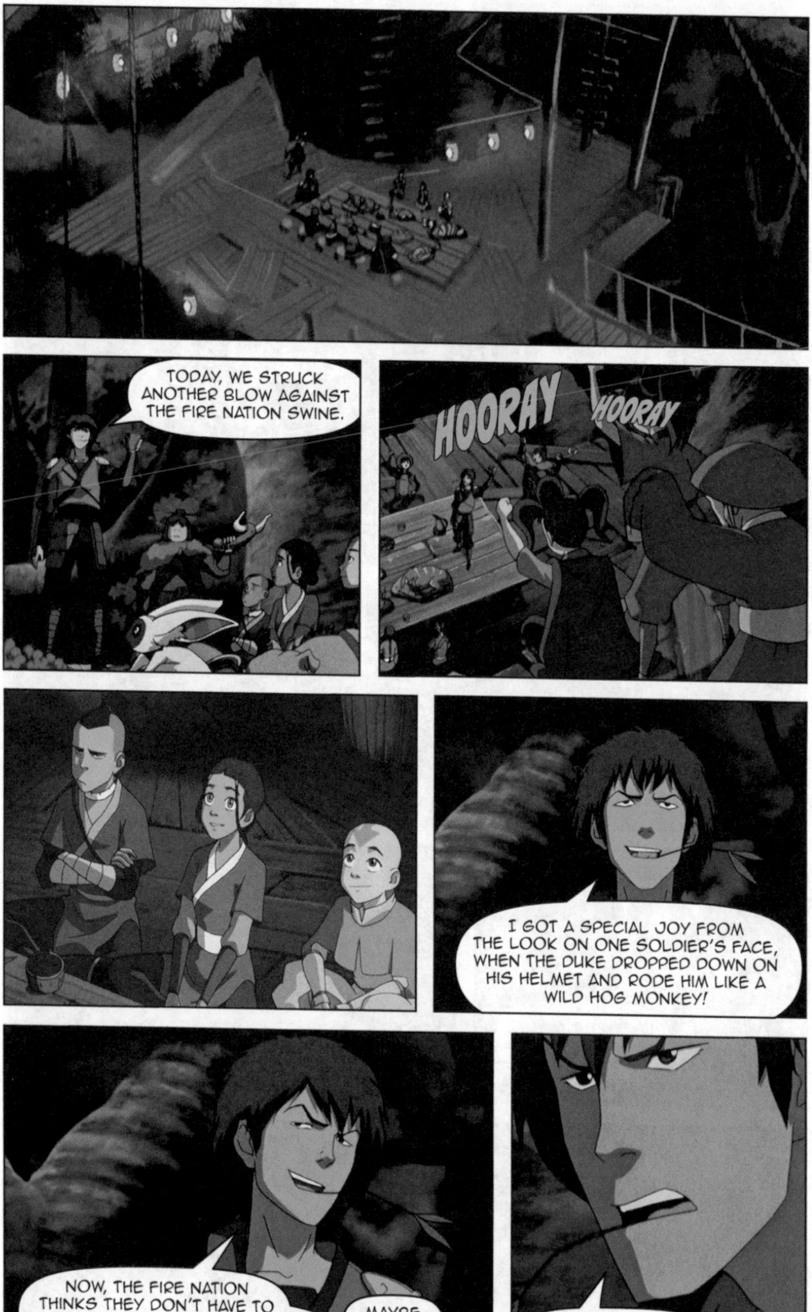
TODAY, WE STRUCK ANOTHER BLOW AGAINST THE FIRE NATION SWINE.
HOORAY
HOORAY
I GOT A SPECIAL JOY FROM THE LOOK ON ONE SOLDIER'S FACE, WHEN THE DUKE DROPPED DOWN ON HIS HELMET AND RODE HIM LIKE A WILD HOG MONKEY!
NOW, THE FIRE NATION THINKS THEY DON'T HAVE TO WORRY ABOUT A COUPLE OF KIDS HIDING IN THE TREES.
MAYBE THEY'RE RIGHT.
OR MAYBE THEY'RE DEAD WRONG.

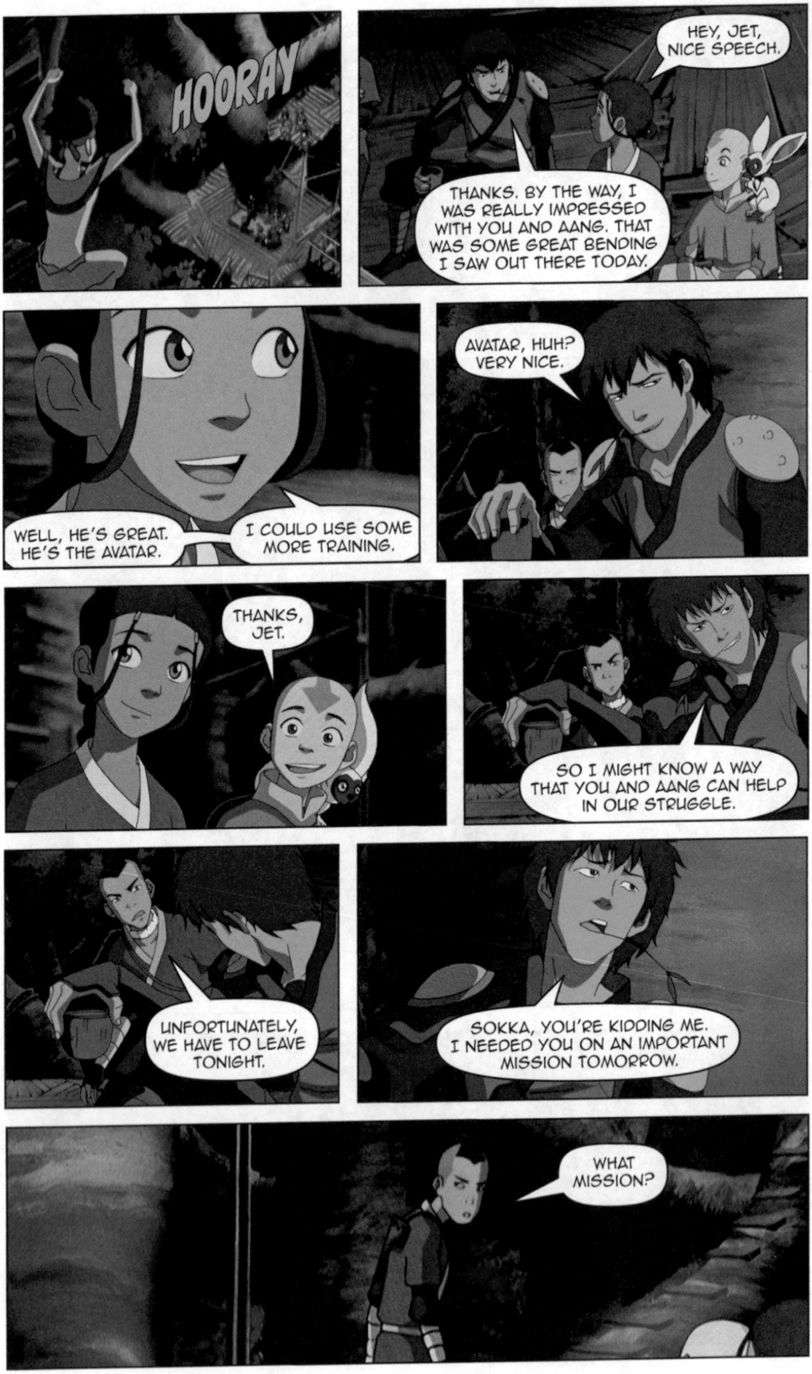
HOORAY
HEY, JET, NICE SPEECH.
THANKS. BY THE WAY, I WAS REALLY IMPRESSED WITH YOU AND AANG. THAT WAS SOME GREAT BENDING I SAW OUT THERE TODAY.
WELL, HE'S GREAT. HE'S THE AVATAR.
I COULD USE SOME MORE TRAINING.
AVATAR, HUH? VERY NICE.
THANKS, JET.
SO I MIGHT KNOW A WAY THAT YOU AND AANG CAN HELP IN OUR STRUGGLE.
UNFORTUNATELY, WE HAVE TO LEAVE TONIGHT.
SOKKA, YOU'RE KIDDING ME. I NEEDED YOU ON AN IMPORTANT MISSION TOMORROW.
WHAT MISSION?

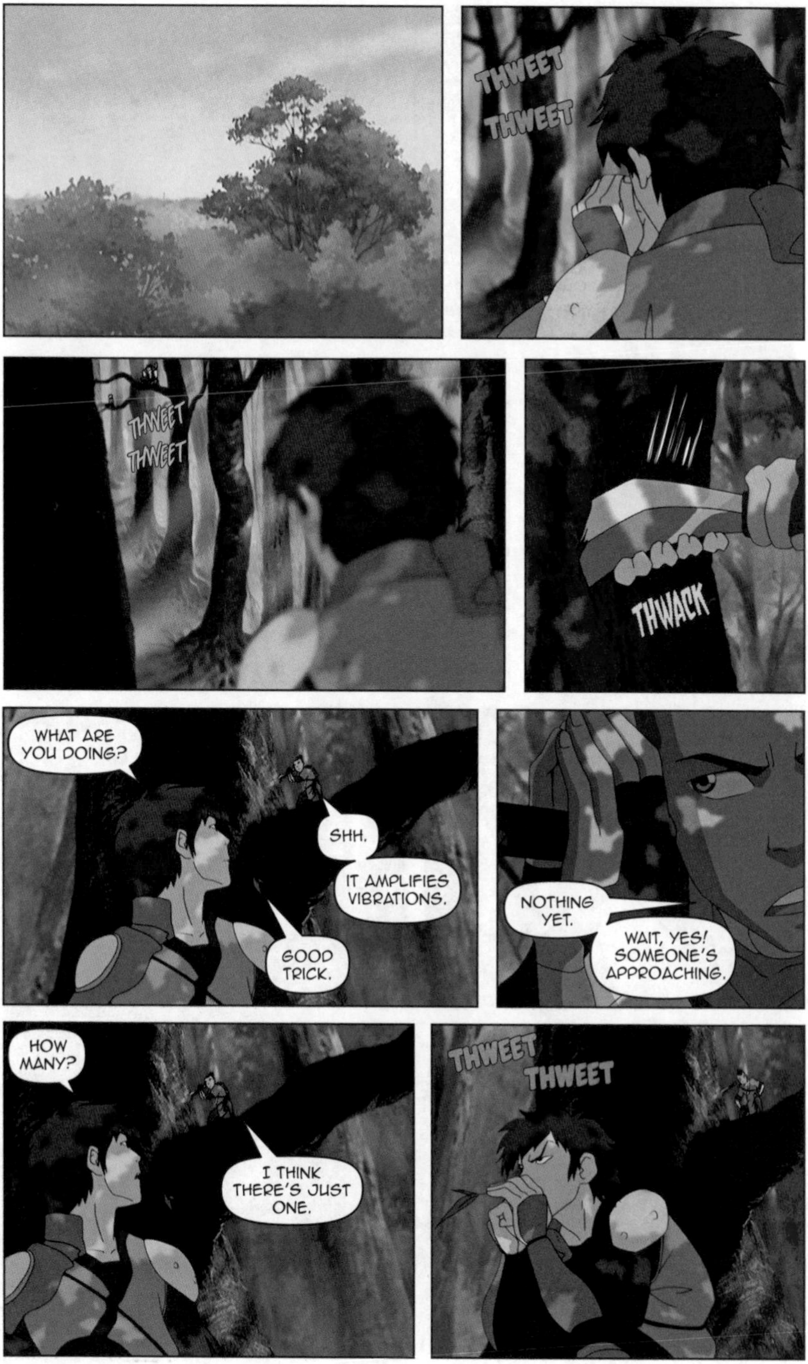
THWEET
THWEET
THWEET
THWEET
THWACK
WHAT ARE YOU DOING?
SHH.
IT AMPLIFIES VIBRATIONS.
GOOD TRICK.
NOTHING YET.
WAIT, YES! SOMEONE'S APPROACHING.
HOW MANY?
I THINK THERE'S JUST ONE.
THWEET
THWEET

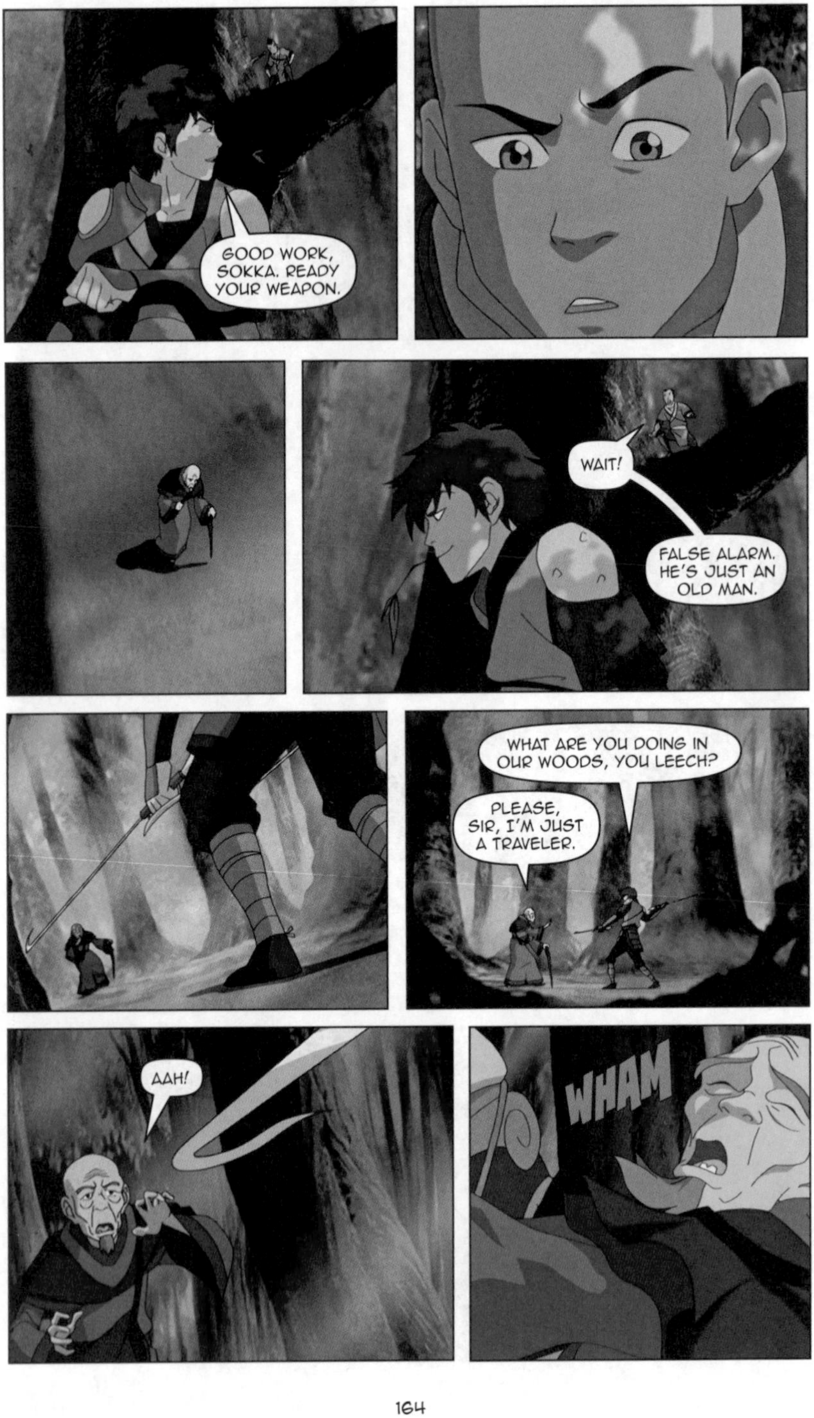
GOOD WORK, SOKKA. READY YOUR WEAPON.
WAIT!
FALSE ALARM. HE'S JUST AN OLD MAN.
WHAT ARE YOU DOING IN OUR WOODS, YOU LEECH?
PLEASE, SIR, I'M JUST A TRAVELER.
AAH!
WHAM

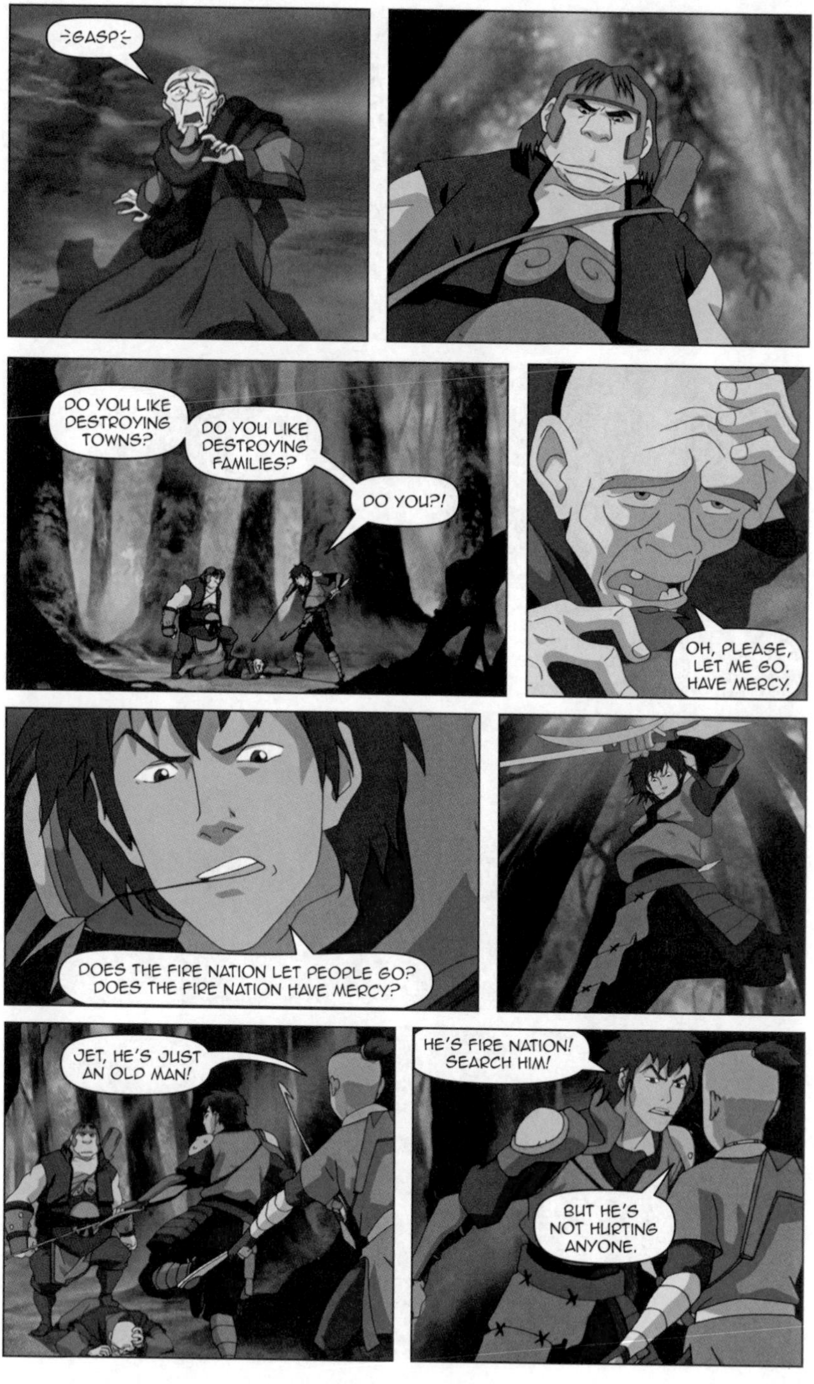

≈GASP≈
DO YOU LIKE DESTROYING TOWNS?
DO YOU LIKE DESTROYING FAMILIES?
DO YOU?!
OH, PLEASE, LET ME GO. HAVE MERCY.
DOES THE FIRE NATION LET PEOPLE GO? DOES THE FIRE NATION HAVE MERCY?
JET, HE'S JUST AN OLD MAN!
HE'S FIRE NATION! SEARCH HIM!
BUT HE'S NOT HURTING ANYONE.

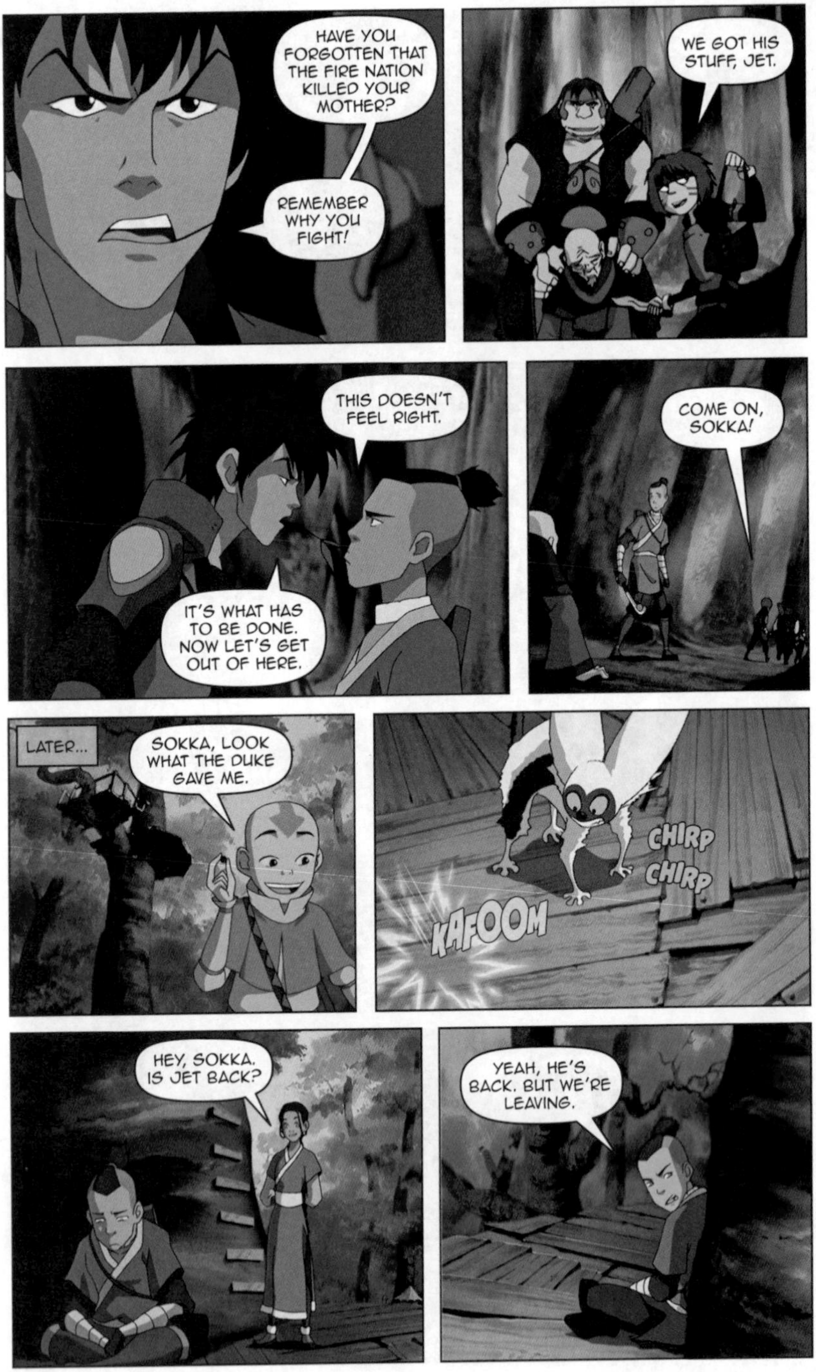

HAVE YOU FORGOTTEN THAT THE FIRE NATION KILLED YOUR MOTHER?
REMEMBER WHY YOU FIGHT!
WE GOT HIS STUFF, JET.
THIS DOESN'T FEEL RIGHT.
IT'S WHAT HAS TO BE DONE. NOW LET'S GET OUT OF HERE.
COME ON, SOKKA!
LATER...
SOKKA, LOOK WHAT THE DUKE GAVE ME.
CHIRP
CHIRP
KAFOOM
HEY, SOKKA. IS JET BACK?
YEAH, HE'S BACK. BUT WE'RE LEAVING.

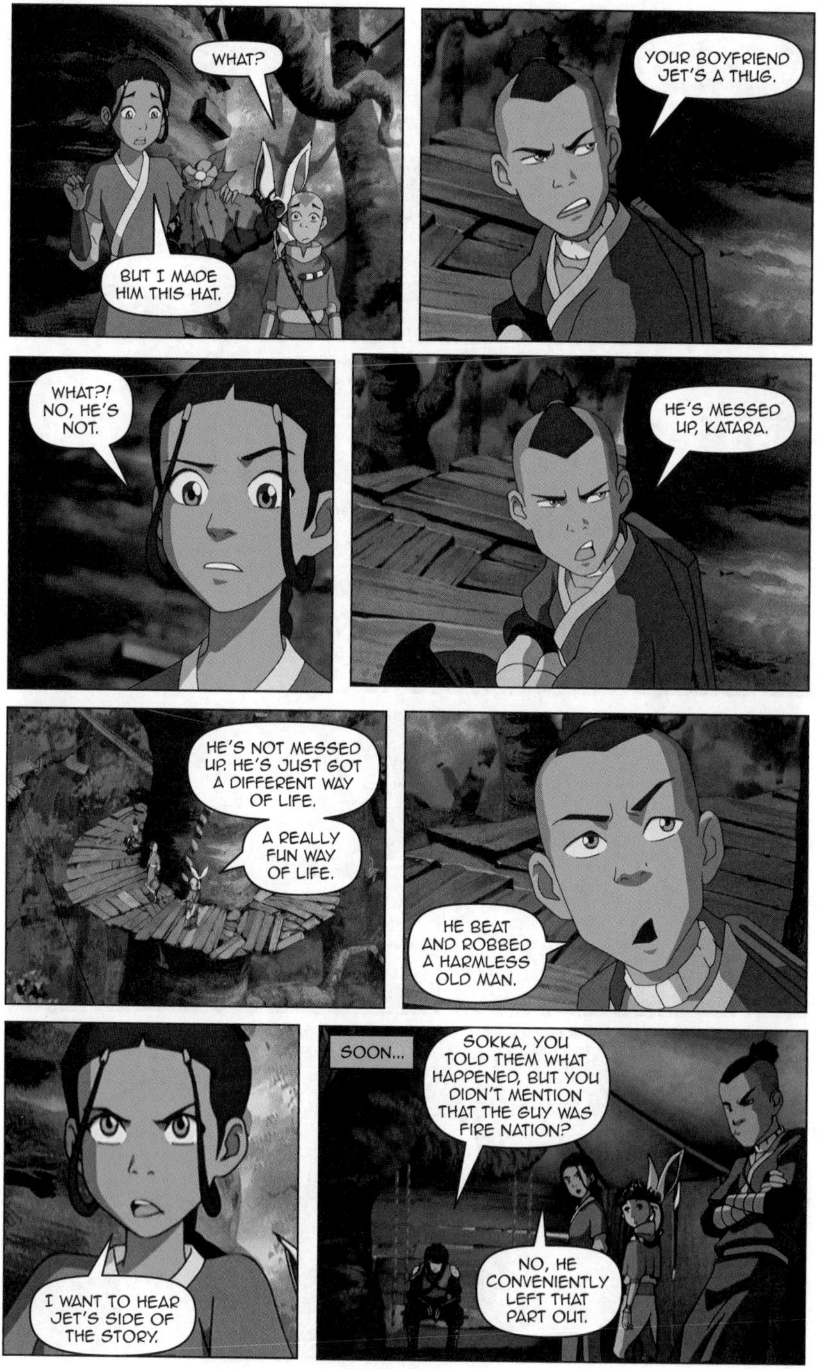
WHAT?
BUT I MADE HIM THIS HAT.
YOUR BOYFRIEND JET'S A THUG.
WHAT?! NO, HE'S NOT.
HE'S MESSED UP, KATARA.
HE'S NOT MESSED UP. HE'S JUST GOT A DIFFERENT WAY OF LIFE.
A REALLY FUN WAY OF LIFE.
HE BEAT AND ROBBED A HARMLESS OLD MAN.
I WANT TO HEAR JET'S SIDE OF THE STORY.
SOON...
SOKKA, YOU TOLD THEM WHAT HAPPENED, BUT YOU DIDN'T MENTION THAT THE GUY WAS FIRE NATION?
NO, HE CONVENIENTLY LEFT THAT PART OUT.

FINE, BUT EVEN IF HE WAS FIRE NATION, HE WAS A HARMLESS CIVILIAN.

HE WAS AN ASSASSIN, SOKKA.

THUNK

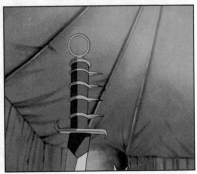

SEE? THERE'S A COMPARTMENT FOR POISON IN THE KNIFE.

HE WAS SENT TO ELIMINATE ME.

YOU HELPED SAVE MY LIFE, SOKKA.

I KNEW THERE WAS AN EXPLANATION.

I DIDN'T SEE ANY KNIFE.

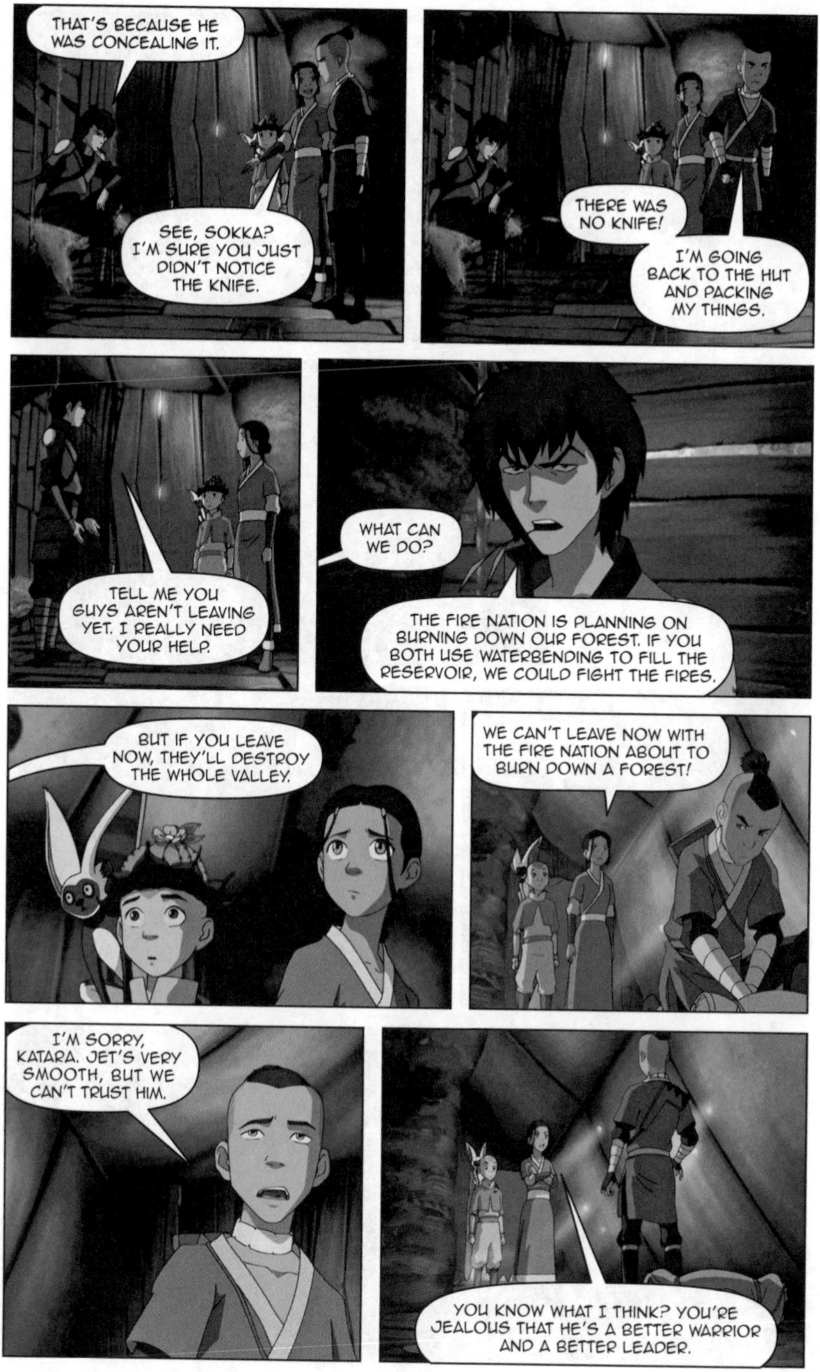
THAT'S BECAUSE HE WAS CONCEALING IT.
SEE, SOKKA? I'M SURE YOU JUST DIDN'T NOTICE THE KNIFE.
THERE WAS NO KNIFE!
I'M GOING BACK TO THE HUT AND PACKING MY THINGS.
TELL ME YOU GUYS AREN'T LEAVING YET. I REALLY NEED YOUR HELP.
WHAT CAN WE DO?
THE FIRE NATION IS PLANNING ON BURNING DOWN OUR FOREST. IF YOU BOTH USE WATERBENDING TO FILL THE RESERVOIR, WE COULD FIGHT THE FIRES.
BUT IF YOU LEAVE NOW, THEY'LL DESTROY THE WHOLE VALLEY.
WE CAN'T LEAVE NOW WITH THE FIRE NATION ABOUT TO BURN DOWN A FOREST!
I'M SORRY, KATARA. JET'S VERY SMOOTH, BUT WE CAN'T TRUST HIM.
YOU KNOW WHAT I THINK? YOU'RE JEALOUS THAT HE'S A BETTER WARRIOR AND A BETTER LEADER.

KATARA, I'M NOT JEALOUS OF JET. IT'S JUST THAT MY INSTINCTS...

WELL, MY INSTINCTS TELL ME WE NEED TO STAY HERE A LITTLE LONGER AND HELP JET.

COME ON, AANG.

SORRY, SOKKA.

LATER...

ZZZZZ

LET'S GO.

HUH?

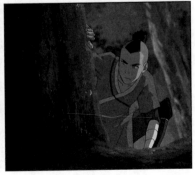

170

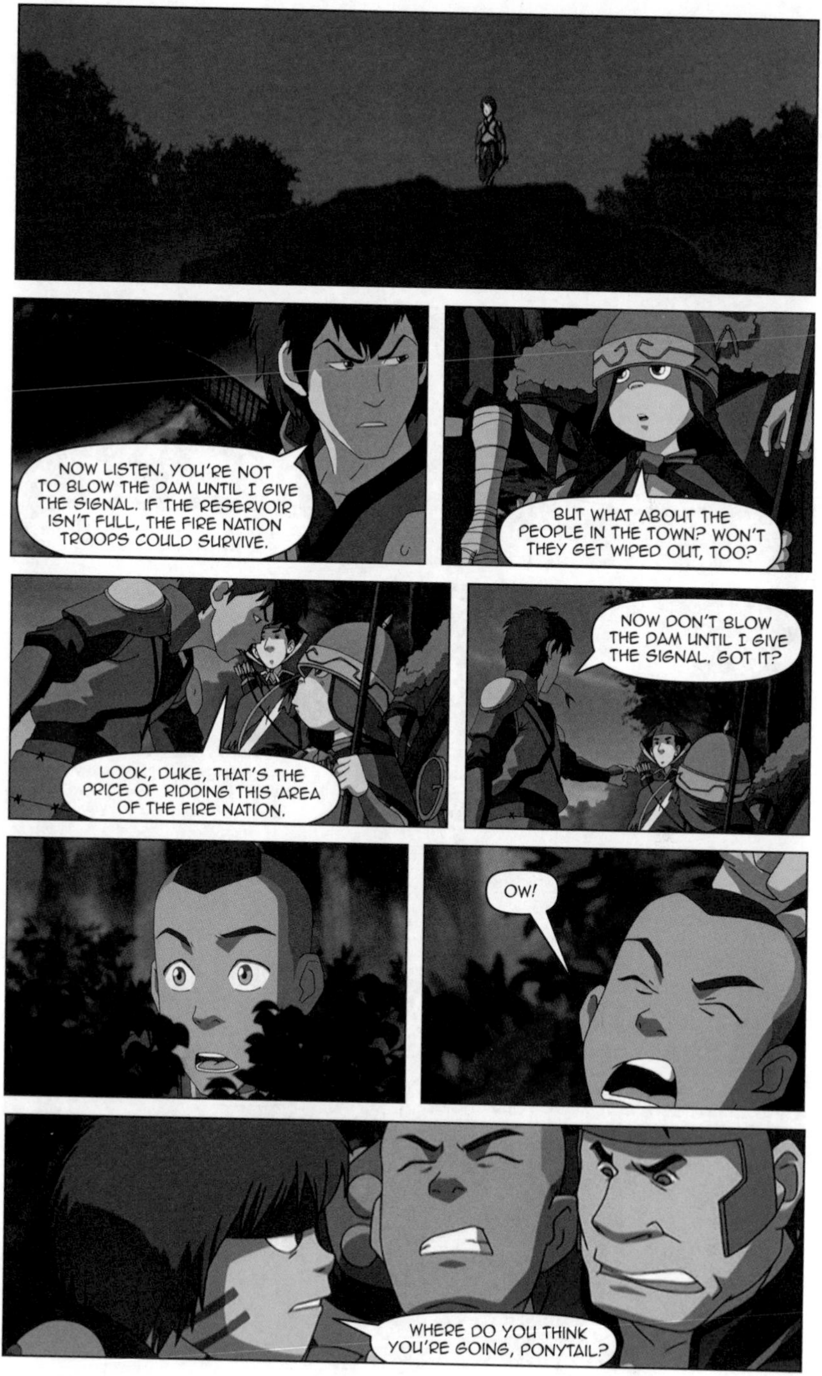
NOW LISTEN. YOU'RE NOT TO BLOW THE DAM UNTIL I GIVE THE SIGNAL. IF THE RESERVOIR ISN'T FULL, THE FIRE NATION TROOPS COULD SURVIVE.
BUT WHAT ABOUT THE PEOPLE IN THE TOWN? WON'T THEY GET WIPED OUT, TOO?
LOOK, DUKE, THAT'S THE PRICE OF RIDDING THIS AREA OF THE FIRE NATION.
NOW DON'T BLOW THE DAM UNTIL I GIVE THE SIGNAL. GOT IT?
OW!
WHERE DO YOU THINK YOU'RE GOING, PONYTAIL?

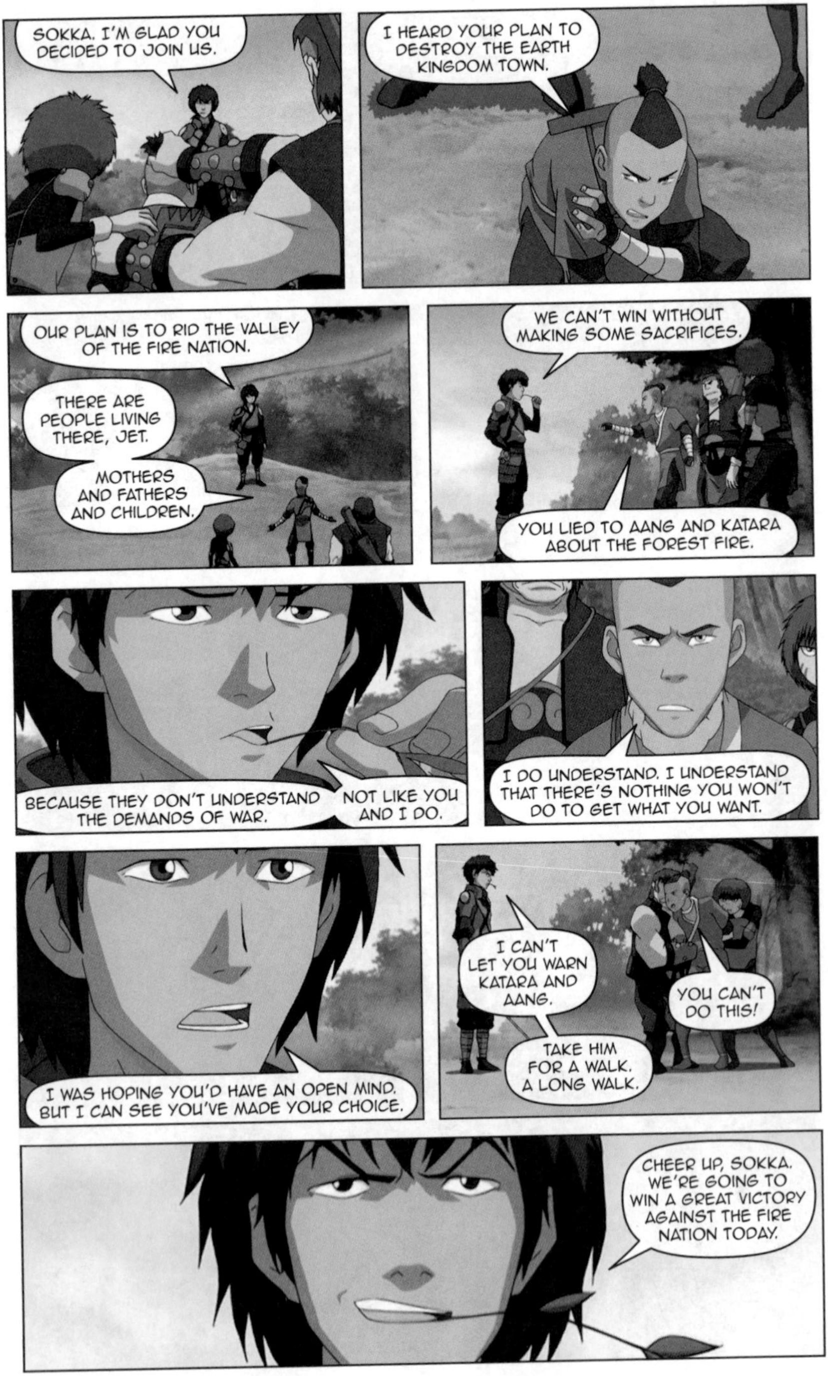
SOKKA. I'M GLAD YOU DECIDED TO JOIN US.
I HEARD YOUR PLAN TO DESTROY THE EARTH KINGDOM TOWN.
OUR PLAN IS TO RID THE VALLEY OF THE FIRE NATION.
THERE ARE PEOPLE LIVING THERE, JET.
MOTHERS AND FATHERS AND CHILDREN.
WE CAN'T WIN WITHOUT MAKING SOME SACRIFICES.
YOU LIED TO AANG AND KATARA ABOUT THE FOREST FIRE.
BECAUSE THEY DON'T UNDERSTAND THE DEMANDS OF WAR.
NOT LIKE YOU AND I DO.
I DO UNDERSTAND. I UNDERSTAND THAT THERE'S NOTHING YOU WON'T DO TO GET WHAT YOU WANT.
I WAS HOPING YOU'D HAVE AN OPEN MIND. BUT I CAN SEE YOU'VE MADE YOUR CHOICE.
I CAN'T LET YOU WARN KATARA AND AANG.
TAKE HIM FOR A WALK. A LONG WALK.
YOU CAN'T DO THIS!
CHEER UP, SOKKA. WE'RE GOING TO WIN A GREAT VICTORY AGAINST THE FIRE NATION TODAY.

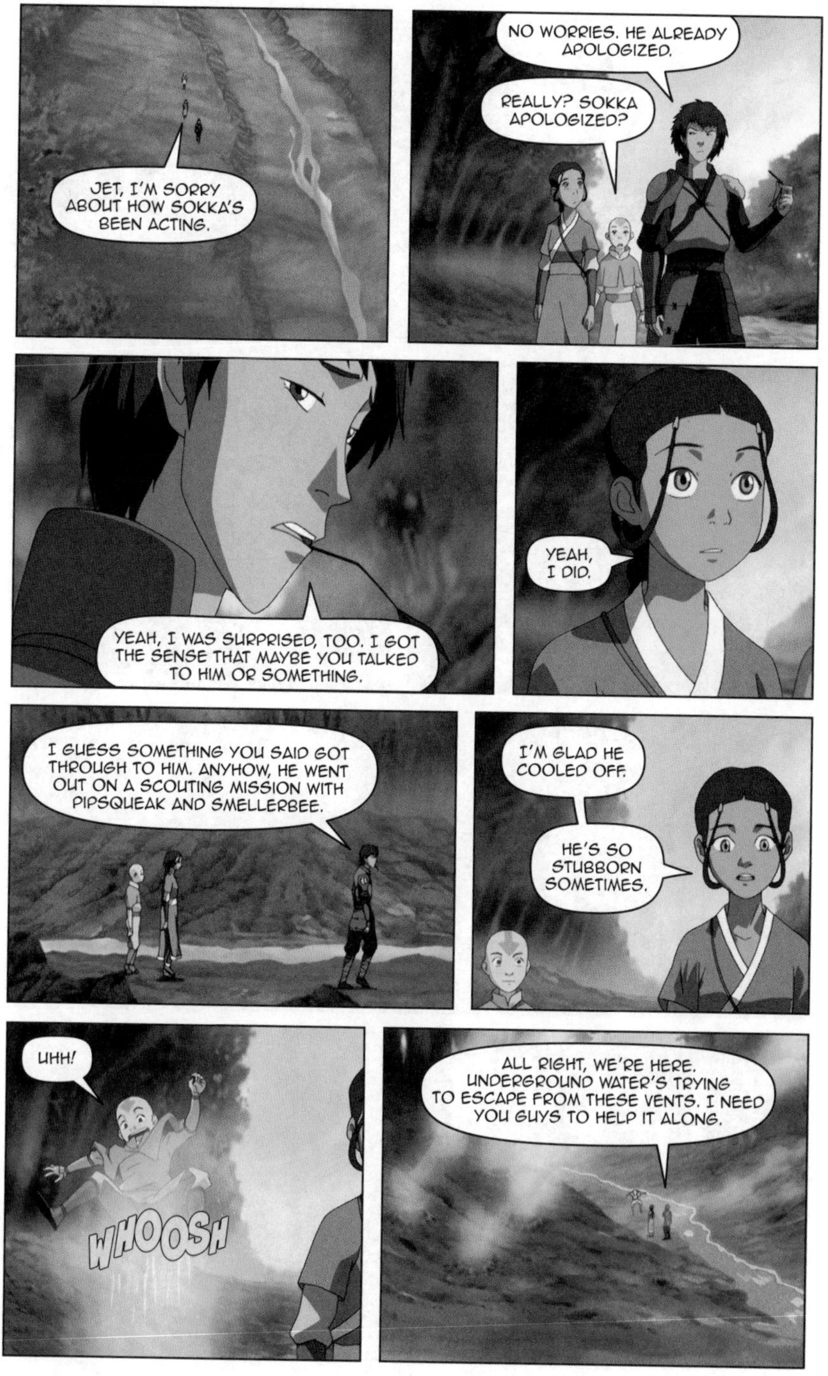

JET, I'M SORRY ABOUT HOW SOKKA'S BEEN ACTING.
NO WORRIES. HE ALREADY APOLOGIZED.
REALLY? SOKKA APOLOGIZED?
YEAH, I WAS SURPRISED, TOO. I GOT THE SENSE THAT MAYBE YOU TALKED TO HIM OR SOMETHING.
YEAH, I DID.
I GUESS SOMETHING YOU SAID GOT THROUGH TO HIM. ANYHOW, HE WENT OUT ON A SCOUTING MISSION WITH PIPSQUEAK AND SMELLERBEE.
I'M GLAD HE COOLED OFF.
HE'S SO STUBBORN SOMETIMES.
UHH!
WHOOSH
ALL RIGHT, WE'RE HERE. UNDERGROUND WATER'S TRYING TO ESCAPE FROM THESE VENTS. I NEED YOU GUYS TO HELP IT ALONG.

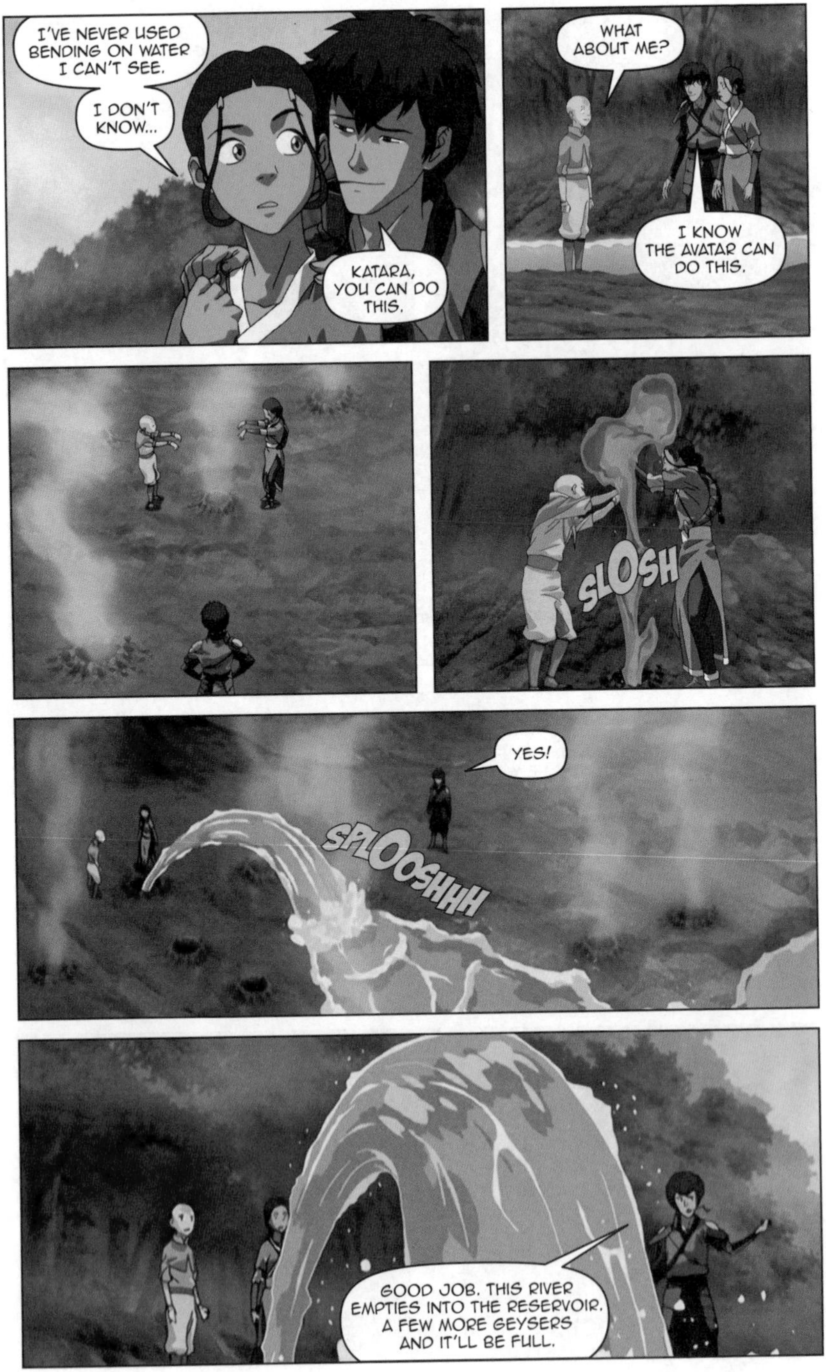

I'VE NEVER USED BENDING ON WATER I CAN'T SEE.
I DON'T KNOW...
KATARA, YOU CAN DO THIS.
WHAT ABOUT ME?
I KNOW THE AVATAR CAN DO THIS.
SLOSH
YES!
SPLOOSHHH
GOOD JOB. THIS RIVER EMPTIES INTO THE RESERVOIR. A FEW MORE GEYSERS AND IT'LL BE FULL.

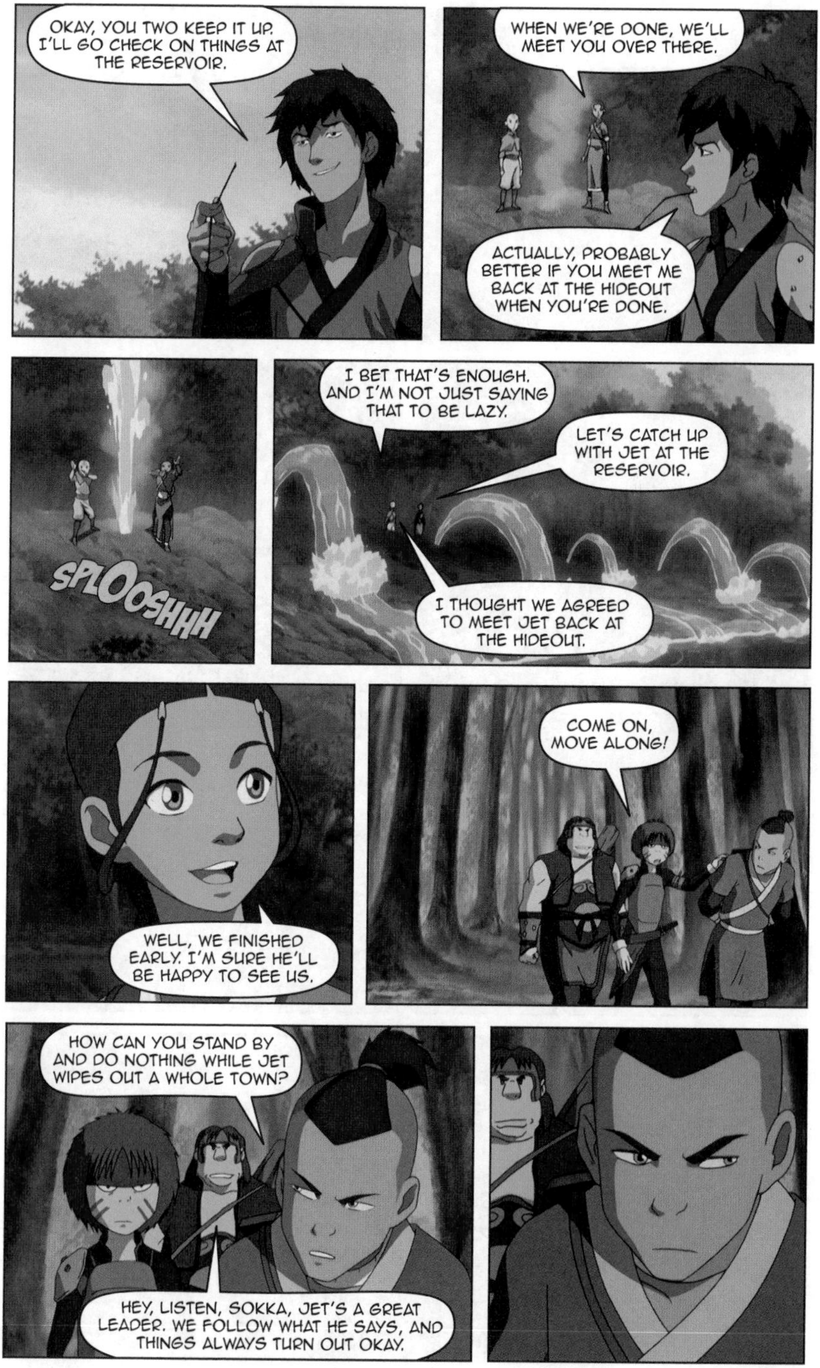
OKAY, YOU TWO KEEP IT UP. I'LL GO CHECK ON THINGS AT THE RESERVOIR.
WHEN WE'RE DONE, WE'LL MEET YOU OVER THERE.
ACTUALLY, PROBABLY BETTER IF YOU MEET ME BACK AT THE HIDEOUT WHEN YOU'RE DONE.
SPLOOSHHH
I BET THAT'S ENOUGH. AND I'M NOT JUST SAYING THAT TO BE LAZY.
LET'S CATCH UP WITH JET AT THE RESERVOIR.
I THOUGHT WE AGREED TO MEET JET BACK AT THE HIDEOUT.
WELL, WE FINISHED EARLY. I'M SURE HE'LL BE HAPPY TO SEE US.
COME ON, MOVE ALONG!
HOW CAN YOU STAND BY AND DO NOTHING WHILE JET WIPES OUT A WHOLE TOWN?
HEY, LISTEN, SOKKA, JET'S A GREAT LEADER. WE FOLLOW WHAT HE SAYS, AND THINGS ALWAYS TURN OUT OKAY.

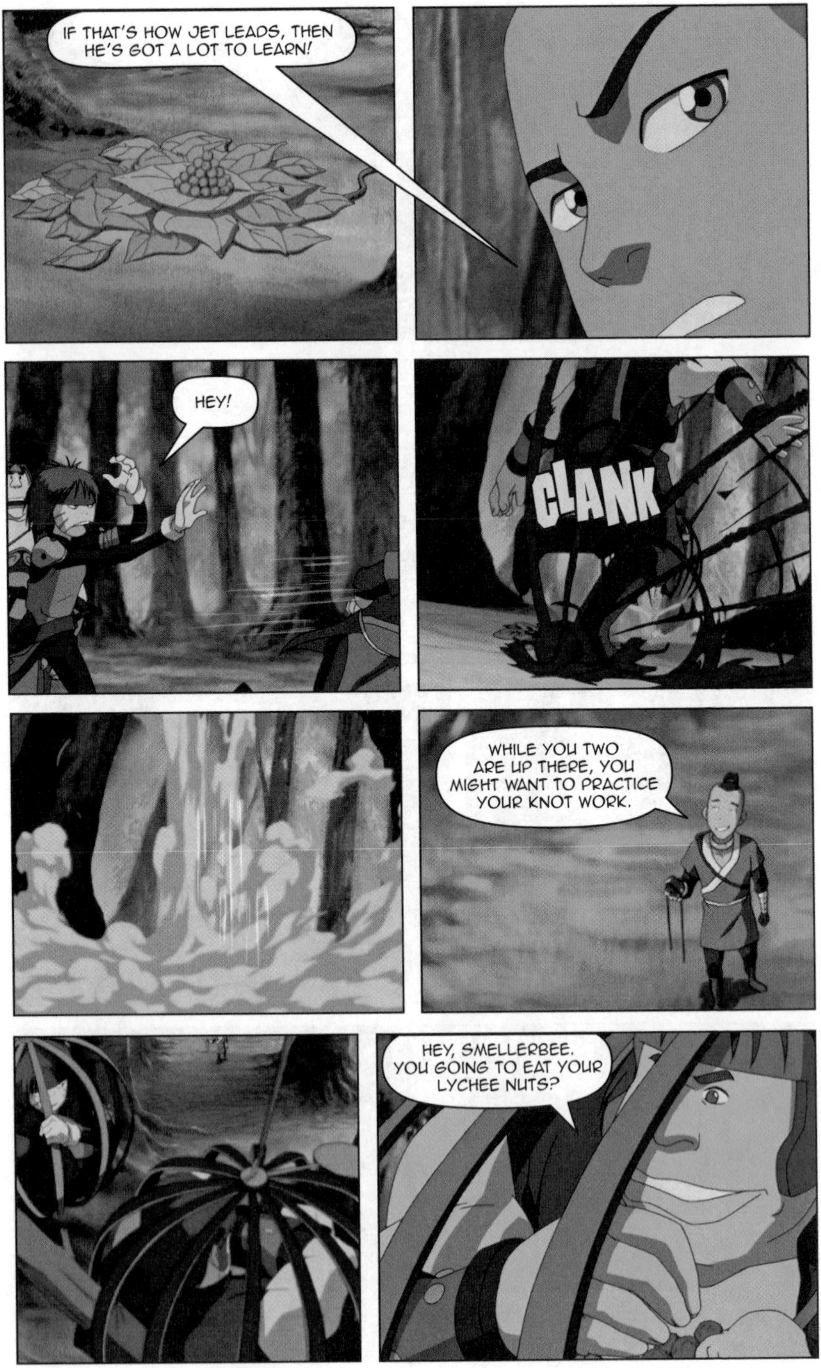
IF THAT'S HOW JET LEADS, THEN HE'S GOT A LOT TO LEARN!
HEY!
CLANK
WHILE YOU TWO ARE UP THERE, YOU MIGHT WANT TO PRACTICE YOUR KNOT WORK.
HEY, SMELLERBEE. YOU GOING TO EAT YOUR LYCHEE NUTS?

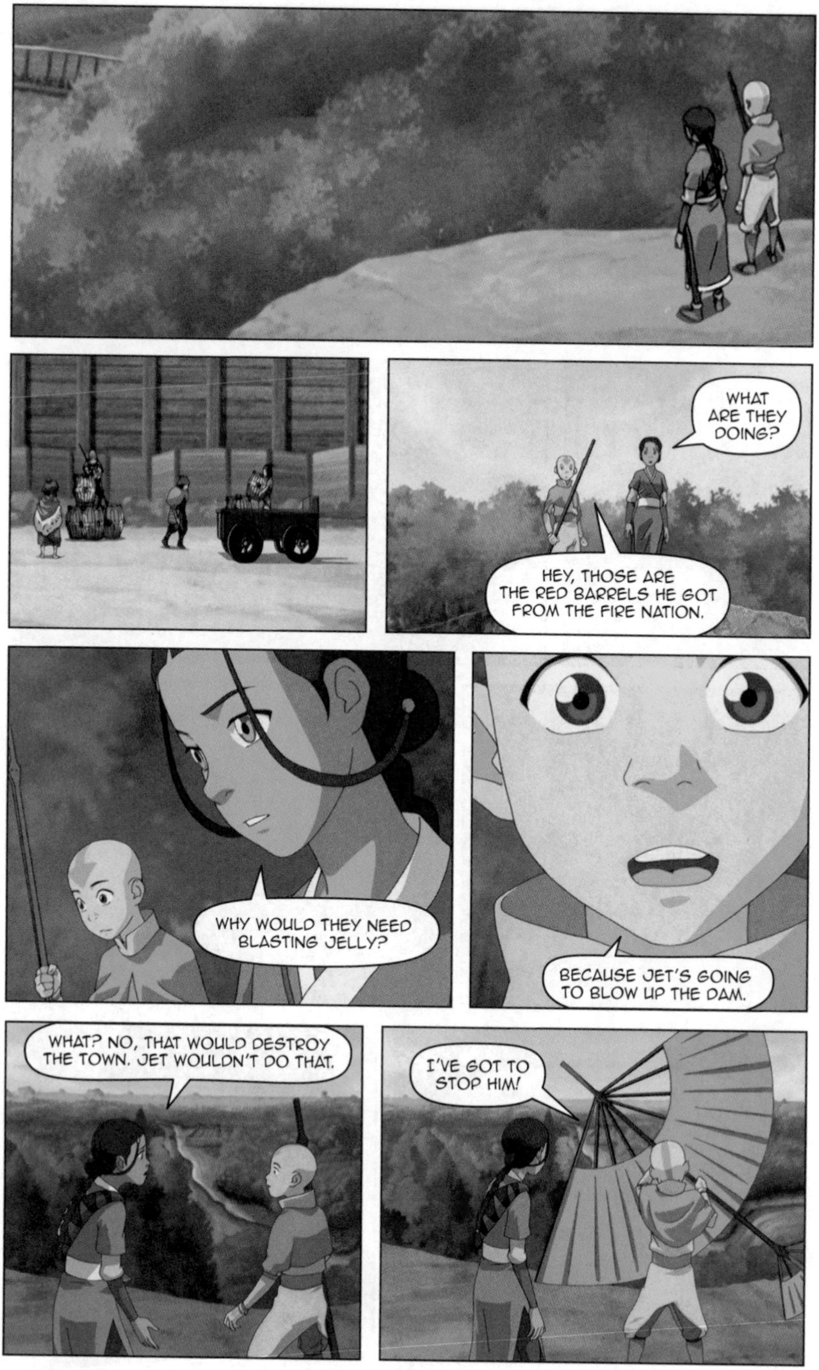
WHAT ARE THEY DOING?
HEY, THOSE ARE THE RED BARRELS HE GOT FROM THE FIRE NATION.
WHY WOULD THEY NEED BLASTING JELLY?
BECAUSE JET'S GOING TO BLOW UP THE DAM.
WHAT? NO, THAT WOULD DESTROY THE TOWN. JET WOULDN'T DO THAT.
I'VE GOT TO STOP HIM!

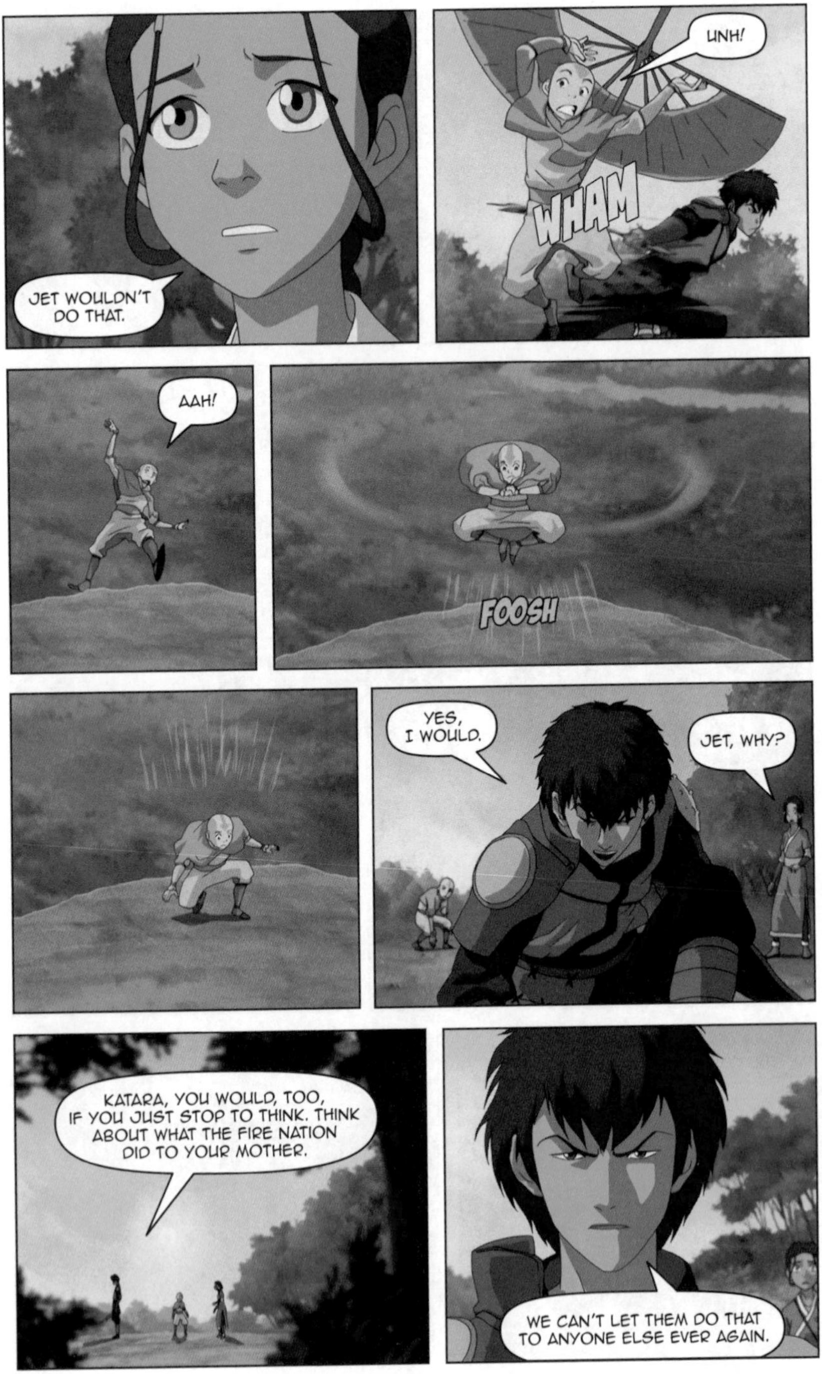
JET WOULDN'T DO THAT.
UNH!
WHAM
AAH!
FOOSH
YES, I WOULD.
JET, WHY?
KATARA, YOU WOULD, TOO, IF YOU JUST STOP TO THINK. THINK ABOUT WHAT THE FIRE NATION DID TO YOUR MOTHER.
WE CAN'T LET THEM DO THAT TO ANYONE ELSE EVER AGAIN.

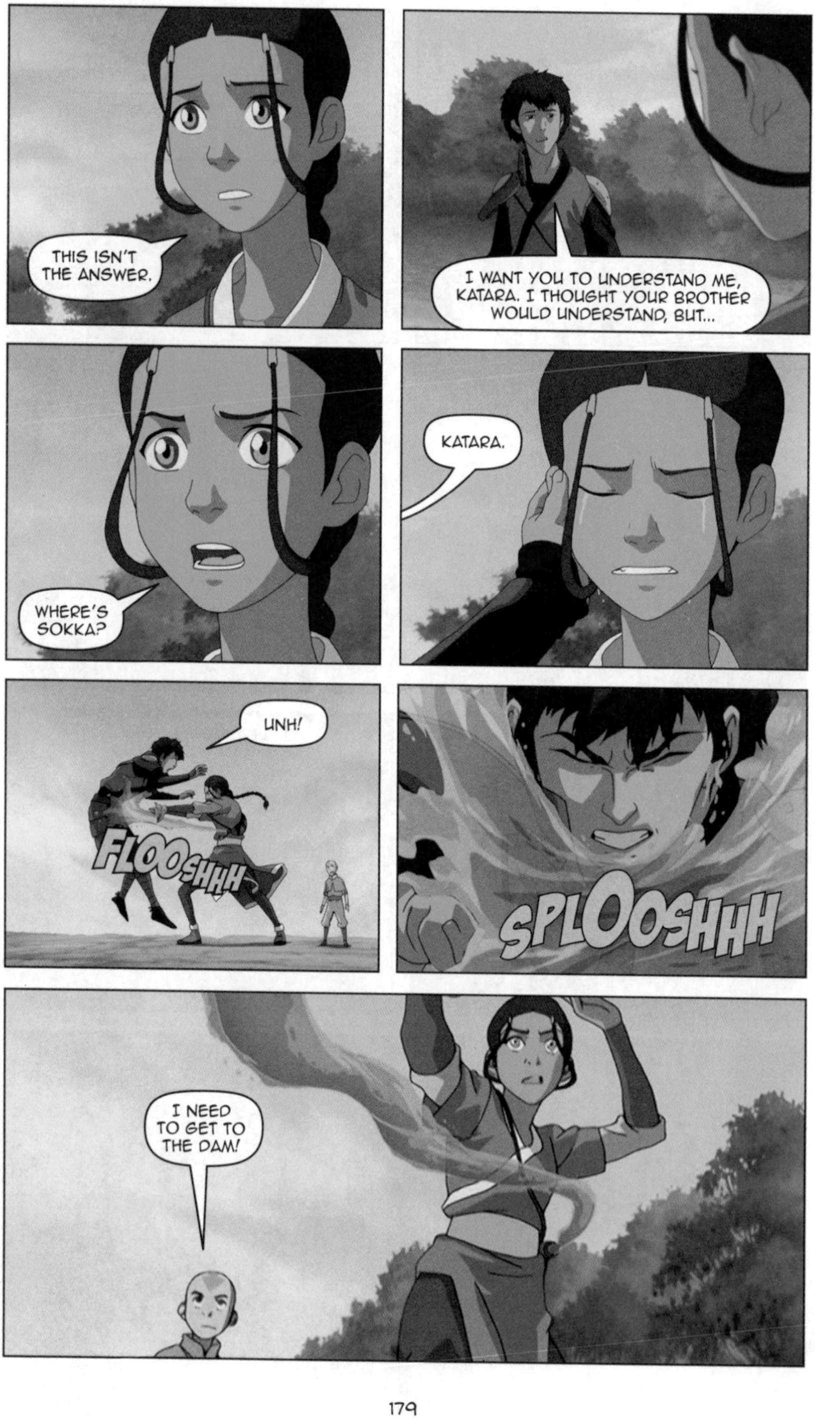
THIS ISN'T THE ANSWER.
I WANT YOU TO UNDERSTAND ME, KATARA. I THOUGHT YOUR BROTHER WOULD UNDERSTAND, BUT...
WHERE'S SOKKA?
KATARA.
UNH!
FLOOSHHH
SPLOOSHHH
I NEED TO GET TO THE DAM!

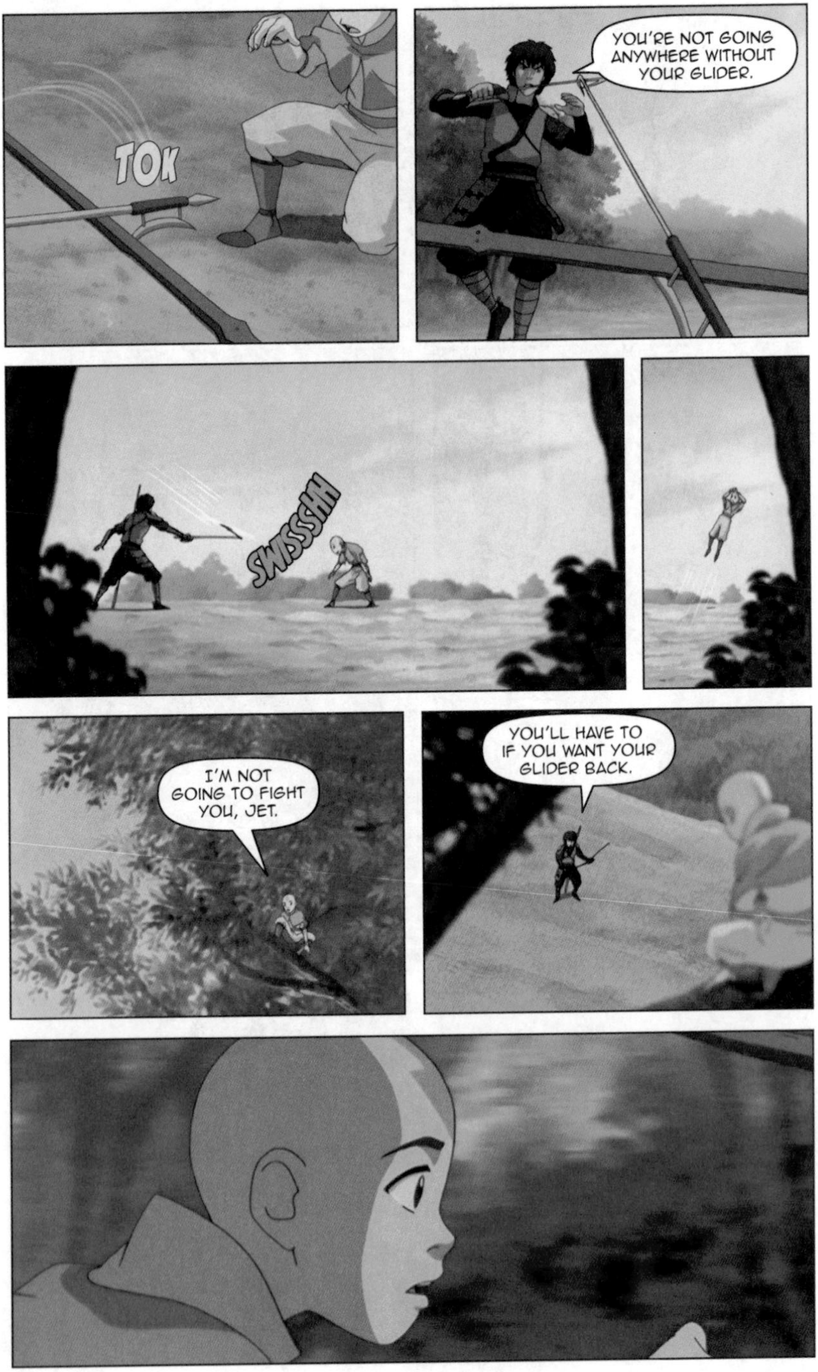
TOK
YOU'RE NOT GOING ANYWHERE WITHOUT YOUR GLIDER.
SWISSSHH
I'M NOT GOING TO FIGHT YOU, JET.
YOU'LL HAVE TO IF YOU WANT YOUR GLIDER BACK.

AAHHHH
THWACK
WHAM
FWISSH
SWISSH
WHOOSH
AAHHHH
TCHNK

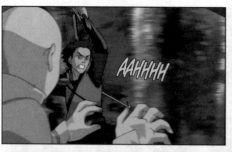

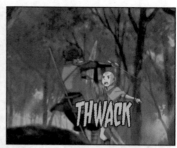

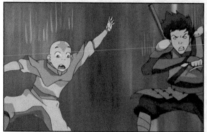

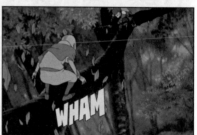

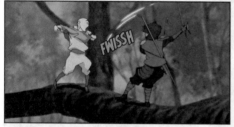

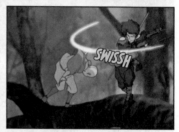

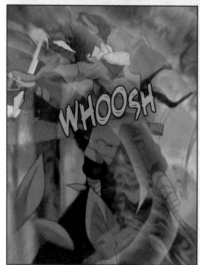

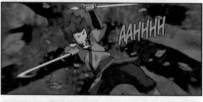

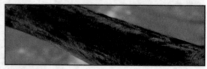

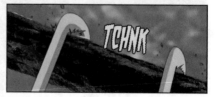

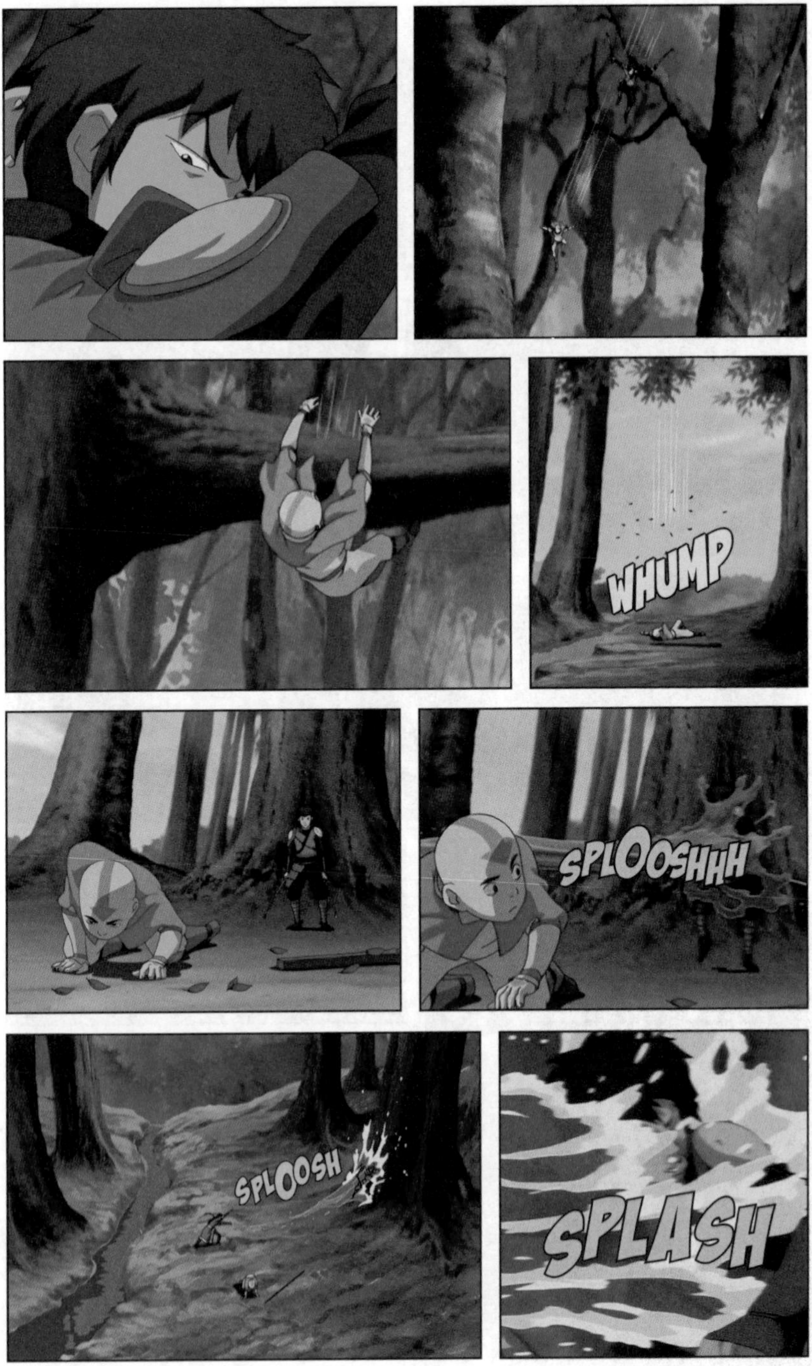
WHUMP
SPLOOSHHH
SPLOOSH
SPLASH

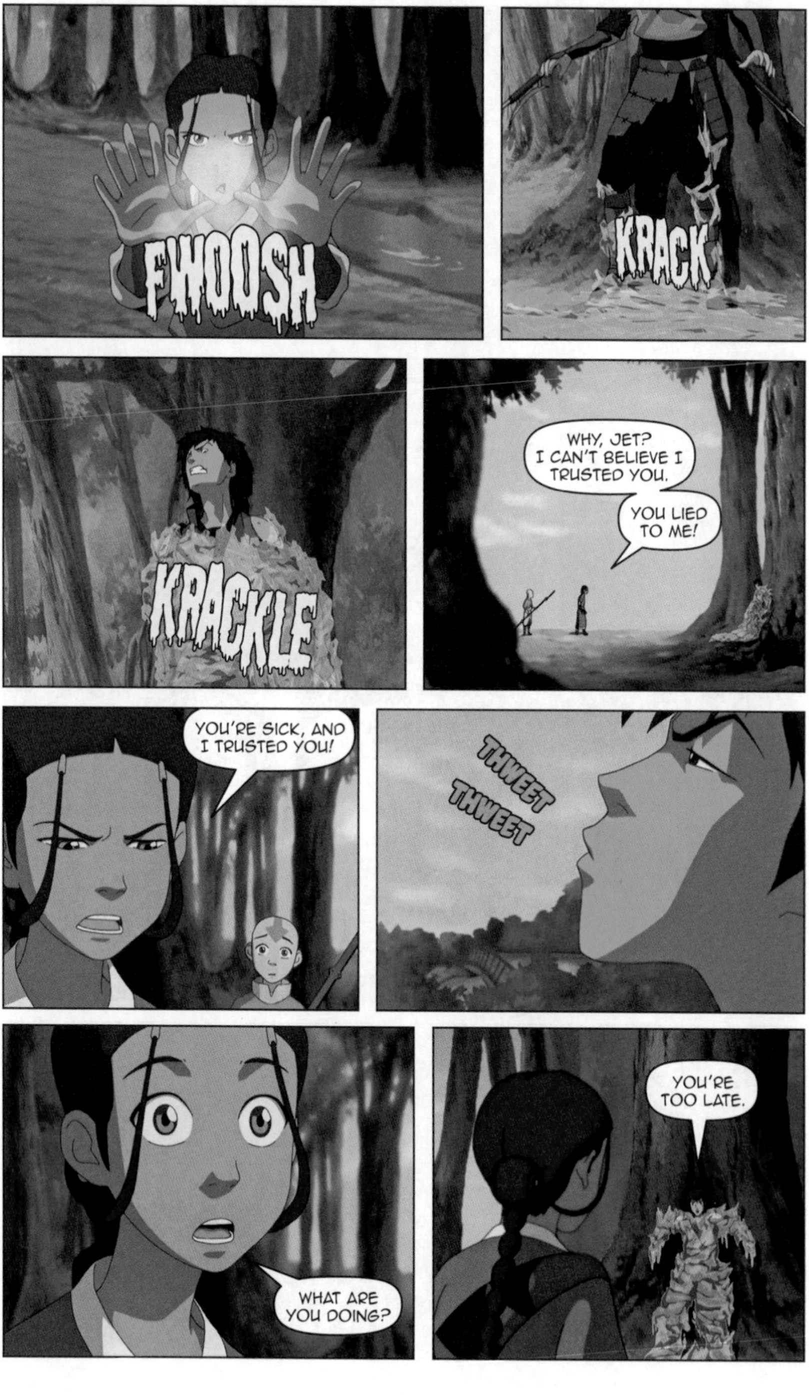
FWOOSH
KRACK
KRACKLE
WHY, JET? I CAN'T BELIEVE I TRUSTED YOU.
YOU LIED TO ME!
YOU'RE SICK, AND I TRUSTED YOU!
THWEET
THWEET
WHAT ARE YOU DOING?
YOU'RE TOO LATE.

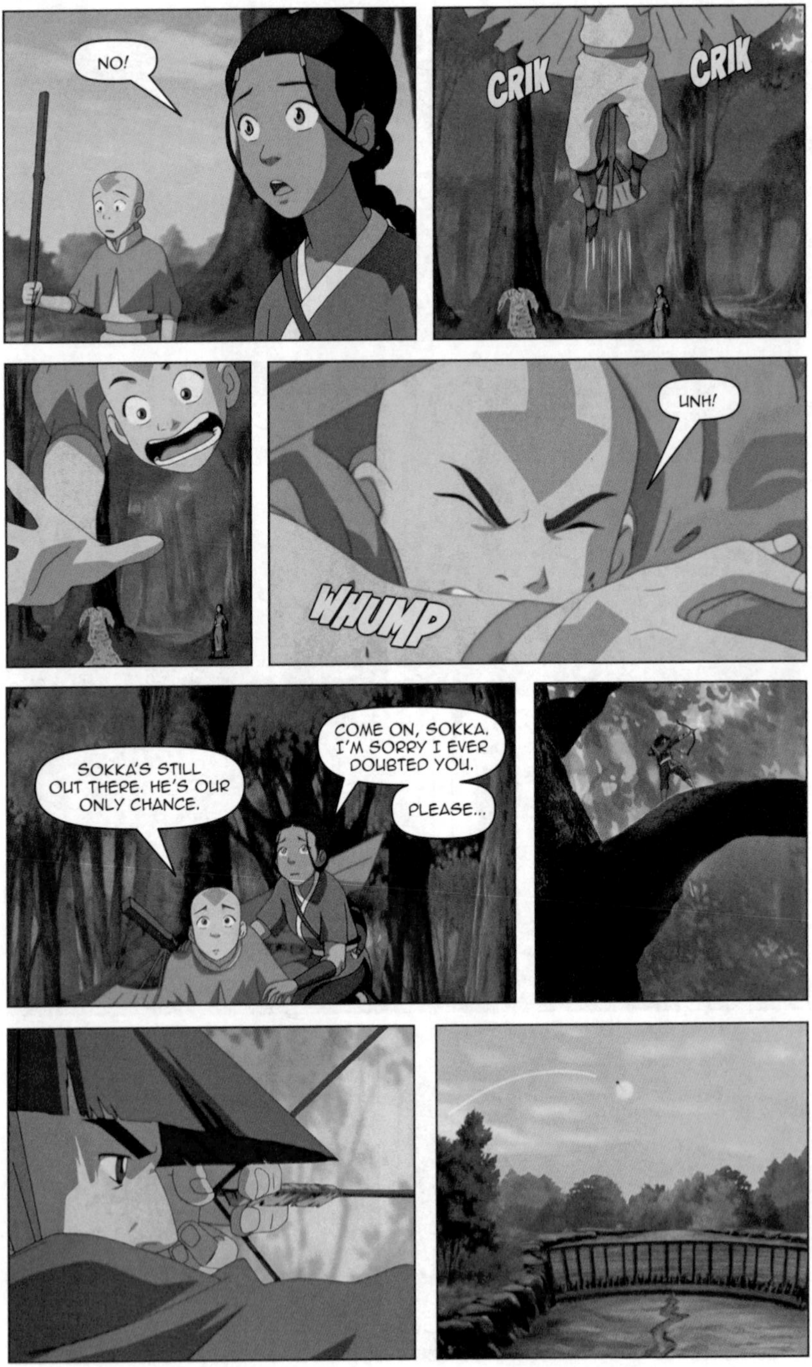
NO!
CRIK
CRIK
UNH!
WHUMP
SOKKA'S STILL OUT THERE. HE'S OUR ONLY CHANCE.
COME ON, SOKKA. I'M SORRY I EVER DOUBTED YOU.
PLEASE...

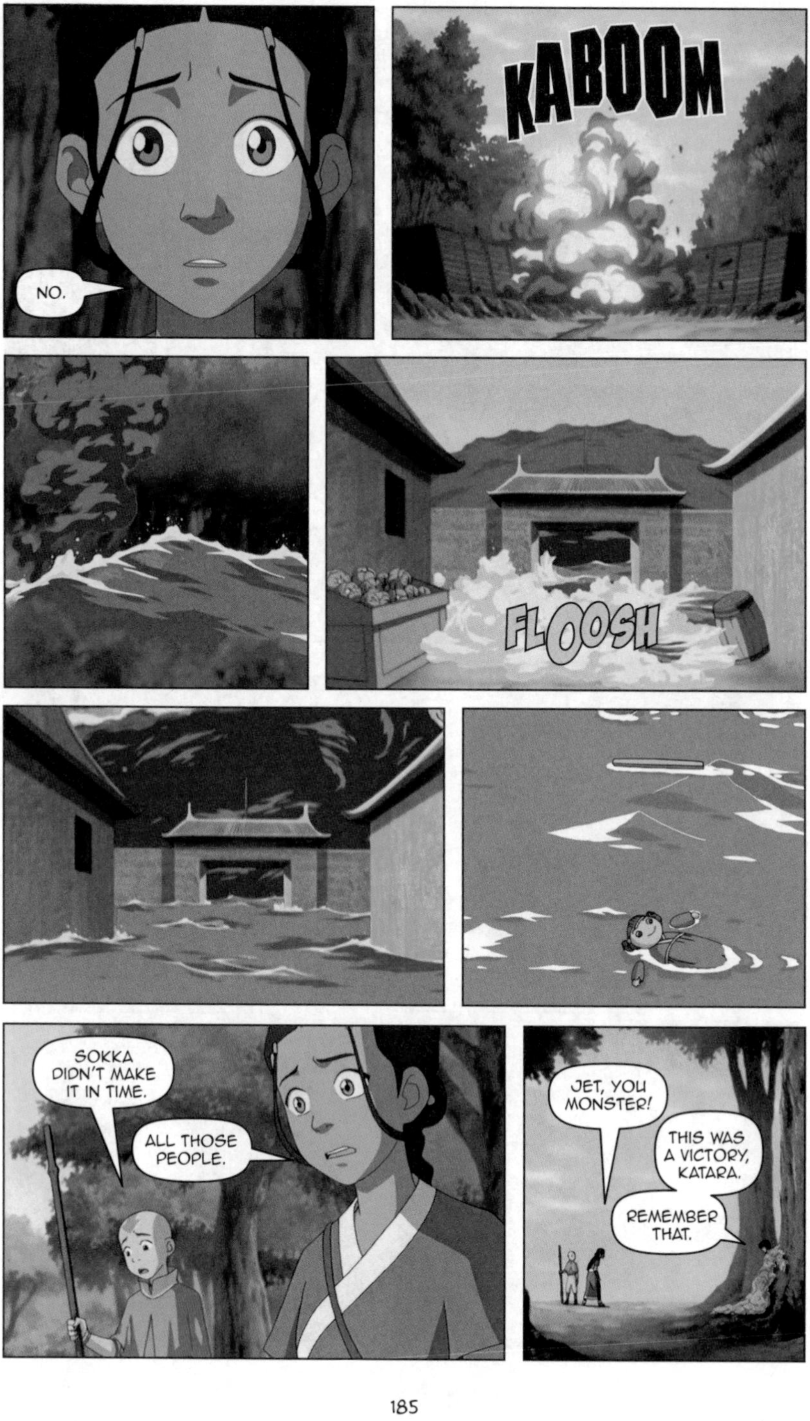

NO.
KABOOM
FLOOSH
SOKKA DIDN'T MAKE IT IN TIME.
ALL THOSE PEOPLE.
JET, YOU MONSTER!
THIS WAS A VICTORY, KATARA.
REMEMBER THAT.

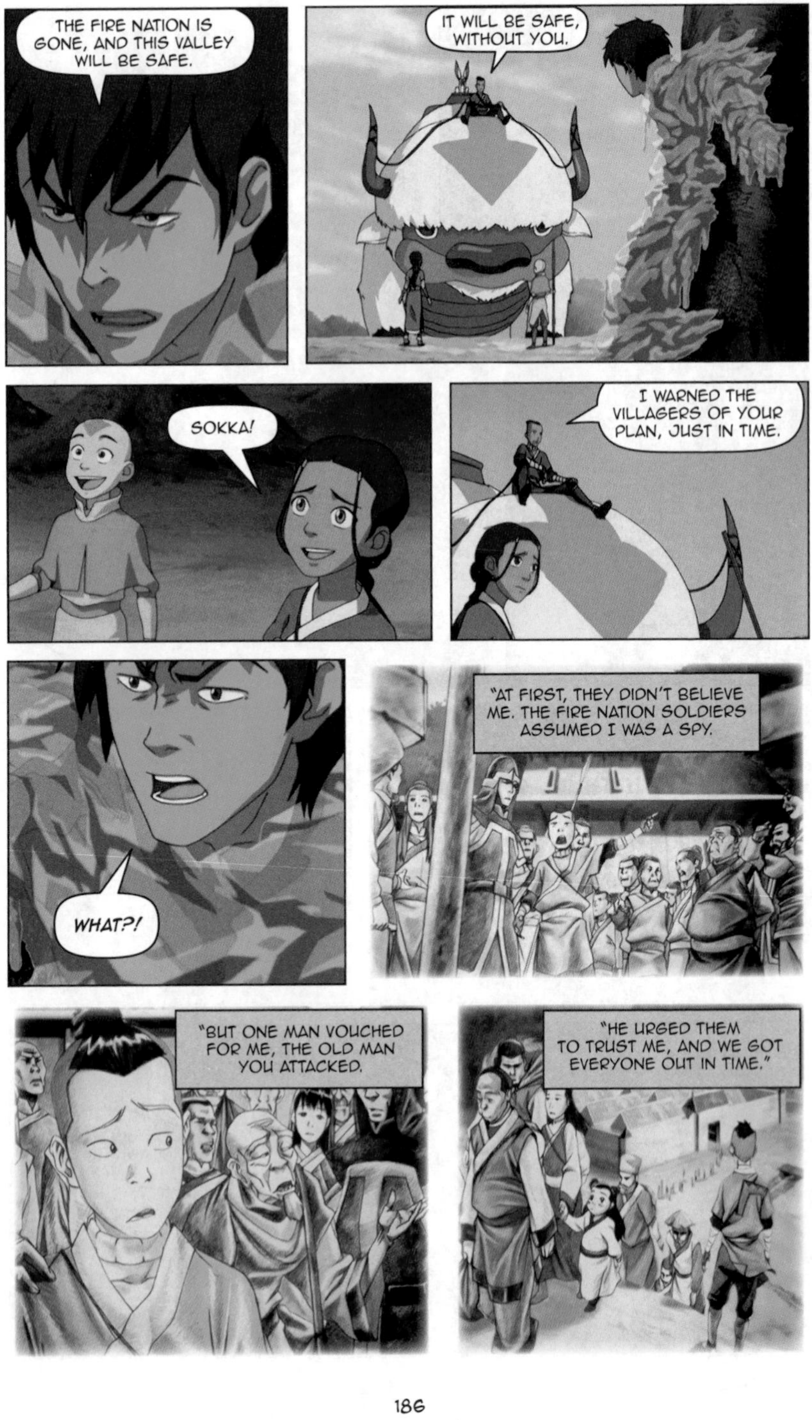
THE FIRE NATION IS GONE, AND THIS VALLEY WILL BE SAFE.
IT WILL BE SAFE, WITHOUT YOU.
SOKKA!
I WARNED THE VILLAGERS OF YOUR PLAN, JUST IN TIME.
WHAT?!
"AT FIRST, THEY DIDN'T BELIEVE ME. THE FIRE NATION SOLDIERS ASSUMED I WAS A SPY.
"BUT ONE MAN VOUCHED FOR ME, THE OLD MAN YOU ATTACKED.
"HE URGED THEM TO TRUST ME, AND WE GOT EVERYONE OUT IN TIME."

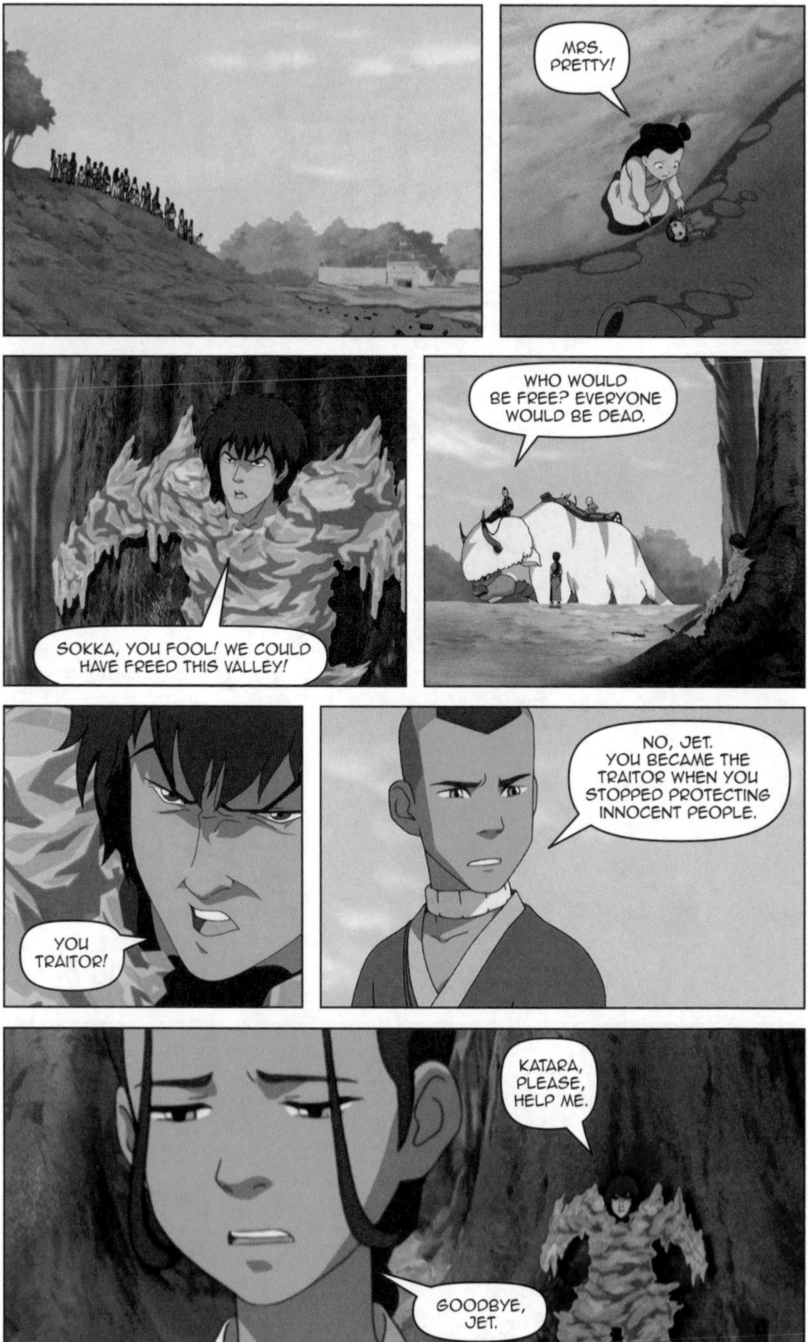
MRS. PRETTY!
SOKKA, YOU FOOL! WE COULD HAVE FREED THIS VALLEY!
WHO WOULD BE FREE? EVERYONE WOULD BE DEAD.
YOU TRAITOR!
NO, JET. YOU BECAME THE TRAITOR WHEN YOU STOPPED PROTECTING INNOCENT PEOPLE.
KATARA, PLEASE, HELP ME.
GOODBYE, JET.

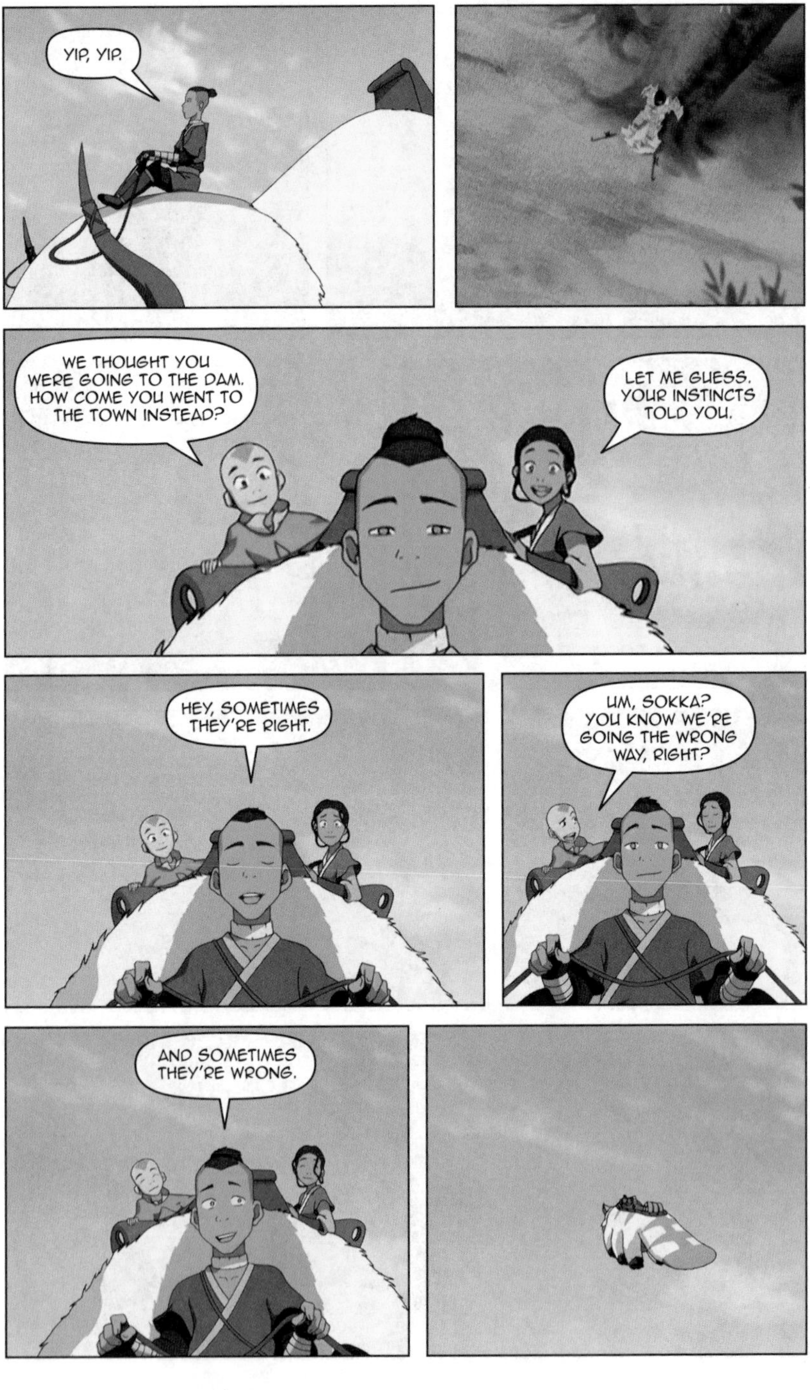
YIP, YIP.
WE THOUGHT YOU WERE GOING TO THE DAM. HOW COME YOU WENT TO THE TOWN INSTEAD?
LET ME GUESS. YOUR INSTINCTS TOLD YOU.
HEY, SOMETIMES THEY'RE RIGHT.
UM, SOKKA? YOU KNOW WE'RE GOING THE WRONG WAY, RIGHT?
AND SOMETIMES THEY'RE WRONG.

CHAPTER ELEVEN
THE GREAT DIVIDE

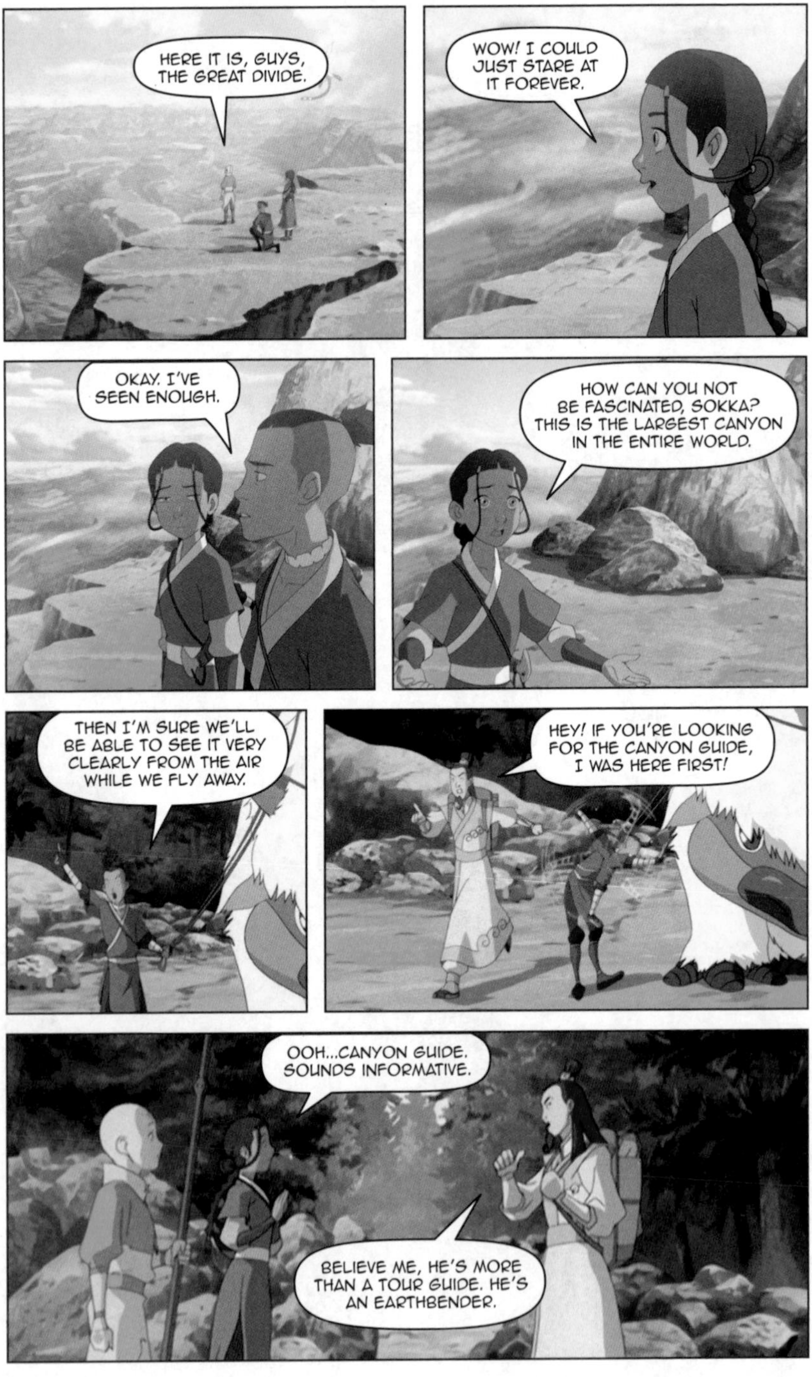
HERE IT IS, GUYS, THE GREAT DIVIDE.
WOW! I COULD JUST STARE AT IT FOREVER.
OKAY. I'VE SEEN ENOUGH.
HOW CAN YOU NOT BE FASCINATED, SOKKA? THIS IS THE LARGEST CANYON IN THE ENTIRE WORLD.
THEN I'M SURE WE'LL BE ABLE TO SEE IT VERY CLEARLY FROM THE AIR WHILE WE FLY AWAY.
HEY! IF YOU'RE LOOKING FOR THE CANYON GUIDE, I WAS HERE FIRST!
OOH...CANYON GUIDE. SOUNDS INFORMATIVE.
BELIEVE ME, HE'S MORE THAN A TOUR GUIDE. HE'S AN EARTHBENDER.

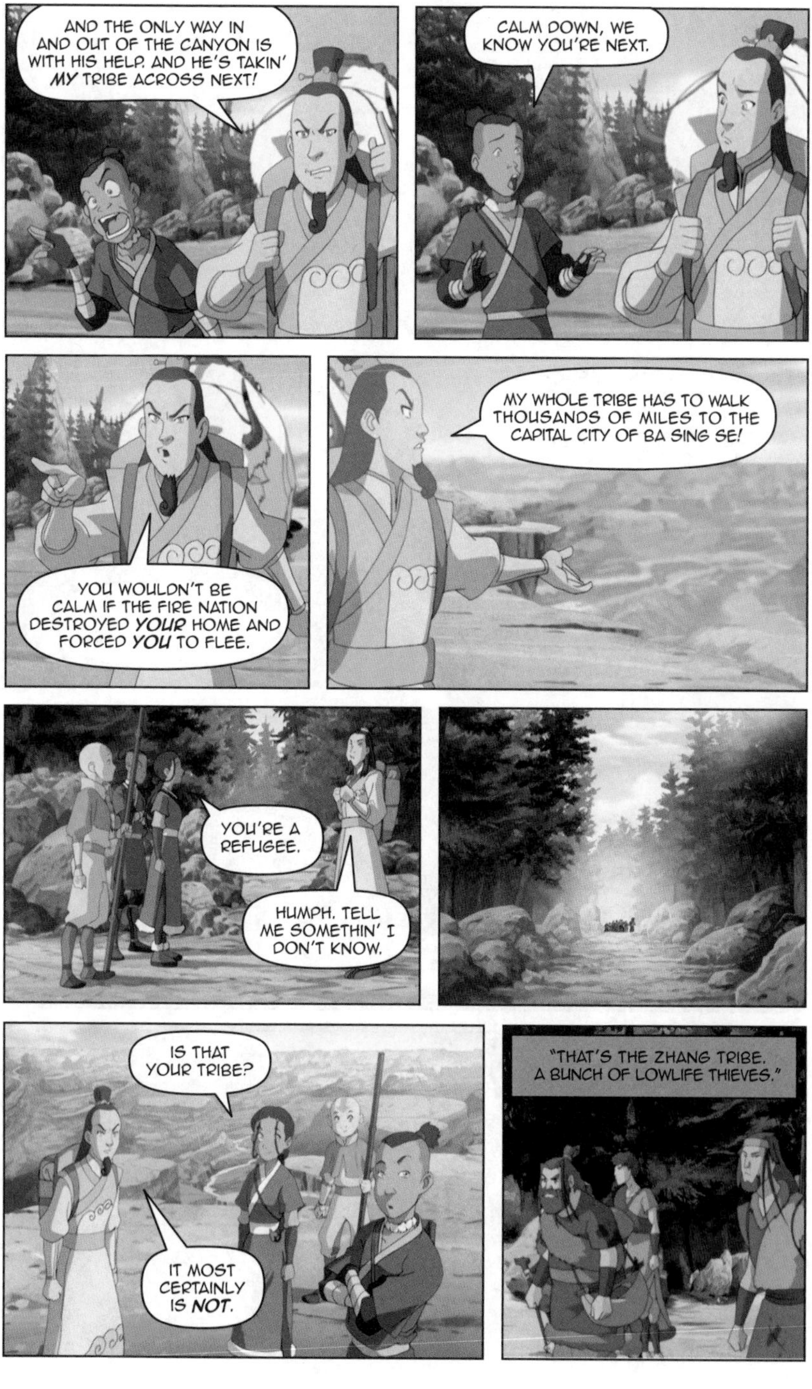
AND THE ONLY WAY IN AND OUT OF THE CANYON IS WITH HIS HELP. AND HE'S TAKIN' *MY* TRIBE ACROSS NEXT!
CALM DOWN, WE KNOW YOU'RE NEXT.
YOU WOULDN'T BE CALM IF THE FIRE NATION DESTROYED *YOUR* HOME AND FORCED *YOU* TO FLEE.
MY WHOLE TRIBE HAS TO WALK THOUSANDS OF MILES TO THE CAPITAL CITY OF BA SING SE!
YOU'RE A REFUGEE.
HUMPH. TELL ME SOMETHIN' I DON'T KNOW.
IS THAT YOUR TRIBE?
IT MOST CERTAINLY IS *NOT*.
"THAT'S THE ZHANG TRIBE. A BUNCH OF LOWLIFE THIEVES."

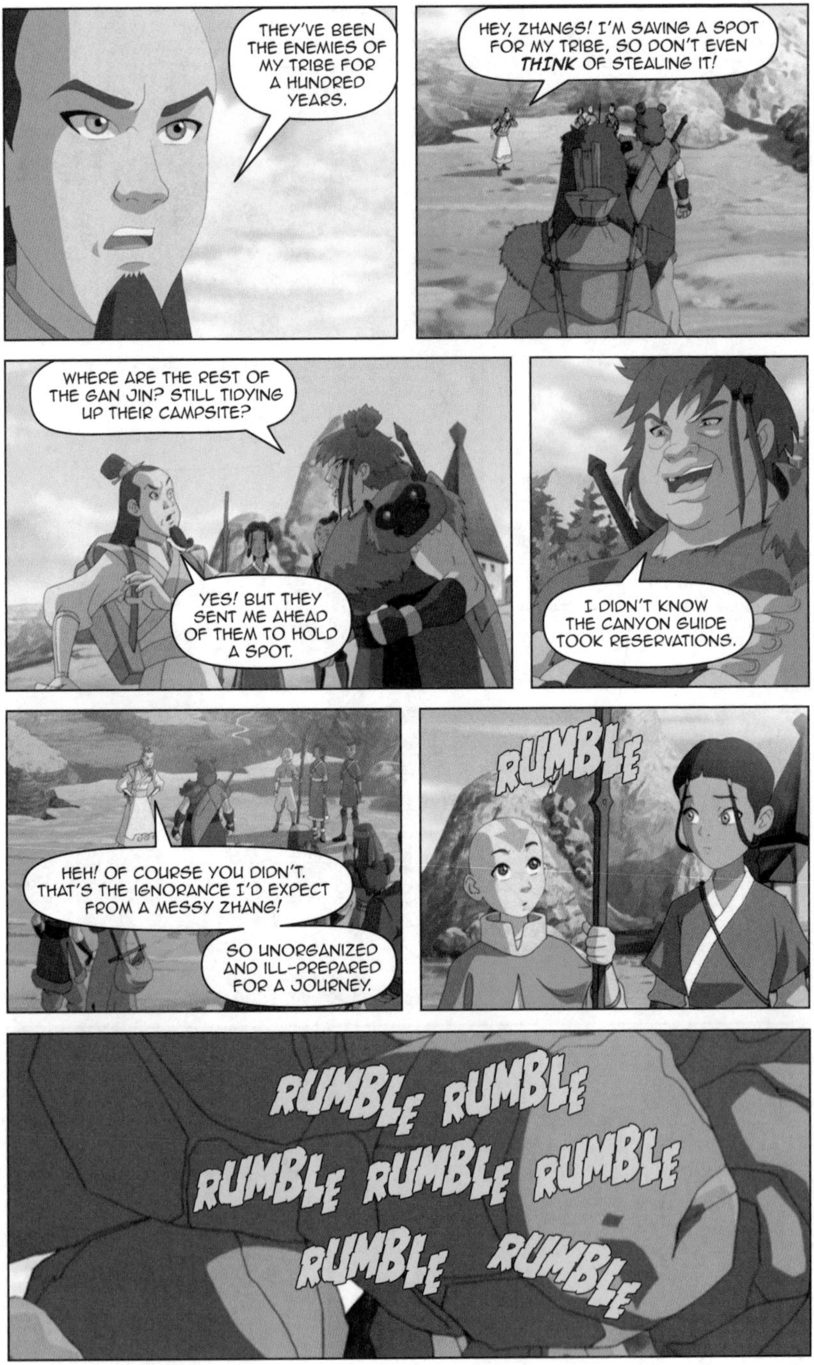
THEY'VE BEEN THE ENEMIES OF MY TRIBE FOR A HUNDRED YEARS.
HEY, ZHANGS! I'M SAVING A SPOT FOR MY TRIBE, SO DON'T EVEN *THINK* OF STEALING IT!
WHERE ARE THE REST OF THE GAN JIN? STILL TIDYING UP THEIR CAMPSITE?
YES! BUT THEY SENT ME AHEAD OF THEM TO HOLD A SPOT.
I DIDN'T KNOW THE CANYON GUIDE TOOK RESERVATIONS.
HEH! OF COURSE YOU DIDN'T. THAT'S THE IGNORANCE I'D EXPECT FROM A MESSY ZHANG!
SO UNORGANIZED AND ILL-PREPARED FOR A JOURNEY.
RUMBLE
RUMBLE RUMBLE
RUMBLE RUMBLE RUMBLE
RUMBLE RUMBLE

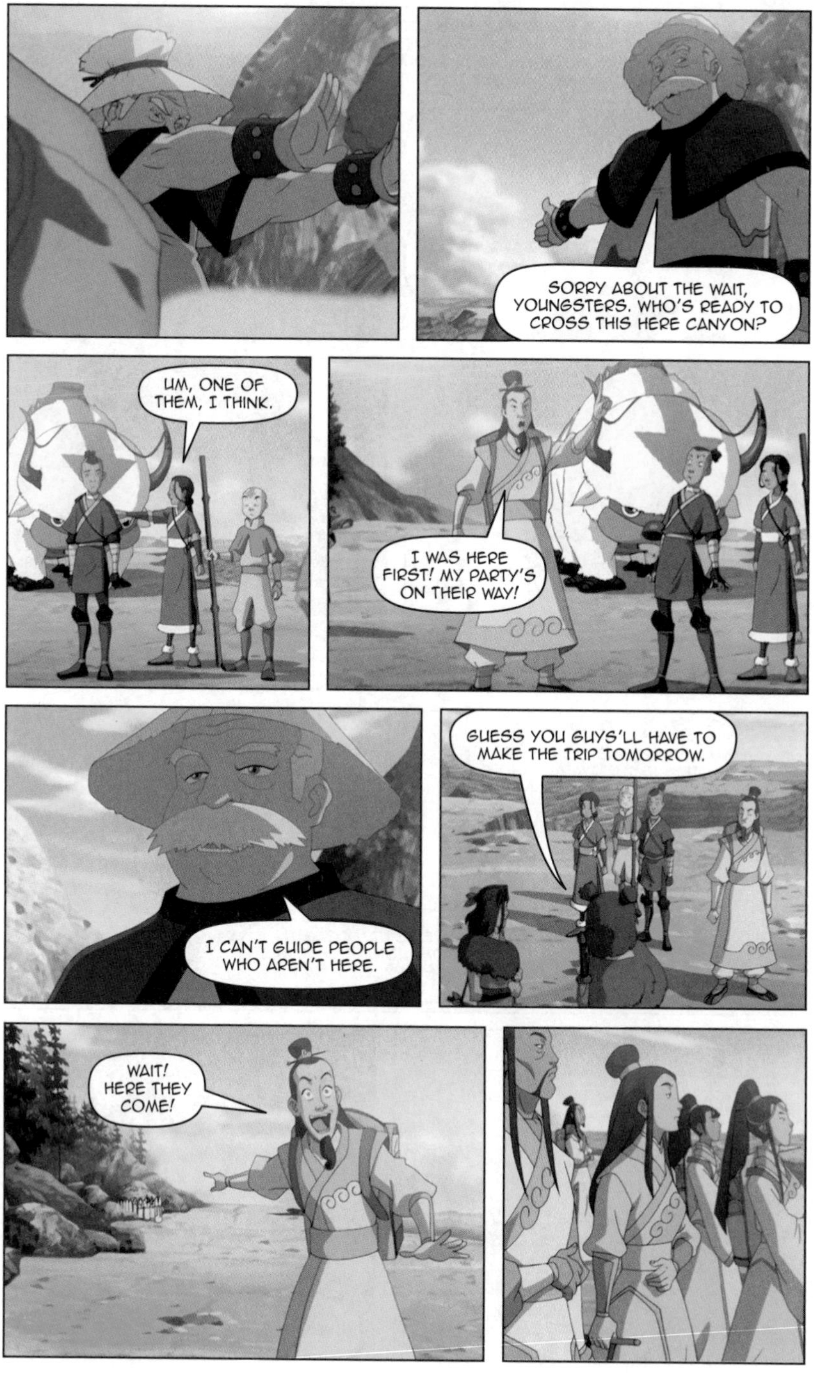
SORRY ABOUT THE WAIT, YOUNGSTERS. WHO'S READY TO CROSS THIS HERE CANYON?
UM, ONE OF THEM, I THINK.
I WAS HERE FIRST! MY PARTY'S ON THEIR WAY!
I CAN'T GUIDE PEOPLE WHO AREN'T HERE.
GUESS YOU GUYS'LL HAVE TO MAKE THE TRIP TOMORROW.
WAIT! HERE THEY COME!

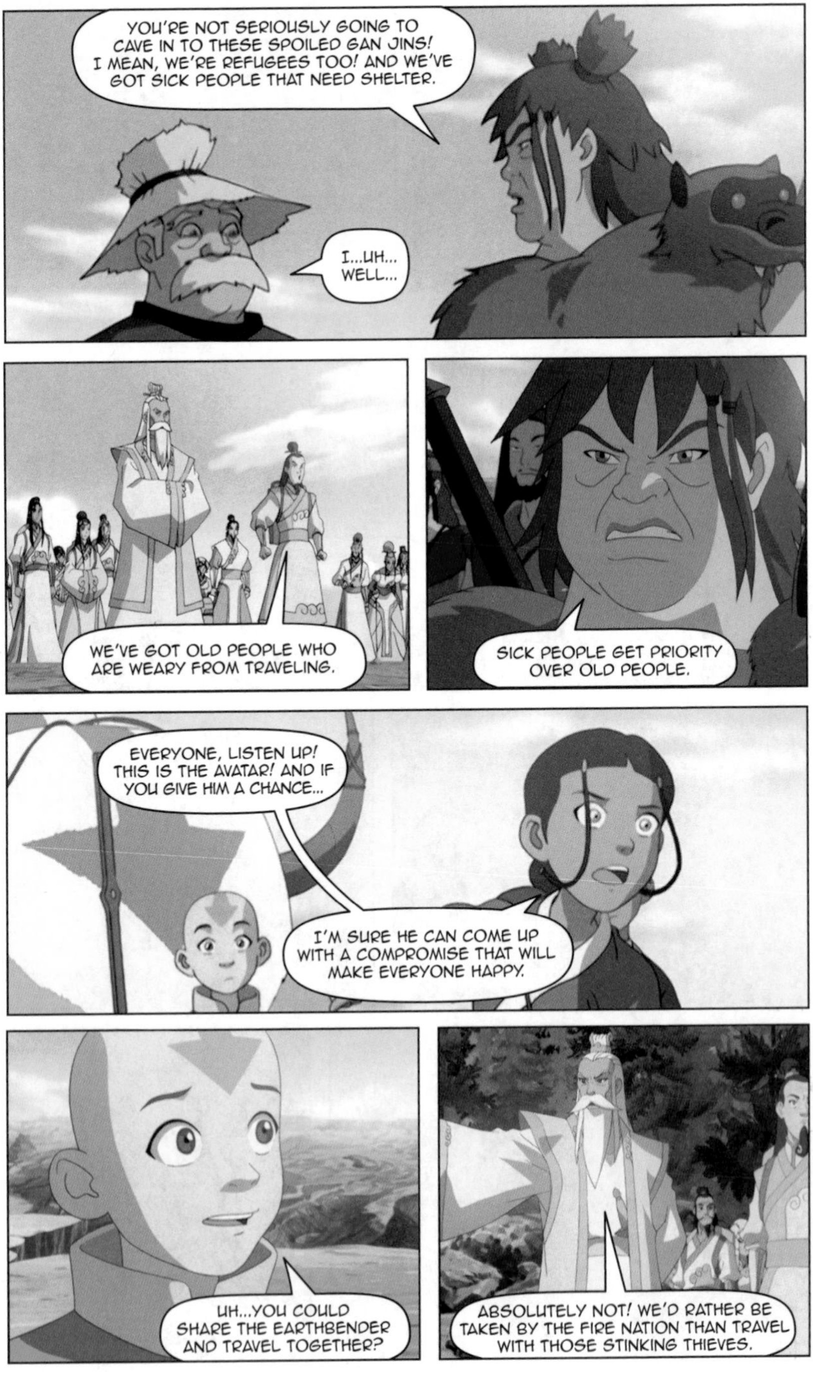

YOU'RE NOT SERIOUSLY GOING TO CAVE IN TO THESE SPOILED GAN JINS! I MEAN, WE'RE REFUGEES TOO! AND WE'VE GOT SICK PEOPLE THAT NEED SHELTER.
I...UH... WELL...
WE'VE GOT OLD PEOPLE WHO ARE WEARY FROM TRAVELING.
SICK PEOPLE GET PRIORITY OVER OLD PEOPLE.
EVERYONE, LISTEN UP! THIS IS THE AVATAR! AND IF YOU GIVE HIM A CHANCE...
I'M SURE HE CAN COME UP WITH A COMPROMISE THAT WILL MAKE EVERYONE HAPPY.
UH...YOU COULD SHARE THE EARTHBENDER AND TRAVEL TOGETHER?
ABSOLUTELY NOT! WE'D RATHER BE TAKEN BY THE FIRE NATION THAN TRAVEL WITH THOSE STINKING THIEVES.

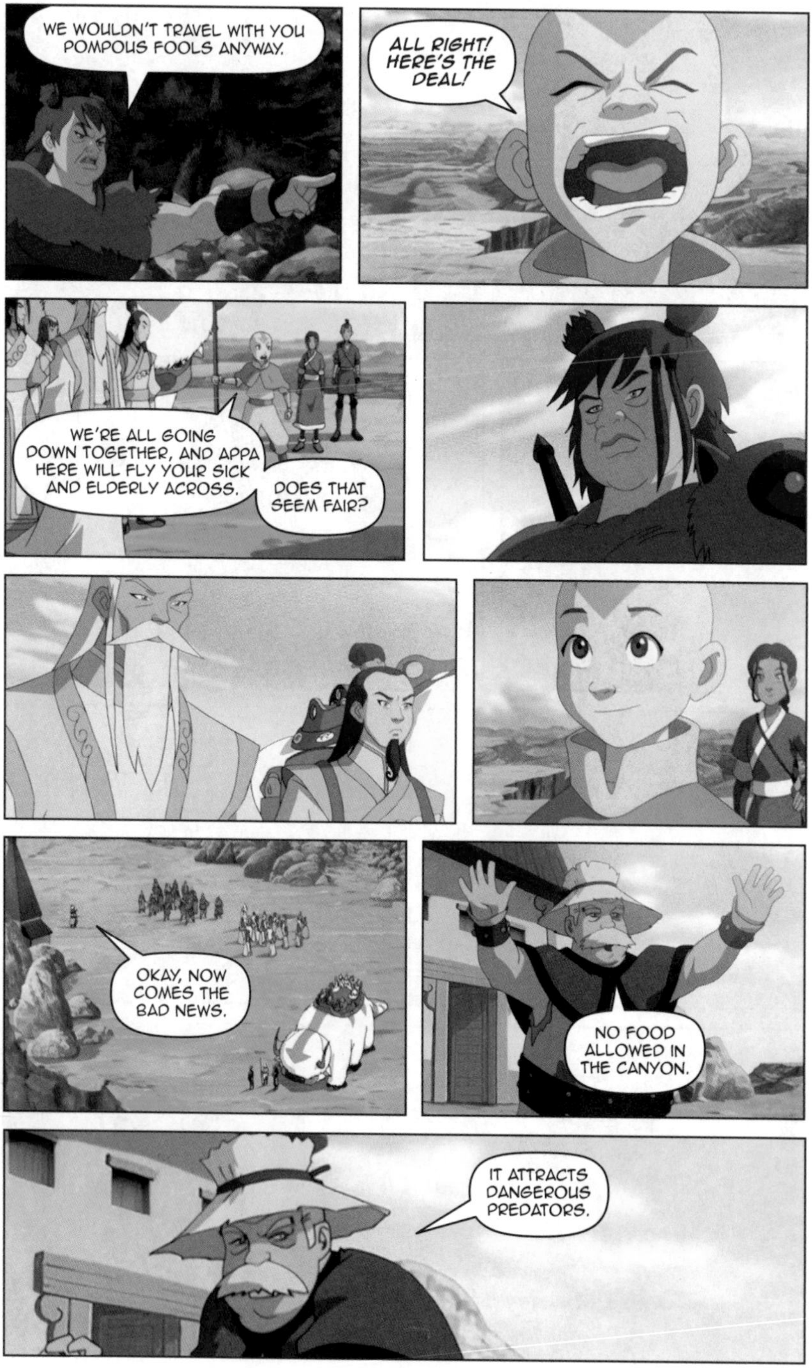
WE WOULDN'T TRAVEL WITH YOU POMPOUS FOOLS ANYWAY.
ALL RIGHT! HERE'S THE DEAL!
WE'RE ALL GOING DOWN TOGETHER, AND APPA HERE WILL FLY YOUR SICK AND ELDERLY ACROSS.
DOES THAT SEEM FAIR?
OKAY, NOW COMES THE BAD NEWS.
NO FOOD ALLOWED IN THE CANYON.
IT ATTRACTS DANGEROUS PREDATORS.

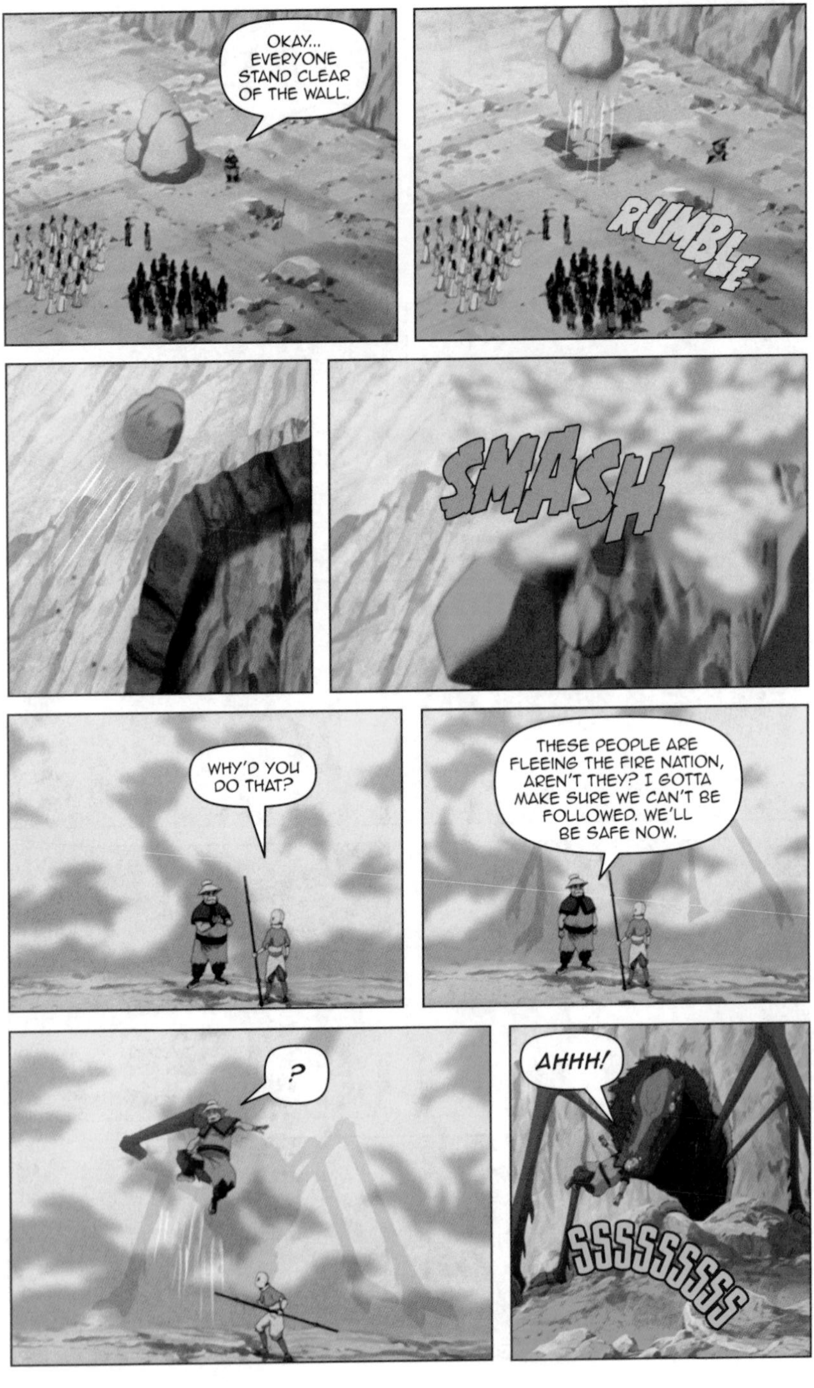

OKAY... EVERYONE STAND CLEAR OF THE WALL.
RUMBLE
SMASH
WHY'D YOU DO THAT?
THESE PEOPLE ARE FLEEING THE FIRE NATION, AREN'T THEY? I GOTTA MAKE SURE WE CAN'T BE FOLLOWED. WE'LL BE SAFE NOW.
?
AHHH!
SSSSSSSSS

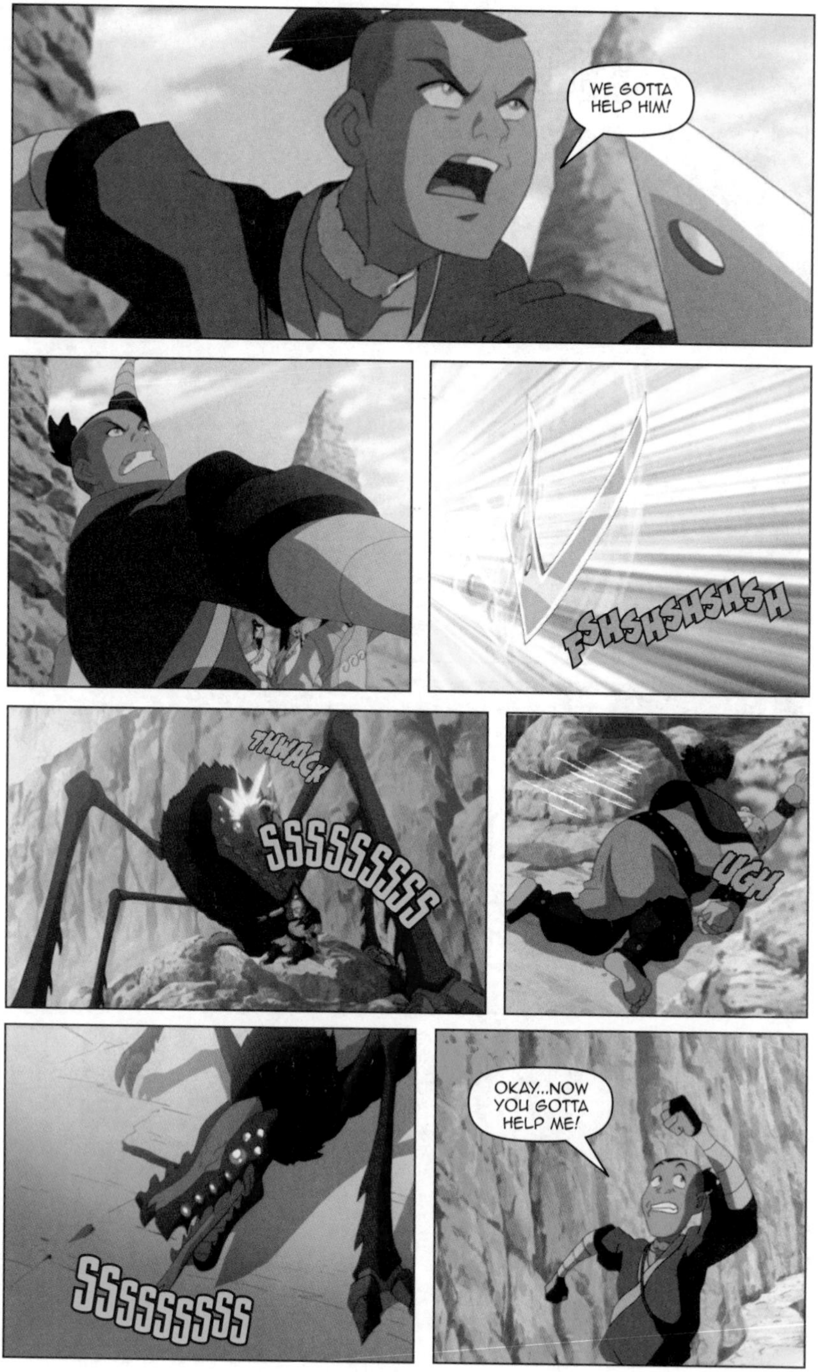
WE GOTTA HELP HIM!
FSHSHSHSHSH
THWACK
SSSSSSSSS
UGH
SSSSSSSSS
OKAY...NOW YOU GOTTA HELP ME!

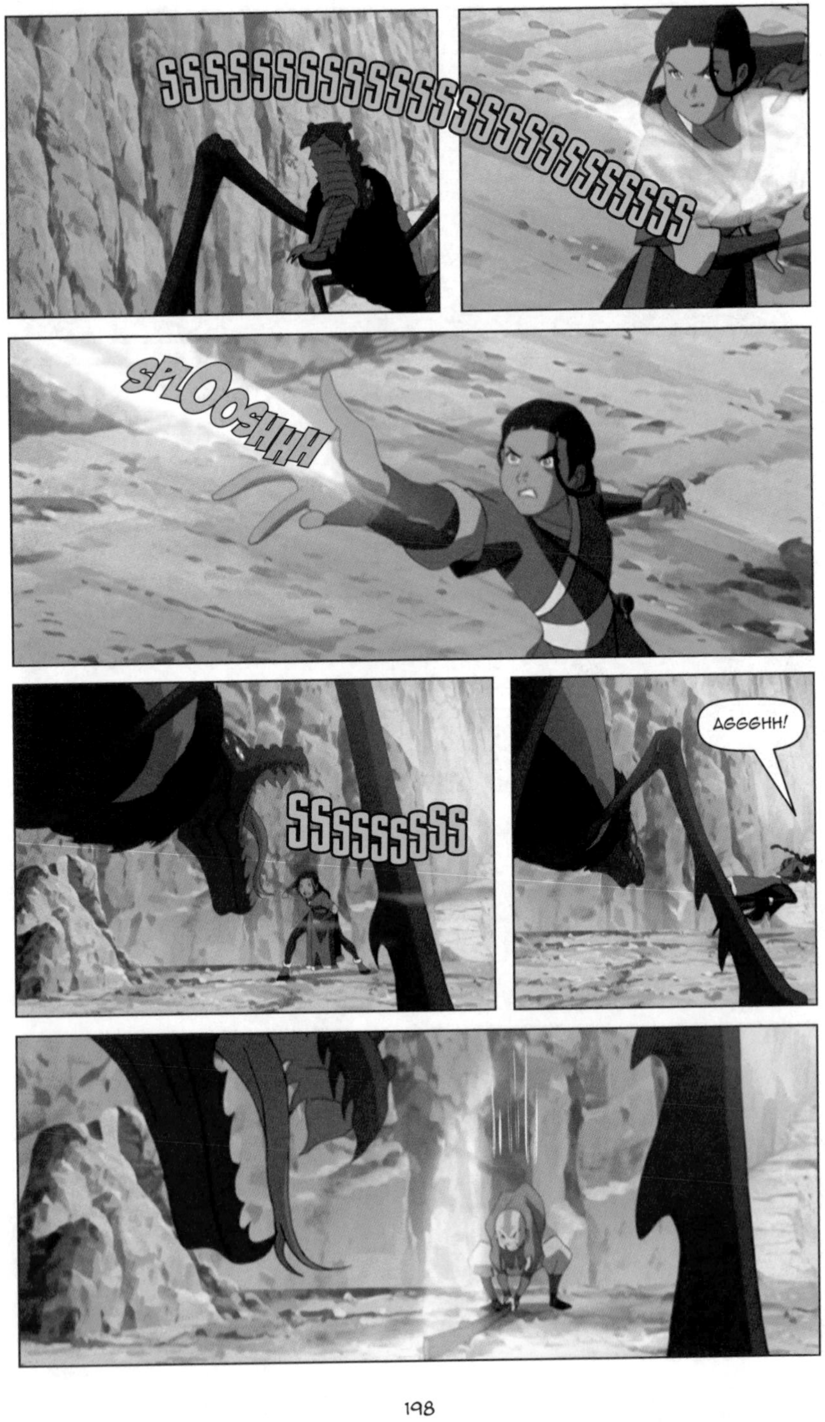
SSSSSSSSSSSSSSSSSSSSSSSSSSSS
SPLOOSHHH
SSSSSSSSS
AGGGHH!

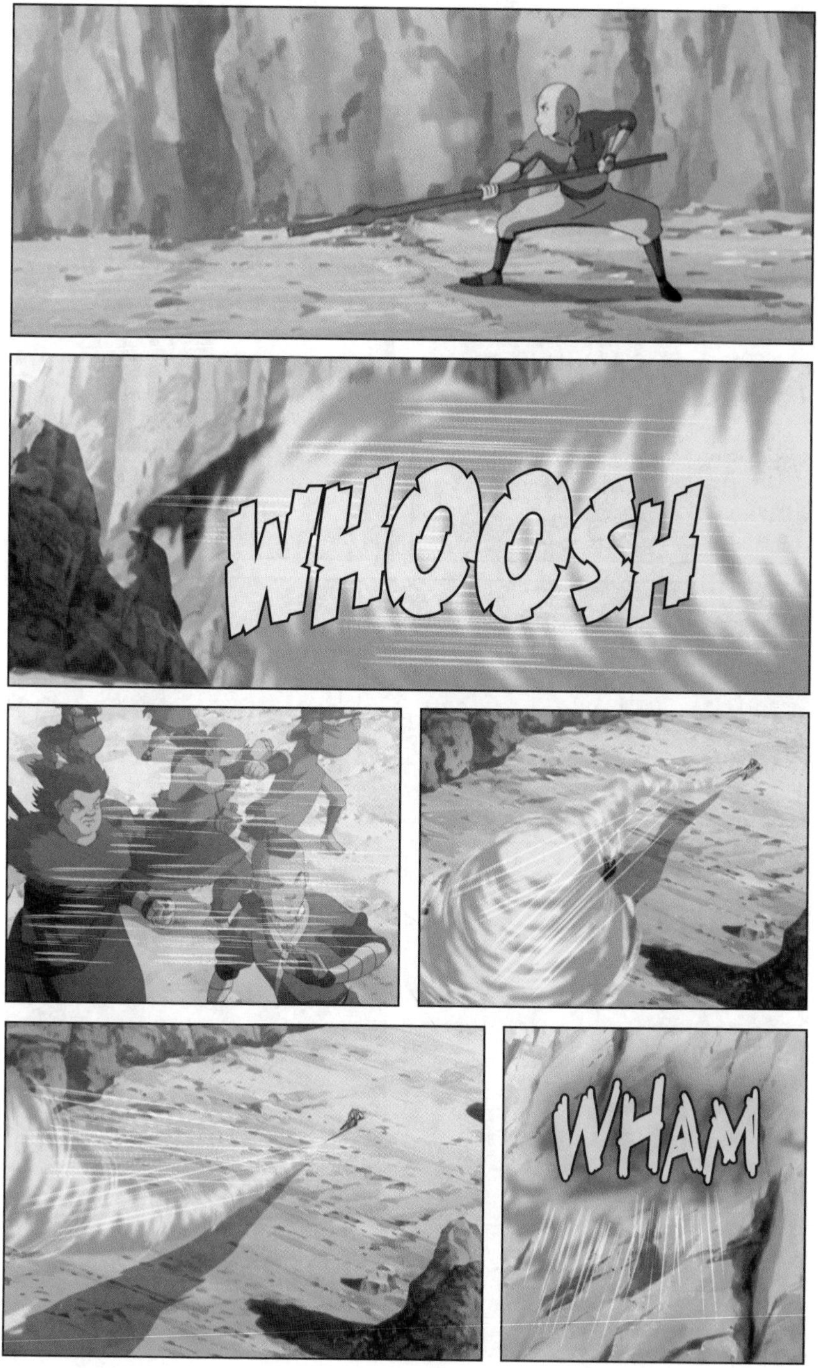
WHOOSH
WHAM

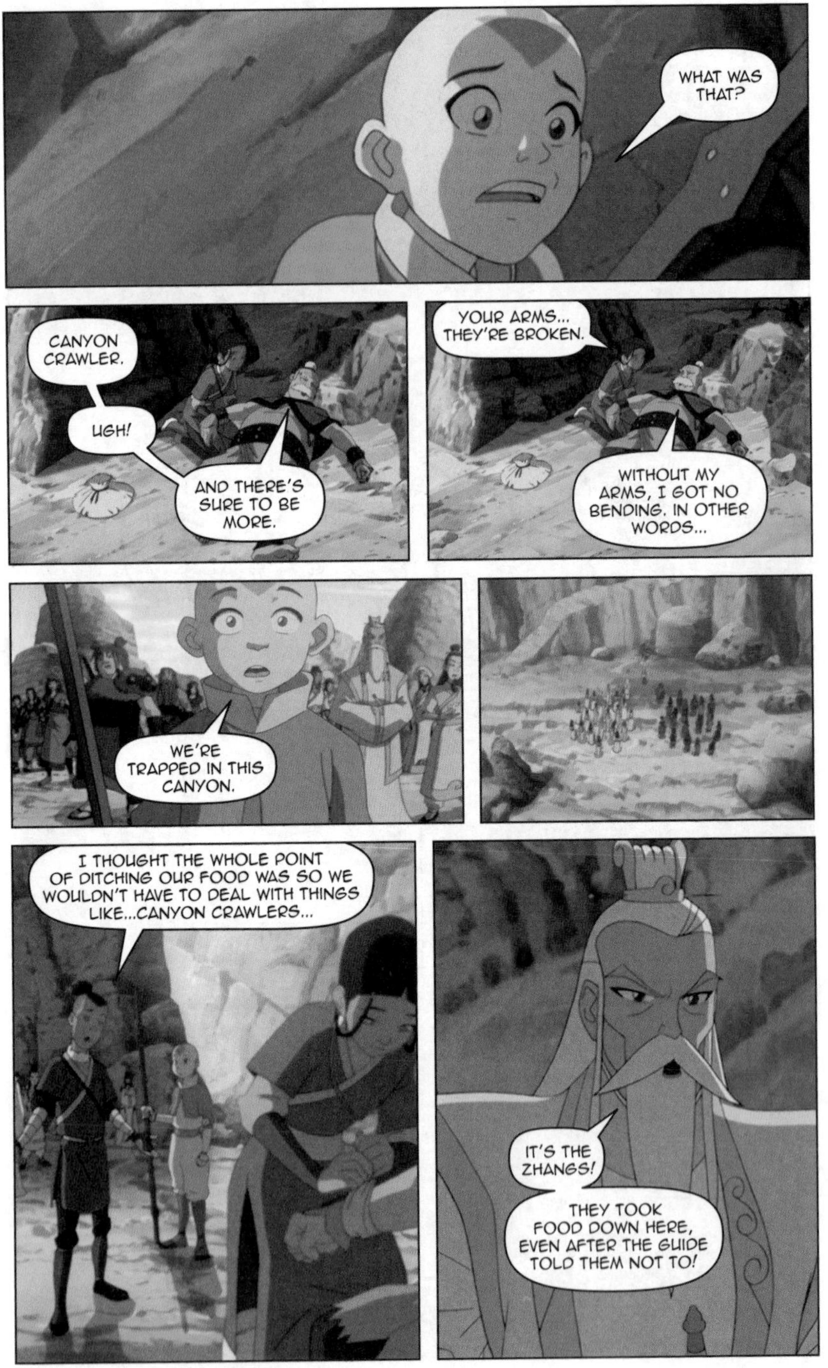
WHAT WAS THAT?
CANYON CRAWLER.
UGH!
AND THERE'S SURE TO BE MORE.
YOUR ARMS... THEY'RE BROKEN.
WITHOUT MY ARMS, I GOT NO BENDING. IN OTHER WORDS...
WE'RE TRAPPED IN THIS CANYON.
I THOUGHT THE WHOLE POINT OF DITCHING OUR FOOD WAS SO WE WOULDN'T HAVE TO DEAL WITH THINGS LIKE...CANYON CRAWLERS...
IT'S THE ZHANGS!
THEY TOOK FOOD DOWN HERE, EVEN AFTER THE GUIDE TOLD THEM NOT TO!

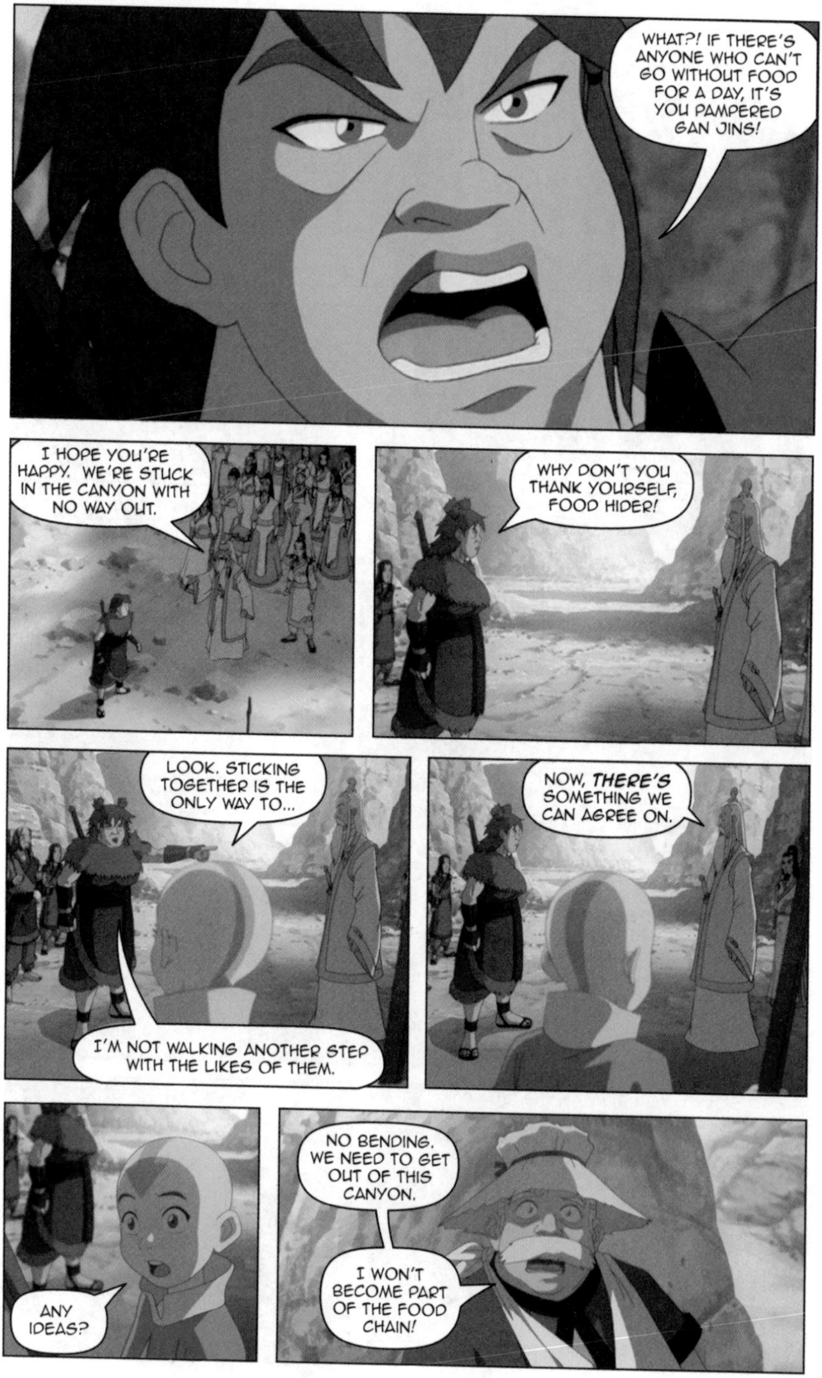

WHAT?! IF THERE'S ANYONE WHO CAN'T GO WITHOUT FOOD FOR A DAY, IT'S YOU PAMPERED GAN JINS!
I HOPE YOU'RE HAPPY. WE'RE STUCK IN THE CANYON WITH NO WAY OUT.
WHY DON'T YOU THANK YOURSELF, FOOD HIDER!
LOOK. STICKING TOGETHER IS THE ONLY WAY TO...
I'M NOT WALKING ANOTHER STEP WITH THE LIKES OF THEM.
NOW, ***THERE'S*** SOMETHING WE CAN AGREE ON.
ANY IDEAS?
NO BENDING. WE NEED TO GET OUT OF THIS CANYON.
I WON'T BECOME PART OF THE FOOD CHAIN!

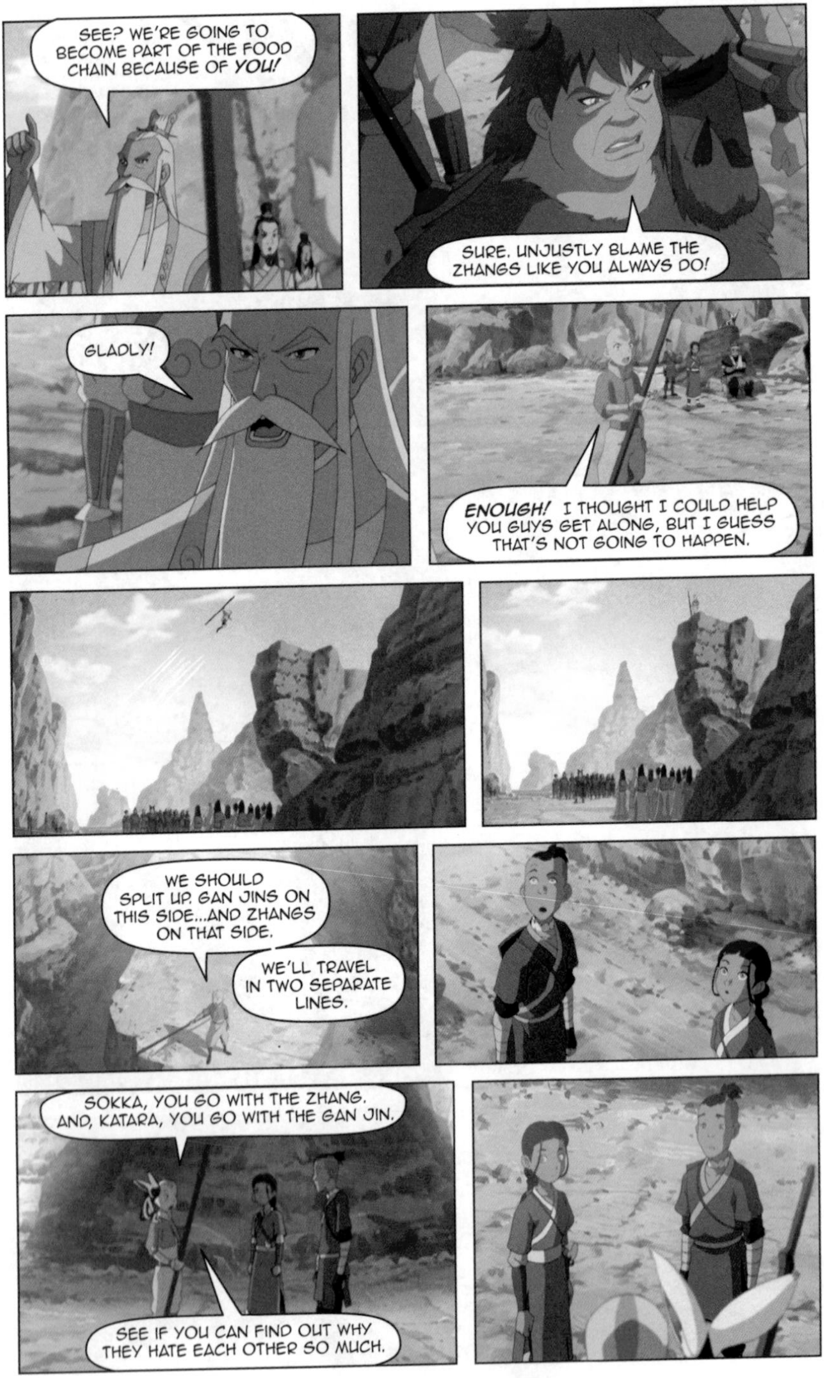
SEE? WE'RE GOING TO BECOME PART OF THE FOOD CHAIN BECAUSE OF *YOU!*
SURE. UNJUSTLY BLAME THE ZHANGS LIKE YOU ALWAYS DO!
GLADLY!
ENOUGH! I THOUGHT I COULD HELP YOU GUYS GET ALONG, BUT I GUESS THAT'S NOT GOING TO HAPPEN.
WE SHOULD SPLIT UP. GAN JINS ON THIS SIDE...AND ZHANGS ON THAT SIDE.
WE'LL TRAVEL IN TWO SEPARATE LINES.
SOKKA, YOU GO WITH THE ZHANG. AND, KATARA, YOU GO WITH THE GAN JIN.
SEE IF YOU CAN FIND OUT WHY THEY HATE EACH OTHER SO MUCH.

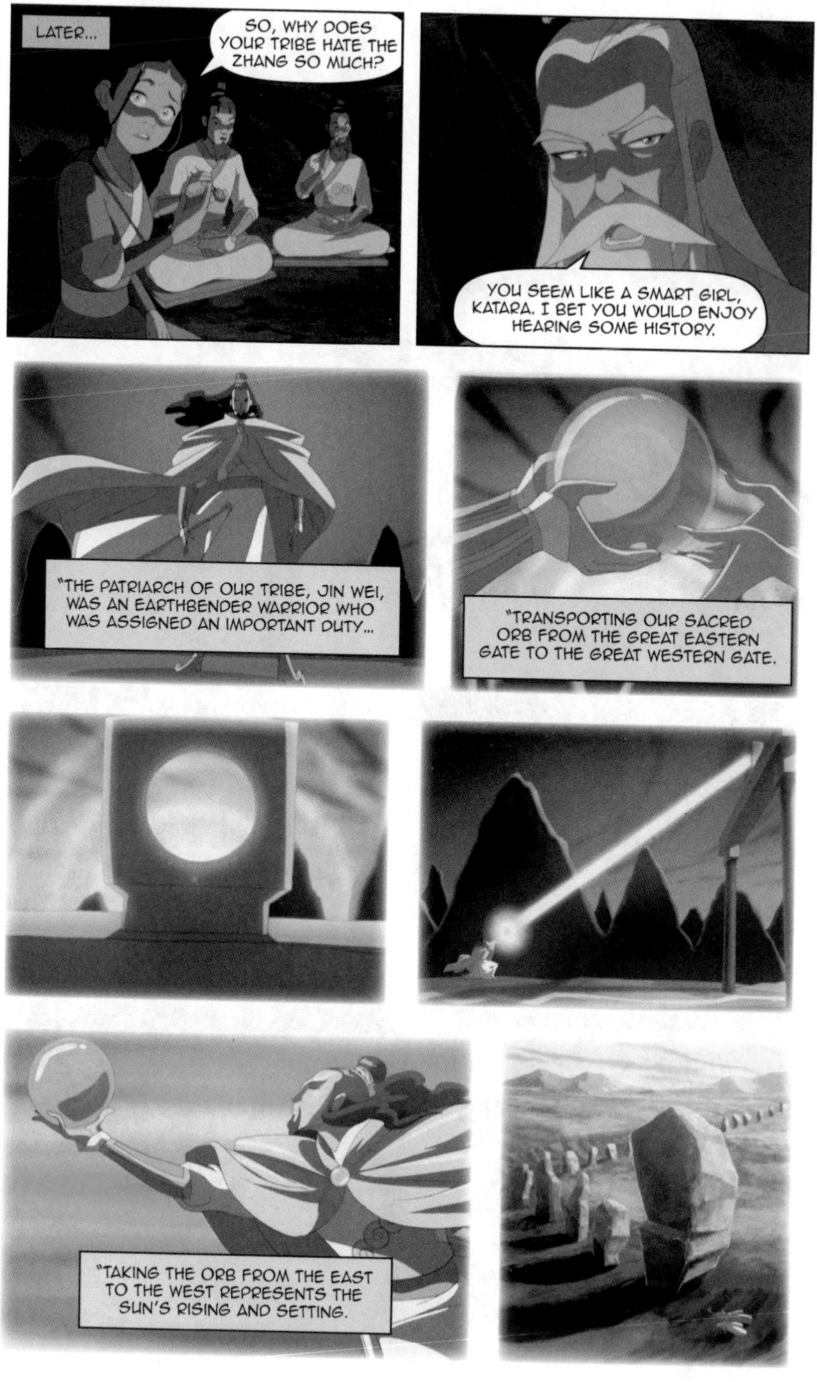
LATER...
SO, WHY DOES YOUR TRIBE HATE THE ZHANG SO MUCH?
YOU SEEM LIKE A SMART GIRL, KATARA. I BET YOU WOULD ENJOY HEARING SOME HISTORY.
"THE PATRIARCH OF OUR TRIBE, JIN WEI, WAS AN EARTHBENDER WARRIOR WHO WAS ASSIGNED AN IMPORTANT DUTY...
"TRANSPORTING OUR SACRED ORB FROM THE GREAT EASTERN GATE TO THE GREAT WESTERN GATE.
"TAKING THE ORB FROM THE EAST TO THE WEST REPRESENTS THE SUN'S RISING AND SETTING.

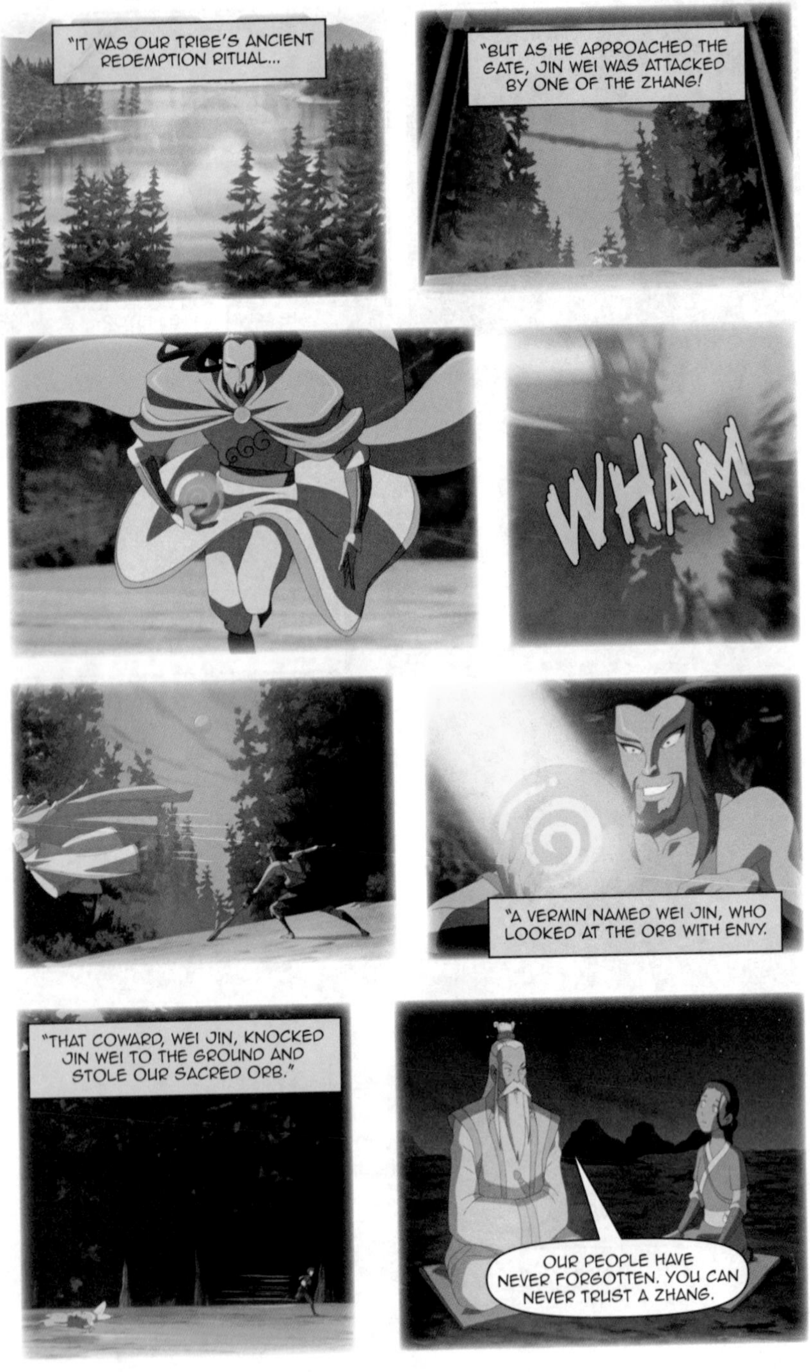
"IT WAS OUR TRIBE'S ANCIENT REDEMPTION RITUAL...
"BUT AS HE APPROACHED THE GATE, JIN WEI WAS ATTACKED BY ONE OF THE ZHANG!
WHAM
"A VERMIN NAMED WEI JIN, WHO LOOKED AT THE ORB WITH ENVY.
"THAT COWARD, WEI JIN, KNOCKED JIN WEI TO THE GROUND AND STOLE OUR SACRED ORB."
OUR PEOPLE HAVE NEVER FORGOTTEN. YOU CAN NEVER TRUST A ZHANG.

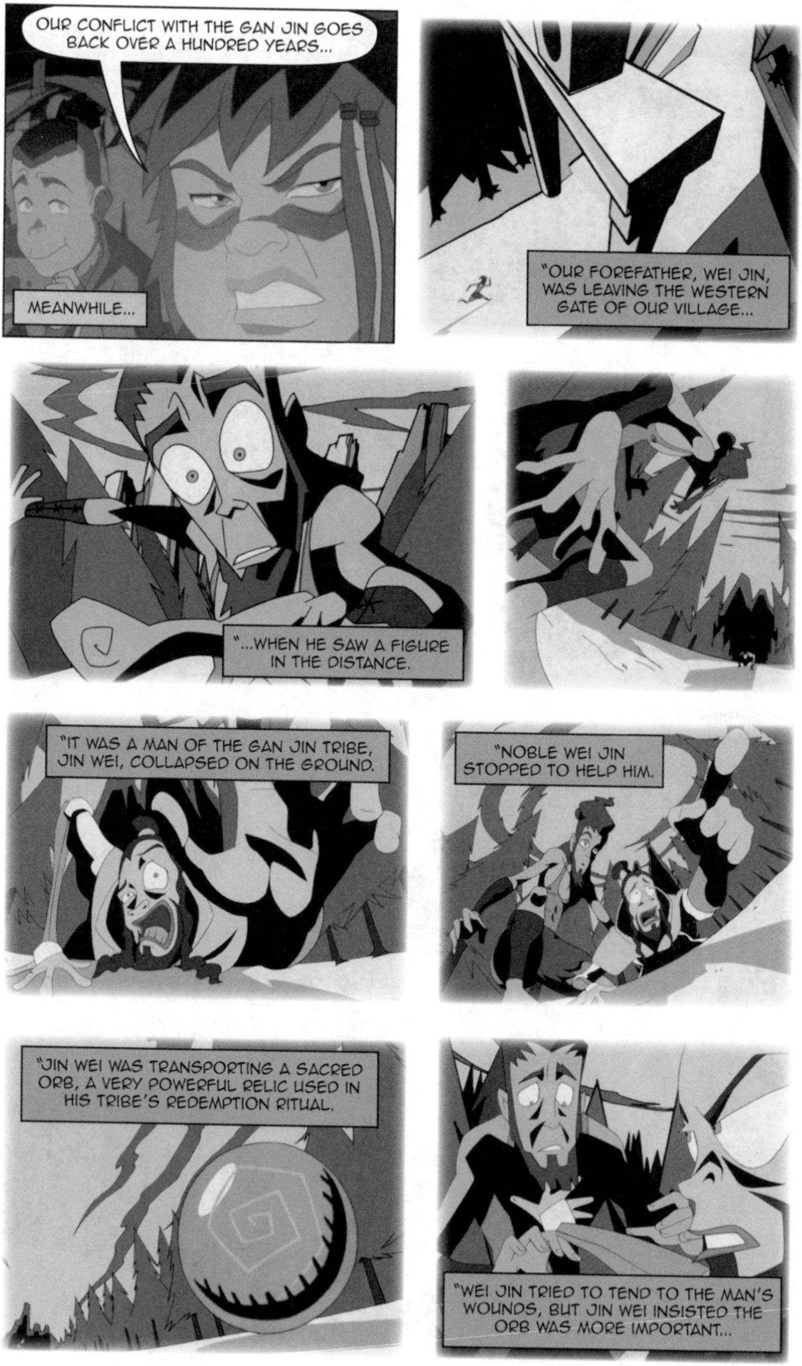
OUR CONFLICT WITH THE GAN JIN GOES BACK OVER A HUNDRED YEARS...
MEANWHILE...
"OUR FOREFATHER, WEI JIN, WAS LEAVING THE WESTERN GATE OF OUR VILLAGE...
"...WHEN HE SAW A FIGURE IN THE DISTANCE.
"IT WAS A MAN OF THE GAN JIN TRIBE, JIN WEI, COLLAPSED ON THE GROUND.
"NOBLE WEI JIN STOPPED TO HELP HIM.
"JIN WEI WAS TRANSPORTING A SACRED ORB, A VERY POWERFUL RELIC USED IN HIS TRIBE'S REDEMPTION RITUAL.
"WEI JIN TRIED TO TEND TO THE MAN'S WOUNDS, BUT JIN WEI INSISTED THE ORB WAS MORE IMPORTANT...

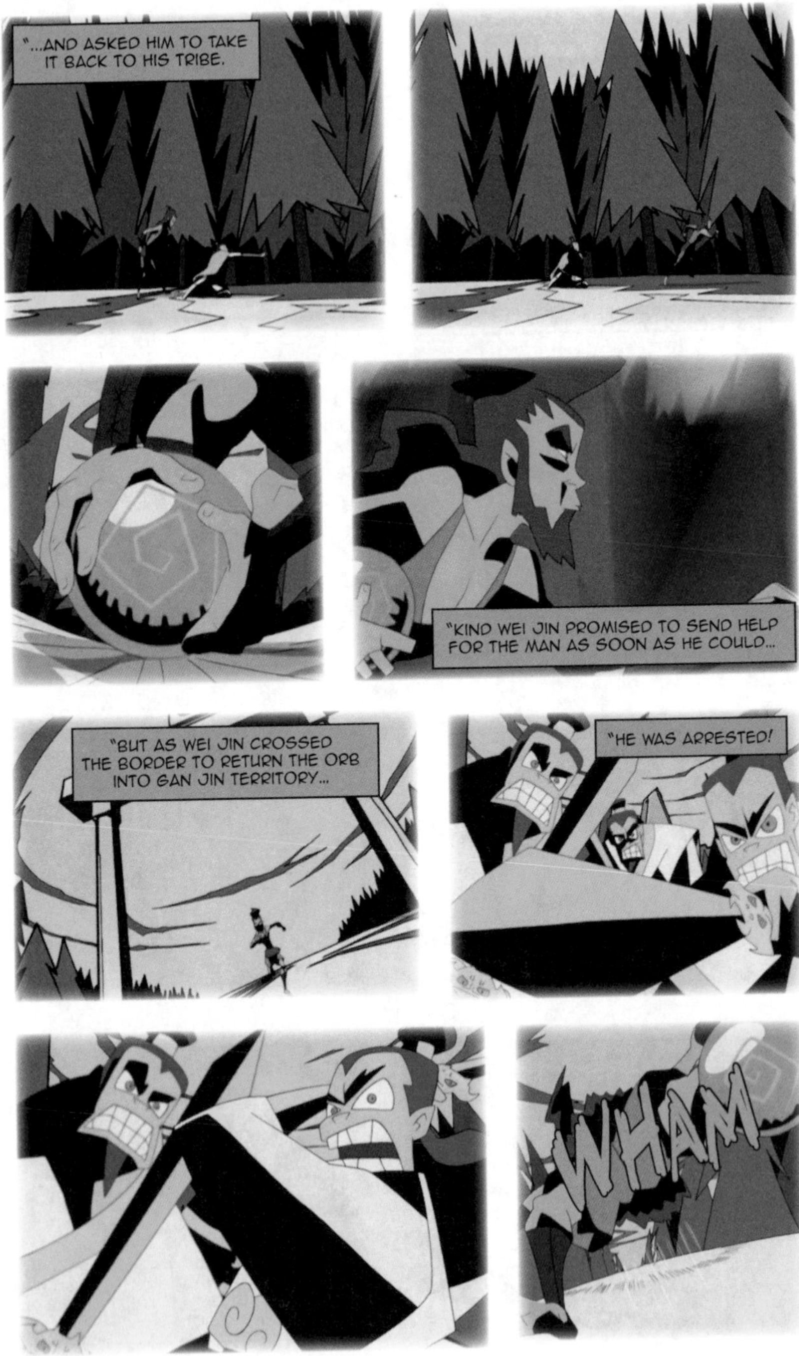
"...AND ASKED HIM TO TAKE IT BACK TO HIS TRIBE.
"KIND WEI JIN PROMISED TO SEND HELP FOR THE MAN AS SOON AS HE COULD...
"BUT AS WEI JIN CROSSED THE BORDER TO RETURN THE ORB INTO GAN JIN TERRITORY...
"HE WAS ARRESTED!
WHAM

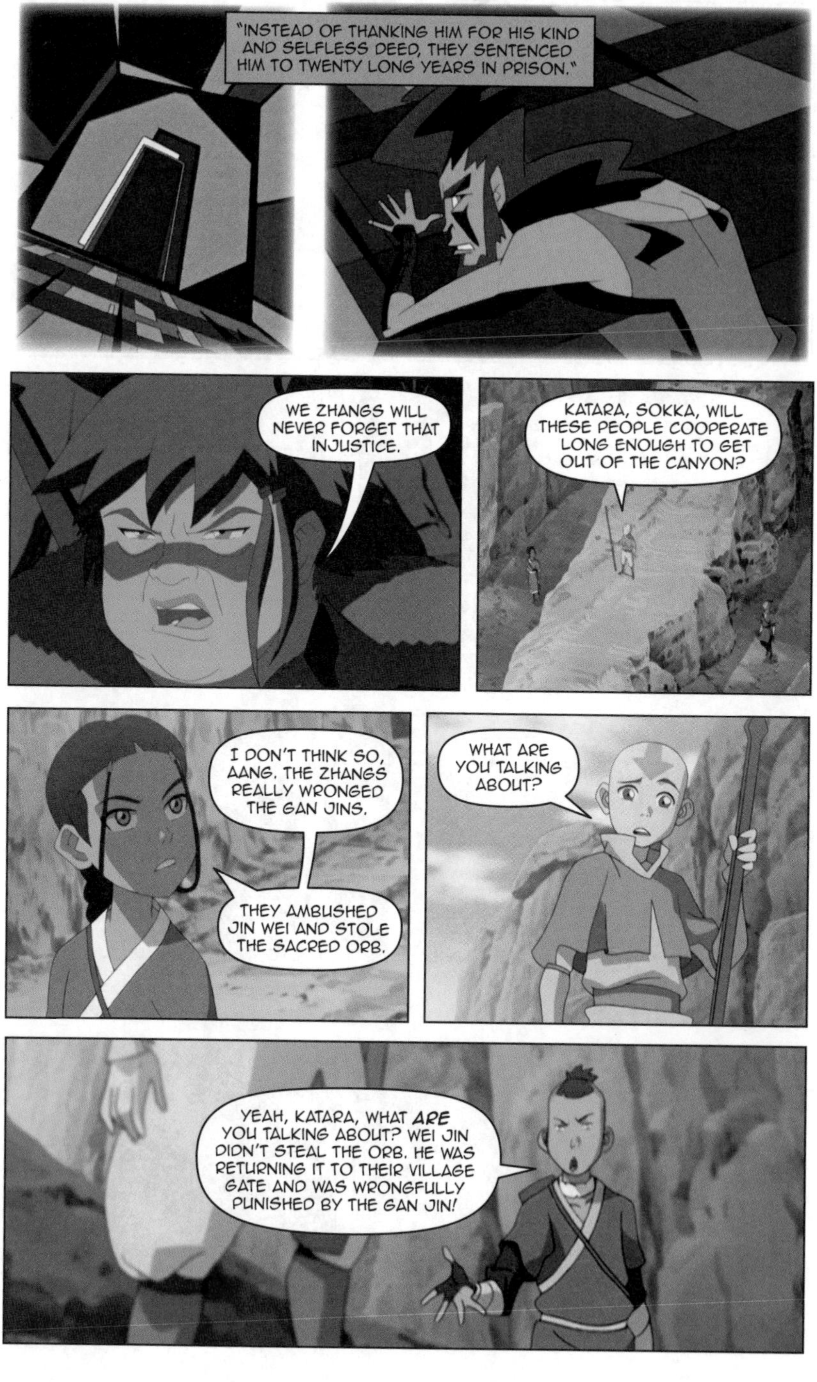
"INSTEAD OF THANKING HIM FOR HIS KIND AND SELFLESS DEED, THEY SENTENCED HIM TO TWENTY LONG YEARS IN PRISON."
WE ZHANGS WILL NEVER FORGET THAT INJUSTICE.
KATARA, SOKKA, WILL THESE PEOPLE COOPERATE LONG ENOUGH TO GET OUT OF THE CANYON?
I DON'T THINK SO, AANG. THE ZHANGS REALLY WRONGED THE GAN JINS.
THEY AMBUSHED JIN WEI AND STOLE THE SACRED ORB.
WHAT ARE YOU TALKING ABOUT?
YEAH, KATARA, WHAT *ARE* YOU TALKING ABOUT? WEI JIN DIDN'T STEAL THE ORB. HE WAS RETURNING IT TO THEIR VILLAGE GATE AND WAS WRONGFULLY PUNISHED BY THE GAN JIN!

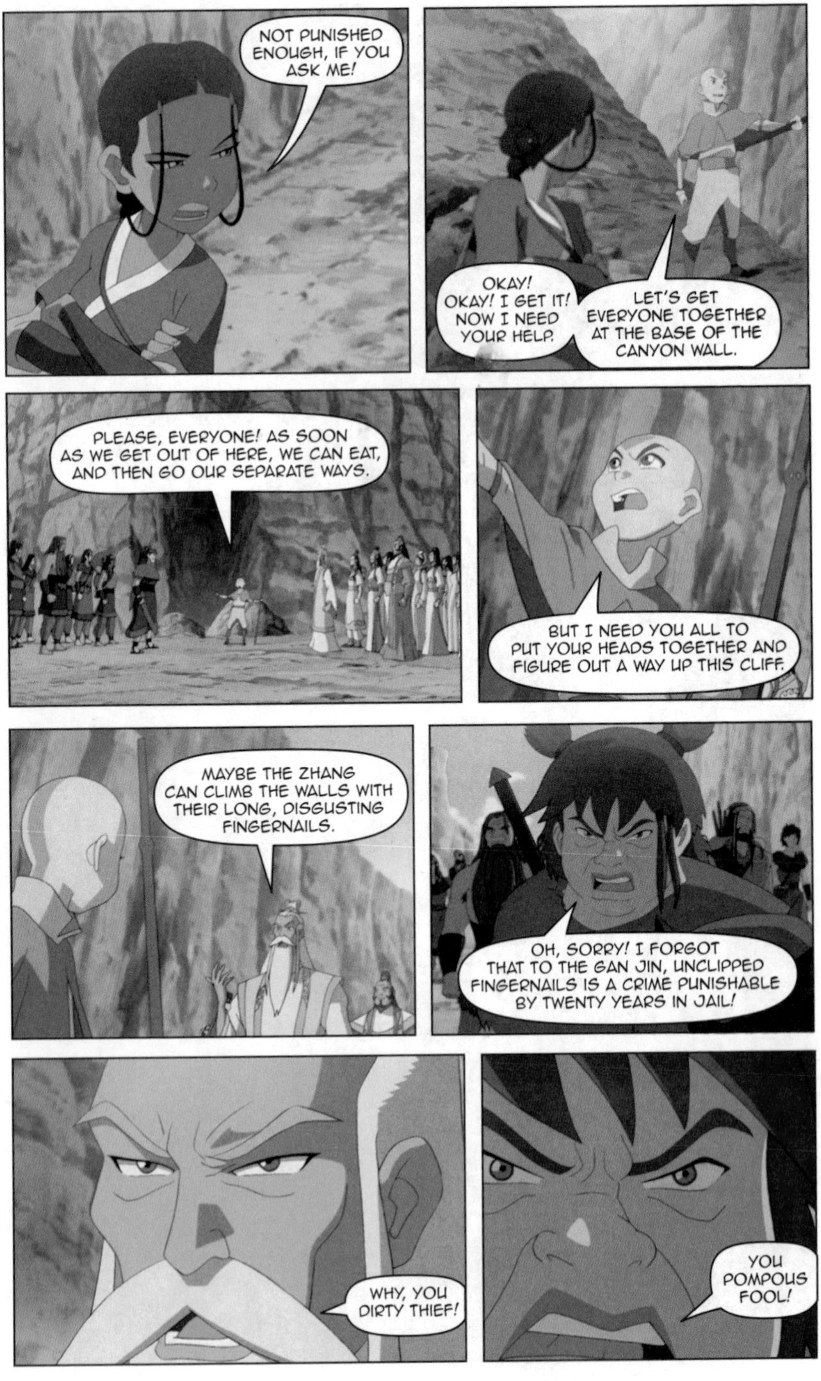
NOT PUNISHED ENOUGH, IF YOU ASK ME!
OKAY! OKAY! I GET IT! NOW I NEED YOUR HELP.
LET'S GET EVERYONE TOGETHER AT THE BASE OF THE CANYON WALL.
PLEASE, EVERYONE! AS SOON AS WE GET OUT OF HERE, WE CAN EAT, AND THEN GO OUR SEPARATE WAYS.
BUT I NEED YOU ALL TO PUT YOUR HEADS TOGETHER AND FIGURE OUT A WAY UP THIS CLIFF.
MAYBE THE ZHANG CAN CLIMB THE WALLS WITH THEIR LONG, DISGUSTING FINGERNAILS.
OH, SORRY! I FORGOT THAT TO THE GAN JIN, UNCLIPPED FINGERNAILS IS A CRIME PUNISHABLE BY TWENTY YEARS IN JAIL!
WHY, YOU DIRTY THIEF!
YOU POMPOUS FOOL!

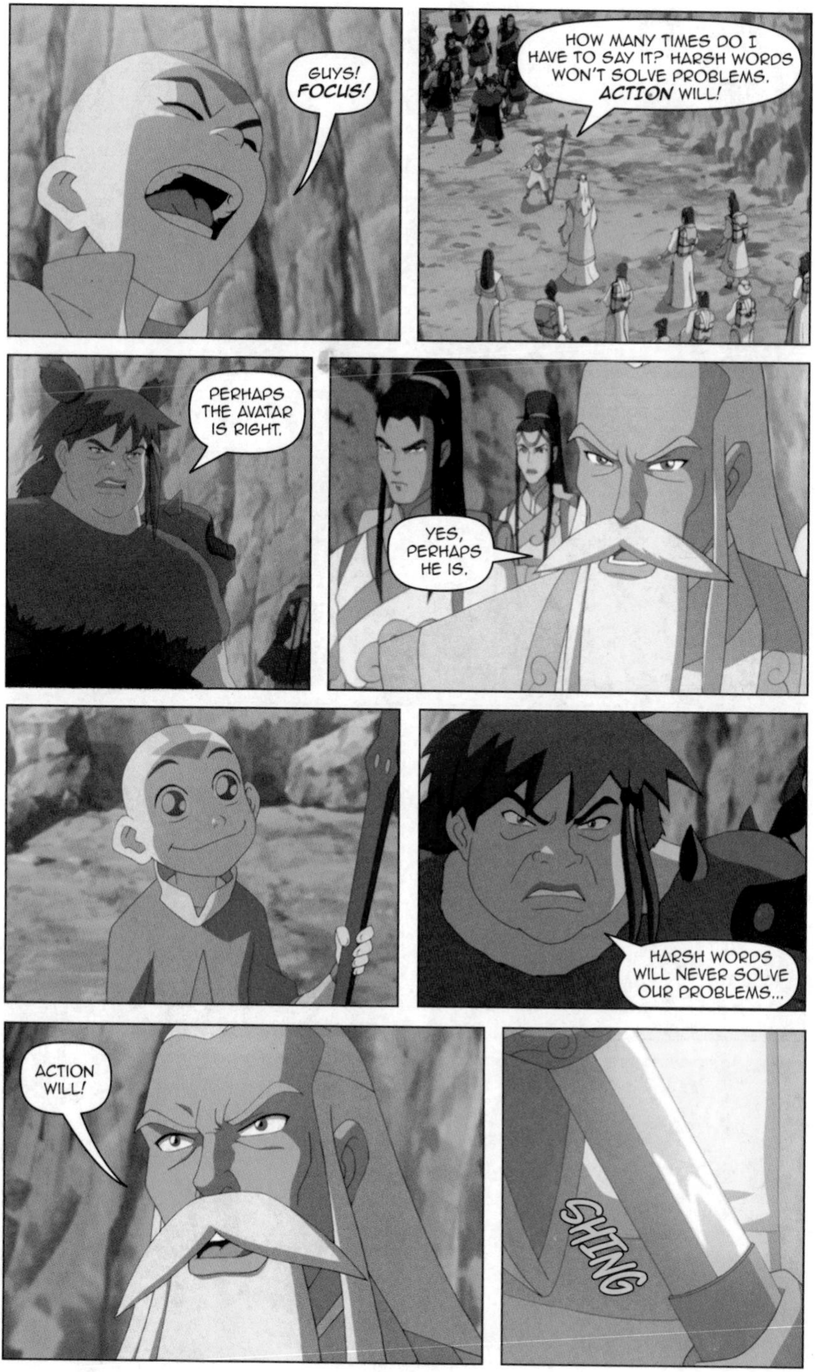
GUYS! FOCUS!
HOW MANY TIMES DO I HAVE TO SAY IT? HARSH WORDS WON'T SOLVE PROBLEMS. ACTION WILL!
PERHAPS THE AVATAR IS RIGHT.
YES, PERHAPS HE IS.
HARSH WORDS WILL NEVER SOLVE OUR PROBLEMS...
ACTION WILL!
SHING

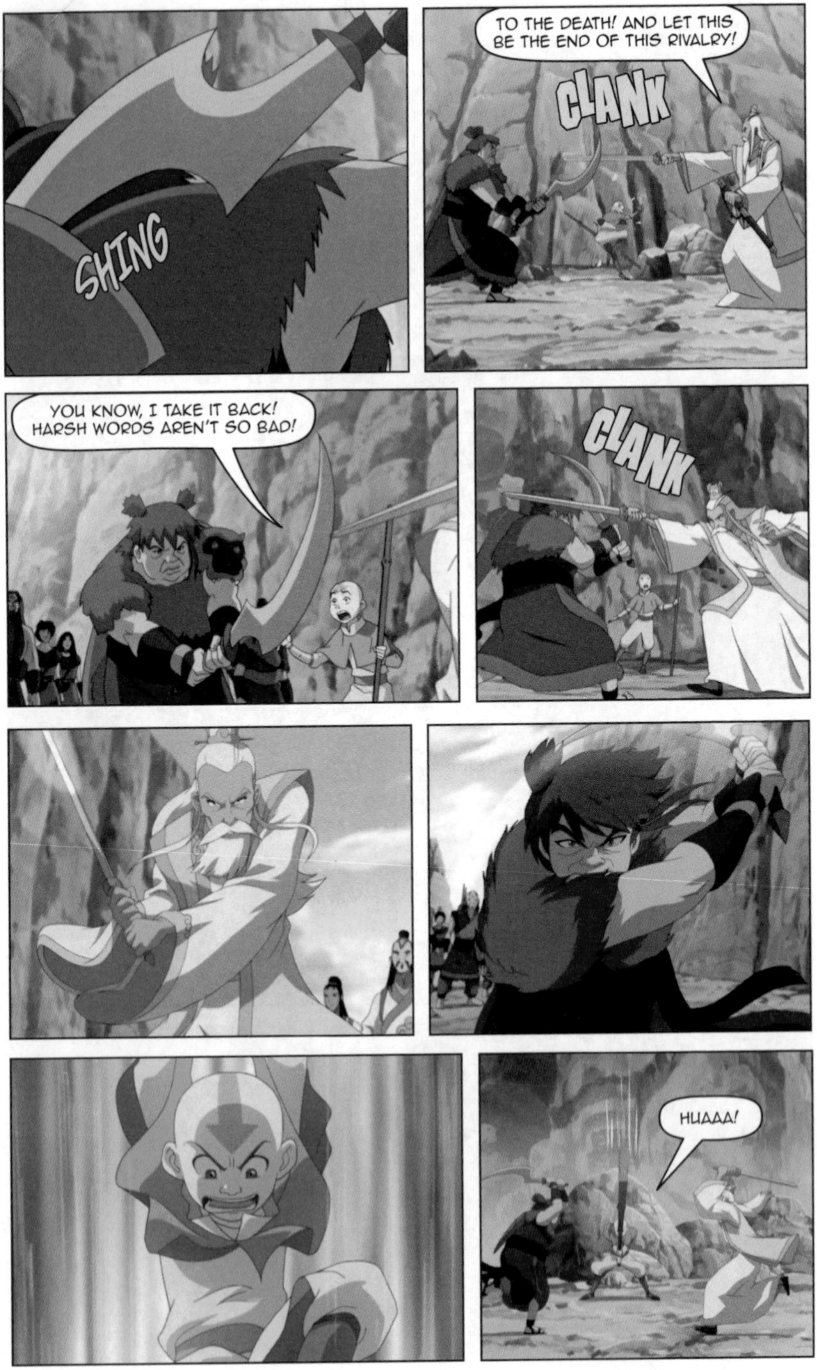
SHING
TO THE DEATH! AND LET THIS BE THE END OF THIS RIVALRY!
CLANK
YOU KNOW, I TAKE IT BACK! HARSH WORDS AREN'T SO BAD!
CLANK
HUAAA!

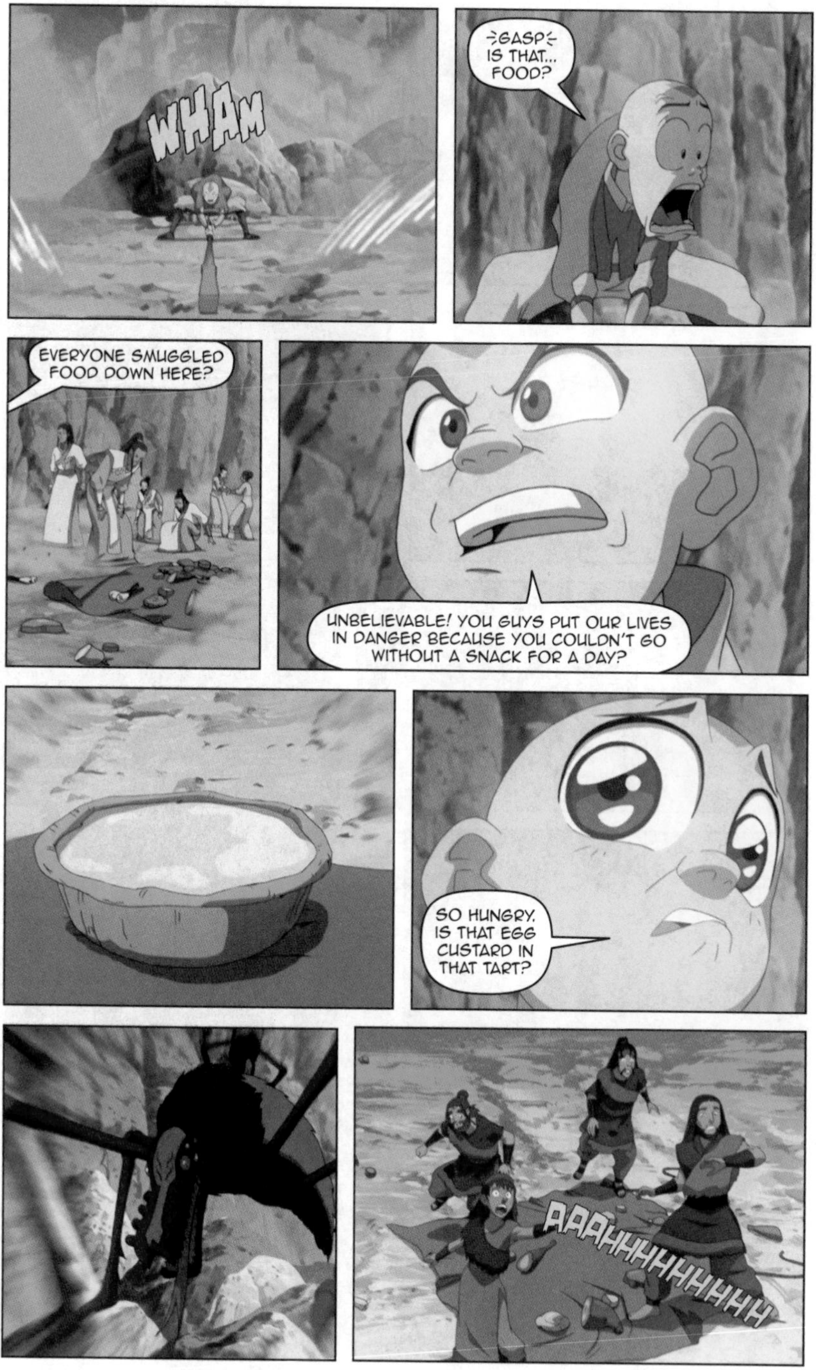
WHAM
-GASP- IS THAT... FOOD?
EVERYONE SMUGGLED FOOD DOWN HERE?
UNBELIEVABLE! YOU GUYS PUT OUR LIVES IN DANGER BECAUSE YOU COULDN'T GO WITHOUT A SNACK FOR A DAY?
SO HUNGRY. IS THAT EGG CUSTARD IN THAT TART?
AAAHHHHHHHHHHH

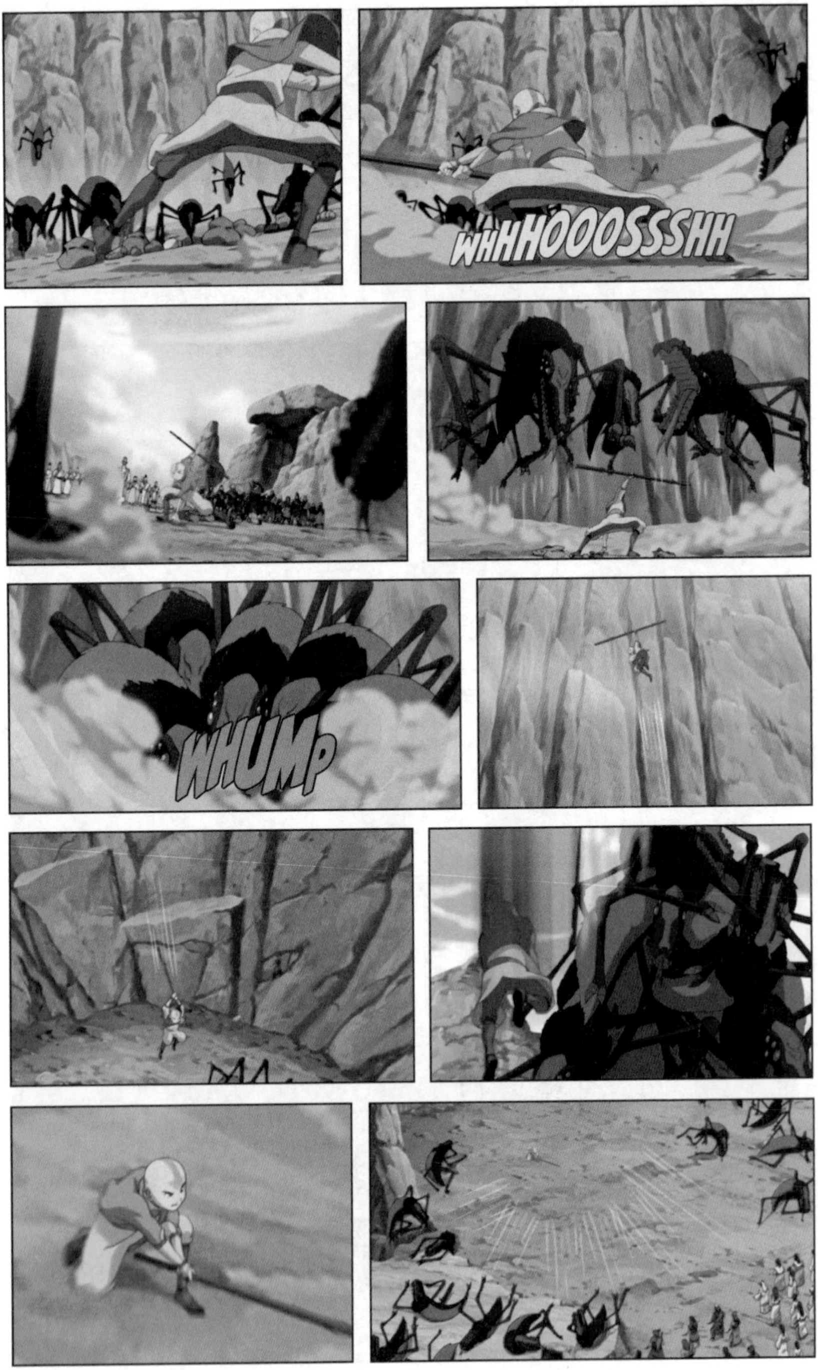
WHHHOOOSSSHH
WHUMP

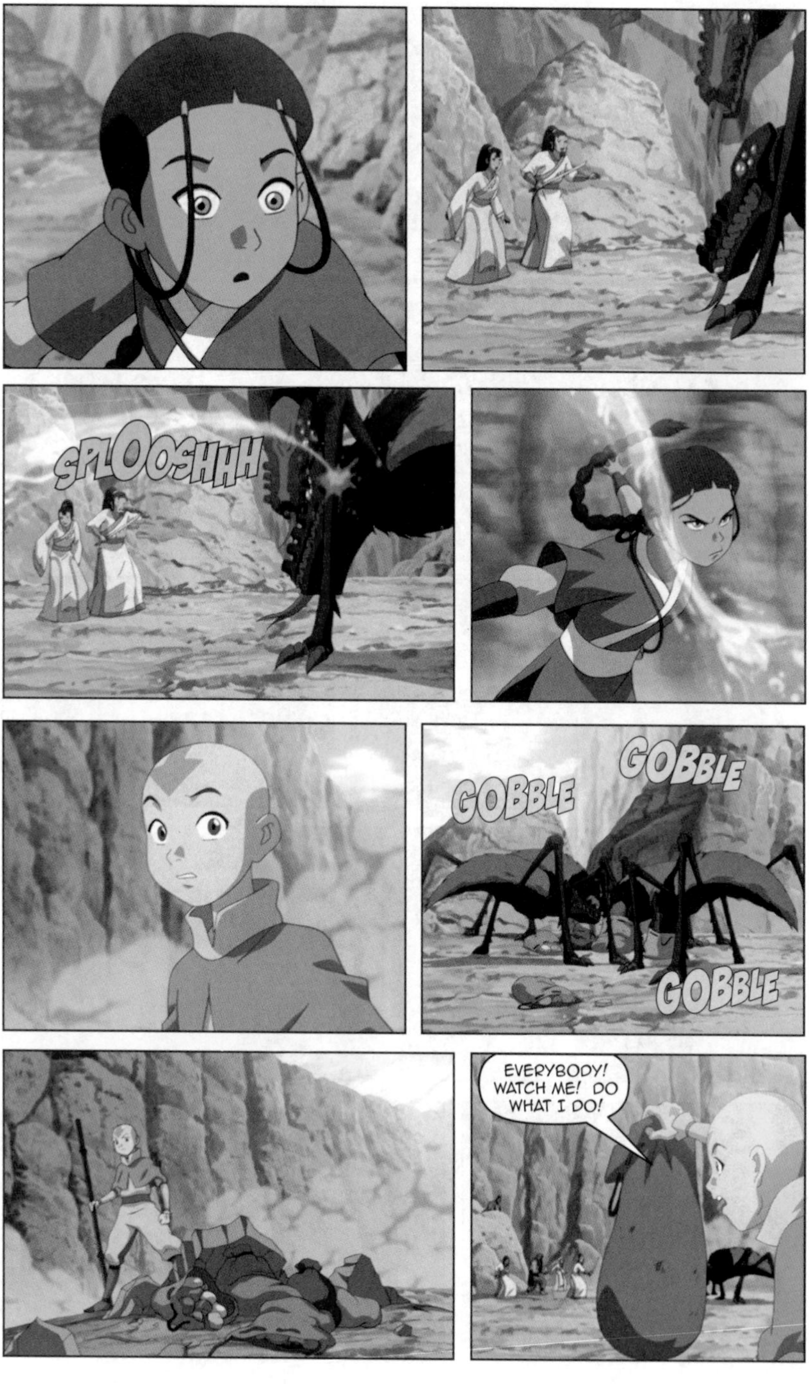
SPLOOSHHH
GOBBLE
GOBBLE
GOBBLE
EVERYBODY! WATCH ME! DO WHAT I DO!

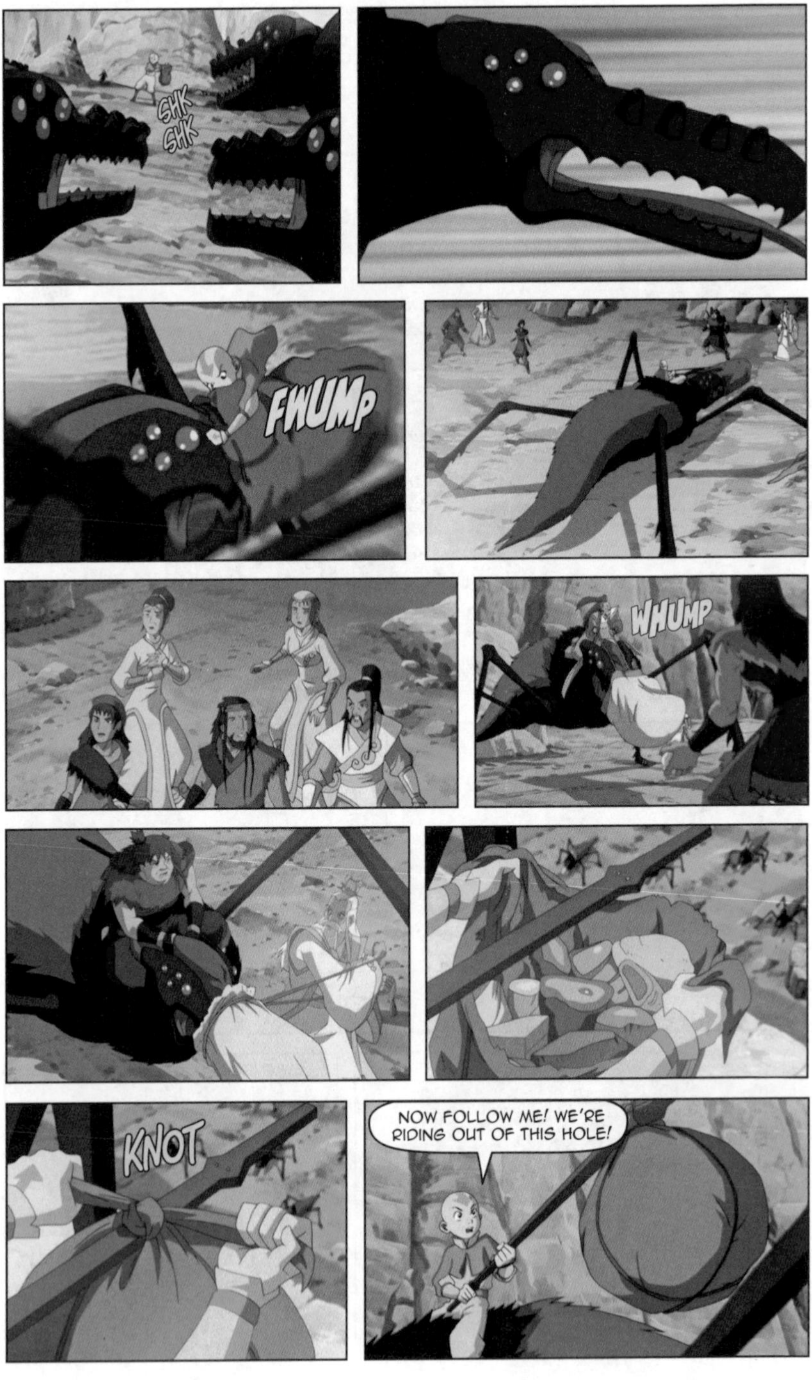
SHK
SHK
FWUMP
WHUMP
KNOT
NOW FOLLOW ME! WE'RE RIDING OUT OF THIS HOLE!

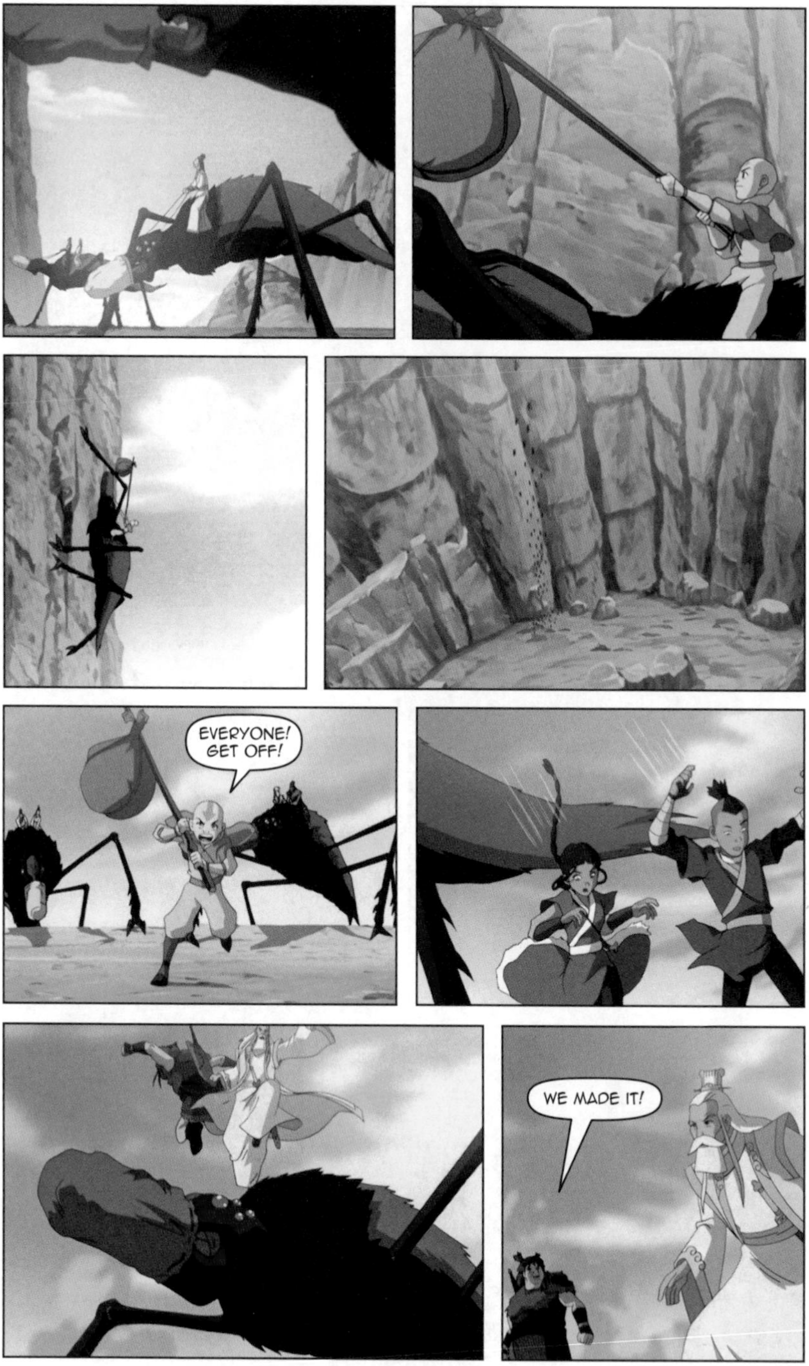
EVERYONE! GET OFF!
WE MADE IT!

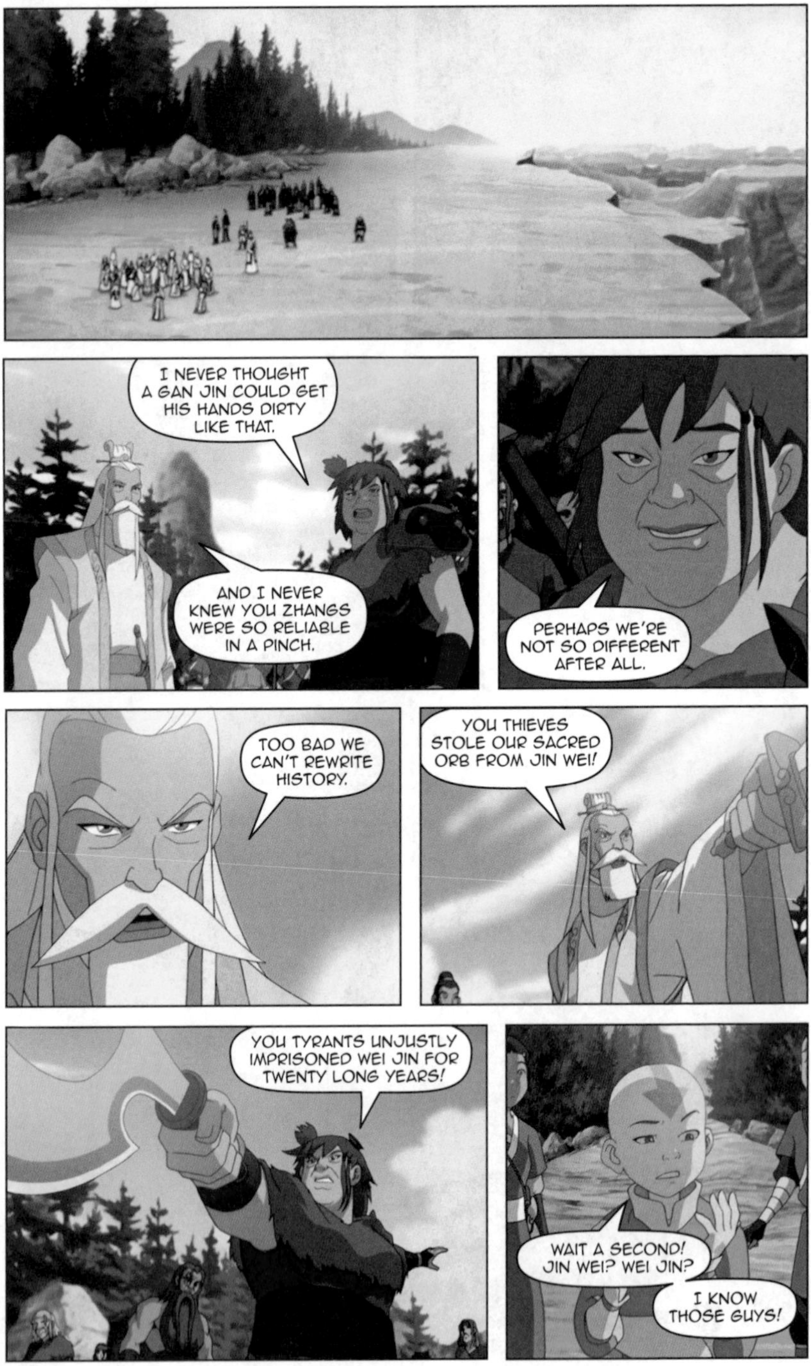
I NEVER THOUGHT A GAN JIN COULD GET HIS HANDS DIRTY LIKE THAT.
AND I NEVER KNEW YOU ZHANGS WERE SO RELIABLE IN A PINCH.
PERHAPS WE'RE NOT SO DIFFERENT AFTER ALL.
TOO BAD WE CAN'T REWRITE HISTORY.
YOU THIEVES STOLE OUR SACRED ORB FROM JIN WEI!
YOU TYRANTS UNJUSTLY IMPRISONED WEI JIN FOR TWENTY LONG YEARS!
WAIT A SECOND! JIN WEI? WEI JIN?
I KNOW THOSE GUYS!

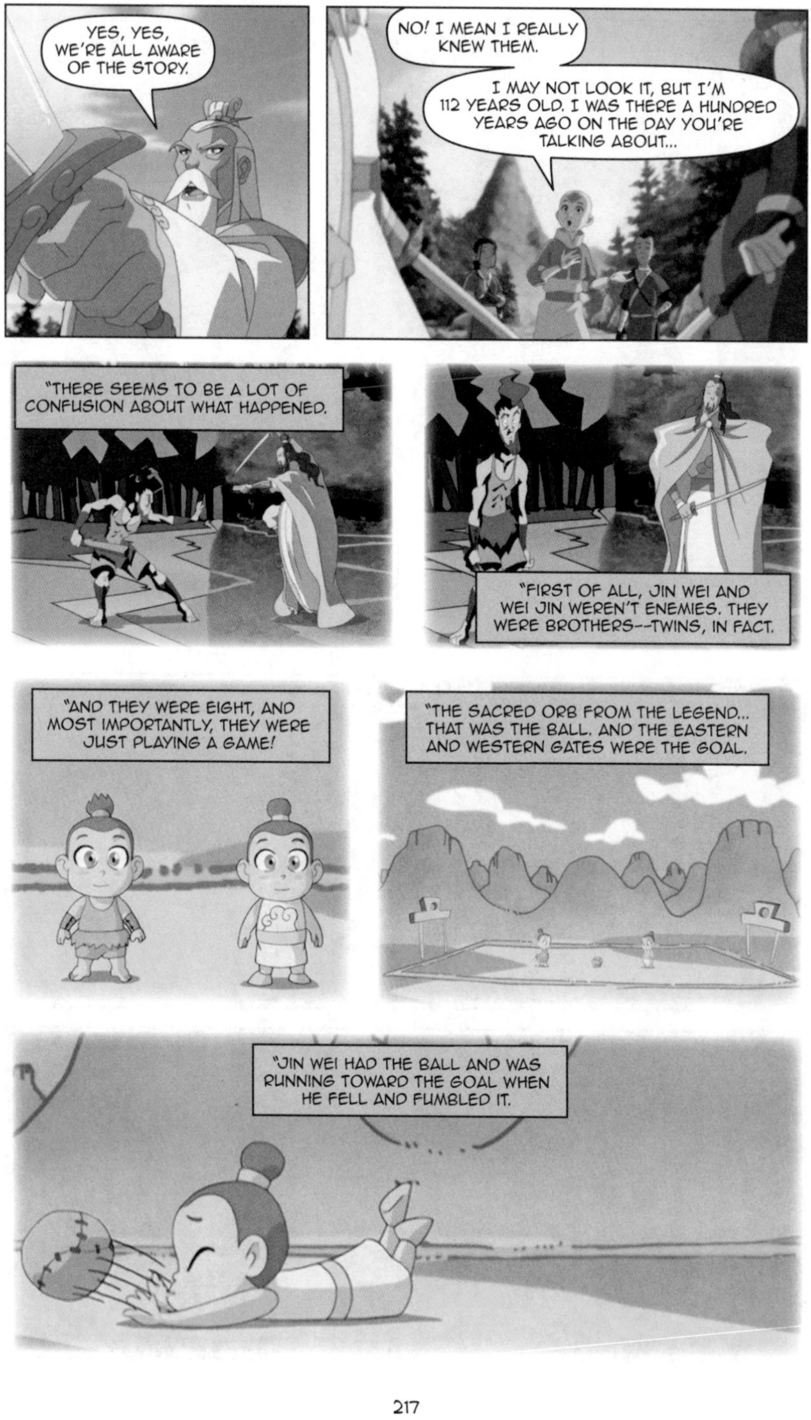
YES, YES, WE'RE ALL AWARE OF THE STORY.
NO! I MEAN I REALLY KNEW THEM.
I MAY NOT LOOK IT, BUT I'M 112 YEARS OLD. I WAS THERE A HUNDRED YEARS AGO ON THE DAY YOU'RE TALKING ABOUT...
"THERE SEEMS TO BE A LOT OF CONFUSION ABOUT WHAT HAPPENED.
"FIRST OF ALL, JIN WEI AND WEI JIN WEREN'T ENEMIES. THEY WERE BROTHERS--TWINS, IN FACT.
"AND THEY WERE EIGHT, AND MOST IMPORTANTLY, THEY WERE JUST PLAYING A GAME!
"THE SACRED ORB FROM THE LEGEND... THAT WAS THE BALL. AND THE EASTERN AND WESTERN GATES WERE THE GOAL.
"JIN WEI HAD THE BALL AND WAS RUNNING TOWARD THE GOAL WHEN HE FELL AND FUMBLED IT.

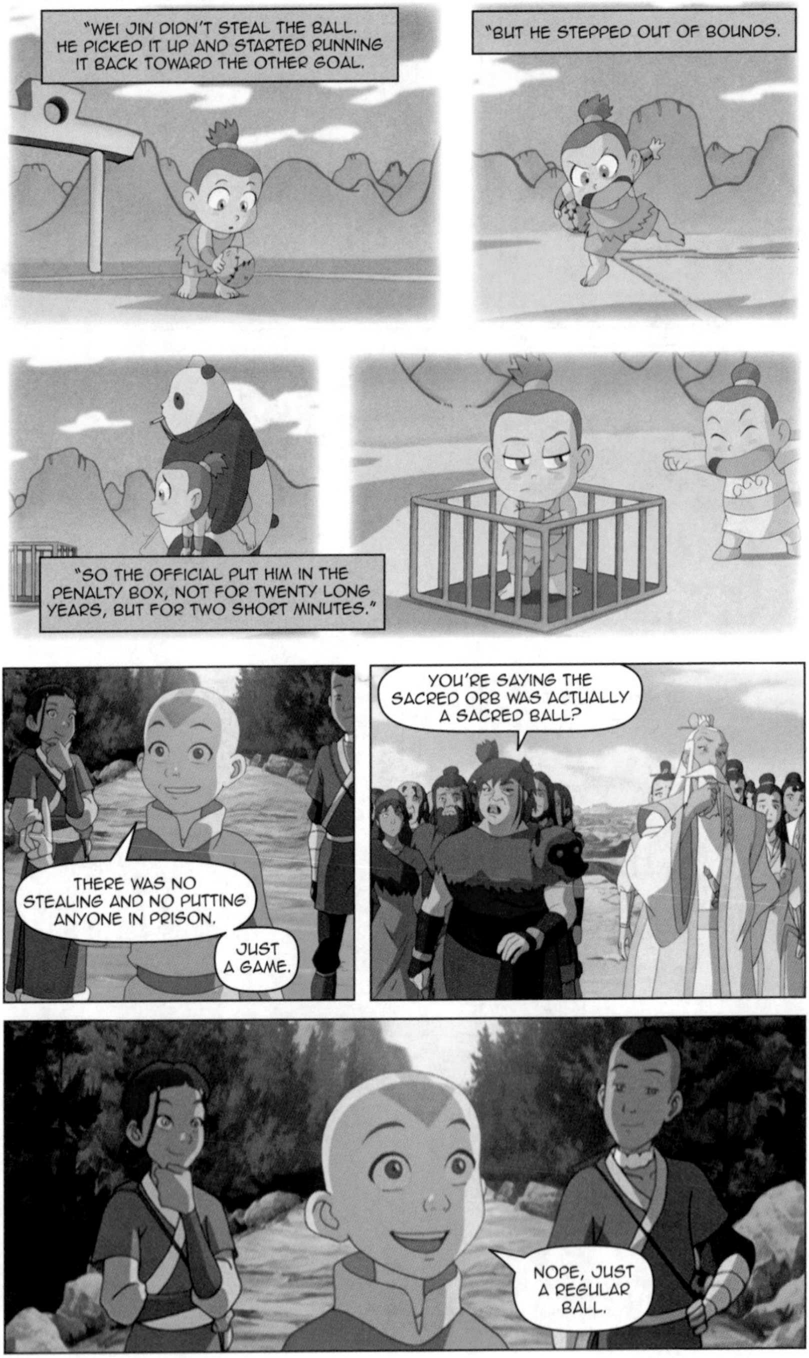
"WEI JIN DIDN'T STEAL THE BALL. HE PICKED IT UP AND STARTED RUNNING IT BACK TOWARD THE OTHER GOAL.
"BUT HE STEPPED OUT OF BOUNDS.
"SO THE OFFICIAL PUT HIM IN THE PENALTY BOX, NOT FOR TWENTY LONG YEARS, BUT FOR TWO SHORT MINUTES."
THERE WAS NO STEALING AND NO PUTTING ANYONE IN PRISON.
JUST A GAME.
YOU'RE SAYING THE SACRED ORB WAS ACTUALLY A SACRED BALL?
NOPE, JUST A REGULAR BALL.

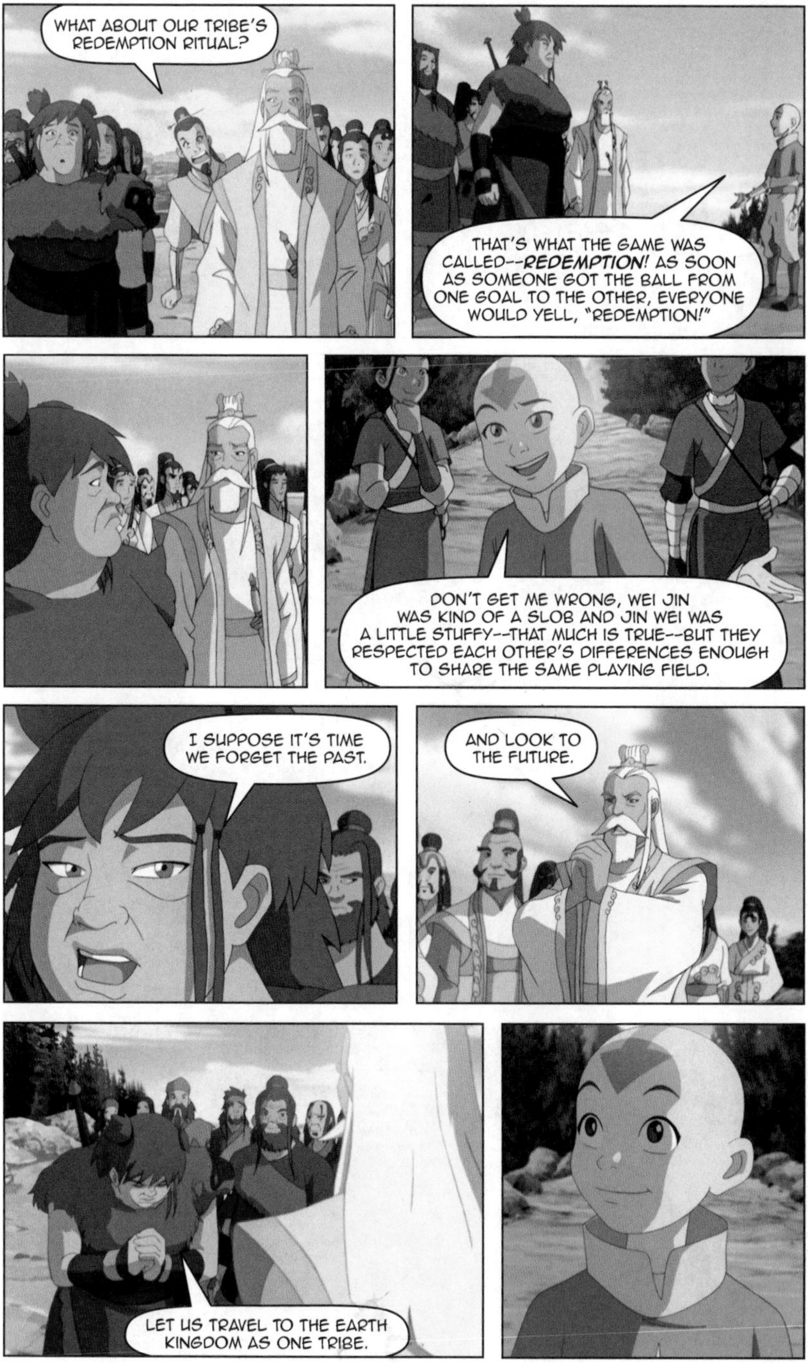
WHAT ABOUT OUR TRIBE'S REDEMPTION RITUAL?
THAT'S WHAT THE GAME WAS CALLED--*REDEMPTION!* AS SOON AS SOMEONE GOT THE BALL FROM ONE GOAL TO THE OTHER, EVERYONE WOULD YELL, "REDEMPTION!"
DON'T GET ME WRONG, WEI JIN WAS KIND OF A SLOB AND JIN WEI WAS A LITTLE STUFFY--THAT MUCH IS TRUE--BUT THEY RESPECTED EACH OTHER'S DIFFERENCES ENOUGH TO SHARE THE SAME PLAYING FIELD.
I SUPPOSE IT'S TIME WE FORGET THE PAST.
AND LOOK TO THE FUTURE.
LET US TRAVEL TO THE EARTH KINGDOM AS ONE TRIBE.

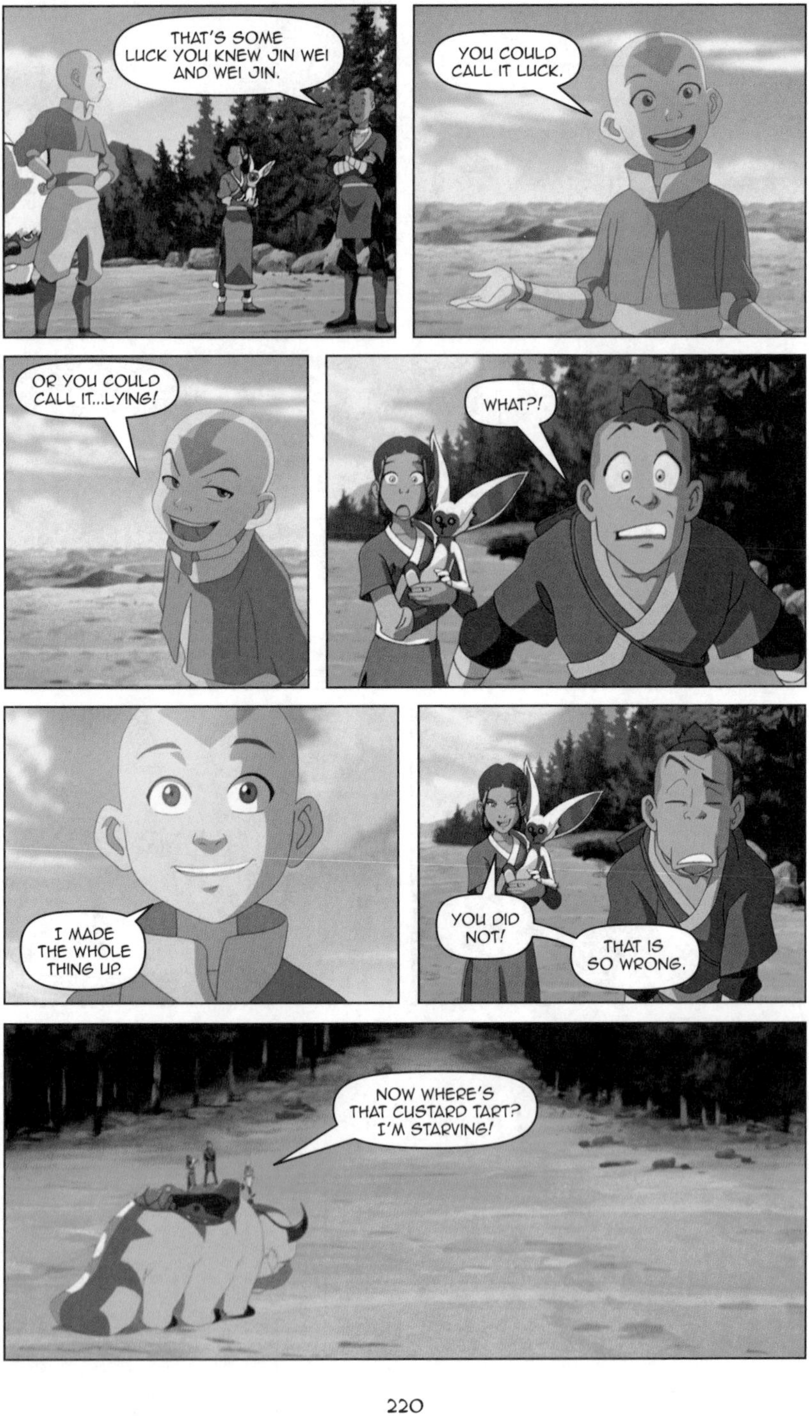

THAT'S SOME LUCK YOU KNEW JIN WEI AND WEI JIN.
YOU COULD CALL IT LUCK.
OR YOU COULD CALL IT...LYING!
WHAT?!
I MADE THE WHOLE THING UP.
YOU DID NOT!
THAT IS SO WRONG.
NOW WHERE'S THAT CUSTARD TART? I'M STARVING!

CHAPTER TWELVE

THE STORM

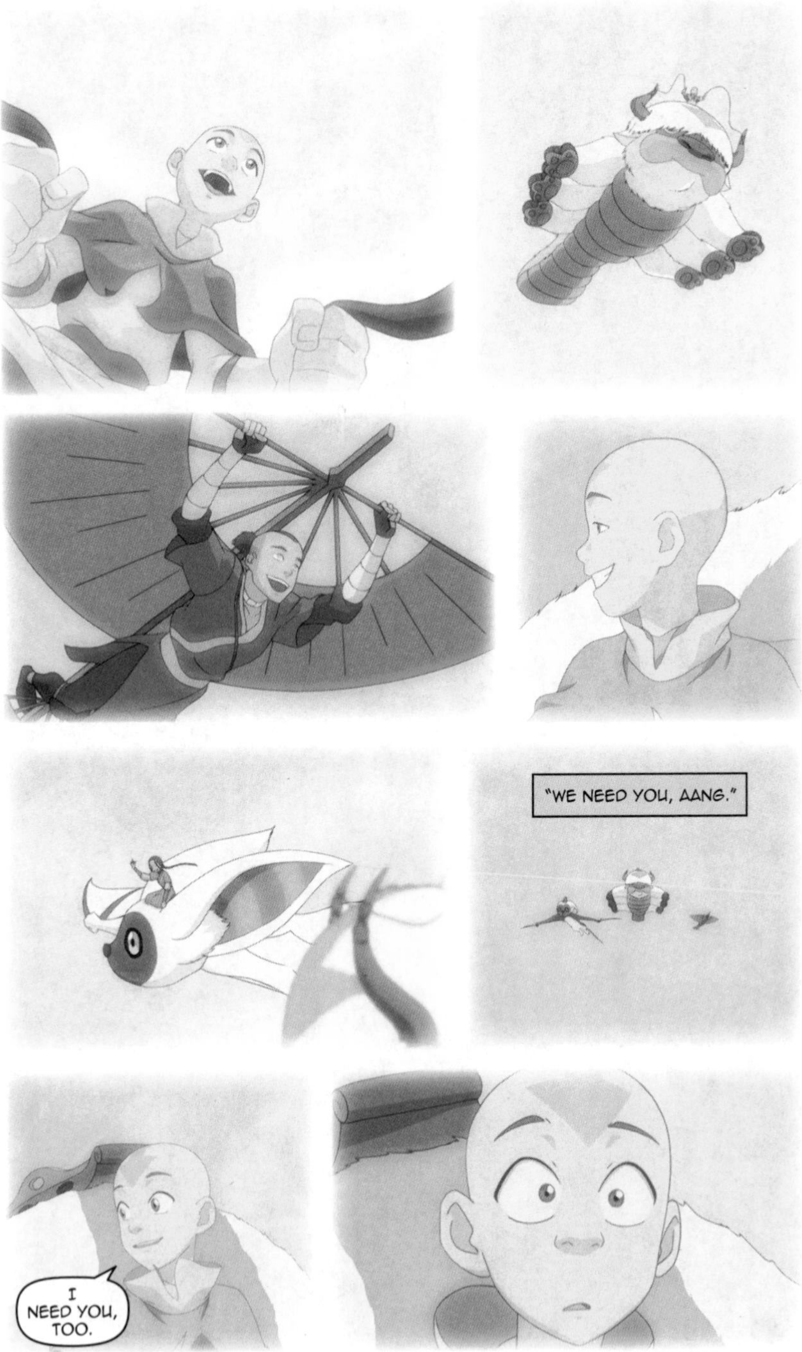
"WE NEED YOU, AANG."
I NEED YOU, TOO.

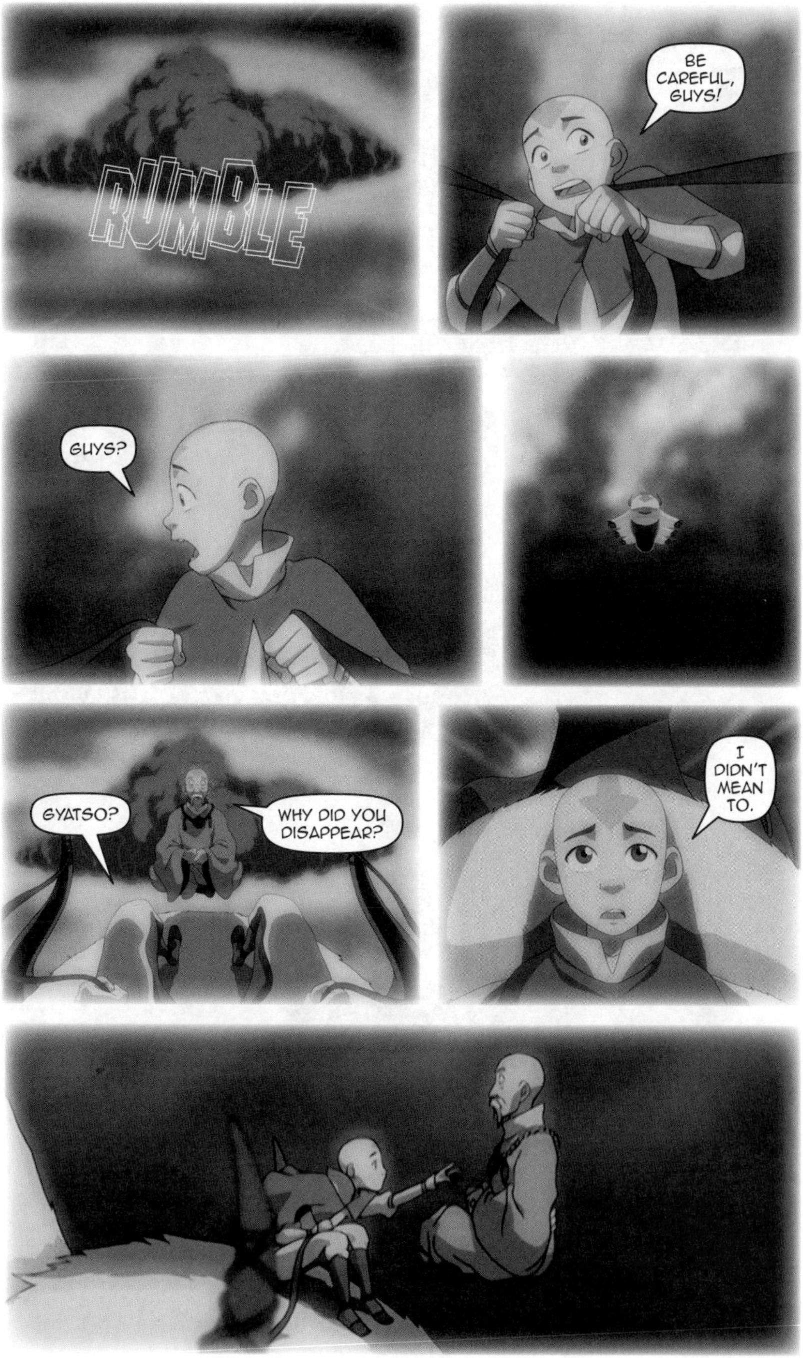
RUMBLE
BE CAREFUL, GUYS!
GUYS?
GYATSO?
WHY DID YOU DISAPPEAR?
I DIDN'T MEAN TO.

"WE NEED YOU, AANG."

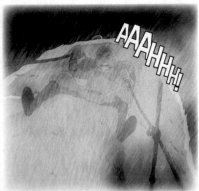

AAAHHH!

SPLASH

WE NEED YOU, AANG. WE NEED YOU.
WE NEED YOU, AANG. WE NEED YOU.

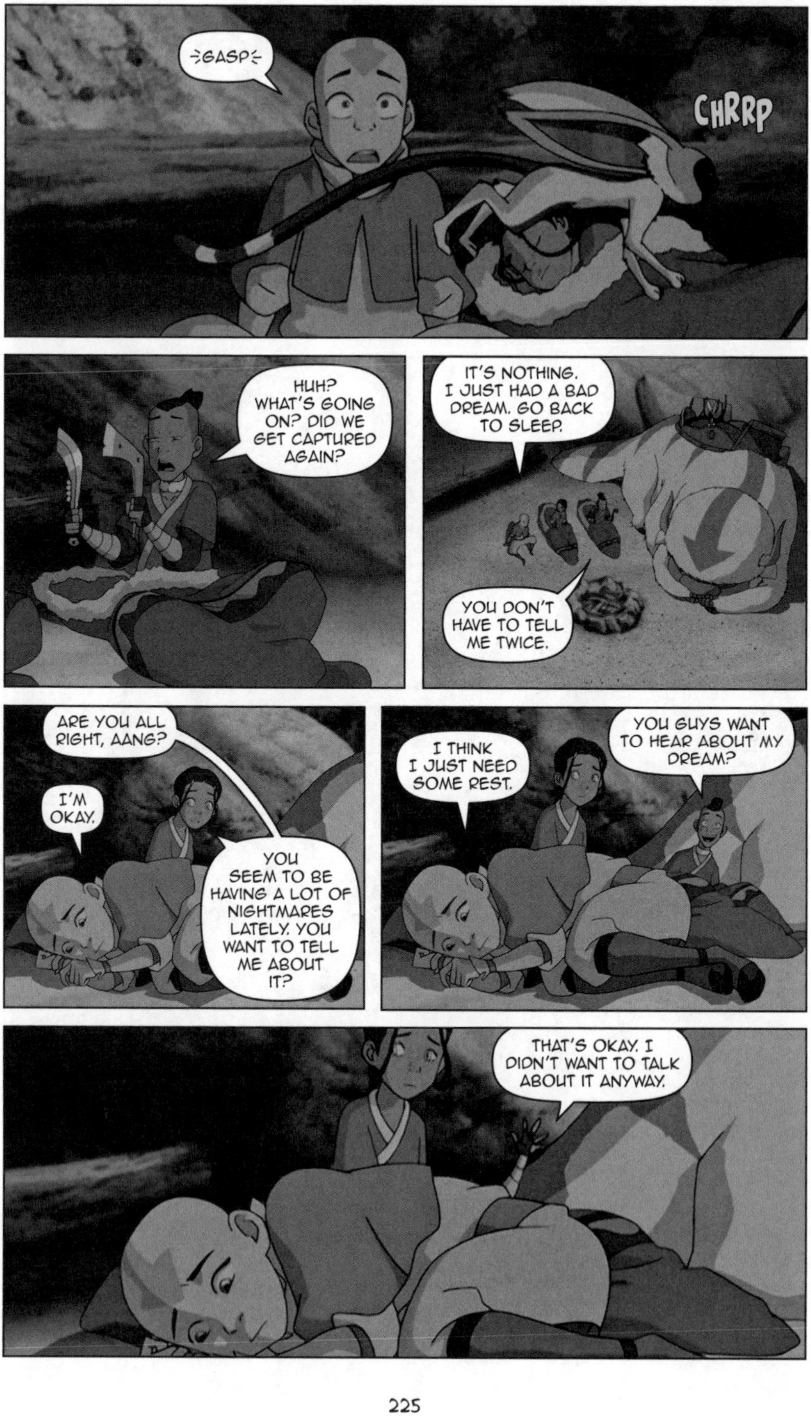
GASP
CHRRP
HUH? WHAT'S GOING ON? DID WE GET CAPTURED AGAIN?
IT'S NOTHING. I JUST HAD A BAD DREAM. GO BACK TO SLEEP.
YOU DON'T HAVE TO TELL ME TWICE.
ARE YOU ALL RIGHT, AANG?
I'M OKAY.
YOU SEEM TO BE HAVING A LOT OF NIGHTMARES LATELY. YOU WANT TO TELL ME ABOUT IT?
I THINK I JUST NEED SOME REST.
YOU GUYS WANT TO HEAR ABOUT MY DREAM?
THAT'S OKAY. I DIDN'T WANT TO TALK ABOUT IT ANYWAY.

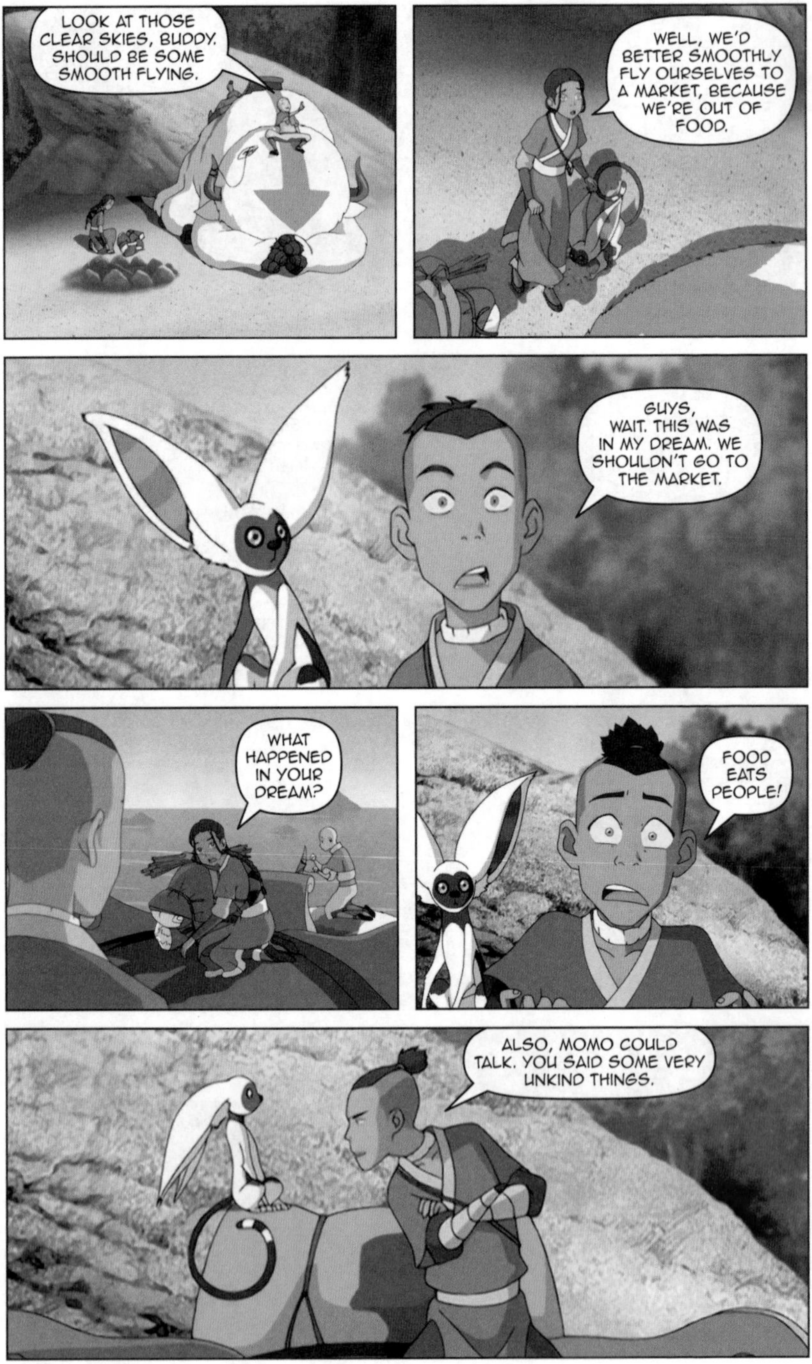
LOOK AT THOSE CLEAR SKIES, BUDDY. SHOULD BE SOME SMOOTH FLYING.
WELL, WE'D BETTER SMOOTHLY FLY OURSELVES TO A MARKET, BECAUSE WE'RE OUT OF FOOD.
GUYS, WAIT. THIS WAS IN MY DREAM. WE SHOULDN'T GO TO THE MARKET.
WHAT HAPPENED IN YOUR DREAM?
FOOD EATS PEOPLE!
ALSO, MOMO COULD TALK. YOU SAID SOME VERY UNKIND THINGS.

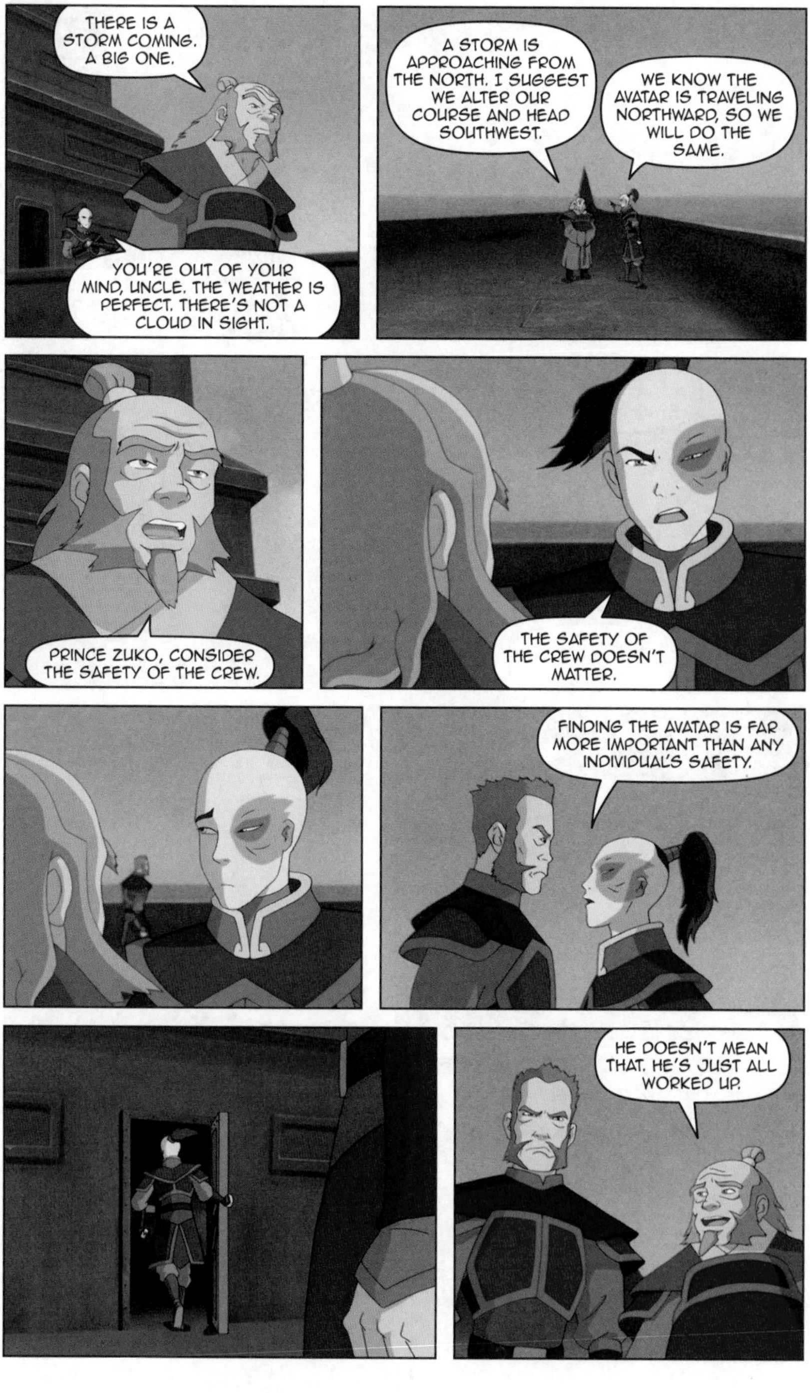
THERE IS A STORM COMING. A BIG ONE.
YOU'RE OUT OF YOUR MIND, UNCLE. THE WEATHER IS PERFECT. THERE'S NOT A CLOUD IN SIGHT.
A STORM IS APPROACHING FROM THE NORTH. I SUGGEST WE ALTER OUR COURSE AND HEAD SOUTHWEST.
WE KNOW THE AVATAR IS TRAVELING NORTHWARD, SO WE WILL DO THE SAME.
PRINCE ZUKO, CONSIDER THE SAFETY OF THE CREW.
THE SAFETY OF THE CREW DOESN'T MATTER.
FINDING THE AVATAR IS FAR MORE IMPORTANT THAN ANY INDIVIDUAL'S SAFETY.
HE DOESN'T MEAN THAT. HE'S JUST ALL WORKED UP.

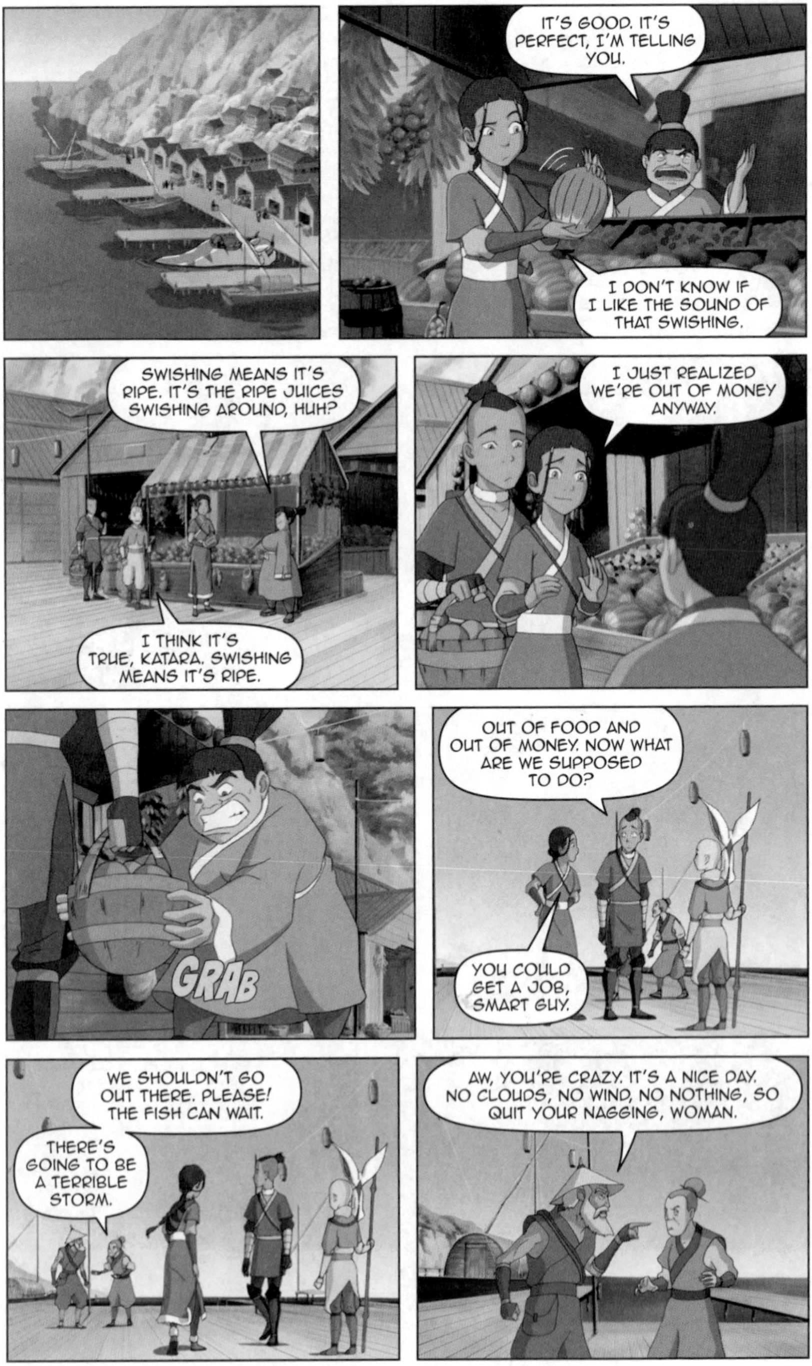
IT'S GOOD. IT'S PERFECT, I'M TELLING YOU.
I DON'T KNOW IF I LIKE THE SOUND OF THAT SWISHING.
SWISHING MEANS IT'S RIPE. IT'S THE RIPE JUICES SWISHING AROUND, HUH?
I THINK IT'S TRUE, KATARA. SWISHING MEANS IT'S RIPE.
I JUST REALIZED WE'RE OUT OF MONEY ANYWAY.
GRAB
OUT OF FOOD AND OUT OF MONEY. NOW WHAT ARE WE SUPPOSED TO DO?
YOU COULD GET A JOB, SMART GUY.
WE SHOULDN'T GO OUT THERE. PLEASE! THE FISH CAN WAIT.
THERE'S GOING TO BE A TERRIBLE STORM.
AW, YOU'RE CRAZY. IT'S A NICE DAY. NO CLOUDS, NO WIND, NO NOTHING, SO QUIT YOUR NAGGING, WOMAN.

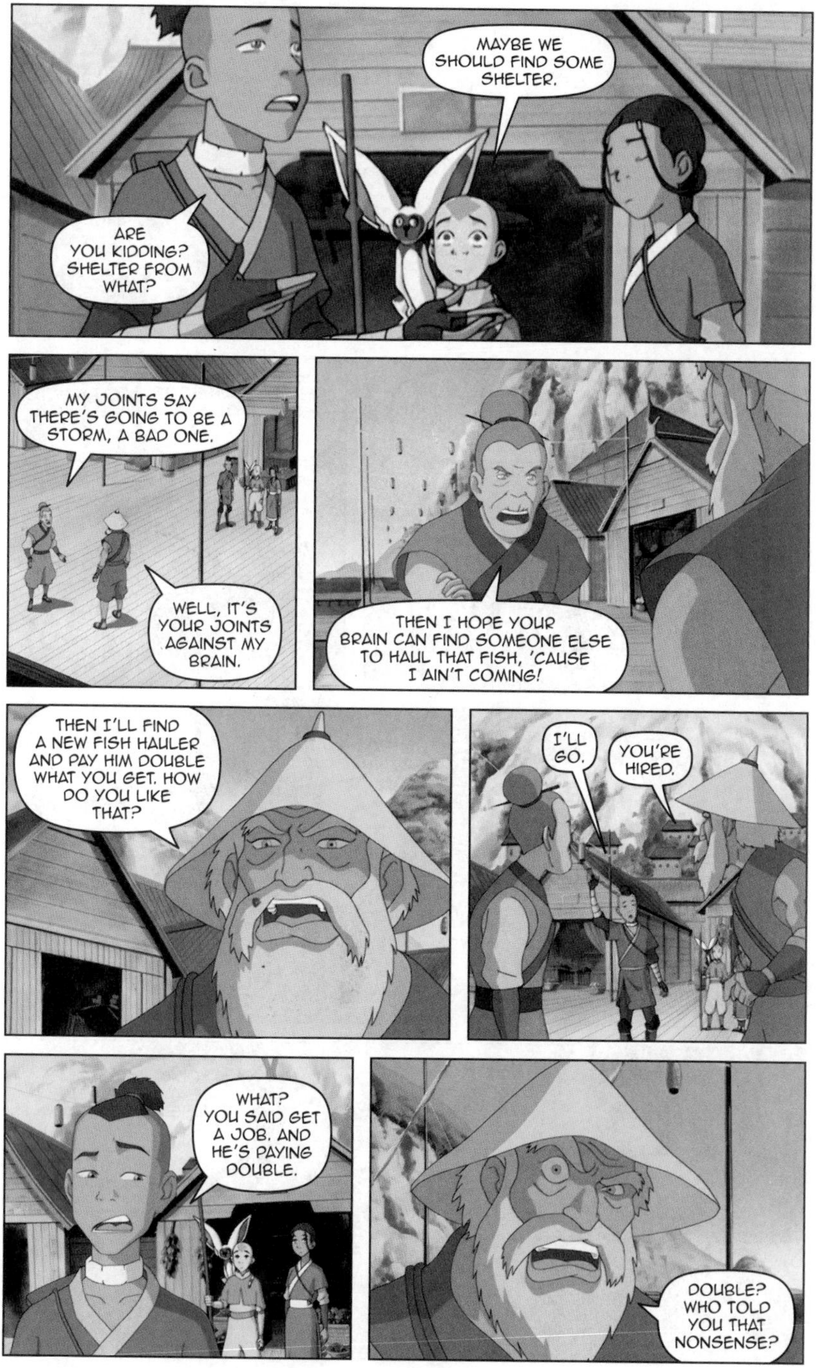

MAYBE WE SHOULD FIND SOME SHELTER.
ARE YOU KIDDING? SHELTER FROM WHAT?
MY JOINTS SAY THERE'S GOING TO BE A STORM, A BAD ONE.
WELL, IT'S YOUR JOINTS AGAINST MY BRAIN.
THEN I HOPE YOUR BRAIN CAN FIND SOMEONE ELSE TO HAUL THAT FISH, 'CAUSE I AIN'T COMING!
THEN I'LL FIND A NEW FISH HAULER AND PAY HIM DOUBLE WHAT YOU GET. HOW DO YOU LIKE THAT?
I'LL GO.
YOU'RE HIRED.
WHAT? YOU SAID GET A JOB. AND HE'S PAYING DOUBLE.
DOUBLE? WHO TOLD YOU THAT NONSENSE?

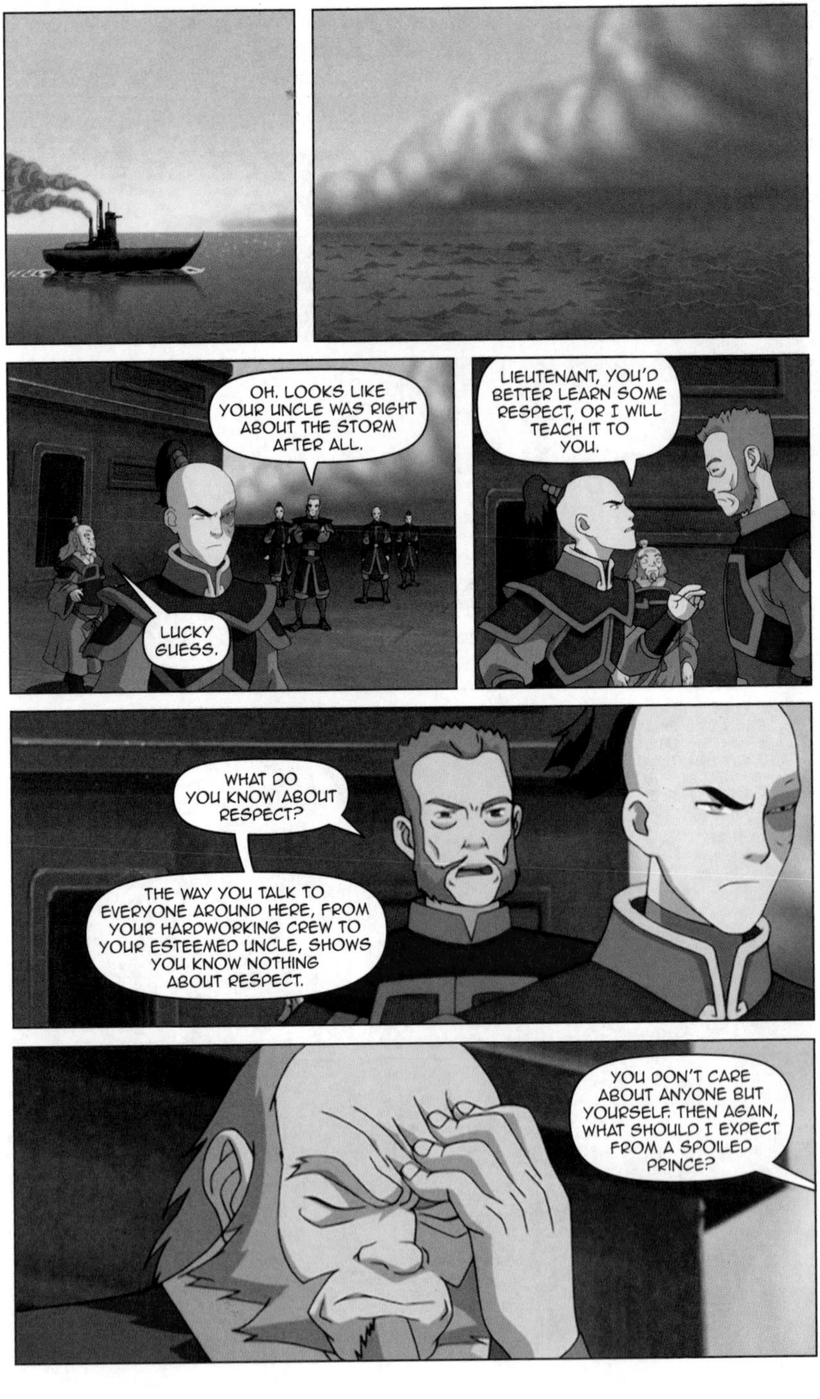

OH. LOOKS LIKE YOUR UNCLE WAS RIGHT ABOUT THE STORM AFTER ALL.
LUCKY GUESS.
LIEUTENANT, YOU'D BETTER LEARN SOME RESPECT, OR I WILL TEACH IT TO YOU.
WHAT DO YOU KNOW ABOUT RESPECT?
THE WAY YOU TALK TO EVERYONE AROUND HERE, FROM YOUR HARDWORKING CREW TO YOUR ESTEEMED UNCLE, SHOWS YOU KNOW NOTHING ABOUT RESPECT.
YOU DON'T CARE ABOUT ANYONE BUT YOURSELF. THEN AGAIN, WHAT SHOULD I EXPECT FROM A SPOILED PRINCE?

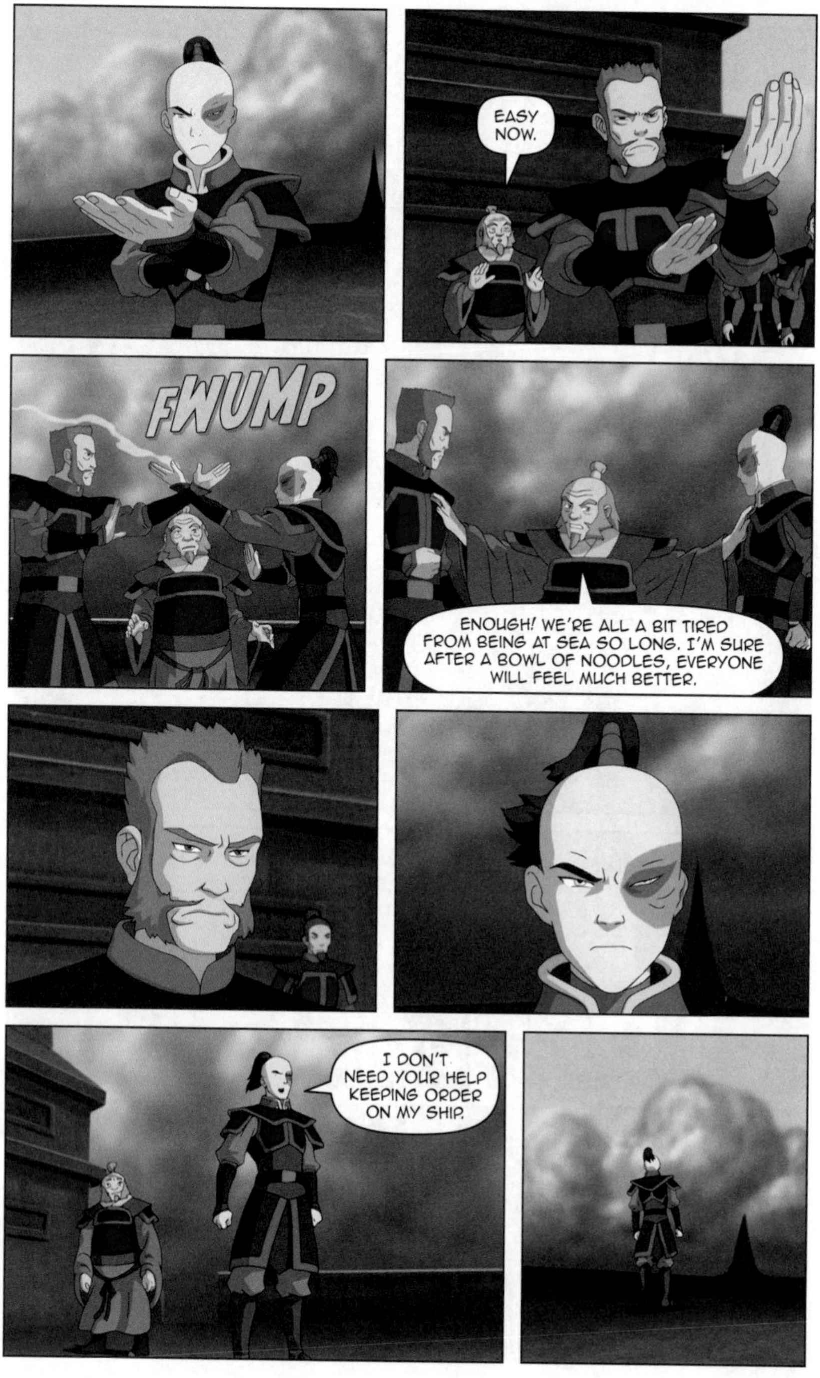

EASY NOW.
FWUMP
ENOUGH! WE'RE ALL A BIT TIRED FROM BEING AT SEA SO LONG. I'M SURE AFTER A BOWL OF NOODLES, EVERYONE WILL FEEL MUCH BETTER.
I DON'T NEED YOUR HELP KEEPING ORDER ON MY SHIP.

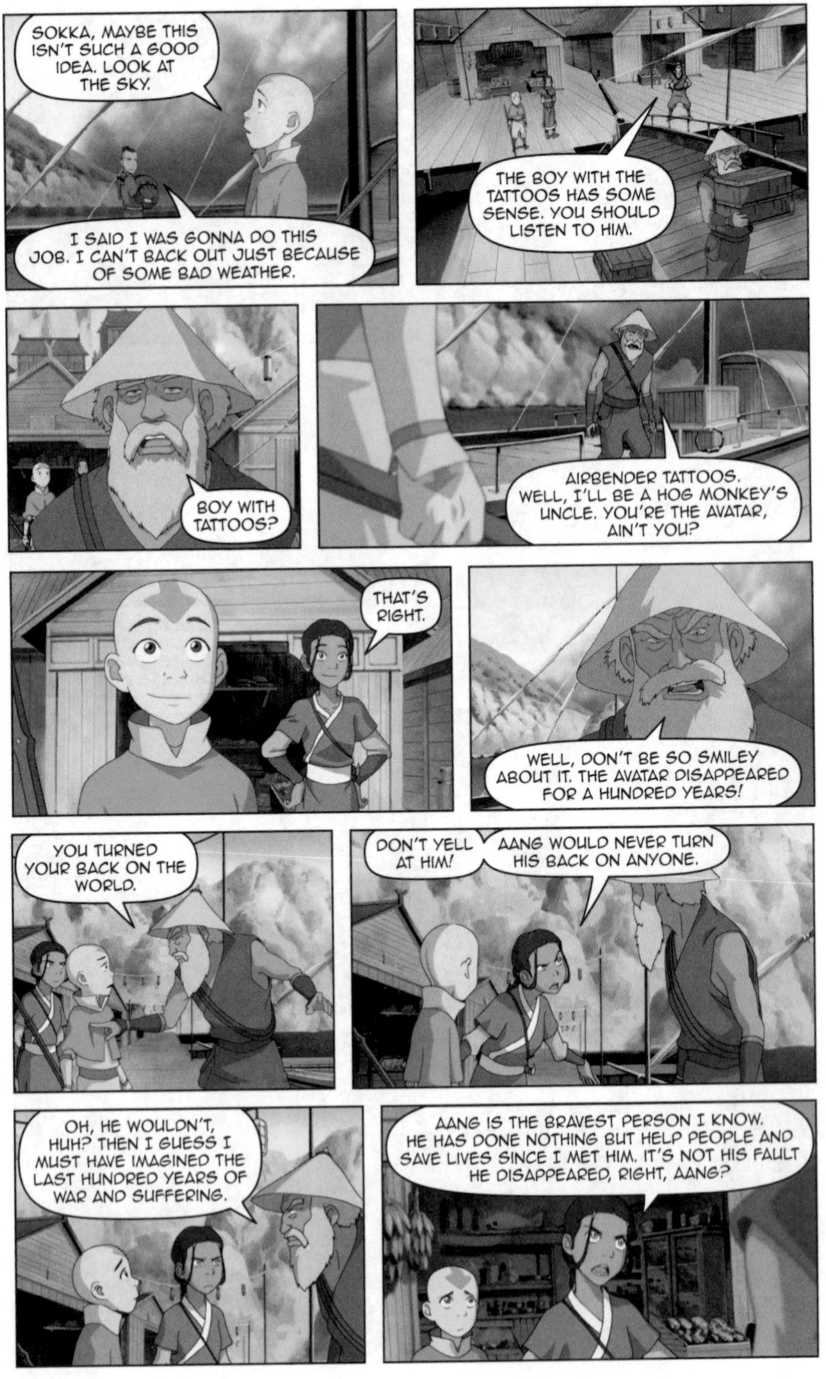
SOKKA, MAYBE THIS ISN'T SUCH A GOOD IDEA. LOOK AT THE SKY.
I SAID I WAS GONNA DO THIS JOB. I CAN'T BACK OUT JUST BECAUSE OF SOME BAD WEATHER.
THE BOY WITH THE TATTOOS HAS SOME SENSE. YOU SHOULD LISTEN TO HIM.
BOY WITH TATTOOS?
AIRBENDER TATTOOS. WELL, I'LL BE A HOG MONKEY'S UNCLE. YOU'RE THE AVATAR, AIN'T YOU?
THAT'S RIGHT.
WELL, DON'T BE SO SMILEY ABOUT IT. THE AVATAR DISAPPEARED FOR A HUNDRED YEARS!
YOU TURNED YOUR BACK ON THE WORLD.
DON'T YELL AT HIM!
AANG WOULD NEVER TURN HIS BACK ON ANYONE.
OH, HE WOULDN'T, HUH? THEN I GUESS I MUST HAVE IMAGINED THE LAST HUNDRED YEARS OF WAR AND SUFFERING.
AANG IS THE BRAVEST PERSON I KNOW. HE HAS DONE NOTHING BUT HELP PEOPLE AND SAVE LIVES SINCE I MET HIM. IT'S NOT HIS FAULT HE DISAPPEARED, RIGHT, AANG?

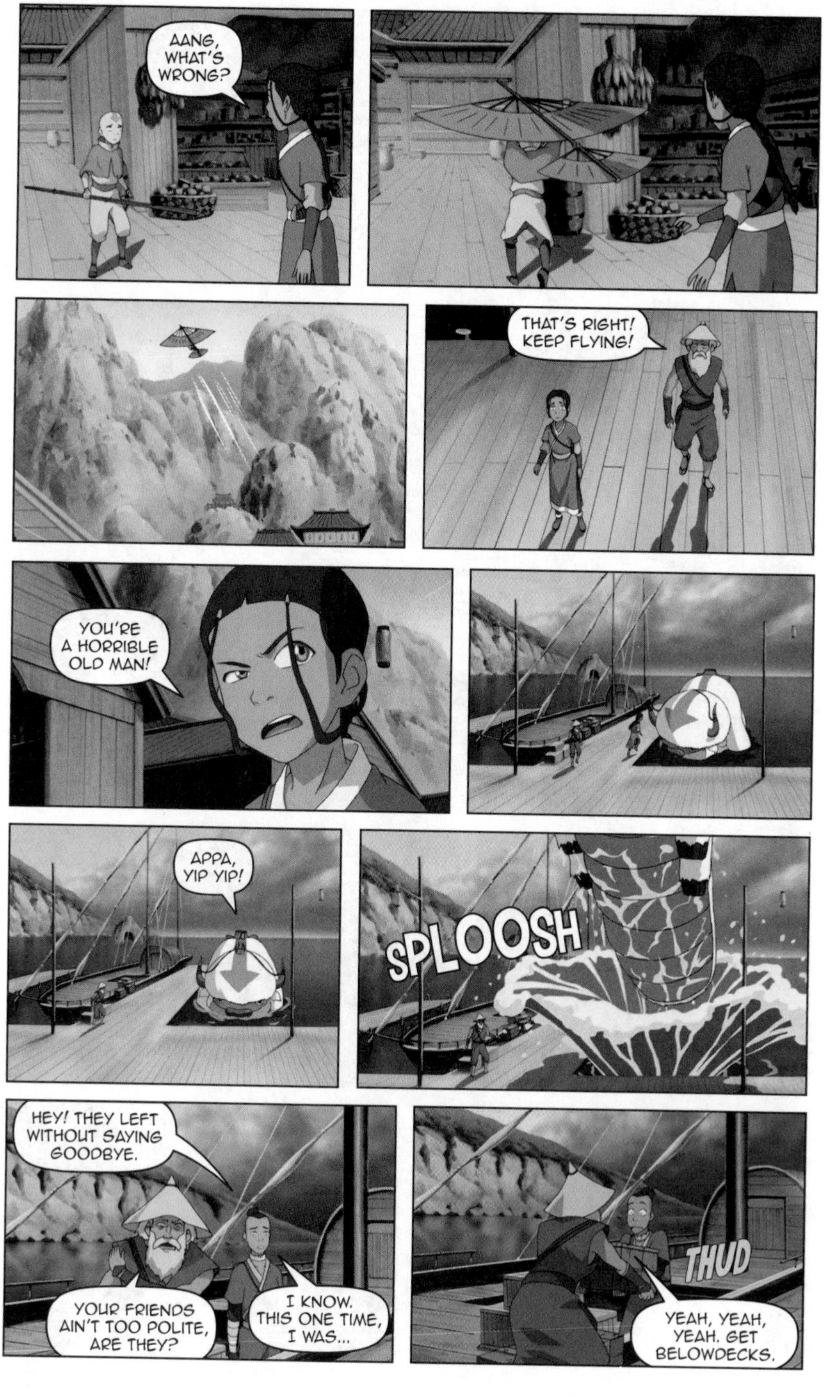

AANG, WHAT'S WRONG?
THAT'S RIGHT! KEEP FLYING!
YOU'RE A HORRIBLE OLD MAN!
APPA, YIP YIP!
SPLOOSH
HEY! THEY LEFT WITHOUT SAYING GOODBYE.
YOUR FRIENDS AIN'T TOO POLITE, ARE THEY?
I KNOW. THIS ONE TIME, I WAS...
THUD
YEAH, YEAH, YEAH. GET BELOWDECKS.

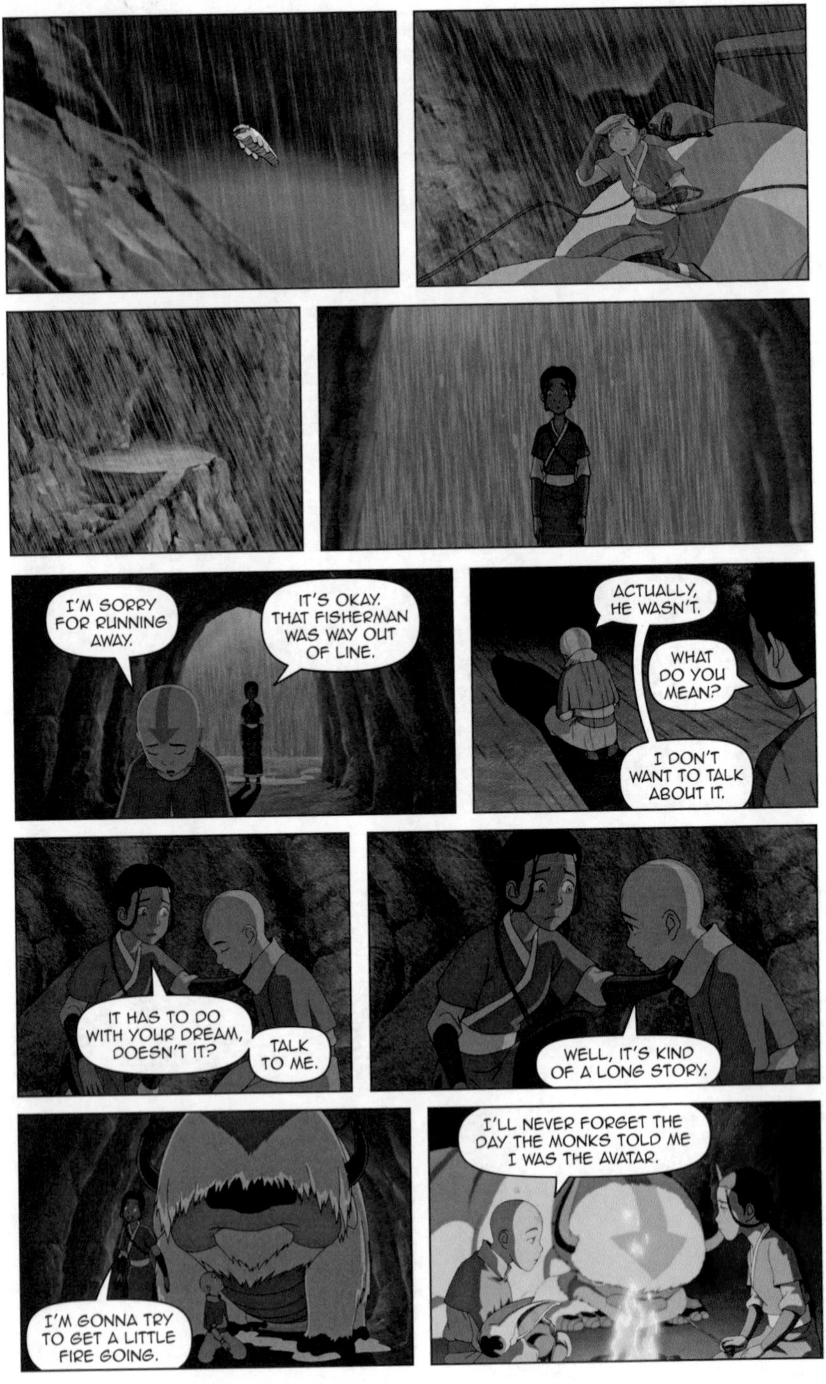
I'M SORRY FOR RUNNING AWAY.
IT'S OKAY. THAT FISHERMAN WAS WAY OUT OF LINE.
ACTUALLY, HE WASN'T.
WHAT DO YOU MEAN?
I DON'T WANT TO TALK ABOUT IT.
IT HAS TO DO WITH YOUR DREAM, DOESN'T IT?
TALK TO ME.
WELL, IT'S KIND OF A LONG STORY.
I'M GONNA TRY TO GET A LITTLE FIRE GOING.
I'LL NEVER FORGET THE DAY THE MONKS TOLD ME I WAS THE AVATAR.

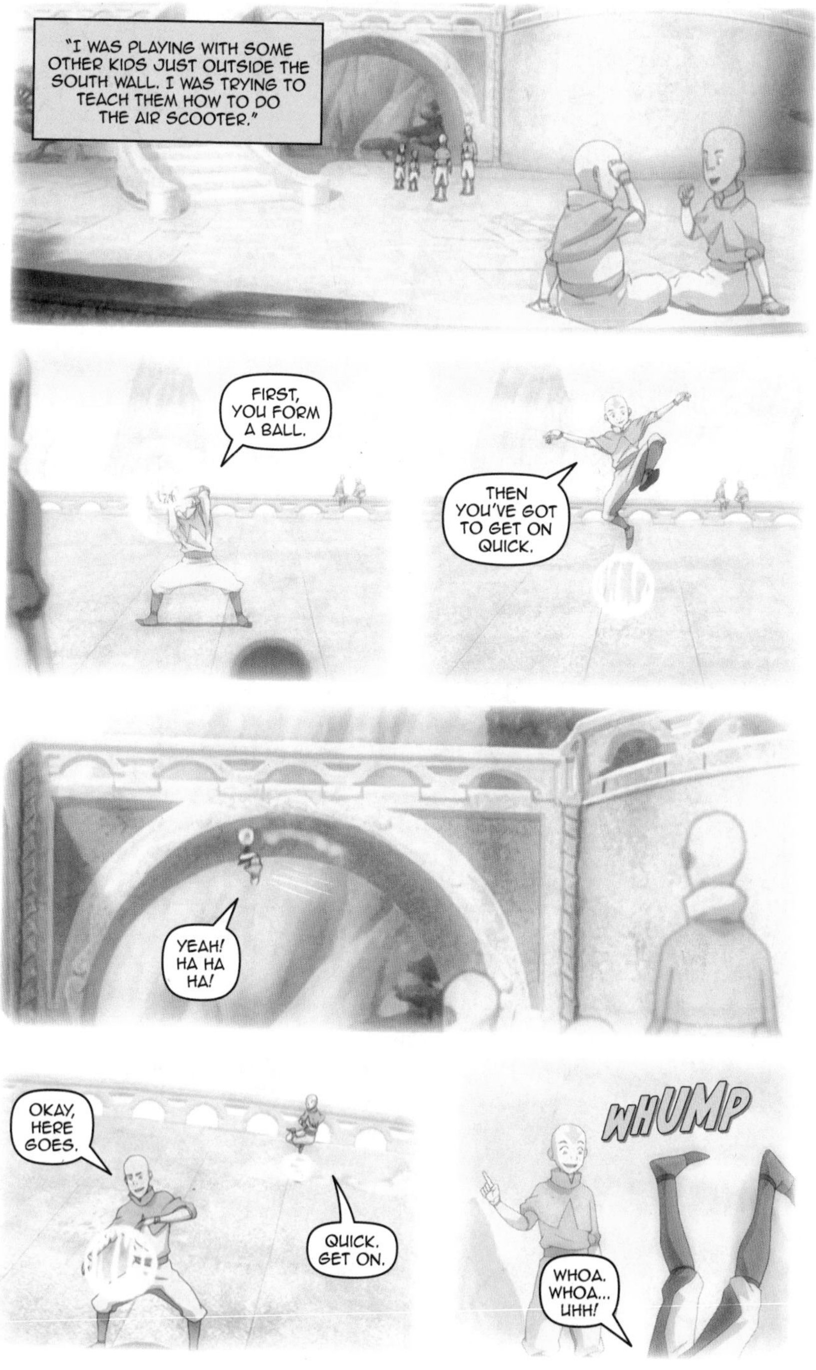
"I WAS PLAYING WITH SOME OTHER KIDS JUST OUTSIDE THE SOUTH WALL. I WAS TRYING TO TEACH THEM HOW TO DO THE AIR SCOOTER."
FIRST, YOU FORM A BALL.
THEN YOU'VE GOT TO GET ON QUICK.
YEAH! HA HA HA!
OKAY, HERE GOES.
QUICK. GET ON.
WHUMP
WHOA. WHOA... UHH!

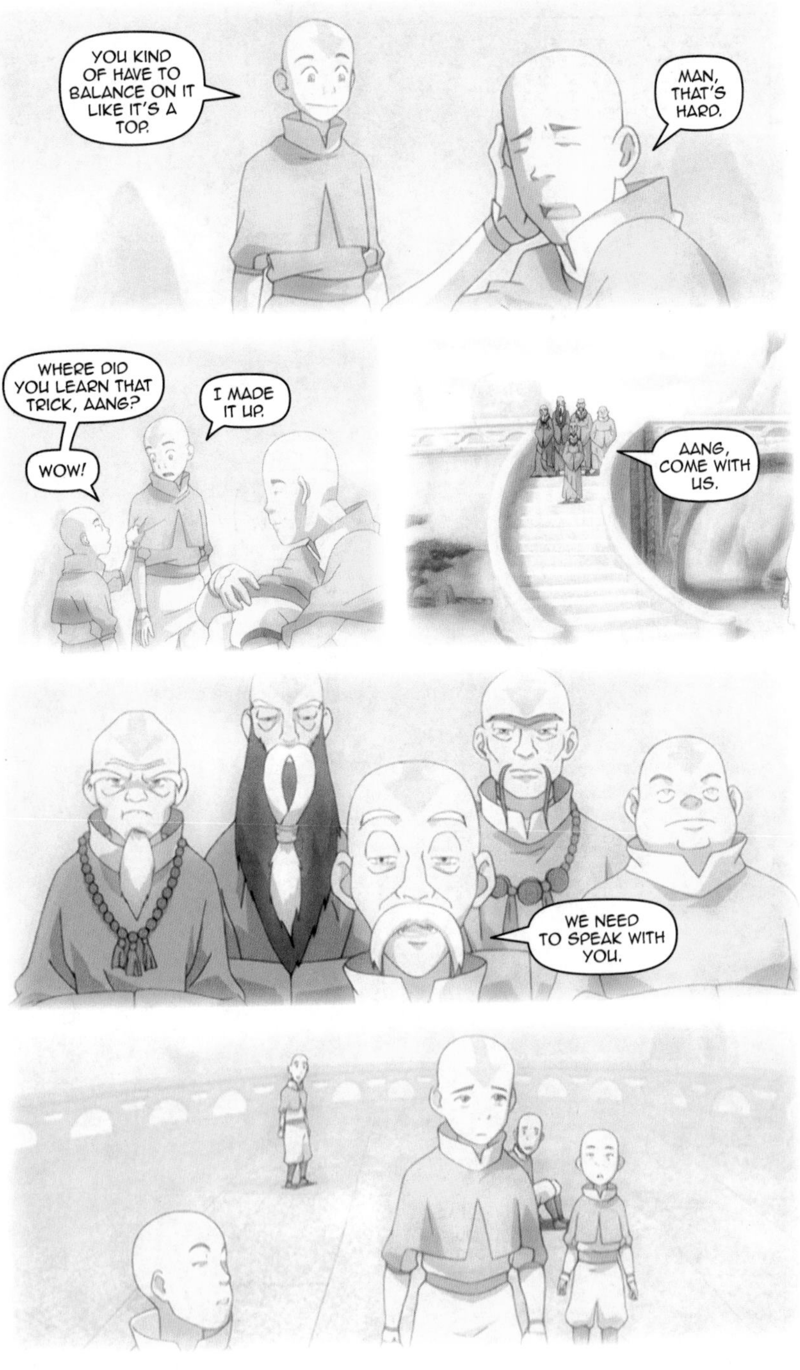
YOU KIND OF HAVE TO BALANCE ON IT LIKE IT'S A TOP.
MAN, THAT'S HARD.
WHERE DID YOU LEARN THAT TRICK, AANG?
I MADE IT UP.
WOW!
AANG, COME WITH US.
WE NEED TO SPEAK WITH YOU.

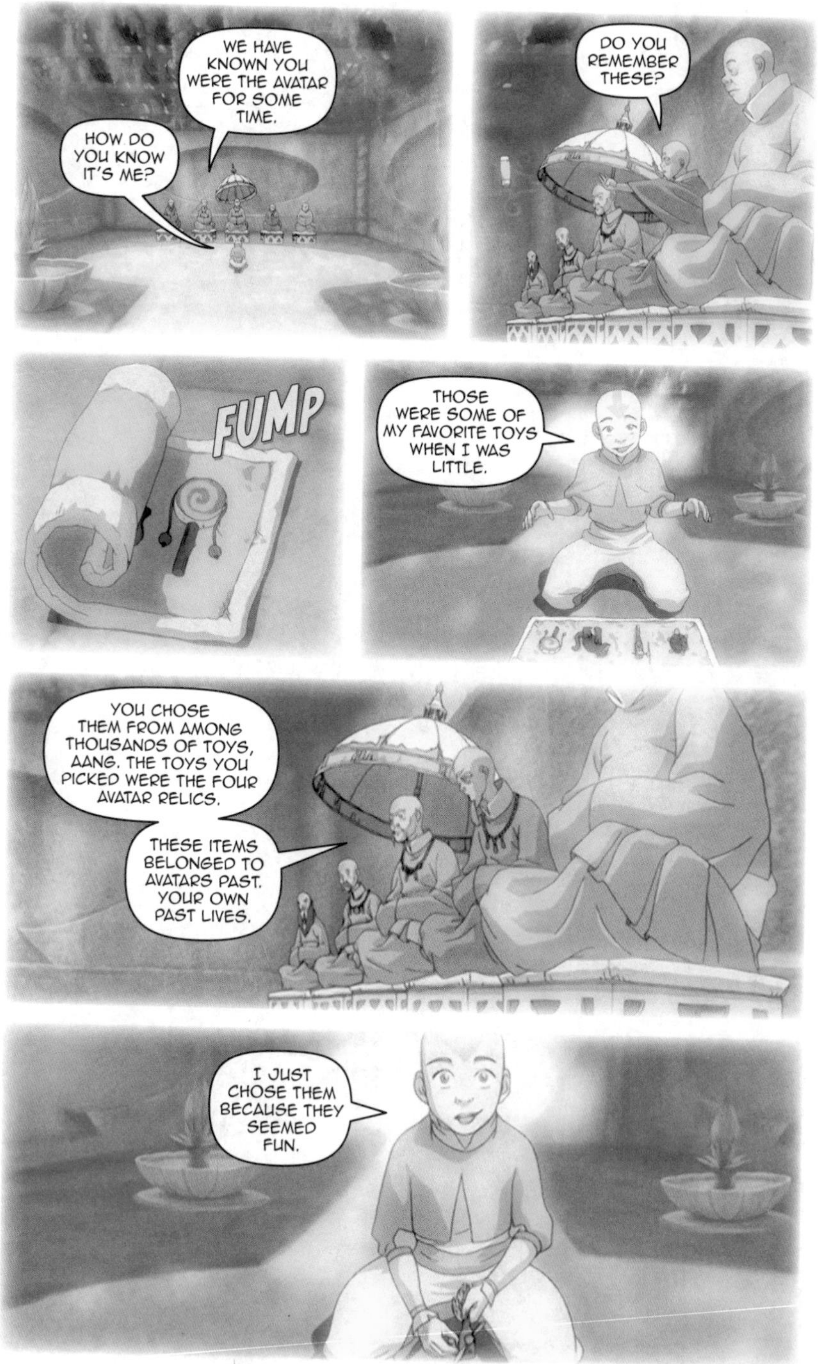
HOW DO YOU KNOW IT'S ME?
WE HAVE KNOWN YOU WERE THE AVATAR FOR SOME TIME.
DO YOU REMEMBER THESE?
FUMP
THOSE WERE SOME OF MY FAVORITE TOYS WHEN I WAS LITTLE.
YOU CHOSE THEM FROM AMONG THOUSANDS OF TOYS, AANG. THE TOYS YOU PICKED WERE THE FOUR AVATAR RELICS.
THESE ITEMS BELONGED TO AVATARS PAST. YOUR OWN PAST LIVES.
I JUST CHOSE THEM BECAUSE THEY SEEMED FUN.

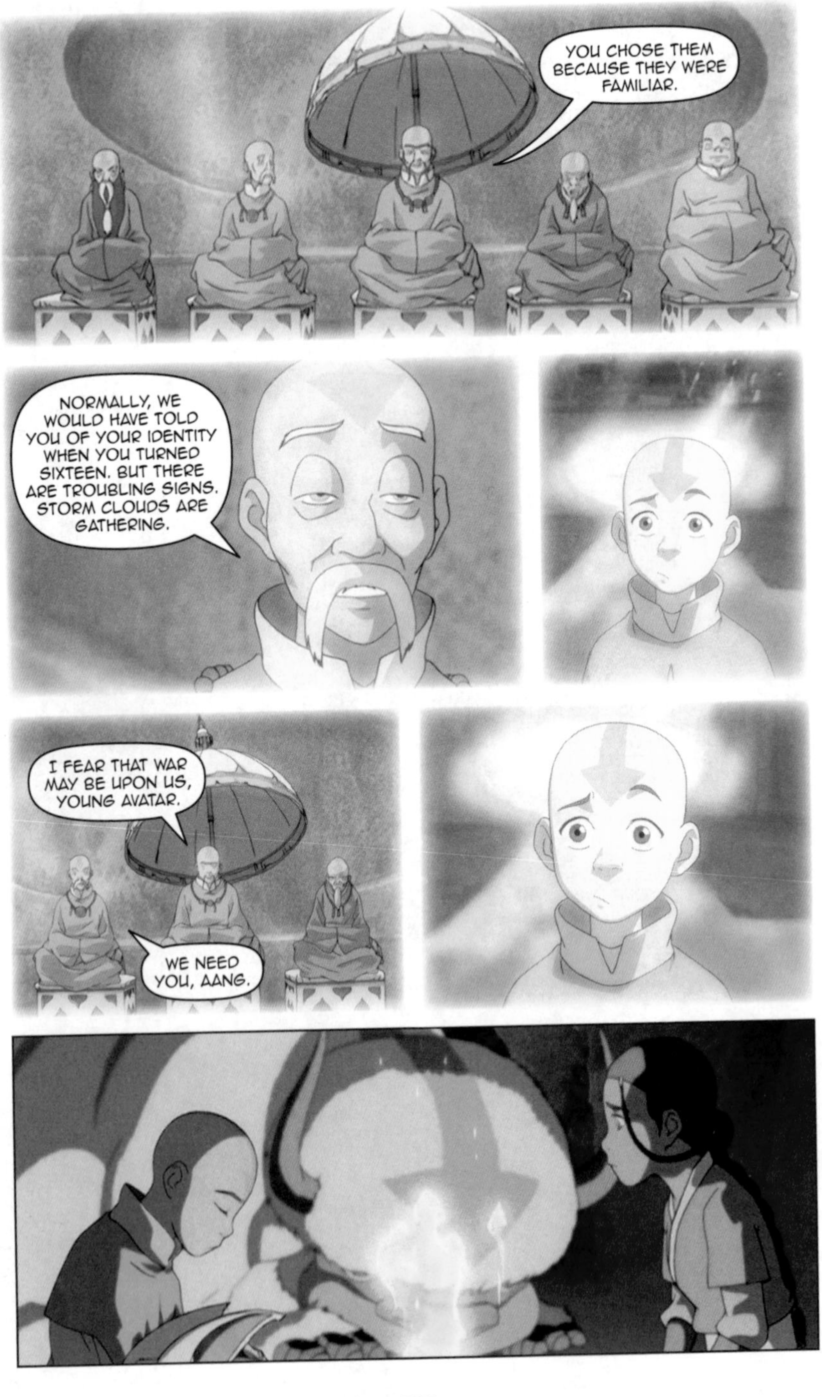
YOU CHOSE THEM BECAUSE THEY WERE FAMILIAR.
NORMALLY, WE WOULD HAVE TOLD YOU OF YOUR IDENTITY WHEN YOU TURNED SIXTEEN. BUT THERE ARE TROUBLING SIGNS. STORM CLOUDS ARE GATHERING.
I FEAR THAT WAR MAY BE UPON US, YOUNG AVATAR.
WE NEED YOU, AANG.

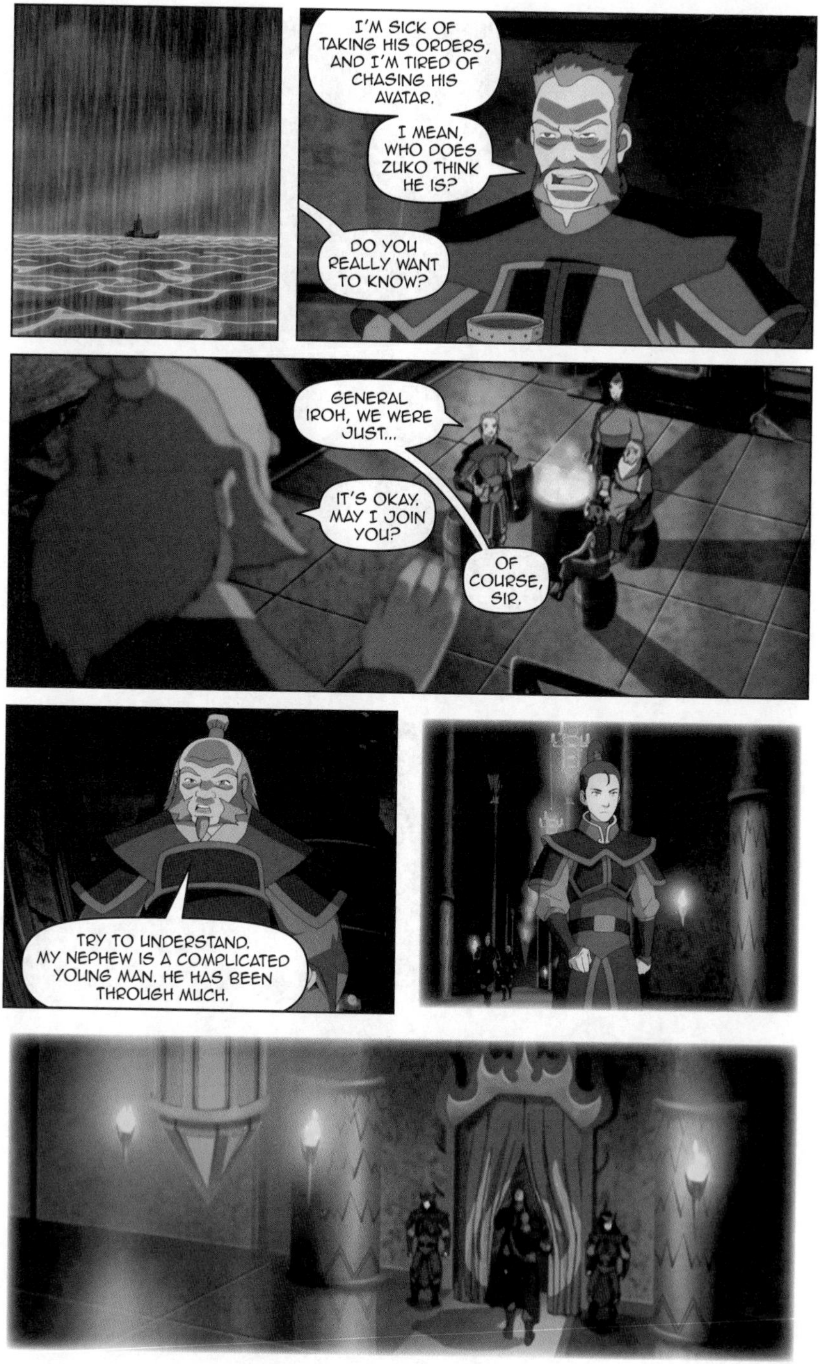
I'M SICK OF TAKING HIS ORDERS, AND I'M TIRED OF CHASING HIS AVATAR.
I MEAN, WHO DOES ZUKO THINK HE IS?
DO YOU REALLY WANT TO KNOW?
GENERAL IROH, WE WERE JUST...
IT'S OKAY. MAY I JOIN YOU?
OF COURSE, SIR.
TRY TO UNDERSTAND. MY NEPHEW IS A COMPLICATED YOUNG MAN. HE HAS BEEN THROUGH MUCH.

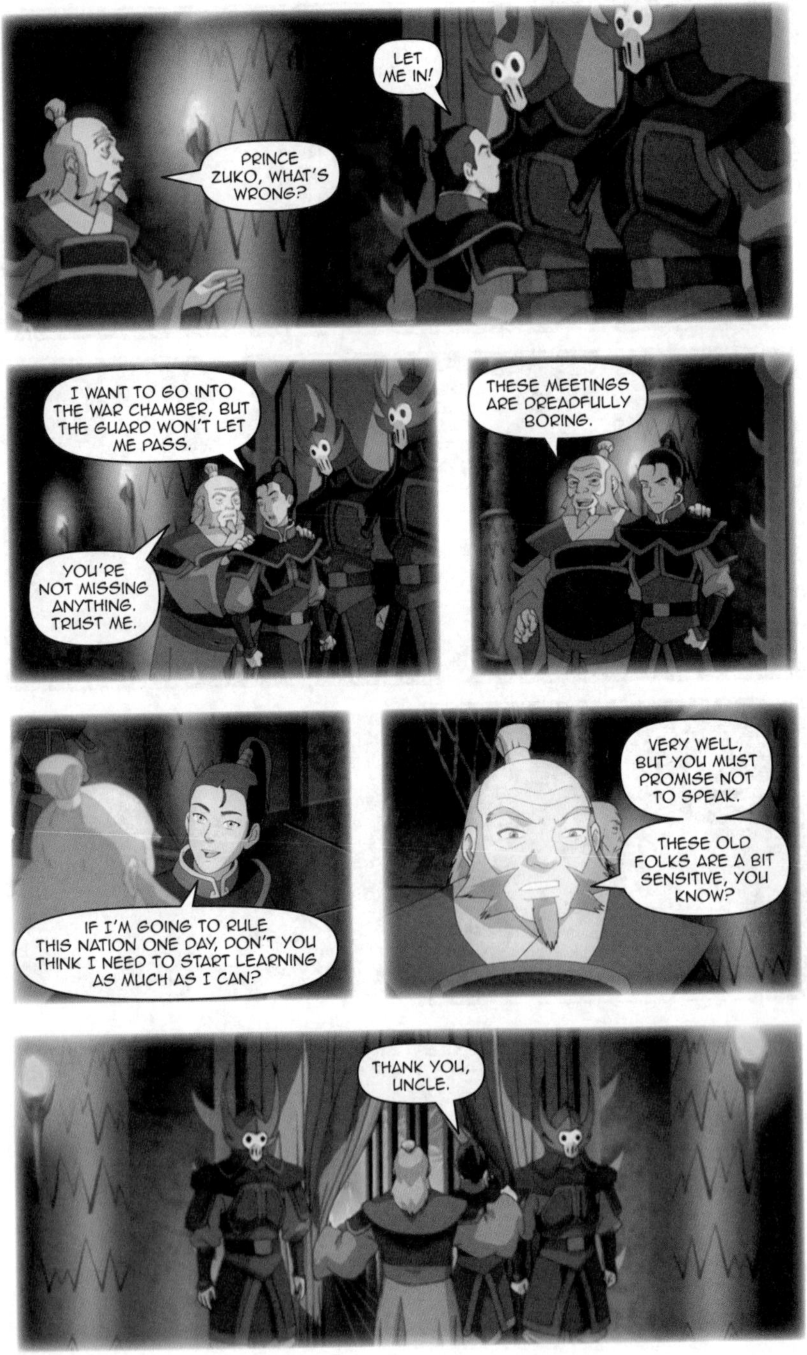
LET ME IN!
PRINCE ZUKO, WHAT'S WRONG?
I WANT TO GO INTO THE WAR CHAMBER, BUT THE GUARD WON'T LET ME PASS.
YOU'RE NOT MISSING ANYTHING. TRUST ME.
THESE MEETINGS ARE DREADFULLY BORING.
IF I'M GOING TO RULE THIS NATION ONE DAY, DON'T YOU THINK I NEED TO START LEARNING AS MUCH AS I CAN?
VERY WELL, BUT YOU MUST PROMISE NOT TO SPEAK.
THESE OLD FOLKS ARE A BIT SENSITIVE, YOU KNOW?
THANK YOU, UNCLE.

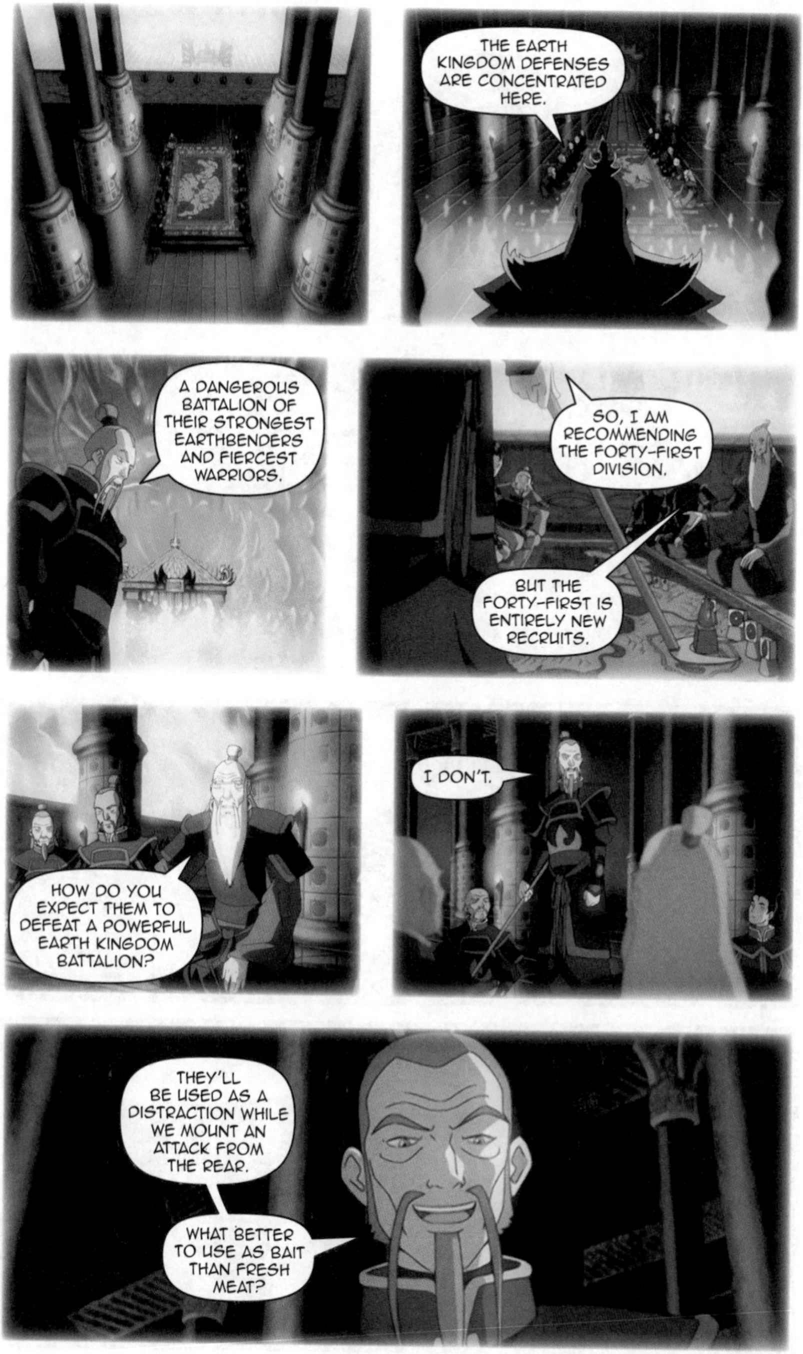
THE EARTH KINGDOM DEFENSES ARE CONCENTRATED HERE.
A DANGEROUS BATTALION OF THEIR STRONGEST EARTHBENDERS AND FIERCEST WARRIORS.
SO, I AM RECOMMENDING THE FORTY-FIRST DIVISION.
BUT THE FORTY-FIRST IS ENTIRELY NEW RECRUITS.
HOW DO YOU EXPECT THEM TO DEFEAT A POWERFUL EARTH KINGDOM BATTALION?
I DON'T.
THEY'LL BE USED AS A DISTRACTION WHILE WE MOUNT AN ATTACK FROM THE REAR.
WHAT BETTER TO USE AS BAIT THAN FRESH MEAT?

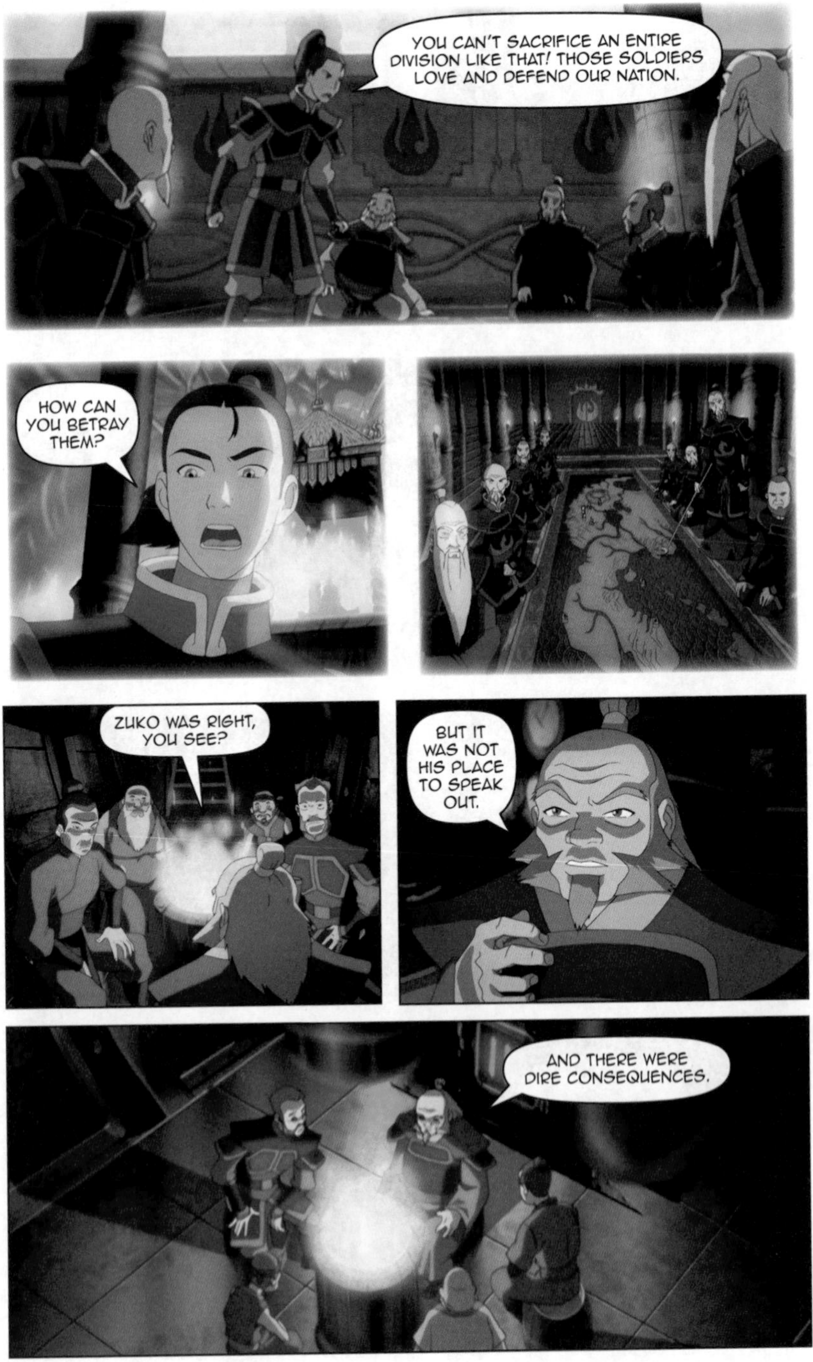
YOU CAN'T SACRIFICE AN ENTIRE DIVISION LIKE THAT! THOSE SOLDIERS LOVE AND DEFEND OUR NATION.
HOW CAN YOU BETRAY THEM?
ZUKO WAS RIGHT, YOU SEE?
BUT IT WAS NOT HIS PLACE TO SPEAK OUT.
AND THERE WERE DIRE CONSEQUENCES.

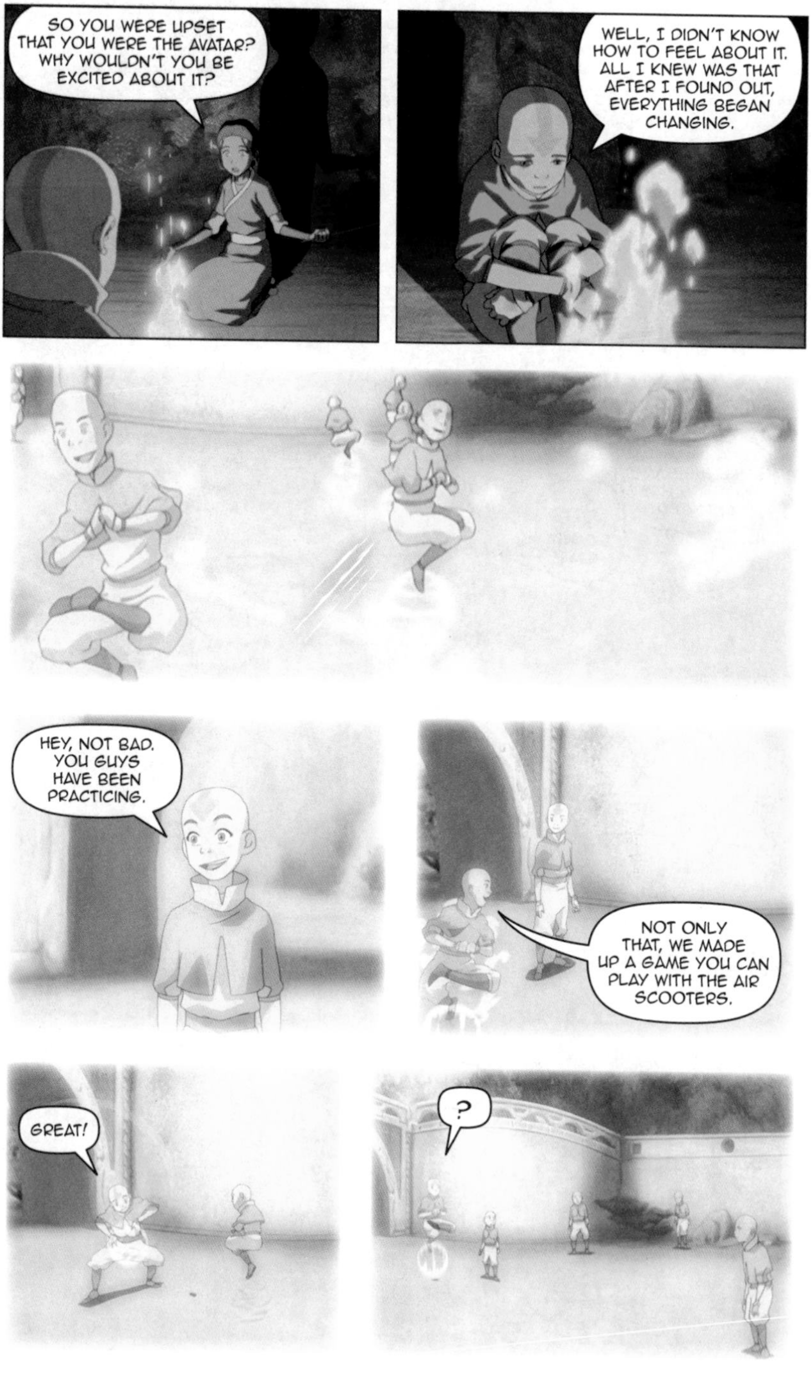
SO YOU WERE UPSET THAT YOU WERE THE AVATAR? WHY WOULDN'T YOU BE EXCITED ABOUT IT?
WELL, I DIDN'T KNOW HOW TO FEEL ABOUT IT. ALL I KNEW WAS THAT AFTER I FOUND OUT, EVERYTHING BEGAN CHANGING.
HEY, NOT BAD. YOU GUYS HAVE BEEN PRACTICING.
NOT ONLY THAT, WE MADE UP A GAME YOU CAN PLAY WITH THE AIR SCOOTERS.
GREAT!
?

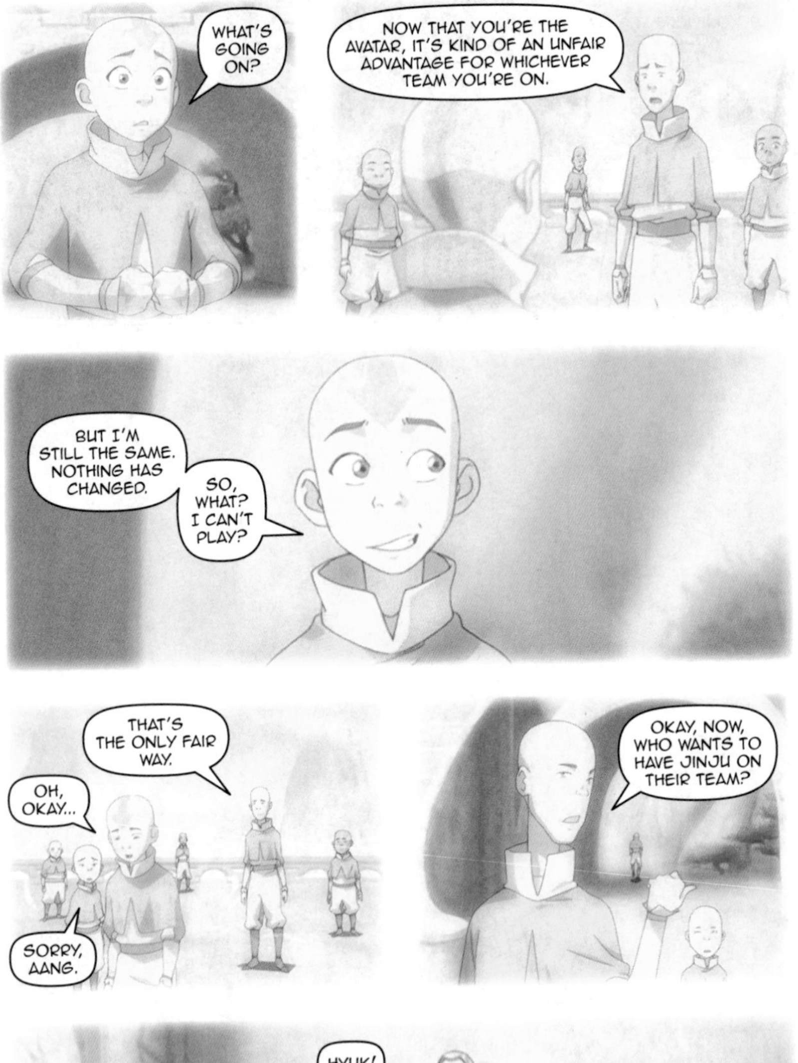
WHAT'S GOING ON?
NOW THAT YOU'RE THE AVATAR, IT'S KIND OF AN UNFAIR ADVANTAGE FOR WHICHEVER TEAM YOU'RE ON.
BUT I'M STILL THE SAME. NOTHING HAS CHANGED.
SO, WHAT? I CAN'T PLAY?
THAT'S THE ONLY FAIR WAY.
OH, OKAY...
SORRY, AANG.
OKAY, NOW, WHO WANTS TO HAVE JINJU ON THEIR TEAM?
HYUK!

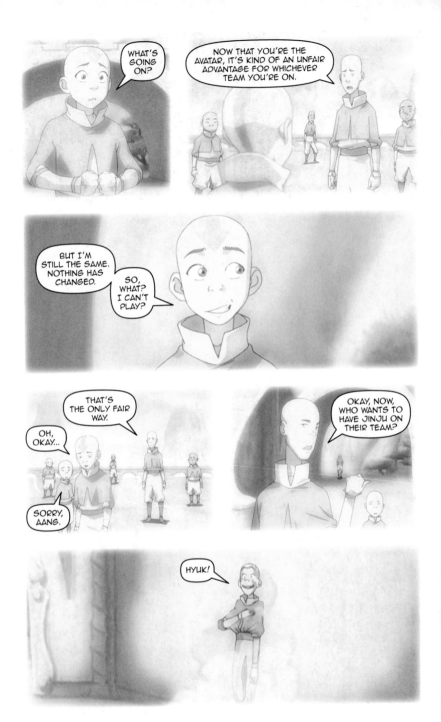

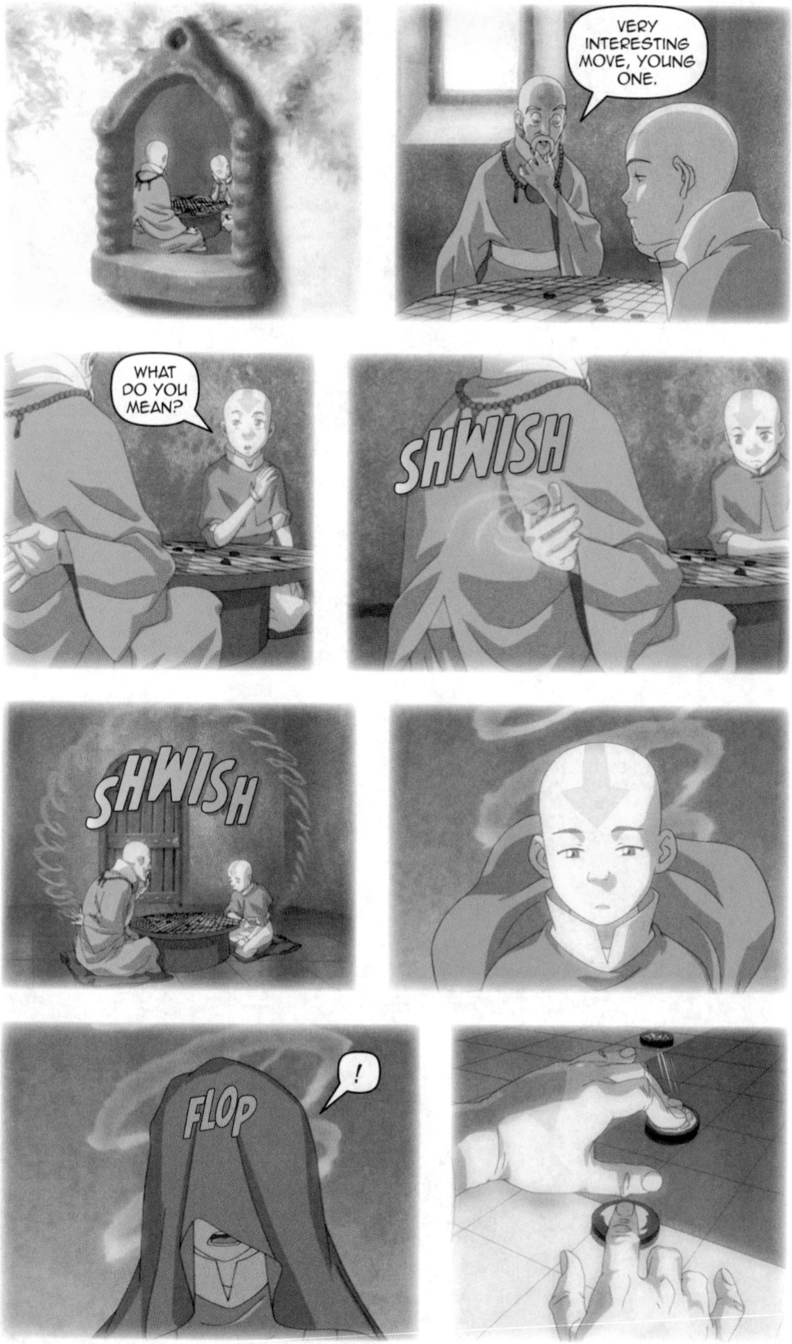
VERY INTERESTING MOVE, YOUNG ONE.
WHAT DO YOU MEAN?
SHWISH
SHWISH
FLOP
!

HEY! HAHAHA!

YOU'RE PLAYING GAMES WITH HIM? THE AVATAR SHOULD BE TRAINING.

AANG HAS ALREADY TRAINED ENOUGH FOR TODAY.

TIME IS SHORT. COME WITH ME. I MUST TEST YOU ON SOME HIGH-LEVEL TECHNIQUES.

NO. AS LONG AS I AM HIS GUARDIAN, I WILL DECIDE WHEN HE TRAINS--AND WHEN HE GETS HIS BUTT KICKED AT PAI SHO.

HMMPH!

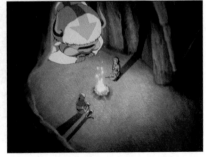

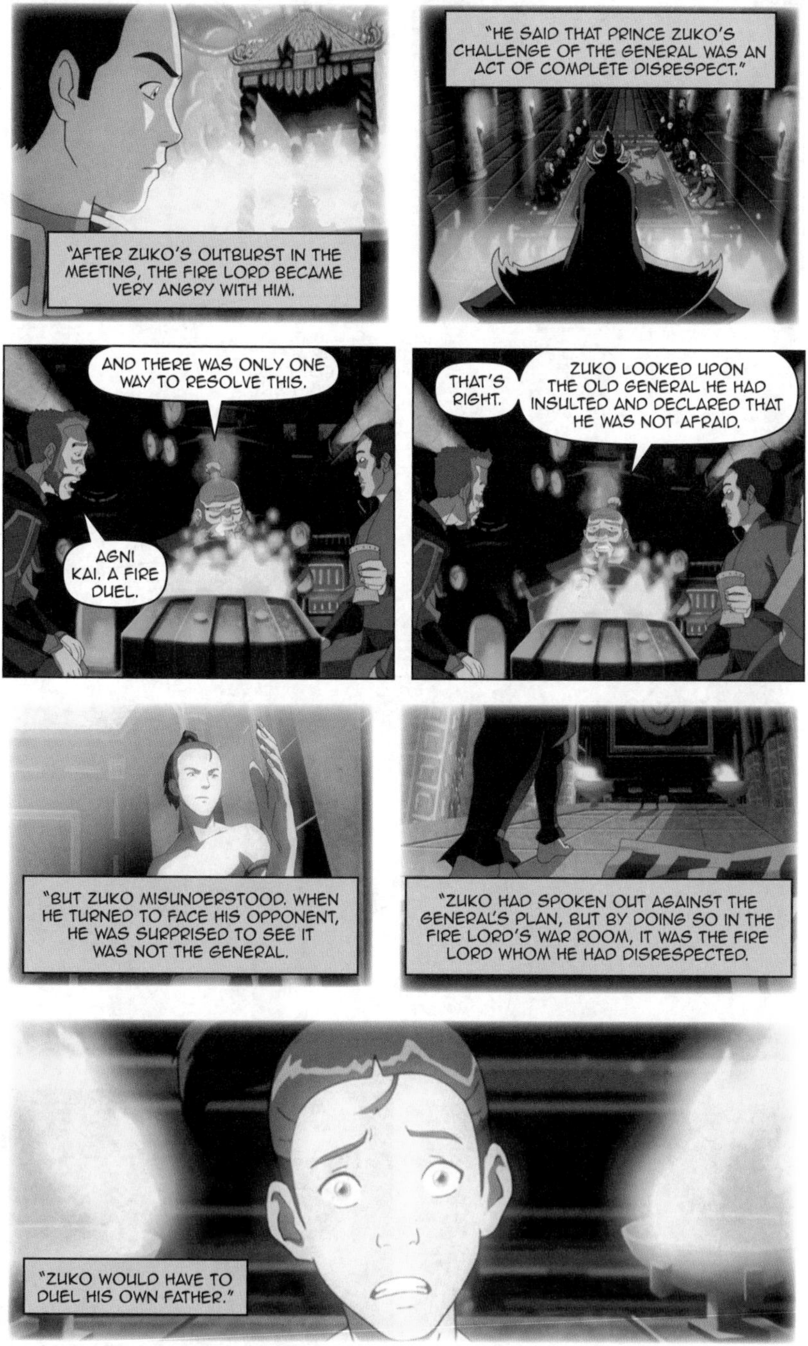

"AFTER ZUKO'S OUTBURST IN THE MEETING, THE FIRE LORD BECAME VERY ANGRY WITH HIM.
"HE SAID THAT PRINCE ZUKO'S CHALLENGE OF THE GENERAL WAS AN ACT OF COMPLETE DISRESPECT."
AND THERE WAS ONLY ONE WAY TO RESOLVE THIS.
AGNI KAI. A FIRE DUEL.
THAT'S RIGHT.
ZUKO LOOKED UPON THE OLD GENERAL HE HAD INSULTED AND DECLARED THAT HE WAS NOT AFRAID.
"BUT ZUKO MISUNDERSTOOD. WHEN HE TURNED TO FACE HIS OPPONENT, HE WAS SURPRISED TO SEE IT WAS NOT THE GENERAL.
"ZUKO HAD SPOKEN OUT AGAINST THE GENERAL'S PLAN, BUT BY DOING SO IN THE FIRE LORD'S WAR ROOM, IT WAS THE FIRE LORD WHOM HE HAD DISRESPECTED.
"ZUKO WOULD HAVE TO DUEL HIS OWN FATHER."

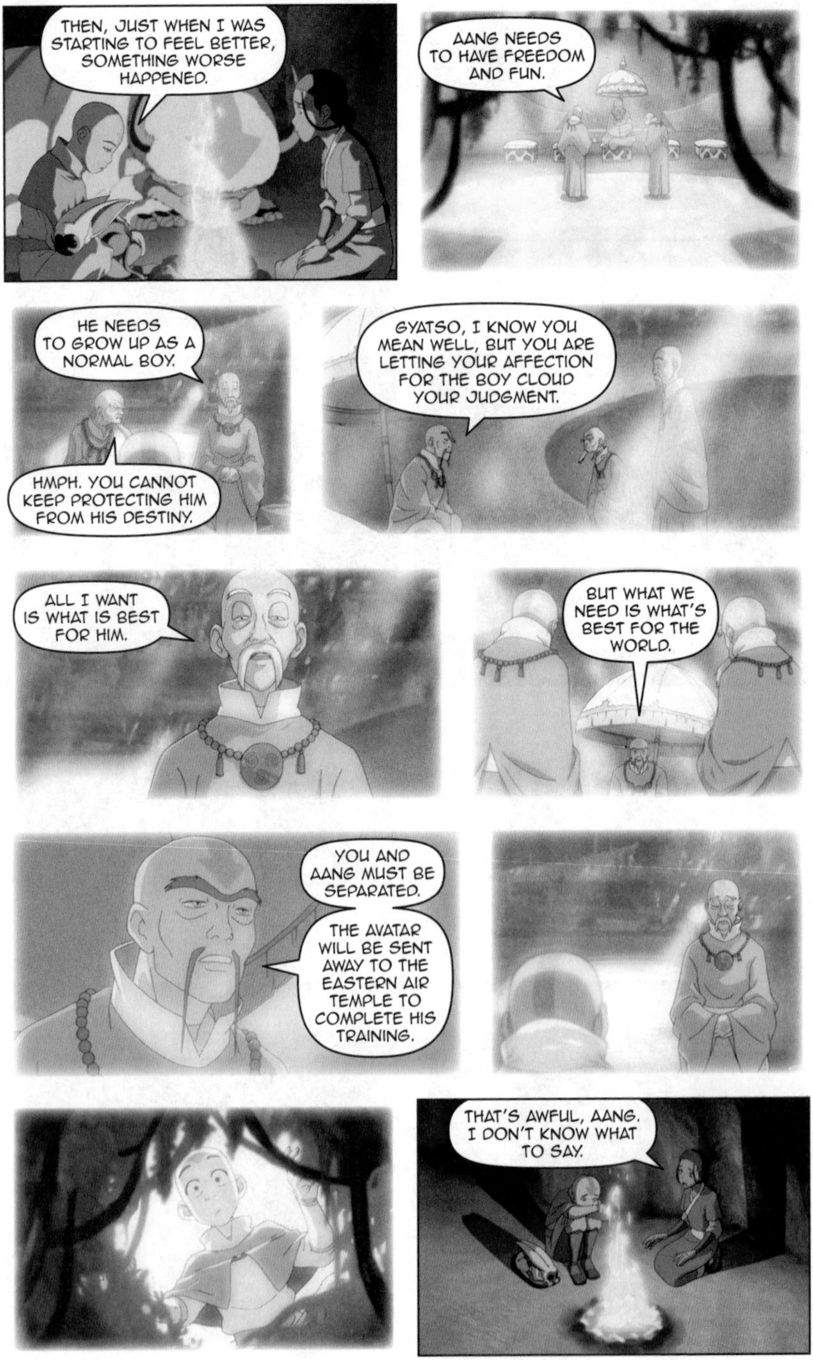

THEN, JUST WHEN I WAS STARTING TO FEEL BETTER, SOMETHING WORSE HAPPENED.
AANG NEEDS TO HAVE FREEDOM AND FUN.
HE NEEDS TO GROW UP AS A NORMAL BOY.
HMPH. YOU CANNOT KEEP PROTECTING HIM FROM HIS DESTINY.
GYATSO, I KNOW YOU MEAN WELL, BUT YOU ARE LETTING YOUR AFFECTION FOR THE BOY CLOUD YOUR JUDGMENT.
ALL I WANT IS WHAT IS BEST FOR HIM.
BUT WHAT WE NEED IS WHAT'S BEST FOR THE WORLD.
YOU AND AANG MUST BE SEPARATED.
THE AVATAR WILL BE SENT AWAY TO THE EASTERN AIR TEMPLE TO COMPLETE HIS TRAINING.
THAT'S AWFUL, AANG. I DON'T KNOW WHAT TO SAY.

HOW COULD THEY DO THAT TO ME? THEY WANTED TO TAKE AWAY EVERYTHING I KNEW AND EVERYONE I LOVED!

WHOA! HOT CINDERS.

FWOOSH

I'M SORRY I GOT SO MAD.

YOU HAVE A RIGHT TO BE ANGRY AFTER THE MONKS SENT YOU AWAY LIKE THAT.

WELL, THAT'S NOT EXACTLY WHAT HAPPENED.

"I WAS AFRAID AND CONFUSED.

"I DIDN'T KNOW WHAT TO DO."

AANG?

I'M NOT GOING TO LET THEM TAKE YOU AWAY FROM ME.

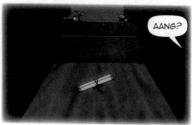

AANG?

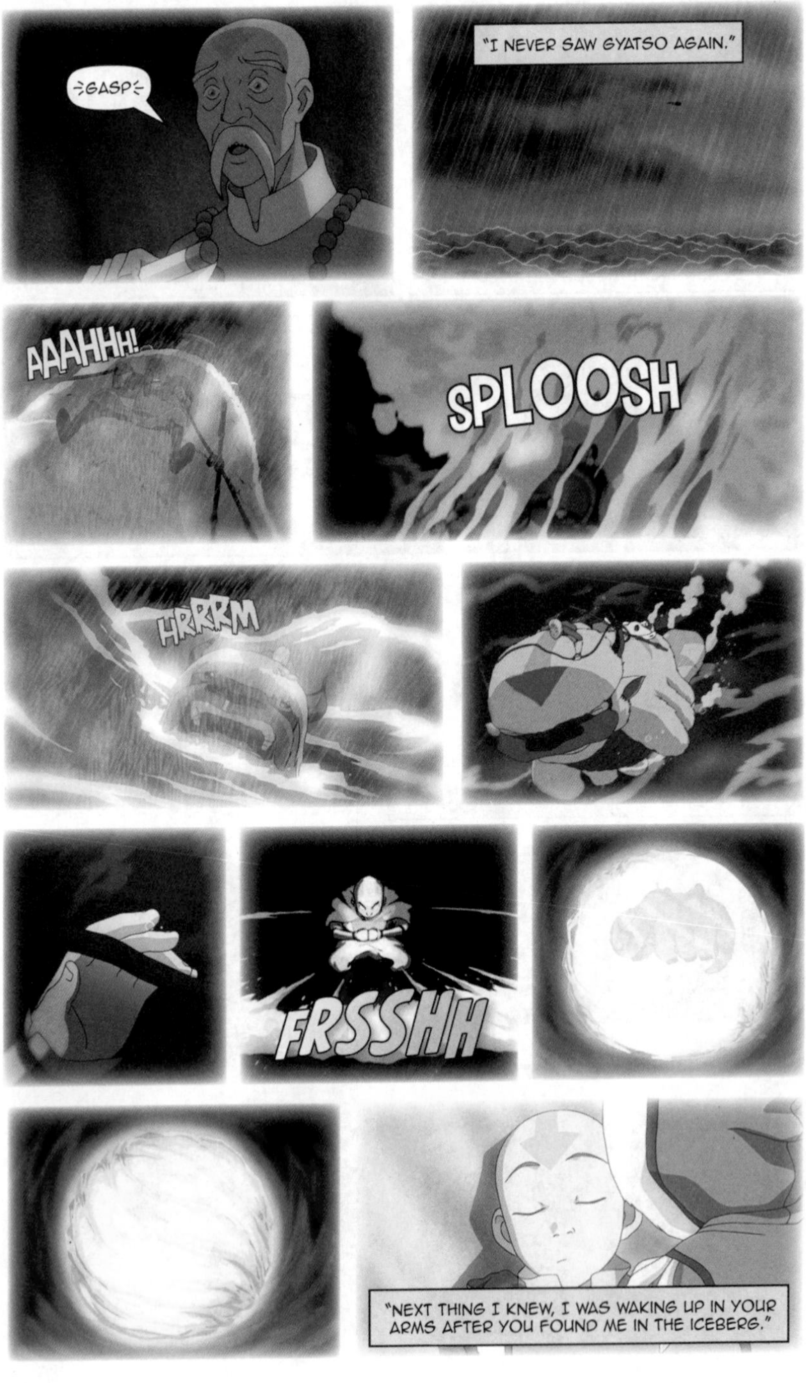

GASP
"I NEVER SAW GYATSO AGAIN."
AAAHHH!
SPLOOSH
HRRRM
FRSSHH
"NEXT THING I KNEW, I WAS WAKING UP IN YOUR ARMS AFTER YOU FOUND ME IN THE ICEBERG."

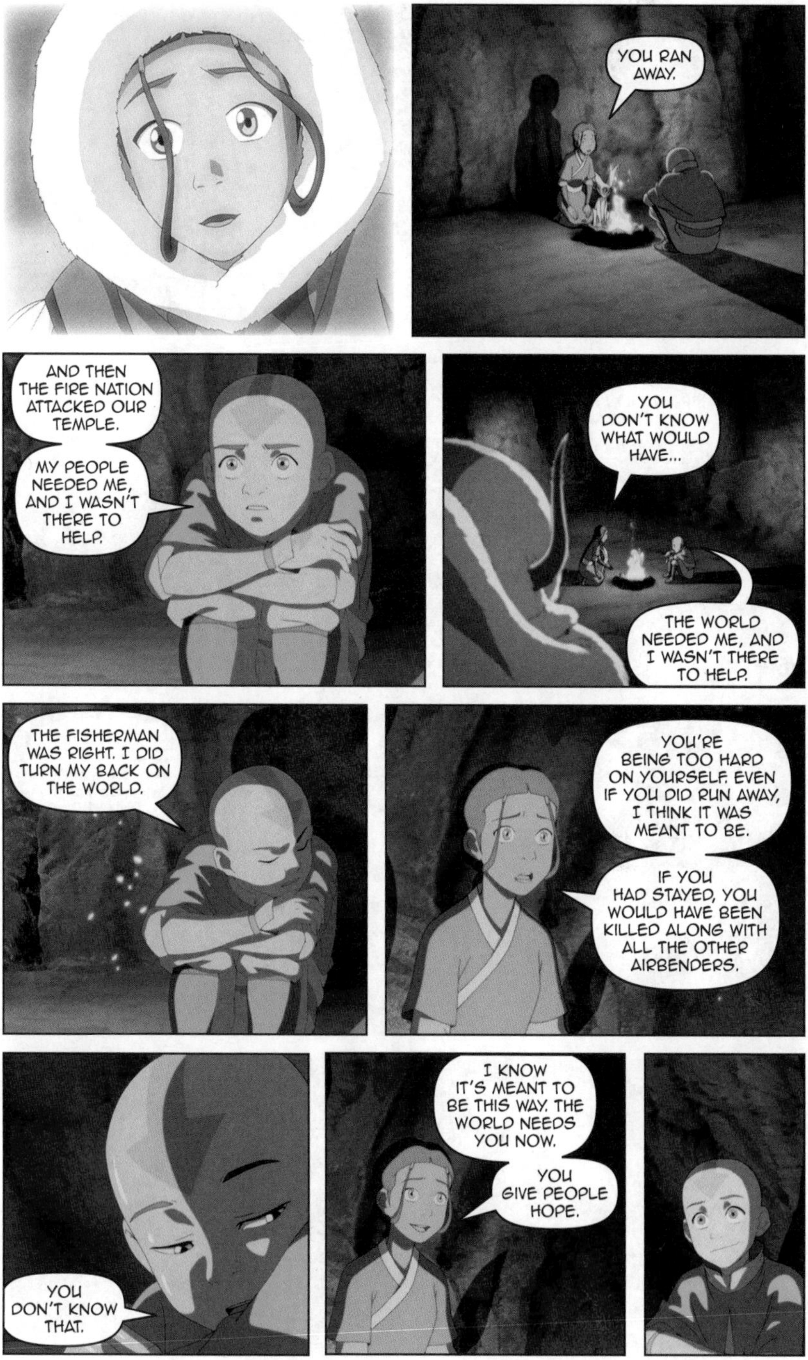
YOU RAN AWAY.
AND THEN THE FIRE NATION ATTACKED OUR TEMPLE.
MY PEOPLE NEEDED ME, AND I WASN'T THERE TO HELP.
YOU DON'T KNOW WHAT WOULD HAVE...
THE WORLD NEEDED ME, AND I WASN'T THERE TO HELP.
THE FISHERMAN WAS RIGHT. I DID TURN MY BACK ON THE WORLD.
YOU'RE BEING TOO HARD ON YOURSELF. EVEN IF YOU DID RUN AWAY, I THINK IT WAS MEANT TO BE.
IF YOU HAD STAYED, YOU WOULD HAVE BEEN KILLED ALONG WITH ALL THE OTHER AIRBENDERS.
YOU DON'T KNOW THAT.
I KNOW IT'S MEANT TO BE THIS WAY. THE WORLD NEEDS YOU NOW.
YOU GIVE PEOPLE HOPE.

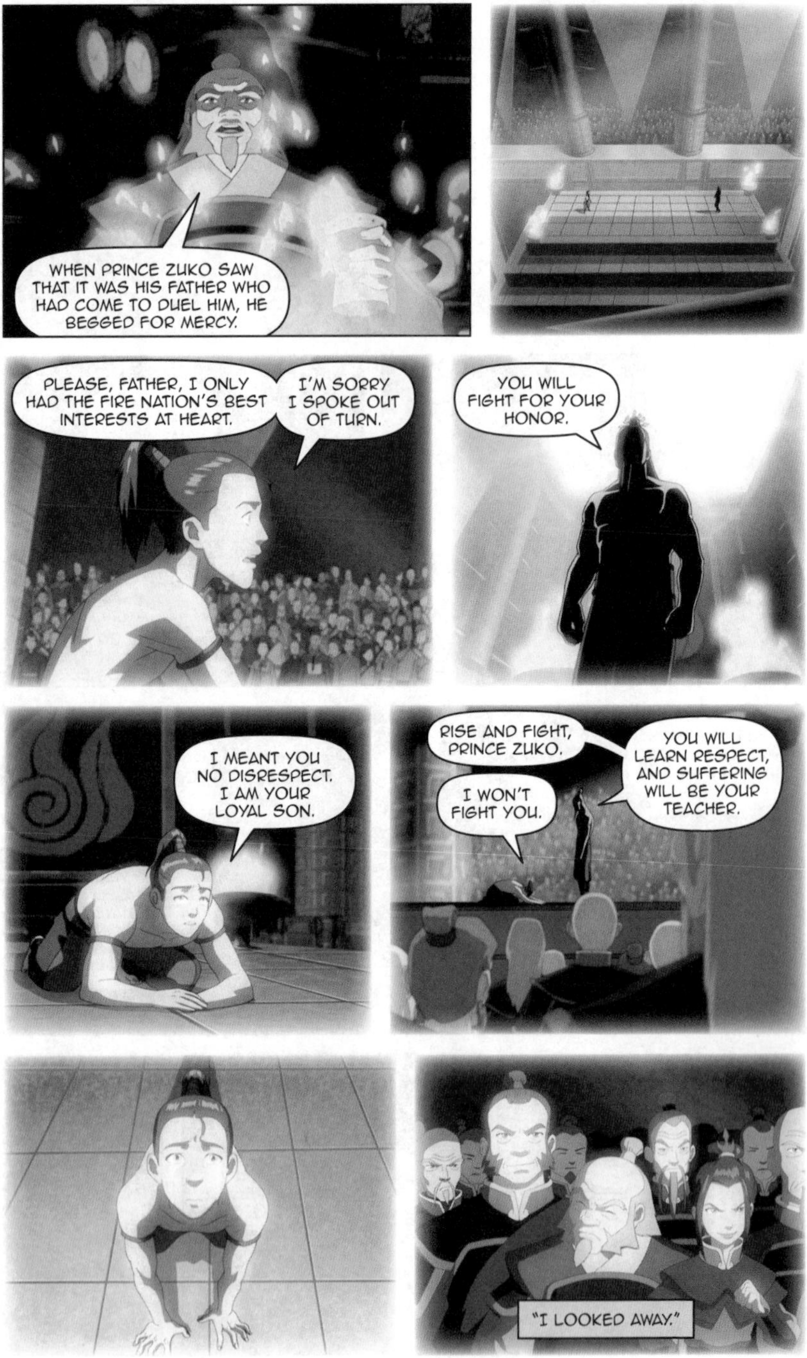
WHEN PRINCE ZUKO SAW THAT IT WAS HIS FATHER WHO HAD COME TO DUEL HIM, HE BEGGED FOR MERCY.
PLEASE, FATHER, I ONLY HAD THE FIRE NATION'S BEST INTERESTS AT HEART.
I'M SORRY I SPOKE OUT OF TURN.
YOU WILL FIGHT FOR YOUR HONOR.
I MEANT YOU NO DISRESPECT. I AM YOUR LOYAL SON.
RISE AND FIGHT, PRINCE ZUKO.
I WON'T FIGHT YOU.
YOU WILL LEARN RESPECT, AND SUFFERING WILL BE YOUR TEACHER.
"I LOOKED AWAY."

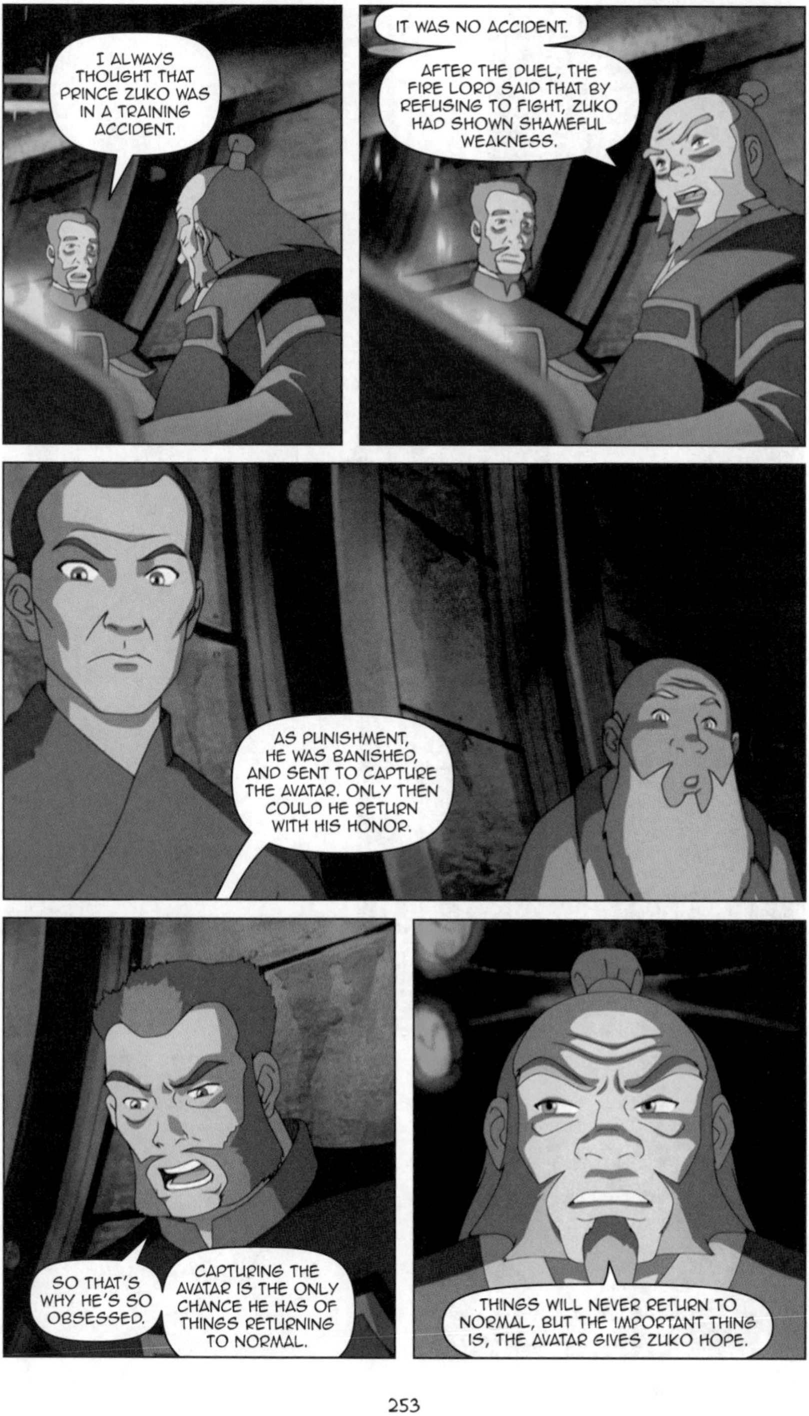
I ALWAYS THOUGHT THAT PRINCE ZUKO WAS IN A TRAINING ACCIDENT.
IT WAS NO ACCIDENT.
AFTER THE DUEL, THE FIRE LORD SAID THAT BY REFUSING TO FIGHT, ZUKO HAD SHOWN SHAMEFUL WEAKNESS.
AS PUNISHMENT, HE WAS BANISHED, AND SENT TO CAPTURE THE AVATAR. ONLY THEN COULD HE RETURN WITH HIS HONOR.
SO THAT'S WHY HE'S SO OBSESSED.
CAPTURING THE AVATAR IS THE ONLY CHANCE HE HAS OF THINGS RETURNING TO NORMAL.
THINGS WILL NEVER RETURN TO NORMAL, BUT THE IMPORTANT THING IS, THE AVATAR GIVES ZUKO HOPE.

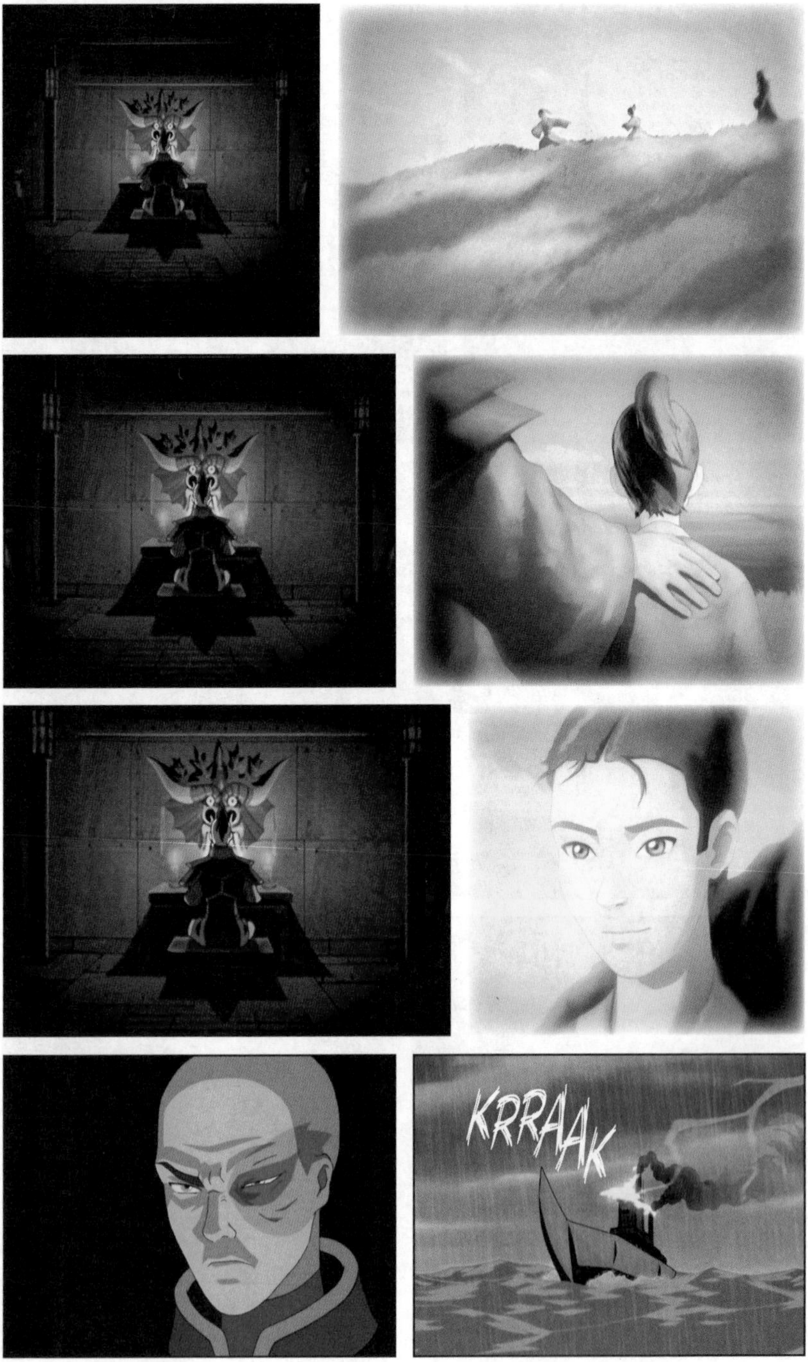
KRRAAK

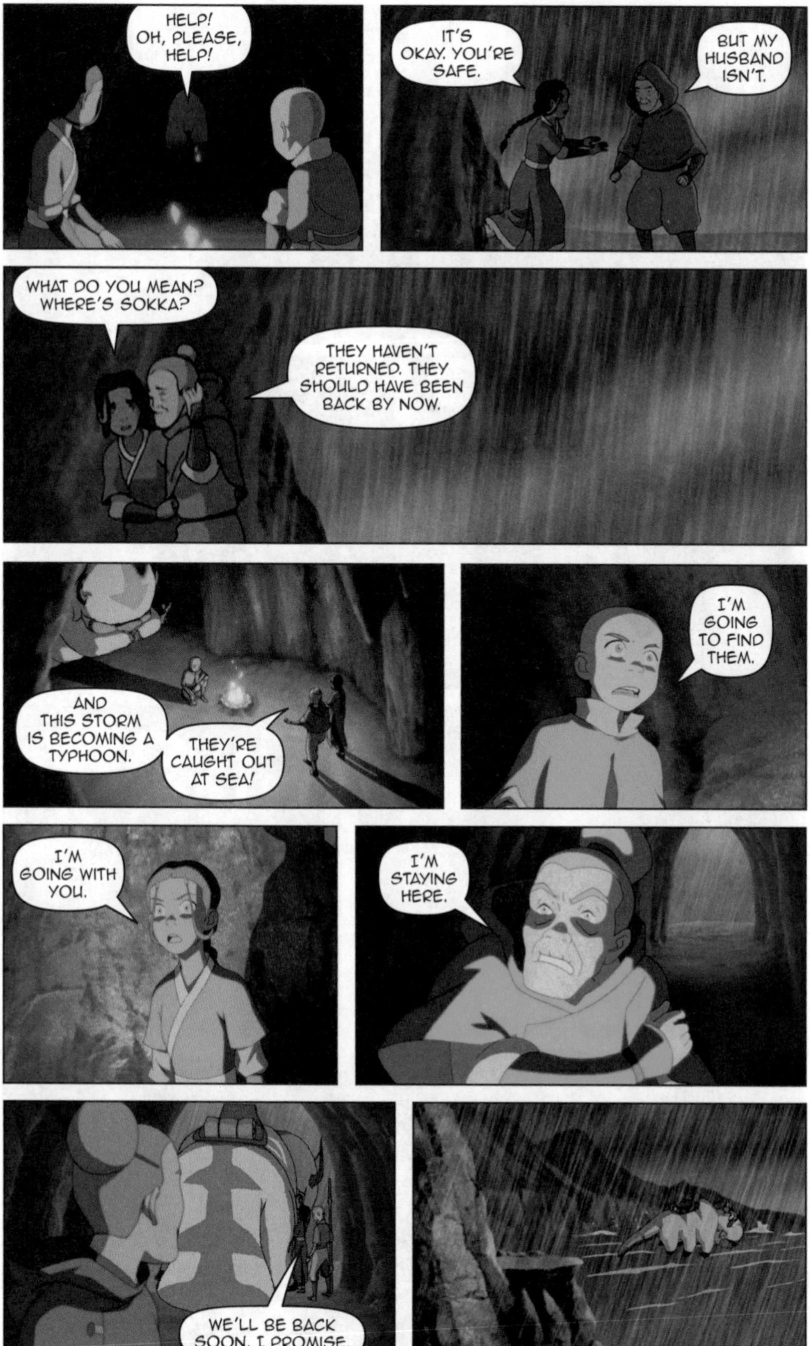
HELP! OH, PLEASE, HELP!
IT'S OKAY. YOU'RE SAFE.
BUT MY HUSBAND ISN'T.
WHAT DO YOU MEAN? WHERE'S SOKKA?
THEY HAVEN'T RETURNED. THEY SHOULD HAVE BEEN BACK BY NOW.
AND THIS STORM IS BECOMING A TYPHOON.
THEY'RE CAUGHT OUT AT SEA!
I'M GOING TO FIND THEM.
I'M GOING WITH YOU.
I'M STAYING HERE.
WE'LL BE BACK SOON. I PROMISE.

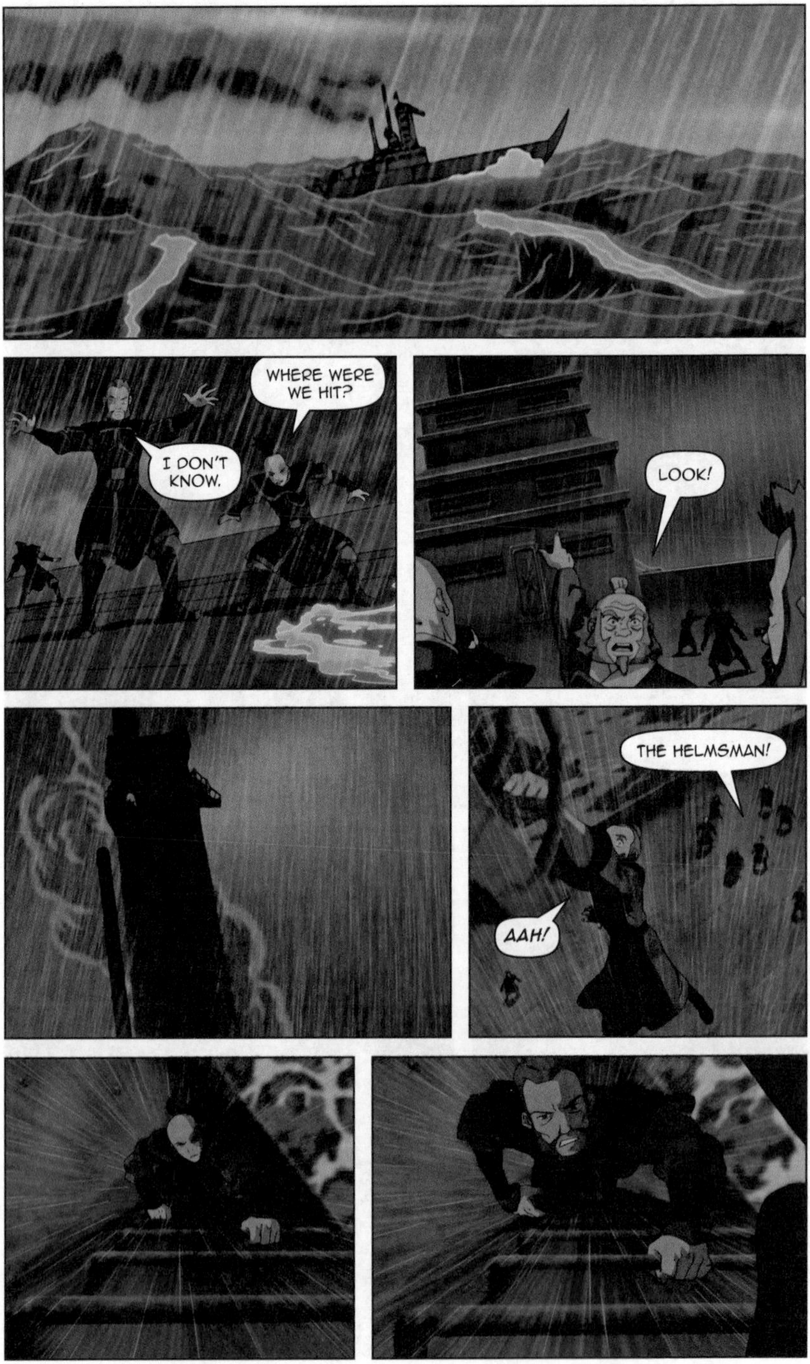
WHERE WERE WE HIT?
I DON'T KNOW.
LOOK!
THE HELMSMAN!
AAH!

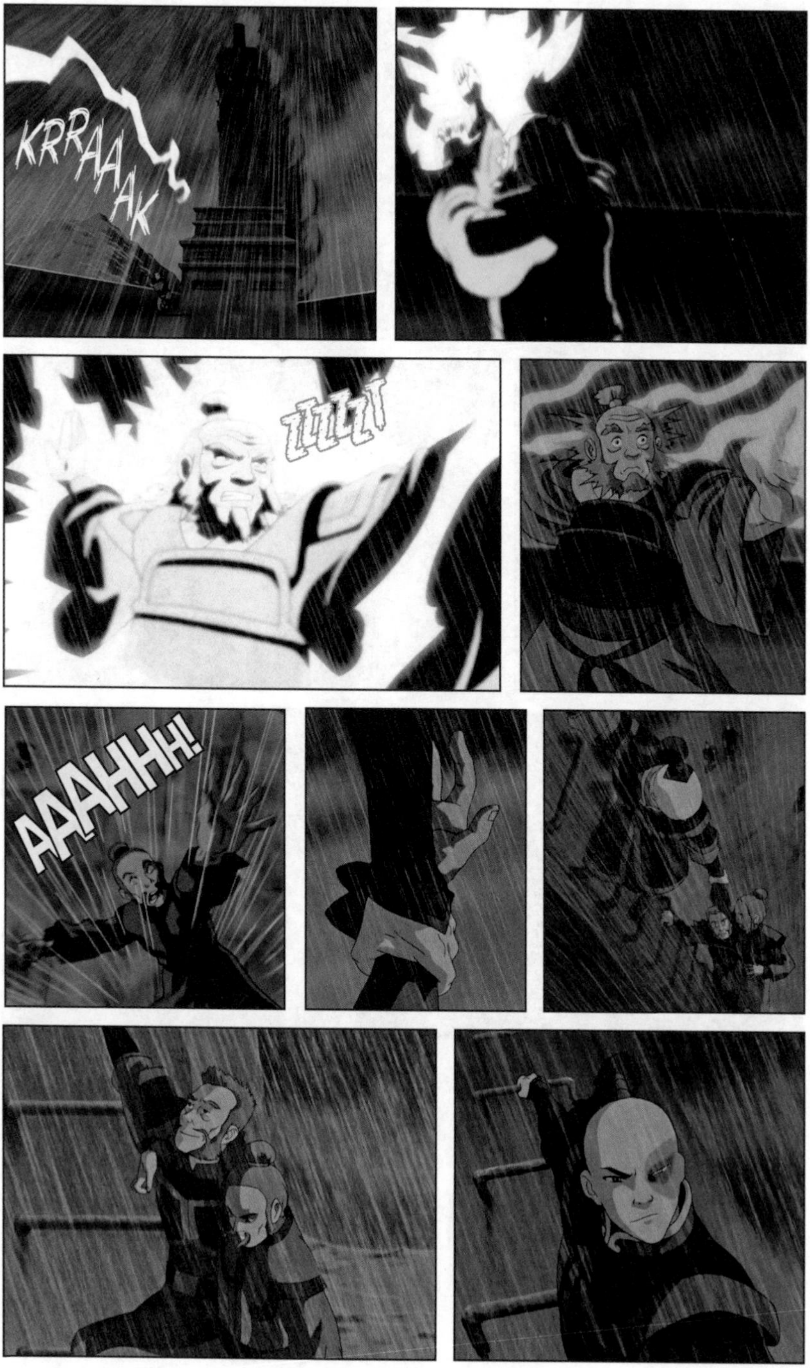

KRRAAAAK
ZZZZZT
AAAHHH!

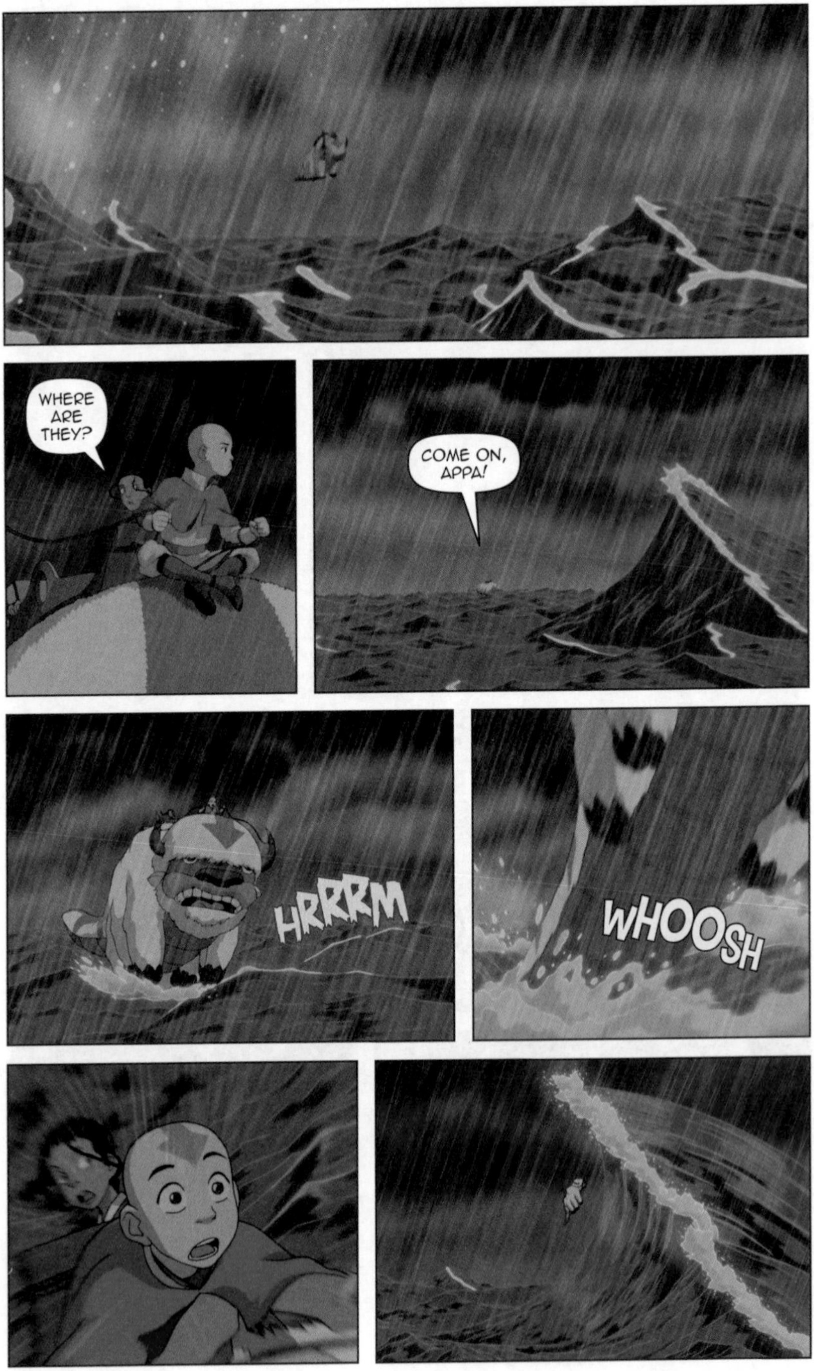
WHERE ARE THEY?
COME ON, APPA!
HRRRM
WHOOSH

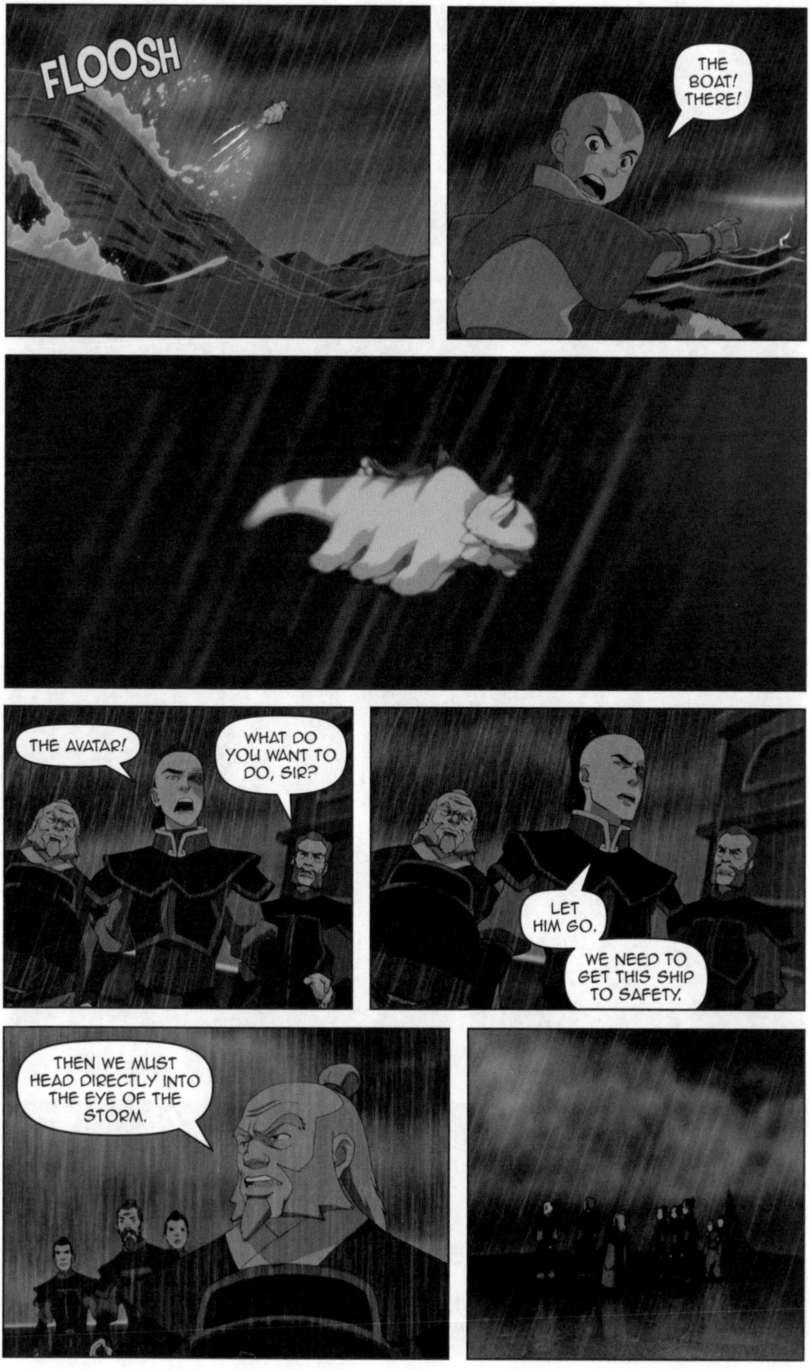
FLOOSH
THE BOAT! THERE!
THE AVATAR!
WHAT DO YOU WANT TO DO, SIR?
LET HIM GO.
WE NEED TO GET THIS SHIP TO SAFETY.
THEN WE MUST HEAD DIRECTLY INTO THE EYE OF THE STORM.

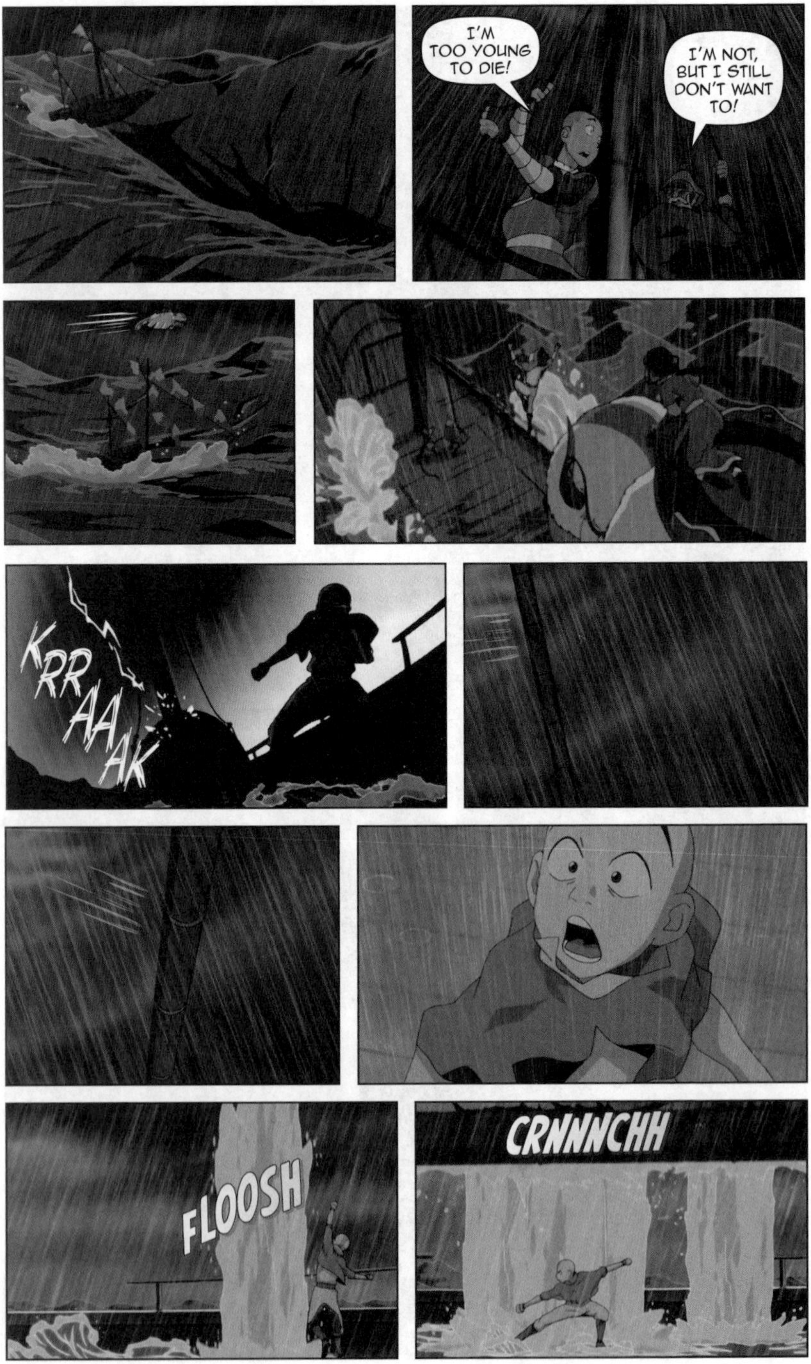
I'M TOO YOUNG TO DIE!
I'M NOT, BUT I STILL DON'T WANT TO!
KRRAAAAK
FLOOSH
CRNNNCHH

HANG ON TO THE ROPE!

WHOA! WHOA!

WHAM

AAAAHH!

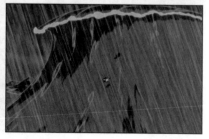

FWOOSH

WHOOSH

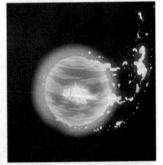

UNCLE, I AM SORRY.

YOUR APOLOGY IS ACCEPTED.

SPLOOSH

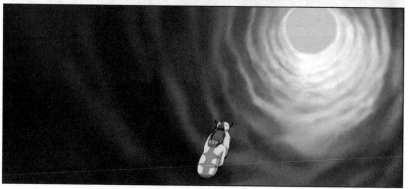

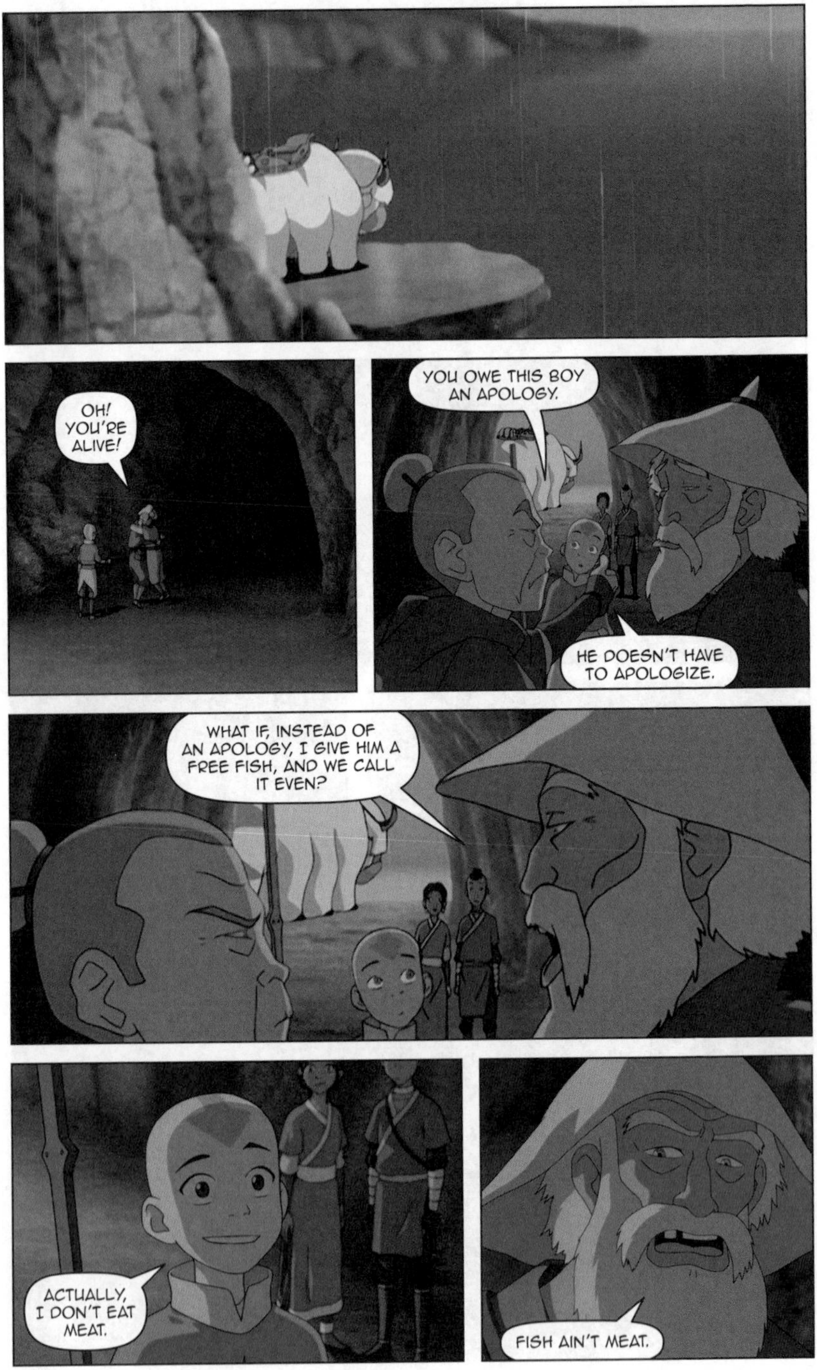
OH! YOU'RE ALIVE!
YOU OWE THIS BOY AN APOLOGY.
HE DOESN'T HAVE TO APOLOGIZE.
WHAT IF, INSTEAD OF AN APOLOGY, I GIVE HIM A FREE FISH, AND WE CALL IT EVEN?
ACTUALLY, I DON'T EAT MEAT.
FISH AIN'T MEAT.

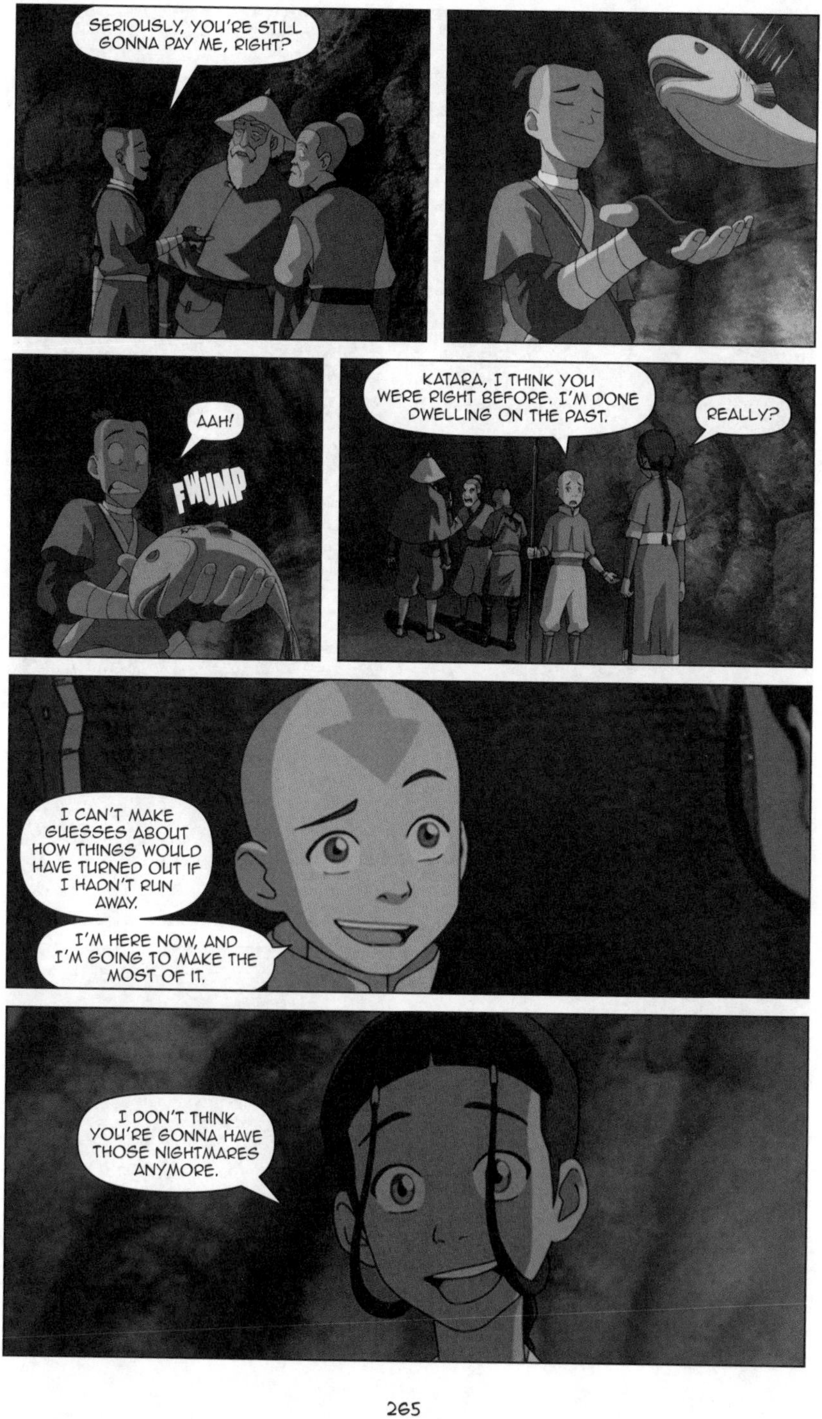
SERIOUSLY, YOU'RE STILL GONNA PAY ME, RIGHT?
AAH!
FWUMP
KATARA, I THINK YOU WERE RIGHT BEFORE. I'M DONE DWELLING ON THE PAST.
REALLY?
I CAN'T MAKE GUESSES ABOUT HOW THINGS WOULD HAVE TURNED OUT IF I HADN'T RUN AWAY.
I'M HERE NOW, AND I'M GOING TO MAKE THE MOST OF IT.
I DON'T THINK YOU'RE GONNA HAVE THOSE NIGHTMARES ANYMORE.

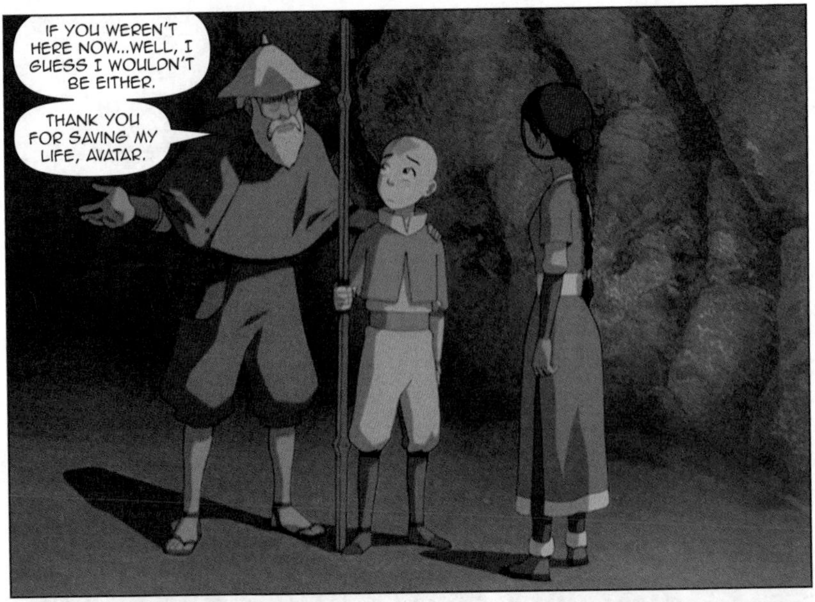
IF YOU WEREN'T HERE NOW...WELL, I GUESS I WOULDN'T BE EITHER.
THANK YOU FOR SAVING MY LIFE, AVATAR.

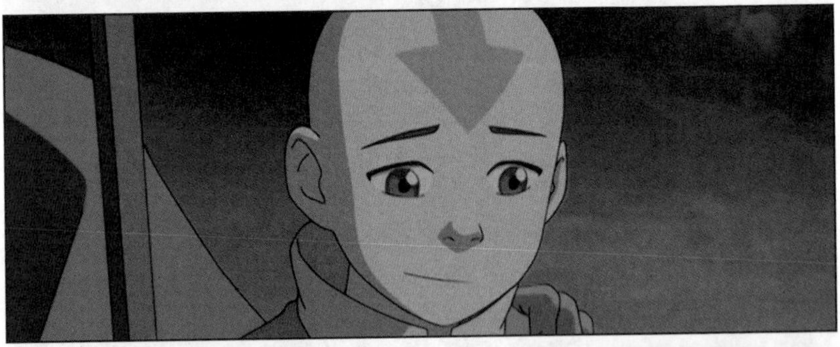

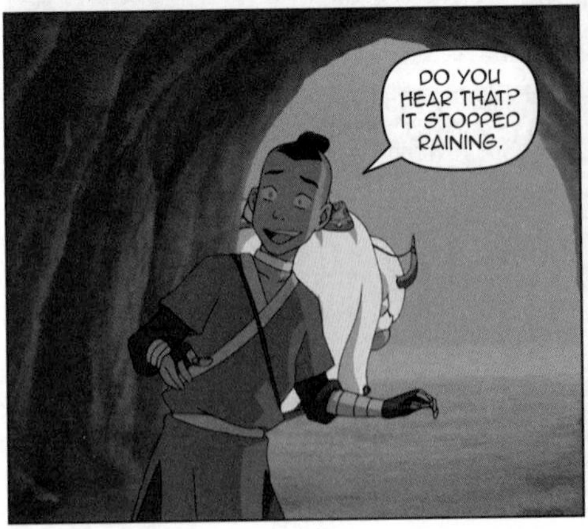
DO YOU HEAR THAT? IT STOPPED RAINING.

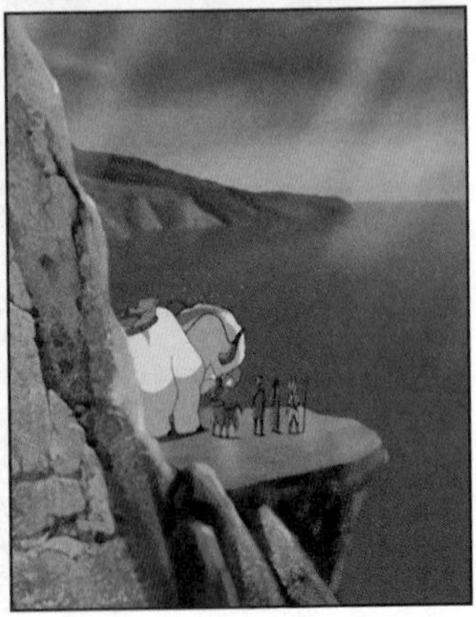

CHAPTER THIRTEEN
THE BLUE SPIRIT

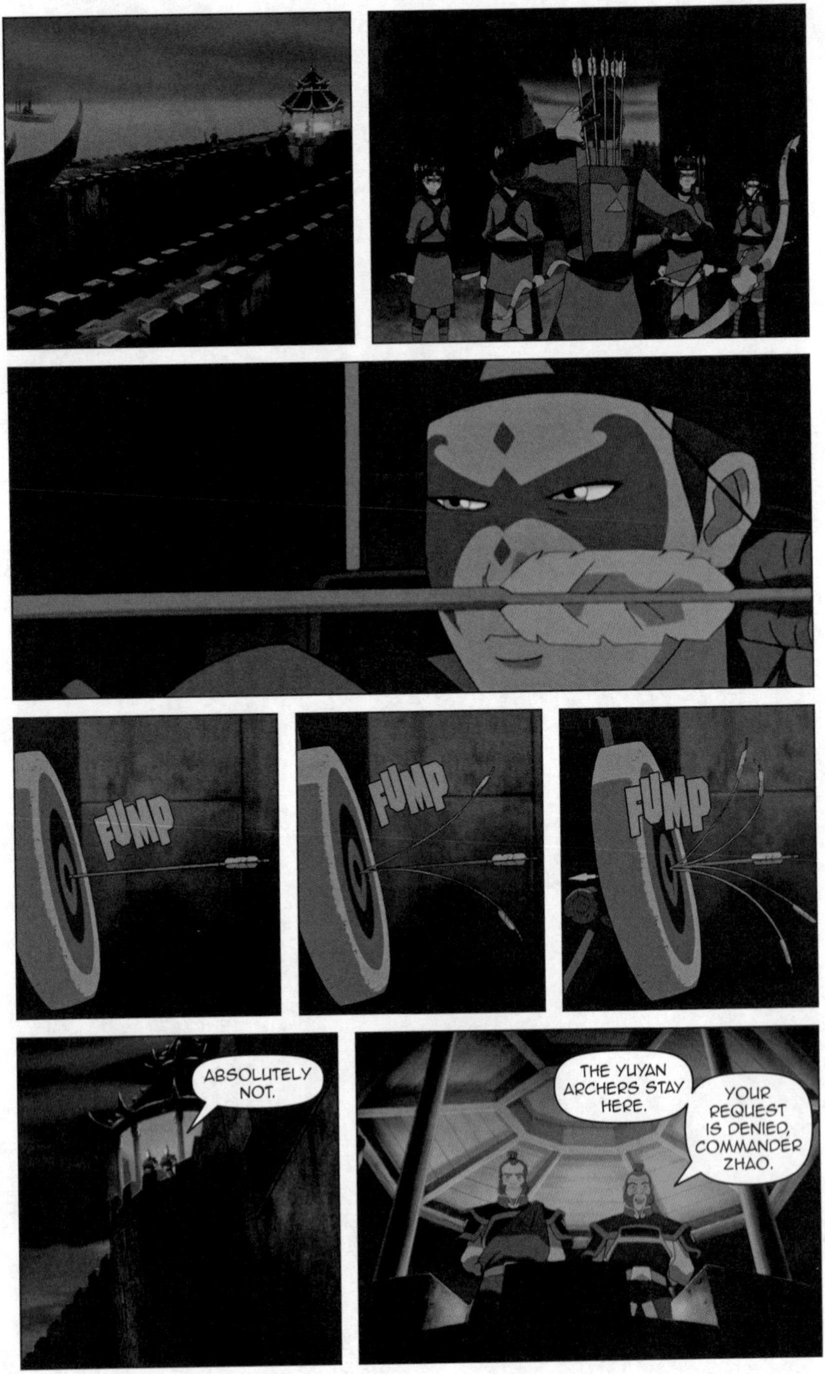
FUMP
FUMP
FUMP
ABSOLUTELY NOT.
THE YUYAN ARCHERS STAY HERE.
YOUR REQUEST IS DENIED, COMMANDER ZHAO.

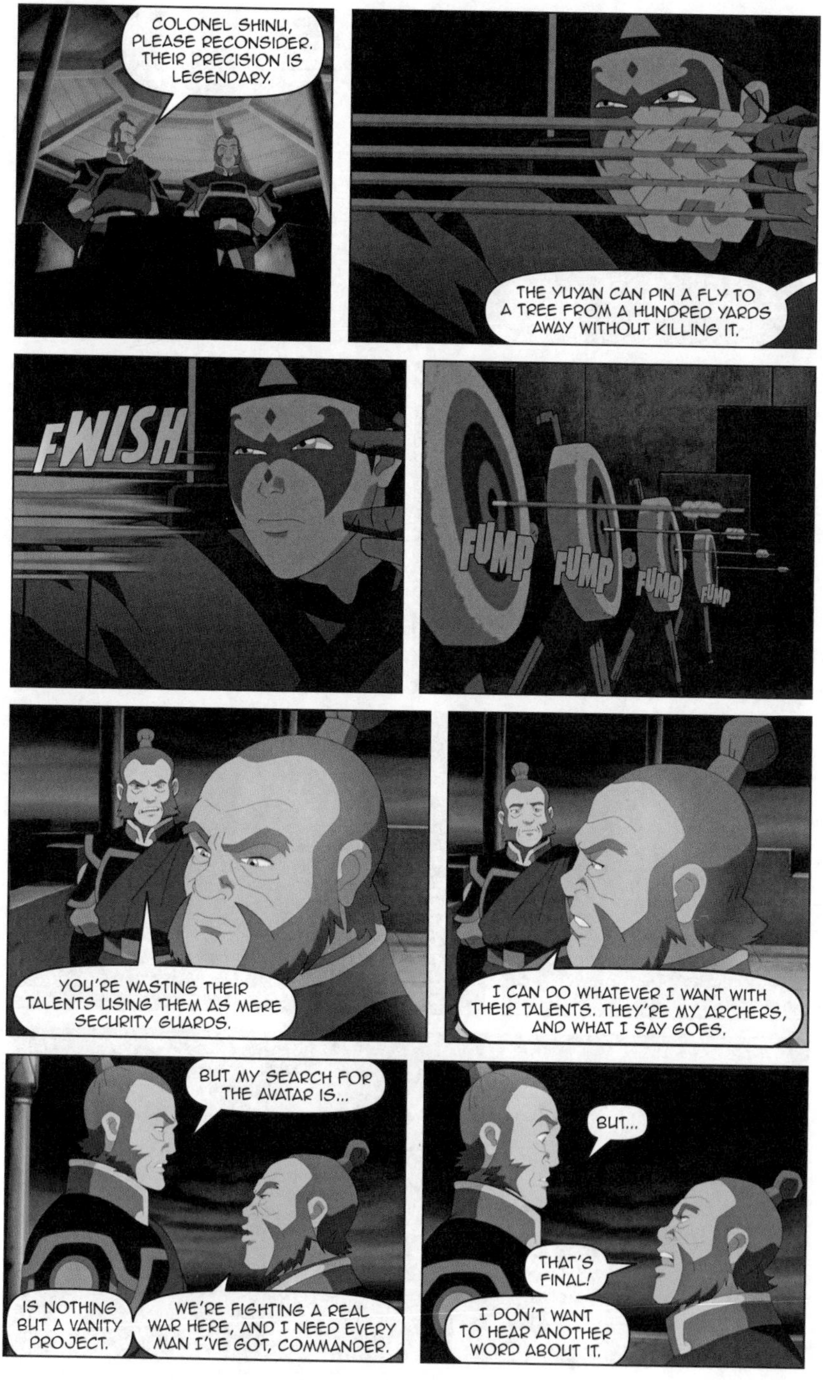
COLONEL SHINU, PLEASE RECONSIDER. THEIR PRECISION IS LEGENDARY.
THE YUYAN CAN PIN A FLY TO A TREE FROM A HUNDRED YARDS AWAY WITHOUT KILLING IT.
FWISH
FUMP
FUMP
FUMP
FUMP
YOU'RE WASTING THEIR TALENTS USING THEM AS MERE SECURITY GUARDS.
I CAN DO WHATEVER I WANT WITH THEIR TALENTS. THEY'RE MY ARCHERS, AND WHAT I SAY GOES.
BUT MY SEARCH FOR THE AVATAR IS...
IS NOTHING BUT A VANITY PROJECT.
WE'RE FIGHTING A REAL WAR HERE, AND I NEED EVERY MAN I'VE GOT, COMMANDER.
BUT...
THAT'S FINAL!
I DON'T WANT TO HEAR ANOTHER WORD ABOUT IT.

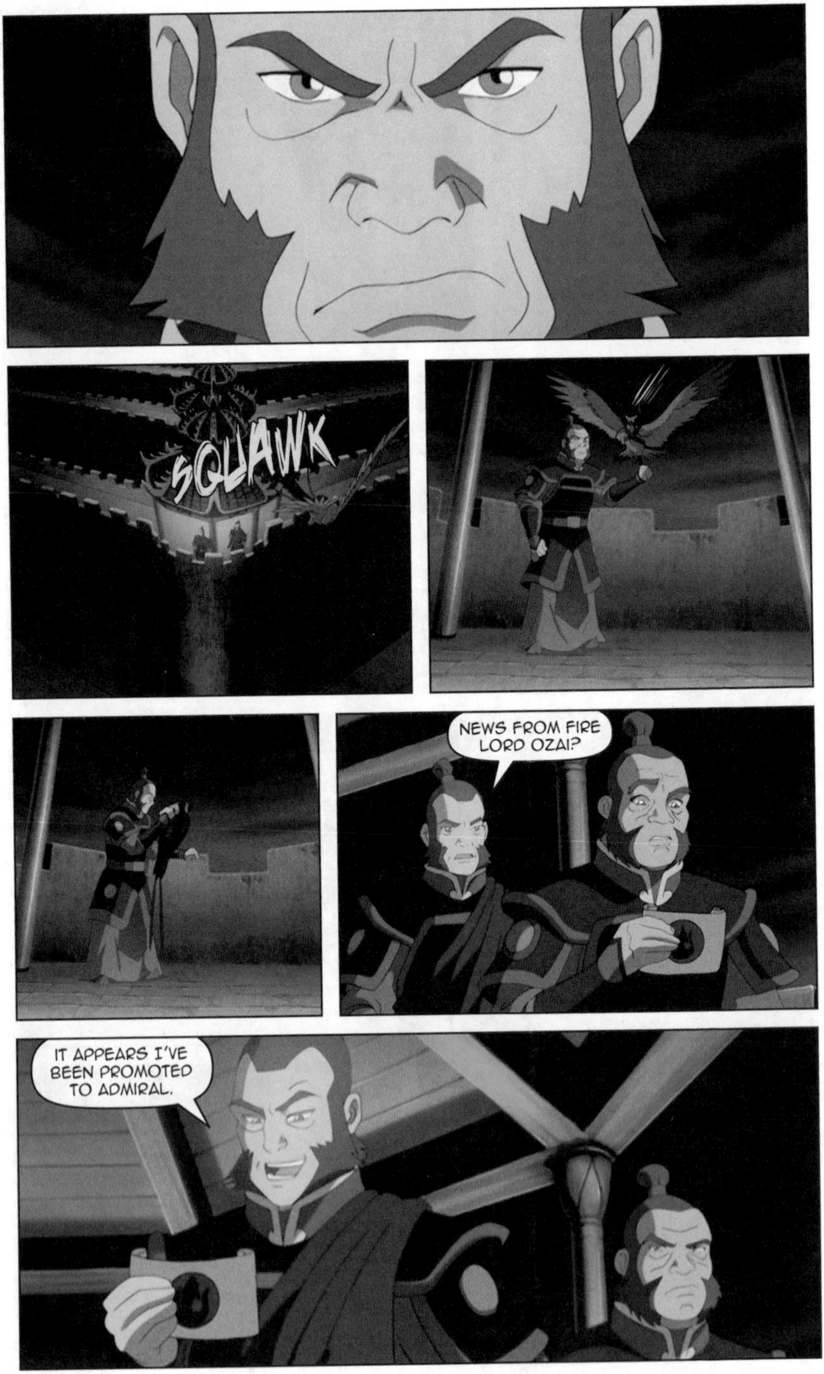
SQUAWK
NEWS FROM FIRE LORD OZAI?
IT APPEARS I'VE BEEN PROMOTED TO ADMIRAL.

MY REQUEST IS NOW AN ORDER.

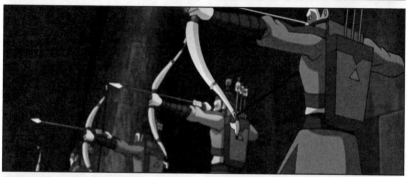

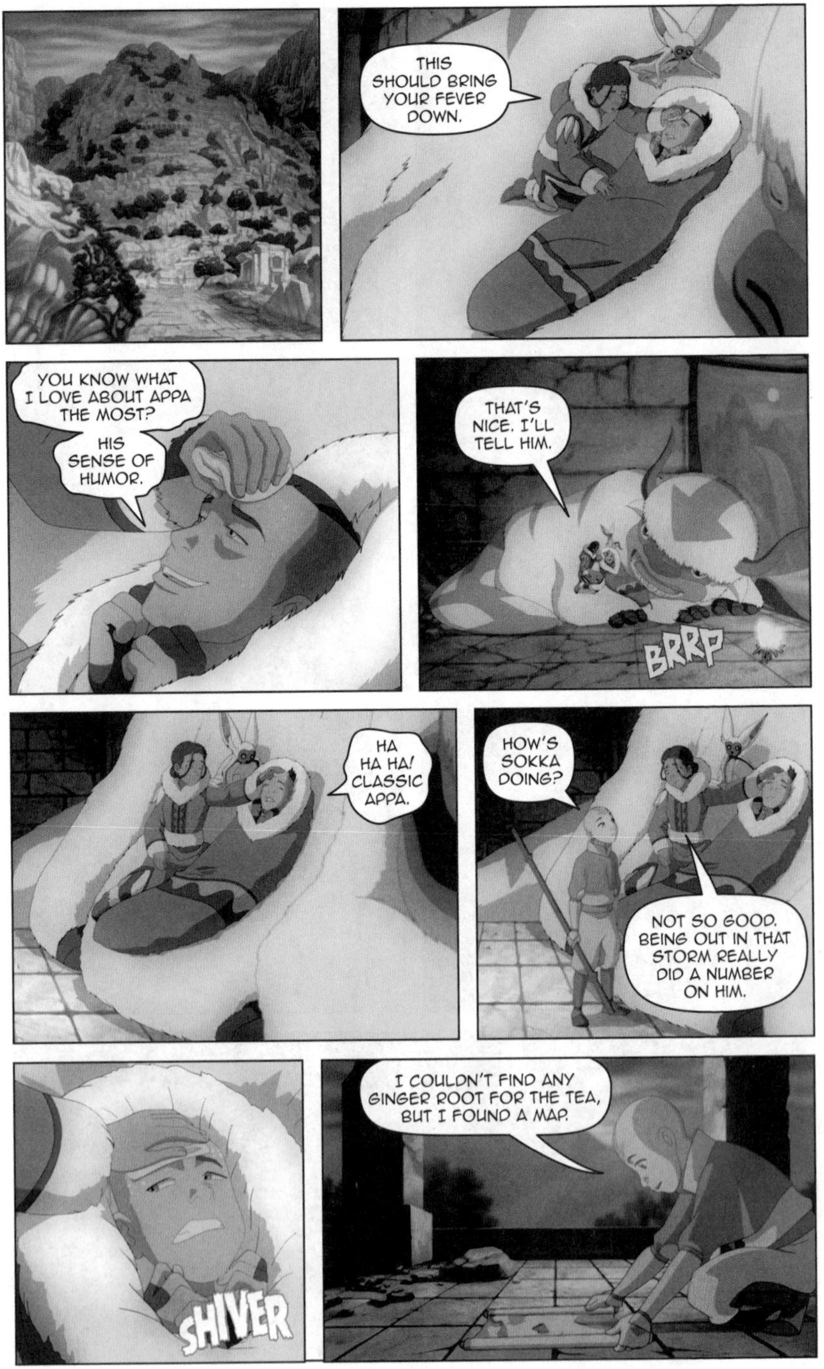
THIS SHOULD BRING YOUR FEVER DOWN.
YOU KNOW WHAT I LOVE ABOUT APPA THE MOST?
HIS SENSE OF HUMOR.
THAT'S NICE. I'LL TELL HIM.
BRRP
HA HA HA! CLASSIC APPA.
HOW'S SOKKA DOING?
NOT SO GOOD. BEING OUT IN THAT STORM REALLY DID A NUMBER ON HIM.
SHIVER
I COULDN'T FIND ANY GINGER ROOT FOR THE TEA, BUT I FOUND A MAP.

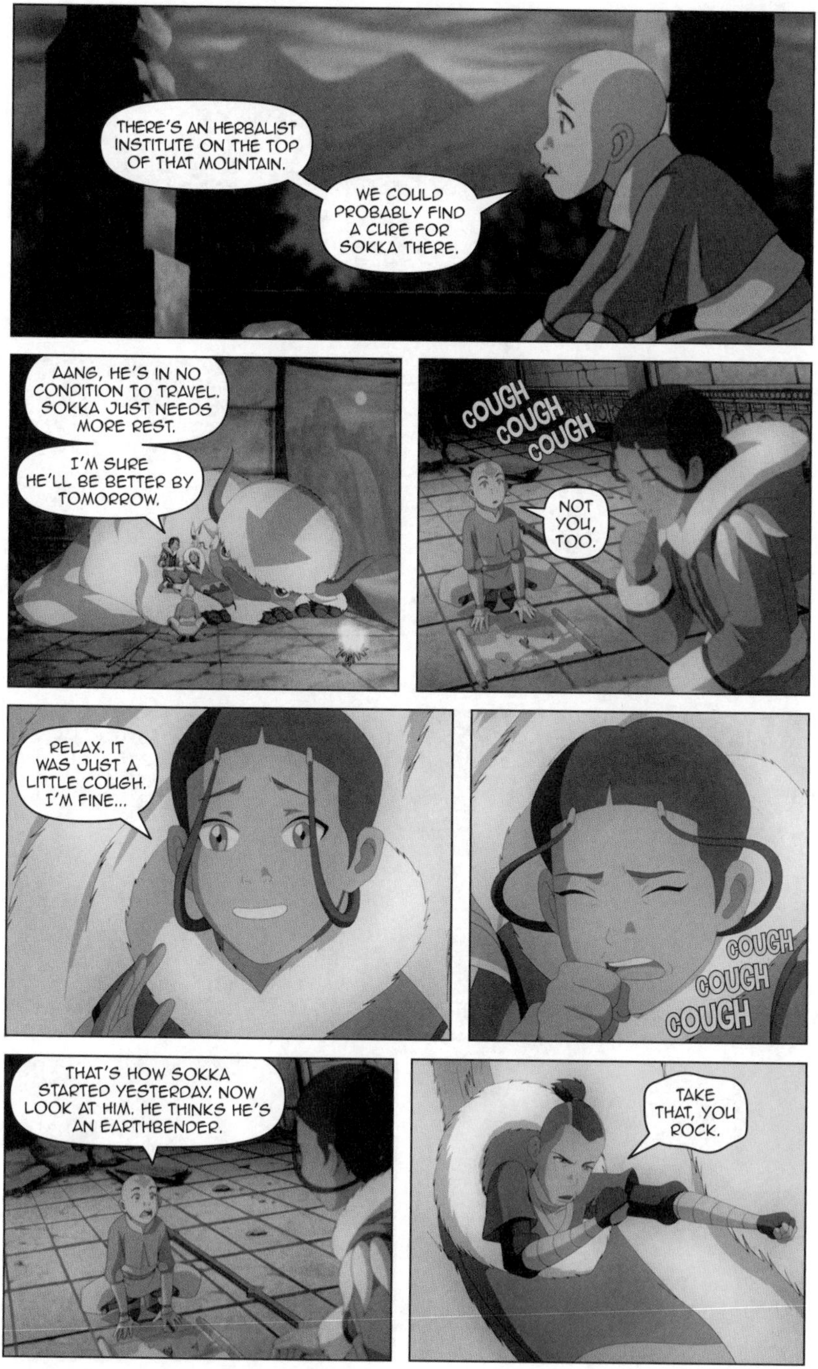
THERE'S AN HERBALIST INSTITUTE ON THE TOP OF THAT MOUNTAIN.
WE COULD PROBABLY FIND A CURE FOR SOKKA THERE.
AANG, HE'S IN NO CONDITION TO TRAVEL. SOKKA JUST NEEDS MORE REST.
I'M SURE HE'LL BE BETTER BY TOMORROW.
COUGH COUGH COUGH
NOT YOU, TOO.
RELAX. IT WAS JUST A LITTLE COUGH. I'M FINE...
COUGH COUGH COUGH
THAT'S HOW SOKKA STARTED YESTERDAY. NOW LOOK AT HIM. HE THINKS HE'S AN EARTHBENDER.
TAKE THAT, YOU ROCK.

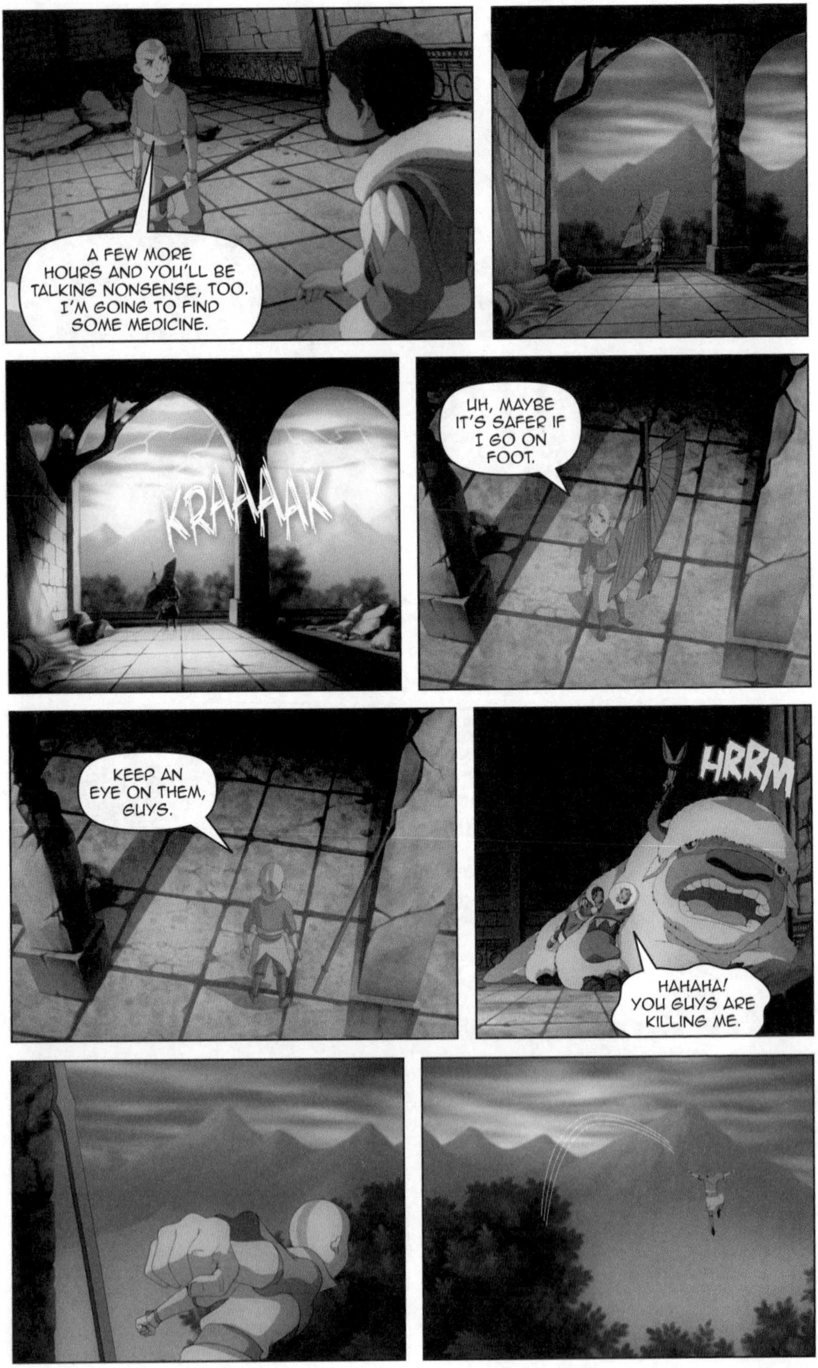

A FEW MORE HOURS AND YOU'LL BE TALKING NONSENSE, TOO. I'M GOING TO FIND SOME MEDICINE.
KRAAAAK
UH, MAYBE IT'S SAFER IF I GO ON FOOT.
KEEP AN EYE ON THEM, GUYS.
HRRM
HAHAHA! YOU GUYS ARE KILLING ME.

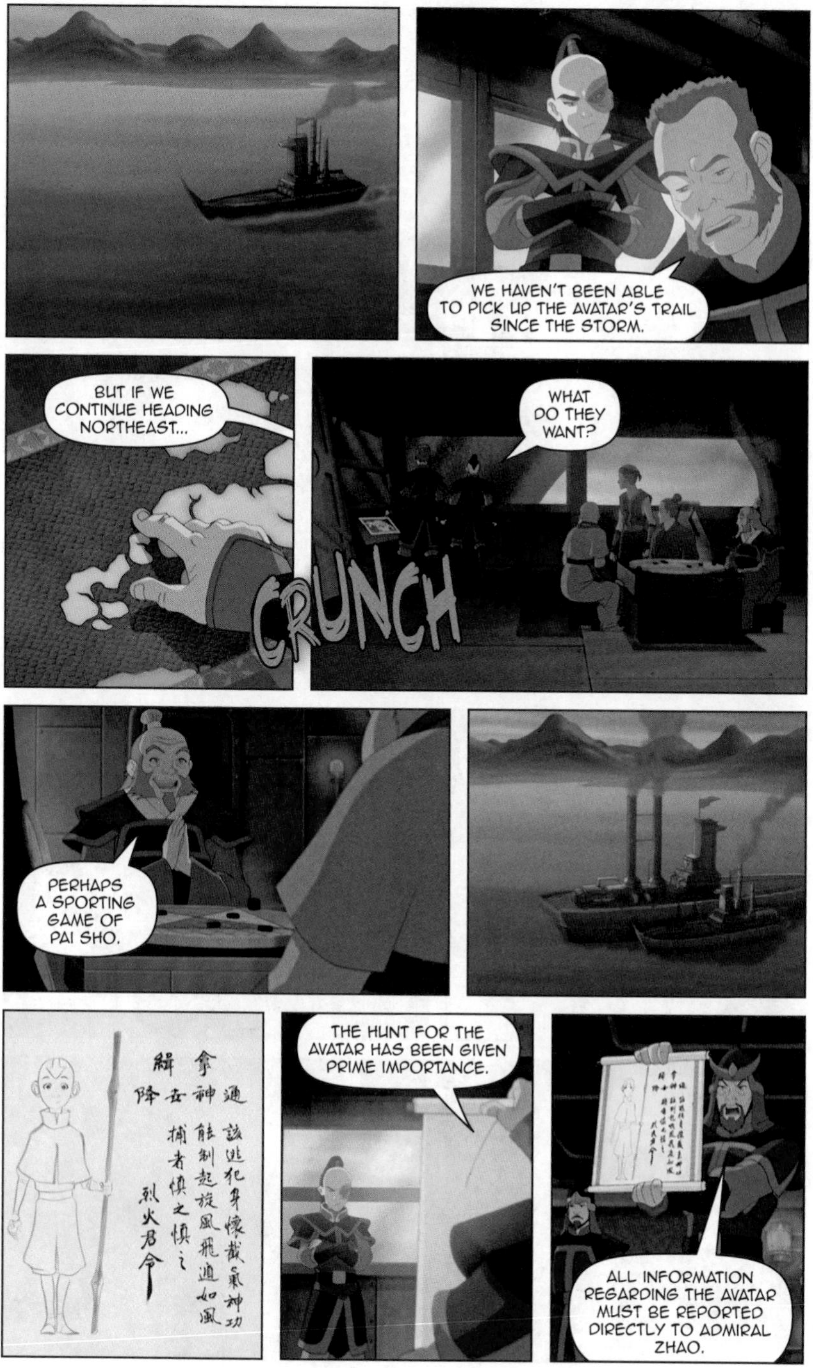
WE HAVEN'T BEEN ABLE TO PICK UP THE AVATAR'S TRAIL SINCE THE STORM.
BUT IF WE CONTINUE HEADING NORTHEAST...
CRUNCH
WHAT DO THEY WANT?
PERHAPS A SPORTING GAME OF PAI SHO.
THE HUNT FOR THE AVATAR HAS BEEN GIVEN PRIME IMPORTANCE.
ALL INFORMATION REGARDING THE AVATAR MUST BE REPORTED DIRECTLY TO ADMIRAL ZHAO.

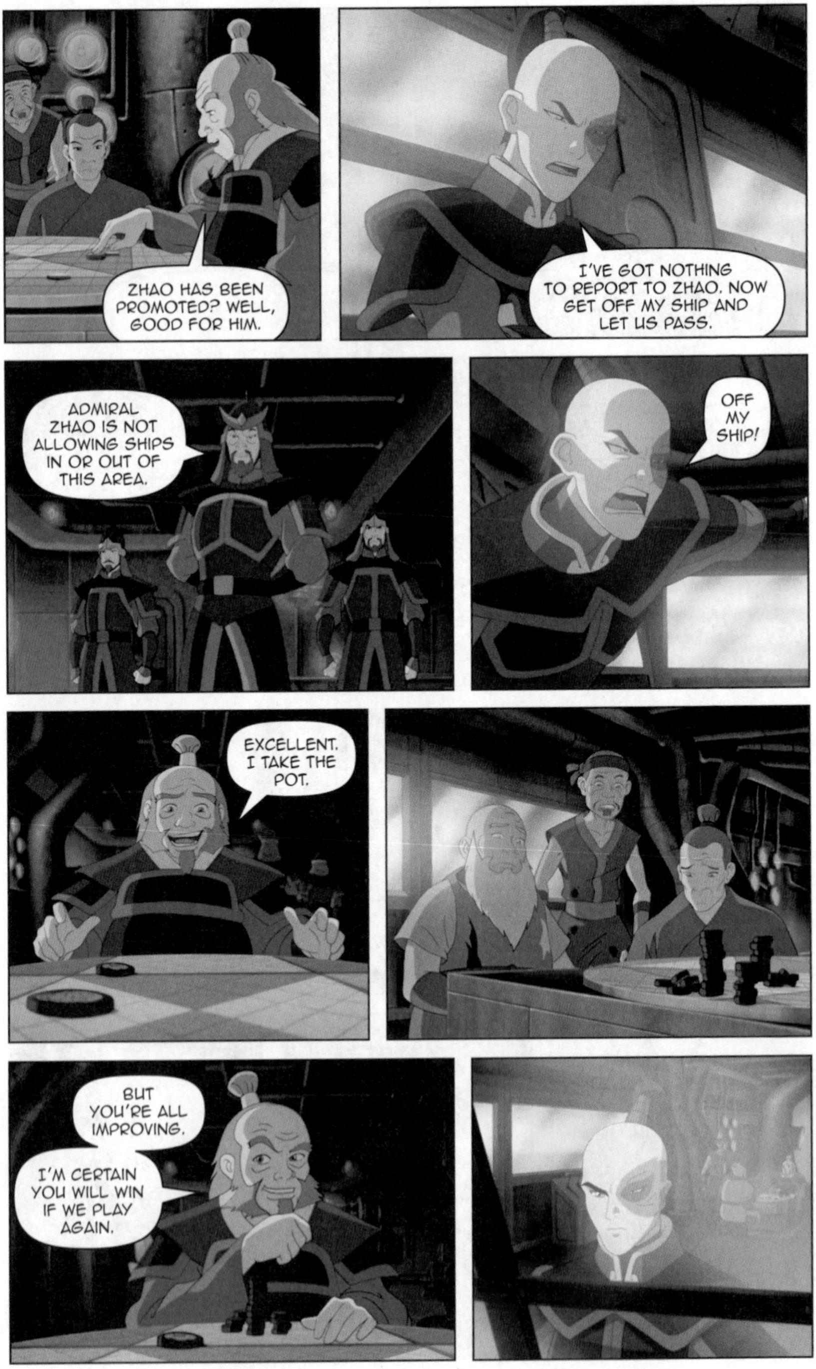
ZHAO HAS BEEN PROMOTED? WELL, GOOD FOR HIM.
I'VE GOT NOTHING TO REPORT TO ZHAO. NOW GET OFF MY SHIP AND LET US PASS.
ADMIRAL ZHAO IS NOT ALLOWING SHIPS IN OR OUT OF THIS AREA.
OFF MY SHIP!
EXCELLENT. I TAKE THE POT.
BUT YOU'RE ALL IMPROVING.
I'M CERTAIN YOU WILL WIN IF WE PLAY AGAIN.

IT SAYS HERE THAT THE AVATAR CAN CREATE TORNADOES AND RUN FASTER THAN THE WIND. PRETTY AMAZING.

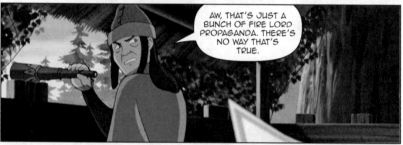

AW, THAT'S JUST A BUNCH OF FIRE LORD PROPAGANDA. THERE'S NO WAY THAT'S TRUE.

WHOOSH

WHOOSH

WHOOSH

WHOOSH

HRRRRN!

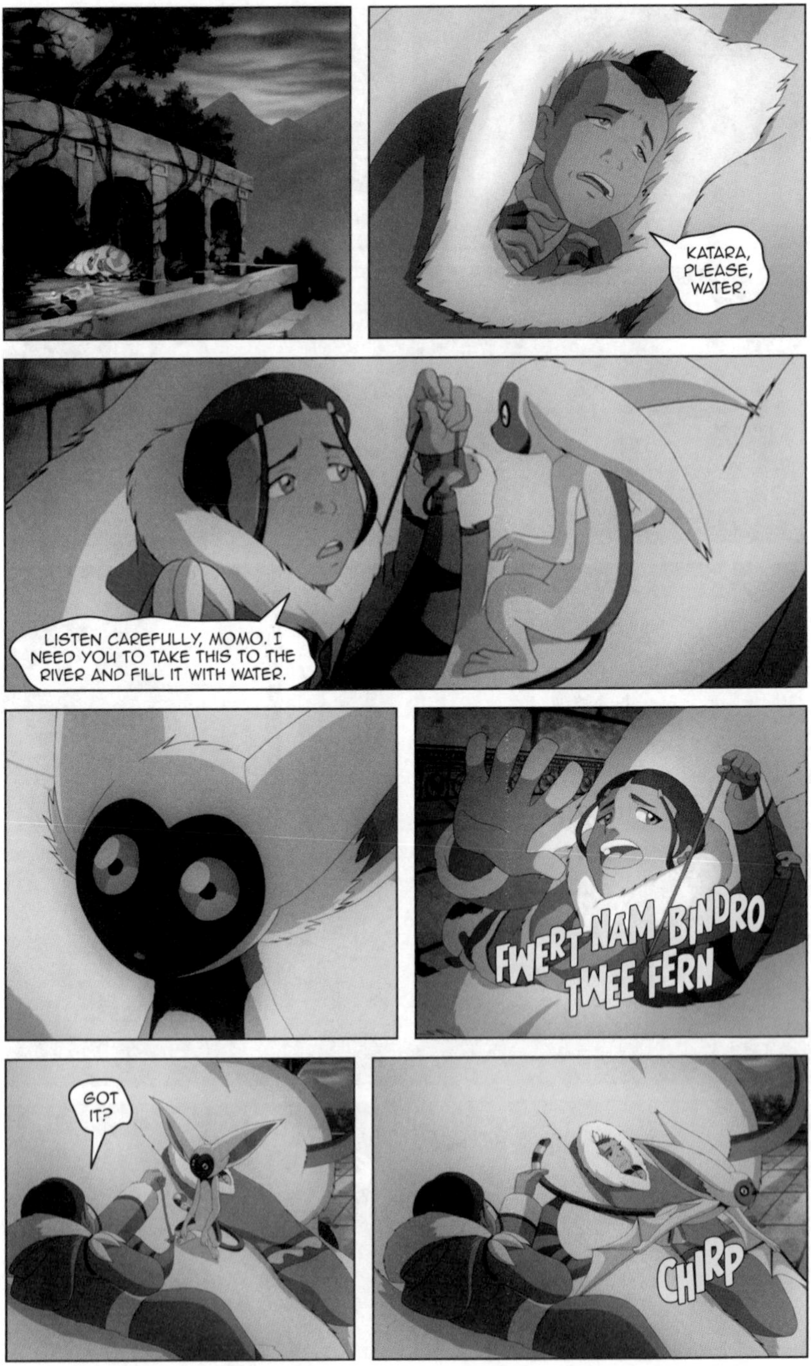
KATARA, PLEASE, WATER.
LISTEN CAREFULLY, MOMO. I NEED YOU TO TAKE THIS TO THE RIVER AND FILL IT WITH WATER.
FWERT NAM BINDRO TWEE FERN
GOT IT?
CHIRP

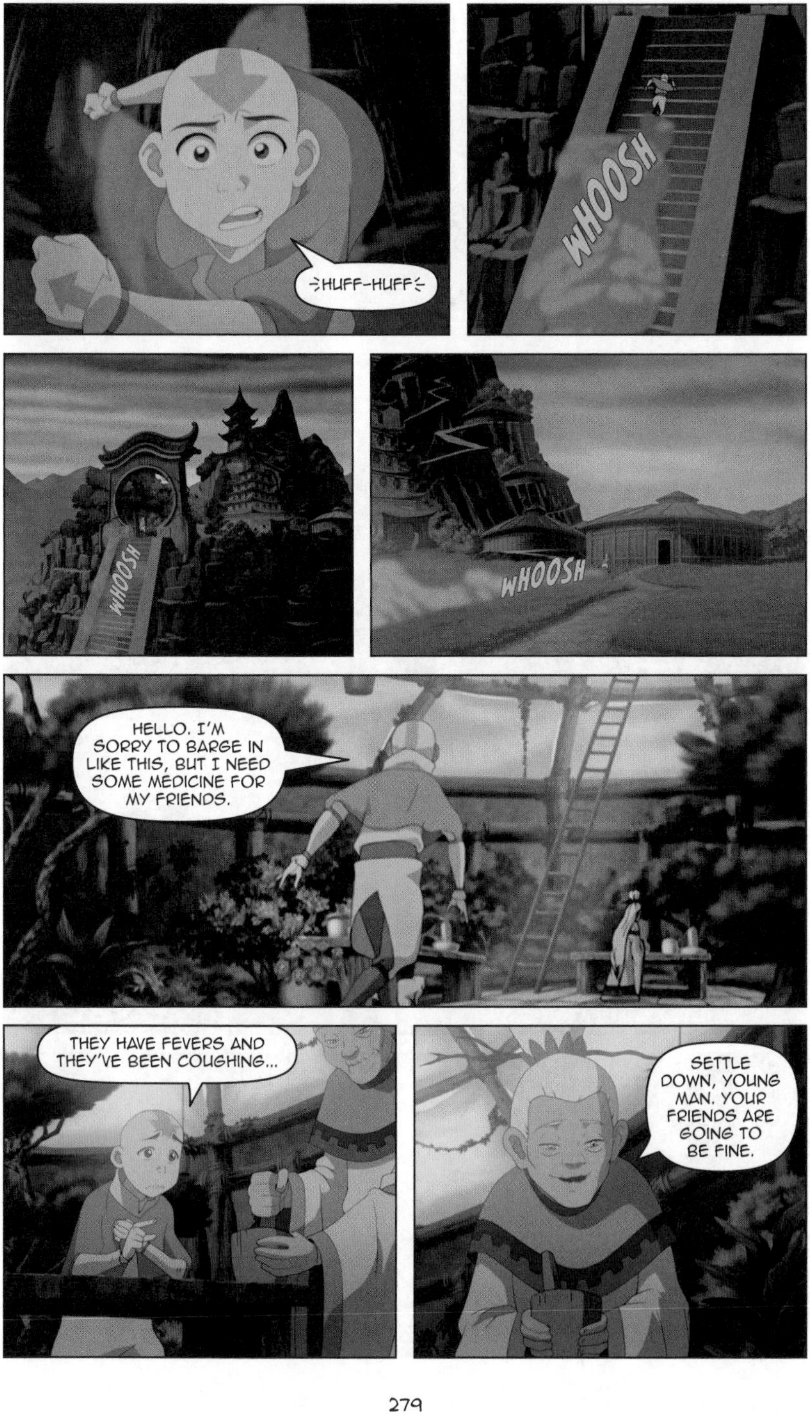
HUFF-HUFF
WHOOSH
WHOOSH
WHOOSH
HELLO. I'M SORRY TO BARGE IN LIKE THIS, BUT I NEED SOME MEDICINE FOR MY FRIENDS.
THEY HAVE FEVERS AND THEY'VE BEEN COUGHING...
SETTLE DOWN, YOUNG MAN. YOUR FRIENDS ARE GOING TO BE FINE.

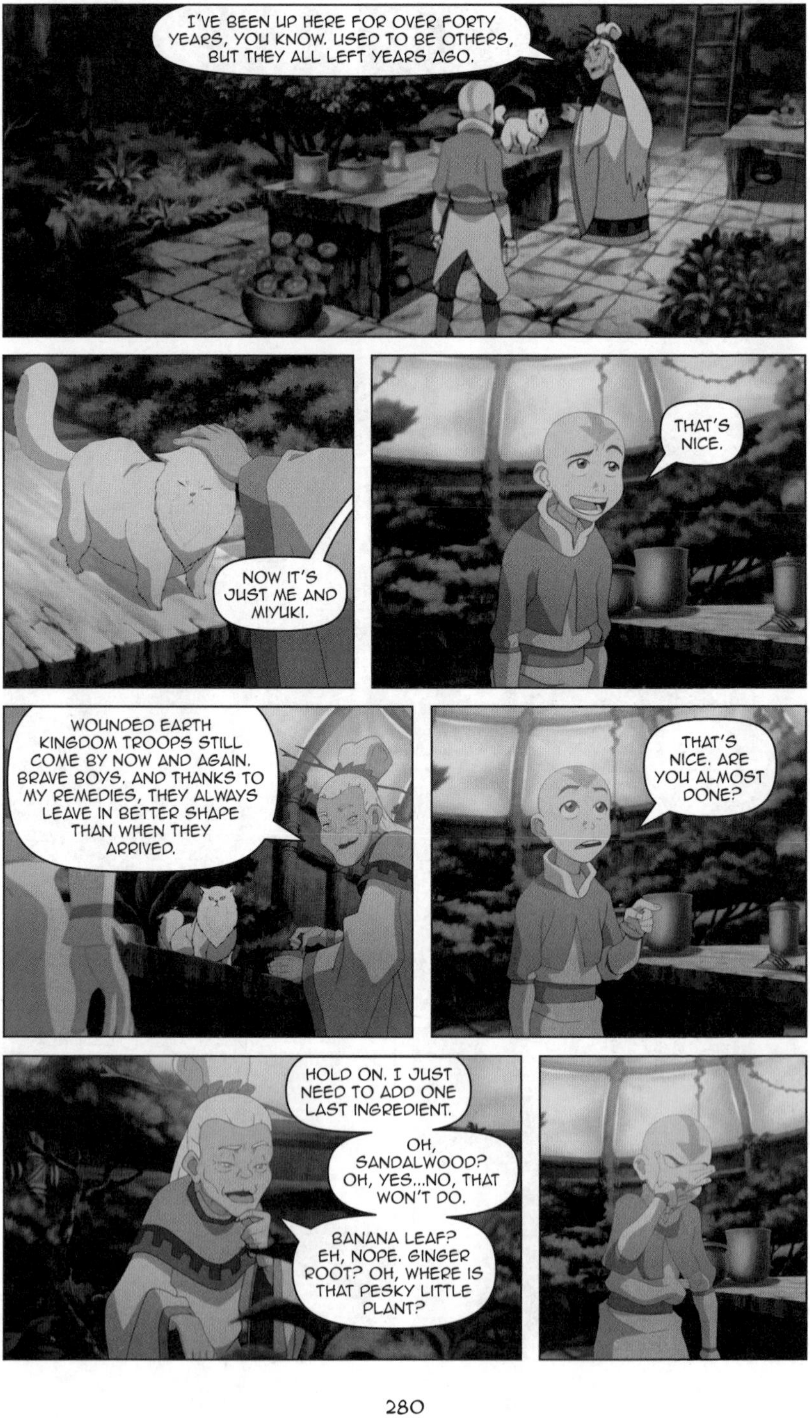
I'VE BEEN UP HERE FOR OVER FORTY YEARS, YOU KNOW. USED TO BE OTHERS, BUT THEY ALL LEFT YEARS AGO.
NOW IT'S JUST ME AND MIYUKI.
THAT'S NICE.
WOUNDED EARTH KINGDOM TROOPS STILL COME BY NOW AND AGAIN. BRAVE BOYS. AND THANKS TO MY REMEDIES, THEY ALWAYS LEAVE IN BETTER SHAPE THAN WHEN THEY ARRIVED.
THAT'S NICE. ARE YOU ALMOST DONE?
HOLD ON. I JUST NEED TO ADD ONE LAST INGREDIENT.
OH, SANDALWOOD? OH, YES...NO, THAT WON'T DO.
BANANA LEAF? EH, NOPE. GINGER ROOT? OH, WHERE IS THAT PESKY LITTLE PLANT?

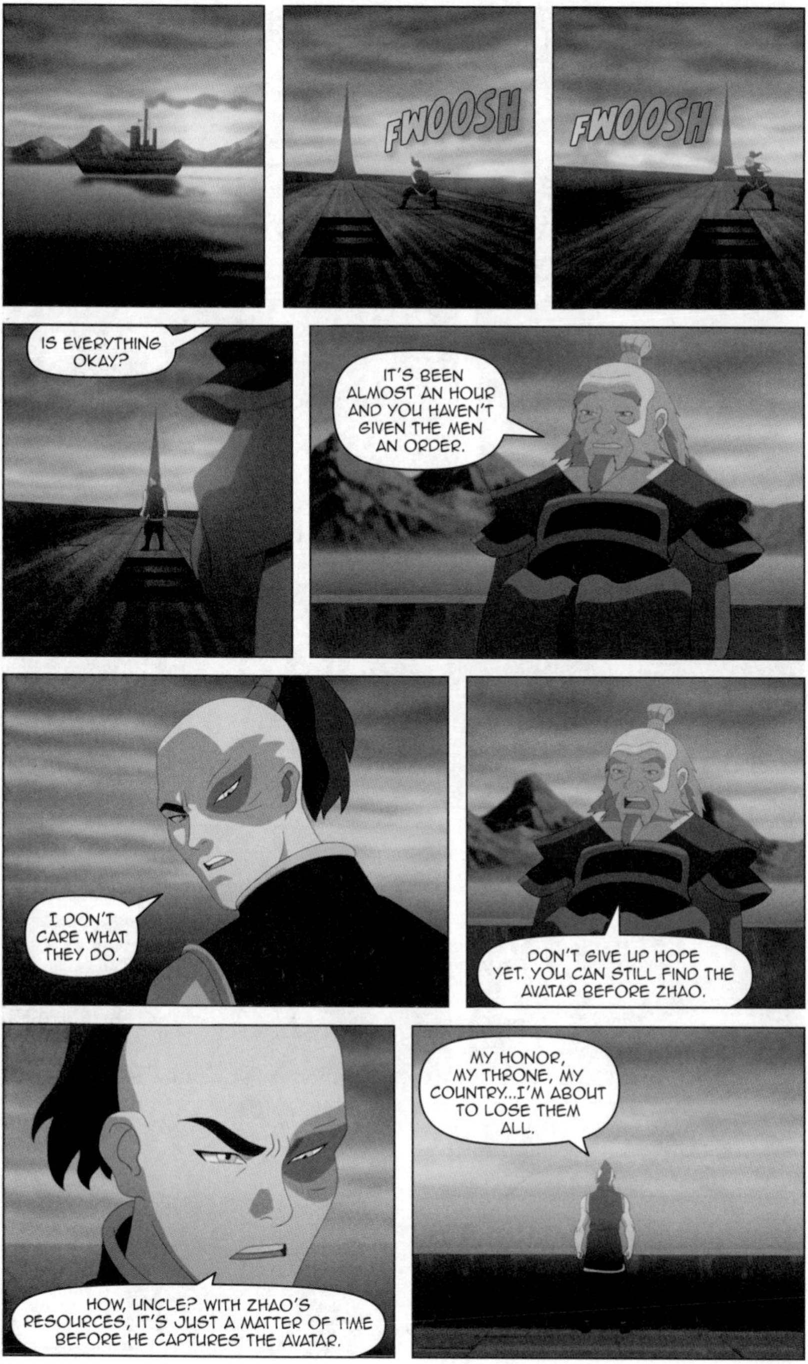

FWOOSH
FWOOSH
IS EVERYTHING OKAY?
IT'S BEEN ALMOST AN HOUR AND YOU HAVEN'T GIVEN THE MEN AN ORDER.
I DON'T CARE WHAT THEY DO.
DON'T GIVE UP HOPE YET. YOU CAN STILL FIND THE AVATAR BEFORE ZHAO.
HOW, UNCLE? WITH ZHAO'S RESOURCES, IT'S JUST A MATTER OF TIME BEFORE HE CAPTURES THE AVATAR.
MY HONOR, MY THRONE, MY COUNTRY...I'M ABOUT TO LOSE THEM ALL.

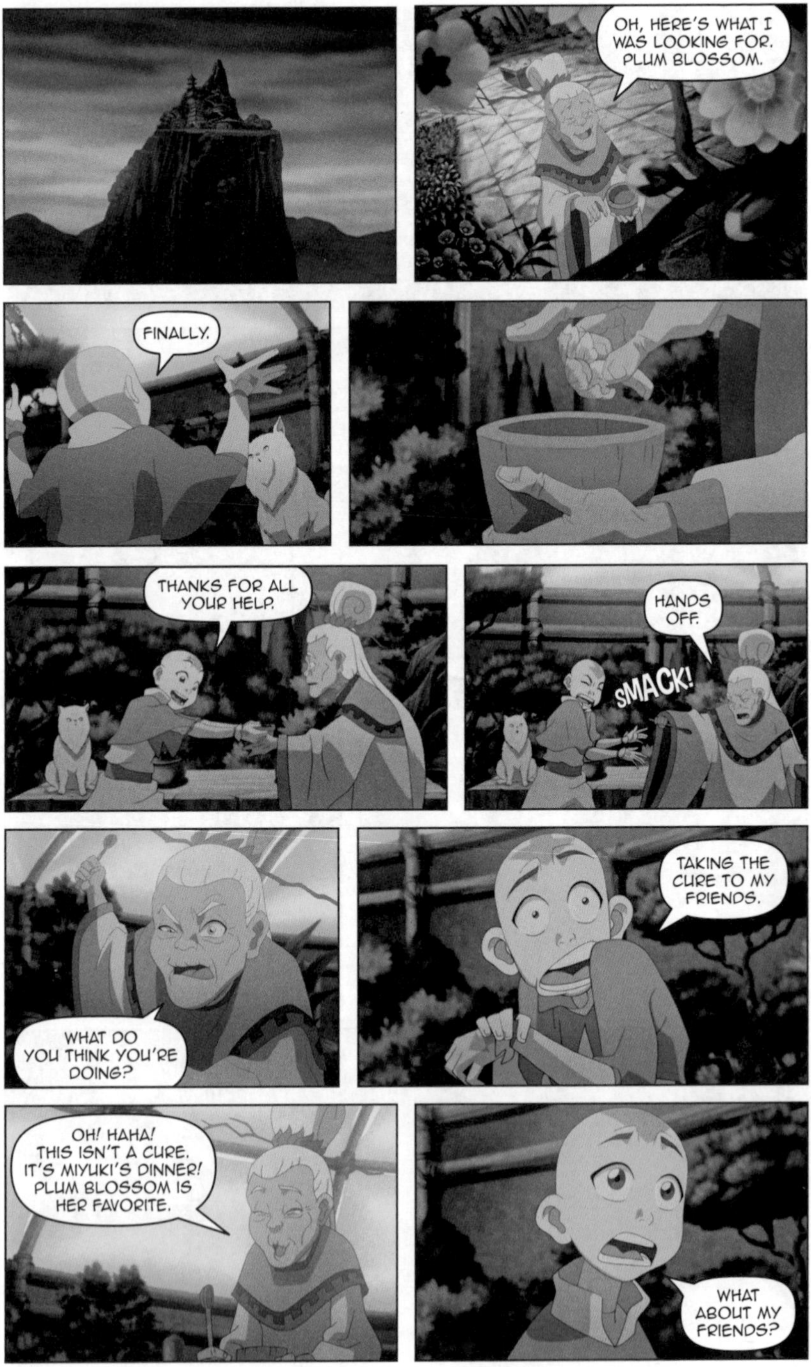
OH, HERE'S WHAT I WAS LOOKING FOR. PLUM BLOSSOM.
FINALLY.
THANKS FOR ALL YOUR HELP.
HANDS OFF.
SMACK!
WHAT DO YOU THINK YOU'RE DOING?
TAKING THE CURE TO MY FRIENDS.
OH! HAHA! THIS ISN'T A CURE. IT'S MIYUKI'S DINNER! PLUM BLOSSOM IS HER FAVORITE.
WHAT ABOUT MY FRIENDS?

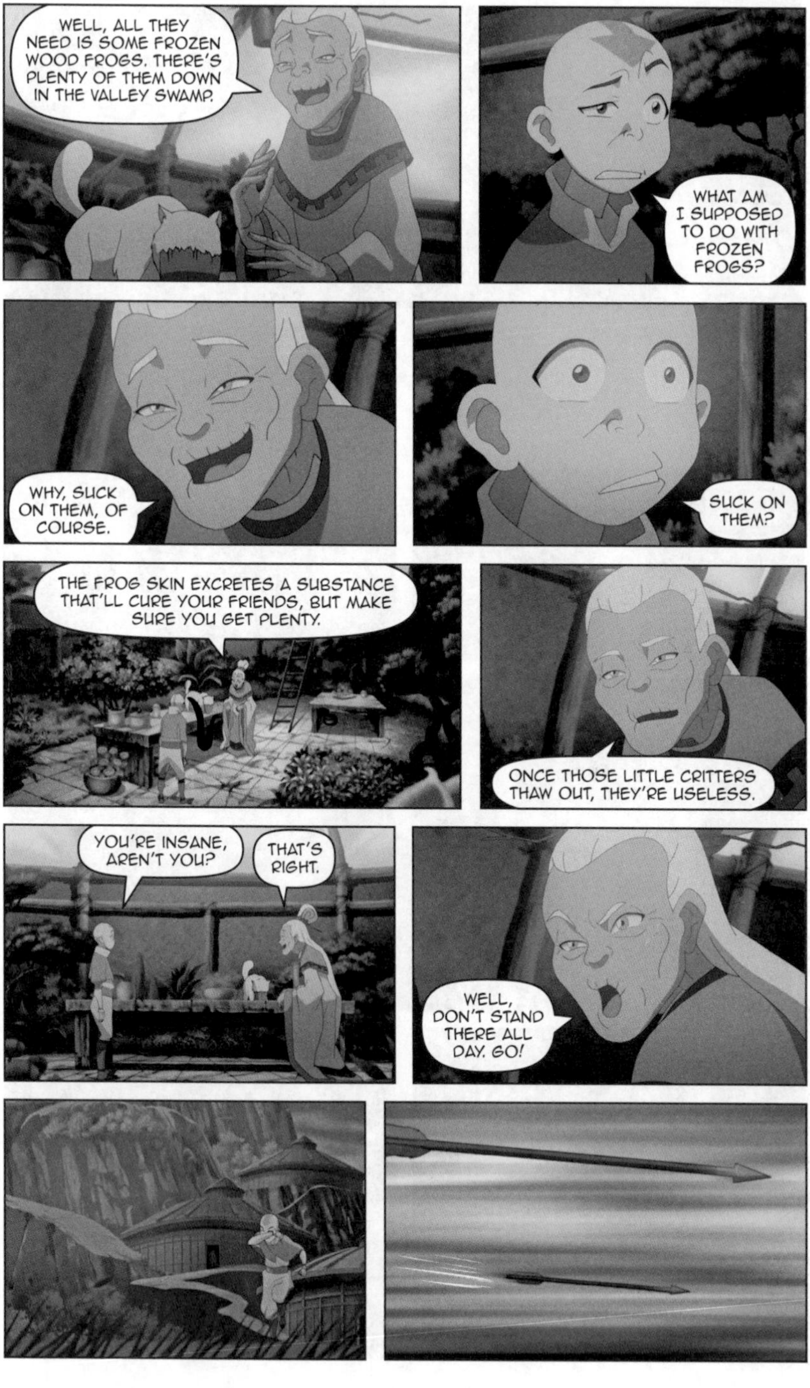
WELL, ALL THEY NEED IS SOME FROZEN WOOD FROGS. THERE'S PLENTY OF THEM DOWN IN THE VALLEY SWAMP.
WHAT AM I SUPPOSED TO DO WITH FROZEN FROGS?
WHY, SUCK ON THEM, OF COURSE.
SUCK ON THEM?
THE FROG SKIN EXCRETES A SUBSTANCE THAT'LL CURE YOUR FRIENDS, BUT MAKE SURE YOU GET PLENTY.
ONCE THOSE LITTLE CRITTERS THAW OUT, THEY'RE USELESS.
YOU'RE INSANE, AREN'T YOU?
THAT'S RIGHT.
WELL, DON'T STAND THERE ALL DAY. GO!

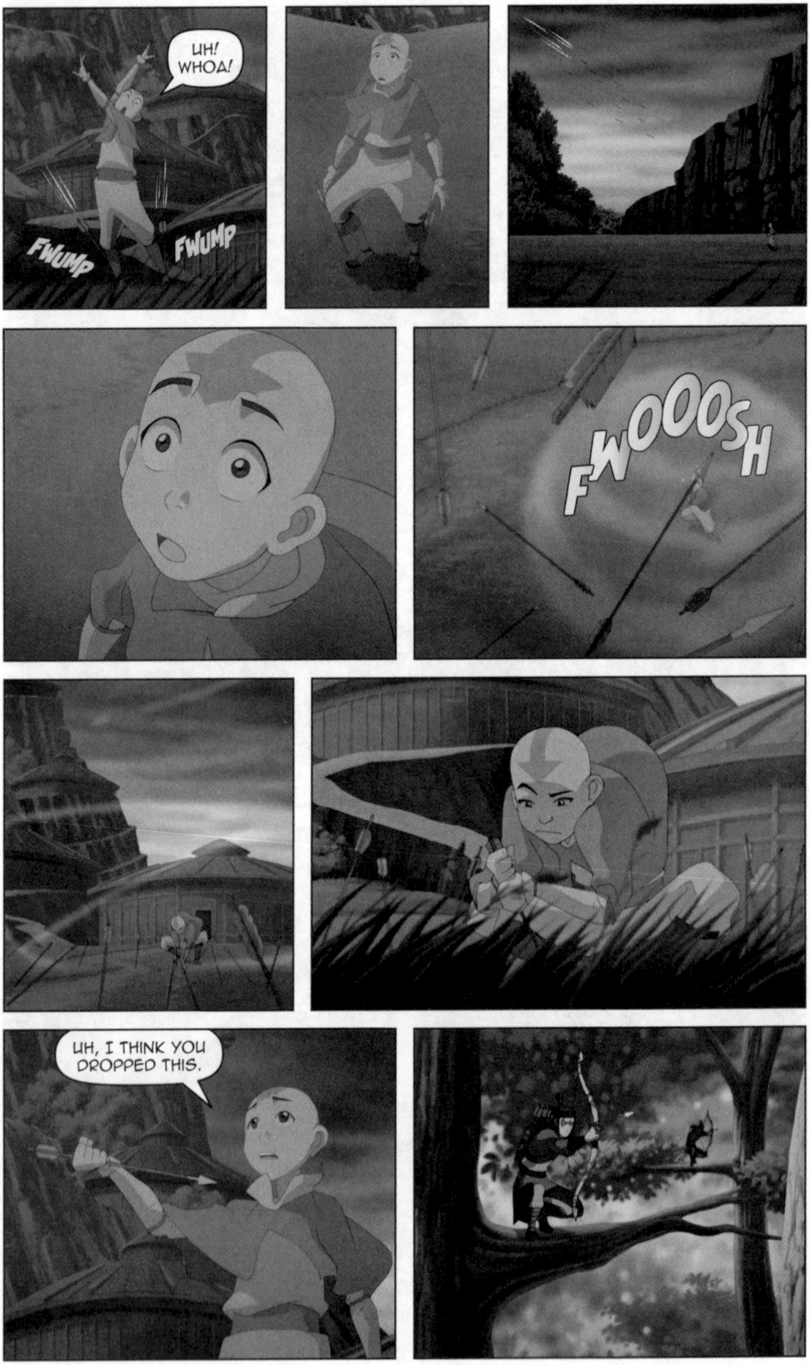
UH! WHOA!
FWUMP
FWUMP
FWOOOSH
UH, I THINK YOU DROPPED THIS.

UGH!

AAAHHH!

FWUMP

FWUMP

FWUMP

FWUMP

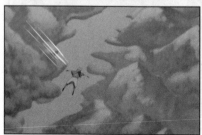

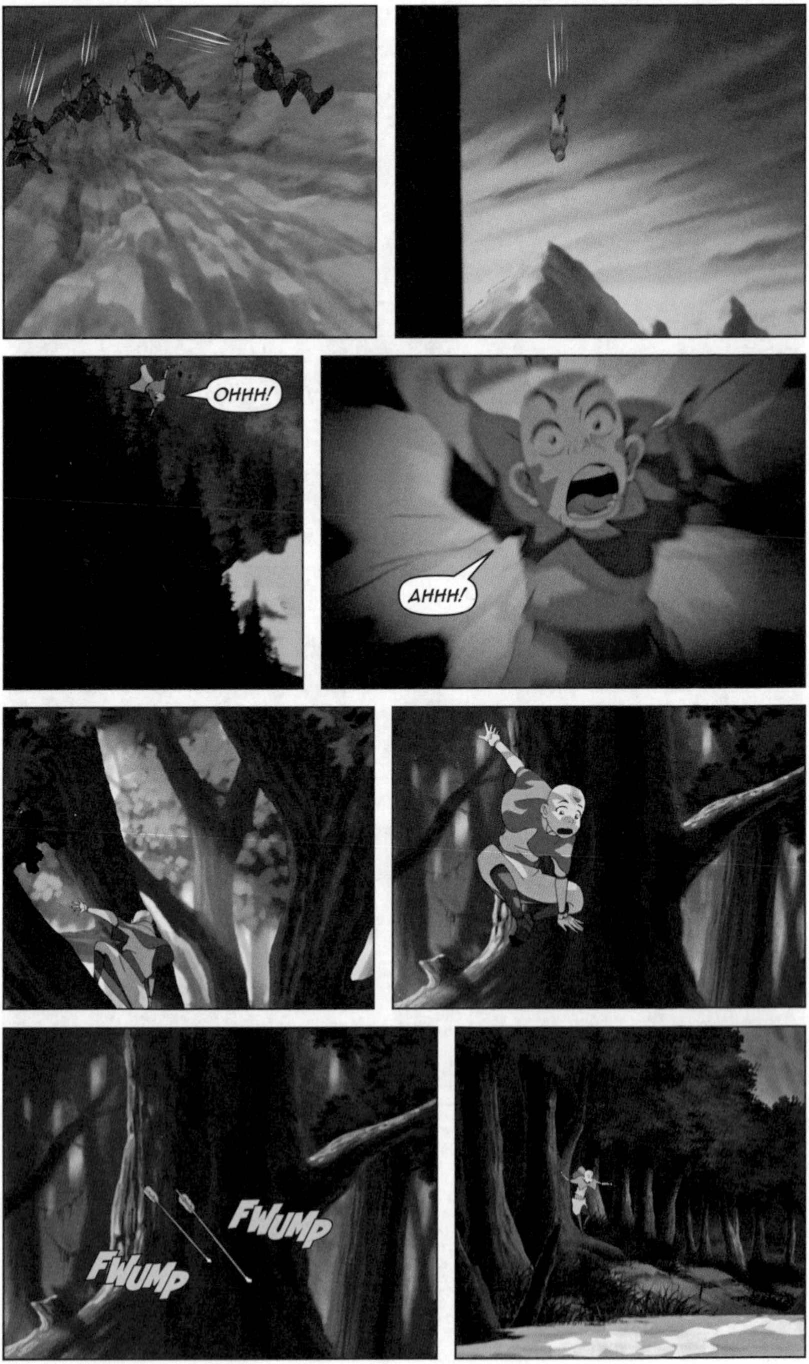
OHHH!
AHHH!
FWUMP
FWUMP

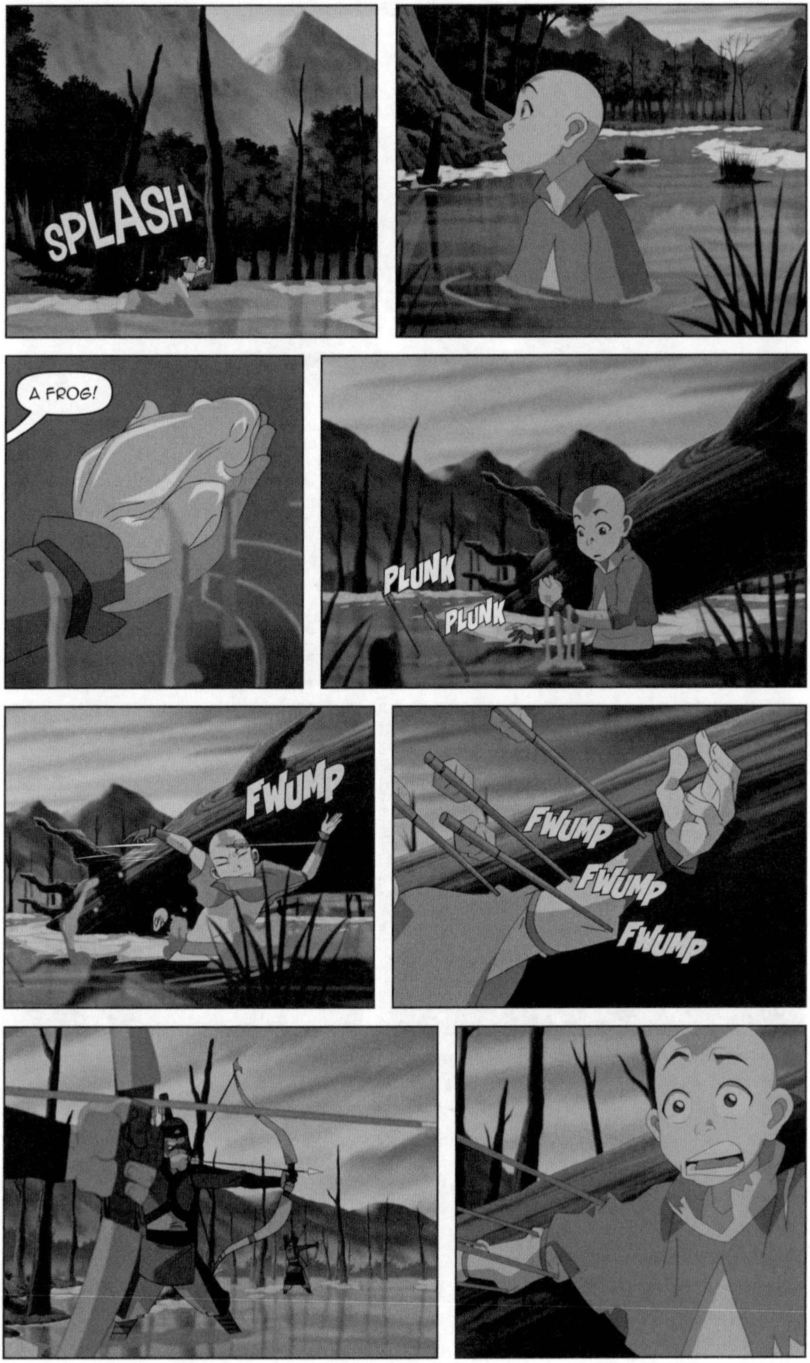
SPLASH
A FROG!
PLUNK
PLUNK
FWUMP
FWUMP
FWUMP
FWUMP

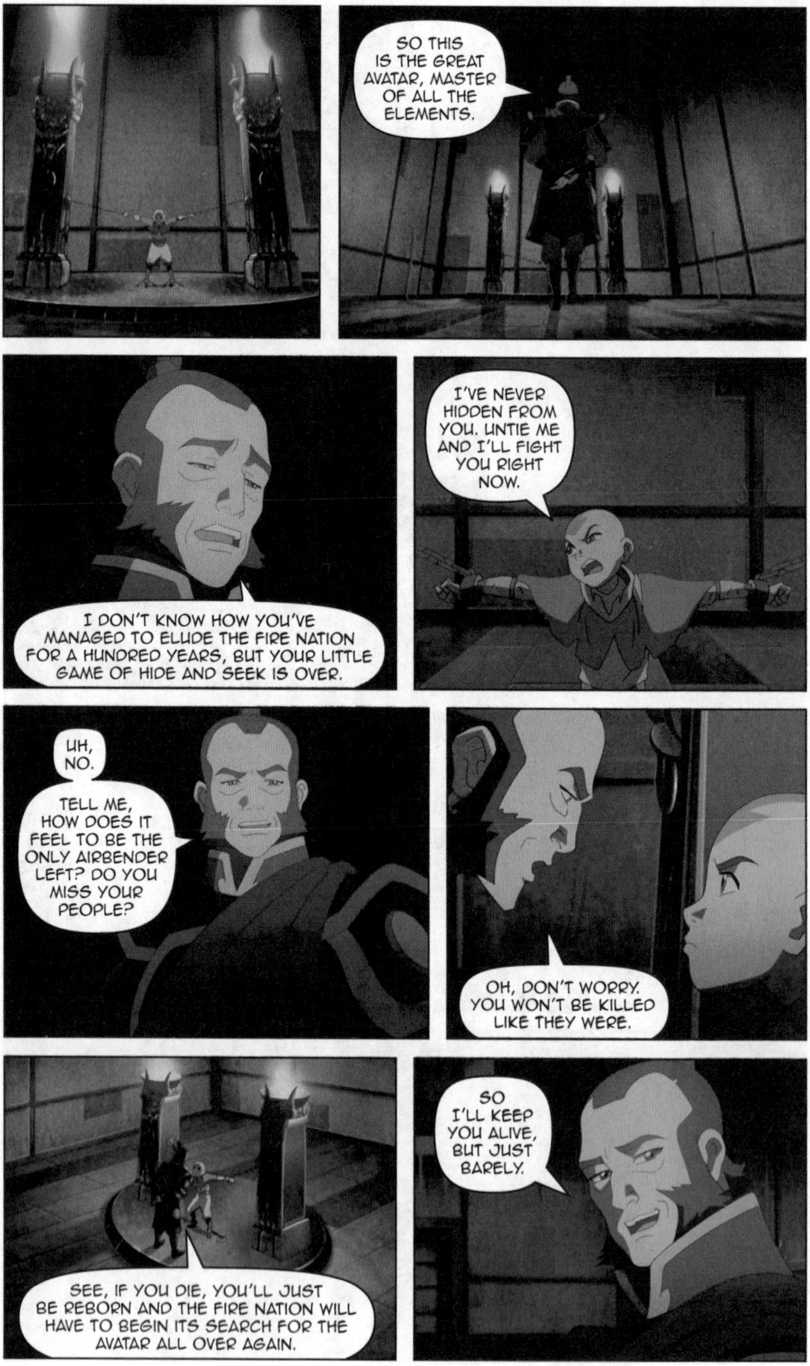
SO THIS IS THE GREAT AVATAR, MASTER OF ALL THE ELEMENTS.
I DON'T KNOW HOW YOU'VE MANAGED TO ELUDE THE FIRE NATION FOR A HUNDRED YEARS, BUT YOUR LITTLE GAME OF HIDE AND SEEK IS OVER.
I'VE NEVER HIDDEN FROM YOU. UNTIE ME AND I'LL FIGHT YOU RIGHT NOW.
UH, NO.
TELL ME, HOW DOES IT FEEL TO BE THE ONLY AIRBENDER LEFT? DO YOU MISS YOUR PEOPLE?
OH, DON'T WORRY. YOU WON'T BE KILLED LIKE THEY WERE.
SEE, IF YOU DIE, YOU'LL JUST BE REBORN AND THE FIRE NATION WILL HAVE TO BEGIN ITS SEARCH FOR THE AVATAR ALL OVER AGAIN.
SO I'LL KEEP YOU ALIVE, BUT JUST BARELY.

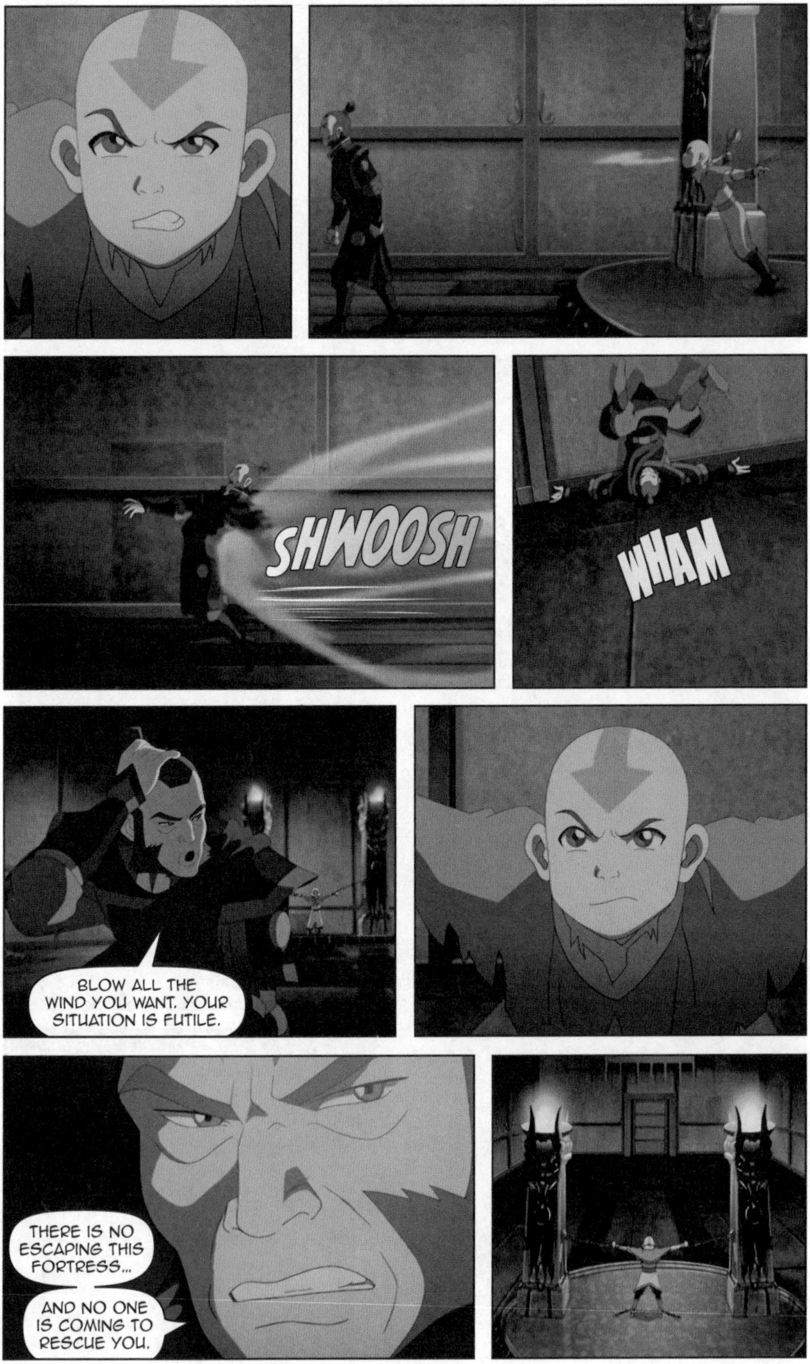
SHWOOSH
WHAM
BLOW ALL THE WIND YOU WANT. YOUR SITUATION IS FUTILE.
THERE IS NO ESCAPING THIS FORTRESS...
AND NO ONE IS COMING TO RESCUE YOU.

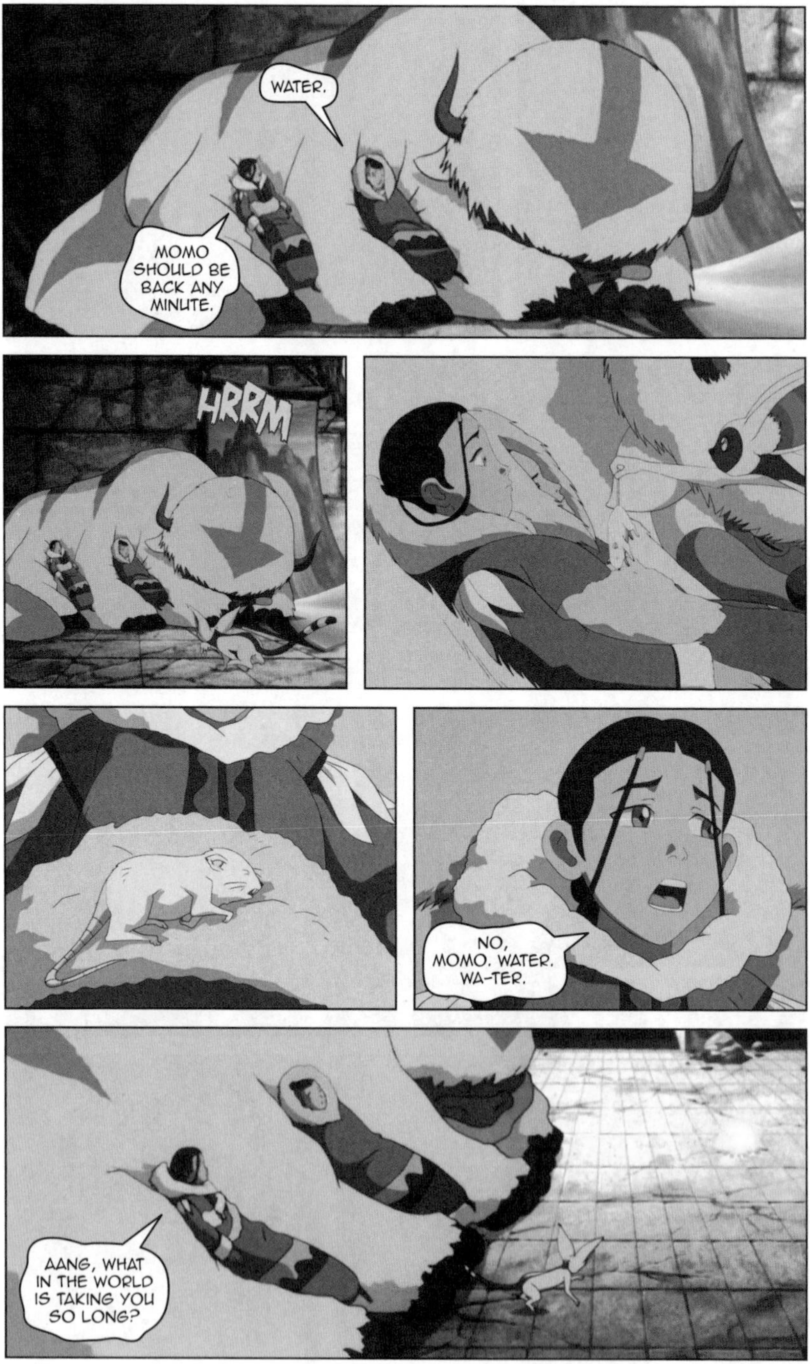
WATER.
MOMO SHOULD BE BACK ANY MINUTE.
HRRM
NO, MOMO. WATER. WA-TER.
AANG, WHAT IN THE WORLD IS TAKING YOU SO LONG?

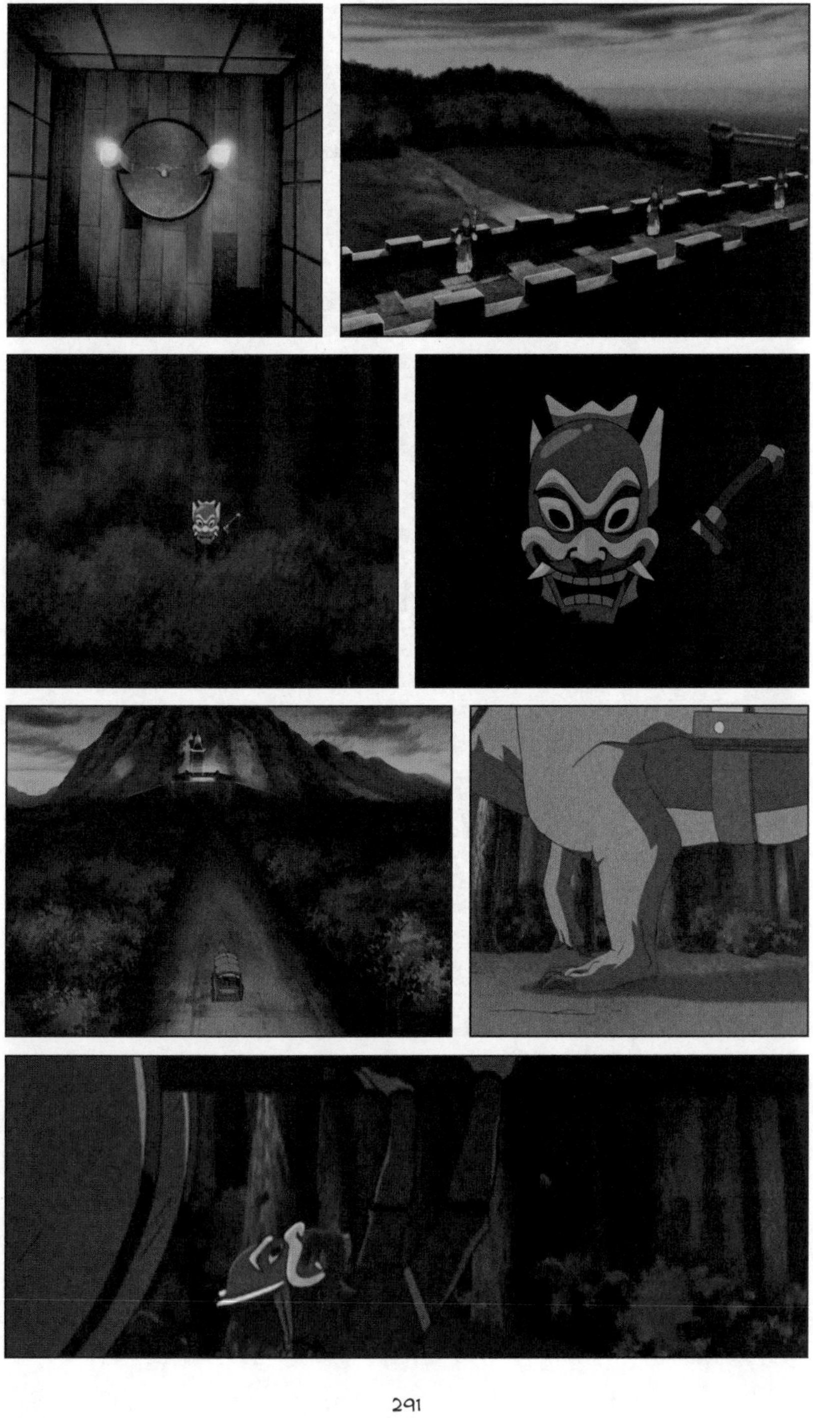

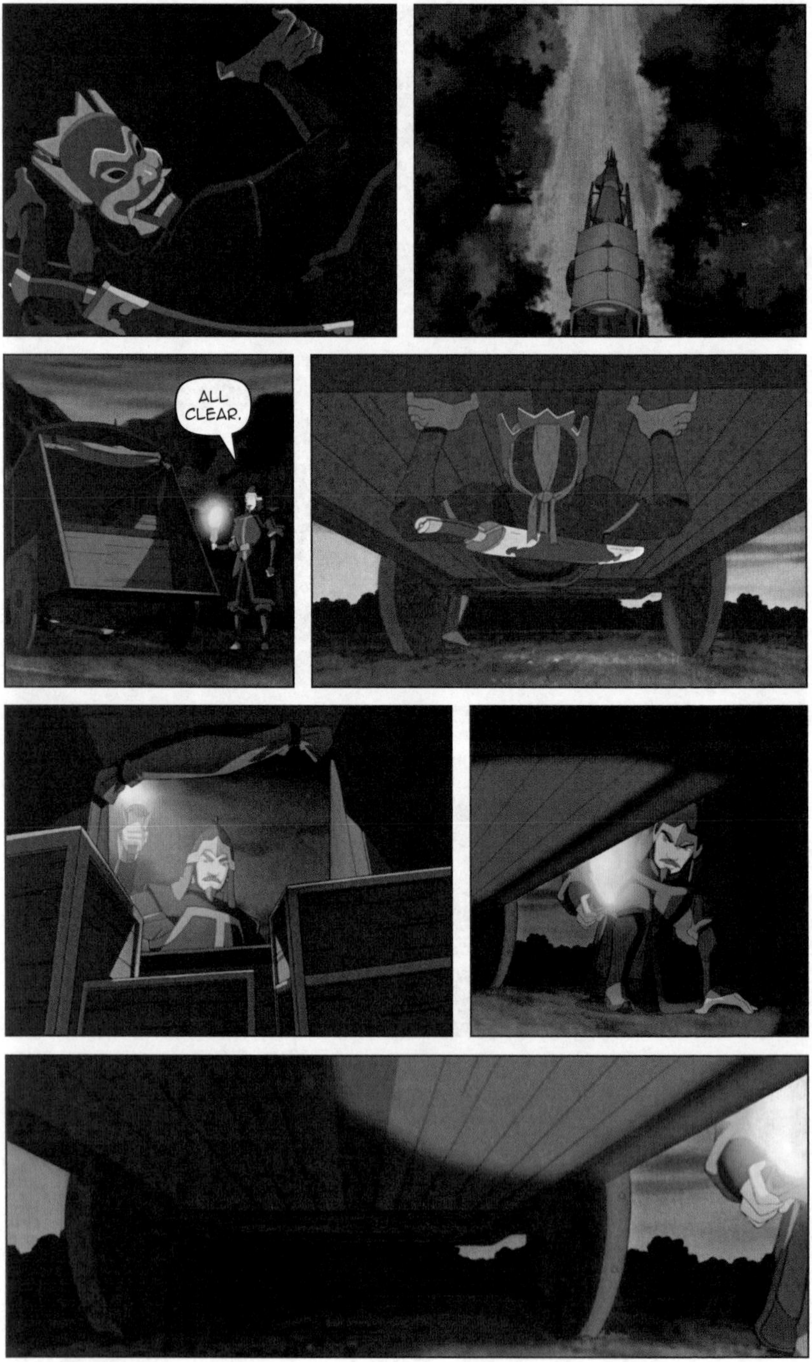
ALL CLEAR.

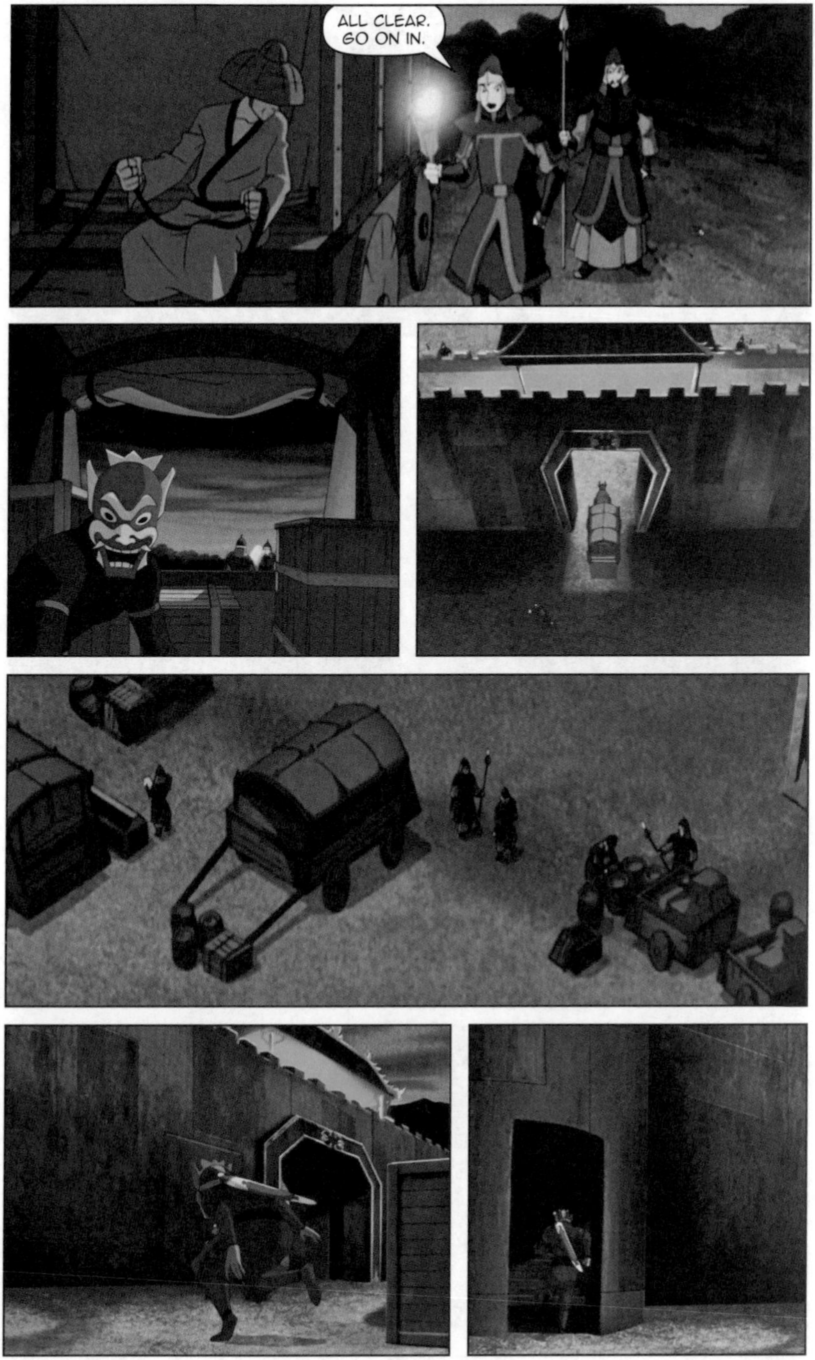
ALL CLEAR.
GO ON IN.

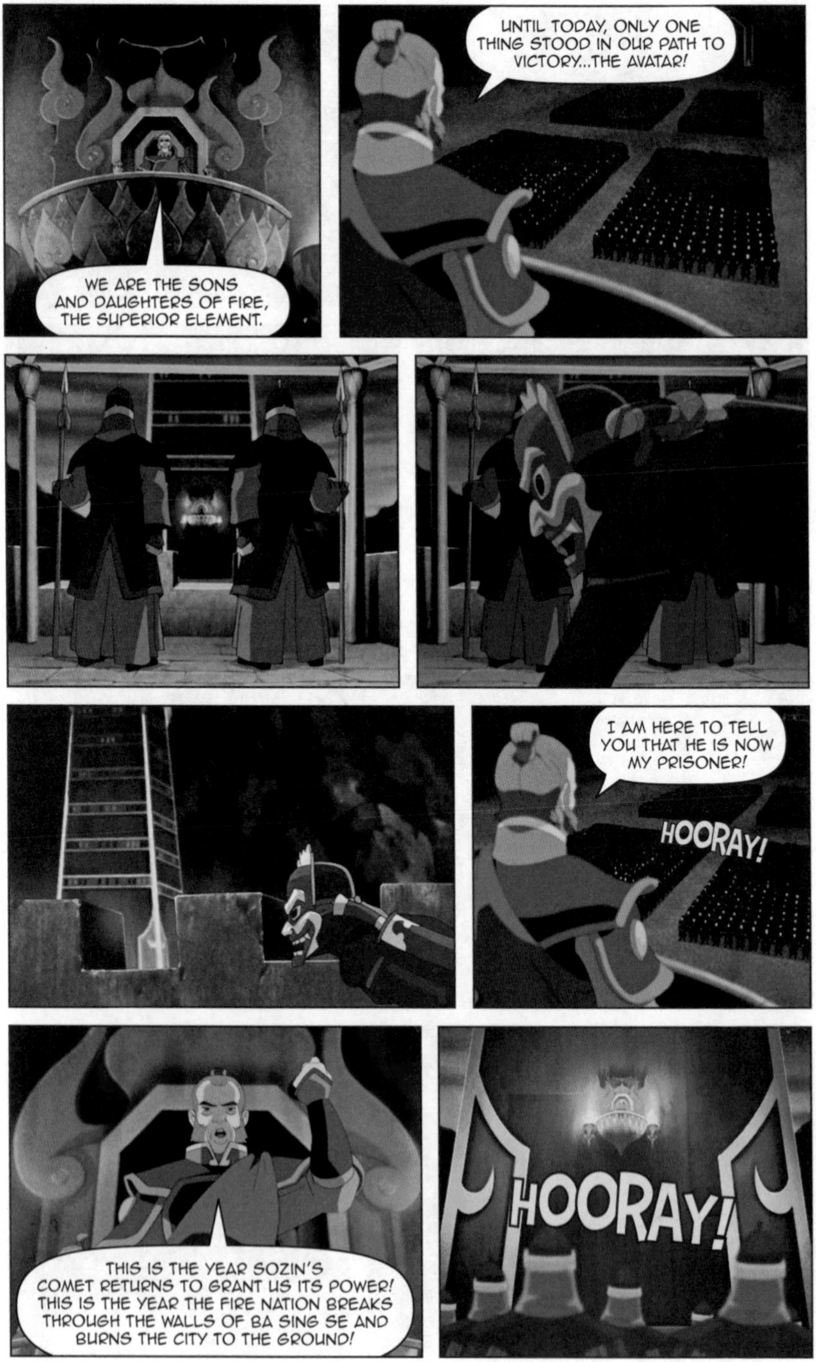
UNTIL TODAY, ONLY ONE THING STOOD IN OUR PATH TO VICTORY...THE AVATAR!
WE ARE THE SONS AND DAUGHTERS OF FIRE, THE SUPERIOR ELEMENT.
I AM HERE TO TELL YOU THAT HE IS NOW MY PRISONER!
HOORAY!
THIS IS THE YEAR SOZIN'S COMET RETURNS TO GRANT US ITS POWER! THIS IS THE YEAR THE FIRE NATION BREAKS THROUGH THE WALLS OF BA SING SE AND BURNS THE CITY TO THE GROUND!
HOORAY!

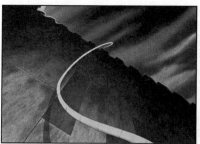

SPLASH

UGH! UGH!

WHAT? NO!

CREAK

DON'T LEAVE, FROGS.

MY FRIENDS ARE SICK AND THEY NEED YOU. PLEASE GO BACK TO BEING FROZEN.

RRBT   RRBT

295

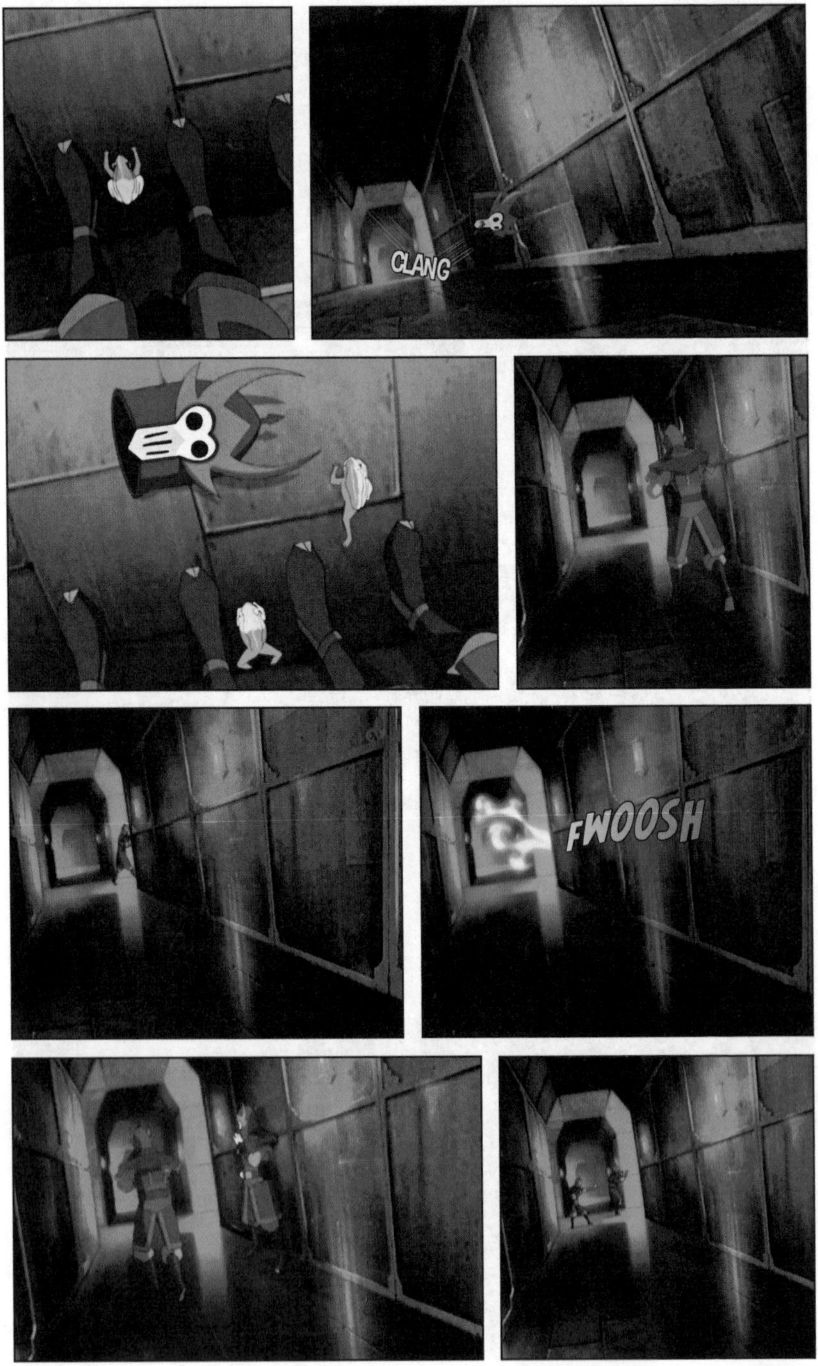
CLANG
FWOOSH

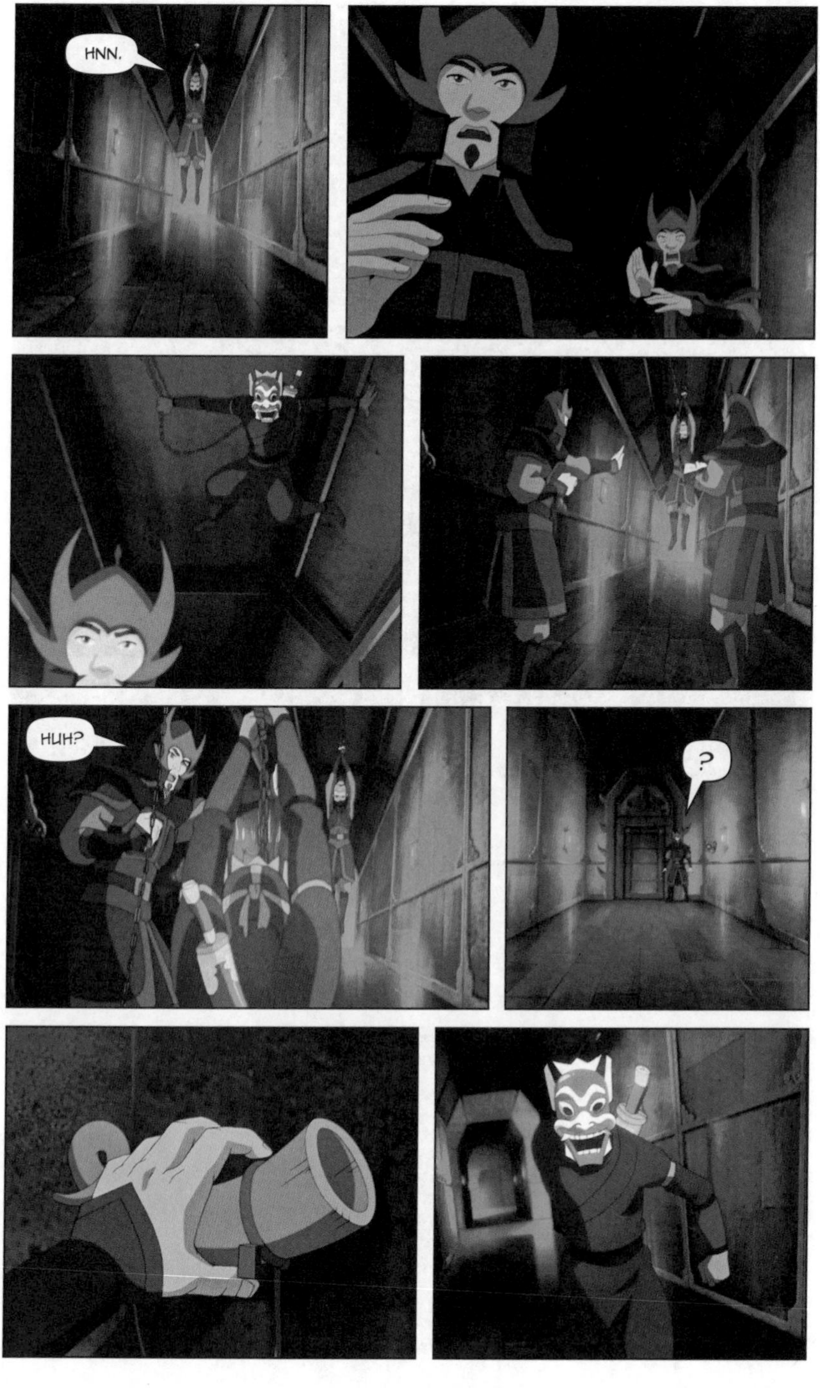
HNN.
HUH?
?

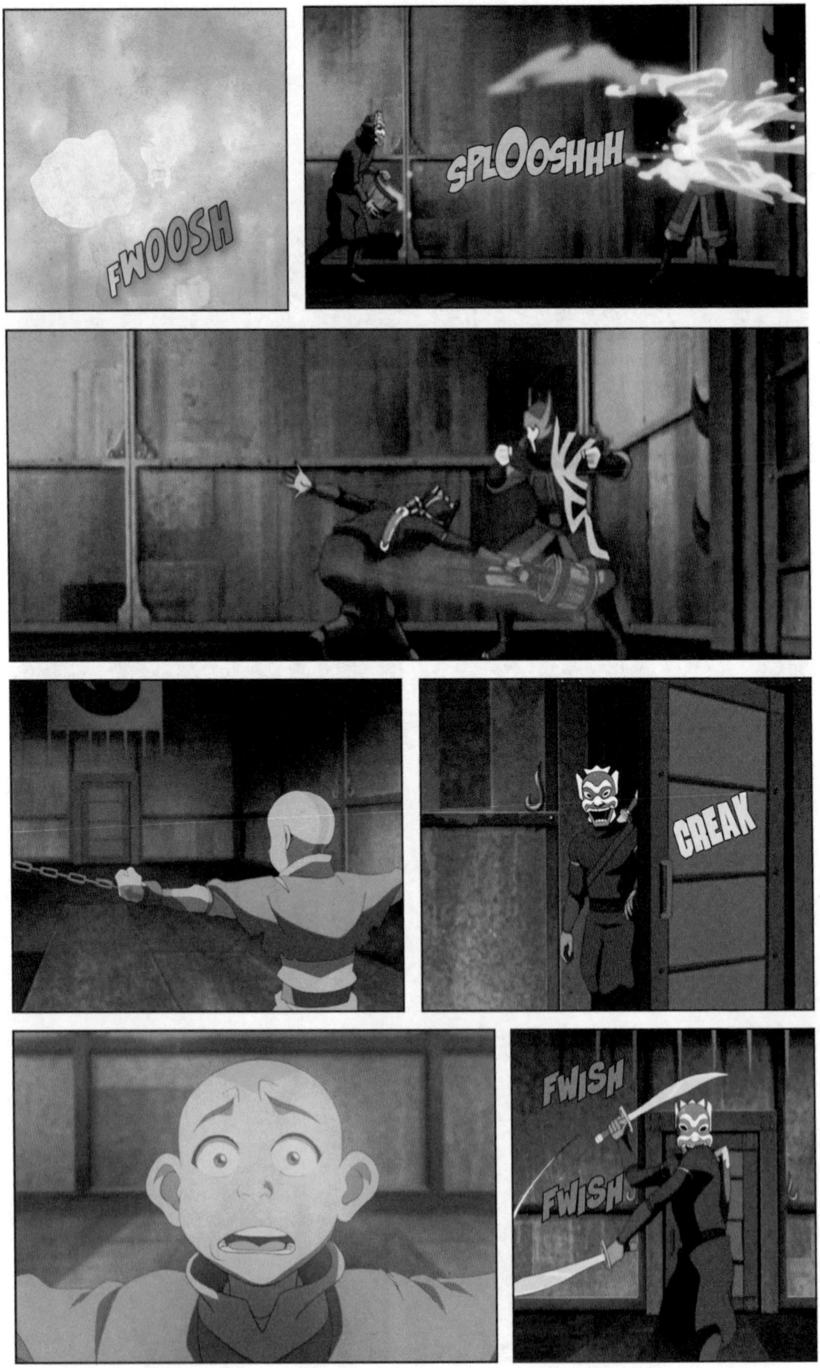
FWOOSH
SPLOOSHHH
CREAK
FWISH
FWISH

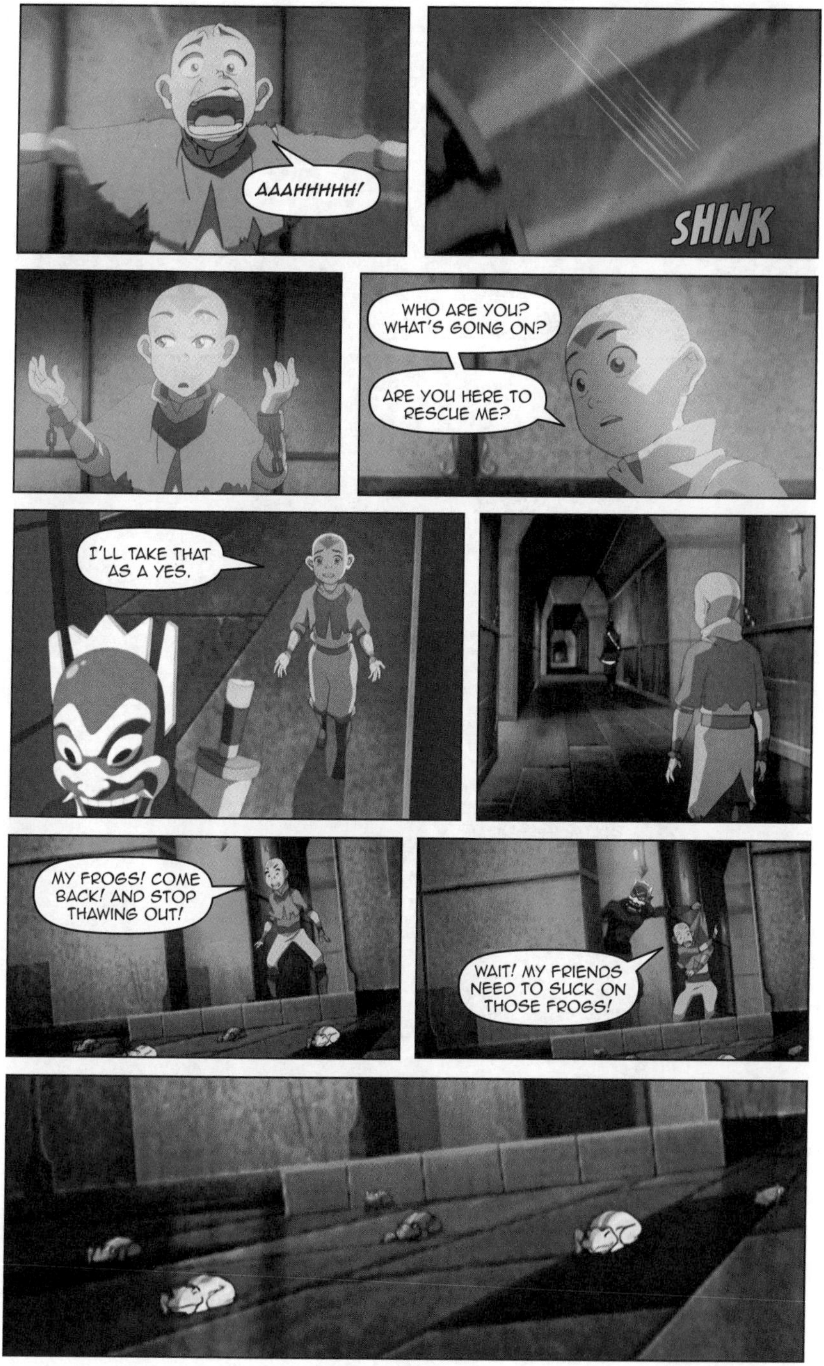
AAAHHHHH!
SHINK
WHO ARE YOU? WHAT'S GOING ON?
ARE YOU HERE TO RESCUE ME?
I'LL TAKE THAT AS A YES.
MY FROGS! COME BACK! AND STOP THAWING OUT!
WAIT! MY FRIENDS NEED TO SUCK ON THOSE FROGS!

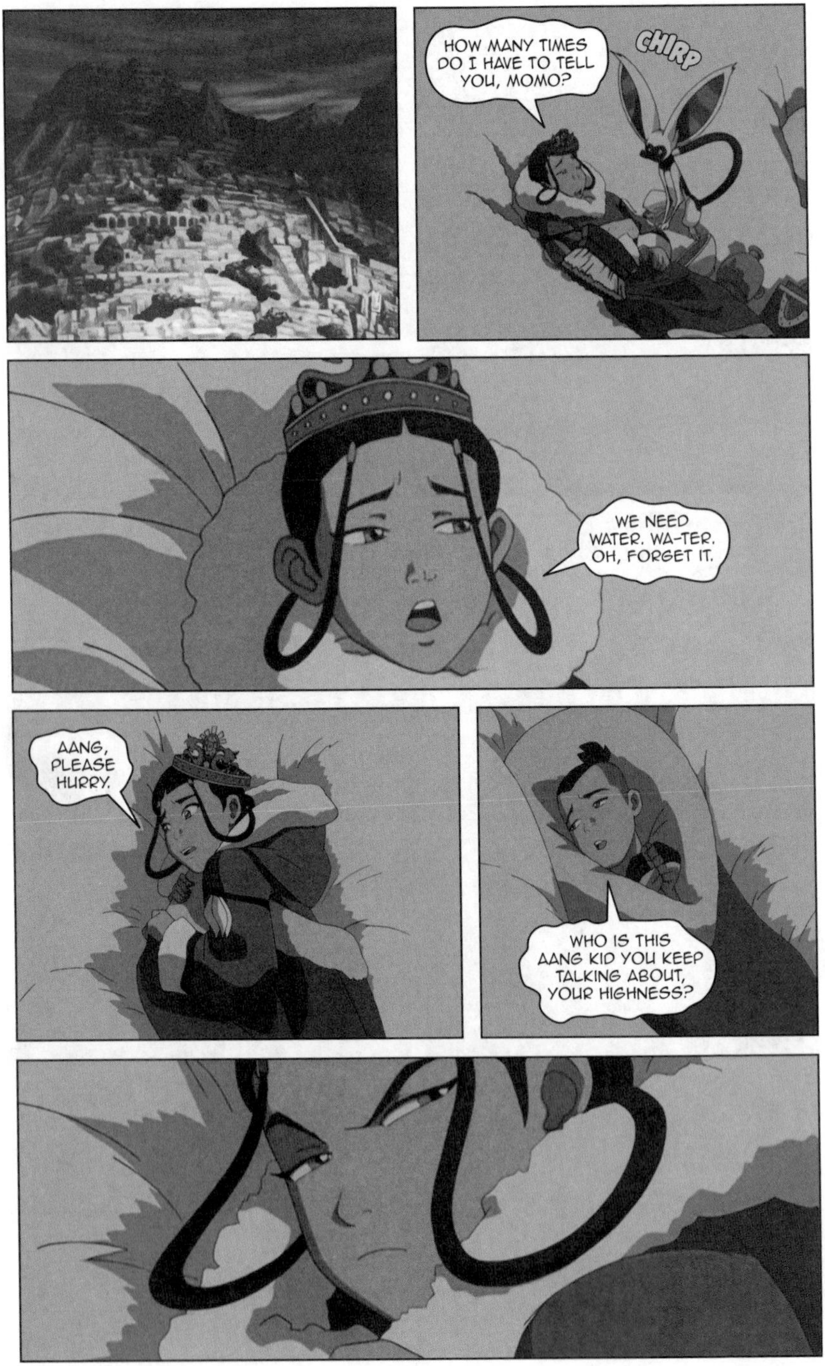
HOW MANY TIMES DO I HAVE TO TELL YOU, MOMO?
CHIRP
WE NEED WATER. WA-TER. OH, FORGET IT.
AANG, PLEASE HURRY.
WHO IS THIS AANG KID YOU KEEP TALKING ABOUT, YOUR HIGHNESS?

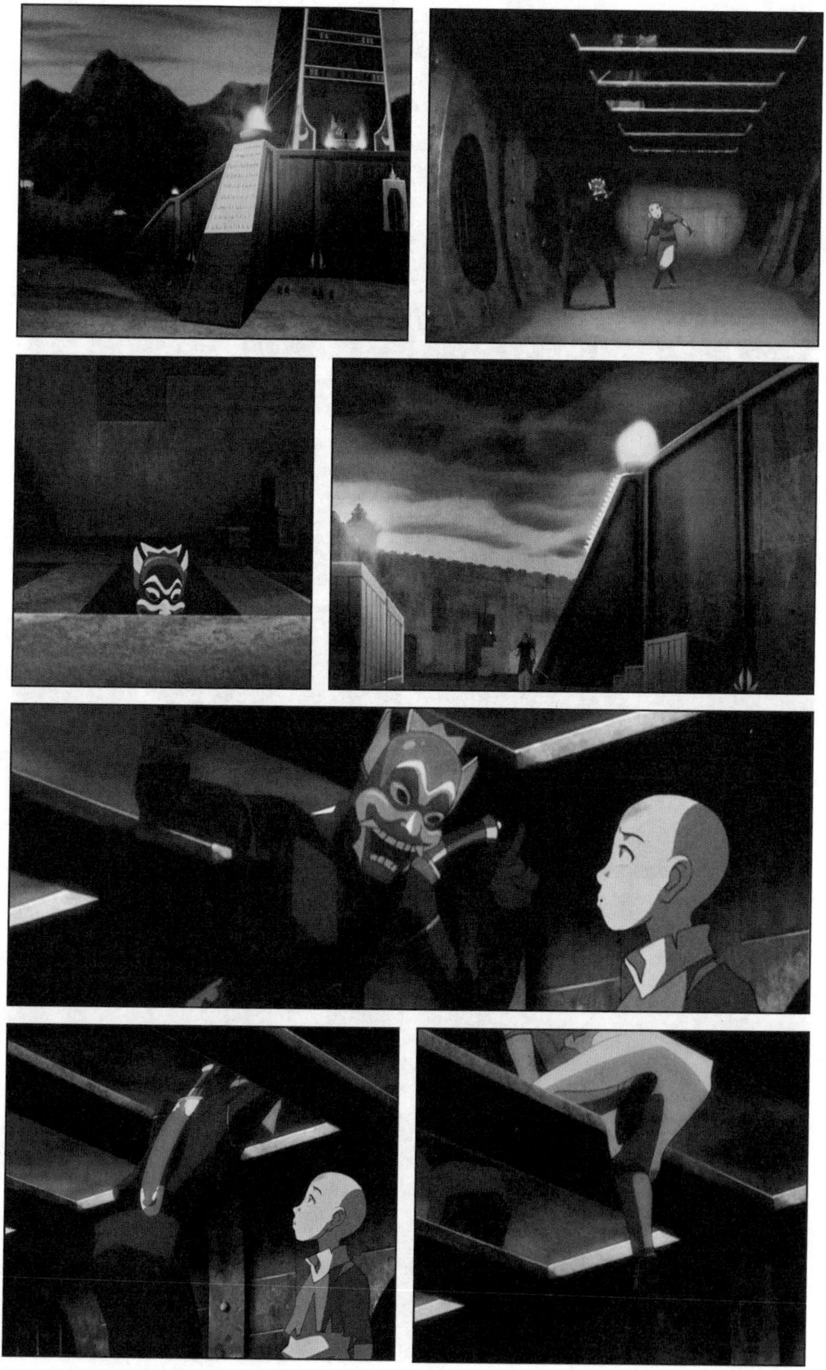

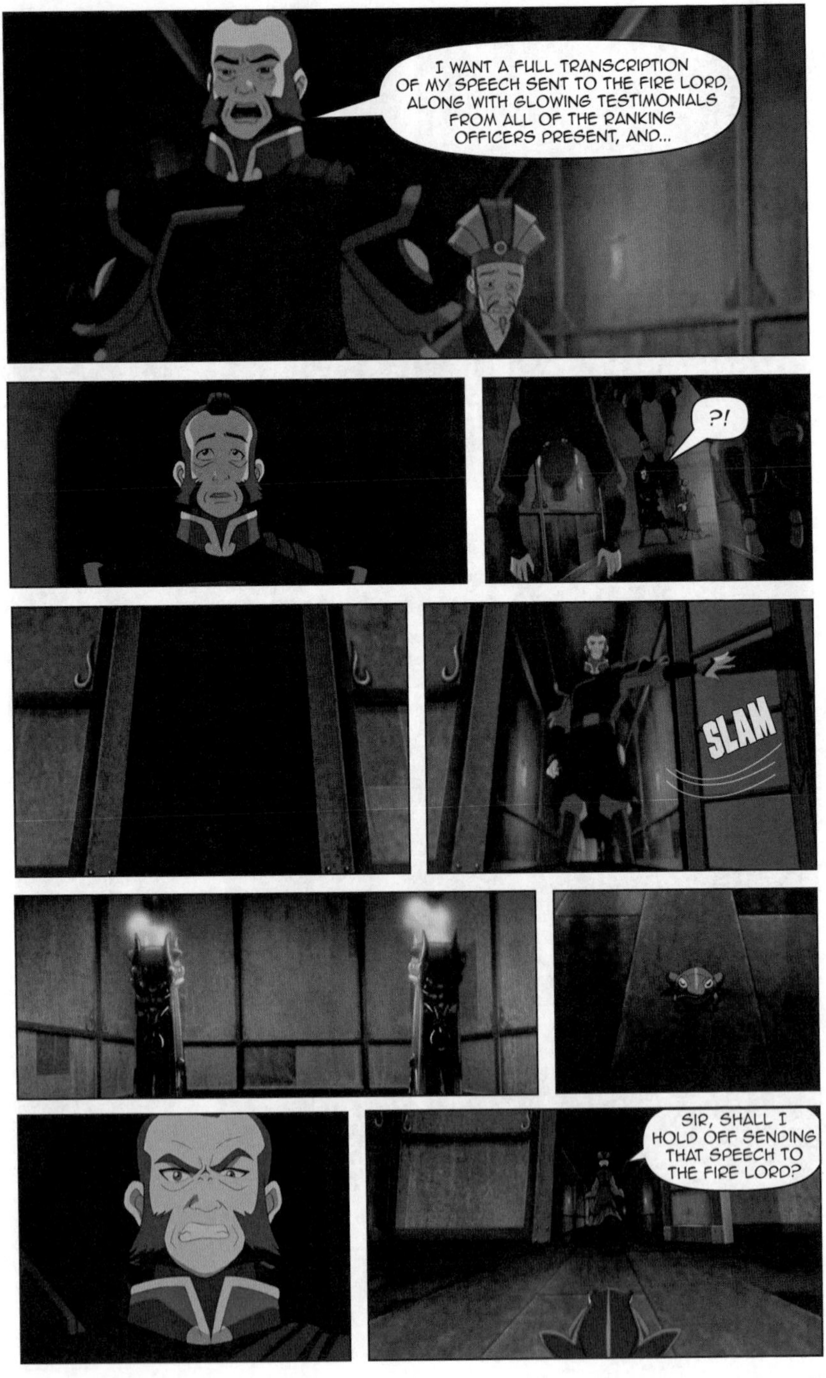
I WANT A FULL TRANSCRIPTION OF MY SPEECH SENT TO THE FIRE LORD, ALONG WITH GLOWING TESTIMONIALS FROM ALL OF THE RANKING OFFICERS PRESENT, AND...
?!
SLAM
SIR, SHALL I HOLD OFF SENDING THAT SPEECH TO THE FIRE LORD?

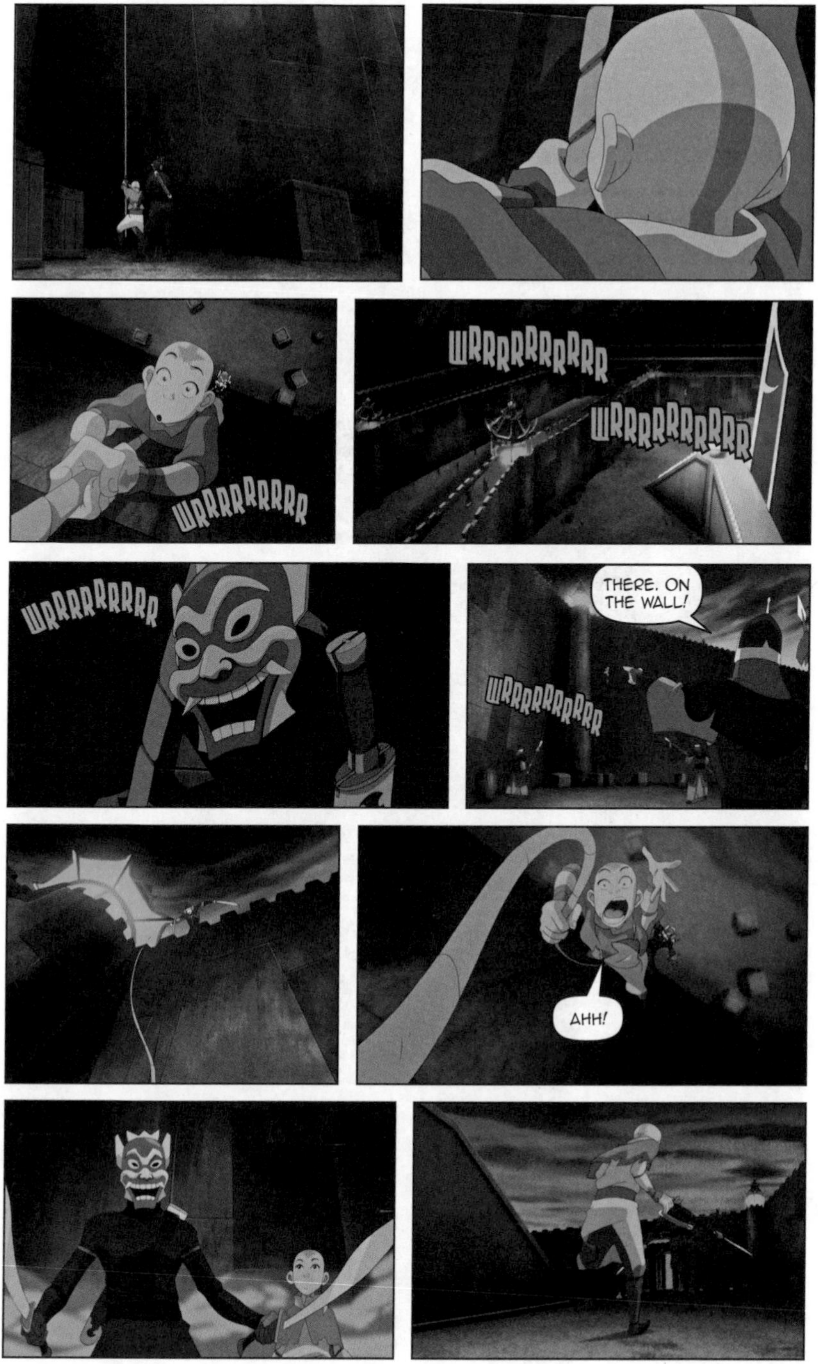
WRRRRRRRR
WRRRRRRRRR
WRRRRRRRRRR
WRRRRRRRR
THERE. ON THE WALL!
WRRRRRRRRR
AHH!

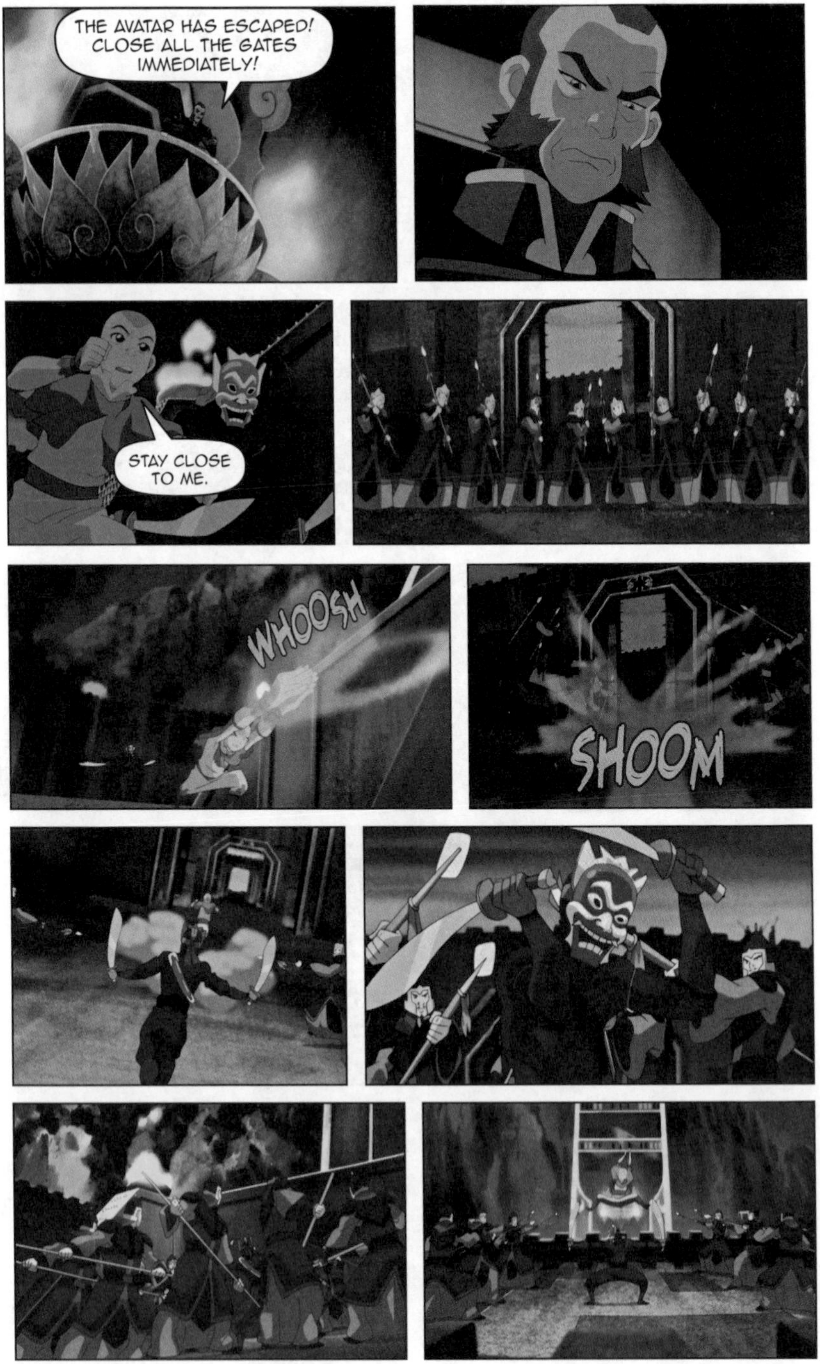
THE AVATAR HAS ESCAPED! CLOSE ALL THE GATES IMMEDIATELY!
STAY CLOSE TO ME.
WHOOSH
SHOOM

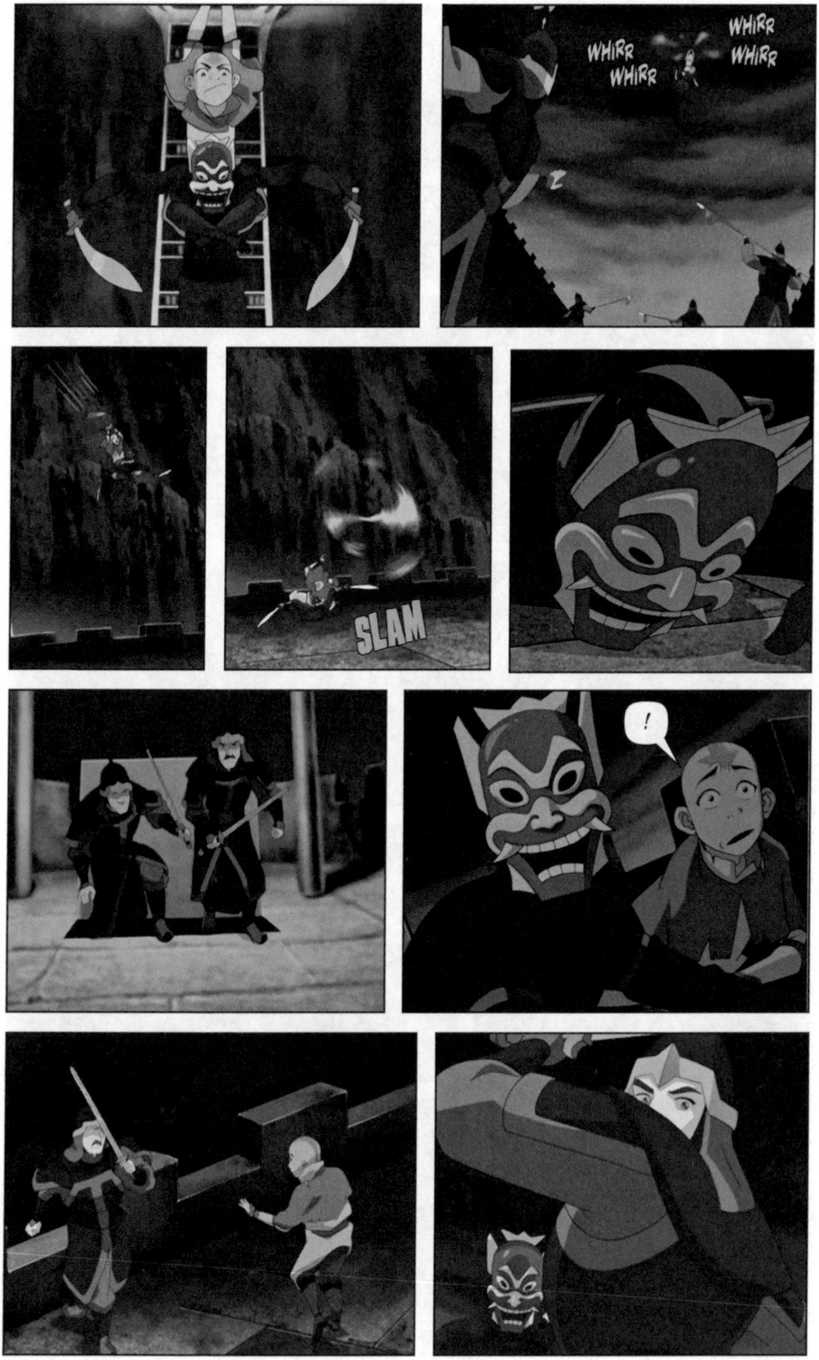
WHIRR
WHIRR
WHIRR
WHIRR
SLAM
!

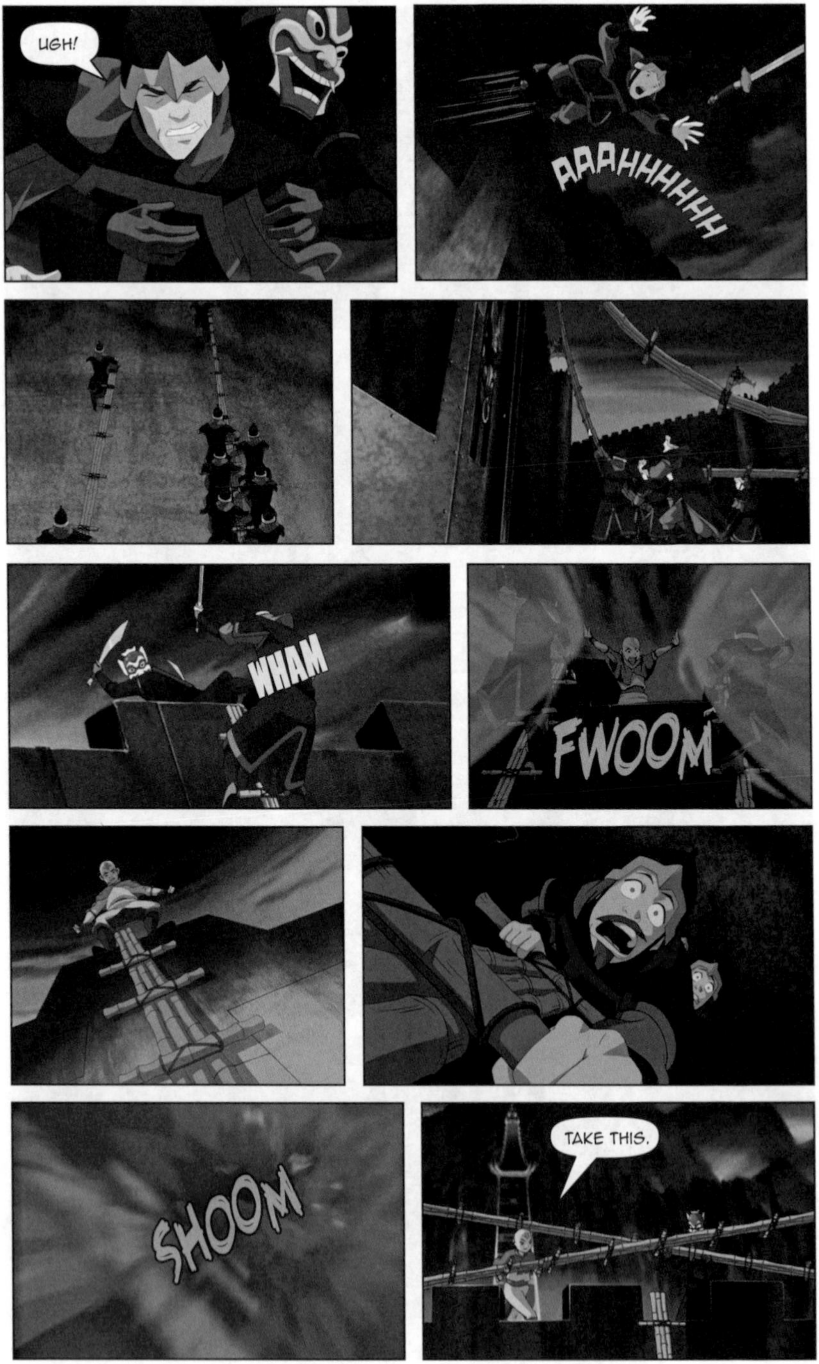
UGH!
AAAHHHHHH
WHAM
FWOOM
SHOOM
TAKE THIS.

JUMP ON MY BACK!
GIVE ME THE NEXT ONE!
FWOOSH
FOOM

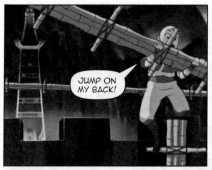

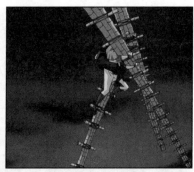

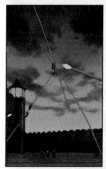

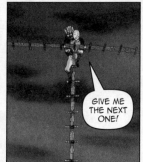

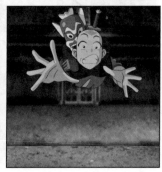

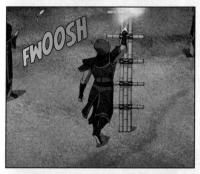

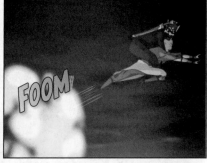

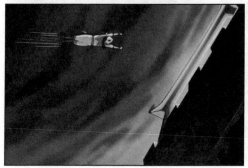

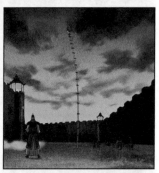

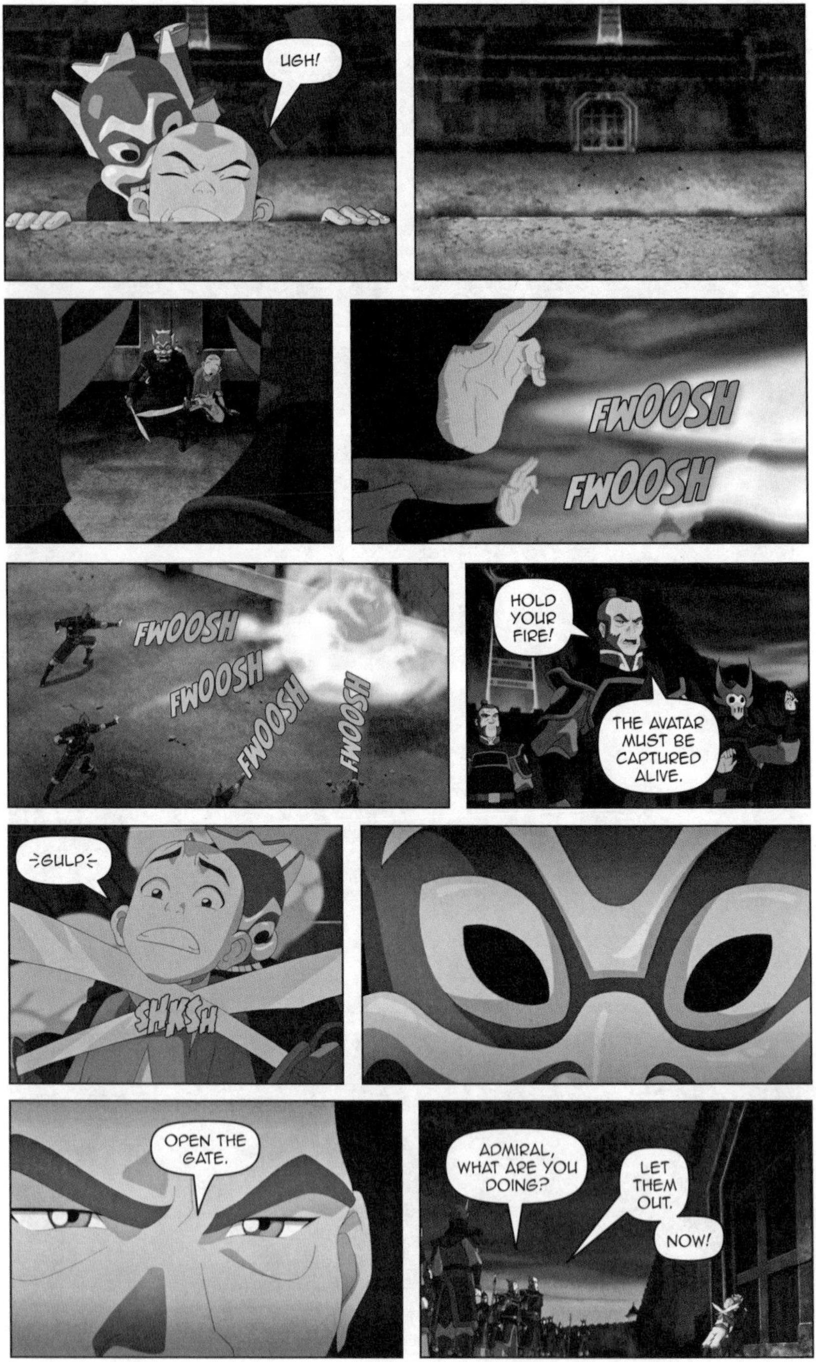
UGH!
FWOOSH
FWOOSH
FWOOSH
FWOOSH
FWOOSH
FWOOSH
HOLD YOUR FIRE!
THE AVATAR MUST BE CAPTURED ALIVE.
GULP
SHKSH
OPEN THE GATE.
ADMIRAL, WHAT ARE YOU DOING?
LET THEM OUT.
NOW!

HOW COULD YOU LET THEM GO?

A SITUATION LIKE THIS REQUIRES...PRECISION.

DO YOU HAVE A CLEAR SHOT?

KNOCK OUT THE THIEF.

I'LL DELIVER HIM TO THE FIRE LORD ALONG WITH THE AVATAR.

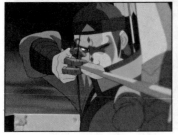

WHUMP

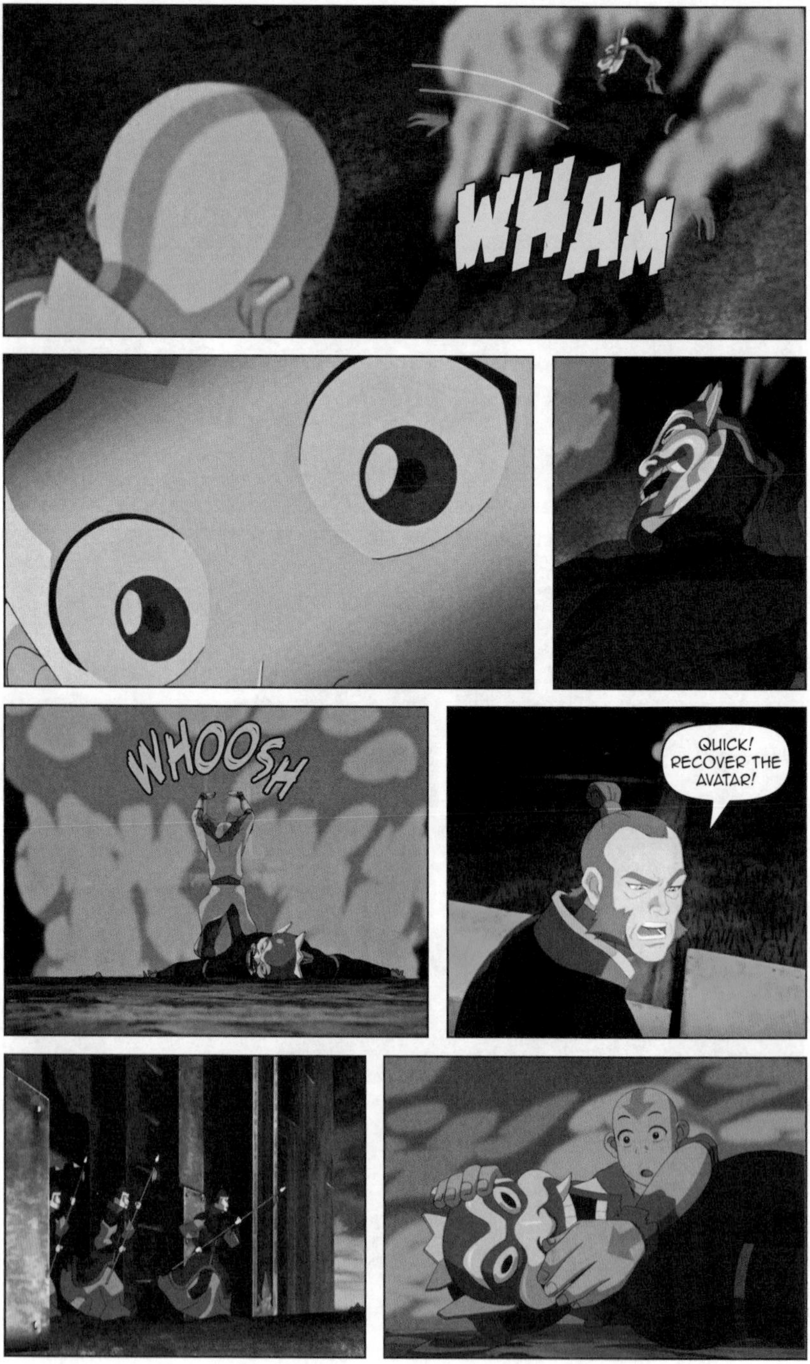
WHAM
WHOOSH
QUICK! RECOVER THE AVATAR!

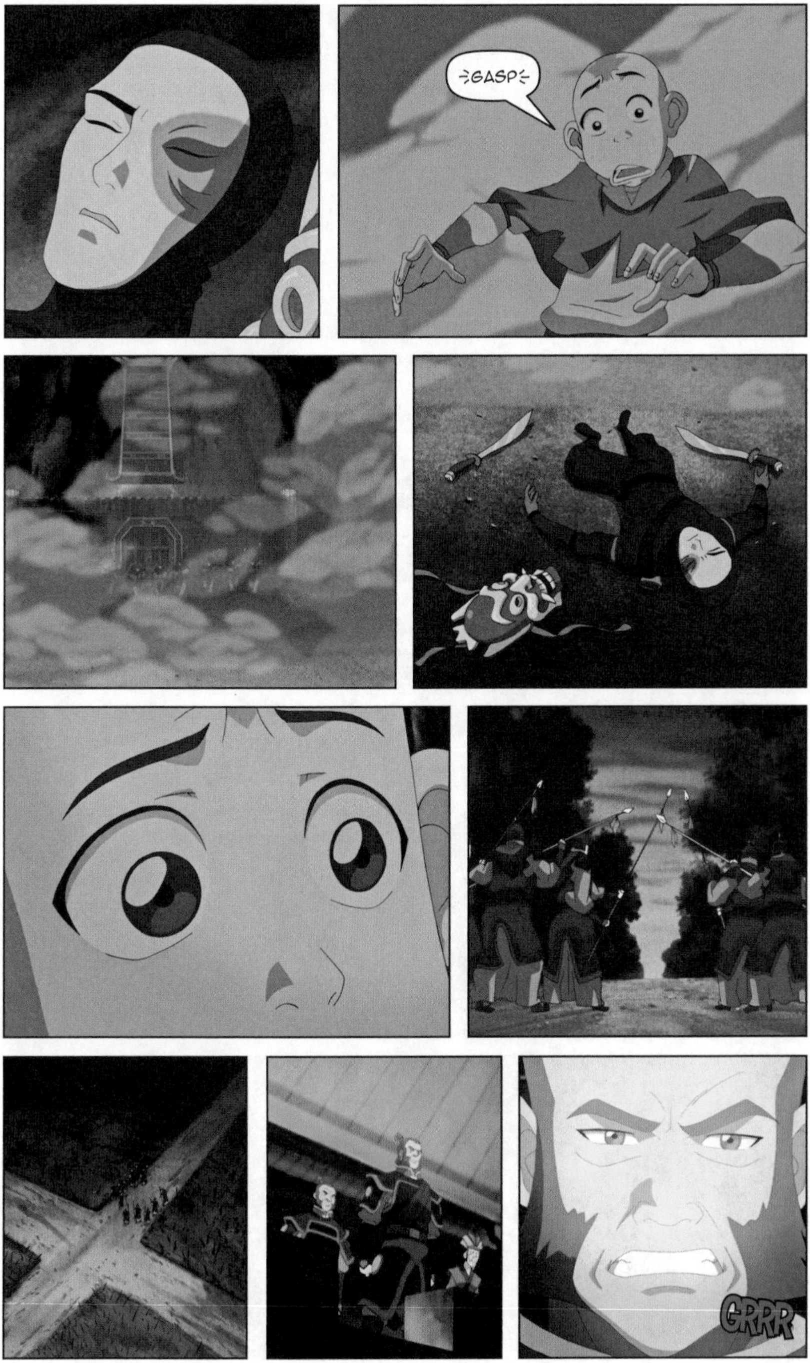
GASP
GRRR

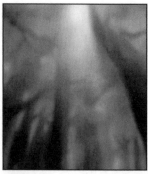

YOU KNOW WHAT THE WORST PART ABOUT BEING BORN OVER A HUNDRED YEARS AGO IS? I MISS ALL THE FRIENDS I USED TO HANG OUT WITH.

BEFORE THE WAR STARTED, I USED TO ALWAYS VISIT MY FRIEND KUZON. THE TWO OF US, WE'D GET IN AND OUT OF SO MUCH TROUBLE TOGETHER.

HE WAS ONE OF THE BEST FRIENDS I EVER HAD...AND HE WAS FROM THE FIRE NATION, JUST LIKE YOU.

IF WE KNEW EACH OTHER BACK THEN, DO YOU THINK WE COULD HAVE BEEN FRIENDS, TOO?

FWOOSH

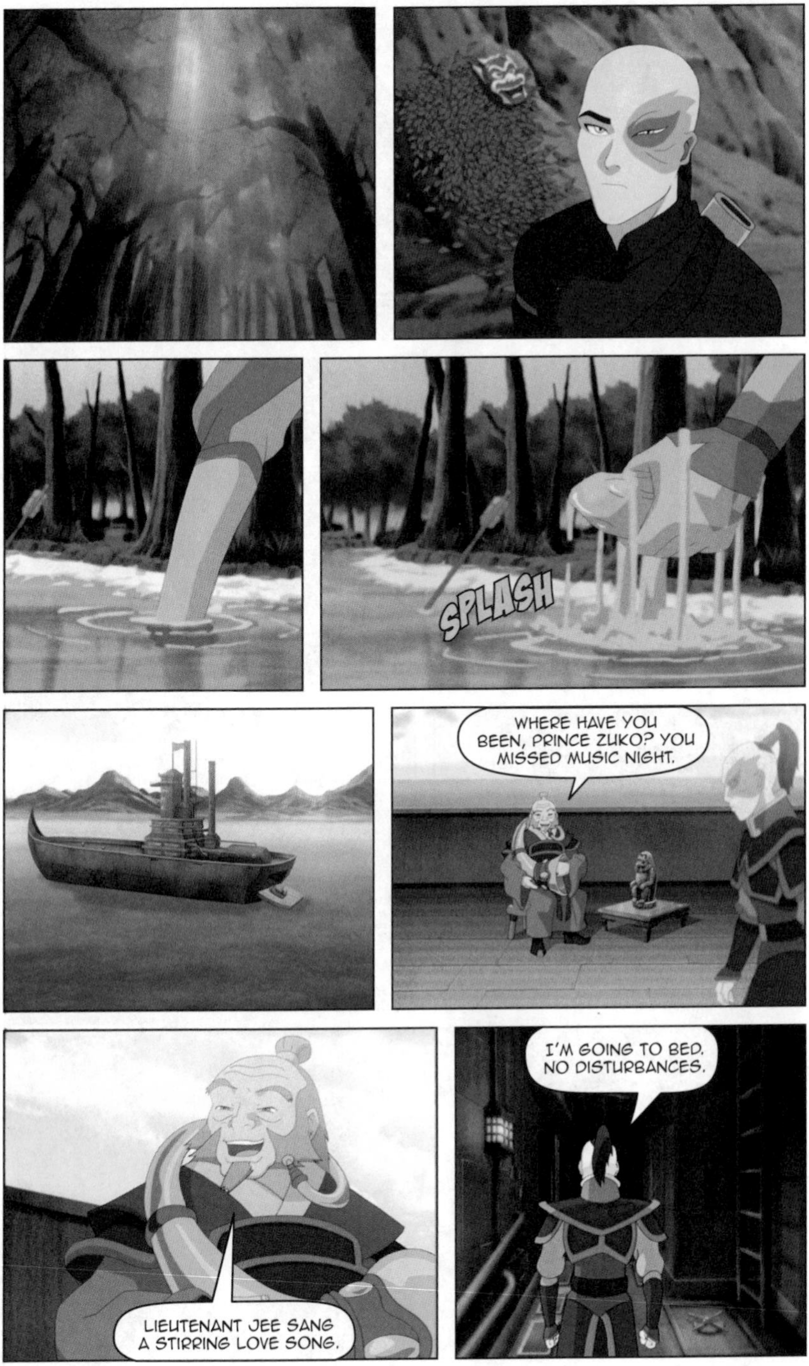
SPLASH
WHERE HAVE YOU BEEN, PRINCE ZUKO? YOU MISSED MUSIC NIGHT.
LIEUTENANT JEE SANG A STIRRING LOVE SONG.
I'M GOING TO BED. NO DISTURBANCES.

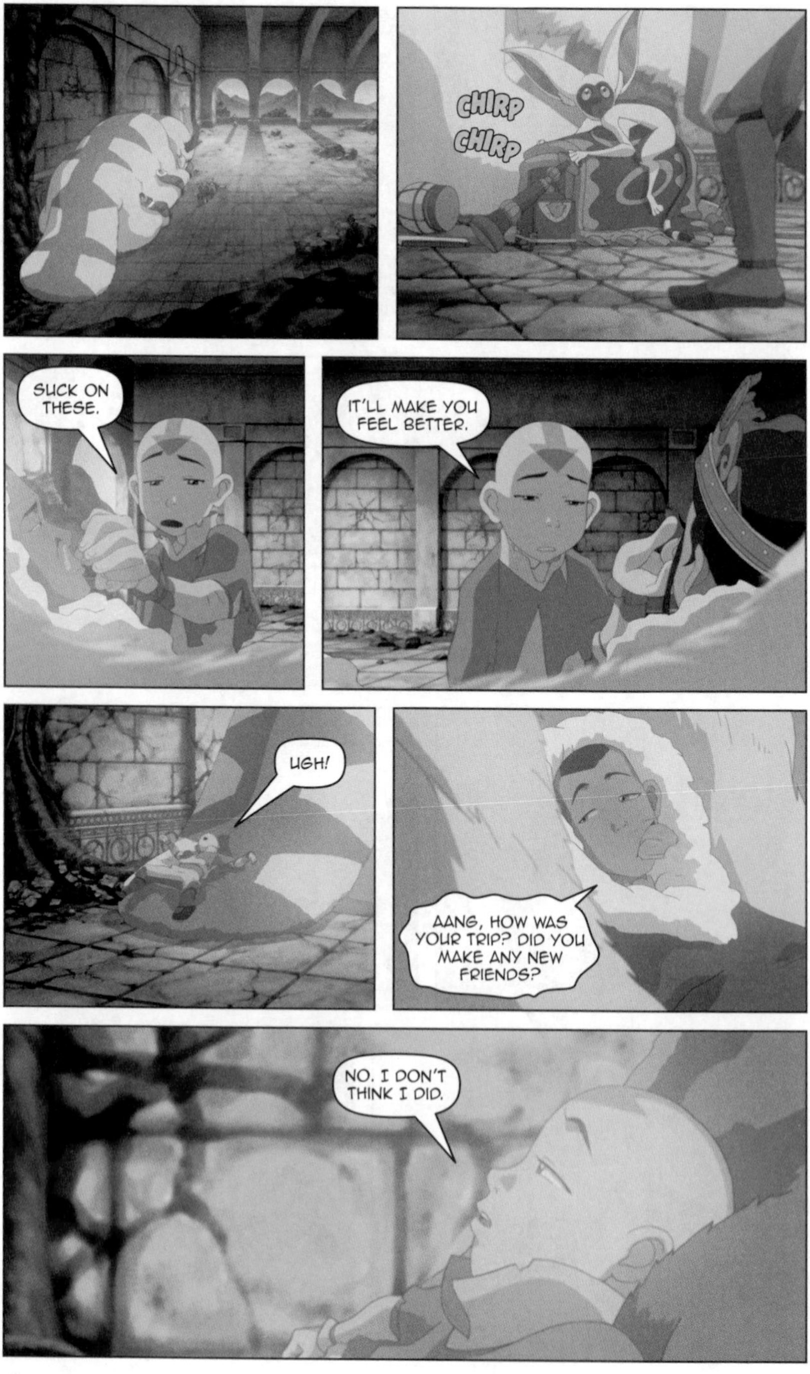
CHIRP
CHIRP
SUCK ON THESE.
IT'LL MAKE YOU FEEL BETTER.
UGH!
AANG, HOW WAS YOUR TRIP? DID YOU MAKE ANY NEW FRIENDS?
NO. I DON'T THINK I DID.

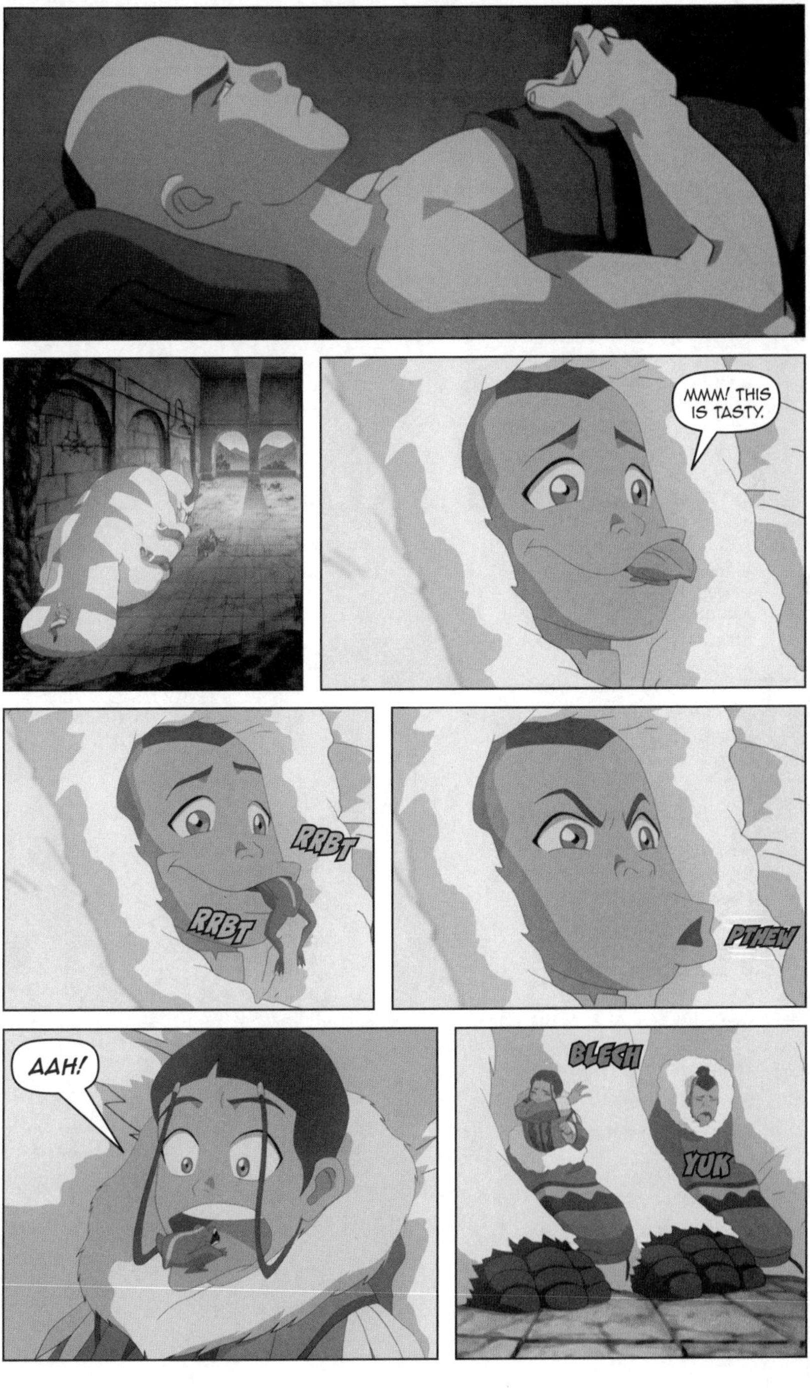
MMM! THIS IS TASTY.
RRBT
RRBT
PTHEW
AAH!
BLECH
YUK

CREDITS

CHAPTER SEVEN
THE SPIRIT WORLD
WRITTEN BY AARON EHASZ
HEAD WRITER
AARON EHASZ
DIRECTED BY LAUREN MACMULLAN
ASSISTANT DIRECTED BY
JERRY LANGFORD
ETHAN SPAULDING
CO-PRODUCER: AARON EHASZ

CHAPTER EIGHT
AVATAR ROKU
WRITTEN BY MICHAEL DANTE
DIMARTINO
HEAD WRITER
AARON EHASZ
DIRECTED BY GIANCARLO VOLPE
ASSISTANT DIRECTED BY
CHRIS GRAHAM
KENJI ONO
CO-PRODUCER: AARON EHASZ

CHAPTER NINE
THE WATERBENDING SCROLL
WRITTEN BY JOHN O'BRYAN
HEAD WRITER
AARON EHASZ
DIRECTED BY ANTHONY LIOI
ASSISTANT DIRECTED BY
IAN GRAHAM
BOBBY RUBIO
CO-PRODUCER: AARON EHASZ

CHAPTER TEN
JET
WRITTEN BY JAMES EAGAN
HEAD WRITER
AARON EHASZ
DIRECTED BY DAVE FILONI
ASSISTANT DIRECTED BY
MIYUKI HOSHIKAWA
JUSTIN RIDGE
CO-PRODUCER: AARON EHASZ

CHAPTER ELEVEN
THE GREAT DIVIDE
WRITTEN BY JOHN O'BRYAN
HEAD WRITER
AARON EHASZ
DIRECTED BY GIANCARLO VOLPE
ASSISTANT DIRECTED BY
CHRIS GRAHAM
KENJI ONO
CO-PRODUCER: AARON EHASZ

CHAPTER TWELVE
THE STORM
WRITTEN BY AARON EHASZ
HEAD WRITER
AARON EHASZ
DIRECTED BY LAUREN MACMULLAN
ASSISTANT DIRECTED BY
JERRY LANGFORD
ETHAN SPAULDING
CO-PRODUCER: AARON EHASZ

CHAPTER THIRTEEN
THE BLUE SPIRIT
WRITTEN BY
MICHAEL DANTE DIMARTINO
BRYAN KONIETZKO
HEAD WRITER
AARON EHASZ
DIRECTED BY DAVE FILONI
ASSISTANT DIRECTED BY
IAN GRAHAM
BOBBY RUBIO
CO-PRODUCER: AARON EHASZ

EXECUTIVE PRODUCERS
MICHAEL DANTE DIMARTINO
BRYAN KONIETZKO